Flight of the Broken
by
Ashley Causey

First Edition ISBN: 978-0-9897089-0-6
Text 2013 © Ashley Causey
Map 2013 © Ashley Causey
Original Cover Concept 2013 © Ashley Causey
Final Cover Artwork 2013 © Phillip Lacson
Edited by Ashley Causey, Sean Sadler, and Nicholas Smith

Second Edition ISBN: 978-0-9897089-2-0
Text 2015 © Ashley Causey
Map 2015 © Ashley Causey
Cover 2015 © Ashley Causey
Edited by Ashley Causey

Map featuring the Lands of the Shadowborn and neighboring territories as visited during the events of Flight of the Broken

DEDICATION

This book is for all writers who ever dared to dream that they could bring their imaginations to life.

AUTHOR'S NOTE

So why come out with another edition of Flight of the Broken? Wasn't the first one good enough? Well, I believe a writer's work is never truly done. I read through the published text for the umpteenth time and while I found it good, it wasn't as great as it could be. Sometimes I doubt that I will ever be truly happy with the text as life changes and new ideas come to light. It is my goal to present the best story possible. I want to give you, the reader, a glimpse into the world I shaped and created. I want to hint at the depth of the entire story of my planned series. I want to deliver a streamlined story from beginning to end. Flight of the Broken: Second Edition will do that for me the writer and you the reader.

So what changes can I expect? The obvious is that I added nineteen new scenes! Some of the scenes were scrapped in the original writing but not thrown away. Some are completely brand new to expand the story. New scenes are notated by a double asterisk in the table of contents so you can quickly go to them. A few of the old scenes have been rewritten to provide a better degree of imagery as I had originally imagined them. These rewritten scenes are notated by a single asterisk in the table of contents. Additional edits have been applied to correct publishing mistakes and to add more detail.

I look at what I do as a life's work for I don't think that I could ever produce anything else independent of the world and story. I put my heart into what I write, crafting characters reflective of who I am and who I want to be. I am constantly asking questions while writing to put myself in the mindset of the reader in order to craft the best story possible. I want to give you my best. I want my passion to inspire others to be creative, to write, and to read. So get out there and get creative!

With this edition, I feel the need to put a disclaimer. In the text, you will find a degree of violence, minor use of profanity, and two scenes of brief nudity. So prepare for a dark tale with a villain ready to take control of the world and who must face a rising courage and hope in its people.

Ashley Causey

TABLE OF CONTENTS

** New scene
* Rewritten Scene

BREAK

A winter wind swept across the high mountain peaks, pushing and pulling snow laden clouds in a swirling torrent. It screamed and hissed like an angry cat. Bare rock was exposed before it was quickly covered again in a blanket of white. Thunder rumbled over the distant grasslands as a storm front began to swell. The air was frigid with a crisp and clean scent. However, one solitary cry rang out above all of the noise.

"Go fetch Lord Avis at once!" The voice trembled, full of fear and desperation, as it carried throughout the peaks. "Hurry!"

The voice echoed inside the mountain tunnel where it reached the ears of a young Airborn man. With the alarming command, the Airborn, dressed in a cream tunic and pants with soft gray leather boots, nearly tripped over his own feet as he turned and bolted from the sacred cavern. Breathing came easy to him at first, but as the tunnel began to ascend, he found himself gasping for air. Whether his exhaustion was the result of physical exertion or fear, he did not know. He spun and leapt around obstacles, careful not to trip and fall. The stone was slick from mountain mist and creeping snow. Breath became frost as his body shivered. For a split second, he was jealous of those who shared the mountain peaks with his people: the mighty Gryphons, their bodies covered in warm fur and sleek feathers that protected them from extreme weather. They were noble creatures with majestic poise and natural ease. The Airborn and the rest of the Spiritborn tribes looked like the Mortal men of the Southlands with

1

bare skin and hair only on their heads. The Airborn shook his head free of the distraction before refocusing his thoughts on his master's command.

The words within the command were in of themselves mundane and an oft familiar sound but the tone in which they were said frightened him. His master was a sensible soul that was never one to raise his voice. In his twenty years of service, the attendant had never heard such fear and desperation from his master before and to summon Lord Avis at this hour meant it was a serious matter. There were very few reasons to wake any Lord at night. The only ones he knew of were war and imminent danger. But he had seen the crack in the stone that had alarmed his superior. He was afraid of what it meant.

He was an attendant to a Keeper of the Truth and what they tended to was the Immortal Truth. It was the law of the Northern Alliance that was written after the Darklands were sealed behind a powerful shield. There was nothing more sacred and important to his world than the words etched in its stone. The stone itself was dark granite with specks of sparkling mica on the surface. But the runes held the true might. Laws, omens, and power scribed in days long past spoke of the noble souls who had been present at its writing. Rumors abound as to its creation, some even believing the codes and portent had been scribed in blood. It was worthy of reverent protection.

The attendant let out a sigh of relief as he exited the deep cavern. Something about being enclosed in rock made him feel trapped and he wondered if the rest of his kin felt the same way. He slowed to a stop at the edge of the rocky outcrop. The open air filled him with a sense of freedom. His eyes glanced about the scenery, his white and black hair floating in the soft breeze. He took a deep breath before diving off the edge of the outcrop. Cliff diving was his favorite pastime and his innate skill made him an expert at it. The air rushed by him, whipping his shoulder length hair around his face. He held his arms rigid behind him as he fell like a diving falcon.

Snow began to fall in a light shower of ice at the high altitude before changing into a frigid rain. A frosty layer clung to him, stiffening his muscles. He closed his eyes and opened them again, seeing the ground rushing at him. He quickly twisted his body and threw out his arms to slow his descent. With instinctual steadiness, he landed perfectly balanced on his feet. He looked up at the high peak, seeing the ledge from which he had jumped. The snow swirled around the mountains with only a few flakes making it to the valley below. At seven hundred feet, the ledge was a smudge in the distance. Not wanting to waste another minute, the attendant took off down the mountain path at high speed.

At the head of the mountain path stood a fortress built of stone, situated at the valley entrance and overlooking the Airborn capital of Tempest on the lower plain. The front wall stretched between the mountains like a dam holding back a river. Thick turrets marked the front gate on both sides. A four story tower loomed behind the wall.

The Airborn attendant drew close to the gate and alerted the attention of the guards with a wave of his arm. Seeing his hurried gait and windswept hair, the two guards rushed to open the gate, raising the portcullis with a wench hidden behind the wall. The Airborn attendant slipped inside just as the opening was wide enough for him to pass through, never slowing his pace. Without a word, the guards closed the gate behind him.

The attendant made a mental note to go back after delivering his message to thank the guards as he slowed his pace in the courtyard. He quickly slid to a stop when a diminutive Screech Owl Gryphon with red plumage came forward to greet him with a head bow. The Gryphon's size reminded him of a large dog. Ear tufts laid back on his round head as his wings were folded against his back. He bowed his head again, puffing out his cream feathered chest.

"Message for Lord Avis," the attendant stammered as he was catching his breath from the jump. He did not want to admit that his fear was getting to him. A few seconds later he added, "It is most urgent that I speak with him."

As required, any night time visit to the Lord Avis' chambers meant that an Owl Gryphon would escort the visitor. They had the best night vision and the sharpest hearing. They also possessed a keen sense of judgement when it came to recognizing the character of the people around them. Only the Dragons exceeded them in this skill as no one was capable of lying in front a creature fearsome enough to devour them. The attendant was thankful that he was greeted by a Screech Owl Gryphon and not the massive Horned Owl and Eagle Owl Gryphons who scared him. He watched as the Gryphon tapped his claws on the stone of the courtyard, staring back at him with big golden eyes. The Gryphon gestured with a twitch of his head towards the flat roof of the tower before opening his wings and rocketing into the air.

The attendant dashed up the outdoor stairs two at a time before sliding to a stop on the tower roof. He bent over with hands on his knees, catching his breath. He then stood up straight with hands on his hips. The Gryphon lighted down beside him, folding his wings and swishing his leonine tail. His ear tufts were now standing up as he held back at the edge. He then slid his front down into a bow and spread out his wings.

Before them on the top of the tower was Lord Proto Avis, an ancient Eagle Gryphon of enormous wisdom and experience. He sat tall and proud with his eyes to the night sky. His wings shuffled as he brought his head down, considering some unknown conundrum.

The attendant quickly went to one knee and bowed his head. "Lord Avis, I bring a most urgent message," he began to say but the aged Eagle Gryphon held up a paw to silence him.

"I know what it is that you wish to say, young one," his voice rasped as he brought his paw back down to a resting position. The attendant then saw how tired and worn the old Gryphon looked. His faded brown wings lay limp out to either side of his body and his shoulders were bent under some great invisible weight. "The stone has cracked," he finally said, his white feathered chest deflating from the released breath. He hung his head in defeat.

To hear the Lord Avis speak in such a manner unnerved the young Airborn. It had always been his impression that this Gryphon above all others was never worried. He looked back at Lord Avis, trying to read his fierce animal eyes. Though the Gryphon was a kind and helpful sage, he was still a deadly beast underneath the smile. He was then distracted by the Gryphon escort's reaction.

The Screech Owl Gryphon shuddered at the admission of Lord Avis. He quickly chirped and chawed in the Gryphon tongue, his posture on the alert. His wings flared out into flight position as his feet tapped back and forth in agitation. Lord Avis responded in his native tongue, his tone commanding in the avian whistles and chirps. The Screech Owl Gryphon immediately shrank down into a sitting position, hanging his head. The attendant wished he knew more of the Gryphon language to understand what they had been saying to each other. To him, it sounded like birds arguing over who got the highest tree branch to perch on.

Lord Avis shifted his position to face the attendant, his movement slow but steady. "I can see the question in your eyes, young one. How could I know if I was not there to witness the event?" He tightened his wings against his back.

"What does it mean? That is what I wish to know, Lord Avis," the attendant said in his own personal confusion.

"Do you know the history of the Immortal Truth? Do you know how it came to be?" Proto asked.

The Airborn shrugged. "I know what I was told when I entered the service of the keeper. Is there something else? Some secret I have yet to be informed of?"

Proto silenced a chuckle. He loved curious minds and questions. "The world was truly a dark and terrible place before the Immortal Truth came into being. Death and destruction were commonplace as Demons ran across the land unopposed. Yes, we tried to mount a defense but it was no use. When one Demon was struck down, four more appeared in its place. Immortal kind could not keep up and soon we were desperate to make a final end."

"The Battle of the North," the Airborn said, being familiar with the event.

"Yes. We are lucky that we are able to even speak of it now. Had it not been for Bane Arlis, we would have had Demons as overlords and Terra would cease to exist as we know it today. Bane gave us courage and thus Immortal kind was able to win the day. Together, the victors formed the Northern Alliance and decided to write a binding code of laws to be infused with the power of souls. The Immortal Truth was given its power by the great sacrifice we dare not speak about," the old Gryphon explained, alternating between despair and hope.

The attendant thought of the Dragons' sacrifice and shuddered. "I have always known the Immortal Truth to be more than just law. I am too young to know the days you speak of but I wanted to serve just the same."

The old Gryphon sighed deeply. "And I am old enough to have seen the dark days of the past. I fear," Proto hesitated. "What the crack means is that a terrible event has occurred that was strong enough to break the bond of blood," Lord Avis said with heaviness. He let out a deep breath as he sat straight up, bringing his gaze to the attendant's eyes. "As I told my kin here, I do not want alarm to spread. Return to your master. Tell him no one is allowed in the cavern until I give the order."

Stunned by the harshness, the attendant hesitated. "Why?" was all he could ask.

Lord Avis looked briefly at his kindred Gryphon before he rose up on all four feet, spreading his wings out in full flare. Each feather sparkled with starlight, glittering like the night sky at the Gryphon's back. To the attendant it appeared as if Lord Avis was youthful and strong again with moonlight for armor wrapped around his supple frame. The attendant fell to his knees in awe. Then a cloud passed over and Lord Avis appeared old and faded, his wings gray with age.

"Because the truth is breaking..."

FEAR

It was as he remembered for the cavern had not changed in a thousand years. If it had changed, Proto Avis did not see it. His bones creaked in the cold air as he stood in the entry way, dew collecting on his feathers. He shivered from the chill and from the inperceptible Spirit energy. This space was a place of ancient power. Proto's eyes swept over the cavern to ensure himself that no one else was present. He needed time alone to think.

The dark stone sparkled in the moonlight that beamed down through a small window like opening in the far wall. It was a silver light that normally Proto Avis found soothing but now it was foreboding. He shook his head to free his mind of such worry but it lingered as his gaze shifted to the rune carved stone in the center of the cavern. A moat of shallow water surrounded the stone in a circular design, four short bridges leading over it at the cardinal points. The only contrast of color to the room was a ring of tall white stone pillars, each carved with artistic designs representing the individual signers. His own pillar portrayed a youthful image of days long past.

"My brothers, my sisters," he uttered in the trademark chaw and whistle of his birth tongue. He bowed his head in reverence. A sudden and fierce wind ripped through the cavern and Proto's eyes snapped open. "What?"

The cavern was filled with shimmering mist that shifted and contorted into fantastic shapes. The lines of every carving glowed with pulsating light and Proto found himself drawn in, his feet moving without command.

"Are we certain of this path? There is no turning back." Proto immediately identified the nervous voice as that of Evander the pacifist Lord of the Lightborn.

"Lord Evander, this is the only way to ensure the peace for Terra's future," came Bane's distinctive stern voice. "Unless you can think of a more binding power."

Proto chuckled at Bane's tone as he remembered where the great war hero stood. Two mist forms stood side by side like sentinels around the stone. He closed his eyes in the mirth of the memory before opening them again. His breath caught in his chest.

The cavern was now filled with a golden light that warmed the entire room. Proto stood slackjawed seeing each of the signers standing where the pillars used to be save Bane and the majestic Shadow Night Silvanus. Shadow Night was as perfect as he remembered, clothed in glistening silver plate armor and a sable cloak lined with wolf fur. His gaze was as sharp as an eagle, his bearing like a ferocious lion ready to be unleashed. He stood with his gloved hands resting on the pommel of his sword. Proto recognized it as the royal blade that would be passed down to his successors. The tall and noble Lord shifted his weight, his expression remaining harsh and unforgiving.

"And what can we hope to gain by signing this in our own blood?" asked the pale blonde Evander. Proto turned to look upon the lean golden cloaked Immortal. Evander pushed back his cloak and stepped forward to get everyone's attention. Only Shadow Night refused to turn and face him, leaving his back to him. "To sign this code of laws, this promise, in blood is to forever bind ourselves to the fate of our people and our world. To lose the memory of Terra's ancient past..."

"Are you afraid, Evander?" Shadow Night interuptted as he sheathed his sword. He turned to face Evander. "Or have you forgotten the meaning of duty?"

The entire room silenced at the sound of Shadow Night's burly voice. The red haired Lord of the Fireborn Forges stopped mid whisper in a conversation with Nereus, the Lord of the Waterborn. Only the golden haired Gaia of the Earthborn in her shimmering forest green gown appeared amused. The white haired Aves in his cloak of feathers remained stoic.

"You insult my courage?" Evander snapped.

"I can do more than that if you wish," Shadow Night stated, betraying no hint of anger.

Proto stood up tall, flaring his wings. A passing thought drove him forward, compelled by the memory. "Enough!" he screeched.

Everyone turned to face him in silence, each bowing their heads in respect. Proto stole a glance at the water in the moat, seeing his youth. He was now deep in the memory. He brought his head back up as he folded his wings. His golden eyes swept across the crowd with utter command. He stopped on Evander, looking deep into his eyes.

"I am sorry, great seer, for my doubt," the Lightborn meekly said.

"I have seen my fair share of war and bloodshed in my years and I will not suffer to see it here," Proto stated firmly, guided by the memory. It felt strange to the Gryphon to be both watching the memory and living it at the same time. He wondered if the crack in the stone was affecting his mind.

"We have all seen too much war as of late," Gaia's sweet but firm voice declared for all to hear. She sauntered forward to gather everyone's attention to her. Standing by Shadow Night and Bane, she was small but no less commanding. "By the swords of these two warriors was our world saved from the Darklands. By the blood of us all did we stem the tide of evil." She clenched her fist and placed it over her heart. "What would we have faced if the Lords of the Spiritborn had failed?"

"Lies, hate, and death," Nereus said as he squared his shoulders. His robes of ocean blue reflected the light as if they were water. Eyes of ice blue made his face look sharp and uncaring.

Proto looked at each of the signers, his present self trying to interpret the meaning of the memory. A part of him reveled in the touch of his youth, his joints no longer aching from age. His reason reminded him that this was only a Living Memory and not reality. But what was it trying to show him?

"The Immortal Truth will guide Terra should the Darklands seek Dominion again. Shadow Night and I have discussed another binding power to ensure the protection of our lands," Bane said as he slowly turned in a circle to address everyone.

Proto realized that the memory skipped ahead in time for now Bane had Evander at attention and listening carefully. He shook his head to better settle his thoughts.

"We agree to seal our bloodlines within the Immortal Truth to stand the test of time as guardians to its word. It will be the lock and key to the newly risen Shadow Mirror. If our bloodlines fail, then the Immortal Truth is broken and the Mirror falls," Shadow Night explained as he held a knife in his right hand. Bane held a similar knife in his left hand, resting the blade on his open palm. "You know my bloodline to be strong and secure with my three sons. The Silvanus family is a line of warriors and we are ready."

"I have walked through the Spirit World and returned. I do not yet have those to follow in my bloodline but I offer my strong heart. I offer my promise to serve the people of Terra with every breath that I take," Bane declared. He and Shadow Night then sliced their open hands. Blood streamed out from between their clenched fingers. "We pledge ourselves by blood to the eternal service of Terra. For the Immortal Truth!"

Proto found himself shouting with approval, flaring his wings and crying out in his native tongue. The golden light grew brighter and brighter to the point of blinding him. He closed his eyes against the stinging shine. When he opened them again, the memory was gone and the room was empty. The soft silver light had shifted to lie directly over the sacred stone.

The sight depressed the old Gryphon for now he remembered why he had come in the first place. Proto could not help but feel a little deflated. His wings drooped over his back, the ragged tips of his feathers dusting the floor. He let out a deep breath to restore what little happiness he had left over from the Living Memory.

He sat up on his haunches, wincing from the extra pressure on his hips. His talons clicked on the stone as his eyes studied the runic text. He tapped the innermost talon of his right paw on the line that started the blood promise passage. Shifting his right paw, he uncovered the crack in the stone. It started out at a thin point, tracing down through the passage until it widened into a small crevice. He reached for the crevice and was immediately overwhelmed with pain and sorrow.

Proto was enveloped in a dark and terrible vision that threatened to tear his soul from his body. He was paralyzed and unable to flee. His wings were pinned against him. A scream formed in his chest but he could not open his beak to shout. His eyes burned so fiercely that he wanted to claw them out of his head. A white foreboding light raced towards him in the blackness.

Suddenly Proto was thrust into a hazy scene, unable to discern any color but that of crimson blood. It was splashed about the wooden floor. At least he thought it was wood for he could feel nothing but pain and fear. To his right, an ornate desk lay overturned and cracked in half, blood smeared across the broken pieces. Proto then managed to command his eyes to follow the smear of blood to his left. In a large pool, shards of glass were spread out in a cruel pattern.

"No! Please! Why are you doing this?" cried a voice that seemed to come from a distant place.

Proto forced his head to turn to look straight ahead. Laying on the floor against the opposite wall was a man in utter panic. The left side of his face was so swollen that his eye could barely open. Black strands of hair clung to his forehead. Bright red blood poured from the corner of his mouth, soaking his chin. His clothes were torn to shreds and hung on his broken frame. His one good eye had no luster to it.

It was only then that the Gryphon saw the hulking dark shadow that loomed over the man. It lurched forward like a predator about to pounce on its prey. The man's breathing was ragged as his chest shuddered from the effort. In his one eye, the look was pleading. But the dark form betrayed no hint of granting mercy. It brandished a wicked blade in its right hand, its left hand twisted into a set of monstrous claws.

He fought with every fiber of his being to jump to the broken man's defense. But Proto could do nothing more than look on with horror. A scream battled its way into his throat as Proto started to recognize who the man was: Shiloh Silvanus.

Shiloh looked nothing like his noble self. His face no longer held the constant expression of kind but firm rule. His grim mouth was now contorted into a wordless scream. He looked small and insignificant before the dark form. He was deathly afraid. His limbs lay limp and Proto realized that he had no chance to defend himself. Shiloh Silvanus was going to die.

"No!" Proto shouted with all the force he had in his body. The dark vision disappeared in an instant and Proto found himself in the cavern clutching the stone. His chest heaved with shock and despair as he struggled to gain control over himself. "No..."

Proto fell to the floor in a heap, sobbing uncontrollably. He keened the death song of the Gryphons when he was able to catch a breath. The grief stricken whistles and shrills bounced off the stone walls. He tried to grab at the floor in a meager attempt to gain control over his emotions. But he could not let go of the fear that he felt from Shiloh.

"Lord Avis!" came a distant shout that was shortly followed by rushing footfalls. But Proto Avis did not hear that cry of concern. All he heard was a dark voice laughing.

VISIONS OF THE PAST

He had not visited Umbra in countless years but Kaiser Adonis found himself on the outskirts of the city's wide territory, staring at three shapeless stones. Umbra was the Shadowborn's great northern city and Cross' rival in importance. Unlike the capital, Umbra sat upon no hill and no wall of rock encapsulated it. A thick high stone wall had been built at the opening of the mountain valley with two looming fortresses, each situated at the natural mountain gateway. No building was taller than the northern wall and there was no farmland beyond it. Only a small rounded hill dared to exist outside of Umbra.

Kaiser had seen this area in its heyday as the last wall between the Darklands and the land of his people. The stones sat upon a grassy knoll that faced the direction of the Daylord's Shadow Mirror as sentinels to the battle that occurred long ago. Kaiser remembered that epic battle against the minions of the Darklands as a flood of Demons raced across the plains towards him. Yes, he once was a warrior but that was a long time ago and Kaiser did not dwell on the thought any longer than necessary. He looked up at the Shadow Mirror, seeing a subtle ripple of energy across its invisible surface.

The three stones had been worn down to almost nothing by time and the elements. The names carved into their surface were barely visible. While it may have been his duty and responsibility as a son of the Adonis bloodline to maintain the graves, Kaiser cared nothing for the bodies beneath the ground. His father had refused a divine legacy. His mother was just as deluded for following her husband. His younger brother had been a complete waste of blood and flesh. Kaiser's lip curled in a sneer as the cool air brushed by in a calm breeze. He hated them. He absolutely hated them. They had to die.

His father Cian Adonis was a legendary general and second in command to the even more famous Shadow Night Silvanus. He was a natural warrior with his broad shoulders and muscular build that hid a deadly speed. Kaiser was born with his father's height and inherited the slight frame of his mother. But he gained his father's powerful gaze that demanded respect and obedience from others. It was naturally expected of him as Cian's firstborn to follow in his footsteps and live in watchful guardianship over the northern reaches. He had been trained as a master swordsman and expert bowman. But being a soldier was not what Kaiser had wanted to be. Especially after he had learned of his family's true nobility.

"I am meant for greater things, Cian," Kaiser stated in a subtle growl. He was not about to acknowledge the decayed husk of flesh as his father. He had not called him Father in many years and only called him by his first name.

The wind whistled in a shrill voice as it blew about the plain between the mountain ranges. It was if the Spirit of his dead father was trying to answer him and ask why he was here. Kaiser scoffed at the imagined reply. He imagined his father's anger and hurt at the betrayal. The last words Cian had said replayed in Kaiser's mind as if they were newly spoken. It was one thing he had never forgotten.

"Oh my son! Is this my fate for doing the unthinkable? Am I to blame for driving you to this? I once thought that my greatest mistake was not telling the truth but it seems now I have unleashed something more terrible on the world than a simple lie," Kaiser quoted, mocking his father's dying words. "Poor witless soul... as if I even cared about your fate. I am an Adonis and you knew that. We are the blood of Begin Anu and we are more deserving of power than anyone. I **am** more deserving and soon I will have everything," Kaiser gloated as he threw his head back to laugh.

The sound echoed in the valley and bounced off the mountains. A flock of foraging crows rose up in a flurry of feathers to escape the tall grass. Kaiser chuckled as he imagined that they were trying to escape the danger he represented. A smirk played on his lips as he considered tapping into his deep reserves of Spirit energy to immolate the birds. It would be simple and easy. Kaiser started to raise his left hand, drawing on the pulse of his heartbeat to generate an electrical shockwave. Black sparks of energy rolled and twisted around his hand. He quickly twisted his body around and threw his hand forward, releasing the Shadow Shock attack. It sizzled quickly through the air and struck the crows. Soon all that was left was a rain of black feathers descending on to the burnt grass.

"You see, Cian! I am more powerful than Shadow Night! I am more daring!" Kaiser shouted as he whirled around to face the gravestones. He spat at them. "I am greater than the Daylord! I am a god!"

Kaiser threw off his cloak and pointed accusingly at his father's grave. A pair of black leather pants and a vest hugged his slim body. His sinewy arms showed no hint of fat. He curled back his finger as he considered what to say. There were so many things he wanted to say to his father, mother, and brother. Cian was the only one he had actually spoken to of the three when he had killed them. He had killed his brother first by slitting his throat from ear to ear before carving out his heart. He was not so merciful to his mother as he ripped her heart out with his bare hand, having her see him as her killer. Kaiser saved his brutality for his father. He pointed his finger again.

"You claimed that the truth mattered! But how was it right that you kept such a secret from your son! By right, I am the heir of Begin Anu, the noble and strong Farlander whom Terra worships! I deserve so much more than the pathetic ideal you thought to make for me!" Kaiser stomped around the hilltop. "Even you cowered before me in the end when you realized that your fatherly love could not heal the wounds you created!"

A swift and strong kick split Cian's headstone in half. Kaiser stood staring at the pieces, fuming. He clenched his fists tightly until his knuckles were white. His vision was blinded by the memory of his father's execution. It was almost as if he was reliving the moment by speaking his father's dying words. His hand gripped the cold steel of an invisible sword. Muscles tightened in anticipation and sweat beaded on his brow. His bones ached from the tension in his body. Usually when his anger got this bad, Rache was there to draw him back to reality. But he had forbidden his Demon servant from following him. This moment with his family was his and his alone.

Suddenly his rage exploded into a terrible storm of long pent up emotion. He slammed his fists on the stone, crushing it from the force of his strength. Kaiser then spun around and smashed his mother's gravestone before turning his attention to that of his brother's. In a final roar so loud that his throat cracked, Kaiser's rage manifested into a Shadow Wolf phantasm that blew through the mess. It stomped and tore with equal fury until it dissipated as Kaiser's rage calmed down. His breath was haggard and raspy as he looked over the rubble. Smoke rose in twisting curls of black.

"See what you made me do?" Kaiser asked quietly as his vision cleared. "I had to kill you. I had to destroy you so I could be free. You understand right?"

Kaiser ran his fingers through his short black hair in an attempt to smooth it down into a more controlled style. A layer of dust dimmed its usual luster and shine. He stumbled back a few steps before falling to his knees.

"I am not sorry for what I did and will be doing. It is all for the right reasons," Kaiser started to say before a long shadow covered him. "Go away, Demon," he growled.

"And miss the show? I think not," Rache answered with a grin, hands on his hips.

Kaiser sneered. "I told you not to follow me," he said as he grabbed his cloak and pulled it back on to his lean body. His muscles ached from the residual tension.

"Well you keep me on a short leash, Boss. Besides, someone has to watch your back," the flame haired Demon replied.

"You never listen," Kaiser growled as he pushed himself up to his feet.

Rache looked down at the broken stone, nudging a piece with his foot. "You might not have liked the guy but he did ultimately give me life... with his own, of course."

"Three hearts for one. A vessel of blood for the dark soul. A shadow of ancients to guide and the will to control. A shield to be born until death comes again. Power rise, life dies to be born again..." Kaiser aimlessly chanted, the horizontal scars on his throat pulsating with the timbre of his voice.

Rache shivered as the words of Kaiser's chant went straight to his core. It felt as if death crept back into his long limbs. The chant was an old one that came from the dark days. How Kaiser came across it and had the power to use it was beyond him. He had yet to ask him as he was too afraid of Kaiser's wrath to invoke the entire chant. Invoking the whole chant again would send him back to the endless Spiral.

There was a long silence before Kaiser spoke again, the chill of the invocation gone. "I cut my own neck and shed my precious blood to bring you forth. But what's done is done and there is still a great deal to do. Let us get back to Cross before my enemies think to get the better of me."

"I forgot that you were from Umbra. Seems fitting," Rache commented as he looked about the valley, seeing the sprawling town in the distance.

Kaiser was beginning to feel annoyed by Rache's presence. He pointed towards the western mountain range, drawing the Demon's attention to a massive fortress that was perched on the rock. "If you are dying to know, I was born in that fort during a lunar eclipse over a thousand years ago. Got any more questions about my childhood?" he snapped angrily.

"Nope. I'm good," Rache said with amusement. His pale skin glowed in the low light as he crossed his muscular arms.

THE DANGEROUS KAISER ADONIS

The room had been untouched for many days following the murder that had occurred among the furniture and finery. It still smelled of blood and death though the gore on the floor had long since been scrubbed away. The air was stale and a fine layer of dust covered the furniture. Sunlight poured in through the windows, dust particles floating in the transparent beams. The dark red curtains smelled musty and old. The gold detail in the chairs and lounge was faded and the maps on the wall were curling in their gold frames. Kaiser dragged his fingers along the edge of the ornate ebony wood desk, frowning at the state of uncleanliness. Looking up at the high ceilings, he expected to find cobwebs in the corners. He grumbled as he rubbed his dust covered finger tips on his pant leg. His freshly shined leather boots creaked as he stepped slowly around the room.

"What are you doing here?" a gruff old voice asked flatly.

Kaiser turned to see Madhuri Coba, High Commander of the Armed Forces, coming in the door. His distasteful frown quickly became an unassuming smile. But his eyes narrowed with simmering malice. "Forgive me, Commander Coba, but I was inspecting this office for my Lord Aku." He slid open a drawer and fingered through the contents.

Madhuri scoffed as he closed the door behind him. "You are not wanted here," he growled, looking like a lion in a man's body with a thick collar of white fur around his neck. His silver armor gleamed in the low light.

Kaiser closed the drawer and tapped the top of the desk. "I have a right to be here. Cross is my home now."

"You are the most hated Shadowborn in Cross. I can't imagine anyone that wants you here. If it weren't for what you pretend you can do," Madhuri growled with disgust.

"So I am more than just a beautiful piece of art to the people. I am wanted for my brain too," Kaiser mused with a grin on his face.

Madhuri growled. "You arrogant," he stopped himself from uttering a curse. "You may think that you can threaten and beat those who disagree with you but I won't allow it anymore. And I believe the Lord Aku will agree with me like his dear father did."

"You are so deluded to think that the Lord Aku will listen to you. I am here on the Lord's command and I do not intend to fail in his service like you did for my dear Lord's father," Kaiser replied, accusation laced in every syllable. He continued to pace around the office, studying the details with a careful eye. His gaze went up and down bookcases, passed over paintings and other extravagant details. "My, my. Not a frugal Lord," he muttered to himself.

"You dare accuse me of a failure to serve the Shadowlord? Unlike you, I am most loyal to the throne," Madhuri fumed, his fists clenched, his bearded jaw locked in barely contained fury.

Kaiser eyed himself in a mirror, running a hand over his slick black hair. He turned to face the old general. "Is the High Commander responsible for the security of the throne or am I mistaken?" he asked.

"And are you not an expert of Demon knowledge? How would you explain the presence of one in Cross?" Madhuri asked in retort.

"What Demon? I have not seen one," Kaiser replied, feigning innocence.

"Don't lie to me," the general snarled, fingers twitching to grab the sword at his side.

Madhuri had heard from secret channels that many Shadowborn in the poorer section of the city had fallen ill to an unknown disease. The illness reminded him of Demon victims who had survived an attack. He himself had investigated and spoke to the survivors who told him of faded memories. All of the details they gave him said Demon but he felt that there was something missing. And every time he tried to go back to speak to the survivors, they had been found brutally slaughtered. He was going to go straight to the Council but Nuru's murder halted everything. How could he burden his Lord when tragedy had just happened. And before he could attempt to speak to Shiloh, he too fell victim. Madhuri had wondered if knowledge of the attacks doomed everyone he wanted to tell. He strengthened his resolve in the aftermath and had sought out Kaiser, hoping the mysterious predator would kill the hated Shadowborn.

Kaiser latched his hands behind him and puffed out his chest. He appeared to hesitate before a pompous grin stretched across his face. "I claim nothing in regards to this knowledge you think that I have. Perhaps the Daylord's Shadow Mirror around the Darklands is not as solid as we have been led to believe."

"Insulting the Daylord is an offense against the Shadowlord, Adonis," Madhuri warned. "You know of their long history."

"Indeed I do since I am old enough to remember those days," Kaiser said with a nonchalant wave of the hand. "Even so, the Shadowlord's own soldiers should have been able to protect him from every danger."

The affront to the old soldier's pride was palpable, but Madhuri quickly gathered himself. "Even so, Master Adonis. How can I be certain that you did not let this Demon in yourself. That you are not responsible for the attacks on the Shadowborn people. Considering your vast knowledge and your sterling reputation."

Kaiser smirked. "Maybe. Maybe not. The attacks are sad but there is nothing I can do to stop them. Only my Shadowlord knows the answer to all of your questions."

Madhuri slid his left hand to the hilt of his sword. "You have no command here nor are you welcome. Get out or I will be forced to remove you myself." He followed Kaiser's sauntering path around the edge of the room and gritted his teeth.

"Why? I brought Lord Aku back from the dead at Lord Shiloh's command. I seem to remember receiving his deepest gratitude and favor," Kaiser coolly answered. "And if you think that Zoras is in command of this realm, you are wrong. He does not have the right to push those of noble nature out of Cross just because he disagrees with them."

"Noble nature? How many times have you been accused of terrible acts? How you continue to save yourself even from the Lords of Crossroads is beyond me. You know what I mean, traitor! You all but admitted your part in Lord Shiloh's murder. And I will not forget what you did to my son Akakios! You are the reason he is dead!" Madhuri shouted in anger. His grip tightened on his sword hilt.

Kaiser chose a high backed velvet chair and sat down, leaning back. He patted his palms on the arm rests. "Contrary to popular belief, your son sealed his fate with his doomed plans for war."

"Plans that you gave him!" Madhuri roared. "If I hadn't been at the borders, I would have stopped everything and thrown you in prison myself! And what of his poor son? He fled because of you!"

Kaiser waved a chiding finger back and forth. "Tsk, tsk, Commander. I thought better of you than to accuse the Shadowlord's humble servant. As for the bastard," he said as he shrugged his shoulders.

The general fought every ounce of his being not to draw out his sword. "You call yourself a good servant?! You who lack any of the qualities of a true servant of the Shadowlord?! You who does not even know the meaning of loyalty, respect, or honor?"

"And yet I am still here so I must be doing something right," Kaiser pointed out, gesturing with his hand towards his presence. He hooked his right leg over the arm of the chair, sliding into a reclined position.

Madhuri took a deep breath to calm himself. "Your presence is no longer needed nor desired and if you even think to step foot in this city again, you will be executed on sight. Let the Daylord find you and wield the executioner's blade if you linger too long."

Kaiser chuckled before snapping his fingers. His masked servant was at his side, slipping out of the shadows like a terrible phantom in tattered tan clothes. He turned to speak with him. "My dear servant, please let this soul know what happens to those who presume to threaten me."

"Would you prefer his head or his heart, Master?" the servant asked as he eyed Madhuri hungrily. The gleam of his gaze burned deep into the Commander's core and Madhuri shook with unrestrained fear.

"Hmm, surprise me," Kaiser replied after some thought.

Madhuri drew his sword and pointed it forward. The servant, Kaiser's unknown aid, caused an unnatural fear to well in his breast. The servant was tall enough to look him in the eyes but thin enough to appear easy to break. "Touch me and I will kill you."

Kaiser gestured towards his servant with an absentminded wave of his hand. "Go ahead and try. You will just end up like the rest."

The masked servant chuckled darkly as he sauntered forward. His steps were careful and calculating as he assessed the Commander's strength. Madhuri stepped back, keeping his sword pointed forward while he contemplated pulling out his hidden knife as a second weapon to defend himself. He laid his left hand on the knife's secreted sheath on his thigh. The servant did not appear to notice the small gesture.

"Oh be done with it. I have a funeral to attend," Kaiser snapped.

Madhuri was thrown back, dropping his sword as Kaiser's servant pounced on him. He lost his grip on his hidden knife as well, pinned down by the overwhelming strength of Kaiser's servant. The lean bodied creature was surprisingly heavy. The servant leaned in close as his clawed hand slid up to Madhuri's neck. Bile rose up in the back of his throat as he smelled the unmistakable scent of death and fire. With his free hand, he ripped back the servant's mask.

"Why hello, Commander," the servant said with a smirk and wink of an eye.

"Rache!" Madhuri said with horror, recognizing the Demon's trademark pale skin and blood red hair.

"Bet you thought I was dead," Rache teased as his fingers moved to grip Madhuri's throat. He briefly stroked his jawline with a finger.

Kaiser got up from his seat as Rache bent down to sniff the throbbing vein in Madhuri's neck. He patted his servant on the back. "Commander Coba, perhaps it is your fault that your bloodline is at an end. As soon as I find the bastard," he chuckled before continuing. "Let's just say he will be no more." Kaiser then stepped back.

Madhuri had no chance to respond as Rache sank his sharp white teeth into his neck. The Commander struggled to break free as Rache gripped his shoulders tightly, snapping his collar bone into pieces. The world around him began to darken as his vision faded. His eyes fluttered before closing, a cold he had never felt spreading through his body.

Ignoring Rache as he feasted on Madhuri's blood, Kaiser walked over to the door and opened it a crack. He gestured towards his two secret guards. They quickly stood at attention. "Clean up this disgusting mess once my servant is finished."

"Yes, Lord Kaiser," the guards said in unison.

Kaiser then pulled out a sealed letter from within his robes. He laid it carefully into the hand of the taller guard. "I want you to take this to Morin Win. I have a mind to make good on a promise."

"Yes, Lord Kaiser," the tall guard stated with a bow. He nodded to his partner before taking off down the hall.

Kaiser pulled himself back inside the office just as Rache rose up, wiping the blood from his mouth with the back of his hand. He licked his fingers, smacking his lips.

"Disgusting," Kaiser grumbled. "Did you learn anything from his blood memories?"

Rache sneered as he stepped away from Madhuri's mangled body. "His memories were clear but sealed. I will need time to sort through them. At least you cared enough to give me a soldier to bleed dry and not a rebel messenger."

Kaiser slid back into the velvet chair. "Then you mistake me for someone else if you think I allowed you to kill him for more than information."

Rache bent down and picked up Madhuri's sword, tossing it between his hands and sweeping the blade in wide arcs. He then broke the weapon over his knee and dropped the pieces to the floor. He glanced back at Madhuri's broken form. "He wasn't much of a soldier."

"He wasn't a Silvanus," Kaiser replied as he stared forward. "But," he raised a finger to keep Rache from interrupting him. "What would that make his dear grandson?"

"The bastard?" Rache asked.

Kaiser nodded. "He is among the last living members of the Silvanus bloodline. Unlike his relatives, he has seen me for what I am and has not lingered around long enough to be killed."

"Thank you."

Kaiser sneered. "As I was saying, Ryder is unique as he is the last Silvanus that is a pure Shadowborn. Aku's brat is half Earthborn. Now does it seem right that a half blood is set to inherit the throne?"

"Oh you know my opinion," Rache drawled. "I'm just here to watch."

"Right, you are here to watch me do all of the hard work. Well sit back and watch like a good Demon. I am just getting started," Kaiser responded with a smug tone.

THE FUNERAL OF SHILOH SILVANUS

It was a somber day in the grand city of Cross, capital of the Shadowborn and home to the illustrious Silvanus family. The sky was pale blue with no clouds in sight. A cold breeze wafted down from the stone hills as white petals rained down from the mountain trees. A sad funeral song rang out in the hallowed valley. The chime ringer was stoic and practiced in his movements, swinging his arm out and back in to strike the bronze chime he carried in his right hand. Sobs and pleading cries started to escape the gathered mourners, dressed in black funeral robes. The robes were lined with a thin strip of silver, clasped at the throat by a crescent moon broach.

People watched anxiously as the first walkers of the procession rounded the corner and appeared into view at the top of the winding mountain path. They kept their hoods up to veil their tears while hands were clasped together in unity. Many of the women and children also held a single white lily in their hands. Mothers and fathers whispered to their charges, answering inquiring questions in low voices. Soldiers stood at salute amongst the crowd in full war regalia with one hand raised to their right eye and a pike in their left hand. Even the pet wolves who sat at their masters' sides kept their heads bowed as owls of all shapes and colors perched in the tree branches.

First into view was the banner bearer, a look of stern unreadable thoughts on his face as his hands were gripped tight around a pole of ebony wood. The banner he carried was the

Silvanus family crest, a silver wolf head on a field of black on the front side and silver on the back side. Two long swords were crossed behind the head. The bearer was dressed in shining chain mail beneath a black leather cuirass with pauldrons that wrapped tight around his shoulders. He wore a helm topped with a small crest of wolf fur that was as silver as the armor. Upon his breast was a crescent moon open to the sky, a trio of stars drawn between its points.

Behind him walked a man with a sheathed sword held in his hands before him. A hood was drawn up around his face while wisps of his dark hair floated lightly along the edges. A single tear wavered at the corners of his eyes. There was no embellishment of thread or jewels on his person except for a silver crescent moon pendent hanging from his neck. Here was the aged Kader Erebus, Lord's Chancellor to the throne and servant to the Silvanus family in all matters of wisdom and guardian to many ancient secrets and legends. He commanded an intense amount of respect for his intelligence and kind nature.

The sword he carried in his hands was an old weapon known at the Silvanus Moon Blade. It was made with a silver steel blade, sharp and clean except for a small gold engraving close to the cross guard. The cross guard had a large white moonstone surrounded by the upturned points of a gold crescent. The hilt was of black leather that molded to each bearer's grip. The gold pommel was carved into a snarling wolf's head. He would use this symbol of office to name the royal successor.

The funeral bier of Shiloh Silvanus passed the onlookers as it was carried by six masked Sabers, soldiers in direct service to the Silvanus family. Shiloh was dressed in his finest war armor. No mark from the murderer's blade could be seen as it was cleverly hidden beneath his silver cuirass and mail. His arms were crossed on his chest, fists tight. A sable cloth trimmed with silver was laid up to his elbows covering the rest of his body. Onlookers turned their focus to his serene face, eyes closed and hair neatly arranged beneath the grand wolf head helm. Shiloh looked like he was sleeping peacefully but his chest did not rise and fall with expected breath.

Next came one that everyone looked upon once the bier of Shiloh passed by: Aku Silvanus, the only son and child of Shiloh and the successor to the abandoned throne. Those on the right side of the path strained to look upon the left side of his face while those on the left side cringed at the sight. Two scars ran jagged from above his left eye down to his jawline, a cruel reminder of the Demon blade that had killed Shiloh. The scars pulled tight against his skin and mangled eye socket. No one dared to imagine what the eye hidden behind the thin lid now looked like.

He walked with heavy steps and bore a listless expression on his face. His funeral garb was a heavy black cloak with no embellishment. His black hair was stringy and messy. With his one good eye, Aku looked forward towards the turn that would take the procession to the hallowed tombs. He was sickly and pale though no one would admit it to him or themselves.

Behind him and almost forgotten walked Aku's own son, Onyx, a boy of twelve years. Unlike his father, Onyx wept openly for his grandfather and could barely hold the stance of a Prince in waiting. He did his best not to cry out as tears ran down his cheek. Every so often, he took the edge of his sleeve to wipe his eyes as the procession continued. He tripped once on the hem of his robe, stumbling into Aku's back. Aku reached a stiff hand to settle his son before walking on. Onyx quickly gathered himself and followed his father, wishing his mother could have been there with him.

Nuru, wife of Aku and mother of Onyx, had been a sweet and gentle presence to all who met her. She had soft, shining dark chestnut hair and silver eyes that showed love and joy. She was considered the perfect match to Aku's more brash and aggressive nature. Though her father Oren, then Lord of the Earthborn, hated to give her up, Nuru knew her duty and had fallen in love with a Prince she considered to be noble and dashing. Many saw the union of Aku and Nuru as a great event, bringing together for the first time the Silvanus and Kano bloodlines. Her compassion for others was only topped by the love for her son. When Onyx had been born, there was cause for even greater celebration. But when she died, it was a time of great sorrow.

The remainder of the procession consisted of the rest of the Sabers, the elite guard led by Sai Parahazur. Sai was a tall large muscled warrior with a harsh expression, his stance threatening and imposing. He looked frequently at Aku, his new liege Lord by the death of Shiloh. Behind the contingent of Sabers walked the members of the noble houses, each member holding a small banner emblazoned with the crest of their respective houses.

Kaiser Adonis, last scion of his house, walked at the end of the procession. He held his head up high and did not carry a banner. His hands were pressed together before him like the point of a blade. As he passed, the crowd eyed him warily. It was well known that he dabbled in Blood Magic. He also had grown up on the borders of the Darklands as the son to a general. No one trusted him and yet his knowledge of Demons was highly valued. He was also one of the oldest Shadowborn at court by many years. At close to eleven hundred years old, Kaiser was ancient and proud of it.

The mood grew more somber and grim as the procession descended down the hill before making the final turn towards the hallowed tombs. The procession halted in a glade, facing an open tomb in the face of the rock wall as the noble houses assembled in a big circle. The banner bearer went to stand at the left side of the opening, fixing the banner pole in the dirt. Kader took his place at the right side of the tomb opening, still holding the sword in his hands. The bier was carried into the darkness of the tomb by the six Sabers who then came out unmasked. At this silent signal, the other Sabers unmasked and knelt in a circle around Aku and Onyx who had stepped forward. Everyone within sight knelt, bowing their heads. The bronzed chime was finally silenced as Kader then moved to stand in front of the tomb, Sai taking his place on the right side.

"In this hour we are moved to lay to watchful rest Shiloh, son of Sin who was the second son of Shadow Night Silvanus. He was taken from us by the powers of the Darklands. Be it now that we call to the everlasting power of the Immortal Truth to give us peace and hope in this time of sorrow. Our hearts call for revenge for the slaying of our leader and the maiming of his son, but we will not seek it thus while Shiloh's Spirit has not been touched by the light of the moon. Tonight he will make the journey to the Spirit World," Kader stated with a soaring yet restrained voice. He looked towards Aku and nodded. Aku shuffled forward within arm's reach of Kader. "Son of Shiloh, you have suffered much in your days and bear a reminder of the attack which took your father's life much too soon. With your remaining sight may you look to the days to come and lead the Shadowborn as your father had before you."

Aku let out a visible breath that seemed like relief as he took the sword from Kader's offering hands. He looked ready to drop it before he found some hidden strength from within. His right hand gripped the hilt tightly as he paused for a short moment. He then quickly drew the sword out, the blade gleaming. He turned it to admire its make, unmarred by many years of war. At a gesture by Kader, Sai stepped forward and took the sheath from Aku, standing off to the side again. Kaiser moved in closer, keeping his eyes on Aku as his hands flexed.

"By taking this blade, the sword of your father and of your forefathers, it passes into your keeping. Use it well for the honor of your family and your people. Let it not fall astray and dishonor the words of the Immortal Truth," Kader said before he quickly looked over at Kaiser who hid his hands in his sleeves. "Tonight, we shall honor the life of Shiloh and lift up Aku as his successor," he then stated, directing his voice towards the crowd.

The crowd looked to see Aku turn around towards Onyx,

who hurriedly wiped his tears away as his father looked upon him. He lightly laid the tip of the blade to Onyx's forehead. "I name my son, Onyx, to be the heir that follows me and that shall serve me as I served my own father," Aku said loudly before his voice cracked.

Onyx nodded his own acceptance while the crowd did as well. In his heart, he had a vague idea of what his acceptance meant. It had been stressed to him time and again that not only was he a Prince of the Shadowborn, he was a direct descendent of Shadow Night Silvanus who was a champion of the Immortal Truth. Growing up, he didn't really understand it as he was more curious about the world than in ruling it. Now, he had to step up and assume his birthright. He just wished it had come at a different time.

As Aku took his spot facing the crowd and began his eulogy in a shaking voice, the six bier carriers began the effort to push the stone door over the opening. They moved in quiet unison as the huge boulder slid into place. Each Saber took turns to face the tomb, bow their heads and cross their hearts as a symbolic gesture to ward off Spirits. They then turned around and lined up together with hands latched behind their backs. Kader pulled Onyx to the side as he saw this as Aku's moment with the Council and the people watching. They knelt beside each other while Aku continued on, sounding tired. He skimmed the crowd again to find Kaiser, hands twisting subtly before him as if he was a puppet master pulling on strings. His eyes narrowed.

"Dry your tears now, my Prince. Everyone is watching," Kader whispered, his hood hiding his moving mouth. "Trust your strength and your heart for you alone can rule who you are and who you will become," he added in a softer tone.

Onyx turned as though to face Kader with a question on his lips but Kader quickly corrected him, silently urging him to keep his face forward. While Aku reflected on the works of his father left undone, Onyx sifted through his memories of Shiloh, using the pleasant thoughts to comfort him. He focused on one that was recent, a special moment between grandfather and grandson. His mother had been laid to rest in the Shadowborn tombs and Shiloh had brought him to a small pond that lay within the palace gardens. There he had taught him a minor custom to honor the dead: placing a white blossom upon a leaf and floating it on the water. This Onyx intended to do to honor the man who had taught him so many small and special things.

THE LIGHT IN THE DARK

At the conclusion of his shaky speech, Aku made the formal invitation to the funeral dinner that would be the final celebration of Shiloh Silvanus' life. Kader directed Onyx to his feet, keeping his hands on the boy's small shoulders to steady him while his eyes looked to Kaiser who closely followed behind Aku. He watched as Kaiser laid a hand on Aku's shoulder. The ancient noble whispered a few words before Aku took his arm. Though Kaiser had redeemed himself to Shiloh, Kader still did not trust him. He knew deep in his heart that no one could bring the dead back to life. To him, Aku seemed unsteady and never left Kaiser's side for more than a few minutes. Doubt and worry began to mix with his sorrow.

Onyx remained silent at Kader's side, wanting to speak, to cry out, but not daring to. He instead concentrated on not tripping again on the lengthy hem of his robes, pushing the hood back enough to see properly. As he did, he felt his damp cheek and the red puffy texture of the skin beneath his eyes. He brought his hand forward, seeing a small tear on the end of his finger. Suddenly a small white cloth was shoved into his view and he turned to see Kader's kind eyes.

"Do not feel embarrassed by your tears, young Onyx. Today is a sad day and thus you are allowed to weep," he said in a soft tone. Onyx silently took the cloth and wiped his eyes. "Death may be sad but there is nobility in it as there is also nobility in living."

"Then why do I have to suffer for I see no light in death," Onyx blurted out as he clutched the cloth tightly.

Kader felt himself tear up at the words but gathered himself before he answered. "You are a child, Onyx and death for Immortal kind is a rare but sad thing. Perhaps we are not as long lived as we would like to believe," he started to say as he concentrated on Aku who walked at the front of the departing crowd. "The future is the darkest I have yet seen."

Onyx sighed as he concentrated on keeping his steps firm on the rising path. Before them, the castle walls rose up with royal banners fluttering at half-mast. It was ominous in appearance with its dark stone and candle lit windows. The only measurable sound was the cascading waterfall to the far left of the path. The air was moist as they passed, the path weaving around the grounds towards the main entrance to the private wing.

Soldiers straightened up with salute as Aku passed, gripping their halberds and trying to look unyielding as door guards with unwavering vigil. The great heavy doors that led into the main left hall of the west wing closed behind them, leaving Kader, Onyx, Kaiser, and Aku to walk past the multitude of tapestries and banners. The flickering light of candle chandeliers illuminated the burgundy runner rug. Aku stopped just as the hall opened into a crossroads with pathways leading left and right to other wings and rooms of the palace. He turned around to face Kader, leaning on Kaiser for support.

"Go to your quarters, my son," he said with a weak voice.

Onyx gave Kader a quick concerned look. Kader gave a subtle nod and Onyx then bent into a quick respectful bow towards Aku. He then strode past him, flinching when Aku brushed his shoulder.

Kaiser then turned his full attention on Kader after Onyx departed. This time his eyes spoke with a severe degree of restrained fury.

"I find you to be a poor teacher and influence to Lord Aku's son and heir," Kaiser said with clarity and authority.

"Stop pretending in front of me. I am not as deluded as others," Kader said sternly. "I am only doing as Lord Shiloh wished. I am still the Lord's Chancellor after all," he added with quiet confidence.

"Or so you think," Kaiser smugly replied.

"The Shadowlord and his family may have forgiven you but I have not. Nor will I ever because I have seen the truth of your actions and it sickens me."

Kaiser growled at the response. "By the command of Lord Aku here, I am now the Lord's Chancellor and you will address me as is proper," he snarled and raised a hand to strike Kader.

Kader didn't flinch away as Kaiser expected and his hand

froze in the air. "Oh really? Do the people know what kind of monster you truly are because everything you do goes against the Immortal Truth," Kader stated with the same quiet tone.

Kaiser dropped his hand, laying it on Aku's arm. "I would be careful what you say, Erebus."

"Just because you are an old rusted out sorcerer does not make you worthy of my position. You are not even worthy to serve at the borders as your noble father did," Kader retorted.

"Do be careful who you speak to in that tone," Kaiser warned with a devilish grin. He patted Aku's arm. "I have the ear of the Shadowlord now and I will do whatever he commands." He turned Aku around, putting his back to Kader. "Come, my Lord. You need your rest before the evening feast," he said in a placating tone. "I am most sorry for my behavior. You do forgive me for I was just doing as you commanded?"

"Yes, as I commanded," Aku answered softly as Kaiser led him away.

*****

Kader watched as Kaiser disappeared down the left corridor with Aku on his arm. He contemplated shouting a curse at the noble and had one on the tip of his tongue. Clenching his fists, Kader held back the curse. It would not have been proper of him as the Lord's Chancellor to be seen or heard shouting such street language even if Kaiser had lowered himself to arguing in front of Aku. It perplexed him that Shiloh and Aku seemed oblivious to the true danger that Kaiser presented. Also, his friend Madhuri Coba had disappeared after an encounter with Kaiser according to rebel intelligence. Remembering his duty, he turned and walked down the right corridor to take the stairs that led to his office.

The Commander of the Sabers, Sai Parahazur, was waiting for him outside his office door. His shoulders loosened as he sighed with relief upon seeing Kader.

"Zoras is panicking and I can't get him to calm down," Sai said as they passed into the office.

Kader closed the door and locked it, leaning back against it. "Kaiser has also seen fit to name himself Lord's Chancellor in my place."

Sai threw up his hands. "Are you serious? Can he do that?"

"It is as the Lord Aku commands and so long as Kaiser holds sway over him, we will be fighting an uphill battle," Kader said as he ran his fingers through his hair. "We need a real and true Shadowlord. Kaiser needs to know that he is not invincible."

"Then what has the world been doing for the last

millennium? Did the war actually end with the Immortal Truth or has it been lurking in the shadows?" Sai cried out. "You're my elder. You tell me."

"I am not the one you need to ask. Yes we all know and believe Kaiser is a bad person but I don't think anyone knows that more than Ryder Coba. You do remember it was Kaiser that revealed him as Akakios' bastard to the Council," Kader explained. "Kaiser has a strange interest in Ryder. Perhaps as Akakios' advisor looking out for his child or he has a twisted plot in mind." He shrugged.

"He has an interest in the Silvanus bloodline. I would like to think that as Commander of the Sabers, I know the reason why but I don't."

The argument had been the same for many years. Kaiser was ambitious and very smart with a deep understanding of life close to the Darklands. People both respected and hated him. Even Kader had to admit to himself that he admired Kaiser's fearless nature. But that nature had become scary as the years went on. Kaiser regularly flouted the law with no care of the consequences. If there ever was an example of a terrible Shadowborn, it was him. Even Shadow Night in his final years hated the man but he disappeared after confronting him. Kaiser told everyone that he knew the truth of what happened to Anu and that their beloved leader left in deep despair. But there were those that doubted him and their trust deteriorated from then on. And Kaiser had only gotten worse.

"We need Ryder Coba to come home," Kader said as he leaned against his desk with his back towards Sai. "We need Sage. We need Aday. We need every Silvanus son to come home. We need a Shadowlord."

The Saber immediately became pale. "You speak treason."

Kader brushed him off. "It is not treason to want a Shadowlord powerful enough to stop Kaiser Adonis from taking over. I know that you are a royal purist but we have to consider other options. Who is left strong enough to take that traitor down?" He shrugged his shoulders. "Who would Bane name?"

"I don't pretend to know the Daylord's mind. I don't think anyone alive could chance a guess," Sai replied as he started to relax.

Moving past the tall Saber, Kader rounded his desk and sat down. He opened the long drawer in front of him and pulled out a folded note, handing it to Sai. "Read this."

Sai took the note and opened it up, reading the scribble. "Zoras is crazy," he stated as he crumbled up the paper and tossed it onto Kader's desk. Kader watched it roll to a stop in front of him.

"He isn't a legitimate son and in case you have forgotten, he left Cross over a century ago. No one knows what or why or where with him."

"But you have to admit that it makes sense," Kader reasoned. "Aku is half dead. Onyx is a child but Ryder is a man of experience. Sage can't be found and Aday is half mad."

Sai held up his hands as though to ward off Kader. "Just stop right there. I cannot bear to hear this doubt concerning my Lord and his son."

Kader knew that Sai would react strongly against Zoras' draft. He himself had concerns over what the noble councilor was proposing. But it made a strange and poetic sense to him even if the Commander of the Sabers could not or would not follow through with such a plan. Either way, they needed a warrior like Ryder.

"I'm worried, Sai," Kader admitted after a long silence.

"We all are," came the short reply. "The people are afraid," Sai stopped himself, not wanting to finish his thought.

"Any word on Madhuri's disappearance?"

Sai shook his head. His broad shoulders slumped under an invisible weight. Kader pinched the bridge of his nose, trying to collect his thoughts. Madhuri had been a valuable ally and his absence was felt everywhere. The soldiers had yet to take the new Commander seriously though duty told them it was right. Morin Win, though a capable officer, was not made of the right substance to lead the entire army. He was too ambitious in Kader's eyes. Kader attributed that quality to Morin's relatively low birth and subsequent rise through the ranks.

"Does it even matter anymore?" he asked Sai directly.

"Of course it does! If we don't stop Kaiser now, who knows what terrible things will happen?" Sai said, ready to jump into battle.

"Then we must be prepared."

AND NOW IT BEGINS

Onyx, upon arriving at his bed chambers, shed the heavy black funeral cloak and it fell in a slump around his feet, leaving him in a white linen shirt and dark wool breeches. He stepped over the small mountain of cloth and went over to the armor stand that stood to the left of the glass alcove. The silver plate armor was shimmering from a recent polishing and the leather straps shone a supple brown color. He laid a hand on the cold metal, sighing deeply. Here was a symbol of strength with his family crest emblazoned on the front of the cuirass and yet he felt wounded to the core.

He fell to his knees, suddenly weak and unable to stand. His knees knocked together as he listed to the side. His breath came in ragged succession as his fingers clawed at the floor, trying to grab on to something. Tears welled up in his eyes and a sob escaped his throat, quickly followed by more weeping. He gripped his heart as he was overwhelmed with sorrow and pain. Within a single month, he had lost his mother and grandfather, two of the most important people in the world to him. It was just too much to bear alone.

His mother's last words to him replayed over and over in his mind: "Let me go fetch your father. The sun will do him some good. Stay here with Master Erebus." Onyx shared a care free smile with her before she bounded off away from him.

He remembered how her chestnut hair seemed to float about her shoulders and how bright her eyes were before the memory began to fade, back to the recesses of his mind. The vision grew faint behind his glassy eyes as he laid on the hardwood floor, arms wrapped tight about his stomach.

"Master Erebus wishes to enter," came the voice of the door warden after a polite knock.

Onyx quickly gathered himself, wiping his face as he got to his feet. He ran his fingers through his hair to smooth it and brushed his bangs back from his forehead. He pulled on his shirt sleeves to straighten the fabric. "Enter."

Kader then entered, the hem of his funeral robes brushing against the floor, his arms drawn together within the voluminous sleeves. His expression was one of warm caring with a soft smile. Onyx couldn't help but feel jealous of Kader's control over himself, for throughout his years, he had never seen the Lord's Chancellor display anger or sadness.

"Come with me. The day ends and the full moon rises," Kader said with a bow of the head. "We must pay our last respects to your grandfather."

Onyx was slow to pick up and put on his funeral robes. He did not want to feel the weight of the fabric again. He kept silent as he followed Kader out of his bed chambers, passing through the long hallway to the stone stairs that led into the private courtyard. Door wardens were quick to open the doors that led to the stairs, allowing the diminishing light into the hallway as Kader and Onyx passed by. The doors closed behind them as they descended the outside stairs. Onyx looked over the courtyard, seeing the central fountain that rose up in a tall spray before the water trickled down the statue of a howling wolf. The statue was the centerpiece to a fountain that stretched twenty feet across the yard. The speckled fish in the waters darted about in mock chase and play, hiding beneath floating white blossom water lilies. The long legged wading birds moved slowly in their hunt along the edges, snatching any stray fish in their spear like beaks.

In the air buzzed a multitude of glow bugs as they appeared to float in place, giving the courtyard a mystical appearance. Onyx sighed deeply as he and Kader kept to the stone paths, passing out of the courtyard to the sheltered entrance of the dining hall. The doors were already opened wide with guards on either side who saluted Onyx as he walked by.

The room was bright with shining gold chandeliers and sparkling candlelight. A drum quartet pounded a lively beat as a flute player whistled a playful tune. Servants flitted about with carefully balanced trays, pausing to offer morsels of food and bubbly drinks. With the full moon high in the sky, the celebration was in full swing. Only the most important of Shadowborn society would be in the hall celebrating, members of the Council and the noble houses dominating the crowd. Onyx was led by Kader to where his father was seated, directing him to sit down. Kaiser sat on the other side of Aku with his ever present servant standing behind him. The servant was fully masked and every inch of him was covered in faded tan cloth.

Aku raised a hand to silence the crowd and all turned to face him as he stood. Gripping the arm rests of his chair, he slowly pushed himself up to his feet. His posture was shaky as he steadied himself.

"The full moon rises upon the beginning of life and at its end. The great Spirit Wolf Omu howls a sad song to guide Spirits to their resting place," he began, keeping to the traditional words. "Shiloh, son of Sin, son of the great Shadow Night Silvanus now makes his journey to the realm we dare not travel in life. He is dressed in his finest armor and bears a steady blade to fight in the war against the darkness as we all do. As we all must." His eyes ran across the crowd for a quick moment. "Tonight we celebrate his life, which was taken before his time by our most terrible enemy, a Demon of the Darklands."

Onyx noticed a small flinch in Kader's shoulders when Aku spoke those words and silently made a point of speaking to him once the speech was done. He watched as Kaiser looked up at his father, a wide smile on his face as he clapped. It appeared as if Kaiser's support spurred his father to continue.

"It was a night such as this when my father ascended to the throne with hope and promise. In him was the nobility of his father Sin and the confidence to rule justly. He took the Moon Blade of office, raised it up high and issued a single proclamation: I will start my reign with forgiveness and mercy." Aku placed his right hand over his heart and looked down. "Thus began an age where a Shadowlord became a friend, a mentor and a true leader to his people." Aku brought his gaze back up to look at the crowd. "But he would not want us to cry at his passing. He would want us to celebrate a new beginning. A new era for the Shadowborn people."

"Here, here!" the crowd cheered as they raised their drinking glasses.

Aku managed a shaky smile. "From Shadow Night to Sin to Shiloh to Aku. The Silvanus bloodline remains strong and unbroken. I ask you now for the same love and support you gave to my father as we celebrate his life."

Kaiser was the first to applaud Aku who slumped back into his seat, looking pale.

"Let me be the first to pledge my fealty to the throne once again in sight of all of you," Kaiser said as he stood up and clapped, leading the crowd in a round of applause. "I know that our Lord Aku will lead us well and I intend to serve his throne faithfully. Now the Lord Aku has asked me to lead a moment of silence in remembrance of his father. If all of you would please bow your heads."

As everyone assembled honored the memory of their deceased Lord, the young heir looked out over the crowd. Onyx noticed the absence of the Rokar family and members of Kader's scholarly order save for Master Erebus himself. He particularly noted the absence of his friend, Soja Rokar, a Saber who had recently been assigned as his guard. Onyx did not have time to question the absences as Kaiser started to direct the crowd in the room to a rousing cry of praise for their new Shadowlord. In the ensuing excitement and cheers, Onyx discreetly made his exit.

Onyx snuck back out to the courtyard, his heart troubled by the missing faces. Soja was one of his closest friends and knew how important attendance was to any state event. He sat on the edge of the fountain's stone rim and dipped his fingers into the water, the fish nibbling lightly at his fingertips. He shook the water free and took the large green leaf he had picked up from the ground, cupping it in his hands. When it took to a boat like shape, Onyx sprinkled a handful of white blossoms he had collected inside and set it to float on the water. The fish followed it with curiosity as it gently floated out into a stream of moonlight.

"Goodbye, Grandfather," he said softly and fighting what tears he had left. He felt a strong hand on his shoulder and he slumped in exhaustion from its weight.

"May the light of the moon guide your way, Lord Shiloh," Kader's distinctive voice said as he sat down beside Onyx. He sighed deeply before speaking again. "Your grandfather will watch over you," he added with an encouraging smile and rubbing Onyx's right arm.

Onyx smiled in return though his smile barely had any joy for life in it. Kader continued with his calm pleasant expression before pulling out a small worn leather pouch from within his robes. He then gave it to Onyx who looked at it perplexed.

"What is it?" he asked as he began tugging at the pouch strings. He pulled them free and the pouch lay open in his hand. Within the pouch was an assortment of small items: a wolf's tooth, a small silver crescent moon and two strange items attached to a thin chain.

Kader gestured towards the two items on the chain. "Those are the emblems of your mother's house. That of the Earthborn. The two leaves are the sign of your Uncle Palani and that small crystal sphere is the sign of your mother's status as Princess Royal.

They are precious symbols for the Kano family," he explained.

Onyx sighed as he fingered the items gingerly. "I wish to do what is right and what is expected of me but I can't lead when I don't know how. Those that can teach me are being picked off by Demons of the Darklands. What if you are next?" he asked, sounding more mature than a boy of twelve.

"It is a lot to expect of a child of your age but I sense greatness in you. Perhaps when the time is right, you can go visit your mother's home on an official state visit. The Earthborn valued your mother greatly for her virtue and they would very much like to see you. I can teach you how to conduct yourself as a proper Shadowborn Prince," Kader suggested before chuckling. "I will not let any Demon take me and I shall continue in my role until you decide otherwise."

Onyx was excited at the prospect of visiting Cascade, the capital of the Earthborn. He had yet to travel beyond the borders of the Shadowborn lands. The very idea of such a trip lifted his Spirits. Ever since he was a baby, his mother and grandfather had told him stories of faraway lands with mighty leaders and beautiful surroundings. His father had even told the story of the time he travelled to Cascade to marry his mother and how grand the city was. But the fond memories brought on a new wave of sadness and Onyx felt himself wracked with sobs. He took a few deep breaths to calm himself as he clutched the pouch tightly in his hand.

Kader put his hands on his shoulders. "Have strength. I will teach you what you need to know. You will become a soldier your grandfather would have been proud of and a leader your mother would have loved," he said. "A Shadowlord that Shadow Night himself could have called his equal."

The approaching strong confident gait of Kaiser disrupted the tender moment in an instant. Onyx shoved his gifted pouch into the folds of his robe. Kader stood up, pulling Onyx to his feet. The tension in the air was immediate as Onyx saw not only Kaiser but the new High Commander Morin Win, a lean sharp eyed soldier, and six Sabers flanking them with weapons drawn. This was not a good sign.

"The Lord Aku has issued a new command that I must in my capacity carry out in his name," Kaiser stated with authority.

Onyx felt Kader's strong hand on his shoulder pulling him closer to his side.

Kaiser chuckled. "Did you not hear me or shall I speak louder? Step back."

Onyx looked over at Morin Win who kept a steady hand within sight of the Sabers. "You have no authority over the Sabers.

That command is for Master Parahazur," he interjected, turning everyone's attention to him. He gulped once he saw all of their harsh expressions.

"The Prince is correct," Kader pointed out as he pulled Onyx to him until their sides were touching.

"We all come under the command of Lord Aku and the Sabers will do as he asks," Morin sneered, his left hand twitching in anticipation.

Kaiser smirked. "If you will not go peacefully then I must resort to drastic measures," he said before snapping his fingers. "Arrest him."

"I wouldn't dare," Kader warned, his free hand reaching for the silver crescent hanging from his neck. The Sabers lowered their swords and relaxed their posture. They were a superstitious bunch despite their fearsome reputation. They knew what the crescent could do.

"Commander Win. Take the Prince to his quarters and see that he does not leave until the Lord Aku commands otherwise," Kaiser barked to the lean soldier at his side.

Morin smirked as he stepped forward, snatching Onyx from Kader's grip. Kader lurched forward but the Sabers quickly laid their hands on him, stopping his progress. He struggled in their tight grip as Morin dragged Onyx away, a look of confusion on his face. Kader then returned his attention to Kaiser and summoned up the fiercest snarl he could muster.

"You will regret every breathing moment you have ever had when I reach the Daylord! You would dare arrest me?" Kader roared with accusing fury as he struggled towards the smirking Kaiser.

"If you can even get past the borders unscathed. Well if you can even get out of Cross unscathed. You don't mess with an Adonis, especially me and you certainly do not out maneuver one," Kaiser said with a warning in his voice. He leaned in closer to whisper. "Maybe what they say about me is true but you will not live long enough to find out."

Kader ripped himself free from the Sabers' grip, watching as they reassembled at Kaiser's side. He rubbed his wrists, anger burning within him. "And you will regret the day that you turned your back on the Immortal Truth," he warned in the darkest of tones.

Kaiser scoffed as he watched Kader rush away towards the main hallway of the palace. "As soon as he clears the city walls, kill him," he ordered softly to the Sabers. They drew their free arms across their chests and bowed before splitting off in different directions, following Kader. Kaiser remained in the courtyard, watching the Sabers depart with arms crossed tight. Rache slipped out of the shadows to stand at his side.

"And now it begins," Rache mused with a hungry tone.

*****

Morin was not gentle as he held a tight grip on Onyx's arm, dragging him up the stairs towards his bed chambers. He kept his eyes focused ahead, completely ignoring the boy in hand.

"Let go of me! What is going on?" Onyx ordered as he tried to tear free of Morin's grip but it was unyielding. "I command you to release me!" he shouted as he then attempted to dig his heels. Again his efforts to stop Morin's pace failed.

They reached his rooms and Morin pushed past the door warden, shoving Onyx inside. Onyx fell to the floor, quickly looking back at Morin who stood in the doorway, hand gripping the iron door handle.

"I take orders only from the Shadowlord, not his whelp. You would do well to follow him like a good loyal son," Morin sneered. He then began to pull at the handle.

"No wait! What's going to happen to Kader?" Onyx quickly asked, fearful for his favorite teacher.

Morin threw back his head, laughing loudly. "Kader will be no more and Kaiser Adonis will take his place," Morin snickered before slamming the door closed. The loud clicking sound of the lock followed. Onyx then heard Morin snapping at the door warden to leave immediately, stating he would take over his post until Kaiser said otherwise. The door warden's hurried steps were the last sounds Onyx heard out in the hallway.

For a long agonizing moment, Onyx did not know what to do next or what to think as he remained on the floor, afraid to move. He sat himself up and smoothed out his hair, running his fingers through it. Something very wrong was happening and it wasn't just that his grandfather had been murdered. To him, Kader seemed to be in some sort of trouble. The Rokars were not present at the funeral dinner despite their high position and noble bloodline. He straightened his shoulders and stood up, his sorrow momentarily put aside. He stomped over to the door and knocked on it with his fist to get Morin's attention.

"What?" Morin snapped from the other side.

"I ask for the Commander of the Sabers. Send him to me at once!" Onyx ordered.

He heard Morin chuckle. "He is busy and cannot attend to you," Morin said in a mocking tone.

Onyx frowned and tightened his fists. "I demand to see him

at once!" he shouted as he restrained himself from banging on the door.

"Listen to me, your Royal Highness," Morin sneered. Onyx could see the look of contempt on his face even through the door. "Things are changing around here and until you wear the crown on your head, I see no reason to even continue talking to you."

Morin's behavior was infuriating and Onyx wanted to rip the door open to yell at him for it. He backed away from the door and flung his arms out in pure exasperation. The small pouch that he had hidden in his robes earlier plopped on to the floor beside his feet. Onyx bent down to pick it and stepped over to the stone and glass alcove. Clutching the pouch in one hand, he pulled open the curtains to let in the moonlight before sitting down on the soft cushions on the bench. He leaned back against the window and opened up the pouch. The contents poured into his hand and he fingered them gently.

"Watch over me, Grandfather, for I need your wisdom and your courage now more than ever. I will find out what is going on," Onyx said aloud to himself as he clutched the symbols and chain to his chest.

A TOAST TO GENIUS

"Come and celebrate with me!" Kaiser said as he reclined on the Shadowborn throne and poured himself another glass of wine. He swirled the dark red liquid around, seeming to admire its color before sniffing. He took a sip and puckered his lips. "This fine drink will do you good."

Rache swirled the contents of his glass, watching it spin. He frowned for he was not fond of the fragrant drink. "Why do you and others like this garbage? I find no appeal in it."

Kaiser pushed himself to sit up straight, setting the wine bottle aside. "And yet, you will drink blood. You have your wine and I have mine. Now help me celebrate the culmination of a finely executed plan!" He raised his glass. "A toast to my genius!"

"A little full of our self aren't we?" Rache asked, hesitating to follow suit. He privately smiled behind his cloth mask when Kaiser frowned.

"Either that or it is the wine talking," Kaiser suggested with a smile, leaning back in the seat. "But you have to admit that I did well," he added as he gestured back towards himself.

Rache pulled back his hood and let the cloth drop down to his shoulders. He examined the wine glass in his hand again before quickly downing the drink. He smacked his lips. "And it only took you what, several centuries of lies, bloodshed, and more lies"

"I never claimed to work quickly. Genius takes time. It is so unsatisfactory to rush through and skip the intricacies of manipulation," Kaiser admitted. He watched as Rache stepped forward and put forth his glass for a refill.

"Then I must admire your patience for I certainly have none. The closer I get to my target, the more heated my desire for the kill becomes. Call me beastly if you must so long as I can call you," Rache said before smirking. Kaiser sneered. "Fine then. You are a genius."

Kaiser poured more wine into Rache's glass before the Demon stepped back. "There are a few that recognize the true genius I am and the wisdom I possess. Yet, dear Sin Silvanus thought that quality unworthy and too dark." Kaiser shrugged as if the thought was an inconvenience.

"Let me guess. Musing on old grudges?" Rache inquired.

"I suppose so."

The snap of the torch flames seemed overly loud in the relative silence of the throne room. Rache wanted to look around but found himself staring back at Kaiser. The master of his unholy bond stared back with an expression that appeared calm yet oddly dangerous. Rache shivered.

"Sin was wrong to ignore me and pass me off as nothing more than a lonely scion for a dead house. Well look where it got his house. Crushed under my thumb," Kaiser declared, raising his glass towards Rache. Rache mimicked him and raised his glass, bowing his head.

"I would say more like you the puppet master and them the puppets to dance for your pleasure," Rache suggested.

"Ah yes. My little game. I have to say that I found great success in toying with those who once thought me harmless. I mean, Mali Silvanus should have been a Prince instead of a Princess. She had the ambition to rule and the backbone to do it. Fortunately for me, she saw that I could teach her son the ways of the world," he stated as he poured more wine into his glass, careful not to spill a single drop.

"She was still as soft as any woman when I took her life," Rache commented as he sipped his wine.

"Of course she was! Her son should have been a Princess instead of a Prince but life has a cruel sense of humor for the Silvanus family. It has a cruel sense of humor for the Shadowborn nation," Kaiser exclaimed before drinking a big gulp of the red wine. He smacked his lips. "It is clear to me that the world refuses to see its true strengths and weaknesses. It is my duty to show them the error of their ways."

Kaiser sank down in the chair, glass in his right hand and his left hand rubbing the engraving of the throne arm. The throne room was cold but Kaiser didn't feel the chill in the air. He preferred it when it was empty. He looked about the large room, imagining his family crest on the banners on the walls.

"Why didn't you let me kill Shiloh? You seemed willing enough for me to kill Aku's bride," Rache asked, breaking the silence.

Kaiser let out a deep breath. "Because I wanted Shiloh to die seeing his son wield the killing blade and Iztal is easier to command in a possession for however short a time," he answered as he set his empty wine glass down by the bottle at his feet. "Imagine being a father about to draw his last breath and looking into the eyes of his flesh and blood. The horror of such truth."

Rache watched as Kaiser chuckled softly to himself, privately reliving some distant memory. "You enjoy what you do, don't you?" Kaiser nodded and smirked. "Good, because otherwise you would be quite boring," Rache said before drinking the rest of his wine.

"In the matter of a month, I have managed to guide this nation into my hands with a puppet Lord and a child Prince. Once they are gone, who is left to rule but myself?" Kaiser said as he settled into the seat.

"Sage Silvanus or perhaps even your ridiculous grandson if you could manage to control him for more than a minute," Rache pointed out.

"You know that I hate it when you state the obvious," Kaiser growled, clutching the arm rests tightly. "I have not forgotten Sage in all my years nor have I ignored my dear grandson. Stupid fool of a boy. I provided for his rise to greatness and how does he thank me? By spitting in my face and that of the grand legacy I so carefully crafted for him."

Rache lifted an eyebrow in question. "Oh mighty Lord Adonis. I thought that you were a master of manipulation. Do my ears deceive me? Have you admitted that you can't control your own bloodline?"

Kaiser twisted his face into a dangerous snarl. "You are not privy to my every thought no matter the strength of our bond."

Rache bent down low into a mocking bow, swinging his arms out to the side. "Oh gracious Lord Adonis, I am most honored to..." A glass hit him in the head and he stood up frowning.

"Mock me again and I'll kill you myself. Then I can summon a better less mouthy Demon in your place," Kaiser warned. "Waste of a good glass," he muttered under his breath as he picked up the wine bottle and drank directly from it. "What do you know of Aday Silvanus?"

Rache laughed. "Him? I wouldn't waste your time with someone who can't be trusted."

"I trust you and you are practically the ultimate in things not to be trusted," Kaiser pointed out. "What do you know?"

"He has long been hiding in the Mortal lands so he is someone else's problem and not mine," Rache replied as he crossed his arms tightly. "Why should I care about him anyway? He is insane and certainly no longer worth your attention."

"So long as he lives, he is worth my attention. I may still have a use for him. If not, well, you know what to do," Kaiser explained.

Rache smirked, the low light casting sharp shadows on his pale face. "And there in lies my genius."

THE ESCAPE

Kader rushed about his living quarters, a sparsely decorated room with a single bed and nightstand, stuffing what precious items he could quickly find into a knapsack. He paused for a moment, counting out what he had left to find on his hand before continuing his frantic packing. His life was in danger; that much he knew if Madhuri's disappearance was any indication of what Kaiser would do to him. He cursed as his unsettled mind tried to sift through his plan of escape in the midst of his unrest. It was something he had planned for when Kaiser returned to favor but he did not account for the need to act on it so suddenly. There was still so much that he needed to teach Onyx about his role and the facts of the world. He collapsed back to sit on his bed, rubbing his temples. His room felt like it was closing in on him as his heart pounded in his chest like a drum.

The worry that Kaiser was going to kill him had always been present in his mind but he had never taken it seriously. It would have been a bold move on his part with Shiloh watching. But now his Shadowlord was gone. His friend was gone. Kader's chest heaved as he thought about Shiloh's cruel death. The job of telling Aku and Onyx was one of the toughest things he had ever had to do in his life. Who would tell them now that he was gone? Kader stood up and took several deep breaths to calm his nerves.

A hard knock rapped at his door and he immediately froze. His eyes glanced at his packed bow and quiver full of arrows, a long knife resting beside them. Were Kaiser and his thugs already at his door? No, they would have burst through the door and struck without hesitation.

"Master Erebus? Are you well? What is going on?" asked the voices on the other side of the wooden door.

A ball of pent up breath rushed out of his lungs as he slung his pack and weapons over his shoulder. Kader pulled open the door and hurriedly pushed past three young students of his scholarly order.

"You are to disband immediately and run to your homes," he ordered as he hurried down the hall, the three young Shadowborn in tow. "No, run to the halls of Evander, Palani, Argos, whomever you can reach. You are no longer safe in the lands of the Shadowborn," he added turning his head back just enough to address them as they stepped out into the stable yard. He didn't stay to hear their response as he hurried towards the barn where a horse stood ready for his own escape. Kader easily slung himself into the saddle and quickly urged the horse in the direction of the gate. "Warn those who will listen about Kaiser."

*****

The students watched with worry as Kader galloped away and out through the gate, the gate keepers barely able to get it open in time. The tallest student with a chain of silver around his neck pushed the other two into the shadows just as six Sabers leapt across the pathway, scaling the walls and rooftops with cat like ease.

"He is being pursued," the tall student said. "You, get to Zoras Rokar and warn him as quickly as you can without arousing suspicion," he ordered to the slender girl who went off with a fast trot. He then turned towards the remaining student, the girl's brother. "You, gather the others in the east wing. I'll get those in the west wing. Meet in the sanctuary," he urged. The boy nodded before the two of them parted.

*****

Kader knew that he could trust Den, the tall student that was followed by the brother and sister pair that were newcomers to his order. He would warn the right people. Zoras and Sai needed to know so Onyx and Aku would still have protection from Kaiser and his machinations. He quickly pushed the thoughts out of his mind, instead focusing on his escape. The horse galloped with pounding hooves, jumping over upraised tree roots and ditches in the dirt road. He had to get to the eastern borders that were patrolled by Palani's famous scouts who knew him well. Not far behind the scouts would be Gryphons that could easily protect him from the hunting party sent after him. But first he had to reach the borders in one piece and if he knew Kaiser, he would send a great party to kill him.

The road he had chosen out of Cross was a side path created to direct the northern trade traffic into the city. At night, it was sparsely populated by late arrivals and guards. It would have been much faster to take the east road directly out of the city but there would be too many people crowding it and Kader wasn't about to use innocents as a shield against Kaiser. This particular road curved through the thickest part of the forest before it split at the eastern edge of the Heights. One path went north towards Umbra and the second path connected to the east road that led to Dusk. Even then, Kader was not certain that he would survive the night if he could not reach the fork.

The piercing sound of howls immediately declared the pursuit for him as hunting hounds thundered alongside the Sabers. The dogs were slate gray shorthaired animals with slender but long muscular limbs. They ran with tails straight out behind them for balance as they picked up speed. White teeth flashed as they barked and snapped their jaws, ears held flat against their skulls. The horse tensed beneath him, whinnying with fright but Kader urged it on. The hounds he could easily deal with on his own but the unrivaled speed and strength of the Sabers was enough to scare him. They needed no horse to cross great distances in short periods of time like he did. They could tear down a tree in their path with a swipe of their swords or a well-placed strike from their bodies. When they were on the hunt, nothing escaped them. And Kader was not a young soul anymore.

A sharp pain exploded from his back as an arrow embedded in the muscle close to his right shoulder. He lurched forward over the horse's neck, swearing through gritted teeth as the horse swerved beneath him. His cloak tangled around his neck before he threw it back with all of his might.

"Damn it," Kader cursed under his breath. He could feel warm blood soaking through his clothes and a dull, throbbing pain radiating from the wound site. "Traitors," he added as he knew that no true Saber would have shot him.

Another shot of pain tore through him again, this time just above his right hip. He felt his right shoulder going numb and that loss of feeling continued down his right arm. Kader could see the arrow shaft poking out of his side and he knew the Sabers were running alongside him, the hounds nipping at the horse's heels. This terrified the already anxious beast but Kader was thankful when it redoubled its pace. Kader painfully reached for his bow, nocked it with an arrow and with a grimace of pain and desperation quickly turned and fired it into the chest of the nearest hound. It crumbled into the dirt, gasping for breath with Kader's excellent shot through its ribs.

He drew his bow and fired again, hitting another hound before a third arrow embedded itself in his exposed chest. Two more arrows quickly followed, striking the horse in the ribs. The horse tumbled forward throwing Kader towards the dirt. Just before he hit the ground, Kader slipped into Shadow Slide.

It was not a smart idea to utilize Shadow Slide in his injured state but Kader had to get away and keep going for the border. The chill of that nether world gripped him as he sped along like an invisible ghost. Through the veil, he could hear the Sabers shouting and the hounds baying though the sound was distorted and distant. Kader zoomed around the trees in a twisting path but he knew that his speed was slowing down and soon he would have nothing left. Coming out of Shadow Slide, he pressed his back to a papery birch trunk and held his breath. His black hair was now a stringy mess.

"You can't hide forever! Your Shadow Slide is nothing compared to ours!"

Kader gritted his teeth and seethed as his wounds pulsated with pain. His entire right side was numb and he knew that running would be useless. But he had to try. He winced as he reached for the arrow embedded in his chest, wrapping his left hand around the shaft. He snapped the wood and dropped the broken piece to the ground. The pain was immense and he resisted screaming out. Kader forced his left hand to work again to break the arrow shaft in his hip but he couldn't reach for the one in his shoulder. He was at least happy to have some feeling in his right side when his muscles twitched. He then noted that the forest was silent and the Sabers were no longer calling out for him.

"Found you!" a brutish Saber shouted before Kader went flying. He crashed into a nearby tree, flexing his jaw and spitting out blood.

The Saber that had struck him stomped forward and lifted him up from the ground by his shirt collar. There was a devious glint in his eyes. He was almost too big to be a proper Saber with a giant's frame that made Sai Parahazur seem small by comparison. And he was impossibly strong.

"What is your name?" Kader managed to cough out, his jaw throbbing with pain. He hoped to use his intelligence to disarm the giant Saber.

"Why do you care?" the Saber snapped. He brought Kader

close to his face. "Now, you are coming with me."

Kader was dragged out of the safety of the trees and back on to the forest path. The giant Saber threw him forward as his five companions approached from behind. Kader gritted his teeth as his skidding body slowed to a stop. He coughed as he squinted his eyes, his vision blurry from the intense pain of his wounds. He heard the growls and the raucous laughter as the six Sabers, dressed in black cloaks and leather armor, and four remaining hounds assembled together on the path a few feet away. The giant Saber stepped back as a smaller Saber stepped forward with a smug look in his eyes.

"Caught like a mouse before a cat, Master Erebus," said the Saber drawing his sword. The others followed and soon Kader was staring at six gleaming blades of shining steel. Each Saber wore their traditional uniforms though the badge of the Silvanus family was missing. "You knew me once. I am Rothe Abendroth and now that Lord Kaiser has shown me the truth, I will truly enjoy killing you. It would boggle your mind to know just how many of us are under his command."

"Truth? What truth is there in flouting the law? Kaiser is a traitor to the Immortal Truth and I will not believe that an Abendroth has sold himself so low!" Kader shouted with as much force as he could, gripping his silver crescent tightly in his left hand. He gasped for breath, trying to draw air in.

"Well you are a traitor to him and therefore sentenced to die," a Saber behind Rothe snarled.

Rothe raised up a hand to silence him. "The truth is not what the Northern Alliance would want us to believe for the world is not so deluded and kind." Rothe pressed the tip of his sword into the dirt at his feet. "I suppose we should grant you last words. What have you to say before I carve out your heart?"

Kader did not say anything but instead blew hard through the crescent's whistle. The note was loud and rang through the wooded path, the trees shaking from the force behind it. The Sabers looked around, their hounds cowering and whimpering at their feet. The distant roar of a great beast permeated the air. A rush of thundering steps and a burst through the trees answered their sudden fear.

Between them and Kader was a solid black furred wolf with eyes of gold and a small path of white on its chest. Muscles rippled under a thick pelt, tightening in fury. Breath was ragged and laced with a deep growl that felt like it came through a thick fog. The growl grew stronger and clearer as the wolf flashed his white fangs. Claws dug into the dirt as he snarled in warning for the attack. The wolf stood at his full height, a threatening beast with hackles raised in anger. He was as big as a bear and as tall at the shoulders as a horse.

Rothe and two other Sabers kicked the hounds to attack the great wolf and with renewed vigor for the fight, they leapt forward. The wolf snapped with massive jaws and struck with strong paws, crushing one hound's back and two others beneath his weight. He threw the last away into the tree lined darkness and stepped forward, lips curling back to reveal sharp teeth. Rothe held the front, gripping his sword tightly while the other Sabers huddled behind him.

"Omu," Rothe said doing his best to hide his fear. He knew that Omu only came to Sabers who were about to die and he was not ready to die.

The wolf growled louder in response. A dark shimmering mist grew in thickness as the growl rose in volume. His eyes turned an eerie white color to match the moonlight beaming down from above.

"Try to strike him and I will kill you," the wolf warned with a deep snarling voice. A roar built up in his chest before it was let loose. It shook the ground with all the force of the Spirit World he came from and with the might of his ancient power. Rothe and the five Sabers bolted down the path, dropping their swords in terror of Omu.

The roar dissipated as Omu turned around to a weakening Kader with three grievous arrow wounds. The mist vanished and the world of the dark forest returned. Kader looked at the beast with reverence and gratitude.

"I am glad you came," Kader said with some strength. Omu came closer and lay down beside him, rolling his shoulders so Kader could grip at the mass of hair at the top of his shoulder blades.

"Do not waste your breath speaking. Climb onto my back and I shall bear you the rest of the way. Palani's scouts will have heard my call and they will be waiting at the border," Omu said, easing his body lower for Kader to get on. Once Kader had dragged himself and settled on Omu's back, Omu stood up and quickly launched into a swift pace towards the east.

THE REBELS BEGIN TO WORRY

Zoras Rokar was bent over his desk in concentration as he scribbled line after line on a dry piece of parchment. When he moved to set the tip of his quill into the inkwell, he considered the tract he was writing. It was treason, he knew, but he had to wonder if it was the only way out of the throne's troubles. For if the throne suffered, the people suffered and he believed that Kaiser was not above stopping at killing those closest to the royal family. He had tried once before without success but maybe, he thought, maybe this time it would work. Letting out a deep breath, Zoras pulled over a leather bound book, flipping quickly through the pages to a section labeled 'Laws of Succession.' He reviewed the laws with a glance before continuing on with his writing. His focus was unwavering as he finished, pausing only to review the succession laws and to ink his quill.

A heavy knock pounded on his door and before Zoras could acknowledge it, a noble looking Saber with shining steel and leather armor came inside. He looked up from his papers to see that Donovan Shunga had burst into his office. He watched as Donovan bent over trying to catch his breath. Setting his white swan feather quill aside in the inkwell, Zoras turned over his papers.

"Normally, I would abhor someone barging into my study while I am working," Zoras said harshly.

"Kader has fled from Cross," Donovan said between breaths. His short black hair clung to his face as he stood straight up, chest heaving.

"What?" Zoras asked as he shot up from his seat. He kicked his chair back.

Donovan wiped his brow. "Kaiser has forced him out, and assumed his mantle as Lord's Chancellor."

Zoras rounded his desk and approached Donovan. "Are you certain?" he asked the Saber plainly.

"Your son told me this after he tried to go see Kader in his chambers. He found Kaiser already there with his... servant," the strong framed Saber replied.

"Every move, every breath that traitor makes is an affront to the Immortal Truth," Zoras growled as he turned away and paced back to his desk. He leaned on the edge, thinking silently to himself. A thought then occurred to him. "Why was my son going to Kader's office at this hour?"

"He had a message from the Lady that could not wait though your son would not divulge anymore details to me," Donovan quickly answered with a bow of the head. He still respected Zoras' former position as leader of the Sabers.

From Zoras' experience, the Lady that Donovan spoke of was a fierce fighter trained by someone he wanted to see again. Any message coming from her offered him hope that perhaps the son of Akakios was coming home. Zoras felt a sense of relief and elation just at the thought.

"I know my son and his propensity to talk especially in regards to you know who. What else did he say to you?" Zoras pressed with an eager voice.

Donovan hesitated, his eyes darting around. Zoras gestured quickly with his hand for the Saber to continue. "He mentioned the Site of Ascension. I swear that he did not say more for fear of unwelcome attention. Who knows how deeply entrenched Kaiser is in the palace."

It always came back to Kaiser and unlike usual, the thought did not bother Zoras. Mixed in with his elation was foolish courage. "Then it is high time that we remove Kaiser Adonis from his power. Permanently."

"If I may say, easier said than done. That servant of his is dangerous and protects him with a deadly power. I myself have tried to eliminate Kaiser through the subtle means of poison and nothing. No poison known in these lands have had any effect," Donovan stated, bringing everything back to reality. "And I am still certain he is responsible for Madhuri's disappearance."

Zoras slid back into his seat, crossing his hands on his lap. "There may be one person who can help us. The one person on our side that knows him better."

"I would be careful. Aku and Onyx are both still in his grasp and he will kill them without a second thought if it suits his purpose," Donovan commented with a heavy heart. "We can't leave our people without a Shadowlord."

"Why not try to take Aku and Onyx away from the city? Why haven't we tried that yet?" Zoras asked, momentarily distracted from his original train of thought.

Donovan was hesitant to answer. "Because Madhuri told me that was what he intended and look what happened to him."

Madhuri had been a close friend to Zoras for countless years. Both shared a dedication to the throne and to the Immortal Truth as well as a distrust of Kaiser. They had both been elevated to their respective Commander positions though Zoras had retired as a Saber to become the Lord's Regent of the Council. Zoras gave Madhuri sanctuary after the execution of his son and the two were as close as brothers.

"There is still Akakios' bastard son and law states that if there is no legitimate son to take the throne, he would succeed in their absence," Zoras said after a moment of silence.

Donovan shook his head. "You mean Ryder?"

"Of course I mean Ryder unless you know of some other royal bastard," Zoras snapped unexpectedly. Donovan startled from the sudden harshness and Zoras quickly realized his mistake. He let out a deep breath. "We may need Ryder Coba before the end of all this. He is a Prince in all but name and a better warrior than most," Zoras said solemnly.

"You know? I don't think that he will come," Donovan pointed out. "He did run away."

Zoras let out a deep sigh. "He will have to. We can't let the throne fall to ruin." He glanced down at the face up papers on his desk. "Make sure that Hayden and Sai keep a close watch over Lord Aku and for Soja to guard the Prince. I will take Kader's place in meeting the Lady."

*****

Like a fleeting apparition, Zoras traversed the streets of Cross under the cloak of Shadow Slide. His long years as the Saber Commander had gifted him with an intimate knowledge of the city layout and thus he was able to exit Cross unnoticed. He knew the secret paths outside the walls that would lead him quickly to his destination.

The Site of Ascension was a historical landmark to the Shadowborn people; it was where Shadow Night Silvanus was named the first Shadowlord. It was a clearing in the Northern

Forest on the other side of the mountains that surrounded Cross. Ancient pines framed the clearing like sentinels. Zoras pulled out of Shadow Slide at the mouth of a small cave watching carefully for the arrival of the Lady. The forest was quiet though he thought that he heard the hoot of an owl in the distance.

As the clouds passed, uncovering the moon, a single beam of silvery light revealed the Lady. Her identity was hidden beneath a thin fabric cloak, her face shielded by a shadow. Zoras knew immediately that she was on edge, obviously expecting to see Kader instead of him. His own sense of caution rose up within his chest.

"Well met, Lady Ombre," Zoras greeted.

The Lady sneered. "Where is Kader?"

Zoras cleared his throat. "His presence or lack there of is still being investigated by those of us in Cross. The more important question is what has brought you so far south of your home in Umbra?"

"That is none of your concern," the Lady snapped, showing her dislike for the old politician.

"Ah, I see that you share your hate of me with one that I hope to hear is coming back. Is that why you have strayed south?" Zoras deftly asked.

Her posture remained tense and ready to crack like a whip. Zoras watched as the Lady pulled back her hood, letting it drop to her shoulders. Even he had to admit that Haven Ombre was a beautiful Shadowborn woman with her smooth skin and slender but shapely body. But as many knew, she was not to be crossed. Zoras had wanted to test his theory though to see if threatening the feisty woman would bring her ferocious partner back. He was certain that he could handle Ryder should it come to blows.

"I came for the funeral," Haven simply said.

"Then let us bow our heads and remember our departed Lord Shiloh in this sacred place."

Both bowed their heads and crossed their hearts with a Spirit Ward. The distant owl hooted again, this time in a lower call. The low timbre echoed among the trees like a rumble of distant waves breaking on the shore. No other night creature dared to whistle, howl or call out to interrupt the song. At the conclusion, Zoras and Haven whispered their private prayers in Shiloh's honor.

"Why come to the funeral and by yourself? Lord or not, you did not know Shiloh personally," Zoras wondered.

"Ryder did. In case you have forgotten, Lord Shiloh was his father's uncle and he bore him great respect and love," Haven promptly answered. "I came here for Ryder."

"Does he know that Lord Shiloh was murdered?" Zoras blurted out. "How does he know if he does know?"

Haven shifted her weight from left to right, leaning heavily on her hip. She lifted an eyebrow, silently indicating that she was not going to reveal an answer to Zoras' liking. "You just do not get it. He is not coming back no matter how great your desperation gets."

"You've talked to him! I have to know how!" Zoras demanded. He felt himself getting angry at her obvious subversion. Reaching into his robes, Zoras pulled out the letter he had written out earlier. He waved it in the air. "I can have him legitimized as a son of the Silvanus family. I have tried once before when Akakios was tried and executed and before our dear Shiloh returned home. As a descendant of our Lady Mali, Lord Shiloh's elder sister, he would have seniority in the line of succession. He would become Peredur Coba-Silvanus, Prince of the Shadowborn."

"Our succession laws have not changed since Shadow Night was named here on this very spot as Shadowlord. Only true born Silvanus sons in patrilineal descent can occupy the throne," Haven stated as she crossed her arms. "So give up on your hopeless dream and leave him be."

"Unfortunately times have changed and the throne needs strength and freedom. Kaiser controls Lord Aku and through him, Onyx. How is that true to the Immortal Truth? Our Shadowlord is supposed to guard against darkness, not be controlled by it," Zoras explained.

"I did not come here to argue about your desires for him. I came here to meet with Kader. Seeing as he is not here, I will not waste my time with you," Haven said before she started to turn around.

Zoras took a step forward and made to reach for Haven to prevent her from leaving. He hesitated. "Haven, please. Kader has fled from Cross."

Haven paused with her back towards Zoras. She slowly turned around, a look of quiet shock on her face. "Fled? Why?"

"I think that you are smart enough to guess why though I doubt Kader fled due to the same reasons as your lover," Zoras challenged. He wanted to get her angry. He had to try.

Haven frowned at the obvious attempt at a threat. Her eyes narrowed as her hand slid down to the sheathed long knife at her side. Her fingers wrapped tightly around the hilt.

"Be careful, Zoras. Your desperation is showing and I am sure that Kaiser will notice. Keep at your pathetic dream and soon, you will not wake to see the next dawn. If his servant does not come for you, Kaiser surely will," Haven warned. She was no friend of Zoras.

"Please, Haven. Hope is all I have. Do not be angry at me

on his behalf for the rebellion still needs you," Zoras pleaded.

"As it needs us all in these dark times," Haven declared as her hand dropped from the hilt of her weapon.

A SCOUT'S REPORT

Branches and leaves shuddered at the quick hard impact of feet, shaking as the leap drew them away. Slumbering birds squawked in anger at the disturbance of their canopy home. The runner did not listen as he leapt across the treetops with unnatural ease and balance. Travelling in this manner ensured the lack of footprints for a suspicious person to follow and his scent would be too high for the sharp nose of a hunting hound to detect.

A sharp glance to his left revealed his companion, Arik Barr, one of the ghostly Barn Owl Gryphons, with limbs tucked into flying position as his great wings beat in a steady rhythm. He was touted as the most silent flyer of the scouting force and many sang their praises. Arik was built perfectly for his role as a Scout. The Scout was from the Earthborn, ruled by Palani, the child of Oren and Willow, from the great city of Cascade.

Arik flew in closer, bending his cinnamon washed wings slightly to maintain speed and a forward direction. His animal face was indiscernible from any expression but that of a creature at ease during the nighttime. Dark eyes lay against a round heart shaped face with a beak of the color of a pearl surrounded by a set of wispy feathers at its base. It opened to utter a chirp like signal. A call of the same note rang back. They were close to their Scout base of operations.

When the trees opened up to reveal a flowing stream bed, Arik tucked his wings in tight against his body and dove into a twisting spiral descending quickly to the exposed shore. At the last moment, he loosened his limbs, flared his wings out to the side and landed easily on his strong furred legs, bending to absorb the force. Landing beside him in less grace was the Earthborn Scout as two guards, a gray and brown Barred Owl Gryphon and an Earthborn, came forward into the torchlight.

"Haro Artemis of the Earthborn," the Scout said, drawing a tight fist across his chest and bowing.

"Arik Barr of the Gryphons," Arik said, bowing his head and bending down on his front limbs as the fur tufted tail swept behind him. His wings flared out emphasizing his greater size.

Gryphons preferred the company of their own kind but had adapted different mannerisms to interact with the human races. They were civilized for a beast race, able to speak in the common tongue if taught though their voices were laced with chirp like accents. Only the older members of the Gryphon race had perfected their speaking enough to converse without the occasional and sometimes embarrassing whistle. Arik was still young by Gryphon standards and thus had a strong rasp to his voice.

"News from the lands of the Shadowborn. I must report directly to Captain Avani," Haro quickly began.

"Go swiftly," the Earthborn guard urged as he and the Gryphon stepped aside to allow passage.

"May the Truth guide you," the Gryphon guard said with a quieted voice as Arik and Haro walked by them into the tunnel of trees.

Arik tucked his wings tightly against his back to avoid snagging limbs tearing at the delicate feathers. He didn't allow his tail to swish like it would if he were walking in less confined spaces. His pace was deliberate and steady with all four feet rising and falling with a regular halting rhythm. Haro walked beside him, pushing back branches to allow his larger companion passage. Though he had been partnered with Arik for several months on multiple scouting missions, Haro was still getting used to the relatively alien nature the Gryphon possessed. How his superiors handled working with Gryphons on a regular basis crossed his mind for not the first time.

The tight tunnel of trees soon opened up into a clearing of tents that lined the edges while a small fire burned in the center. A pavilion was the center point of the tents with a single banner to each side of the entrance. Arik nodded with encouragement as he sauntered over to a bare patch of ground set aside for the large Gryphons to rest upon. Haro cleared his throat as the Gryphon left his side and he slowed to a halt in front of the pavilion. He was quickly ushered in once he showed his Scout emblem, a pendent bearing a small silver disc etched with a leaf blade.

Haro stepped inside of the tent, straightening his posture as he looked about the interior. A single woven carpet covered the grass and dirt of the natural ground. A large oak table sat before him with a map staked down at the corners with rusty daggers. Leaning over the map was his scout team leader, a tough as nails golden blonde who took her job seriously when on duty. Haro knew her as Scout Captain Avani. She was only as tall as Haro's shoulder but she was all muscle and faster than a falcon in a dive. Her skill with a knife was unparalleled. Beside her was a small Forest Hawk Gryphon who followed her hand over the map with a keen eye, reaching out once to point to a landmark with a talon.

"No, Stria. Whisper said that bend in the river wouldn't suit us well for an outpost. It is too open even at night," Avani argued with a restrained voice.

"That blasted owl doesn't know what he sees. It is a good launching site for my Day Scouts and the rapids would hide any noise," Stria corrected.

Avani rolled her eyes. "Well we don't have the order yet to pack up this camp," she stated putting both of her hands on the edge of the table. She then looked up to see Haro who quickly drew his left arm across his chest in a motion of respect. "Speak your piece and be done with it."

Haro cleared his throat. "I bring news that the Lord Shiloh Silvanus of the Shadowborn has died."

Avani and Stria both straightened up and stared at him in shock.

"How?" Stria asked, finding his voice first.

Shifting his gaze to Avani, Haro continued. "I could discover nothing concrete regarding the nature of his death. There seems to be this barrier, a darkness that I cannot see through. But the earth does not lie. Its sorrow sang to me in a way that gave me concern and an urgency to speak to you," Haro stressed with his best imitation of his earlier concern.

"The earth never lies," Avani stated. She crossed her arms and looked away from Haro, muttering to herself.

Haro shifted his weight. "I tried to get in closer but I couldn't cross the river. Arik listened as best as he could and caught wind of a dark whisper." Haro paused for a moment, trying to remember what he and the Barn Owl Gryphon had told each other before reaching the station. "A name: Kaiser Adonis."

Stria and Avani looked at each other before turning their attention back to Haro. "We will need closer inspection as this barrier allows. Avani, I will have Whisper send out a messenger at once to each of the other Lords. A Feather Whisper to keep such news from spreading before it is ready to," Stria proposed.

Avani nodded. "We have been watching Kaiser for quite some time. I did not think he would move against Shiloh so quickly after the death of Nuru. But how can one tell with the border sealed against us? I shall redouble the watch on the river to see what else we can learn. We cannot have him moving unchecked. The Owl Gryphons have been a vital asset with their excellent hearing and I hope they can learn more. Dismissed."

Haro repeated the arm across the chest motion before turning around to exit the tent. Arik waited for him, laying on a small patch of grass with front limbs crossed over each other. He cocked his head as he watched his teammate.

"Still so many questions, Arik. I know everyone here has suspicions but I want to know the truth so we can act," Haro said with a defeated tone as he sat on a nearby downed log.

"Well what do we know? Perhaps I can help you sort out your thoughts so your mind is clear again," Arik suggested.

"I almost have to go back to the beginning. Are you sure about that?" Haro asked.

Arik thought for a moment. "Perhaps we need simple words and not a history lesson," he rasped as his Gryphon accent broke through.

"Well then. Who are we really watching?" Haro asked. He then threw his hands up in the air. "You know what? I think we spend too much time thinking and talking about our problems," he stated as he leaned back to look at the night sky. He always appreciated the beauty of a clear night.

Arik let out a deep breath before twisting his head around to pick at his wing feathers. He took each one delicately in his beak, moving up the feather shaft until reaching the tip. With precision, he cleaned and set his flight feathers into position with his sharp beak. Taking a small rock in one paw, Arik rubbed his talons back and forth on the hard surface to sharpen them. He repeated the maneuver on his other paw.

"Scout Haro? Your captain wishes that you go the North Bend. Scout Arik, Captain Stria says to use your watching eyes," a black and gray Eagle Gryphon reported after a quick bow of the head.

Haro knew that as a diurnal Gryphon, the night restricted him to running messages around the station. The Gryphon looked uncomfortable whereas Arik, being an Owl blood, was in his element. Even his own sight was nothing compared to Arik's. What he lacked in the Gryphon's superior senses, he could read the earth by placing a hand on the ground. He placed a hand on the ground, feeling the magnetic ebb and flow of energy. Arik pushed himself to his feet as Haro removed his hand from the dirt, brushing it on his pant leg. Arik chirped a few Gryphon words before the young messenger departed from their presence.

"To North Bend," Arik said dutifully.

WHAT NEXT?

The sun was starting to rise as Arik and Haro reached the bend of the river. The rapids roared as water splashed and collided with the broken rocky wall. As Avani had argued, the piece of land was too open to prying eyes but as Stria disputed, it was also a perfect launching and landing space for the Gryphons in their Scout teams. The trees ended with the grass and left an open clearing overlooking the river rapids.

Arik landed in a small clearing in the stand of trees as Haro slid to a stop beside him. The dirt beneath his feet was cool and smelled of pine needles. Arik folded his wings close to his body as his eyes swept the area. The dark orbs squinted as his brow furrowed. He gestured towards the spray of mist that covered the open ground beside the river.

"The air feels unnaturally cold," Arik dared to say as his shoulders shivered.

Haro agreed. "This is no normal winter chill."

Arik frowned as a Gryphon could, turning down the corners of his beak. He rustled his wings as his feathers stiffened along his spine. His claws dug furrows in the dirt beneath his paws. They both looked to the land across the river, seeing the dark trees of the Shadowborn that somehow let no one pass.

The border had been a thing of strange happenings for nearly ten years. The lands of the Shadowborn were already imposing with broken mountains and ancient pines. But an impassable border was worrisome. The Scouts struggled in their long held duty to watch over their neighbors, frequently left staring at the dark land across the river.

"This doesn't feel right," Haro said, pointing to the opposite bank. "Why can't we enter a land that we can plainly see?"

The Gryphon shrugged. "My kin and I have tried to interpret its power." He shook his head, feeling uncomfortable. "I remember the days when I could fly over that river. There is a town just beyond the trees called Dusk that guards the river crossing." He threw his head towards a southern direction.

"I have never been to the lands of the Shadowborn. What is it like?" Haro asked.

Arik considered his answer with a tilt of the head. "I was last there as a newly named scout. I delivered my assignment papers to the mayor of Dusk. It was..." He bent his head for a moment.

"Wait. What is that?" Haro asked, interrupting Arik's quiet thoughts.

Arik studied the prone dark form Haro had pointed out. He then froze and backed up a few steps. He mumbled in his native tongue, chirps and rasps escaping his beak.

"I don't speak Gryphon. What is it?" Haro asked more directly. He bit back a disrespectful comment as Arik ignored him.

After what felt like a painful wait, Arik answered. "This space has been touched by a mighty Spirit."

Haro now understood Arik's hesitation and quickly crossed his heart in a Spirit Ward. When he saw Arik stepping out of the tree line, he reached to grab his tail to pull him back, missing by a hair's breath. It would have been rude to pull a Gryphon's tail but Haro could think of nothing else to stop his companion. He stomped his feet before following cautiously behind Arik.

With wings flared out, Arik was prepared to take flight as he took slow steps forward. Haro put a hand on his small knife, ready to fight if called to. As he drew closer to the form lying on the ground, Haro began to feel the Spirit energy that Arik had sensed. He fought the urge to run back to the safety of the trees.

"Wolf paws!" Haro shouted when he spotted the familiar footprints. "It is Omu's presence!"

Arik tucked his wings back down as he relaxed, knowing the stories of the benevolent Wolf Spirit. He watched as Haro knelt down to inspect the form.

"Be careful. Omu had reason to leave a signal here," Arik stated.

Haro rolled the form over and jumped back when the person coughed. He pulled his knife as a knee jerk reflex. Arik leaned in to see the person's face, wings raised again in uncertainty.

"Sanctuary," the person said weakly before falling unconscious. His right arm fell flat out to his side, hand opening to reveal a silver crescent.

"Kader Erebus!" Arik shouted. He erupted in a whirlwind of motion and was soon in the sky with Kader on his back. Haro ran under him with all possible haste and speed. The two headed back to the border station as fast as they possibly could.

*****

Arik had not moved from the bare patch of ground, sitting up on his haunches, tail wrapped around his paws. His wings were laid out limp, resting from the speedy flight. He picked at a stray feather at his elbow gingerly pulling it back into place with his talons.

"I don't think the others will care if a feather is out of place," Haro said as he paced with hands on his hips. He looked around to see several Gryphons and Earthborn looking anxiously towards the pavilion.

"It is important for my kind in flight for feathers to be taken care of. You and the rest of the two legged races look rather naked in comparison," Arik replied with a turn of the head.

Haro sighed deeply. "All is in the eye of the beholder. I wonder how Kader was hurt and how he came to be at the North Bend.

Arik stopped preening. "Clearly he summoned Omu under extreme danger and the great wolf brought him there."

"I only know of what others say of Kader but to summon a Spirit must have taken a great deal of power. But surely he would not have done it on a whim," Haro said before pausing for a moment. "He said sanctuary and Omu came to his call. Spirits just don't come whenever someone cries out for them."

The Gryphon tilted his head in thought. "True. A Spirit has to have purpose to leave the Spirit World."

The nature of Spirits was unpredictable as countless generations were taught. And to walk in the Spirit World was even more uncertain than its residents. Since Haro was a small child, he had been told that Spirits were something to be wary of. His grandmother had even showed him a Spirit Ward to guard his heart though sometimes, Haro wondered if it even worked.

Haro was startled out of his mind's wandering when a fast beating sound and cloud of dust disrupted his senses. He turned to glare at Arik but quickly fell into a fit of laughter.

"You've never seen a dust bath before? It's quite relaxing," Arik stated matter of factly as he continued to rustle his great wings in the dust, flipping it onto his body. Haro did his best to contain his humor, wiping tears from the corner of one eye. Seeing such a large predatory beast roll in the dirt just seemed so silly to him and Haro was soon taken by another bout of laughter.

Arik stood up and shook his body, shoulders rolling before he folded his wings back in. "Considering the seriousness of what is going on inside of that..." he paused trying to think of the word. "...covered nest, laughter is not appropriate."

Haro steadied himself as his laughter calmed. "I'm sorry. It's just that I forget that you are of the Beastborn."

Arik clacked his beak. "We have more important things to worry about than the differences between our races."

A nearby guard shushed them as Avani came out of the pavilion with Whisper and Stria weaving around from their entrance on the back wall. Everyone looked at them anxiously for news.

"A dark message was delivered to me just this night past but I will not trouble you with its details. Many questions have been raised into the conduct of the one named Kaiser Adonis, a name that I know all of you are familiar with," Avani stated, sounding tired. She briefly rubbed her forehead. "We must trust our Lords to decide our path and direct us with great wisdom and strength. As such, we must do our part to make sure that they are properly informed. But I must warn you now, Kaiser is more dangerous than we all realize."

As the Night Leader for the Gryphons, Whisper spoke in his native tongue while Stria translated for the remaining Earthborn. "Kaiser has thrown the first strike of war and we will not stand for it. The Shadowborn are in danger and it is our duty to protect our neighbors from the," Stria spat as did Whisper before going on. "...darkness that surrounds them. We will look into the condition of Aku and the safety of Onyx and the people."

Arik leaned in towards Haro. "I've never heard Whisper curse before."

"What did he say?" Haro asked. He had a hard time trying to understand the whistles, chirps and chaws of the Gryphon tongue.

Arik hesitated for a moment. "A curse from our tongue that I dare not say in this company but it equates to traitor of truth in yours. To get that curse is dark indeed."

Whisper and Stria continued their tandem speech until the whole group was riled up and ready to march. Gryphon-Earthborn scout pairs eagerly waited for assignments from the captains. Arik and Haro were less inclined to go back out, having seen firsthand what Kaiser's influence produced. Also with it being daytime, Arik was an Owl Gryphon and best suited for night missions.

Relieved to get some rest, Haro and Arik departed the gathering that was now being organized by Avani and Stria. Haro could hear the orders being shouted out as they left the pavilion. He stretched and rolled his shoulders as Arik paced behind him. Once at his tent, Haro collapsed on his bed roll.

"You need food," Arik said as he poked his head in the entryway. His dark eyes peered around the interior.

"There is too much to think about to warrant getting back up and going to the supply tent for rations," Haro said turning onto his side away from Arik. The Owl Gryphon eased himself down to the ground.

"I worry about my family too. If the Demons of the Darklands are indeed coming back, I don't think we have the same heroes we had a thousand years ago," Arik stated, voicing Haro's thoughts.

"There is still Bane," Haro commented.

"But he does not come where he is needed most. If we Immortals fall, who is left to protect the Mortals?" Arik replied.

Haro sat up to face him. "It seems everyone keeps saying that about him. If you really think about it, what is more dangerous than someone like Kaiser to keep the Daylord occupied?"

Arik shrugged. "I'm not going to debate on an empty stomach. I'll bring something back," he said as he scooted away from the tent entrance and stood up.

"Please don't tear up your meal near mine! Last time, you left a piece of chewed up fur!" Haro quickly shouted as Arik walked away.

THE MORNING AFTER

Onyx sighed deeply as he hugged his feather pillow, bed covers bunched around his shoulders. He looked out the window as the sun light beamed into his room. He was worn out and exhausted despite a full night of sleep. Rolling over onto his back, he stared at the molded pattern on the ceiling, trying to make sense of the whimsical curves and designs. After a few minutes of staring, Onyx got out of bed. He stepped into his sitting room, setting his hands on his hips. He glanced over at the small table and chair by the fireplace where a bed of coals and wood ash burned a dim red. On the table was a silver tray with a bowl of honey porridge, a small plate of fresh berries and a glass of milk. He sat up when he saw a folded note with his name on the front.

Bypassing the food, Onyx grabbed the note and sat down to read it.

"My good and dear Crowned Prince, I am deeply saddened by the losses this family has suffered as of late. As Lord's Chancellor, your father has instructed me on this morning to offer my guidance for your future. If it pleases you, I ask you to join me in the solar when you have broken your fast," Onyx read aloud.

He dropped the note back on the table, knowing it was from Kaiser and wishing it was from Kader instead. Kader was always so kind and caring to him, acting as a teacher and friend. But now his presence was gone and Onyx felt alone. He tried to figure out why Kaiser acted so harshly against Kader. Perhaps he was angry in the wake of his grandfather's death. Maybe he was just too overwhelmed. Onyx decided that he would be direct with Kaiser and ask him once he arrived at the solar.

Kader had been like a second father to him while his own father lingered in a sick and listless state. He had stepped up to the role as mentor and teacher right after Aku was brought back mortally wounded. Onyx slumped back in his black velvet chair, gripping the arms of the chair as the memory of that terrible day came over him. He remembered every word and every sensation from what he saw and from what others told him. All of the emotion he had bottled up inside simmered on the edge.

*****

Onyx slid into the seat next to his grandfather, grasping the crimson cushion with both hands to keep it from slipping. After assuring himself that it would not move, he looked up and smiled. His grandfather smiled back, lines forming around his gray eyes. Onyx watched as his grandfather made a gesture towards a tall uniformed servant that stood by the open terrace door. The servant bowed, keeping his left arm bent to avoid dropping the cloth laid across it, and twisted around to disappear inside.

"I am glad that the weather has warmed sufficiently enough for us to take breakfast outside," Shiloh commented as another servant pulled out a chair for Nuru to sit down. Once seated, the servant pushed it to the edge of the ironwork table. She politely thanked the servant before he stepped back.

"Spring must be upon us. Onyx said he already saw several flowers budding in the courtyard," Nuru stated in a sweet tone. She briefly set a hand on Onyx's shoulder. "Tell your grandfather which ones you saw."

"I saw the moon roses and the dawn glories," Onyx said excitedly, his head bobbing up and down. He looked to his mother for confirmation. She nodded and silently mouthed one he had missed. "Oh! And the thistles!"

Shiloh chuckled softly. "Perhaps after our meal, you can show me."

Onyx's smile broadened as he swung his legs back and forth. "I want to show Father when he comes home. When is he coming back?"

"I suspect by the next full moon to announce his victory," Kader stated as he stepped onto the terrace. He paused by Shiloh to bow before taking the seat to Nuru's right. "My apologies for coming late. I had hoped to receive the messenger from the Waterborn but she has yet to arrive."

"The Waterborn are not particularly known for their speed

on land. Give it time, Master Erebus. I'd rather Lord Marinus give proper consideration to my message than to hastily answer it without much thought. These are peace talks, not declarations of war or an invitation for a grand state visit," Shiloh explained as the first course for breakfast was laid out on the table.

Onyx unfolded his napkin and laid it across his lap as a servant leaned over to set down a bowl of honey porridge. Two sticks of cinnamon were arranged in a X shape in the center of the creamy mound. He leaned forward to savor the smell.

"I hope that Aku does come in time to meet with the Waterborn messenger. I worry about him so," Nuru admitted as she pushed back a stray lock of her chestnut hair.

"The entire nation worries. We most of all as his family," Shiloh said as he set out his own napkin with a flick of the wrists. "He is a Silvanus and is well prepared to hunt and kill a Demon. Such an act will assure your family of his strength and worthiness to be your husband."

Onyx swallowed a mouthful of porridge, savoring the delicate sweet taste. A team of four servants flitted about the diners at the table, delivering food and refilling cups in tactum silence. His porridge bowl was soon replaced with a plate of venison sausage and maple syrup glazed apples. Breakfast had to be his favorite meal of the day. It was when he didn't have to be dressed up or greet an endless parade of people. He enjoyed the more intimate settings of the terrace. He and his grandfather had spent many afternoons on the ivy choked porch, talking about all sorts of things.

"Have you ever fought a Demon, Grandfather?" Onyx asked in between bites.

"Now, good Prince. Such talk is not appropriate for the breakfast table," Kaiser said as he strode out onto the terrace. He snatched a biscuit from a nearby tray and began picking at it.

"Ah, Master Adonis. I was wondering when you would join us this morning," Shiloh said, turning in his seat towards the slender noble. "Onyx, there are few alive who have fought more Demons than can be counted. Master Adonis is one of those souls and he has gained a mass of experience from those encounters."

Kaiser paused and bowed his head. "You flatter me, my Lord."

"I respect your experience. My family and you have not always seen eye to eye but your knowledge is greatly valued," Shiloh said before taking a sip of his hot tea. "In this day and age, knowledge is just as powerful as brute strength."

Nuru leaned over to whisper something to Kader but Onyx didn't hear it. He suspected their short private conversation was about Kaiser. It was obvious that they did not feel the same comfort and respect as his grandfather did for the ancient noble. Onyx looked over at Kaiser, studying his face. The noble's expression was brooding but calculating. It was clear that he was very intelligent. Onyx remembered that Kaiser was the son of a general, whose name he could not remember at the moment, but he did not look like much of a warrior. He knew that Kaiser was older than his grandfather though it surprised him how unaffected he was by age.

"Master Adonis, you examined the scene of the Demon's attack. What can you tell us of its nature? I find that the Crowned Prince being away this long troubling," Kader suddenly asked as if to put Kaiser on the spot.

Kaiser stopped pacing around the edge of the terrace. Onyx watched as he sprinkled a handful of crumbs on the ledge that was immediately set upon by three gray songbirds. "It is a young and stupid creature but driven by the desire to please. That makes it lethal." Both Nuru and Onyx shuddered but Kader leaned in to reassure them. Shiloh remained focused on Kaiser, waiting for him to continue. "But its youth will be its downfall. The Crowned Prince's greatest effort will be expended in the hunt but the actual encounter should be short."

"Donovan Shunga is with him," Kader reminded Nuru as he leaned towards her. "And I made sure that Hayden Abendroth accompanied them," he added in a lower voice.

Nuru pressed a hand to her heart and sighed with relief. Onyx returned his attention to the meal before him. The conversation between the adults turned to state matters and the planning of an upcoming state visit. Kaiser did not participate in the conversation, remaining silent as he continued to break apart the biscuit in his hand. More gray songbirds flitted down to the ledge to feed on his offerings.

"Master Adonis, can you go check on the messages? I want to have at least something to present to the Council this afternoon," Shiloh stated as he took a biscuit from the servant's tray.

"Of course, my Lord," Kaiser said as he dropped the last of his torn up biscuit on the ledge. He turned towards Shiloh, latched his hands behind his back, and bowed. He then spun on his feet and departed inside.

"If I may ask, what exactly did you say in your last message to Lord Marinus?" Nuru asked before taking a bite of glazed apples.

Shiloh set aside the butter knife and sighed. "I made the recommendation that we meet on his terms to discuss a new alliance. I expressed my hope to restore the Waterborn's confidence in the Shadowborn though I doubt I could ever get them to trust Akakios' bastard. It's probably a good thing that he is long gone from Cross otherwise I suppose Marinus would spit in my face."

Onyx's attention immediately switched to his grandfather. Barely anyone spoke of his mysterious cousin in great detail and he doubted that he could get his mother, Master Erebus, or his grandfather to tell him more. So instead of asking why the Waterborn hated his cousin, he decided to ask his grandfather about the terms in the message.

"Well, I merely asked Lord Marinus to make his own terms. I of course suggested we meet in Lough. That is the capital of the Waterborn nation," Shiloh said as he leaned back in his seat.

"What is Lough like?" Onyx asked.

Shiloh looked over at Kader to explain. "I suppose I can tell him since I was there just last month," Kader said with a smile. He turned towards Onyx. "It is a beautiful and bright city where the buildings are made of white stone and gold trim. The palace rises up out of ocean waves so blue and clear that it reflects back a perfect image. Just like a mirror."

"Cool! Is it cold like it is here?" Onyx asked with delight.

"Actually the winter there is a bit mild though the ocean breezes keep it cool enough," Kader replied.

Before Kader could continue, a blood curdling scream cut through the calm of the morning. Shiloh's posture immediately tightened as he jumped up from his seat. Before he could walk two feet from his chair, Sai Parahazur flanked by six Sabers stepped onto the terrace. All seven slapped clenched fists across their chests and bowed quickly. Sai bent in close to whisper something to Shiloh that immediately caused him to blanche.

"Master Erebus, take the Lady Nuru and my grandson to my private quarters. Now," Shiloh ordered with absolute control.

Kader gathered Nuru and Onyx from their seats as Sai barked an order to three of his Sabers to escort them. Onyx clutched his mother's hand as Kader led them away from the terrace, the Sabers taking up positions around them. They left Shiloh and Sai in uneasy silence. Onyx's thoughts were so scrambled that he barely noticed the details in the hallway that led to his grandfather's rooms. Who screamed? What had his grandfather so frightened? Was there a Demon in the city? Is that why the Sabers were on high alert? He had so many questions but he did not know where to begin.

His grandfather's quarters reflected the combined nature of a military scholar with a worldly perspective. Normally, Onyx would run over to the globe by the window and spin it until he found an exotic place for his grandfather to describe. Now, he just sat next to his mother as Kader nervously paced back and forth by the door. The three Sabers darted about the room, checking each window and door. Everyone whispered to each other in low voices.

"Master Erebus, what is going on?" his mother finally asked.

Kader stopped pacing and dropped the hand that he was scratching his chin with. "I wish that I had a solid answer to give you. As long as I have known Lord Shiloh, I still do not know his mind." His black robes, normally crisp and unwrinkled, were unsettled on his thin body. He had pushed his sleeves back to expose his forearms.

"Is is a Demon?" Onyx asked as Nuru held him tight. He could tell that she was shaking.

"Whatever it is, the Shadowlord will destroy it," one of the Sabers stated with absolute surety. His two companions agreed.

Kader stayed the three Sabers with a pressing gesture of his hand. "We must trust in Lord Shiloh to do what is right."

No one seemed to want to speak and speculate anymore on what was going on. Kader resumed pacing, mouthing to himself in a private conversation. Nuru kept her arms tight around Onyx as if to protect him from some unseen danger. The wait was agonizing and it only served to further agitate the three Sabers. Their hands never left the hilts of their belted on swords. Onyx knew that he should be just as worried as everyone else but he did not know what to think or feel. After a while, the couch he and his mother were sitting on felt hard and uncomfortable but he didn't want to move away.

Sai then stepped into the room and went to stand close to Kader. "The Lord Shiloh wants to see you," the Commander of the Sabers said in a low voice.

Kader nodded. "Stay here. I know that Lord Shiloh would want to be certain that his grandson is well protected."

"No one will be allowed to pass without me to deal with," Sai stated with confidence. He nodded towards Kader before the Lord's Chancellor disappeared into the hallway beyond the door.

The tone of Sai's voice unnerved Onyx and when Kader left the room, he started to feel just as worried and scared as his mother. Sai stood with his back to the door, left hand gripping the hilt of his sword tightly. He was just as tense as his underlings. Onyx watched as Sai's eyes darted back and forth between the three Sabers. The big Saber Commander was practically unreadable underneath his intense gaze. The only thing that Onyx could tell was that Sai held a tight posture and constantly looked back at him as if to reassure himself that his Prince was still before him. Onyx immediately thought of his father and shuddered.

In reaction to her son's shudder, Nuru held Onyx tighter

and rubbed his back. He appreciated the comforting touch as fear threatened to overwhelm him. Minutes passed in agonizing silence with only the occasional word between Sai and the three Sabers that paced near the floor to ceiling window on the other side of the room. Onyx fought with worry as his mind dared to think that the source of the scream was his father. As he thought about it, he had never heard his father scream though he was apt to shout during combat matches. So if it was his father, why was he screaming so terribly?

Kader reappeared an hour later, looking somber and tired. Once the door closed behind him, he fell back against it as if burdened by some unseen weight. He pinched the bridge of his nose, closing his eyes tightly. Sai looked to him as if to offer help but Kader then quickly stood up straight. The Lord's Chancellor stopped the Saber Commander from speaking as he made his way over to Onyx and Nuru. He pulled a footstool forward to sit before them. He leaned forward, elbows on his knees with his hands clasped together.

"I will be plain with you. His Royal Highness has suffered a grievous injury that was inflicted upon him during the hunt. The Lord Shiloh has asked me not to say more for fear of frightening you but I can not hide the truth. The wounds are terrible and may very well take Aku's life," Kader said frankly though he struggled with his delivery.

Onyx wailed at the thought that his father might die while Nuru rested her chin on the top of his head, tears streaming down her face. She held him tightly to her as they both wept. As stoic as the Sabers were in their duty, they too felt the pain of Onyx and Nuru. Each one of them drew closer to their royals in a protective circle.

"I want to see my husband," Nuru said before her voice broke. "If he is to die, then he should have those he loves at his side."

Sai put a hand on Kader's shoulder but he brushed it away. "If it is your wish but I would not lose hope just yet. Master Adonis is tending to your husband even as we speak. I will take you to him now."

Onyx remained tightly latched to his mother's side as they followed Kader through the halls. More Sabers and palace guards surrounded them, hands at the ready on their weapons. The mood in the castle was somber and anxious. Onyx held on to his mother's hand as if he was still a small child and not a young boy of nearly nine years of age. He could barely see through the tears as the group walked with Kader in the lead. Sai walked at Onyx's left side. They eventually turned down a hallway that led into the eastern wing of the castle. Onyx began to recognize the various office doors to the Shadow Council members. He picked out Kaiser's office once he saw the mixed line of guards and Sabers flanking the door.

Kader paused before the closed door and turned around to bend down to Onyx's eye level. He set a hand on the Prince's left shoulder, giving it a squeeze. "Do you wish to come inside? If you do not, Commander Parahazur will remain at your side."

He looked up to see Sai nod and confirm the statement. Onyx considered the idea for a moment before nodding himself. He liked Sai well enough but he did not want to leave his mother's side. Kader sighed deeply before standing up straight. He turned around and with a gesture of his hand, the door to Kaiser's office was opened.

The inside of the office was surprisingly luxurious though furniture was in disarray. Chairs and tables were pushed into each other at strange angles with all spare pillows and cushions piled up around a bench. On the bench laid Aku with a deathly palour in his skin. His personal Saber guard Donovan Shunga paced back and forth nearby, chewing on a fingernail. Kaiser knelt by Aku's side, sleeves rolled up to his elbows. What horrified Onyx was that Kaiser's forearms were coated in bright red blood. His grandfather sat with his back towards the door, clutching Aku's hand.

"The wound is so deep. Can you save him?" Shiloh struggled to ask as he looked towards the noble.

"It will take time, my Lord, but I am certain that I can bring him back to us," Kaiser said with utter calm as he washed his hands in a basin sitting on the floor by his knees. His eyes darted up to indicate to Shiloh that Onyx and Nuru had entered the room.

Shiloh nodded before he stood up slowly. He turned around to embrace the both of them. "Please do not be frightened," he said over and over again as he held onto them.

"Is it true, Master Adonis? Can you save him?" Nuru asked, looking over Shiloh's shoulder.

Kaiser looked up, lifting an eyebrow. "I have my talents, Princess. No son of Umbra grows up without training in the medical arts and the treatment of Demon wounds. I have suffered my own wounds at the hands of a score of Demons. I more than anyone understand the pain your dear husband is going through at this moment."

"Choose your words carefully, Adonis," Kader warned in a voice that made Onyx turn to look at him. He wondered why the Lord's Chancellor said what he did.

With a roll of the shoulders, Kaiser brushed the statement off with cool confidence. He bowed his head. "Let my healing of the

Crowned Prince restore the people's faith in me and my loyalty to the throne. I will bring him back even if I must stay awake through the days and nights." Kaiser turned his gaze to Onyx. "Do you trust me to save your father?"

*****

Onyx hated that the memory still hurt him after four years when his father had survived. Kader had promised him the hope that he would. At the time, Onyx would have done anything to have his father back and though Aku was not the same, Onyx still had him. And he was thankful. But now Kaiser had pushed away the man that had been his comfort in all of his time of sorrow. He did not know whether to hate him or accept the truth. With mixed emotions, Onyx left his rooms.

The solar was situated under a glass dome on the only point of the castle that was higher than the Heights. A black iron cage held the glass in place to the stone walls. It was a wide room, centered on a massive oak table with a map of the known world painted on its surface. Along the walls were shelves of compasses, astrolabes, scrolls, books and other tomes dedicated to knowledge and history. From the center of the iron cage hung an iron wrought chandelier.

Onyx stepped over to the table as soon as he entered the room, seeing that Kaiser was already there. He glanced over the expansive map and quickly spotted his home city of Cross. He reached out towards it, jumping back in surprise when the map moved under his fingers and zoomed in closer to Cross.

"It is a Living Map. See how the rivers are flowing and how the wind moves across the grasslands," Kaiser said with a wave of his hand. The map returned to its original state.

Onyx returned to the side of the table and eyed the map warily. With Kaiser watching, he reached out to touch the map again. A smile came across his face when he felt the cool air of the high mountains on his palm. "How is this possible?"

Kaiser chuckled as he stood back. "There are many powers in this world. This is but a minor one." He latched his hands together and cleared his throat. "Your father has asked me to speak to you as his heir on his behalf this morning. He is not well after the trials of yesterday."

The mention of his father's infirmity took Onyx's attention away from the map. He then remembered Kader and how they parted. He stood up straight and faced Kaiser from across the table. "Then as my father's new Lord's Chancellor, you will tell me what happened to Kader," Onyx said firmly.

Kaiser sighed deeply. "As my young Prince knows, I serve your father with the utmost loyalty. It was his decision to dismiss Master Erebus from his position when I brought to him some troubling evidence of treason." He cleared his throat. "Your Master Erebus was planning to spirit you away from Cross to keep you from your father."

Onyx could not believe Kaiser's words. "The Master Erebus I know is an honorable man with a sterling reputation. I may be young but I am not blind to what is said about you," he retorted.

"That is because your father sought to protect you from the truth but I found out that Master Erebus was planning to kidnap you. Yes, many things are said about me but many do not understand the loyal ambition to serve the greater good. And I was the son of a border general after all," Kaiser deftly explained. "I am a warrior of subtlety, not swords."

It was well known that Kaiser was the son of celebrated general Cian Adonis who fought at Shadow Night's side until his death. And history spoke of his unwavering loyalty. Onyx remembered his grandfather telling him war stories by the fireside when his mother was not looking. His favorite story had been when Cian led a battalion of Shadowborn to rescue Shadow Night from the advance of a Demon general. In that story, the general was brave, noble and fierce. Onyx began to doubt his feelings, thinking that maybe he didn't understand loyalty as he once thought. He then remembered Akakios.

"You were arrested after the fall of Akakios. You were convicted of treason," Onyx said.

"I did counsel our dearly departed Lord with poor advice and I was not able to save him from his own madness. I had thought it best to protect his memory and not say certain truths," Kaiser solemnly replied by hanging his head. "But I did hope to redeem myself by answering your grandfather's call to rescue your dear father from death."

Onyx fought back the memories of fear when his father was brought back by his personal guard, a hole ripped in his chest. "And I had wished that my father would live no matter what."

Kaiser rounded the table and bent down to his eye level. "The art I used is not perfect and I have cursed myself day and night for not bringing him back to you whole. Can you find it in your heart to forgive my failure, your Highness?" Onyx nodded slowly, fighting back tears. Kaiser reached into his pocket and pulled out a small handkerchief. "Take this and wipe your tears. I do bear some good tidings on this morning."

The wounds of loss were still fresh but Onyx gathered

himself, wiping his eyes. Kaiser gestured towards the map and waved a hand over the southern borders of the Northlands. The image sped from Cross to the white walls of Crossroads.

"This is a grand city that will host a majestic and lavish celebration soon. It is my hope that we all go and celebrate the investiture of the Immortal Truth with our friends and neighbors," Kaiser started to say as he watched Onyx lean over the table edge. "It is celebrated every one hundred years; truly a grand occasion and one of the few times we gather in such numbers."

"Tell me more," Onyx said looking up at Kaiser.

The Chancellor smiled as he bowed his head. He then waved his right hand across the map, setting it to run to a new place. The image shifted and transformed beneath his palm in a flurry of colors.

"There is so much more in the world than what you have been told. The truth is more than just the walls of Cross. I can show you everything that you want to know and more," Kaiser stated with a pleading voice as if he was begging Onyx to listen. "I can even take you myself to the Mortal lands. To look across the sea to the Farlands."

It was like a living dream as Kaiser directed the map down to the Southlands with a waft of his left hand. He then spread out his fingers and the map zoomed in to view the docks of Arken where sailors, fisherman, and harbor masters shouted greetings and business deals. The ocean waves lapped up against the hulls of ships as seabirds darted in and out of the water for fish.

It surprised him how much the men of the docks looked like every Shadowborn Onyx had seen. The sailors had sinewy muscles that reminded him of the fastest Sabers though he doubted that they shared the same ability for speed. The fishermen had eyes as bright as any Immortal, full of a zest for life and enjoying it to the fullest. Onyx felt like if he were to stand among them, he would blend right in.

"Yes, the Mortals are joyous and free of the long years that we as Immortals bear witness to. It is ultimately our duty to guide them and protect them from harm," Kaiser said as he watched Onyx's curious expression. "Now, do you see the fog that covers the sea here?"

Onyx watched as he pointed to a shady gray line of mist that wavered over the sea. The Living Map then refused to move further past it. "What is beyond the fog?"

"The Farlands. The land that Begin Anu hails from. It is said that he was the last of the Farlanders to escape their war torn land for reasons left to history. But that is a lesson for another time, good Prince," Kaiser said as he drew his hand back and the map quickly returned to a paper like appearance. "There is so much for you to learn."

"Have you ever been to the Southlands? Seen the Farlands?" Onyx asked with mesmorized curiosity.

Kaiser chuckled. "Yes, I have been to the Southlands though my visit was ages ago. No one alive has seen the Farlands though. Its existence is now only within books and our memories. I shall teach you the lessons needed to become a good Prince and worldly Shadowlord. I would give a lesson today but I have business to attend to in Eclipse. I also still wish for you to get proper rest and have time to grieve."

"You are kinder than I had thought for so many paint you in a poor light," Onyx pointed out.

Kaiser smiled briefly. "I understand the pain of loss, good Prince. Very few of us truly do."

THE PIRATE

"This place stinks," Rache groaned as he wrinkled his thin nose. He covered his mouth to avoid gagging.

"Says the Demon who drinks blood and has a taste for man flesh. The smell of briny seawater and waste bothers the likes of you?" Kaiser asked as he turned a rusted iron key in the lock. The old door creaked in response.

Rache snorted. "And it doesn't bother you?"

Kaiser smirked as he pushed the door open. He gestured for Rache to take a torch from its holder on the stone wall. The Demon obeyed, using his free hand to reset the cloth mask over his face. He dutifully followed Kaiser into the hallway.

The hallway was on the bottom level of a prison that housed the criminals of Eclipse. Eclipse was a sea side city on the northeastern shore of the glassy Mirror Sea. It was the largest settlement west of the capital and was subject to attacks by pirates. This particular prison held the most infamous of Shadowborn raiders. It was a stone fortress that was built half on land, half in the water.

Rache did not want to admit it but he hated the small of salty seawater. It left a sour taste in his mouth whenever Kaiser forced him to go to places near the ocean. He was a creature of fire and shadow that could make it rain blood. He was terrifying, brutal, and dangerous but he hated the ocean for it was filled with uncomfortable memories. Rache sucked in his breath as he followed Kaiser through the winding tunnel. Soon he was able to hear the subtle thump of heartbeats.

"You have been rather quiet," Kaiser casually said, breaking the silence. He halted and turned around, pressing a hand to the center of Rache's chest.

"I hate the ocean," Rache grumbled as he tightened his grip on the torch.

"Of course you do. My illustrious ancestor and you toppled into the seas by the West Gatelands. He left you to die beneath the waves and yet you managed to irk out some degree of survival," Kaiser mocked with a tilt of his head.

Rache frowned, knowing that Kaiser was trying to sense the rhythm of his heart for hints of fear. He hated the control Kaiser had over him with their unholy bond.

Kaiser chuckled as he removed his hand, pointing a finger at the spot over Rache's heart. "Do not worry. Your presence is worthwhile here. The warden asked for me to... clean out the riff raff. I dare not get my hands dirty but you are more than welcome to."

"The warden knows of me?" came Rache's concerned reply.

"Well, let's just say he knows that I have a dangerous weapon. I bought his loyalty decades ago by securing him this vaulted position. Seems people will do anything for the hope of my protection against pirates and raiders. And why not trust me? I am the son of a powerful general so I must be just as capable as he had been," Kaiser reasoned though his cunning grin never left his face. He patted Rache's cheek before turning around. "At least that is what I told them."

The prospect of slaughter excited Rache's appetite for blood and he found himself smiling. Though the strong salty odor of the sea still unnerved him, Rache focused on the faint heartbeats of the prisoners. He spotted an unlit line of torches on the wall to his right. He wafted his free hand, taking control of his torch flame. Kaiser watched his Demon servant manipulate the flame into a concentrated ball, mimicking his clenched fist. He grinned as Rache released the flame, lighting the torches and illuminating the long hallway.

Almost immediately, hands and arms sprung through the iron bars of multiple cell doors. Their owners stretched and reached for any form of contact. Shadowborn prisoners were kept in an absolute darkness in below ground cells in accordance of their offense. The prison in Eclipse had the added barrier of being partially submerged. As such, prisoners were starved for light and for attention. The condition was meant to break the hardest of criminals. Both Kaiser and Rache told themselves in the quiet of their own minds that they would never be broken. The stretch for attention was accompanied by cries and desparate words.

"I repent! I repent! Let me go! Get me out of here!" were just some of the pleading cries. Hands swiped the empty air.

Rache's body began to tingle with anticipation. He stretched his hands to free his fingers of tension. All of his focus intensified the bloodlust that was now transformed into a thumping pulse. He was a predator ready to pounce. Bouncing on his heels, he looked to Kaiser for any indication of a command or permission. He frowned when Kaiser only gestured for him to follow.

"Can I just have a taste? You can't just dangle prey in front of me and expect me to do nothing," Rache asked with the hint of demand.

"You can't just kill everyone and waste your precious talent for reading blood memories on trash," Kaiser stated as he paused. "Even if you are good at killing."

The Demon puffed out his chest with pride. He was good at killing as it was something he enjoyed. His mind briefly touched on the memory of his fall into the ocean, locked in his titantic battle with Begin Anu. Beneath the churning waves, Begin Anu had struck him so hard on the chest that the impact had crushed his heart. He remembered gasping for breath only to suck in a torrent of salt water. He remembered the look of superiority and power in Begin's eyes and how it frightened him. A brief glimpse of his own fear at dying beneath the waves was quickly enveloped by the return to life by Kaiser's command. The feeling of a new chance to take on the world that had tried to give up on him. All of those emotions only intensified his bloodlust.

"You will have your chance. First, I need to find someone," Kaiser stated. Rache knew that he did not care in a genuine sense. Rache was smart enough to know Kaiser only cared about himself and in the end, he could not be trusted.

"Who?" Rache asked, clenching his fists. His crimson hair gleamed in the torch light. Amidst his desire to kill, he was starting to feel gross from the sea air settling on him. Even he had pride in how he looked.

"The one I would have named High Commander had he not been caught," Kaiser replied as the two continued down the hallway, ignoring the cries for attention.

Rache was about to press for an answer when a prisoner reached out and grabbed a fold of Kaiser's long coat. In a flash of movement, Kaiser grabbed the arm, pulled his coat free, and ripped the prisoner's arm forward. The prisoner slammed chest first into the iron bars, groaning from the impact. Kaiser growled an inaudible warning before pulling hard. He broke the prisoner's shoulder and tore the arm until the skin and muscle ripped down to the bone. Kaiser shoved back and the prisoner wailed in pain. Kaiser scoffed before continuing on down the hall towards a solid iron door with a small window. Rache looked in to the cell, seeing the copious amount of blood squirting all over the floor. The injured prisoner continued to cry as his cellmates had backed themselves up against the far wall. Three frightened men stared from their injured cellmate to Rache.

Now Kaiser's answer did not matter. "Can I?" Rache asked eagerly looking to his master. He pulled his mask away from his face.

"Start there and work your way back towards the entrance. I have business to attend to," Kaiser said with an absent flip of the hand.

Almost immediately, Rache rushed forward and tore the door from its hinges, tossing it aside. It hit the wall with a loud clang. Rache balanced against the stone archway that threatened to crumble at any moment. He licked his lips as his bone white fangs flashed in the low light. The four prisoners cowered in fear, unable to scream. Rache lurched forward, blocking any chance for escape. He crouched down to the injured prisoner, looming over him. His bones and muscles began to shift beneath his taut pale skin as his blood vessels swelled. "You're first."

Kaiser smirked as he heard the blood curdling screams and the rendering of flesh. He chuckled as he unlocked the door before him. With a flick of the wrist, a spark of fire alighted from the closest torch and settled over his open hand. The door creaked open with a shuddering sound. As soon as he stepped inside the cell, he threw the door closed.

"Welcome to my humble abode," came a low voice in the deep black darkness. Kaiser raised his flame wielding hand, revealing a tall, lean man sitting on a wood frame cot. He had a thin, knotted scar that ran from his right temple across the front of his face, and down to the edge of his left jaw. His eyes were a haunting gray and it looked like his nose had been broken and healed improperly. His black hair, tied back with a leather band, melted into the shadows.

"My good Loran Win. Your cousin asked about you," Kaiser said as he sat down on the only available chair. It was crudely made from old driftwood.

Loran spit on the ground. "Like I care about that worthless prick. Our fathers may have been brothers but we only share blood and a name. Nothing more." He tossed several pieces of broken wood on the floor and gestured for Kaiser to light the pile. Kaiser brought the flame down low and let it go. Soon a small fire was crackling and burning. "He is a pretender of power and courage."

"That may be true but he serves his purpose for the time being," Kaiser stated as he pulled on his sleeves. "He is like a dog eager to please his master. You however are a wolf, savage and wild."

"Then why name him High Commander?" Loran asked.

"I have other plans for you. Besides, it would have been difficult to get the nobles to accept the notorious pirate of the Mirror Sea as the leader of the armed forces," Kaiser replied as he pulled his seat forward. "I need powerful allies that can move outside of the border unseen. I know and understand what you are capable of and it is unfortunate that you were caught." Kaiser bowed his head.

"Blame Shiloh Silvanus. I was this close to taking the city but the mighty Prince rolls in," Loran began, clenching his fists. "Well here I am." He slapped his knees.

"I seem to remember when Akakios had been executed and the throne sat empty. The Shadow Council was in an uproar. Akakios' bastard was the only Silvanus blood in Cross while Shiloh was away dealing with you. And I'm sure you know that Sage Silvanus can't be found and Aday is lost in his insanity," Kaiser explained.

"What of Aku? Wasn't he of age?" Loran asked as he sorted through Kaiser's explanation.

Kaiser laughed. "The Council did not even consider him. He was unproven, inexperienced. It was down to the bastard and Shiloh."

The fire snapped as the wood burned red and hot. "Seems like the royal bloodline is falling apart," Loran stated as he nudged another piece of wood towards the fire with his foot. He then smirked as he turned his gaze to Kaiser. "But that is your plan is it not?"

"Ah you are as smart as I had hoped. Tell me, Master Win, where do your loyalties lie?" Kaiser asked as he crossed his arms tightly.

Loran grinned. "To the one who sets me free from this place and gives me purpose again."

The answer pleased Kaiser and he proudly squared his shoulders in response. Loran had proved as he hoped. Even clad in the thin roughspun cotton shirt and faded, worn wool breeches, Loran was as lethal as the rumors had told him. Kaiser admired his hunter's bearing though Loran was no match for himself. Off in the distance, he heard the loud crash of another iron door and the resulting screams of terror. A roar boomed down the hallway.

"You hear that roar? That is who will destroy you if you prove false to me. My reach goes so deep that if you try to run away, I will find you and I will kill you. There is nowhere you can hide from me," Kaiser warned in a dark tone. The fire seemed to diminish as the room grew utterly dark. Loran shivered from the chill in the air. "Do you understand?"

"I am not my cousin. I go into battle without fear. With no name in my heart but that of my master. Lord Kaiser, if you free me from this miserable place, I will serve you with utter loyalty. I will die for you," Loran intoned with unwavering certainty. He meant every word that he said.

Kaiser waved his hand and the fire sparked back to life. The darkness in the room disappeared with the cold. "Good. We have an understanding. First, I only wished you had kept Shiloh away long enough for me to talk to the bastard."

"What is the bastard to you?" Loran quickly asked.

"He is of my blood though he airs on the side of his Silvanus relatives. He is my dead daughter's son," Kaiser stated with no emotion.

Loran laughed out loud. "That does explain a lot about Ryder Coba. He is like a diluted version of you with the glimmer of an actual heart."

Kaiser frowned. He debated on striking Loran even though he bore no familial love for Ryder. He only viewed him as a weapon and potential ally. Someone he had invested a lot of time and energy in. The chair creaked beneath him as he leaned forward. "He is of my blood and is none of your concern unless I command it to be. Got it?" Loran put his hands up in surrender. "I am not here to discuss the failings of the Silvanus bloodline. I am here to present an opportunity."

Loran put his arms out to the side. "I am yours to command."

Kaiser's faith in the man was renewed. Unlike his cousin, Loran did not press for answers or ask more questions when a tender subject was broached. He clenched his jaw as he heard the dying gasps of yet another prisoner. Rache was being thorough. He only hoped that the Demon would learn some useful information from the blood memories.

"I need you to go to Cascade and deliver a message. Remind Lord Oren of how precious his silence is and that if he harbors anyone who speaks ill of me, I will have him and his entire family slaughtered." Kaiser reached into his coat pocket. "This is a Blood Seal with my coat of arms. It will allow you to pass through the Shadow Mirror at the border at will. Do not lose it."

Loran took the palm sized silver pendent and turned it over to examine the coat of arms. Traced in shining red metal, the design was of a crowned eagle in mid flight, clutching a curved sword in its talons. "Never knew that this was the Adonis coat of arms. It's not like eagles rank high in the Shadowborn culture."

"It is a homage to the Anu name and bloodline. Adonis was the birth name of Begin Anu's eldest. My surname comes from his birthname," Kaiser answered.

"Fair enough. I think mine is a pair of crossed scimitars. So when do I begin?" Loran asked as he closely examined the blood seal.

"RACHE!" Kaiser roared. In a heartbeat, Rache had ripped Loran's cell door from its hinges and stepped inside. He was covered in blood and gore with the red liquid dripping from his chin. "Stage an escape. Kill whom you wish. Destroy what you must." Kaiser stood up to face the Demon and pointed back at Loran. "Make sure he gets out alive."

Rache nodded. "I'll do what I do best."

Kaiser smirked and turned his head to look back at Loran one last time. "Do not disappoint me or you will have to answer to him."

THE JOURNEY TO CASCADE

Haro stood beside his Gryphon partner, gripping the sturdy leather straps of his traveling pack tightly. He anxiously waited, shifting his weight between his feet. It was nerve wracking to be standing around so Haro turned to look at the setting sun for comfort.

"I wonder why the captains chose us instead of waiting for an armed escort." Haro asked, speaking out of the side of his mouth.

Arik shook his head and shoulders, trying to get rid of his own tension. "We did find him at North Bend," the Gryphon replied as he pawed the dirt. He stretched out his talons, carving furrows as he relaxed.

"We are scouts, not escorts," Haro grumbled as he looked down at his feet. He was ready to get moving.

"Our captains seem to think otherwise," Arik stated in reprimand. "And did you forget that you are from Cascade?"

Haro sighed deeply as he thought of his sister back home. Before he could respond, Avani and Whisper exited the pavilion with Kader Erebus. Kader was drowning in a forest green cloak, a hood pulled low over his face. His steps were shuffled as he clutched a crudely carved staff in his left hand. Avani whispered a few words, placing a hand on his back and directing him towards Haro and Arik. She then looked up and snapped her fingers towards two Earthborn guards who promptly brought forth two slim chestnut horses.

Haro took the reins of his horse while the two guards turned to assist Kader. Avani took the reins while the guards lifted Kader up into the saddle. Kader slumped forward, dropping the staff and grabbing the saddle horn with his left hand. When he settled, a guard handed him the dropped staff.

"The path shall lead you to safety in the halls of my Lord," Avani said as she settled the horse. "I would advise you not to speak of what you told me to anyone else but Lord Palani," she added as she stroked the horse's neck.

Kader weakly nodded. "I take your counsel in good faith, Captain."

Whisper finally stepped forward and bowed his round brown head. "Ride true," he stated in halting words. The Night Captain of the Gryphons was not a confident speaker of the common tongue.

Avani turned to look at Haro as he mounted his horse, pulling back on the reins to steady the mare. "I do not anticipate trouble but be on your guard," she stated firmly.

"I shall watch the sky while he watches the forest," Arik promised with a bow of the head. He stood up on all fours and opened his wings. Whisper chirped a short sentence, his tone stern. Arik replied in kind with a confident whistle.

Haro eased his horse beside Kader's as Avani and Whisper stepped back to give them space. With three quick flaps, Arik was air born and rose quickly into the sky, twisting his body to gain speed. Haro watched as his Gryphon partner turned into a small white speck above the treetops. He let out a deep breath before turning his gaze towards the path that led deep into the eastern forest.

"Go and be quick about it. I suspect that war is once again upon us," Avani said sternly as she stepped forward again to secure a lead line between the two horses.

Haro nodded as he urged his horse forward, Kader's horse following dutifully behind. There was no fanfare and no applause as he passed under the eaves of the tree branches. Already he missed the warmth and comfort of his tent with its small blazing camp fire. He shook from an imagined chill as he went over in his head the different Gryphon calls Arik had taught him.

The horses plodded along in silence and ease, swishing their tails to slap at biting insects. Haro began to wonder as the sun continued to set about lighting a torch. The smoke would at the very least discourage the insects from getting too close. Being an Earthborn, he did not have the night vision of a Shadowborn but with Kader weak from his injuries, Haro did not want to push him to help.

Arik whistled a sharp note from above his head that was

clear and abrupt. That was their prearranged signal for night approaching and close flight as Arik had put it. His Gryphon partner would be flying close to the tree tops. Haro whistled his best imitation of the call to let his partner know that he had heard him. He looked back to check on Kader, seeing him slightly bent over in silence. The heavy cloth hood hid his face from view.

"I am not bereft of my ability to speak," Kader said suddenly. "The shadows of the night are a comfort to my wounds."

"Avani told me not to bother you too much," Haro answered, feeling like a child in the old sage's presence.

Kader chuckled softly. "Just don't ask me to walk. I know that Cascade is a good distance away from the border river." He coughed for a few seconds. "It is the River Shadow in my homeland. What name do the Earthborn give it in theirs?"

It was nice that Kader was making conversation so Haro happily replied. "The same as the Shadowborn. The River Shadow."

"It has been a few years since I travelled in the lands of the Earthborn though I had the pleasure of hosting your Lord and his family in mine," Kader stated.

Haro thought that Kader would happily continue into a story about the grand event. Instead, Kader fell silent. He waited before he responded. "My homeland is better to see in the daytime and especially in spring when the flowers are blooming."

"Yes, I remember the golden fields before Cascade. Seeing the wind brush across the wheat was so soothing and beautiful," Kader replied. He sighed deeply.

Every time Kader fell silent, Haro began to wonder if he was fighting back a wave of pain. "Have you seen the gardens of Cascade?"

"I have," Kader said with a smile. "My Lady Nuru brought a glimpse of them to Cross. As I am sure that you have been taught, my land is that of a mountain forest so fields of wheat and flowers are a rare sight. Lady Nuru thought that our use of black was too serious and depressing." Kader chuckled. "Within a single growing season, red roses, white lilies, and pastel daisies bloomed all over Cross."

"May she rest in peace," Haro said upon hearing the Earthborn Princess' name. He wanted to ask so many questions regarding her death as very little information had reached his people. She was beloved throughout the lands of the Earthborn for her gentle nature and kindness.

Arik whistled two short chirps as a check in. Haro replied back with his own chirps, still having a hard time wrapping his tongue around the sound.

"That is one thing I never mastered. How difficult is it to speak the Gryphon tongue?" Kader asked in interest.

"I am actually not fluent in speaking it. Arik has taught me a few words and sounds as scouting signals but I have yet to master any subtly as he tells me," Haro explained with a shrug.

"May I? I know a few words," Kader asked. Haro nodded and Kader did his own check in chirp. Arik excitedly whistled back before regaining his quiet composure. "How did you come to have him as your partner?"

Haro could tell that Kader was deliberately avoiding any conversation that reminded him of his home. But he did not mind keeping the Shadowborn at ease. "Arik is a little older than me but in a Gryphon's lifetime, he is mentally my age. We are both young in the grand scheme of things so when I graduated from my training, I was matched with him. Nothing exciting I'll admit."

"You two have a similar temperament. Very eager to learn and loyal to your duty," Kader pointed out.

"Thank you," Haro graciously answered. "I am proud to serve my Lord Palani."

Kader nodded. "True loyalty is hard to come by these days. Everyone is out for themselves," he seethed for a rare moment of anger. "Forgive me."

Haro only shrugged though questions raced around in his head. He wanted so many answers but Avani's orders roared back to the forefront of his mind. He returned his gaze forward, trying to remain focused. It was difficult and he couldn't stand it any longer. "What happened to my Lord's sister?"

Kader cleared his throat. "This is not a light matter for me to discuss though I know you wish to learn of your beloved Princess's fate. Do trust me for the time being."

His answer spoke volumes even if he did not say many words. Haro sunk down in the saddle as he tried to consider what all of his scouting observations have meant. The questions in his mind threatened to overwhelm him and he shook his head to break concentration. He felt like he was standing on the edge looking into a deep and dark abyss. All he could see was a terrible shadow with glowing white eyes.

RYDER COBA

The Gryphon messenger beat her pointed wings as fast as she could, gliding when the air currents allowed for a moment of rest. She was not an endurance flier but she was young and fast, the best qualities for a Falcon Gryphon messenger. She knew that endurance would come with time. This was her first major mission and she had no intentions of failing. Strapped around her chest in a leather tube was a Feather Whisper meant for the Lord of the Fireborn, Argos.

She spotted the Fireborn capital of Coal in the distance, a spread out collection of sandstone buildings. It was as she remembered from her first visit with her mother where a large white stone building sat in the center of the sandstone architecture with a long set of stairs leading up to its entrance. She banked to the left, turning up her right wing to change her direction. The ground came closer as she descended over the outer buildings, coasting towards an open courtyard. The people below her shouted in welcome and she puffed up her chest in response, knowing how revered her kind was. She could not help but feel a little proud.

Flaring out her wings and stretching out her legs, the Desert Falcon Gryphon landed in a cloud of dust. She promptly shook the dust off her back, not wanting to look dirty. Her sharp eyes looked around the courtyard.

"Mistress Gryphon," a Fireborn said as he stepped forward and bowed. He was clean shaven with short crimson hair and he wore white linen that billowed in the breeze.

"I bear a message for Lord Argos of the Fireborn," she said as she plucked the leather tube from her chest. She repeated the words in her head, checking to see if her language practice had paid off. She straightened her posture and threw back her shoulders with pride.

The Fireborn took the leather tube and read the words scratched into the side. "You may follow me, Mistress Lana. My Lord is in the practice yard with Ryder Coba."

Lana had heard of Ryder Coba many times before. He was a son of the royal Shadowborn family though not a legitimate one by their laws. People spoke of him in pity for he grew up in Umbra without a father who ruled in distant Cross. When Akakios waged his unjust war and was later executed, the bastard son was lopped in with his father, facing scorn and hate as if he committed the same crimes. It was sad as Ryder was truly a shining example of what his ancestor Shadow Night Silvanus had been during the height of his power. Lana had even heard from several Gryphon leaders back home that Ryder would have made a fine Shadowlord and that none of the troubles that had recently beset the throne would have happened. She had not expected to meet him here in Coal.

The Fireborn court official guided her through the winding streets to the palace stairs. Lana hesitated as she had no experience climbing stairs for Gryphons did not have them in their own homeland. Thankfully, the Fireborn gestured for her to fly to the top. She jumped into the air and with a few quick wing beats, landed at the top of the stairs. Again, she had to shake the dust from her body with a roll of her shoulders. Coal was quickly becoming her least favorite place and she hoped that she could get a proper bath before leaving.

The practice yard was a short distance to the right of the palace stairs and outside of the palace walls. Lana groaned when she saw how sandy the area was. Desert Falcon Gryphon or not, she did not like to get dirty. She chose a thick woven carpet that had been laid out to sit on while the court official approached a tall flame haired man with tan skin.

"My Lord Argos. Mistress Lana of the Gryphons has brought you a message," the official said, handing over the leather tube.

Lana glanced over at the tall man that the official handed the tube to. Sweat glistened on his brawny arms as a dirty brown vest clung to his chest. His red hair fell down to the middle of his back in a messy ponytail that exposed streaks of black strands. She grimaced to see such a noble Lord dirty and unclean.

Argos twisted off the cap and pulled out a golden feather

that gleamed in the sunlight. He looked briefly at Lana who quickly sat up straight. He held the feather next to his ear. "A dire message indeed," Argos stated after he put the feather back in the tube and returned it to his official. The official bowed and stepped back.

"My Owl kin heard the words of the wind..." Lana said as she tried to think of the correct translation between her native tongue and that of the Spiritborn. "...and brought forth dark whispers..." Her eyes widened as she whistled sharply in the middle of talking.

Argos chuckled softly. "You have flown strong and true, Mistress Lana," he chawed in his limited knowledge of the Gryphon tongue.

Lana let out a sigh of relief that she had not embarrassed herself before the Lord of the Fireborn. She then watched as Argos directed her attention to the circle of sand. In the center stood a Shadowborn with his head down and a long wooden stave held tightly against his body. There was something about him that moved Lana's heart to hope and reverence. She fought the desire to bow down and lower her head. But there was a wild nature about him that she could not place. He bore himself with great control, his muscles relaxed but ready to fight. There was no hint of fear that he might fail in his endeavor. Lana then realized that the Shadowborn was completely aware of his great power. He betrayed nothing and he knew that he was dangerous. Around him in a circle were five Fireborn soldiers, stripped down to their pants and brandishing their own poles. Their muscles twitched in anticipation.

Argos moved to stand at Lana's side. "Ryder has seen fit to prove that my soldiers are powerless before his might. But let us see how does against greater odds." He whistled one sharp note.

Two of the soldiers leaped forward towards the Shadowborn, spinning their weapons around and kicking up dust. In a flurry of motion, the Shadowborn twisted his waist and flung the stave up into attack position. He spun under the first attacking Fireborn's pole, swinging his staff down low. Ryder swept the Fireborn off his feet and finished the spin up to his own feet to take the strike of the second Fireborn. As he sparred with the second, two more Fireborn charged forward. With a swift kick, he pushed his second opponent back and spun the wooden stick with both hands to take on the double attack.

The first Fireborn that had attacked him charged forward with the intent of using his weight to knock Ryder off balance. He nodded towards his companions, initiating a private attack plan. Ryder's eyes narrowed as he assessed the changing battle tactics.

The charging Fireborn lowered his left shoulder and angled his arm like a battering ram. The other four Fireborn split off in two pairs to surround Ryder again. Ryder smirked as he stabbed his staff into the ground. The Fireborn stopped in their attack, wondering if he had given up.

Only Lana could feel the imperceptible shake in the ground through her paws. She picked up her right paw, wiggling her talons before setting it down again. The shake was growing stronger and she looked up towards Ryder. The five soldiers could now feel the movement in the ground and their eyes darted about trying to determine a source. Just as they looked at Ryder, he cocked his head and an invisible wall of energy rushed out of his body. Each Fireborn was thrown back violently, crashing on the ground fifteen feet away. The wall of energy then withdrew in a rush and Ryder politely bowed.

"He is quite the warrior for very few outside of the Airborn can do what he just did," Argos declared as his five soldiers groaned in pain. "If there had been any shadows, he could have used his Shadow Slide to slip in and out of attack. I guess he made due with the circumstances."

Lana tried to figure out on her own what technique Ryder had utilized. It looked like the Airborn technique of Air Push where the wielder controls a gust of wind to push and pull an opponent but she could not be certain. Ryder was a Shadowborn so how could he use Air Push? It was now clear to her that the Shadowborn bastard knew that he was going to win the match from the beginning. She decided that it was a smart move on his part to lead his opponent on with thoughts of victory. It was an odd idea as Gryphons stalked and watched before attacking at the last moment. They did not fight with trickery. She shook her head, telling herself that the Spiritborn never ceased to confuse her.

"You've brought news from my homeland?" he asked her directly in a flawless command of the Gryphon tongue.

Lana was momentarily startled. She nodded after she gathered herself and straightened her posture. "I came with haste," was all she found herself able to say.

"Shiloh Silvanus has died from unnatural means and his ill son has taken his place. Once again, a choice is laid before you," Argos said aloud. "Will you remain in my city or will you go back home?"

Lana immediately saw the frown on Ryder's face as he turned his back to Argos. She thought the Fireborn would gasp at the affront like she did. In her homeland, turning your back to the Lord was a deep insult. The courtier who had led her to the yard and the five soldiers Ryder had just defeated did indeed gasp.

Argos frowned at the sign of disrespect.

"I wait for the Lord Avis' return to Coal and then I will go back to Crossroads," Ryder replied curtly as he handed his stave to one of the soldiers. "The decision of who sits on the throne of the Shadowborn is not mine to make and I will not take away what is rightfully Aku's."

Argos sighed deeply as he crossed his arms. "Lord Avis will be arriving at noon time tomorrow and you can then be on your way, Master Coba," the Lord of the Fireborn said formally. He then snapped his fingers at the official who promptly handed him a wooden rod.

Lana watched with sharp eyes as Argos burst forward. Ryder immediately turned to defend himself, taking his staff back and banging it against Argos' weapon. Argos attacked with the famous ferocity of the Fireborn people, driving hard against Ryder's strong defense. She found it odd that they appeared evenly matched as she considered their age difference.

Ryder flipped backwards, landing on his feet with stave pointed forward. Argos twisted around, whipping up a powerful Flame Shot. With the end of his stave, he threw it towards Ryder. Spinning his weapon around in a rapid succession of circles, Ryder dispelled the small blaze. Argos snorted like a charging bull before shooting off Flames Shots one by one. Ryder expertly dispelled each fiery bullet with quick jabs of his stave.

Piece of gray ash floated down to the sand like slowly falling snow as both Argos and Ryder stood on opposite sides of the practice yard. Argos stood with a frown on his face and stave pointed down. Ryder looked composed and equally stern. It was a standoff between two strong personalities. Lana tried to decide who looked fiercer. Argos then charged forward with a roar as loud as any lion she had heard. The two warriors collided with a smack of wood. Argos pressed his strength forward, keeping a tight grip on his long weapon.

"You are a heartless bastard, abandoning your people in their time of need! Everyone knows that Aku wavers on the edge of death and his son is still a child!" Argos snapped before shoving all of his weight forward. Ryder stumbled back a few steps but managed to stay on his feet. Seeing the challenge, Ryder returned with equal ferocity.

Lana could see that Argos now fought with a simmering anger that seemed to accuse Ryder of some unknown slight. Argos and Ryder traded blows with neither landing a strike. Their feet scuffed and pounded around the practice yard with their focus only on each other. After a forward push, Ryder spun around to Argos' right side, wrapped his right leg around Argos' leg and kicked forward. Argos fell onto his stomach but quickly somersaulted forward and jumped up to his feet. He reached for his pole but Ryder kicked it away. Argos sneered before cartwheeling towards his weapon, grabbing it and flipping up to meet Ryder's counter attack. He slid under Ryder's staff and then quickly stood up flipping Ryder up over him. Instead of falling flat on his back, Ryder twisted his body to land perfectly balanced.

"You do not have the power to command me. No one does," Ryder growled as he tightened his grip.

"But I do have the power to judge you," Argos barked as he circled him.

Ryder watched Argos, barely turning his head. "Since when? I have no Fireborn blood in me. I am pure Shadowborn through and through."

"You have a duty to Terra as a son of Shadow Night Silvanus and you chose to run away," Argos retorted as he came around to face Ryder. "You have sins to atone for," he added in a low and threatening voice.

Ryder got up in Argos' face. "I have done nothing," he growled before shoving the Lord of the Fireborn back. He threw his staff to the ground and pointed at him with fuming anger. "Do not think for a second that Akakios' sins are mine to share. I did not fight and I did not kill so my head should not roll."

If Lana could compare their stand off to something in Gryphon culture, it appeared as if Argos had insulted Ryder's honor. If they were indeed Gryphons, they would be hissing and screeching with hackles raised. It wasn't really a fight but a brawl that threatened to turn violent. And to Lana, that was unbecoming behavior for two Spiritborn of noble blood.

"Then you would watch the throne of your ancestors fall to ruin? Certainly no true Silvanus son in his right mind would run away from his birthright, bastard or not!" Argos mocked in a high and mighty voice.

Ryder then hit Argos so hard in the jaw that the Fireborn was knocked to the ground, the right side of his face swelling immediately. Lana was speechless as she watched Ryder approach Argos. "I am not Shadow Night. I am not Akakios. Their fate is not mine."

Argos looked like his pride had been wounded as he rubbed his jaw. He glanced at his fingertips looking for blood. All of the Fireborn at the edge of the yard were ready to pounce on Ryder but Argos stayed them with a gesture of his hand. He slowly got to his feet. "Had you been a Fireborn, I would have you whipped and thrown in prison."

"I have had worse," Ryder declared. "Evander threatened to

have me banished from his Dominion when I broke his arm."

Lana choked as her eyes widened in shock. "How did you manage to keep your head?" she chawed in the Gryphon tongue. She had managed to keep her silence until now and immediately regretted the question.

Ryder laughed. "I took out half of his royal guard until Vorin intervened on behalf. So much for the Lightborn's dislike of war." He then repeated the statement to Argos in the common tongue.

"Indeed," Argos stated as he squared his shoulders, flexing his jaw. "Mistress Lana, would you care to join me and Master Coba for an evening repast? It would honor my table to have the presence of a Gryphon," he asked as he looked over at Lana sitting on the carpet. Argos' eyes narrowed as his gaze returned to Ryder.

It was a kind invitation, Lana thought. She nodded, not confident enough to reply with her limited language skills.

*****

Lana watched as Ryder was seated at Argos' right hand, looking more like a stern dignitary than a bastard in his posture and expression. She sat slackjawed at the sight. This would have been unacceptable to her strict parents. Especially since Ryder had knocked Argos to the ground. Her father was a no nonsense courtier in the entourage of Lord Paladon who accepted nothing less than perfection from his peers. Her mother was equally as stern and never cared for the squabbles of the Spiritborn. From her bench at the opposite end of the small table, she watched Ryder carefully. She had to learn what she could about him. Her golden eyes squinted as her muscles tightened.

"How is the meat, Lady Gryphon?" Argos asked politely, breaking the silence.

Lana nodded before tearing off a morsel. She did not want to seem rude as she used a talon to slide a strange looking brown lump over to her plate.

Ryder chuckled from his seat, setting his glass of wine down. "That is a potato," he told her in the Gryphon tongue. "I suppose this setting is unfamiliar and rather strange."

It was strange but not for the reasons he hinted at. Lana had studied the cultures of the Spiritborn extensively before her flight to Coal. "I am trying to decide, Master Coba, how you earned Lord Argos' honor of right wing," she confidently stated in her native language.

"The Lord Argos and I finished our conversation in a less combative manner while dinner was being prepared. I am also the guest and confidant of the Lords of Crossroads. Why shouldn't I receive this honor?" Ryder mocked, showing his lack of appreciation at the insinuation she had made. "At one point in this world's history, we were all equal."

"Back when Terra was newly hatched but that was thousands of years ago," Lana retorted. She did not like his abrupt way of speaking.

Argos laughed as he watched the exchange with curiosity. "Are you speaking of secret Gryphon matters? I can leave if need be."

"She is trying to understand Ryder Coba the Shadowborn Bastard," Ryder teased as he looked back at Lana, her feathers bristling.

That was enough! "I can see why you were kicked out of your nest!" Lana chawed. Her hackles bristled in anger.

"I left on my own accord," Ryder said with no hint of anger or amusement. "You are young, Lady Gryphon. I will forgive that."

Lana quickly did a series of breathing exercises to calm herself before she did something unbecoming of a messenger to a royal court. She closed her eyes and bowed her head.

Argos leaned over to whisper to Ryder. Ryder nodded before repeating what he had said in the Gryphon tongue. "Lord Argos states that I am a royal bastard with the confidence of Lord Proto Avis. I am also one of the few Spiritborn that can speak your tongue currently in Coal."

"Then you should know that in my culture, I am granted a free question when a matter befuddles me," Lana declared underneath bubbling tension.

Ryder downed the rest of his wine. "Go ahead. I have already offended Argos so why not add a befuddled Gryphon to the mix?"

"Why will you not return home? Your people need you," she asked, referencing his less than polite response from the practice yard.

Ryder frowned. "My question to my so called people would be is why does everyone think I am the one to sit on the throne? A wasted question." He pushed himself up from his seat, bowed his head once towards Argos before leaving the room.

"You will have to forgive him as he is a typical Shadowborn in his demeanor. What did you ask him?" Argos asked her. Translating the question took a long time for Lana but Argos nodded when she finished. "History has not been kind to him and the world, myself included, has a hard time looking past his birth."

"The world can learn," Lana replied haltingly.

HOPE FOR THE FUTURE

The arrow landed with a thud, embedding itself in the swinging straw target. The target swung into its neighbor, shaking the bar it was attached to in between two thick posts. Haven looked at the bull's eye shot with a grin before pulling another steel tipped arrow from the quiver across her back. Her thick braid of black hair bounced on her shoulders. Just like before, she set the arrow in place, pulled the bowstring back and sighted her target with her sharp eyes. With a subtle move of her finger, the arrow flew forward and landed on the same target.

"I've still got it," she said proudly as she brushed her ebony bangs from her face. She swung her long limbs around only to see Zoras standing on the edge of the practice yard. In the blink of an eye, Haven notched another arrow and pointed it at him. "You know what happened to the last person who snuck up on me here?"

Zoras laughed as he came forward, his cape brushing the ground. The oiled leather armor's scent permeated the air. He looked every bit the old Saber with his warrior's stance and manner of bearing. "I'm sure Ryder still bears that scar as a cautionary reminder."

Haven relented and slid the bowstring back, dropping her arms. "Why have you strayed so far north to my little city?" she mocked, remembering their last conversation.

"I had business for the Council in Umbra and thought to check in on those important to my cause. Perhaps ask a few questions if you are willing," Zoras stated politely as he latched his hands behind his back.

"Why? You have received the secret reports and I would be foolish to exclude anything of importance. You have nothing to ask," Haven snapped back, tightening her grip on her curved bow.

"But is that completely true? You who know the object of my desperation better than anyone else. One of the reasons I have conducted my cause," Zoras challenged with a bow of the head. "I want to talk to you about Ryder."

Haven rolled her eyes. The old man had alterior motives to their meeting. That much she was sure of by the tone of his voice. He wanted confirmation of some truth that he believed only she knew. She was not about to tell him anything. She watched closely as Zoras took a few more sauntering steps towards her. She hated the way he stood, the typical calm and confident stance of an experienced Saber.

"Back off or I'll shoot," Haven warned as she raised the bow and arrow again.

"I am not here to threaten you. I just want to talk," Zoras replied, still calm as ever.

"You were a Saber Commander and privy to the secret knowledge of our world. You have known Ryder longer than me. For his entire lifetime in fact," Haven said cautiously as she turned around to glance at the straw target bar at the other end of the practice yard. She took several cleansing breaths to calm her simmering anger towards the old politician.

"What does Ryder see in you?" Zoras started to say.

Haven whirled around and fired her arrow at Zoras' head. With a lean to the left, the tall Saber politician avoided injury. But Haven did not remain still. She bounded forward, wielding her bow like a blunt weapon. Zoras slid his feet and dodged each strike with the agility of his younger days. Haven was relentless in her attack, becoming more daring with each passing moment. When she drew close for another stab of the bow, Zoras deftly tore the quiver free from her back and tossed it aside. He didn't want to risk getting an arrow shot at him. He then grabbed her left arm and twisted it behind her back. Almost immediately, Haven threw her head back and broke Zoras' nose.

"You little," Zoras groaned as he pressed a hand to his nose, trying to stop the bleeding.

"Then learn well not to challenge Ryder's best and only student!" Haven said proudly.

Zoras stretched his jaw as he slid his broken nose back into place. He wiped the blood from his face and shook his head. "Fine if you want to talk that way."

Haven watched as Zoras threw off his cape and turned to a rack of swords. He considered the array of blunted blades before picking out two. He flipped one in his right hand before tossing it towards her. A deft swipe of her hand took the sword out of the air.

"I'm not talking," Haven said sternly.

"Why not?" Zoras asked in a commanding tone.

"What goes on between me and Ryder is my own business," Haven answered as she tossed her bow aside.

Zoras nodded as he fingered his blade. "I hope that Ryder has taught you well for as you so cleverly pointed out, I am older and more experienced."

"I would expect nothing less from a former Saber Commander," Haven stated as she studied Zoras carefully. Ryder's old tips for how to overcome a more experienced opponent raced in her mind. She was not going to embarrass herself in front of the highly trained Zoras.

Retirement did not change Zoras' appearance. Every inch of his tall frame was hard muscle. He still wore his black hair in a short soldier's cut. His expression was always cool and calculating with a watchful look in his silver eyes. It reminded Haven of Ryder though Ryder had a thicker muscular frame typical of a Silvanus. She was slender and tiny in comparison.

"This is silly. We should not be fighting each other and I would not be winning any points with Ryder if I harmed you," Zoras finally admitted as he tossed the sword aside. "I had thought to test a theory that by fighting you, your lover would come running to defend you."

Suddenly, a black burst of energy shot into view. Zoras and Haven watched as it curved back in a sharp turn. The energy burst slowed quickly and floated before Haven as if it was waiting.

"I would be careful," Zoras urged. He was wary of the sentinent energy and kept his distance.

Haven ignored him and reached out for it. The black energy cleared and revealed a letter with a red design drawn on the front seal. Haven's heart started to flutter in a combination of shock and excitement as she grabbed the letter. A broad smile spread across her face: it was Ryder's seal. She caressed the letter, trying to draw out any sense of Ryder's presence through the folded parchment. Closing her eyes, she imagined his masculine scent and the touch of his hand. Letting out a deep breath, Haven opened her eyes and proceeded to read the letter to herself.

"Care to read it aloud?" Zoras asked politely.

"No. It's personal," Haven replied, her entire body on edge. It had been over a decade since she last got a note from Ryder and she was not about to share.

"Why not? If it is from Ryder, I would surely like to know if he intends to come back," Zoras started to articulate.

"I already told you! He won't come back! Not even for me!" Haven shouted before she realized that she had said too much. Zoras looked at her with an inquiring eye. Haven then relented and handed him the note.

Zoras cleared his throat. He skimmed over the lines before settling on the final passage. "The years continue to linger on and the war for the throne remains at home. Yes, I know what they say of me. That I am the second coming. But I am not Shadow Night Silvanus and until the world believes that, I will not come home to Cross. I can only hope that you will come to join me and together we can see the world of Terra. There is so much more out there. We can go see the lands where Mortals live. We can travel to the wide forests of the Eastlands. We could be free. I only hope that I will see you again in more than just my dreams. Always yours, Ryder."

Haven took the note back. "Now do you believe me?" She felt vulnerable in both body and mind now that Zoras was privy to her and Ryder's once secret exchange of letters. She wondered what Ryder would say of the matter.

"I had hoped that Ryder would declare that he was returning home. Instead he remains afraid of the possibilities," Zoras said shaking his head in dismay. "You do know what this means. If Ryder ever becomes the true Shadowlord, you would be his Queen. Can you handle that idea?" Zoras frankly stated.

"If that is what the Immortal Truth wants of me, then I will gladly step up and support Ryder," Haven replied as she bent down to collect the discard swords. She returned them to the weapons rack and went to retrieve her bow from where she dropped it. "But he does not want to be the Shadowlord."

The practice yard became quiet except for the creaking of the target bar and the snapping and cracking of the torches. The smoke rose high into the dark night sky. A wind gust brushed across the dusty ground. Haven was slow to pick up her quiver as if she was considering a deep and very upsetting thought. Zoras realized that he had broken through her tough shell and her inner soul was laid bare before him.

"Are you afraid?" Zoras started to ask but he was not sure why he was asking.

On the verge of tears, Haven was slow to answer him. "He fears the throne more than he fears never seeing me again. I hate him for that. I hate you and Kaiser for forcing him out of Cross."

"I didn't tell him to leave!" Zoras shouted in his defense.

"You did not have to keep pushing the throne on him. He

does not want it! He did not want it after Akakios was executed and he does not now. He'd rather see it fall to ruin by Kaiser than come claim it for himself!" Haven cried out.

"I highly doubt that Ryder would be so stupid as to let Kaiser have the victory," he stated. Zoras wanted to feel sorry for the young Shadowborn woman but something stopped his heart from reaching out to her. And he hated himself for it. He drew himself up proudly. "Then Ryder Coba left his home and everything he cared about for selfish reasons. He has turned his back on the Immortal Truth. But I have hope for him and for the future. He may not see it but he will be the greatest Shadowborn the world has ever seen."

WHAT IS A SABER?

"Why do I need to learn how to be a Saber?" Onyx asked as he fidgeted with the black leather cuirass. He had never worn anything this scuffed and damaged before and he wondered if Sai had dragged the cuirass out of a long forgotten closet.

Sai chuckled as he finished tieing his boot laces before standing up straight. "Because you are a Prince of the throne. It would not suit your family legacy to be an ill-trained warrior for as Shadowlord, you must appear strong. You will become the defender of your people much like your ancestor Shadow Night. From a more practical perspective, the training regimen shapes your body and mind to handle all sorts of dangers and tough situations. Take Master Rokar, Lord's Regent of the Council. He once led the Sabers and was one of the finest warriors of his day and now he serves as Lord's Regent," he replied. He threw his arms back and forth to loosen up his shoulders. "Of course most Rokar sons become great Sabers."

Onyx smiled as he thought of his friend Soja who was fun loving and excited to continue on with his family's legacy. He started to mimic Sai's actions. "Did my father go through the same training?"

The Saber Commander nodded as he crossed his arms. "Every Shadowborn goes through some degree of battle training. Even the women."

Shadowborn were a tough and serious group of Immortals. Their nature was a reflection of the hard mountain landscape of their homeland and their proximity to the borders of the Darklands. Clad in black and never without a sword close at hand, they commanded the darkness of shadows as fiercely as they fought. The Sabers were considered the most elite of Shadowborn warriors.

"Well then I am willing to learn as my father did," Onyx stated firmly as he set his fists on his hips. "Do not go easy on me."

Sai knew that Onyx would eventually say that in the training sessions. "Well now that is out of the way, in here and in my presence, I am the teacher and you are the student. In here, I outrank you as the Commander of the Sabers." Sai pointed to the closed iron doors set in the dirty whitewashed walls. "Out there, you are my Crowned Prince. Understood?"

"Yes," Onyx said excitedly. A fierce look from Sai made him drop his shoulders. "Yes, Commander," he quickly corrected himself, now realizing how serious Sai was being. He let out a deep breath and regained his posture.

Sai nodded with approval. He hated being so harsh as he looked over the young Prince before him. A young Prince who would one day grow into a powerful Shadowlord. "See the circles on the floor? I want you to stand in the centermost circle." Sai directed him to a circular target design carved into the gray stone. He watched as Onyx backpedaled to stand in the center of the design. "My lesson today: the more you know your target, the closer you can get and overcome them. If you answer my questions correctly, you may take a step towards me."

"Yes, Commander," Onyx answered quickly, loosening up his arms.

The Commander of the Sabers began to pace around the room at the very edge of the floor design. He kept his arms crossed as he took slow and deliberate steps. "Who founded the Saber order?"

"Sin Silvanus in honor of his elder brother Anu," Onyx replied. He took a step forward when Sai nodded that he was pleased with the answer.

"Why?" Sai prodded as he continued walking around the room.

Onyx thought for a moment, trying to remember what Kader had told him. He looked down to focus his thoughts. He grinned and puffed out his chest. "Sin believed that the skills of his brother..."

"No!" Sai immediately interrupted. He rubbed the bridge of his nose as he felt Onyx flinch from his tone. "Again."

Onyx honestly thought that he had the right answer in his mind. Was Kader wrong? He bit his lip as he tried to sort through the history again. At least Sai did not motion for him to take a step back. "When Anu was taken and killed, Sin believed that had there been a secret guard to protect him, his brother would still be alive. So to protect the Silvanus family, he founded the Saber Order that would be trained in the same skills of swordsmanship, discretion, and loyalty reminiscent of a Shadowborn Prince."

Sai nodded. "You may take a step forward." He waited to continue until Onyx stepped to the next circle. "Anu Silvanus was the eldest of the three sons of Shadow Night. In those days, he was his father reborn with the dedication and skill to match his illustrious parent. And your great grandfather looked up to his brother and loved him very much. The loss of Anu was terrible and ultimately led to the disappearance of Shadow Night from Shadowborn civilization. Sin was suddenly the leader of his people, had lost his father, and had his own young family to guide in the wake of sorrow. Thus the Sabers were born. Now who can be a Saber?"

Onyx wanted Sai to continue for he loved learning about the Silvanus family history. He loved hearing stories about his famous ancestors. Kaiser was old enough to have known Shadow Night. He decided to go find the Chancellor after his lesson with Sai. "Nobles?"

"Wrong. Take a step back," Sai stated. Onyx frowned as he stepped back. "Try again."

The young prince tried to figure out why his answer had not pleased the Saber Commander. As far as he knew, nobles made up the order. "Anyone?"

"I see your uncertainty with your answer but it is correct. Anyone is eligible to join the order if they have the right skill and countenance. In fact, many want to join but only a few graduate into the ranks. Since nobles can afford the best trainers, they predominate but there are a few from lesser means and backgrounds. If your bastard cousin was still in Cross, he would have made a fine Saber and would have probably been in my place as Commander," Sai explained as Onyx took a step forward. "Women are also allowed to become Sabers. They make the fiercest and most deadly fighters. I have five Shadowborn ladies under my command and my predecessor was considering a sixth. Her name escapes me but she was from Umbra and bore a feisty personality."

Onyx had never seen a lady Saber and realized that he really did not see any Sabers save Sai and Soja. "Then the Sabers are good at what they do for I never truly see them during my day to day life."

Sai chuckled. "We are the worst kept secret of the Shadowborn. The people know that we exist but they never see us.

It is one of the rules of the order: act with discretion. Can you name the three basic rules?"

His brow furrowed as Onyx thought long and hard on the right answer. He knew that the Sabers operated with a set of rules like any other organization. Even he as a Prince had his own rules to follow related to his position. Onyx dared to look up at Sai who only patiently waited for his response. "Act with discretion. Defend the throne. Honor the Truth."

The Saber Commander nodded with approval and gestured for Onyx to take a step forward. He took slow and steady steps, his arms tightly crossed. "Who are the commanding officers of the Sabers?"

The question seemed silly as Onyx already knew that Sai was the Commander of the Sabers. But one thing was quickly obvious to him: all Sabers answered to the Shadowlord. "My father and you, Commander."

"Good. You remembered that the Shadowlord is our High Commander even if he does not live his life like a normal Saber. Continue with the four captains," Sai stated.

Naming the captains was more difficult for Onyx as he only knew the names of four other Sabers. He knew that Zoras was retired from the Order and now his son served with the Sabers. Donovan Shunga was the equivilant to Soja for his father. Hayden Abendroth was an officer; that much he was sure of. "Hayden Abendroth?"

Sai chuckled. "I will be lenient in this answer. Yes, Hayden is a Captain of the Sabers. He is originally from Dusk so he is the Captain of the East. There is a Captain for each of the four cardinal directions. Below them are the lieutenants that serve in each of our cities and villages. All are answerable to me and ultimately the throne. When you rise to the throne, you will learn all of their names as they come forth to pledge their loyalty to you."

The question and answer session continued with the same back and forth banter. Sai was pleased at Onyx's answers, correcting him when the reply did not please him. He paced around Onyx, studying him and his features. The Prince had the build and frame of his father though he was still growing into it. But Sai could see a softness and grace in the way Onyx stood that reminded the Commander of his Earthborn mother. His eyes showed a deep intelligence and curious nature. It was different from the usual Shadowborn he trained to become Sabers.

"Normally, your training would have begun at age sixteen and ended at age twenty eight. You are twelve now so I have an early start. You will end your instruction at eighteen... if you can pass my trials for then you must focus more on matters of state,"

Sai teased. He waited for the inevitable question but Onyx remained quiet. "I shall have you ready by the time we go to Crossroads."

"Have you ever been there?" Onyx asked, remembering what Kaiser had told him of the great city.

Sai fell silent as he remembered the last time he went to Crossroads. "I went not for leisure but for the delivery of justice on behalf of your grandfather. I shall be frank for this moment: I went to pick up the order of execution for Akakios Coba."

Onyx wanted to find out more about the fallen Akakios Coba but he had a feeling that it was a subject not up for discussion. Not yet at least, he decided. "When do I get to learn how to use a sword? A bow and arrow?"

That question pleased Sai. He held up a finger before turning around to a wooden weapon stand that leaned up against the wall. He considered it for a moment before pulling out two blunted swords. With a flick of the wrist, he tossed the weapon over to Onyx. Onyx fumbled to catch it by the hilt and the blade clattered to the floor. He looked up embarrassed before quickly retrieving it from beside his feet.

"Dexterity takes practice. We may be Immortal but we still must learn technique and how to master our bodies and minds. Now," Sai said as he came forward, holding out his sword to where Onyx could see how he was holding the hilt. Onyx quickly adjusted his grip. "Watch first. You will learn how to hold and guide this weapon before you can use it."

Onyx nodded as he checked his grip on the sword. He wiggled his fingers to avoid cramping. Sai slowly guided him into a simple form, pushing his limbs into the correct position. Onyx paid close attention as Sai then showed him how to get into the position once the sword was drawn. The Commander nodded with approval as Onyx was quick to learn and demonstrate each form he was taught. By the end of the session, Sai showed Onyx how to greet a higher ranking officer by clenching his right hand into a fist, crossing his heart, and bowing. Onyx repeated the motion with enthusiasm.

THE PRANKSTERS

Onyx walked down the hallway with hands pressed to his lower back. A long runner rug of various red shades shimmered in the light that beamed through the high rounded windows to his right. He mumbled Sai's teachings to assure himself of his memory. He knew it would do him no good to forget the basic forms and proper way to handle a sword. And he did not want to look bad before his teacher in the next training session. Onyx wanted to make his father proud and impressing the Commander of the Sabers would do that. A smile crossed his face as he thought about becoming a noble warrior and a respected Shadowlord.

"Hi, your Highness!" Soja greeted as he suddenly came up from the floor in front of Onyx.

Onyx fell back onto his rear end in surprise. How did his Saber guard and friend suddenly appear before him? Was Soja following him and he just did not see him? Sabers were supposed to be the unseen guards of the throne. He did not think that this was what everyone meant.

"What... how did... where..." Onyx stammered as he tried to figure out the mystery.

Soja extended a hand towards Onyx to help him up from the floor. "It's called Shadow Slide. I use it to follow you around and look out for potential threats without being discovered," he answered in his characteristic upbeat tone.

"Shadow Slide?" Onyx asked as he got to his feet. He smoothed out the wrinkles on his pants. "Is that something all

Shadowborn can do?"

"Every single one. And the Sabers are experts. Didn't Commander Parahazur tell you this?" Soja inquired.

"He was more focused on making sure I knew how to hold a sword. Should he have?" Onyx answered back. "I think Kader mentioned something about our innate powers but warned me not to try anything before I learned how to use them."

Soja chuckled as he patted the young Prince on the shoulders. "Come on and I'll show you Shadow Slide."

The calm and cool demeanor was such a sharp contrast to Soja's appearance in the Saber uniform. A cloak lay open to reveal a simple leather armor cuirass that was molded to Soja's tall and lean body. Onyx felt like he could have worn the uniform with equal grace as the royal Prince. Unlike most Sabers that Onyx knew, Soja walked around with his head uncovered and his identity plain for everyone to see. Onyx knew that Soja was an unconventional Saber despite being a Rokar. The Rokars were famous for producing great warriors, many of whom joined the noble order.

"Is it really your place to show me?" Onyx asked, doubtful of Soja's suggestion. He began to think that confidence was one of the Saber's many weapons.

Soja waved him off. "Trust me. It will be a lot easier training under the Commander if you already know Shadow Slide. Plus I won't be a hard ass like him."

His bold nature at insulting his ranking officer was a shock. Onyx began to wonder how Soja passed his training regiment with that kind of attitude. Of course with a former Commander for a father, Soja was brought up to be a Saber before he was even of age to begin training. Zoras Rokar was also the Lord's Regent and had plenty of political pull to advance the status of his family. But still, a large part of him wanted to learn Shadow Slide with Soja as his teacher. Sai was too serious for his tastes.

"Ok. Show me," Onyx finally replied with an emerging smile.

"Good," Soja said as he grabbed Onyx's arm.

The world around him suddenly became dark and chilling to the core. Onyx felt that he was moving but he could not tell where he was going. He looked towards Soja, seeing a glow about his body. Onyx then realized the same glow covered him as well. His center of balance was in complete disarray and he felt himself getting sick. Just as he thought that he couldn't take the nausea any longer, the light returned. Soja had brought him to the kitchens.

"Oh god," Onyx managed to say as he bent over, hands

pressed to his knees. He shivered from the cold of whatever Soja brought him through.

"You'll survive," Soja stated as he leaned towards the kitchen doors. They had been thrown open for the preparation of the evening meal. Soja sniffed deeply. "Apple pie. My favorite."

Onyx looked at him with a confused expression. How could the Saber even think about food when he felt like throwing up? Another wave of queasiness came over him and he groaned. Soja turned around and bent down to his eye level. He smiled encouragingly and helped Onyx to steady himself.

"Shadow Slide can be unsettling. I recommend not eating a big meal before entering it until you've had a little practice," Soja explained with a kind voice.

"It? What is it?" Onyx managed to ask in between shivers and waves of nausea.

"How best to explain," Soja considered for a moment. "Ah!" He grinned as he steadied Onyx again, hands holding the young Prince up. "To enter Shadow Slide is to enter the veil between the world of the living and the Spirit World. That's why you are feeling so cold. The nausea is a result of not being centered. But don't worry. I will teach you how before I give you a little test."

The warm light from the kitchen fires began to warm Onyx as he and Soja looked inside from the dark hallway. Preparation stations were set up on both sides of the kitchen. A single aisle appeared uncluttered by tables and cutting blocks with staff running about in a practiced frantic dance. Soot from the roasting pit blackened the wall to the right of the doors. The high ceilings were coated with years of smoke. The smell of cooking food was intoxicating to Onyx as the nausea disappeared but the energy in the kitchen was wild. The head chef was shouting and barking orders. People hustled to and fro, carrying ingredients and utensils. Soja then pointed to a bowl of red apples that sat on a table piled high with fruits and vegetables that had yet to be sorted.

"Your objective: steal an apple without getting caught," Soja said with a wink. "To properly center yourself for Shadow Slide, close your eyes and settle your breath. Listen to your heartbeat. Feel the warmth of your core. Without opening your eyes, push out your senses and seek out the cool of a shadow. It will pulsate until it matches your heartbeat. Once you have that connection, pull yourself towards the shadow."

"Then I will be in Shadow Slide?" Onyx asked as he felt the excitement rising within him.

Soja nodded. "Focus on that pulse but remember, don't lose your focus or you will immediately become visible." He suddenly disappeared into Shadow Slide like it was second nature.

Onyx watched as Soja reappeared briefly to snatch an apple before disappearing again. Soja then reappeared on the other side of the kitchen, leaning against the open door and biting into the apple.

"Ok. I can do this," Onyx told himself. He was a descendent of Shadow Night so how hard could this technique be? He repeated that thought over and over in his head.

He stood up in the doorway and brushed back his black shoulder length hair. Deciding to stand in the low light that beamed out into the hallway, Onyx closed his eyes and focused on his heartbeat. He took deep breaths to calm himself as he reached for the heat of his core. It was an earthy warmth and he embraced it completely. The warmth was comforting and reminded him of his mother. When he connected with the cool pulse of the shadow, it was unnerving. But Onyx pulled himself towards it anyway.

His first attempt at sliding was a disaster from the start as Onyx realized he couldn't feel the even pulse. He thought that he was pulling himself towards the shadows that Soja had pointed out but he found out that he was only walking. He was in clear view of everyone. A voice shouted towards him and he returned to his senses. The head chef was barreling towards him, pushing past the workers with his thick arms. Onyx squeaked and ran towards Soja who was laughing hysterically in the doorway.

"Run!" Onyx shouted towards the Saber as he bumped into him. They both scrambled and ran as fast as they could away from the angry shouts of the head chef.

The laughter continued as Onyx and Soja ran through the castle, joking and jostling along the way. Servants and officials looked at them perplexed as they passed but only chuckled before continuing on. Onyx tried to mimic Soja's nimble movement and footwork, tripping into a servant carrying linens. The servant tried to apologize profusely for making a mess but Soja grabbed Onyx and pulled him back onto his feet, preventing him from explaining. They kept running until they reached a balcony overlooking a private garden and slid down to rest and catch their breath. Both were grinning.

"Not bad for your first try despite completely blowing it," Soja teased.

Onyx was in too much of a good mood to even care. Soja was his friend and that was all that mattered to him right now. He shoved the Saber who promptly fell over onto his side, a wide grin on his face. Onyx stifled a laugh when Soja held up a hand for him to be quiet. He curled a finger and pointed down into the garden. The young Prince shuffled his body over to Soja's side and spied Kaiser sitting on a bench, reading a book. Standing nearby was his ever present masked servant. Soja then got a devious look in his eyes.

"See that fountain?" Soja whispered in a low voice. Onyx nodded. Soja then reached into a hidden pocket in his robe and pulled out the pilfered apple. "I'll show you how later but watch this."

Onyx watched as Soja held his half eaten apple in his left hand. He could see Soja pushing himself into a crouching position, apple clutched tightly. Soja then leaped up to his feet and hurled the apple, now veiled in a tight ball of darkness. It landed in the fountain with a terrific splash, soaking Kaiser completely. Soja dropped down out of sight beside Onyx barely able to control his laughter.

"You disrespectful, insolent," Kaiser raged as he dropped his book to the grass at his feet. He kicked it across the yard as he flung water from his sleeves. He glared briefly at his perpetual companion. His servant was bent over in uncontrollable laughter. He growled in fury. "When I find you, I'll make sure you are beaten within an inch of your life!"

"If he yells anymore, his face will be redder than the apple you just threw at him," Onyx giggled. The suggestion was just too much as he and Soja burst out laughing. The fact that Kaiser's servant was laughing just as hard made everything even more hilarious. Onyx could hear Kaiser shouting at his servant to get him a towel and the servant gasping for breath and laughing in response.

THE COURT OF THE EARTHBORN

Haro sighed with a sense of belonging when he, Kader and Arik passed out from under the eaves of the forest onto the fields before Cascade. The smell of growing wheat was pleasant and a welcome change from the wet scent of leaf litter and moss. He looked to his left to see Arik padding beside him, pausing to rustle his wings and stretch them out to their full length.

"The forest is so cramped. It feels good to be in the open again," Arik said. He had started walking for the last stretch of their journey to rest his weary wings.

Kader sat quietly on his horse, surveying the land before him. "Fly ahead and alert the guard for an escort. Though we are before the city, I do not trust this land entirely."

Haro wanted to jump to the defense of his home but thought it better not to. During their journey, he had learned that Kader was a cautious Shadowborn who had rarely left Cross on his own. It was peculiar to Haro as he had travelled the bounds of the Earthborn lands before he reached his twenty eighth year. Most of that was due to his scout training but part of it was because he wanted to know and see all corners of his nation. He was too curious to sit still for long.

"I shall return," Arik said before bounding into the air. With four strong pumps of his wing muscles, he quickly became a white speck in the distance.

Haro settled in the saddle. "An escort will draw attention."

"Better protected and known than vulnerable and hidden,"

Kader replied. He coughed and cleared his throat.

The Shadowborn's eyes drifted over the farmland before them, watching the city for the inevitable contingent of soldiers. Within the hour, Arik came at the head of a column of four mounted Earthborn guards in light chainmail armor and green tunics. The lead guard barked the positions to his companions before each one took up point. With a guard on each side, Haro looked over at Kader who visibly relaxed. He then looked up to see Arik wheeling around back towards the city, hovering above them. They nodded to each other before the escort moved forward.

In the early morning light, the fields of wheat shimmered with a soft golden glow. The smell was earthy and pleasant. Haro took a deep breath, taking it all in. He closed his eyes and thought back to childhood memories when he ran with his friends through the fields with no bound and the farmers shouting angrily at them as they passed. Laughing to himself, Haro opened his eyes.

Cascade emerged before him like a grand and noble symbol of Earthborn power. The palace loomed over the crest of the hill with its high stone walls. Greenery and flowers were blooming from every available space not occupied by buildings or streets. The air had a pleasant and homey scent. Haro breathed in deep as he stepped foot on the streets of his home. He looked around to see the street cleaners at work, brushing away fallen leaves and dirt to make ready for the day. Each one that looked up quickly looked away when Arik glared at them. The Gryphon was doing his best to keep inquiring eyes away from their party.

The guards kept close to Kader and Haro as Arik led the pack, his size clearing the street. City folk were slowly waking up and preparing for the day so the crowd was light. Haro sighed deeply as he spied a bakery that sold his favorite sweet buns. He wished that he could stop to get one for breakfast but pouted when the group kept going forward. The smell of cinnamon permeated the air and it made his mouth water. The four guards led them up to the palace gate where the lead guard whispered a few short words with the gatekeeper. The gatekeeper nodded and soon the cranking sound of levers was heard. The gate slowly opened.

"Scout Haro Artemis, I know that you are familiar with the palace. You may proceed," the lead guard said as he turned his horse away. With a nod, the other three guards followed him.

"Well they were a serious bunch," Haro commented as the gate closed behind them. He dismounted and brushed the horse hair from his legs. A groom came forward to lead their horses away.

"Indeed," Kader quietly said. Haro helped him dismount and handed him his wooden staff. "Where to, Master Gryphon?"

Arik puffed up his chest. "Lord Palani Kano is touring in the southeast so we will meet with his noble father."

"Well, follow me. I know the way to his study," Haro said. "And don't worry, Arik. His quarters are spacious enough for you."

Haro led the way through the palace, showing his scout seal when needed for passage. He kept his eyes open for his sister until he heard from a courtier that the Ladies of Flora were with Lady Willow in the gardens. Seeing her would have to wait. Arik kept his head held high and his wings tightly folded against his back. If a servant's gaze lingered too long in their direction, the Gryphon stared them down until they looked away and went about their business. Haro laughed privately with himself at seeing his Gryphon partner's actions. As calm and educated as Arik was, he still held on to his wild and animalistic nature.

After a twisting path from the front gate and up a flight of stairs that frustrated Arik, the three arrived in the wing of the palace that housed government offices. The straw haired Oren stood outside his office doors speaking to a secretary in a forest green coat. The secretary held a leather bound file in the crook of his left arm as he pulled out a paper to hand to Oren. Oren graciously nodded and indicated that he no longer had any questions. The secretary bowed before turning away and disappearing down a spiraling set of stairs at the other end of the hall.

"Ah, I was told that a scout pair was escorting a gentleman to see me. Please come in and let us talk," Oren graciously welcomed, swinging his arm to gesture for them to come inside. "I was just about to send for some breakfast. Would any of you care for a drink or something to eat?" he asked once the door closed behind them.

"I have flown for many hours. Perhaps your cooks could prepare a bowl of minced venison and boar for me?" Arik politely asked with a dip of his head.

Oren smiled. "Anything for our Gryphon friends. We might still have some dried basil and oat mash from when Lord Paladon visited. I was told it has restorative properties."

"It serves to settle the stomach after a long flight," Arik explained.

Haro placed his breakfast order for sweet buns and pork sausage after making Arik promise that he would try the treats. Arik rolled his eyes in response at his partner's eagerness. Once Haro had calmed, Oren turned to look at a cloaked Kader who had remained silent through the entire exchange.

"I have been most impolite focusing on a meal when I have yet to learn your name, good traveler," Oren apologized as he looked hard at Kader. He took a step forward to try and look under Kader's hood.

"Kader Erebus of the Shadowborn," Kader stated as he pulled back his hood, revealing his identity. Even though he was a Shadowborn, he still bowed deeply to Oren. "It is an honor to speak with you."

The look of shock on Oren's face was unsettling to Haro. He had expected Oren to be surprised at seeing Kader but there was something deeper in his expression that worried him. It was if seeing Kader brought out a sense of fear in his Lord's father. He watched as Oren took a deep breath and let it out slowly.

"This is most unexpected. I was not aware of a coming visit from the Lord's Chancellor of the Shadowborn. I have indeed heard of the passing of Lord Shiloh and offer your nation my heartfelt condolencenes," Oren said respectfully with a bow of the head.

"We have much to discuss." Kader looked around for a chair. Oren quickly pulled his own desk chair around and offered it to Kader. The Shadowborn slowly eased himself down into the seat as Haro took his wooden staff. "Pardon me for my infirmities. I am not as young and whole as I used to be."

Arik positioned himself in a reclined posture before the door. Though he stretched out to rest, the Gryphon was capable of bouncing up to his feet in the span of a heartbeat. Inside, Haro was grateful as he was certain that Arik's presence gave Kader a sense of safety. No one else seemed to want to speak as Oren stepped outside of his office to place his breakfast order with a passing servant. He came back inside, this time with a forced smile.

"Was your journey eventful? Perhaps I should send a contigent of soldiers to inspect the path from North Bend to Cascade," Oren supposed as he pulled around a seat for him and Haro. Both men sat down, facing Kader. "Scout Arik, you did not mention any trouble to the gate messenger."

"Because there was none to be had, good sir," Arik replied. "I told your messenger that Master Erebus here requested an escort though I did not reveal his name at the time."

Oren nodded before he returned his gaze to Kader. "I can assure you of my silence, Master Erebus, for I sense that what you have to say is private."

Kader relaxed slightly in his seat. His right hand gripped the head of the arm rest as his left arm laid across his lap. "I am no longer the Lord's Chancellor. It seems that the traitor has seen fit to take the first strike against the Truth. Kaiser Adonis sent Sabers to kill me as I fled from Cross just a few nights ago. I have this pair to thank for my survival," Kader said as he bowed his head towards Haro and Arik with a generous smile. Haro dropped his head sheepishly in response.

"I will make a recommendation to Captain Avani," Oren proposed. He pressed a finger to his chin before quickly pointing at Kader. "You said Sabers were sent to kill you by Kaiser's command. How can that be possible? They only answer to the Shadowlord and they would never attack a fellow Shadowborn."

A polite knock alerted them to the arrival of their breakfast. Oren quickly got up to answer the door and thanked the servant before pushing the cart inside. This time he locked the door. Haro helped him distribute the food and drink before everyone settled back down. Arik held his bowl in his paws, securing the rim with his talons to make sure it did not topple over as he ate.

"There is much at work in my homeland and very little of it good. The death of Lord Shiloh is just a small though no less important loss for my people," Kader stated as he took a cup of tea and sipped the warm drink.

"The Lord Shiloh bore a heavy burden after the execution of Akakios. I knew him well enough to know that he had hoped to never come to the throne. I remember him telling me how he begged Akakios' bastard son to remain in Cross instead of going north to fight the Mirror Sea Pirate," Oren revealed, having once kept the nature of his conversation with Shiloh private.

If Kader was surprised by the statement, he did not show it. "Much death and sorrow has plagued Cross and the Silvanus family. First to my mind is the injury and subsequent illness of Lord Aku. Then the departure of Akakios' bastard to parts unknown." Kader shook his head. "And then to lose Lord Shiloh? I feel as a man who has lost a dear friend. But his poor son Aku is not strong enough to hold his father's throne and young Onyx is just that. Young and inexperienced. My people are absolutely leaderless."

"It seems that Kaiser has placed himself at the head of your nation once again and this time, his position is stronger. If I could, I would ride at the head of the Earthborn army and march across the River Shadow but your border is sealed by some strange power. Has the Daylord's Mirror grown to shield your homeland?" Oren asked as he stirred a spoonful of sugar into his cup of tea.

"The Daylord's Mirror is indeed inpenetrable but I have it on good authority that he did not raise it to seal my homeland from our allies. I have gone to inspect the Daylord's work and found it to be sound and unmoving. I suspect that Kaiser has something to do with the trouble at the border though how, I do not yet know," Kader stated with deep thought laced throughout his words. He shook his head.

"A Shadow Mirror!" Arik suddenly exclaimed.

Everyone turned to look at the Gryphon. Arik quickly brushed off the crumbs of food from his face and straightened his neck. Both Kader and Oren set down their tea cups and even Haro stopped picking at the sweet bun in his hands.

"What exactly is a Shadow Mirror?" Oren asked, first looking at Kader for an explanation. Kader shrugged.

"Around the nest, my grandfather told me stories about the Shadow Mirror that Begin Anu spoke of to the First Alliance. He said that in his escape from the Farlands, he and his eldest son Adonis raised a Shadow Mirror to stop his kinsmen from following him. It is why the Mortal sailors can not go past the Stormlands," Arik explained.

"Then I suppose that it is no coincidence that Kaiser's surname is Adonis. I had heard many rumors over the years regarding his family's legacy. I did not want to believe them but perhaps they were true after all," Kader mused as he looked out the window behind Oren's desk. "It does explain his high and mighty nature."

Haro slid forward in his seat. "What do you mean, Master Erebus?"

Oren set a hand on the young Earthborn's shoulders. "It means that Kaiser is a descendent of Begin Anu through his eldest son Adonis."

"So Kaiser raised a Shadow Mirror?" Haro asked, looking between Oren, Kader, and Arik.

"It would seem so," Kader replied as he studied the bustling city outside. "A very powerful Shadow Mirror."

Outside, the markets were just getting into full swing. Produce vendors set out their fruits and vegetables, being careful not to place their carefully grown items in the direct sunlight. City guards walked among the growing crowd, offering assistance when asked. Kader sighed deeply as if he had been drawn into a distant dream. "Why should Kaiser's relation to Begin Anu make a difference?" Haro asked still confused.

"A Shadow Mirror can only be opened or closed by Kaiser and those in his bloodline. Seeing as he had no children, the border is completely sealed save on his whim," Arik stated, suddenly the authority in the room. "It explains why we had so much trouble trying to... trying to... oh what is the word in this tongue?" Arik added in slight frustration.

As the Gryphon mulled over the proper translation for his thoughts, Kader, Haro, and Oren continued their conversation. Oren and Kader listed many of Kaiser's supposed atrocities and acts that went beyond the law of the land.

"So we have been sitting around for centuries waiting for a reason to risk open war against Kaiser? What are we so afraid of? Maybe I am too young to understand but what have we been waiting for? You two have made it very clear to me that he has lied and cheated his way through the years. People obviously question his character and loyalty. I say we call the banners and march on Cross right now!" Haro declared, charged up by his words into jumping out of his seat. He sat back down when Oren, Arik, and Kader stared at him. "Sorry."

"The boy makes a very good point, Oren. We have been languishing in uncertainty for far too long. I can not myself call my people to act but I think that I can tell you that there is a rebel movement in my homeland ready to act against Kaiser. Call your banners and join us," Kader proposed with growing confidence. He looked to Oren to see if he had the same attitude.

"I can't," Oren said meekly.

"Why not?" Kader asked. "Even if your son now leads the Earthborn, you still have authority in this land and an obligation to Onyx who is your grandson by blood," Kader challenged as he set his empty tea cup down on the edge of Oren's desk.

Oren looked to Haro with a hint of worry in his eyes. "What I am about to say, you will speak of to no one." He then looked at Arik. "I am not your Lord so I can not order you to keep to the same promise but I beg you to do so."

Arik nodded deeply. "You have my word."

"I did not pass my throne to my son because I had been called to a different purpose," Oren started to say after a long moment of uneasy silence. It was clear that he was struggling with whatever he was going to say. He dropped his head for a few seconds. "When the Demon murdered my two eldest grandchildren, I was ready to charge into the wilds after the creature. I had even pulled on my armor and strapped on my weapons. Kaiser then came to me in this very office at first to offer his condolenscenes for my loss. I thought nothing of his presence for Lord Shiloh had sent him to inspect the murder scene for insight into what kind of Demon was responsible. I asked him for his thoughts and in that moment, his true nature was revealed to me."

The Earthborn royal's resolve broke and he dropped his head into his hands, fighting back tears. Kader slid his chair forward and took Oren's hand. Oren looked up at the Shadowborn with tears in his eyes. "He threatened to destroy all that you hold dear," Kader suggested. When Oren's sad wide eyed expression questioned the statement, Kader continued. "Because that is what he does. That is what he will continue to do unless we stop him here and now. I know that you are afraid. We all are but we can no longer let our fear paralyze us. Let us use Kaiser's weapon of threats against him."

"We have to have hope," Arik said softly. "It is what Proto Avis would tell us."

Kader sighed deeply. "We have to assemble the Northern Alliance, gather the Silvanus bloodline, and strike Kaiser down once and for all. With such a force, Kaiser will crumble before us and we will bring his terror to an end."

YOU'RE BEING WATCHED

Oren found himself smiling, filled with a deep sense of hope. It was an honest and true feeling that radiated from the sadness in his heart. He leaned over the front edge of his desk, pushing aside an ivory inkwell. The gray goose feather quill toppled onto the desk top and splattered black ink over a thin pile of parchment. He didn't care about the mess. There was hope! Hope to avenge his family! Hope to protect his people! Hope that the world can be saved! He was going to support the Shadowborn rebellion with all of his might.

He looked up when the crystalline tones of the noon bell sounded, signaling the midday meal and break. It was a policy he had implemented in the early days of his reign to encourage conversation and peace during a busy work day. It had been difficult convincing people to relax and that society would not collapse if they took a break but in the end, it proved successful. People were friendlier, more pleasant, and worked more efficiently when given a chance to rest. The city bakers had even come up with a variety of sweet treats to pass out as a way to promote themselves while conversing with the people. The atmosphere in the city was always more relaxed during the hour break.

Looking towards the window, Oren hoped to see a Falcon Gryphon winging past but only saw a speeding flock of pigeons flapping away. He laughed to himself as he bent over to clean up the mess of ink. His thoughts began to stray towards the message the Falcon Gryphon would carry to Crossroads.

"My Lord Proto Avis of Crossroads," Oren said out loud as he wiped away the ink and replaced the quill in the well. "I bring you news that requires your utmost attention. No, that doesn't sound right." He straightened the papers. "What to say?"

The message had to convey everything he wanted to say, everything Kader had said, and a plea to the Gryphon sage. He also knew that he had to reveal the threat of Kaiser's reach in Cascade. There were too many words to convey in a Feather Whisper. Oren glanced at the shadowbox on the far wall that held a pair of mounted Gryphon feathers. Not for the first time he wondered how the Gryphons ensourced their feathers to carry voices. The carefully laid barbs and shafts were some how capable of carrying the sound and timbre of a whispered message. Whatever the method used, Feather Whispers were a valuable form of communication with the Gryphons.

"Oh, Proto Avis, for the first time in a long time, I feel a sense of true hope," Oren declared, still staring at the mounted feathers. He rounded the desk, dragging his fingers along the surface of the finished wood. "I have been in the haze of despair for far too long. I have been running from the bare truth but no longer." He put a fist to his chest and bowed his head. He fought back tears.

A gust of wind hit him in the back and Oren turned back towards the floor to ceiling window. The curtains flapped in the breeze. One of the side panes stood open. Despite the bright warm sunshine, the room felt cold. Oren let out a deep breath and strode over to close the side pane. He locked it tightly by its brass fittings. The curtains settled back into place and he turned around.

Standing in front of the shadow box was a tall, lean figure dressed in black. The stranger held a steel dagger in his right hand, turning the blade slowly. The cold metal gleamed as he twisted it. There was no hint of color on the black clothes other than a frayed band of silver brocade on the coat collar. The man's long black hair laid across his shoulder. A long scar ran diagonally across his face. Oren gulped.

"Go ahead and shout for your guards," the man dared.

"Who are you? Oren asked, clenching his fists and reaching within himself for his innate Spirit energy.

The man chuckled as he waved his dagger back and forth. "I am the shadow."

The answer infuriated Oren as he took hold of the Spirit energy. He slid the tip of his boot to stand over the wooden floor. He needed just a moment to send a signal through the natural magnetic field to alert his guards. He began to concentrate his thoughts.

"And what is a shadow doing in my city?" Oren growled as he hardened his heart. The call was almost ready.

"Keeping an eye on you of course. Checking in on your precious living family," the man replied with an eerie smile. His gray eyes studied Oren carefully. "You wouldn't be thinking of talking and endangering them now would you?"

Oren slid his entire left foot onto the wooden floor to strengthen his call for help. He steadied his breathing to bring his respiration in line with his heartbeat. His eyes briefly glanced to the pole arm on display on a nearby cherry wood shelf. The carved wooded haft had been broken in two but to Oren, it would be a suitable defense weapon. He stared hard at the man before him, betraying none of his thoughts and observations.

"He sent you, didn't he? Has Kaiser lost confidence in my silence? Does he doubt the love I bear for my family?" Oren demanded. Just a moment longer and he would be ready.

"So you are a smart man. For a moment there, I had lost faith in you," the man replied, casually brandishing the dagger. He rolled and tossed it between his hands. He snatched it out of the air and pointed the dagger at Oren. "Strange thing is I do not believe you. Tell me who the man in the forest green cloak was. The man brought in by the scout and Gryphon pair."

Oren realized that the shadow man had been watching him for quite some time but not long enough to identify Kader. He vowed not to give Kader up. He quickly calmed his nerves and began to listen to the syncing of his respiration and heartbeat. Once the natural pulse became consistent, he put feelers out for the magnetic field around him. He latched on quickly and sent a signal. Unexpectedly, it hit a wall and made him take a few steps back.

"Tsk, tsk. Did you not think that I would come before you the least bit prepared? Unlike my predecessors, I have a much deeper understanding of the abilities of an Earthborn. Be glad though that when you hit the shield, you only stumbled," the man explained with a mocking tone. "Consider Shadow Shield a simpler, more tame Shadow Mirror. Don't think you were the only one silently preparing Spirit energy."

The Shadow Shield had been unexpected. It was a Shadowborn technique that could cut off the connection of Spirit energy to the natural world. In theory, the effect was temporary but the older a Shadowborn was, the longer its power could be maintained. Oren gritted his teeth, knowing that it would be a waste of energy if he continued to test his Earth Call against the Shadowborn. He made a daring leap for the broken pole arm and ripped it from the display. He spun around and pointed the weapon at the Shadowborn. The man appeared unmoved.

"Do not think that my age has diminished my skills as a warrior," Oren warned.

The Shadowborn laughed. "Seriously? It will be so easy to kill you even without the dagger. You see, I have a weapon that you do not see. I know where each of your beloved family members are and with one word." He drew a finger across his neck in a kill motion. "I will drop them dead."

Oren gritted his teeth as he tightened his grip on the broken pole arm. "You are as treacherous as your master," he growled.

"I actually find him to be quite merciful. I mean the fact that you are still breathing is proof of that. Now, who was that man?" the Shadowborn demanded in a low voice.

Oren let out a tense breath. If he could kill this Shadowborn, his hope would be restored. "A noble." It was a true enough answer that Oren hoped would be good enough.

It was not as the Shadowborn stepped forward in a threatening manner. Oren followed, keeping his weapon between him and the Shadowborn. The rug bunched up under his feet, threatening to trip him. With a split second thought, the Earthborn lord commanded the ivy latched to a white deer statue in the corner to rise up and shoot towards the Shadowborn. The statue crumbled and Oren immediately summoned the stone pieces to fly up. It was clear by the expression on the Shadowborn's face that he was caught off guard and it pleased Oren. Earth Command was one of his favorite Spirit energy techniques.

The Shadowborn was not caught off guard for long as he immediately bounded for Oren. He utilized Shadow Slide to move quickly and avoid the grasping ivy and flying stone. Just as he came back out of Shadow Slide, a large chunk of stone hit him in the back. The Shadowborn fell to the floor in a stupor. The ivy and stone fell beside him. Much to Oren's shock, the body disappeared and he immediately knew he had been duped.

"Shadow Shade. Even better than your Earth Call," the Shadowborn growled as he perched on the desk like a predator. He pointed to the ivy and stone on the floor with his dagger. In a heartbeat, he slipped into Shadow Slide and quickly threw Oren into the bookcase on the wall. He pressed a dagger to his throat. "Who was that man?"

Oren could not swallow past the lump in his throat. He winced at the icy cold touch of the steel blade. But he could not bring himself to reveal Kader. "The scouts escorted one of my nobles from the western border." He gasped when the blade was pressed tighter against his throat. "He came from Agin, hoping to resign his post as mayor and retire! I swear!"

The Shadowborn frowned. "You're lying." He bent in close, their noses almost touching. "I certainly hope that for the sake of your family, you would not risk their lives to protect a noble."

Oren wrinkled his nose at the smell of the Shadowborn's breath. It was a salty, sickening smell. He felt his stomach lurch. "I would risk my life before theirs. Kill me now if that is your wish."

The Shadowborn studied him for a moment longer before pulling back and relaxing the pressure of the dagger. "It is clear that this noble is important to you. Well, consider my master merciful for he will not harm your family... this time. But be warned that he is always watching. I would not do anything that risks those of your precious bloodline, including your daughter's son."

Oren's body went limp at the mention of Onyx. The pain of losing his daughter roared back into his heart and his desire to see his grandson filled his mind. He closed his eyes as he fought back tears, his chest tightening. Crying in front of the Shadowborn would show how weak and fragile his resolve was. He opened his eyes only to discover that the Shadowborn was gone. Oren collapsed to the floor in a heap, wrapping his arms around his knees, and sobbing at the memories of his lost daughter.

RACHE AND THE SABERS

Rache perched in the high tree tops, his right hand against the trunk of a massive pine. He sniffed the air and knew his prey was coming closer. He briefly glanced down at the pile of rocks and leaf litter at the base of his hiding place. A smile began to form on his lips as his senses told him that his prey was not alone. The excitement began to build as his muscles tightened in anticipation. He was hungry and two Sabers would be a pleasing meal. The branch creaked beneath his weight.

The heartbeats of his prey grew stronger as they came in closer. Sabers were too smart to talk out in the open unless absolutely necessary. But Rache did not need to hear words to know what they were planning to do. The smell of their blood rushing through their veins told him everything he needed to know. Their steps were light and careful, a sign of caution. But it was all too predictable to the Demon's senses. Sabers were notoriously wary when it came to Spirits and the dead. And the grave they came seeking would certainly give them reason to pause.

Kaiser had stated that the body of Madhuri Coba should be discarded in the wild, out of reach but not completely hidden. Rache was not going to argue as the opportunity for easy prey was there. Madhuri was a rebel and he had plenty of friends who would come looking for him. Or what was left of him. It was a thought that made Rache laugh softly.

The two Sabers came into view, eyes darting around for danger. Each held a long curved sword in their hands, prepared for attack. Rache thought that they were right to fear the burial space but he wondered what they hoped to achieve by finding Madhuri's mangled corpse. Knowing that he was dead would mean nothing. What hope could come from knowing the truth?

As he continued to watch the Shadowborn warriors, Rache's mind drifted to his most ancient memories. He had just crossed the border into the lands of the Shadowborn, eager for opportunity and to prove himself. But he encountered a Shadowborn whose name he had long forgotten and who he only remembered as the First Saber. He had been in the retinue of Shadow Night's eldest son Anu and fought with a tenacity he had yet come across. Rache grimaced as he thought about the deep cut the First Saber had laid upon his back. The scar pulled tight across his skin as he shifted his feet. It was a constant reminder that Sabers were dedicated and deadly, when driven to be.

The two Sabers began whispering to each other in low voices, careful not to speak too loudly. The one to Rache's left directed his companion with a subtle sweep of the sword. They broke apart and began to circle the area. Rache then saw his opportunity to attack. He licked his lips as his eyes focused on the left Saber. He waited until his target was out of sight of his companion.

Like a black wind, Rache leaped down from his hidden perch in the pine tree. The Saber turned around at the rustle of air but saw nothing. Rache smirked as he kept himself hidden from sight, ready to toy with his prey. Every time the Saber turned, he zipped around to stand behind him. It became a game to Rache as he watched the Saber's tension rise. He could tell that the royal guardian was fighting a shout to his companion. It was amusing for him to see the struggle.

Just as the Saber turned to call out, Rache struck hard and fast. He leaped forward, tackling his prey. His full weight pressed down and pinned the warrior to the ground. He pressed a hand over his mouth and bent in close to whisper in his ear.

"Time to join your kinsman."

The Saber's face turned bone white. It was rather pathetic considering the order's fearsome reputation. Keeping one ear open to the movements of the second, Rache sank his teeth into the fleshy neck. The muscle was hard but had a tender taste and Rache could not help but savor it.

Searing pain suddenly cut across his back and Rache whipped around to face the second Saber who held a bloody sword. The only way he could have sneaked up on him was by Shadow Slide. This Saber was smarter than he originally anticipated.

"Come to defend the bones of the Commander?" Rache

sneered as he jumped backwards. He narrowly avoided tripping over the broken body.

"I seek the truth," the Saber growled.

Clearly this one was an officer by his attitude, Rache thought to himself. A soon to be nameless dead officer. He pointed to the pile of rocks. "And you think that you will find truth there?"

"You are Adonis' servant are you not?"

Rache chuckled. "Does it matter?" He pulled back his cowl and mask. "I would say you are his servant too after all he has done for the throne."

"I am not the fool you think me to be," came the confident reply.

The Saber's demeanor was infuriating but Rache kept his cool. "I have killed hundreds of Sabers in my lifetime. You will be no different."

The Saber's face was unreadable. It was an expression of utter calm and control. Determined to rip his prey apart, Rache did not wait for a moment longer. He unleashed his full might without hesitation.

A scream tore through the night signaling the Saber's blood curdling end. Rache stood over the second corpse, covered in gore and blood. The blood slowly dripped down the front of his torso, leaving a sticky mess. His skin now matched his hair in color as his eyes burned through the crimson red. With a snort of disdain, he bent down to strip the corpses of their uniforms. Wrapping the equipment up in a cape, Rache carried the spoils back to Cross.

He found Kaiser lounging on the throne, laughing and drinking with courtesans that were catering to his vanity. One buxom raven haired woman sat on Kaiser's lap and pulled open his shirt to run her fingers over the muscles of his chest. Another woman of equal beauty fed him grapes one by one, giggling. Kaiser grinned as he savored each bite before grabbing the girl's chin and pulling her in for a kiss. A third courtesan poured more wine into his glass as Kaiser leaned his head back laughing. The second bent down to pick up more grapes. Rache stood at the entryway, scoffing at the debauchery. He had long thought that his master was indeed full of himself but this was open and brazen. He strode forward, catching everyone's attention with his gruesome look.

"My dear Rache!" Kaiser crooned, clearly on the edge of drunkenness. The buxom beauty moaned as she draped herself over him.

Rache did not bow but instead tossed the uniforms at his feet. The folds of the cape parted to reveal the equally dirty leathers and armor. He did not like Kaiser in this state and hated their unnatural bond more than ever at this moment. Resisting the urge to strangle Kaiser, Rache clenched his fists tightly. When the wine pouring courtesan sauntered up to him, he snapped his fangs and frightened her away.

"Darling, he cares nothing for the heat of a lover's flesh except to drain it of blood and tear skin from bone," Kaiser said as he comforted the scared woman. He kissed the top of her head.

"You disgust me," Rache growled.

Kaiser shot him a scowl that sent shivers down everyone's spine. A twitch of his hand was the silent order for the courtesans to leave his presence. The three women groaned at the thought of leaving him and blew kisses at him. Kaiser gestured towards the messy pile of armor and gear in front of Rache. They picked up the Saber equipment and left. Soon only Kaiser and Rache were left in the throne room.

"I should say the same to you considering your state of filthiness," Kaiser stated with utter sharpness.

Perhaps his master was not quite as drunk as he thought. "It seems the rebels have discovered the grave of the dearly departed Madhuri Coba. You have a leak in your... circle of allies," Rache pointed out.

"And I suppose you wish to kill him or her. Keep doing that and I will have no one left," Kaiser snapped.

"Oh are we frustrated about something?" the Demon teased. "Should I have let those two Sabers live?"

Kaiser sneered. "There are many things I am frustrated about. Some of them a minor inconvenience coming from my role as Lord's Chancellor. Tax complaints, charitable donations to help the pathetic, trade negotiations. More importantly, wayward Silvanus sons that I still have to bring home. The missing Sage and my wayward grandson. The Sabers are still not wholly under my control and you waltz in here covered in their blood!" He gestured with his hand towards Rache. "At least I have the nobles too terrified to act against me. Oh I just love wringing their fragile necks until they break." Kaiser mimicked the deadly twisting motion with his hands.

"Why is Sage Silvanus so important if he is either lost or dead? Why do you care so much about Shadow Night's third son?" Rache asked as he crossed his arms tightly.

Kaiser wafted his hand back and forth in a private rhythm. It was if he was having an entire conversation with himself before he dared to speak a word out loud. "When Shadow Night left this world, he left his two younger sons to deal with the mess of a post war land. Sin took up the mantle of the throne. I remember how he stared upon the seat with great reluctance to sit upon it. You see, the eldest of the three sons, as noble and grand as he was, was a stupid little shit who knew nothing of subtley. Sin was more somber and careful than his older brother. Sage, the youngest, was not the warrior his brothers were. He was a scholar, a lover of books. He was Sin's first Lord's Chancellor."

"Did not know that. Probably because I don't care," Rache said before gesturing up with a finger. "Why not you? I am not so uneducated on Shadowborn politics to wonder why you did not become Lord's Chancellor. Wasn't Adonis Anu Shadow Night's Chancellor before retiring to Umbra?"

"Good. You are not stupid," Kaiser chuckled softly. "Sage convinced his brother that they should, how you say, stick together until the world settled. I was young but I was angry and rather aggressive. I was angry about a lot of things. And then you came!"

The Demon rolled his eyes. "And yet for some reason, you sent the Pirate on this expedition to find Sage Silvanus. I am a superior hunter to him."

"Oh, are we jealous?" Kaiser snickered.

"Like you aren't. Shouldn't the grand Kaiser Adonis find Sage Silvanus himself and claim the throne by throwing down the last of Shadow Night's sons?" Rache boasted with a forced laugh.

"Shut up," Kaiser growled. "Sometimes I am so close to smacking you."

Rache stuck his chin out towards Kaiser. "Go ahead. I'll give you a free shot."

Kaiser sneered before reclining across the throne. His legs dangled over the right hand arm rest as his head and arms were thrown over the left hand arm rest. His eyes closed as his breathing settled into a steady calm rhythm. The throne room became so quiet that the gentle rocking of the iron chandelier above their heads seemed unusually loud. Rache pulled himself back as he studied Kaiser, trying to discern a hint of what he was thinking about.

His eyes snapped open. "I think it is time for a rest. Let people believe in their own security."

"Why? Have the rebels gotten under your skin?" the Demon asked, lifting an eyebrow.

Kaiser waved him off. "I have only survived this long because unlike you, I do not fight every second of every day. Even I need a break to expand my mind. To search the world with my thoughts. Maybe even entertain bedding a few women."

"You're over a thousand years old. You honestly think a young Shadowborn lady will want to be your bed warmer?" Rache doubted that Kaiser was as irresisitable as he thought he was. He shifted his weight between his feet, leaning heavily on his right leg.

"Do I look like an old man to you?" Kaiser asked, closing his eyes again.

Rache shrugged. "You look like you. Where I come from, age is weakness but experience is power. I have never seen what your people would consider an old and wrinkled Demon."

Kaiser chuckled. "Well if a lady displeases me, you can have the spoils. Just don't make too big of a mess. I don't want a repeat of your gross appearance."

"You and your kind place so much value on crisp clean looks. Blood is power, not something to be ashamed of," Rache argued.

Silence fell between them. Kaiser then eased himself up to sit properly on the throne, resting his hands on the arm rests. "You're right. Blood is power."

A DRAGON'S JUDGEMENT

Ryder took a deep breath as he stepped out onto the outdoor Arena floor. He slowly released the breath as he turned around in a circle, seeing hundreds of empty seats. The Arena was completely deserted of spectators though he spotted a pair of stonemasons inspecting a broken stair. He smiled as the smaller of the two angrily pointed at another crack that had been poorly repaired. He raced several rows down the stairs to emphasize a point. The sight was amusing as Ryder figured the smaller stonemason was the boss and the taller bald man was the hired worker. The argument over the poor repair continued for a few minutes longer until it appeared that the tall worker conceded.

The Crossroads celebration would not be happening for another six years but preparations for it had already begun. As the capital of the Northlands, the city had to look its best for the thousands of visitors that were due to come. As Ryder saw with the stonemason pair, repairs were reviewed and damage was examined with careful eyes. Nothing but the best would be acceptable. In time, the Arena would be decorated with finely woven banners, some to be hung by the royal viewing boxes and others by the floor entry ways. Iron poles had already been welded down along the top row of seats to eventually hold strings of lanterns for the nighttime events.

He bent down towards the dusty floor, leather boots creaking. The scabbard strapped across his back rose up towards his neck. He took a handful of dirt and stood back up, brushing the mess between his palms. The dust fell back to his feet in a thin cloud. This was how Ryder had always prepared before practicing his combat skills in the Arena. The dust prevented his hands from becoming too slick from sweat and blood. Studying one's surroundings was one of the earliest lessons Ryder had been taught. Being aware of the environment presented possible advantages in battle that could be utilized in the spur of the moment.

Ryder popped his shoulders to loosen the steel sword in the scabbard strapped across his back. He reached behind and pulled the sword loose before quickly flipping it to his right hand. He swung it around in a wide circle, testing the weight and balance. It was no great weapon but it would do. Ryder then dropped the leather straps and scabbard to the ground. He rolled his neck and shoulders to stretch out the muscles. He loosened the muscles of his bare arms with a good shake. Tension before a fight would lead to poor decisions and muddled actions.

Ryder was a Shadowborn who fought with absolute surety. Bastard though he was, he wanted to fight as well as any legitimately born royal son. It was easy to hide behind a warrior's fierce veneer as people whispered and accused with unkind words. But they were less likely to do so in his prescence if they feared him. The conversation about him was mixed with awe, praise, and harsh accusations and it was something he had lived with his entire life. This would all end once he claimed victory during the Crossroads Arena.

With eyes closed, Ryder focused his remaining senses into one strong cohesive unit. His heartbeat slowed into a careful rhythm, ready at a moment's notice for Shadow Slide. All it would take for a Shadowborn of Ryder's skill was a quick thought and a sliver of shadow to activate. He opened his eyes again, the calm anticipation of an imaginary battle upon him. He slid his feet apart into a wide stance, bending his knees and pulling his weight into his thighs. Tightening his grip on the sword hilt, he drew his right arm back and brought his left hand forward. He wiggled his fingers.

He burst into action, jumping high into the air in a forward leap. Coming down to land on his feet, he spun, swinging his sword with cutting force. With the downward arc, he continued his spin low to the ground, kicking out with his leg to knock an imaginary foe off their feet. He quickly flipped the blade around and stabbed downward in a killing maneuver. Using his sword as a pivot, Ryder balanced himself as he kicked up from the ground. With a powerful spin, he got up to his feet and ripped his sword free of the ground. He steadied his limbs as he settled into another ready position. Ryder twisted his body, keeping his front to the side but his sword pointed towards yet another imaginary enemy in both offense and in defense. This time, both of his hands gripped the hilt.

His focus was intense as Ryder imagined five armed swordsman casually approaching him. His eyes darted around as the Shades surrounded him, their ghost like swords gleaming with an eerie light. His mother had taught him as a young man how to conjure misty Shades in his own image to serve as distractions in a fight. He chose to use Shadow Shade to hone his battle skills in the absence of an opponent. It was strange to look at five mirror images and Ryder found himself smiling. Too bad, he thought, as he usually liked to exchange disarming insults. A good jab at one's character was all it took to cause doubt. A shadow passed over him with a loud thunderous sound just as the energy in Ryder's muscles began to surge.

Vorin wheeled around, tipping his left wing down and his right wing up at a sharp angle. The sunlight shimmered across his wine red scaled hide, giving him the color of a blood red ruby. The heat of the sun was soothing. Normally, Vorin would have been sunbathing, stretching out his large sinewy length across a bare rock face. As a Dragon, it was his favorite leisure activity but before his stomach could touch the hot stone, he heard that Ryder was going to go practice in the Arena. The news spread like wildfire but he was the first to arrive. He flapped his wings in short bursts, his hind legs touching the dusty floor of the Arena first before he brought his front down with a shudder.

Ryder twisted his body around to meet the first attack of the shades. He brought his sword up to block a heavy handed strike, the collision of steel loud and shrill. He shoved his weight forward and spun around on his feet, ducking underneath the first shade's counterattack. His left hand quickly dropped from the sword hilt as Ryder stretched out his right arm in a wide slashing cut. Two shades swung their swords with brute force, coming at Ryder from his left and right side. Seeing the attack, Ryder launched himself forward, clutching his sword close to his body. The shades' swords passed over his chest and under his back as he passed through the small opening between the blades. As soon as he was free, he rolled in a somersault up to his feet.

The Dragon watched with fevered anticipation as Ryder dodged and leaped around with the circle of shades. It amazed him that the shades resembled Ryder in both appearance and movement. It was a clear indication that in all of Crossroads, Ryder felt like the strongest person he could practice with was himself. Any other Lord would have thought the Shadowborn bastard arrogant but Vorin was fond of him and he understood the decision. The ancient Dragon also knew the Shadowborn to be among the fiercest and most tenacious warriors. Ryder was a shining example of his people.

Steel blades sang a high metallic peal as they banged into each other with furious force. The shades followed Ryder's every move with unwavering accuracy. Ryder fought with equal tenacity, his sword darting in and out. He charged towards a shade that was separated from the group. His outline started to fade as he rushed towards the target. He lifted his sword for the attack, the blade glowing with a silver light. His body faded even more while the blade glowed with greater intensity and brightness.

In a flash of silver light that even Vorin had to turn away from, Ryder cut down the shade. He slid in the dirt, sword held out to his right side. He slowly turned his head to look over his shoulder with a mischievous grin. With a twisting jump up to his feet, he readied himself for the counterattack of the shades. The four remaining shades charged forward, angry snarls on their faces. Ryder rolled his shoulders as he tightened his grip on his glowing sword. He dodged the first attack to spar with the second. He traded blows for a few short seconds before kicking the shade in the chest, dispersing it into a blurry mist. Ducking under another attack, Ryder spun around and sliced through another shade with a backhanded cut.

Vorin began to realize as the sparring match dragged on, Ryder's sword began to smoke. Wisps of gray twisted around the blade as Ryder spun and slashed. The fight drew closer to Vorin's resting spot on the Arena floor. The Dragon lifted his head, arching his neck, as Ryder moved to dispatch another shade. His sword had now caught fire and blazed hot with a red flame. The air hissed wherever the sword passed, sizzling loudly. He chased after the two remaining shades, bursting in and out of Shadow Slide as he drew closer. One of the shades darted away towards the far wall. Instead of giving chase, Ryder hurled his sword at the escaping shade. The melting blade tore through the shade's head before crashing into the wall, shattering into pieces.

The last shade looked around in a panic, completely unaware of the Dragon close by. Vorin thought the panic was not characteristic of Ryder even though the conjured shades looked just like him. It was the fear of the Spirit World in the shade's eyes. Ryder was dangerous. The shade scrambled to figure out an escape as Ryder slowly approached. His arms hung at his sides as his eyes bore an incredible focus. The shade seemed paralyzed with pure fear.

The exchange was entrancing to the old Dragon. It was a

stand off between Spiritborn and a shade brought forth from the Spirit World. Ryder was already quite young to have such a strong command over his innate Spirit energy but part of Vorin was not surprised. If there ever was a more perfect example of Spiritual heir, it was the bastard of the royal Silvanus line. Vorin took the rumors and comments about Ryder's striking looks to heart. Everyone he knew of the older generation said that Ryder looked like Shadow Night reborn. He was tall and strong like his famous ancestor with the battle skills to match. But Vorin felt that there was something more and he finally saw it when Ryder leapt for the shade, his right arm drawn back in a burning inferno.

Ryder tore at the shade with his fire licked arm, ripping it to shreds. He landed with a proud smile, shaking his arm to snuff out the flame. A round of applause erupted, interspersed with cheers and shouts. Ryder turned around to see a sizable crowd in the stands on their feet and clapping. He bowed his head to acknowledge their praise.

"What a fantastic preview to the Crossroads Arena!" Vorin's deep voice rumbled. His golden eyes were warm like a proud mentor to his talented student.

"It was only practice," Ryder stated as he brushed his right palm on his roughspun cotton sleeveless tunic. A smear of dirt and ash appeared on the light colored fabric.

Vorin gestured towards the excited crowd with a bow of his large serpentine head. "And yet your practice inspires them to cheer with praise. You should be proud."

Ryder shrugged as he held the Dragon's gaze. "Pride does not suit me."

The Dragon's expression softened as the rustled scales on the top of his crown settled back into place. His eyes returned Ryder's gaze with equal expression. He shook his massive shoulders, loosening the tension in his leathery wings. "It is not wrong to feel some pride. You are a shining testament to the blood that flows in your veins."

"Then you are truly the only one who thinks so. To everyone else, I am Akakios' bastard," Ryder stated with no emotion but shimmering anger. He clenched his fists tightly at his sides.

"But that is not all of who you are is it? The looks of the Silvanus royals, the air of command from the Coba generals, the quiet nobility of the," Vorin started to say before he was ferociously and very quickly interrupted.

"Don't say it," Ryder growled in warning.

A roar built up in the depths of Vorin's broad chest. His large claws gripped the ground. He was not used to anyone being so bold as to interrupt him. His lip curled revealing a row of aged yellow teeth. The crowd quickly dispersed upon seeing Vorin's reaction to whatever was being said between him and Ryder. They did not want to bear witness to any display of wrath. Soon the Dragon and the Shadowborn were alone.

"How dare you think to interrupt me! I should roast you!" Vorin snarled. Ryder was unmoved. Vorin lifted himself towards Ryder in a threatening manner.

"Go ahead and save the world its pain," Ryder dared without a qualm.

Vorin got in Ryder's face, snorting a plume of black smoke from his nostrils. He growled, lips quivering. "You have your grandfather's blasted arrogance. Some would mistake that for confidence." He loosed a loud growl before drawing back. He drew himself up in a proud pose, keeping his eyes on Ryder. "You have yet to ask how I knew of your relation to Kaiser."

"You are the Dragonlord. I do not doubt your ability to read and judge people. For who could look you in the eyes without fear," came Ryder's knowing reply.

"Begin Anu could. Of his six children, only Adonis could match him with the same intensity. How could I not see the same true bearing in you? As you are purely Shadowborn, and your father's family is well known, your connection must come from your mother's family which the world knows little," Vorin explained as he was slow to relax his fury. It was a difficult task for a Dragon. "Only a true line descendent of Begin Anu can manifest the Spiritual energies of more than just his birth."

A breeze brushed across the large dusty floor of the arena. The sun beamed down, not a cloud in the sky. A flag at the far end of the sandstone stadium bearing the city seal flapped in the wind. The early peace returned as Vorin sat up, lifting his wings and stretching them out. His wing tips touched the walls of the floor as he moved to take advantage of the sun.

"I am no one but myself and one day, the world will see that. Until then, they are not my friend or my enemy," Ryder stated firmly. He then bowed his head in respect to Vorin. "Only then will I allow myself to be judged."

THE DANGER IN THE SHADOWS

The heat of the rising sun on his back was soothing to the Falcon Gryphon's aching muscles. He yawned, stretching his jaw, before clacking his gray beak shut. He shook his head to displace the dust that had settled over his raptorian brow. Stretching out his forelimbs before him, the Gryphon arched his back. He then leaned his weight forward, kicking out each of his two rear legs to unlock his knees and ankles. A couple of flaps followed by a rustle of his slate gray wings finished his morning stretch.

A pair of brown and white songbirds flitted over the Gryphon's head. He looked up to watch the creatures, his dark eyes following their movements until they disappeared into the branches of a nearby oak tree. The forest that the Gryphon had settled in was full of birds both big and small. As the sun continued to rise, a chorus of avian voices erupted with a glorious sound. The Gryphon smiled, turning up the corners of his beak. He thought about adding his own voice to the mix. His voice was not musical though and would not have complemented the shrill chirps and whistles.

The Gryphon sauntered over to a slow moving brook and dipped his face into the water. He snorted once before pulling his face back out. The cold water dripped from his face and trickled down his neck. His stomach began rumbling. The Gryphon looked around to see if there was any quick prey to get his energy going for the remaining flight south. His senses sharpened suddenly and he bolted into action. He leaped over the brook and pounced on a large rabbit. With a practiced stroke, he slew his prey and began feasting on it.

After finishing his meal, the Gryphon dug a small hole with his talons. He nudged the remains of his kill into the hole and quickly covered it with dirt. In a low short series of trills, the Gryphon spoke a song of parting to the rabbit. He may have been a predator but even the Gryphon respected the sanctity of life.

With a deep upward and downward flap of his wings, the Gryphon lifted into the air. He flapped his wings again in quick succession to gain altitude. The wind was light so it did not hinder his ascent. The rising thermal of heated air gave him enough lift to fly above the forest canopy. He coasted for a few moments, spreading out his gray flight feathers to take advantage of the thermal. The current of air tickled him across his furred back and down to the tip of his leonine tail. He smiled again, enjoying the touch of warm air.

He loved flying under a clear, sunny sky with a sturdy breeze. There was something incredibly soothing about the clean air ruffling his feathers and fur. Being up in the sky allowed him a clear view of his surroundings that could not be found if he was on the ground. The dark mustache marks under his eyes shielded them from the bright morning light. In the far distance behind him was the edge of the Red Desert. He was glad to be away from the sandy expanse of land. He was immensely glad that he had not been assigned the flight to the Fireborn capital of Coal. Only another day's flight and he would reach his assigned destination: Crossroads.

The Gryphon twisted his great body around and charged towards the direction of the great capital city. He knew that the forest would thin out soon. Then, he planned on following the curving course of the East Shadow River. The river would easily lead him to his destination. As he flew, the Gryphon thought about the lush farmlands before Crossroads. He smiled as he remembered bounding through the fields, catching quails with his nestmates. The varied fields of growing crops were always succulent with fruit, vegetables, and grain year round. A tingle went down his spine as he thought about the treats made in the city markets specifically for the Gryphons. He whistled out loud with delight.

The forest soon turned into open grasslands as the East Shadow flowed to his right. He spotted a herd of deer grazing by its bank. The deer looked up and bolted when they saw him. The sight amused him. He tipped his right wing to soar away from a twist in the river to avoid flying over the water. He repeated the motion with his left wing to resettle his position in the air. He tucked his limbs closer to his body to avoid any drag that would slow his flight down.

As he flew further south towards Crossroads, the Gryphon's mind began to drift to the Feather Whisper he had been given. It was currently inside a leather tube that was strapped to his chest. At first, he tried to avoid thinking about what message had been ensourced within the barbs of the feather. Normally, he would have been given some hint as to the message's contents should the feather be lost or destroyed. This time, he was told nothing other than it must be delivered to the Lord of Crossroads. It could only mean that the message was of absolute secrecy.

To get his mind off of the seriousness of the thought, the Gryphon refocused on his early days training in Crossroads to be a messenger. One of his favorite training memories was the first flight lesson over the Wall of Crossroads and how Vorin the Dragon Lord joined them. Gryphons and Dragons were both masters of flight and his teacher relished in having the mighty beast fly with his students. His teacher had been a gristled old Falcon Gryphon that had become stark white with age. Thinking about his mentor made him feel sad for only last winter was he laid to rest. As a messenger trainer in Crossroads, the old Gryphon had been buried by the city cliffs so his Spirit could fly free.

> To my brothers and sisters,
> Fly free forevermore.
> Up into the sky,
> And beyond the shore.
>
> Soar to the stars,
> And glide to the moon.
> Climb with the wind,
> Escape the sun at noon.
>
> Remember that you are loved,
> So dearly missed.
> Remember the Spirits,
> Of the ones you once kissed.

The simple song had been composed by Aves, Lord of the Airborn for his mentor's funeral. The Gryphon would have continued to sing it but he had forgotten the remaining verses. Losing his mentor had saddened him greatly. He once asked one of the Airborn courtiers how they handled death and sorrow. The Airborn hesitated to answer him and only relented after much prodding. The Gryphon remembered the Airborn telling him that death and sorrow were the same in any culture. Ever since then, he sang the verses of Aves' song to put his mind at ease.

A flock of crows cawed as they joined him, following in his wake. He cried back to welcome them. He loved shared the wind with other birds and masters of the sky. The crows continued to cry out in a raucous song that sounded more like noise than any pattern of communication he knew. He pumped his wings forward to put some distance between him and the crows. The flock only sought harder to catch up with him. Their presence was starting to unnerve the Gryphon and he stooped into a sharp dive. No crow would be able to keep with a Falcon Gryphon once they dove.

He leveled out several hundred feet closer to the ground. The cawing of the crows was now a distant sound though it seemed more shrill and desparate than before. The Gryphon looked up over his shoulder, contemplating on flying back and dispersing the flock with a loud hiss. He never heard the twang of the bowstring before an arrow buried itself deep in his chest. He immediately lost altitude and fell towards the ground. He crashed and skidded over the brush and stones, sliding to a stop in a broken mess. His vision steadily grew darker and darker until a hiss of breath escaped his beak. On the edge of his hearing, the Gryphon heard footsteps and the scrap of a steel sword being pulled out of a scabbard.

*****

SIX YEARS LATER

It was his first Saber trial, a confirmation of his training after six hard years of work. He was no longer a child Prince but a warrior: taller in frame and possessing broad muscled shoulders. His hands were rough and callused from constant weapons drills. He was not an expert fighter like Sai and even Soja but he was now more than capable of defending himself. As a child, Onyx had not given much thought to how he appeared to others but now he was being noticed by more than just the members of the court. The people of the city remarked on his strong Silvanus looks and the kind eyes of his beloved mother. The women of the court whispered about how a betrothal must be in the works. He had to smile at the thought as he walked slowly through the city square, dressed in the Saber black and leather.

The castle Onyx called home rose up over the north side of the city, the great mountain wall of the Heights behind it. The moon shined brightly in the clear night sky, surrounded by blinking stars. He took a deep breath, taking in all of the smells of the marketplace. All around him, people were closing up their stalls, sweeping the debris and packing unsold merchandise. A vegetable stall owner shouted nighttime farewells to a neighboring meat vendor. The meat vendor promptly invited his neighbor for a drink and the two laughed and carried on about the day's customers. The night watch looked about for any hint of thieves. Taverns buzzed to life as men shouted how the sales went and women gossiped about court fashion. Every sight, smell, and sound put Onyx at ease with the city he loved and called home.

Onyx slowly came to a halt and closed his eyes. He pushed his senses out all around him, crossing into the world of auras and Spiritual energy. The world turned black until bursts of light erupted like the stars in the night sky. They pulsated with each one of his heartbeats until they settled into their own rhythm. His eyes snapped open when he found his target.

With a quick spring, he leaped up to a nearby rooftop, thumping down on the wooden slats. Another jump and careful landing brought him to a neighboring rooftop. His target was quickly moving away so he slipped into Shadow Slide. Just as swiftly, his target slid into his own Shadow Slide. Now the hunt was truly on.

Together, hunter and hunted weaved throughout the city in a shadowy dance, leaping across rooftops and speeding down alleyways. In the dark of night, people barely noticed the chase as they focused instead on going back home. Onyx felt himself drawing closer to his target and was almost within arm's reach until his target surged forward and climbed the Heights. Oynx was quick to follow.

The Heights was a tall mountain wall that wrapped around the northern border of the city. It was an imposing natural defense to the castle that was carved into its stone face. It also served as the perfect spot to finally confront his target. With a final surge of energy, Onyx charged out of Shadow Slide and tackled Sai to the ground. Sai broke free with a push and Oynx rolled onto his back. He flipped up to his feet to face him.

"Very good. Tracking auras and energy signatures are a highly prized skill for a proper Saber," Sai said as they circled each other. "But as one knows, it is easy enough to hunt someone. It is often much harder to subdue them."

Onyx pulled out his steel short sword, holding it loosely in his right hand. He rolled it with his fingers, the excitement building in his body. "Then do you surrender?"

Sai smirked. "Not a chance, my Prince!" he challenged as he revealed out a long shafted staff with a sharp blade attached at both ends that he had hidden behind his back.

The Saber Commander was taller and broader in the shoulders than Onyx and far more experienced in the ways of combat. He was nearly four hundred while Onyx was a mere eighteen years old. Sai's martial strategy was often to overpower his opponent and knock him off his feet before slicing off his head. His large size belied his deadly speed and agility but Onyx had not been idle in his lessons. He had studied Sai's combat style and adapted his own to compete with it. And youth always had its advantages.

"You have cornered your target and he is prepared to fight to his last breath. Your Commander has ordered you not to kill but to subdue. Show me how you would go about making sure your orders are obeyed," Sai instructed as they started to circle each other.

Onyx took careful steps on the uneven stone beneath his feet. His eyes studied Sai's posture, looking at how his limbs were positioned. He sought out any catch or weakness that he could exploit. He could not find anything and it frustrated him. His grip tightened on his short sword. As soon as he did, Sai leaped forward and swung his bladed staff down low. Onyx managed to jump backwards out of range before the Commander could knock him off of his feet. Before he could regain a strong balance, Sai came forward again aiming for his legs. Onyx stumbled back and fell but managed to catch himself with his left hand before hitting the ground. Sai spun his weapon around and stabbed down. The young Prince quickly rolled to the right and spun up to his feet.

The Commander was not giving him a second to rest before he twisted his body and swung his bladed staff out in a wide arc. Onyx bent backwards towards his right, barely avoiding the weapon from hitting him in the head. He followed Sai's momentum and danced towards the left. Their movements were interlocked until Onyx rolled around Sai's back to slash at his dominant right arm. He cut a shallow gash through the leather bracer of Sai's forearm. He was immediately elated that he had landed a hit.

Suddenly, stars danced before his eyes and Onyx fell backwards with a splitting headache. He gritted his teeth and slammed his eyes shut as he laid sprawled on the stone. The screech of steel next to the left side of his head forced his eyes back open. Sai was leaning on the staff, looking down on him .

"You think too much. You need to trust your instincts and just feel," Sai admonished before he pulled his weapon back. "Get up and try again."

It hurt to move but Onyx forced himself back up to his feet. He was grateful that he did not lose his grip on his short sword when Sai had cracked him on the side of the head. He shook his head and massaged his jaw. Pressing his finger tips to the corner of his mouth, he found a spot of bright red blood. The sight shocked him. He had never shed blood before except when he skinned a knee or had a hard fall off of a horse. No one had ever struck him like Sai had just struck him.

"That is a taste of what a real fight is like for a Saber against a live or die opponent," Sai said as he pointed towards Onyx's bleeding mouth. "In a real fight, you can not think. You have to just do. You have to trust in what you know and you have to believe that you know it. Now try again and stop thinking about a scratch on your face."

Onyx gathered his resolve but his mind refused to listen. With extreme mental effort, he forced his mind to cooperate and focus on the fight. He got into ready position and decided to just go for it. Onyx charged forward, his right arm drawn back like an arrow on a bow. Sai stood waiting for his attack, his weapon pulled behind him and the blade pointed to the ground. Just as Onyx came within range, Sai swung the bladed staff around to block. Onyx pressed his short sword against the wood of the shaft with as much force as he could muster.

"Good, now you are acting without lingering on what your mind is telling you but do not expect to best me so easily. I have had many years of trials and tribulations to learn from. Do not let that deter you from fighting with everything you have," Sai said with a proud smile.

The praising words made Onyx's confidence grow and he smirked. He decided to wrestle Sai's weapon from him. He continued to press his weight forward with the short sword in his right hand as he gripped the staff with his left hand. The two of them struggled against each other but Onyx soon felt that Sai was not giving his all in their small contest. He quickly switched his left hand onto the hilt of his short sword and pushed forward with all of his weight. The staff cracked under the pressure before eventually shattering. Sai stumbled back with Onyx stepping forward with a heavy foot to avoid falling into him.

"Not bad. Breaking a weapon such as a staff or a pole axe into two pieces will force your opponent to change fighting styles. If they are experienced enough, they can easily adapt. If they are not experienced enough, I would say you are one step closer to claiming victory," Sai explained as he settled his balance. He readjusted his grip on each piece of his broken weapon and spun them around.

Even though it was clear that Sai was not defeated, Onyx was excited to see how their fight would progress with the change. He threw himself into the close combat fight with fervor. Sai kept the bladed piece in his right hand, using it to attack, while swinging and blocking with the other broken piece in his left hand. Onyx began to have fun as he felt his training finally being applied against a more than worthy opponent. He did not even mind that Sai had struck him. He was going to wear any cut or bruise he received from Sai with honor.

He flipped backwards, swinging his legs up over his head to kick Sai in the chin. Sai stumbled back, wiggling his jaw. Onyx quickly pushed off on his feet as soon as he landed and launched himself back towards Sai. As Onyx drew in close, Sai spun into him with a high kick that slammed into his side and sent him flying. He skidded across the stone and slowed to a stop just before the edge dropped off on the Heights to the city below.

"You are making progress," Sai said as he stepped over and offered a hand to help Onyx up. Onyx graciously took it and Sai pulled him up to his feet.

"So do I pass my first trial?" Onyx asked as he sheathed his short sword.

"You definitely get high marks. The point of the first trial is to get a Saber in training to stop thinking if you catch my meaning," Sai stated as he helped Onyx to brush dirt off of his shoulders.

"A Saber needs to act by instinct. Even a second spent in thought means life or death for their charge or themselves," Onyx answered with a confident smile.

Sai waved a finger to emphasize a point. "Exactly. A truly experienced Saber, even a normal fighter, to be great acts with an instinct he trusts in. He doesn't think about the end result of an encounter though the idea of victory or defeat may flash in his mind. He doesn't dwell on it."

"Is that why everyone seems to think my bastard cousin is some force to be reckoned with? Don't look away. I know what is said about him. I am not blind or deaf to it," Onyx said with a degree of command when Sai tried to turn his head.

The Commander let out a deep breath. "I do not pretend to know his true mind. Few do. From what I do know, he fights to survive and that makes him dangerous. I have said it before. Your cousin would make a fantastic Saber"

"Do you think he would make a better Shadowlord than me?" Onyx asked.

The question obviously unnerved Sai and he stammered for a few seconds. It was clear that he did not either know what to say or how to answer without offending Onyx. "He is an illegitimate son. He can not inherit the throne when a legitimate son is waiting."

The answer was expected as Onyx had received the same response from Zoras many times. "Do you think I will make a good Shadowlord?"

This time, Sai did not hesitate. "You have a good heart reminiscent of your noble grandfather. The Shadowborn need that more than the skills of a hard core warrior."

Onyx nodded as he stepped away from the edge with Sai watching him carefully. "I am not blind to my father's condition. I want you to announce my intention to take the throne to the

Shadow Council at the next meeting. I know that my father will support me in this and he will find peace in seeing me rise to his throne."

Sai fell to his knees and grabbed Onyx's hand. He bowed his head deeply. "Long have I waited to hear you speak those words and now, I hear the confidence of a future leader that I would be happy to serve with all my being. I will tell the Council on your behalf."

THE SON OF CIAN

Kaiser sat, legs crossed, in a worn oak wood chair. He picked at his fingernails with the tip of a steel dagger, frowning whenever he found a speck of filth. He flicked his fingers, tossing the debris away. Strands of midnight hair hung over his forehead as his eyes were locked in deep concentration.

"I have better things to do than watch you scrape dirt from under your nails," Rache grumbled as he sat before Kaiser on the stone floor.

"Like what?" Kaiser asked in a harsh tone. He stretched his right hand out to admire his work. He then drew it back and shifted his attention to his left hand.

"Maybe ripping a few throats out. You haven't let me kill in days!" Rache answered. He lay back on the floor and closed his eyes.

Kaiser scoffed. "You do not need my permission to kill."

Rache shot back up. "Really?"

Suddenly, the Demon felt a burning pain across the back of his left hand. He looked down to see an emerging cut across his bony knuckles. A sickly glob of blood oozed out of the wound. The deep red color was a sign that Kaiser had touched upon their unholy bond. Rache snarled as he tore a length of cloth from the bottom edge of his shirt.

Kaiser chuckled as he flashed the back of his left hand towards Rache. The impression of the mirrored cut disappeared within a few seconds. He flexed his hand, laughing. "You are not to kill unless I command it. If I point to a man and say 'kill him,' you are to wait until I tell you how. Otherwise, you shall continue to wait until it pleases me to shed blood."

Rache snorted as he tied the torn tan cloth over his left hand. It was a crude makeshift bandage that did little to halt the bleeding. Soon it was soaked through.

"Don't you dare bleed on my floor," Kaiser growled as he picked at the fingernails of his left hand.

"Don't invoke the bond," Rache growled in equal fury. Kaiser only laughed.

The room they sat in was part of new quarters that Kaiser had assigned himself. When the Shadow Council complained that he was overstepping his rank, Kaiser played the members with a half promise about leaving them as soon as his old quarters were renovated. Zoras the Lord's Regent was annoyed and prepared to force Kaiser to obey the Council's order. Clever as he always was, Kaiser said he only answered to the Shadowlord and he would report the Council's behavior to Lord Aku. Rache had laughed when Kaiser had told him the tale of how he had manipulated the Shadow Council yet again. Kaiser had only claimed the sparsely furnished room just to prove he could. He enjoyed manipulating the Council and threatening them with the Lord Aku's retribution for disobedience.

"I am thinking of a wolf skin rug right there," Kaiser stated, pointing to the center of the room with the dagger. He threw his legs over the arm of the chair and reclined back. "A foot stool and my coat of arms. Yes, that could work," he mused to himself.

"Why not just skin the bastard and carve your coat of arms in his hide?" Rache suggested. "Drape a Silvanus skin over your chair for an enhanced effect," he added as he gestured with his hands.

Kaiser tapped his chin with the tip of the dagger as he looked up at the ceiling. The heels of his leather boots clicked together as he wiggled his feet. He hmmed and hawed in private consideration. "What I wouldn't do for a Dragon skin or the wings of a Gryphon."

"Why?" Rache asked. "Dirty, filthy beasts."

"The great generals of the North sat on Dragon bone chairs gilded with silver. Am I not afforded the same luxury as a general's son?" Kaiser asked as he closed his eyes. "Yes and cushions stuffed with Gryphon down. Banners of the finest cloth sewn with gold and silver thread. Sometimes I can not believe how dark and depressing the Shadowborn are."

"Aren't you a Shadowborn too?" Rache asked. It was obvious that Kaiser was with his dark hair and propensity to be aggressive.

"I am not entirely Shadowborn am I? The blood of a Farlander runs through my veins too," Kaiser pointed out. He twisted his wrist around, swinging the dagger blade.

Rache knew full well that Kaiser was a direct descendent of the Farlander Begin Anu. Though he did not always press that piece of information, the Demon could see it in Kaiser's eyes. The same eyes that had witnessed destruction though in Kaiser's case, it was destruction he caused. There was a fire in the eyes of a Farlander no matter how true his blood ran. It was dangerous. It was alluring. Looking any deeper risked falling into an abyss that could never be escaped.

He lay back down on the gray stone floor, bored with just sitting around. His limbs itched for action and to tear flesh from bone. Something about the wet ripping sound excited him into a frenzy. The splash of warm flowing blood, the crack of brittle bones beneath his grip. He licked his thin lips, enticed by the memory. Rache then frowned as the bare stone cooled the heat in his body.

"Let me lay waste to just one village! Something besides this mind numbing boredom!" Rache griped as he pounded the floor with his right arm.

"Are you saying that I bore you?" Kaiser asked flatly as he stopped twirling the dagger.

Rache immediately flipped up to his feet and dropped his head. He clenched his fists tightly. His breath caught in his chest as his heart fluttered with dread. The tone in Kaiser's voice frightened him to the core. Kaiser calmly eased himself out of the chair, his woolen coat falling into place at his back. His boots padded the floor at a slow pace. Rache began to tremble as Kaiser drew closer, the dagger gripped in his right hand. A bead of nervous sweat trickled from his brow and down his neck. He gulped.

"I asked if you said that I bore you," Kaiser demanded with a hiss. He stood before Rache and lifted up the Demon's head by the chin.

The look in Kaiser's eyes was awful. It was the deadly calm Rache had seen once before. Only this time, he saw danger and not acceptance. Kaiser may have been Begin Anu's blood relative but he was a terror all his own. It was what he did not say and do that caused the greatest damage. The wheels in his mind were always turning.

"I," Rache started to say past the lump in his throat.

Kaiser struck him hard across the jaw and Rache crumbled to the floor. His chest hit the stone, cracking two ribs. He spit out a globule of dark red blood as he bit back a cry of pain. Kaiser came to stand over him, the look in his eyes even more dangerous.

"I told you not to bleed on my floor!" Kaiser roared before he struck Rache again. He hit the Demon in the left side with a hard kick, cracking even more ribs. Rache slid across the floor, leaving a smear of blood.

"Master," Rache tried to plead before coughing up another mouthful of blood.

His heart suddenly tightened with pain and Rache gasped for a breath. His mind rushed back to when he had entered the void of death and the great blackness that threatened to smother him. He remembered the sense of desperation as he writhed on the floor. He remembered the promise he shouted to the emptiness.

"Three hearts for one. A vessel of blood for the dark soul. A shadow of ancients to guide and the will to control," Kaiser chanted as he drew closer to Rache, stepping over the streak of blood.

The silence that followed was even worse to Rache. Would Kaiser continue with the ancient chant or was he just content to watch him writhe in pain? Rache tried to reach for the warmth of Kaiser to drag himself from the edge of the cold void his being teetered on. He forced his arms to reach out towards his master. His bloody left hand touched the tip of Kaiser's boot. Kaiser snorted as he jerked his foot away and brought it down on Rache's arm, shattering the bone. Rache pressed his face to the floor, nearly biting his tongue in half from the effort to not scream. Kaiser shook the drip of Rache's blood from his foot before he crouched down. He bent over the Demon in a strangely benevolent manner.

The heavy ebony wood door creaked open and in stepped the lean Morin Win. He was about to say something when he spotted the broken Rache in a pool of blood on the floor. His steel plate armor jingled against him as he came to a dead stop.

"What?" Kaiser asked calmly as he remained crouched over Rache.

Morin swallowed hard before answering. "You asked for me to report when the Prince's Saber trial was over."

"Is it?" Kaiser asked as he reached down to turn Rache's head to look up at him.

"Yes sir," Morin quickly answered with a nervous bow.

Kaiser nodded before he looked down into Rache's eyes. He held the Demon's chin in his right hand, the dagger blade pressing against Rache's jaw. "Now if you had been patient, I would be sending you out to do my bidding instead of Commander Win. You could have had the chance to kill Sai Parahazur but no, you had to question my command and insult me. Pity, you would have done such a splendid job tearing that worthless Saber to pieces."

"I will not question you again," Rache whispered through a mouthful of blood.

"Good," Kaiser said before roughly dropping Rache's head, his dagger slashing a line along his jaw. Kaiser then stood up tall. "Commander Win."

Morin quickly stood at attention, giving Kaiser a salute with his fist over his heart. "I am at your command, Lord Kaiser."

Kaiser slowly strode over to Morin, hands latched behind his back. "In truth, I would prefer to send your cousin to do this task but I guess you will have to do." When Morin started to open his mouth to speak, Kaiser held up a finger to silence him. He smirked. "Your cousin is busy doing my work in Crossroads and he is preparing for my arrival during the celebration. Of course, I can't let my influence suffer here in Cross while I am gone. Make sure the Commander of the Sabers understands the retribution I would bring down upon him should he seek to usurp my position."

"Shall I kill him for you, my lord?" Morin asked, a devious expression on his face.

"Oh no," Kaiser said, patting Morin's cheek. "In a true fight, I believe Sai would destroy you. He didn't get to where he is just because he is of noble blood. He does have some talent as a warrior. You however have been risen to your position because I chose you. Still, make me proud or you will end up like dear Rache here. Understand?"

Morin briefly looked over his shoulder to see Rache struggling to breath, spitting out mouthfuls of blood. He returned his gaze towards Kaiser. "Understood, Lord Kaiser."

Kaiser smiled though the ferocity never left his eyes. "Did anyone accompany you to this room?"

"Yes sir. Two foot soldiers," Morin answered. He gestured towards the closed door. "They are at your command.

"Have them clean up this mess. I do not want to see a single drop of blood on this floor when I return in the morning," Kaiser calmly ordered.

Morin snapped his fingers loudly. Within seconds, two small foot solders stepped into the room. They saluted and bowed before Kaiser without a word. Dressed in a crude version of Morin's more refined armor, the foot soldiers appeared to be a pair of new recruits. Kaiser stepped past them towards the door, pausing to hear Morin issue his command in a barking tone. He chuckled when he saw the foot soldiers look back and forth between Rache and Morin.

"Did I stutter? Lord Kaiser wants this mess cleaned up at once! Get to it!" Morin snapped.

"Yes sir! Right away sir!" the foot soldiers squeaked. They

joustled amongst each other for a minute before the taller soldier shoved his companion towards the open door. They took off down the hallway towards a distant washroom to fetch cleaning cloths and a bucket of soapy water.

Kaiser gestured for Morin to go ahead of him. Morin saluted and bowed before he followed the soldiers. Instead of turning right towards the washroom, he strode on past and disappeared down a left corridor. Kaiser found himself smiling, knowing that his jabs at Morin's character and worth would push him to fight harder against Sai.

"Are you alive, Rache?" Kaiser asked from the doorway.

Rache took a long time to answer. "Yes, my Lord."

"You have my permission to kill in the manner that pleases you. Just be sure to clean up," Kaiser stated. He then heard a weak chuckle from his Demon servant.

The foot soldiers returned, carrying a bucket and two cleaning cloths. Kaiser stepped aside and gestured for them to go inside. As soon as they crossed the threshold, Kaiser pulled the door closed and locked it. He dropped the key into his coat pocket. Just as he started to walk away, a pair of blood curdling screams blasted from inside the room. Kaiser smirked as he paused briefly to listen. He chuckled, shaking his head before he continued on.

A WARNING

Back at his house that was located in the southwest section of Cross, Sai pulled off his uniform and rubbed his elbows vigorously. Though they ached, Sai was proud to bear the pain. Onyx was growing stronger by the day. Now, he wanted to take his father's throne. Sai was more than ready to support his claim. But he was worried.

Sai glanced at his face in the mirror, eyeing the tired expression in his eyes. The wrinkles of his skin made him look as old as he felt. He bent down and splashed cold water from the wash basin on to his face. The water was refreshing as it dripped off his chin. He grabbed a wash towel and wiped his face dry. Though the cold water woke him up, it did nothing to ease his heavy heart. He dropped his head and stepped away, a secret anger burning up deep inside of him. A sense of hopelessness and a feeling of abandonment raged in his heart.

"Where are you, Daylord? My Prince is preparing to take his father's throne from a Demonic shadow of a man that holds on to it tightly," he asked himself.

Ever since Kaiser Adonis had returned to favor, a sense of uncertainty and doubt fell upon the royal supporters. In his mind and those of his fellow rebels, Kaiser was a danger to the Silvanus family and the Shadowborn people and needed to be stopped. With Kader gone, Sai promised himself that he would assume the role as mentor and protector of Onyx. He wanted to make sure that the young Prince could defend himself both physically and mentally, but eluding Kaiser's gaze and suspicion was growing difficult. Soon Onyx would be alone if Kaiser had his way.

In frustration, Sai threw a tight fist forward and broke the mirror. Glass shards fell into the wash basin and on to the floor. He glanced at his bloody knuckles, flexing his hand, hoping for some new insight. With a deep sigh, he leaned forward to wash the blood away.

He felt a strong and tight grip on his right shoulder and he wished he hadn't broken the mirror to see who was standing behind him. Sai was forcibly flung around to face forward, catching a glimpse of Morin before he was thrown through the walls of his home, crashing on to the street. Morin stepped through the rubble, his fists clenched tightly as Sai shook the dust from his head. In a swift motion, he was on his feet ready to fight.

"Surprised to see me, Parahazur? I bet that you never thought skinny me could toss you through a wall," Morin smugly taunted as he stopped moving forward.

Sai growled. "What the Hell was that for? Are you still angry that I was given command of the Sabers?"

Morin spat in Sai's direction. "I am Commander of the mightiest army in the North. What could be a more proud position to hold?"

"People are watching and will report your actions to the Shadowlord!" Sai snarled.

"Please, Kaiser has the nobles in his pocket with promises of great wealth and prestige. It is truly amazing what people will do for power," Morin laughed as he glanced back. A watching street cleaner shivered with fear before bolting in the opposite direction. "You have no idea how deep Kaiser's hold is on the Shadowborn. How tight his grip is over the Shadowlord himself."

It was incredulous to think that so many people could turn against their Lord and sovereign. Sai wondered if perhaps the Shadowborn had lost faith in the Silvanus family after the execution of Akakios. Maybe Shiloh's peace was not a peace after all. "Just what exactly is Kaiser promising everyone? Aside from promising not to kill them?"

"Yes the threat of death does wonders for compliance. The people want to believe in their Shadowlord again and Kaiser can deliver that faith to them. He is an Adonis after all," the sly army Commander explained.

"What does being an Adonis have to do with all of this foolishness?" Sai asked, confused at the statement.

"Oh then you don't know. Sad considering that the masterful Commander of the Sabers does not recognize a direct descendant of Begin Anu when he sees one. Kaiser is that descendant and he can bring the people what they want: peace," Morin mocked as he started to step forward, his posture threatening.

As much as Sai did not want to believe Morin's claim, the idea that Kaiser was descended from Adonis, Begin Anu's eldest child made sense. It explained Kaiser's confidence and constant air of nobility. Sai clenched his fists tightly. "If your claim is true, then Kaiser has done nothing to honor the bloodline of a most righteous hero. You are a fool to believe that he can deliver you to greatness!"

"Oh but he already has!" Morin shouted. "It is because of him that I became the Commander of the Armed Forces. I have the numbers under my command that you wish you had. No more will I be subservient in my ability to a Saber! I am now more than the street peasant you beat out for your position!"

Morin sounded completely deluded in his reasoning and it was perfectly clear to Sai that the Commander had turned his back on the rightful Shadowlord. And that did not sit well with him at all. Sai took a deep breath and focused all of his energy towards Morin, allowing his anger to guide his senses.

Morin launched himself at Sai, revealing a strength and speed that had Sai on the defensive immediately. No obstacle could shield him long enough before Morin was again on top of his every move. Morin moved and attacked like a Saber with all the strength and endurance from years of experience. Sai even wondered if Kaiser had worked some bizarre magic to enhance Morin's physical attributes. They sped through the streets and up across the rooftops, citizens scrambling to get out of the way. Parents jerked their children inside as the two fighters passed while city police could nothing to hinder them. Halting Morin would incur the wrath of the High Commander and none of them were brave enough to do so for Kaiser's wrath would soon follow. Helping Sai would also lead to the same consequences. Their quarrel was a matter for the throne to deal with.

Sai spun to avoid Morin's next charging attack and with a leap, using the Army Commander's back as a step up, he jumped up to the rooftop of a closed tailor's shop. His feet slapped down on the slate and wood roof. A scrawny black cat screeched at him before leaping into a nearby tree. Morin then appeared landing with less weight.

"I always knew that you were ambitious but to sell yourself to Kaiser? I did not think you were that desparate for respect," Sai reasoned as he gestured with his hand towards the castle.

"The noble Saber Order promised me greatness," Morin sneered and spat. "I trained and studied until my eyes bled and my bones broke into a thousand pieces. I fought twice as hard as anyone and what did I get for it? Nothing! But a son of the mighty Parahazur family waltzes in and everyone loves him. Why bother with a street rat Win from Eclipse?"

It was incredulous to think that Morin had held on so tightly to a sense of jealousy. Sai laughed out loud. "You think I did not have to work as hard as you to become a Saber?"

"Really? Once you came, I was pushed into the background, forgotten because I did not have some rich father paying my way," Morin asserted as he slowly paced towards the roof's edge. His left side faced Sai, his right hand hidden from view. "I have had to fight since the very beginning. First to get out of the shadow of my cousin and now to break free of yours!"

Shadow Shock was an electrifying bolt of black lightning that Sai had only seen once during his Saber training. The then Commander of the Sabers had asked Kaiser to come demonstrate the higher Spirit techniques of the Shadowborn. Kaiser had at first declined the invitation until Sin Silvanus intervened and convinced him to accept. Even then, Kaiser's personality was a force to be reckoned with and before an audience full of young Sabers in training, he summoned up a terrible storm of Spirit energy. It cracked and sparked around his left arm as he pointed towards the Saber Commander with a smirk on his face. He knew how to entrance an audience. The Commander then dared him to hit him with Shadow Shock to better show its effects and Kaiser seemed all too happy to oblige.

Sai's chest burned horribly as he was thrown back by the force of the technique. He crashed through a wooden horse cart and hit the street back first. Although his limbs refused to work, Sai pushed all of his strength out from his core to stand. Morin had followed after him and their hand to hand combat chase through the streets resumed.

The two arrived in the main city square. Sai stumbled back from a hard hit to his chest, clutching the spot as his backwards motion slowed to a dusty stop on the stone. The Army Commander was relentless in striking the spot where the Shadow Shock technique had hit his body. Morin glared at him as he straightened his posture, giving himself a commanding appearance. He then spun around in a leap forward and slammed Sai again in the chest, sending him flying into the square fountain. Water splashed over the rim as Sai came to a stop, his body soaked. Morin came to stand over him for a moment before reaching down, pulling him up by the collar of his tunic. Sai then grabbed his arm and threw Morin over his head and into the water. Morin fell flat on his back, gasping for breath as the wind was knocked out of him.

Sai rolled over to right himself just as Morin was spitting out a stream of water. "You want a fight? I shall give you one and then you can go crawling back to Kaiser like a wet dog!" He grinned before charging forward. He would not let his old rival best him.

The Army Commander turned his head to see Sai rushing forward, weaving in a zig zag pattern. Morin flipped up to his feet to meet him, chest still burning from the lack of breath. He blocked Sai's first punch with his left forearm and shot his right hand forward, grabbing and twisting his fingers in Sai's chest wound. Sai immediately collapsed to his knees. Morin released him and pressed his foot to Sai's torso to push him down.

"I may not have your bulk but I more than outmatch you in smarts. And I have seen where the world is heading. The past is done and Kaiser is the future. If you want to see what is going to happen, I would recommend following my example or you will end up like Kader: dead. Consider yourself warned," Morin growled. He walked away without further word, shaking the water from his hands.

A few witnesses peered out of their windows before quickly closing the curtains. No one dared to approach to help him, eyes watching the direction Morin took. Off to the side, Sai saw one of the young Sabers under his command, Soja Rokar, watching with concern. The Saber rushed over to his side and leant his strength to balance a rising Sai. "Just get me to a healer," Sai growled as he managed a glance in Morin's direction.

Soja helped Sai up to his feet, keeping his thoughts to himself. Sai stumbled as he attempted to walk, his chest hurting him badly. He gripped the spot Morin had last struck him, finding a gruesome mess of torn flesh, blood, and bone.

"If I may ask, Commander, what was your quarrel with Morin Win about?" Soja asked, unable to stay silent. He shouldered Sai's weight by wrapping his arm around his own neck.

Sai grumbled to himself before answering. "We need to be more careful. Our movement is being watched."

THE SHADOW COUNCIL

The seat of government for the Shadowborn nation was in a modest size stone building. Two pillars held up the slate roof at the front entrance. A large banner with the royal crest was tied between the pillars, a sign for all to see who controlled the throne. Inside the building were two rooms, one being the interior entryway and the other being the council room. A long rectangular table dominated the council chamber with fourteen chairs placed around it. At one end of the table, the chair remained vacant while Zoras Rokar sat at the other end of the table. Six pairs of chairs sat across each other and their occupants were busy chatting about current events. Only Kaiser leaned back in his chair watching the conversation with a smirk on his face.

"As Lord's Regent, I call this Shadow Council to order," Zoras said as he pounded the gavel on the table. The conversation between the councilors continued. Sai Parahazur and Donovan Shunga immediately stopped talking. The other councilors looked to Kaiser. Kaiser lifted a hand and everyone quieted down. Zoras eased himself down into his seat once he was certain the silence would last. "We are here to discuss matters of state in the absence of the Shadowlord during the Crossroads celebration. Before this Council session is over, we will finalize the logistics of the journey to Crossroads and the subsequent regency of our homeland while the Shadowlord is away."

A thin Shadowborn man with a tuft of facial hair on his chin glanced at Kaiser before he stood up. "The Master of Trade wishes to speak." Zoras nodded and the man cleared his throat. He began to wring his hands. "I have concerns regarding the East Road Bridge over the River Shadow. There are reports of unfriendly eyes from the Master of Roads' agents in Dusk."

"I hardly see the Gryphon and Earthborn scouts as unfriendly eyes. I have been meaning to thank Lord Palani for his assistance in monitoring our borders," Zoras stated as he leaned back in his chair. "Master of Roads, why are you not making this proclamation in council?"

The thin Master of Trade sat down for the Master of Roads to take the floor. The beefy councilor rose with the same trepidation. "Lord Kai..."

Zoras shot up from his seat. "Sit down and rethink what you are about to say!" The Master of Roads sat down immediately and looked away. "There is only one person in this land to be addressed as Lord and that is Lord Aku!" he said harshly. Zoras allowed for the shock of his anger to subside before he sat back down. "Master Adonis, you seem to have the councilors looking to you for permission to speak. Why?"

Kaiser laced his fingers together. "As Lord's Chancellor, I am the voice of the Shadowlord in his absence during Council."

"That may be true but the Council is not answerable to you under my direction. Now, Master of Roads, you may continue," Zoras pronounced with a sweeping gesture of his hand.

"Even with Lord Palani's help, I feel that security should be increased while the Shadowlord is in Crossroads. I trust only Shadowborn to protect our lands," the beefy councilor stated, his voice still shaky.

"Too bad Commander Win did not find time to attend. Perhaps we shall move on to the trip details until the Commander arrives," Zoras said as he rubbed his temples.

Sai then stood up taking the floor. He looked around at his fellow councilors that sat at the large oak table. "A contingent of Sabers will accompany the Shadowlord on his journey. The Prince will have his personal guard Soja Rokar and I will see to the Shadowlord myself. In my place, I have asked Donovan Shunga to serve until I return."

Kaiser cleared his throat, interrupting Sai and taking attention away from him. "My Lord Aku has expressed a different set of desires regarding his Sabers," he said calmly.

The air in the Council room suddenly became very tense. Zoras clutched the gavel handle tightly as several of the councilors looked between him, Sai, and Kaiser.

"And what does our Lord command?" he tersely asked, running his fingers along the handle.

Kaiser sat up in his seat. "He expresses that Commander Parahazur remain in Cross to see that his throne is properly protected. High Commander Win will accompany him to Crossroads instead."

Sai frowned. "And who will command the soldiers while Commander Win is away, Lord's Chancellor?" he seethed.

"Why Master Rokar of course. If our law is true, he shall be Regent until Lord Aku's return," Kaiser stated with a smug grin.

"I was a Commander of Sabers, not soldiers," Zoras stated firmly. "If Commander Win was a part of his decision, why is he not here as a member of the Council? His predecessor never missed a meeting."

Murmurs broke out among the councilors. Zoras hushed them again with a light tapping of his gavel. Everyone then waited for Kaiser to reply.

"He is seeing to the security of our borders as we speak. I had felt it best that he have all of his focus there instead of in this stuffy room," Kaiser said as he pulled at his collar.

"I seem to remember how impenetrable our borders have been for the last ten years. I thought that you were supposed to fix any issue," Sai asked as he stood up from his seat.

"I wasn't aware that there was an issue to be fixed. Trade has been going smoothly as far as the reports have been telling me," came Kaiser's cool answer. "Besides, I am Lord's Chancellor now."

"We can argue such later. The Crossroads journey must be sorted out in the meantime," Zoras said, growing annoyed with Kaiser. "If our Lord Aku does indeed command for Master Parahazur to remain here and Commander Win to go, it will be so. And as our law states, I will serve as Regent until the Shadowlord returns."

Each councilor nodded their heads except for Kaiser who seemed lost in his own thoughts. Zoras frowned as he glared at the Lord's Chancellor until he finally looked in his direction. Kaiser smiled as if nothing was wrong.

"I suppose you have a route that takes the caravan safely to Crossroads and that doesn't tax the health of our dear Shadowlord too harshly," Kaiser said as he leaned back in his seat.

Zoras narrowed his eyes but kept his control. "The Master of Roads and myself have chosen a proper route for all Shadowborn travelling to Crossroads. Of those on this journey, you have the greatest knowledge of the lands ahead. I would hope that you will provide direction in the event of a change."

Kaiser scoffed. "I suppose I could act as a living map should those of the Master of Roads fail. It is at least one thing this old soul is good for despite whatever you are thinking."

His attitude infuriated Zoras to no end. "Let me remind you and all who sit in Council that the Crowned Prince, though young, has the authority to speak in the Shadowlord's name and represent him if called to do so. No one speaks more for Lord Aku than his own son." He waited to continue until everyone had nodded in acceptance. "Have all the necessary funds been raised to support this journey?"

A Shadowborn with a black and gray beard stood up and pressed his hands to the table before him. "As Treasurer for the realm, I have managed the raising of funds since the last trek to Crossroads. Each of the great cities have made good on their pledges so long as a representative of their city accompanies the caravan. I found no fault in the request and thus each of our cities will follow the Shadowlord and be represented." He gestured towards Kaiser who nodded. "Though he has not lived in Umbra for many years, the Council of Umbra has elected Master Adonis to represent them." He continued to name people from each city until moving on to his next topic. "Tax collection for the recent quarter will be used to support the realm during the regency of Master Rokar as is per law."

Each of the Councilors gave their individual acquiesce to the report that the funds raised were acceptable and good.

Sai then stood up, gathering everyone's attention. "If I may speak plainly in front of all of you, it is my express desire that upon the return, we consider supporting the Crowned Prince in his rise to the throne. As we all know, our Lord Aku is ailing..."

"You speak of treason, Commander Parahazur," Kaiser interrupted with a warning.

"Lord's Chancellor, you of all people should know our laws towards succession. You alone of us remember the ascension of Sin to his father Shadow Night," Zoras stated, taking command before an argument broke out. "I will speak to the Prince and the Shadowlord upon their return regarding the matter." He then looked directly at Kaiser.

Kaiser let out a deep breath. "Then I will remind you of the need of my attendance to the Shadowlord. Not only am I his most loyal servant, I have also attended every Crossroads ceremony since the beginning. I will accompany His Majesty with my servant. You may decide the rest."

Zoras looked to the other councilors who nodded their acceptance. He then unrolled a map onto the table with a bold line drawn from Cross to Crossroads. He stood up and planted his finger on the marker for Cross. "The caravan will leave from our city and move east to the border. It will pass through Dusk before entering the lands of our neighbors, the Earthborn. It will continue in a southern direction towards the Fireborn's great western city of Lavan," Zoras described in detail as he dragged his finger over the line.

"Alerts have gone out ahead of the caravan to each stop on the journey," a slim, pale faced councilor said with a glance towards Kaiser.

"Though the movement of the Shadowlord is never truly unannounced, I had felt it best to alert our hosts ahead of time," Kaiser said. "Our messages were passed along the trade routes and preparations are already underway."

Zoras wanted Kaiser to shut up and not say another word. He glanced over at Sai and nodded. "All who take this journey are representative of the Shadowlord and will conduct themselves accordingly. Failure to do so will result in immediate punishment in accordance to the Immortal Truth."

Kaiser sat with a pleasant smile of his face, ignoring the warning. "Lord Aku expects the same of those who remain behind. I will carry out justice on his behalf."

"Fine," Zoras said, tired of hearing Kaiser talk. "The path has been established and the funds have been raised to support the journey. Regency will be as the law states. Upon the return of the Shadowlord, we will meet with both him and the Crowned Prince present to discuss the matters of succession. We must also consider finding a match for the Prince."

"I shall see to a royal match during the Crossroads celebration as per the Shadowlord's instructions. He wishes his son to find a suitable partner," Kaiser stated.

Sai chuckled. "What do you know of betrothals or marriage? You are no Kader Erebus who planned the match of Lord Aku to the Lady Nuru. Nor have you ever been married."

Zoras expected Kaiser to rise out of his seat and curse Sai. He didn't even flinch.

"Perhaps I should have in my youth, and then I would have sons to support me and defend the Adonis name. Sadly, I am what is left and I am past my prime," Kaiser deftly replied. "I expect to see Argos and Aves with their graceful daughters in Crossroads. Commander Win and I shall determine each daughter's suitability to become a Queen of the Shadowborn."

"Both you and Morin can make your lists if you please. I will ask my son to introduce the Crown Prince to the youth and gather notes for my own perusal," Zoras said. He stood up from his seat with each of the councilors. "The caravan will depart by the time of the next full moon. May the truth protect and watch over the journey to Crossroads."

INTO THE NIGHT

"Here you go, sir," the server said in a polite voice. He set down a plate of roast chicken and vegetables. He stepped back, bowed his head, and turned around to go back inside the tavern.

Ryder slid his wooden chair forward until the edge of the table was six inches from touching his torso. He unfolded his cloth napkin with a snap of the wrist. He then laid it across his lap and proceeded to pick apart the small chicken on his plate. All around him was the vibrant nightlife of one of Crossroads' many taverns. Patrons of all sorts settled down to a meal just like him. Several families were seated at nearby tables, making loud conversation as they waited for food. Ryder had arrived just before the dinner rush and was thankful he had been seated at his favorite table. It was situated on the edge of the tavern's front yard. Usually, he avoided the crowds but with the celebration fast approaching, the city of Crossroads was burgeoning with people.

He had debated on staying in Crossroads for the celebration. When the previous celebration had occurred, Ryder travelled far to the northeast in a desire to stay away from any Shadowborn contact. Even as he sat and ate his dinner, he thought about the Shadowborn caravan that was now on the move from Cross. He paused and sat back in his seat. He laid his right hand on the table, scrapping his fingers together. Part of him hoped that his long time love Haven would accompany the caravan but he knew that she would not leave her family behind. But he worried more that Kaiser would be with the caravan. Ryder did not want to deal with him.

A burst of raucous laughter brought Ryder out of his deep thoughts. He glanced over his shoulder to see a pair of gray Screech Owl Gryphons animatedly telling a series of jokes in the common tongue. They purposely thickened their beastial accents and exaggerated their movements to garner laughs from the tavern crowd. Ryder found himself amused by their display. He had always appreciated Gryphon humor. It was simple, respectful, and fun.

The Gryphon that had thick white brow feathers was animatedly telling a story in a purposedly thick accent. He waved his taloned paws and rustled his wings. "The gathering went on long into the night until it was far too late to fly home. Well, the young Gryphon declared that he would fly no matter what and no matter how many servings of spun berry juice he had consumed."

The storyteller's partner crossed his eyes and dropped his beak open. He ruffled his ear tufts until they appeared messy and frayed. "There ish no skyz that I can'ts flyz."

"Well as any proper Gryphon knows, there is no flying with a stomach full of drink and WHACK!" The storyteller's partner then contorted his face and groaned. "For a tree will always stand in the way." The partner tumbled backwards, falling in an exaggerated manner until his back hit the ground.

Ryder laughed as the crowd did, amused at the fallen Gryphon's vain attempts to get resettled on his feet. He clapped as the Gryphon pair bowed again and again amidst the round of applause.

"Ah, did I miss it? Did I miss the wandering tree tale?" a deep voiced Gryphon asked, coming up to Ryder's table.

Ryder turned in his seat to see a tall, broad shouldered gray and black Gryphon. The Eagle Gryphon was as tall as a draft horse with talons long enough to disembowel a man in one swipe. But Ryder knew this Gryphon would never hurt a fly.

"Harper, I did not think you would be coming to Crossroads. I thought you did not like the smell of city life," Ryder said, greeting his old travelling friend.

"I still have my duties to attend to. My father was left in Ornith as Regent whilst the Lords Paladon and Stellaris travelled here. I came in my father's place," Harper stated with a degree of pride. He sat down on his haunches and rolled his shoulders. "Surely someone like you understands the matter of duty and obligation."

Ryder scoffed before he popped a morsel of chicken in his mouth. "Indeed I do." He then offered a large piece to Harper who gladly snapped it up in his beak.

"You know. You promised to come back to my homeland after your visit here in Crossroads. How long has it been now since you have settled in this city?" Harper asked once he swallowed the morsel.

"In your eyes, it would be too many years to count. You never were that patient to begin with," Ryder commented as he leaned back in his chair. He rested his arm across the back of the neighboring seat.

Harper reached forward with his talons, pinching off another piece of chicken from Ryder's plate. "And you are quick to insult others. You always have been."

"Must run in my family," Ryder replied as he looked off into the distance. He studied the comedic Gryphon pair, seeing that they were now joined by several others of their kind for dinner. "So the Gryphon caravan is the first to arrive."

The Eagle Gryphon nodded. "The Lords Paladon and Stellaris led my people into Crossroads not an hour past. Lord Proto Avis himself greeted us! I had forgotten how grand the Lord of Crossroads was!"

Ryder gestured for the server with a twitch of his hand. The lithe apron wearing Airborn man jogged over and bowed when he saw Harper. Harper placed his order for dinner, gesturing towards Ryder's plate.

"I shall return swiftly with your meal, mighty Gryphon," the server stated before bounding away towards the kitchen.

"My sweet Razila would have enjoyed the city greatly," Harper commented after a long pause.

Ryder turned his full attention to Harper. "She did not come with you? Since you two have bonded, I was under the impression that you rarely left her side."

Harper at first appeared to act sheepish before a large smile appeared with the upturned corners of his beak. "She has a more important duty to attend to: our first egg child!"

"Congratulations. When will the egg child hatch?" Ryder asked.

"Oh I don't know these things. I am just thrilled that my mate and I were blessed with an egg child. The Spirits must think well of our union," Harper said, sounding like he was embarrassed for not knowing. He shrugged his shoulders. "What of you and Haven? Do you think the Spirits will bless your union with a child?"

Ryder fell silent, unwilling to answer. He tapped the table with his fingers. For a long time, Ryder listened to the sounds of the dinner crowd around him. A family of six Fireborn sat two tables over. The four children were all under ten years of age.

Each of them were taking turns in talking about seeing the great Dragon Vorin. The oldest of the children was a lanky boy who waved his arms in the air to emphasize Vorin's large size. Both parents were laughing at the excitement of their children.

"I would not know the first thing about being a father. I only had my mother growing up," Ryder finally said as he returned his attention to Harper.

"But surely you have entertained the idea. You have been with the lady Haven for so long," Harper reasoned. He briefly looked up when the server returned with his food. He waited to continue until the server had stepped away. "Surely you have thought of the future."

Ryder let out a deep breath, pulling his fingers back into a fist. "The world has seen fit to decide my future for me. Why should I waste my time worrying about what is to come?"

"Or what could happen?" Harper asked in between bites and tears of meat with his talons. He watched as Ryder dropped a handful of gold coins on the table.

"Another time, Harper. That is for another time," Ryder said once he stood up. He bowed his head and stepped away from the warm light of the tavern.

Ryder strode through the city streets, hands shoved into his pockets. He kept his head down to avoid eye contact with passersby. His entire body was tight and standoffish for he did not want to talk to anyone. He wanted to lash out and punch a wall. Inside, Ryder knew that Harper meant well. The Gryphon always meant well for it was inherent in his nature.

He was genuinely happy for Harper and his mate's egg child. In their last trek towards the northern coast, Harper had spoken endlessly about courting Razila and his plans to ask her to be his mate. During a drunken night around a campfire, Ryder told him all about Haven. He profressed his deep and unwavering love for her. The rest of the night was a blur but he did remember the feeling of happiness and peace that clung to him when he woke the next morning.

Haven was the love of his life and Ryder missed her terribly. But he could not force himself to return to Cross and face the very thing that drove him away. Every mention of his royal blood or any push for consideration of his future caused him near physical pain for it forced him to think about what he was giving up. Ryder had once thought to ask her to join him in his self imposed exile but in his heart, he knew that she would never abandon her family. He thought not for the first time about making one last secret trip to Umbra to say goodbye.

The scuff of a boot against a small stone alerted Ryder to a presence behind him. The sound was so slight that if Ryder had not trained his senses to be on constant alert, he would have never heard it. He paused and listened carefully. His eyes narrowed and he tightened his fists. With a great shout, Ryder whirled around and slammed his follower up against the wall. He lifted the lean Shadowborn man, his feet dangling off the ground.

"My, my. You are strong," the Shadowborn said, the diagonal scar on his face pulling at his skin.

Ryder tightened his grip on the Shadowborn's tunic collar. "And you are far from the waves of the Mirror Sea, Pirate," he snarled in warning.

"I am not the only one far from home. Sometimes, one's duty and loyalty takes them to distant places," Loran replied with a cavalier grin.

Ryder dropped Loran and stepped back, keeping his fists clenched. Loran rubbed his throat as he sat on the ground. He then looked up at Ryder, smirking. He got up to his feet to stand up tall. Ryder frowned as he looked back at Loran, his entire body on high alert.

"I know he sent you ahead of his high and mighty arrival for the celebration," Ryder snarled.

Loran shrugged. "Maybe he did. Maybe he didn't but surely I needed to look upon the man that he has so highly thought of." Loran looked Ryder up and down with a careful eye. "You kind of look like him."

Ryder slammed Loran back up against the wall. "I am nothing like him," he snarled harshly.

Loran chuckled. "True. He would have taken my head off but then, you are not far from the action." A wide grin crossed his face. "Is it so wrong for a grandfather to inquire after the health and well being of his only grandson and only descendant for that matter?"

"Enough of your bullshit, Pirate. I know first hand that what Kaiser says and does is never what it appears. I do not know what he promised you but he will never grant it. He loves no one and cares only for himself," Ryder snapped quickly.

"Maybe I like that quality in a master. At least he is always going to be a conniving and aggressive son of a bitch to everyone and never false. He speaks the truth more than anyone in the Northlands," Loran admitted as if the fact was obvious.

Ryder frowned. "You are as stupid as the rest of his pawns. He will destroy everything and everyone you hold dear."

Loran then smirked. "You mean like that girl from Umbra that holds your heart so dearly? She is quite the ravishing beauty for so low a birth. How did she manage to capture the heart of an unnamed royal Prince?"

"You do not know of what you speak," Ryder growled as he pressed Loran harder against the stone wall.

"I think I do, mighty Peredur. I am the Pirate afterall. I know very well the value of treasure. So I would not do anything to endanger her precious life," Loran said cooly.

Ryder released his grip on Loran and turned away. He paused to issue a warning. "If he so much as looks harshly in her direction, I will tear his eyes out of his head and rip his black heart from his chest." He did not stay to listen to Loran's smug reply.

He stomped off towards his city home, ignoring everything around him. The pain of his thoughts was now amplified into a fully manifested physical sensation. Once he arrived at his home, Ryder locked the doors and went into his modest study. He ripped open a desk drawer to pull out a stack of blank pieces of paper. Stray pieces floated back to the floor, completely ignored. Ryder slapped the parchment down on the desk top and began furiously writing a letter. He wrote long into the night, scratching out lines and rewriting the words. When the sun began to rise, Ryder finally stopped, his letter to Haven an unfinished mess. He crumpled up the latest draft, closed his eyes, and pressed the paper to his forehead. With one deep breath, Ryder settled himself. He looked up towards the window, sunlight streaming in through the glass.

"It is a new day and all I see is the approaching darkness."

KAISER'S MIRROR

The sun was setting when the Shadowborn caravan stopped to make camp for the night. The sky had turned into a warm rainbow of orange, red, and blue. The thin wispy clouds were now a faded purple, the glow of sunlight illuminating them from behind. Tree tops shifted and churned in the breeze, leaves dry from heat clattering together in a strange autumn song. Shouts of command went up and down the road as a team of mounted riders began to organize the myriad of servants and officials into a manageable order. Foremost of the riders was the ranking Saber, a harsh Captain named Hayden Abendroth. He wheeled his chestnut horse around to snap at a small group of forest drifters, hired to watch beyond the firelight and scout the deep forests.

"Why not send the scouts? Surely they would be more reliable than a bunch of vagabonds," Onyx commented as he handed his horse's reins to Soja. He watched as a particularly dirty man crept out of the shadows of the trees.

Soja settled the horse with a reassuring pat on its neck. The horse leaned into his shoulder. "Forest drifters wander the wilds and know every rock and blade of grass between here and the Mirror Sea. They may be strange but they have their uses." He looked back over his shoulder to look at Hayden. "Captain Abendroth is likely saving the scouts for when we cross the borders. Forest drifters tend to stick close to home."

"Oh," Onyx said. He watched as Soja led his horse away. Behind him, two young foot soldiers worked to set up his personal tent, first by clearing a level space of open soil. They then began pounding in the stakes and poles that formed the frame.

The camp settled into a rhythm of tents being erected and wood being arranged for a large fire. Foot soldiers and servants went about with light feet, carrying and retrieving amidst a torrent of shouts and loud voices. Bawdy jokes and tall tales became the topic of everyone's conversation. Older men and the scant few women told the younger generation about Crossroads, the great capital of the Northlands. The experienced soldiers slapped their younger comrades on the back, laughing at their expense when they talked about the city's pretty girls.

"Come on, your Highness! Come hear a few stories with us!" shouted Morin as he raised up a flagon. The pale ale sloshed out over his hand.

Onyx sat in front of his tent, eating a meal of venison stew and bread. He looked up at Morin and lifted an eyebrow. Soja stood a short distance away watching the exchange, left hand on his sword hilt. Morin didn't seem to pay him any mind as he tossed back the flagon, downing the rest of the ale in three big gulps. He then looked down at the empty flagon, frowning. He swayed on his feet.

"You're drunk," Onyx stated before taking a spoonful of stew.

Morin stumbled two steps, pointing at his empty flagon. "I'm not drunk. I'm just," Morin fumbled to say. "I'm just in a good mood." He then started snickering like a fool.

"The Commander of the Armed Forces should not appear before his Prince as a bumbling fool," Soja stated firmly.

"Oh, piss off!" Morin snapped as he stumbled backwards. He waved Soja off with an exaggerated gesture of his arm. "I was talking to his Highness." He tried to bow before Onyx and nearly fell over. "You two are..." he started to say before bursting into a fit of manic laughter. "I'm going where there is some fun."

Onyx watched as Morin stumbled away, barely keeping his balance and laughing at a loud volume. An equally inebriated officer slapped Morin on the back before refilling his flagon. The officer then began to babble about the stories by the fireside.

"I do not see how Morin is still the Commander of the Armed Forces. Shall I report his behavior?" Soja asked as he picked up Onyx's dinner tray.

"Let him embarrass himself. I don't want my father to be burdered with any more than necessary," Onyx said as he wiped his hands with his dinner cloth.

Soja took the cloth from Onyx and dropped it on the tray. He then summoned a lithe kitchen servant who promptly took the tray, bowed his head, and left in the direction of the kitchen tents. The young Saber then took up watch beside Onyx's tent. Onyx stood up, dusting off his coat. He nodded once towards Soja before throwing the tent door open and going inside.

A crowd of soldiers, camp servants, and officials assembled around a large firepit where a bonfire burned brightly. Drinks were liberally passed around as people smacked their flagons together and cheered. Morin was in the midst of a group of young officers, laughing at a captain's dirty joke. He became the butt of another's joke when he spilled his ale all over the ground. As he stared at the mess, he was slapped on the back and he tumbled forward into the dirt. The crowd roared with laughter as Morin rolled onto his back, giggling like an idiot with a big grin.

Kaiser sneered before popping a morsel of salted pork into his mouth. He grimaced at the taste and spit it into his napkin. He snapped his fingers for a masked Rache who stood behind him, holding a decanter of deep red wine. Kaiser lifted his wine glass and Rache filled it halfway. He took a small sip, hoping to wash the taste of salt pork from his mouth.

"This food is disgusting," Kaiser said as he waved his hand for Rache to take the dinner tray away. "And Morin's drunken behavior is revolting."

"I say let the fool act like the lowborn waste of blood and flesh he is," Rache stated, glancing over at Morin who climbed back onto his seat. He wavered as he continued to laugh.

"I say my merry lads! How about a grand tale?" Morin called out, slurring his words. He raised up his flagon, drawing attention to himself. "Hey Kaiser! You're the oldest soul on this trek. How about telling us a story?"

Kaiser frowned at hearing Morin's drunken shout. The crowd seemed to agree with Morin's request and began clapping and cheering for Kaiser. Rache refilled Kaiser's wine glass and took the tray from his lap. He stepped back from the fireside.

"Alas, I was never the noble warrior. My tales would certainly bore you fine lot," Kaiser mocked, lifting his glass. He forced himself to smile pleasantly. He then downed the contents of his glass in a single draught. Rache returned to stand behind Kaiser and quickly refilled his glass. "I'd have to be as drunk as them before I start spinning a story," he whispered to the Demon.

"Shall I fetch the wine from Umbra then?" Rache asked in a low voice. Kaiser waved him off and the Demon returned to standing behind him like a servant waiting for his master's next command.

The crowd continued to beg and plead for Kaiser to tell a story. Kaiser gripped his glass even tighter in annoyance. He was ready to smack Morin for the suggestion. One of the low level soldiers began a rousing song as a way to encourage Kaiser to participate. Very soon, the drunken crowd shouted out the words.

"Here is the song of the howling dog,
Who wails and sings all night long.
He paces the yard from east to west,
Begging for the meat that he likes best.
The juicy flesh, the nice white bone,
The kind that makes his belly groan.
All he asks is for a bit of meal,
Maybe some chicken, maybe some veal.
Or perhaps a filet of mountain fish,
Something to make a nice hot dish!"

It was a simple but loud tavern song that the assembled crowd sang with drunken joy. They slapped each other's backs and clapped with the quick beat of the lyrics. Kaiser hated the song for his long dead younger brother used to sing it before every meal as a child. His grip became so tight on his wine glass that it finally shattered with a resounding crack. The song immediately ended and everyone fell quiet. All that could be heard was the snapping and crackling of the fire.

Kaiser slowly stood up, brushing the glass pieces off of his hand. The wine left a sticky, fragrant residue. Rache held back as he watched his master step away from his seat. No one dared to say a word. The strong, tight posture of Kaiser's body commanded everyone's attention. His coat was a finely woven wool garment that reflected the firelight. The black fabric made it appear that Kaiser had shifted out of Shadow Slide and yet still straddled the mysterious line between the veil of death and the light of life. It was an eerie sight.

"You want a proper tale?" Kaiser snapped as he glared at Morin. The Commander gulped and trembled. "Then I will tell you one."

The light of the roaring fire dimmed as Kaiser approached it. He held his right arm behind his back while extending his left hand towards the flames. The fire shrank away from his touch as if it had a life of its own. It hissed like a cat and lashed out at Kaiser's hand. Kaiser's interaction with the fire was mesmorizing to the crowd that eagerly awaited his story.

"It was the six hundred and thirty eighth year since the recording of time. It was the Second Dominion of Terra's mightly life. It was my fifty eighth year in this world," Kaiser said ominously as he stared into the fire. The light casted sharply across his cheekbones. "The Battle of the North was yet upon us."

The camp settled into silence. Not a drink or morsel of food was passed around. Even the picketed horses stood still. The trees loomed over the crowd cloaked in shadow. No one dared to move as they waited for Kaiser to continue.

"I remember when the Demon horde had been spotted, bearing down on the northern reaches. Like a massive swarm of locusts, nothing stood in their way as the Demons tore through the forests and across the green fields. Oh how I remember riding with wild abandon across those fields. I rode to the very limits of our people's domain to look upon the desolation of the Darklands, safe in the knowledge that I could ride on back through those beautiful fields," Kaiser stated as he weaved a vivid image for the listening camp. He drew his left hand back. "Their very steps burned the ground, leaving a poisonous blight where ever they went. The grass turned to ash and the air suffocated with every breath. Upon the foothills north of Umbra, I was able to see their approach on the horizon. It horrified me how the Demons moved like life sucking parasites and in that instant, I knew I had to alert my illustrious father, Cian Adonis the great General of the North."

Young and old, everyone knew the name of Cian Adonis. They had long been told the tales of his great deeds as Shadow Night Silvanus' second in command. Everyone sat with anticipation for what they now knew to be the story of how Cian died. It was a rarely told tale, mostly out of respect for Kaiser and fear of his wrath for telling it.

"By nightfall, the Demons broke upon the walls of Umbra like a crashing wave. They tore through the defenders on the northern fields, simply joyous in shedding Shadowborn blood. My father led those still alive with a slash of his sword and a courageous shout on his lips. His voice boomed through the approaching night like a beacon of hope. But what hope could there be when there was no end in sight," Kaiser described before his voice faltered.

In that moment, the remote idea that Kaiser was capable of any feeling became real. He was known for his stoicism and self assured courage. Even Rache thought his master was about to weep before the entire crowd.

Kaiser covered his eyes as if to shield everyone from the sight of his tears. His hand dropped from his face and his posture tightened. "My brother Khan and I were charged by my father to gather the people of Umbra in the safety of the citadel. We ran through the streets, pounding on doors to relay my father's order. Children screamed with fright as their parents cradled them tightly, running towards the citadel. By now, the Demons had fired flaming missiles beyond the walls and homes were burning on every street. They had cast some sort of unearthly spell on stone they had cut from the walls to bathe them in a fire that could not be squelched. One flaming stone crashed into a home I had just entered, throwing me through the street facing window. A shard of glass sliced my arm from shoulder to wrist. I knew I was bleeding but I could not stop to tend to myself. I had to protect my city."

The fire grew tall as the flames reached for the stars in the night sky. Within the twisting flames, shadows of people could be seen, their screams of fear and desperation growing with the volume of his voice. The wind tore through the tree tops as if the very earth was screaming in pain. Kaiser lifted his hand towards the fire, slowly twisting his arm. The flames tentatively reached out to him as if he was a lifeline to the shadow people trapped inside. The dark clouds rolled in, blinking like terrible lights as bolts of lightning charged within. Thunder boomed with increasing power. People grabbed onto their coats and gripped their seats for fear of the storm pulling them free from the ground. Banners snapped in the bursting wind, threatening to tear free.

Kaiser swiftly drew his hand back towards himself and in an instant, the storm stopped. The fire died back down to a burning bed of hot coals. Everything was quiet.

"In the end, I could not even protect my own family from the terrible slaughter. The gates had been breeched, blown asunder by one of the flaming missiles. The dead lay in gruesome ruin at every turn. In the back of my mind, my sense told me to rush to my father's side at the wall but my heart begged to find my mother and brother. I was weak but not diminished by my bloodloss. I slew every Demon that dared to cross my path. Until I found them," Kaiser's voice trailed off into a barely contained sob. He took a deep breath and let it out slowly. "My brother lay dying in my already dead mother's arms. His last words spoke of the chill of death and I knew there was no saving him. As the breath of life left him, I remember closing his eyes. No brother should ever have to experience that."

The crowd was fully drawn into his tale, feeling the pull of Kaiser's vivid emotion. Many of the soldiers bit back tears of shared sorrow while others comforted them. Kaiser turned away from the fire pit, now barely burning. The look on his face was that of restrained fury and a desire for retribution.

"I broke upon the invaders with all of my rage. I tore into every Demon that dared to stand in my way for if I was going to die this night, I was going to do it at my father's side," Kaiser promised, pointing down in a quick gesture. He gripped an invisible sword in his hands and made play with slashing and cutting movements. "I showed the Demons the same slaughter they had showed me! I ripped everyone of them to shreds like they had done to my people! They deserved it and I would have banished them all to Hell if I could!"

The fire roared back to life as the volume of Kaiser's voice grew. The returning light glinted off of the soldiers' armor. It was if Kaiser had brought forth the very flames of Hell with his strong declaration. The heat was intense.

"But I was too late," Kaiser suddenly said and the fire died back down in response. He dropped his imaginary sword as his arms hung limp by his sides. "I arrived just as a Demon delivered the killing blow, cutting my father in two. Suddenly, only I was left to defend Umbra. I had to push my sorrow aside to fight. I fought long into the night, the fires of war burning all around me. I bled from countless wounds. My body ached from the blows. The dawn came and I was found lying over the burnt remains of my father by Sin Silvanus. He and his father had arrived to drive the Demons back."

"Praise the Shadowlord," Hayden stated as he stood at the edge of the circle of people. Similar praises were murmured.

Kaiser scoffed. "I was now the last of my bloodline. I was all that remained of Cian Adonis' legacy. I left Umbra that day and I never went back. So forgive me for my character but had you seen what I saw that night, you might begin to understand what it is like to live with the memory."

No one dared to applaud Kaiser for his story as he bowed and turned towards his seat. They watched as Kaiser snapped his fingers at his ever present servant. The servant set the wine decanter down on his master's chair and followed him into the shadow of the camp.

Rache followed Kaiser as he left the ring of tents and entered the forest. Leaf litter and twigs crunched beneath their feet as they headed east towards the border. Soon, the sound of the rushing River Shadow could be heard in the distance. Kaiser turned towards the south, coming upon the massive stone bridge that spanned the banks. He came to a halt just as the western bank fell away into the churning water.

"Do you see it?" Kaiser asked as he pulled a steel dagger from the small scabbard at his waist.

Rache turned on his feet and looked around. "See what?"

Kaiser chuckled as he sliced the meat of his left thumb. Blood beaded along the cut. "This."

He stretched his fingers and pressed his hand forward. At the end of his reach, his hand hit an invisible wall. Energy rippled out from his touch in slow pulsing waves. He pressed his bleeding thumb to the energy ripple and it immediately turned red. The ripples stopped as each of Kaiser's fingertips started to glow. Veins of energy crept out from his touch, going from blood red to fading black. Strands of silver reached out towards Kaiser, wrapping around his hand and arm. They continued to crawl down the length of his arm, curling around his shoulder, and stretching towards his heart. A strand reached up and tapped his chest before plunging deep. Kaiser's back arched in response, a smile on his face.

"Won't those in the camp see this?" Rache asked, glancing over his shoulder towards the west.

Kaiser chuckled. "My lie of a story has likely set them to tears and my little show of command over the fire has them too frightened to look in my direction."

"You told your lie so well that you had even me believing it to the be the truth," Rache commented as he returned his attention to his master.

"My tongue is my greatest weapon, Rache. Yours is your ferocity," Kaiser stated as he began to slowly turn his arm. The strands immediately tightened with a taut snap. He looked up at the Shadow Mirror before him and smiled with a dark expression. "With this blood of mine, I open the gate. Let those pass that is in my will to allow. Let none pass that seek to destroy me. Let none pass without my command of blood."

With an audible crack, Kaiser pulled free of the silver strands and all hint of energy from the Mirror disappeared. Kaiser then turned to Rache and gestured for him to step forward. Rache took a deep breath before proceeding. He immediately hit a wall and was thrown back. He shook his head after the jarring impact and snarled at Kaiser.

"Do you seek to destroy me, Rache?" he calmly asked.

"No, master but I would like to get my hands on your bastard grandson," Rache spit out. He got up to this feet and brushed the dirt from his legs.

"In due time, my Demon. We are about to step out into the wide world, all eyes upon us. Tread lightly and carefully for we are one step closer to destiny," Kaiser stated as he looked towards the other river bank.

A LOOK TO THE LAND BEYOND

The rolling green plains of the Southlands spread out from the high rock Wall of Crossroads. On the horizon, it met with a dark brown and green forest. A sparkling, slow moving river meandered around the hills as it flowed. On its left bank was the sleepy village of Garhune. It was a small fishing village with a collection of farms and vegetable gardens that the Mortal inhabitants tended. This was the sight before Proto Avis the Gryphon and Vorin the ancient Dragon as they searched the plains for any sign of the Daylord.

"The wind is quiet and the river no longer speaks to me," Vorin's deep voice rumbled. He let out a heavy breath as he lifted his reptilian head to study the land with his golden eyes. "The forest is veiled against my sight."

"A dark power is at work in the Mortal homeland and I would rush to break it if we did not have our own troubles," Proto said with a heavy heart. "You know of what I speak."

"Or who," Vorin stated as he turned a golden eye to his old friend who laid at his right side. "We are under attack from all sides with no place to mount a defense."

Proto shook his head. "Do not lose hope. A light will reveal itself in this darkness. I have always believed that since my people did not see this coming."

"It is easy for a person to lie in front of someone they are not threatened by. Do not blame your good nature," Vorin said as he squared his shoulders. "Though if I was the first to meet Kaiser, I would have seen right through him. People find it hard to lie in front of a beast capable of swallowing them whole."

A harsh rustle of feathers and tapping of claws disrupted the calm watch. Both Vorin and Proto looked back towards two Tawny Eagle Gryphon guards who bared the path forward. A slate feathered Falcon Gryphon snapped and argued with the guards in rising panic. His wings were flared in preparation to leap over the Tawny Eagle Gryphons despite their brutish size. A fight looked ready to break out.

Vorin glanced over at Proto who nodded, knowing he could not give the command without the Gryphon's sage's permission. "Let him pass!"

The Dragon's booming voice echoed across the rock and the guards immediately stood down, bowing their heads in shame. The Falcon Gryphon snorted towards them as he passed. He hopped up onto the rocky perch, limping on his right rear leg. Blood soaked the gray fur from a ragged wound. His feathers were unkempt and tattered from a long journey.

"I bring a secret message from Cascade," the Gryphon said, easing himself into a bow. "Though I beg forgiveness for my appearance and interruption of your conversation."

The statement immediately caught of Proto and Vorin's attention. "A secret message?" Proto asked in confusion.

The Falcon Gryphon raised his head. "The roads and skies are hunted by a dangerous force. No messenger is safe and it takes great stealth to travel with any note of importance." He spoke with a confident tone with only a slight whistle.

"I have not seen a single threat on my many journeys to the Earthborn capital," Vorin exclaimed with concern.

"You are a mighty Dragon, Lord Vorin. Respect for positions aside, you have the breath of fire and great strength in your arsenal. I am the son of General Grinus and I was chosen to fly so that this message would reach you," the messenger stated. He then plucked a thick scroll from a leather tube attached to his chest by a harness.

"This is in Oren's hand. I would know his elegant script anywhere," Proto said once the scroll was laid out. "See his careful and elegant lines. There is a second style of writing here. Vorin, my eyes are not what they used to be. Can you read this?"

Vorin's wine red scales rustled as he shifted his massive bulk. He pointed at the first line with a blackened claw. Line after line was devoured under his intense gaze. "This is most troubling. To suggest that Lord Shiloh of the Shadowborn was murdered in his own city is inconceivable. And the troubles of Lord Oren? I am truly saddened by the truth of his abdication."

"You are dismissed. Have your wound tended to and rest," Proto calmly ordered. The Falcon Gryphon messenger bowed his head and departed. "My guards will keep their peace," he told Vorin to assure him.

The Dragon nodded. "Oren speaks of the attack that killed his two grandchildren and maimed Aku. He accuses Kaiser of involvement by using a Demon! True blasphemy!"

"Kaiser has always been suspected of such friendships but as the Immortal Truth demands, proof must be obtained," Proto started to quote.

Vorin snapped his jaws. "I am tired of fear and wondering with him!" He spit out a line of fire and incinerated the paper. He stamped his paws. "He has proven to be a danger for too long and I do not need to see more evidence of his crimes! He had his part in the downfall of Akakios and surely is working to do the same again."

"But even I was able to see that Oren warned us against open war. The moment we mobilize, he will kill Aku and Onyx and the Immortal Truth will collapse. We will be plunged into a war that we will not be able to win," Proto argued, feeling himself getting heated. He would suffer no insult to the Immortal Truth. He eased himself away from his Dragon friend to avoid getting singed by his flame. His feathers and fur were damaged enough from age. His cloudy eyes fluttered closed in thought.

"Have you forgotten? There are still members of the Silvanus bloodline left. The bastard, the lost son, and the mad one?" Vorin pointed out. He gestured to the plains with a toss of his head. "Aday Silvanus is still alive even in his madness."

Proto scoffed. "Would you put a mad soul on the throne? You do remember how well that fared when Akakios was Shadowlord. You do remember how we both signed the order of execution."

A growl rumbled deep in Vorin's broad chest. His lips curled revealing a line of sharp yellowed ivory teeth. "Don't mock me, Gryphon," he warned.

For a long agonizing moment, Vorin and Proto stared at each other with bristling anger. The Dragon's tail twitched in tension, thumping the dusty rock. The sun beat down on them, adding to the heat of the moment. Both then let out a deep breath, calming their bunched up nerves.

"Madness would not suit the throne and we must be assured that an occupant can be found. That leaves the bastard of Akakios as our choice," Proto stated with formality.

"I would not count out the young Onyx though I do not really know him or his nature," Vorin pointed out as exhaustion settled over his heart. He laid his big head on the ground and sighed deeply.

Heavy thoughts and feelings made the sunny afternoon seem dark and bleak. It was if gray storm clouds had rolled in to douse the land with a shower of cold rain. The green grass of the lower plains appeared faded and dead to their eyes. The river looked to have dried up and the earthy bed cracked. Long had this vision of death and utter ruin overwhelmed them when terrible thoughts claimed their minds.

"There has to be hope. I will not let this world fall to him. To that traitor. But neither will I let the Immortal Truth fall and see the darkness of my youth again," Proto stated as his broad wings lay limp to his side.

"I too feel the same and in order to achieve a future of light, a strong hearted and sound minded Shadowlord must be seated," the wine red Dragon admitted. He crossed his paws and rested his chin on the top.

"So what do we do?" Proto asked after a pause.

Vorin considered an answer. "The celebration is coming soon. We can use it to assess where we stand. Both the young Prince and the bastard will be in attendance. Perhaps we can offer a push to the Shadowborn nation and bless a new Shadowlord."

"Or we can use the distraction of the celebration," Proto suggested.

"Indeed," Vorin replied solemnly. He hated how often that his conversations with Proto turned depressing and melancholy. "I miss the days of peace."

Proto agreed. "Do you remember the nobility of the great Shadow Night and his general Cian Adonis? The courage they had?"

"Cian could speak the Dragon tongue and roared as fiercely as any Dragon did in battle. Him and Shadow Night... what a mighty pair. It was a sad day when Cian was killed," Vorin mused as he thought about the past. "But then came Bane out of the eastern wilds and born on the battlefields was the greatest partnership Terra had ever seen."

The old Gryphon sage had to smile. "My youth if I could call it that. I am glad that my sight lasted long enough to see that momentous event." He felt his Spirit getting lighter.

Vorin turned his gaze to his longtime friend. "Has Bane ever told you where he came from? Anything about his origins?"

"He has kept most things hidden from me in the years I have known him. From what told me, he came from a now abandoned village in the Eastlands. His father was a farmer and his mother kept the household. No brothers or sisters. Beyond that, you will have to ask him," Proto answered as he shuffled his wings. "Why the curiosity?"

The Dragon twisted his head to look south. "Because I find it unusual that he does not come. We are left without a champion to face Kaiser," he grumbled as he shifted his gaze back to the city. He thought about the last time he saw Bane and he felt that him leaving was a bad idea. The Immortal Truth had just been set into law and the wounds of war were still fresh. Why did he leave?

Though Vorin dwarfed him by his mass, Proto felt no fear or unease. Even when he threatened to explode with his temper. Proto understood his friend's frustration. "We will find our champion again. We will give Oren his justice. We will have peace once more."

A silence fell over the two friends as they returned to looking out over the Southlands. Both pair of eyes searched the land like an unbreakable watch. This had been their routine every time they were both in the city of Crossroads. Even when they were apart, they always looked to the south.

The excitable chirps and whistles of a group of Gryphon children lifted the heavy mood in their air. Proto and Vorin turned to see five bright-eyed Gryphon fledglings, all from a Falcon bloodline. Each one still bore the fuzz of their nestling days. A sleek and dangerously beautiful Falcon Gryphon sauntered forward with her charges at her side. Her pale brown and cream body added to her animalistic beauty. A darker feathered Desert Falcon Gryphon followed behind her. Proto immediately recognized the darker Gryphon as Lana, the messenger he met in Coal.

"My Lord Avis," the pale Gryphon said with a bow of the head. She glanced at her charges to make sure they too were showing respect. "My Lord Dragon," she added.

"Mistress Savanna, what brings you to the cliffs?" Vorin asked, amused at the energy of the children. They too were eager and full of curiosity, teasing each other with playful nips.

"A flying lesson for these future messengers. A very honorable role. If it pleases my Lords, may we continue the lesson in your presence?" Savanna asked politely with her sultry voice. She spoke with no accent in the common tongue.

Vorin smiled for he loved children with curious minds. He glanced at Proto before pushing himself off of his belly. "If it pleases you, I would like to join in your lesson."

"It would be an honor," Savanna replied. She repeated Vorin's words to the Gryphon children.

Proto laughed as he thought the children could not be more excited. They bounced around, flapping their wings before Lana quieted them down with a curt chirp. Vorin vaulted off the edge and unfurled his broad leathery wings. Savanna led the Gryphon charge as she followed the Dragon. The five children took off without hesitation. Lana followed close behind, repeating the teaching commands. Vorin's heavy wing beats buffeted the Gryphons and the children whistled and laughed as only they could.

"Lord Avis! Watch me!" one child squeaked.

Proto nodded and called out comments in both the Gryphon tongue and common tongue as the children flew and twisted around Vorin. The Dragon's laugh was deep and booming as he teased in mock play. It was a surprising sight to see the ancient soul play as if he was young again. Only Proto could see and understand the longing in his friend's golden eyes, knowing the sacrifice the Dragons made for the Immortal Truth. He pushed the sad memory into the back of his mind just as Vorin soared past with seven Gryphons on his tail.

BY THE FIRESIDE

"What are you doing?" Onyx asked when he came upon Kaiser pacing around a watchfire. He paused to watch the ancient Shadowborn stare into the flames with great intent.

"Shadow is the absence of light. Even something as bright as this fire can not illuminate every nook and cranny of the world," Kaiser replied, keeping his eyes on the heart of the watchfire. "The Fireborn know this best but perhaps a Shadowborn such as you or me can rival them in understanding."

Onyx stepped into the small dirt space that had been specifically cleared for the watchfire. He looked around for any hint of the guards that he assumed would have been present instead of Kaiser. On the dusty ground to Kaiser's right were a set of footprints leading into the forest. "Where are the guards?"

Kaiser finally looked up and smiled pleasantly. "They are still here, watching out for you from the shadows. I am also keeping a careful eye to the world around us." He tapped the side of his head. "Nothing shall come upon the camp without me knowing."

"How can you know what is coming if you can not see it?" Onyx asked as he stopped on the other side of the watchfire. He looked at Kaiser through the flames.

"When you get to be my age, the ability to sense auras and energy trails is quite near perfect. Unlike a youth such as yourself, it takes just a flicker of thought to sharpen my focus and see what can not be seen," Kaiser explained, sounding like a teacher talking to a student.

Onyx nodded, silently agreeing that Kaiser's logic made sense. Kaiser was after all nearly eleven hundred years old. There were probably many things he knew and understood about the world that only came with his age. Onyx scuffed the tip of his boot in the dirt, looking down as he traced a short line. He forced out a deep breath before looking up again. Kaiser had returned to studying the heart of the flame, the light casting shadows across his sharp features. At first glance, the sight was frightening. But then Kaiser's features softened as he looked up at Onyx.

"Is something on your mind? You should be resting. Tomorrow, we enter the Red Desert and the heat can be quite draining," Kaiser asked in an inquisitive tone.

"I couldn't sleep," Onyx admitted with a shrug. He scratched his forearm, the cloth of his wool jacket irritating his skin.

"Perhaps I can ease whatever fears you have about the road ahead. You are welcome to stay awhile with me," Kaiser said. He gestured for Onyx to come over with a wave of his hand.

Onyx hesitated at first. His hesitation did not escape Kaiser's notice. The noble persisted with his gesture until Onyx finally came to his side. Kaiser laid his right arm around Onyx's shoulders, giving him a reassuring squeeze.

"Come now. Tell me your worries," Kaiser encouraged as his arm dropped away.

"The further we advance, the more I feel the chill of a history I don't think I can begin to understand," Onyx finally admitted.

Kaiser nodded. "This is your first time away from home. You are moving towards a world that exalts the blood of your ancestor to near divinity. That would make any young man nervous and uncertain."

"What was it like for you the first time you left our homeland?" Onyx asked, looking Kaiser in the eyes.

Kaiser kept his expression soft and warm. "In my youth, I was a rash and daring soul. I have travelled many times beyond our borders. The most enlightening time was just after the sealing of the Darklands. Your noble ancestor asked me to accompany him to Crossroads in what would be the beginning of what was to become the Immortal Truth. Would you like to hear the tale?"

Onyx nodded. He followed Kaiser over to a downed tree trunk. Kaiser brushed his hand over the wood to get rid of the dirt and debris before gesturing for Onyx to sit down. Onyx slowly sat down, avoiding a patch of damp green moss. Kaiser then sat down beside him. He looked back towards the fire as he crossed his legs. He wafted his left hand towards the flames, awakening them with the pass of his hand.

"How can you do that if you are only a Shadowborn? I thought only Fireborn could command a fire to their will?" Onyx asked looking back towards the fire. He watched as the flames jumped and crackled, reaching for the stars in the night sky.

Kaiser smiled. "Look at the fire. See how the flames twist and move. Even in their ever present dance, shadows are intermingled amongst the spirals and curves. Now it is a challenge to learn but I can teach you how manipulate fire by capturing the shadows within." He patted Onyx's left shoulder. "I have learned a great deal in my long life and I am willing to pass on my knowledge."

Onyx had to admit that Kaiser was probably the smartest person in all of the Shadowborn lands. For the last six years, the lessons with his father's Chancellor had been intense but very informative. "You can do that?"

"I have been educating you in the finer arts of statecraft for these last years. If you wish to learn more about your Spirit energy, you will find no better teacher than me," Kaiser said with confidence. "Use every opportunity to learn more about the world whether from the advice of an elder or through personal exploration."

The young Prince stared into the fire, trying to pick out the shadows that Kaiser had mentioned. Each time he thought he had spotted one, the sliver of darkness disappeared in the blink of an eye. He sighed deeply. "Is the Daylord like everyone says?"

Kaiser let out a deep breath. "More or less. I first saw him on the fields north of Umbra but he left for Crossroads before I could truly meet him face to face. I jumped at the chance to join your ancestor in his trek to the capital. Even with the sealing of the Darklands, the road south was fraught with Demons. It was an absolute honor to fight at your ancestor's side and show him that despite my father's death, he still had a loyal warrior to fight for him."

"You really are a warrior?" Onyx asked in disbelief.

"I was trained to be one by my father. Now I pursue more scholarly endeavors in my old age," Kaiser replied with a grin. "Now as I was saying, the road south was dangerous but the convoy made it to Crossroads in due time. The city was celebratory but no where near what is waiting for you. The Northern Alliance had just won a hard fought war so there was still a great deal of damage to be healed. To give you an idea, do you remember visiting Umbra on your sixteenth birthday?"

Onyx nodded. "You showed me the old fortress in the mountains. The one that had been torn apart by some great beast."

"Even a thousand years after the end of the war, the scars of it remain. That was only a taste of the destruction the war caused. In its aftermath, the great Lords of the North met in Crossroads. Shadow Night personally introduced me to the Daylord while we were waiting for the rest of the Lords to arrive," Kaiser explained in a voice that changed from reverence of the past to awe. "I remember exactly what he wore: a dark brown leather cuirass trimmed with gold, an ocean blue tunic, red bracers and waistband, midnight blue pants, and dark gray boots. His hair was chestnut brown and his eyes were a haunting sky blue. He was built more like a man who had grown up on a farm, strong but light in frame. Quite similar to myself."

"Really?" Onyx asked. He slid back to look Kaiser up and down.

Kaiser chuckled at his reaction. "A man can be more than he appears and Bane was such a man. I do not think there is any word that truly describes him. But such is the countenance of a man with Farlander blood in his veins. It is not widely known for any discussion regarding the Farlands is met with uncertainty but several groups migrated to the Spiritlands long before you or I were even born."

The fire popped loudly, diverting Onyx's attention away from Kaiser. He watched the flames for a few seconds. "Barely anyone speaks of the Farlands. How do I know that you are not lying?"

"Speak to the Dragonlord. He will confirm my story," Kaiser stated. "Bane is a great man for what he has done for the Spiritlands. I am certain that to this day, he fights to defend the innocent. He is noble yet humble. Quiet and strong. The right kind of man that the Northern Alliance named as the High King. That fact, I know I have told you before."

"For as long as I can remember, the Daylord has had this air of mystery for there are so few alive that have seen him. Will I understand him better when I get to Crossroads? Is there more you can tell me so I am prepared?" Onyx asked, starting to feel uncertain about the road ahead.

"The city of Crossroads will show you things you have never seen. Inspire feelings you have never felt before. The celebration is a transformative experience for all who attend," Kaiser said as his gaze went back to the watchfire. "Like this fire, you will encounter twists, turns, and a light that even the shadows can not touch. Now, get some sleep. We move at dawn."

LAVAN

Onyx wiped the sweat from his brow with the back of his hand. He flicked his hand off to the side, grimacing at the sticky mess. He was beginning to hate the heat of the Fireborn lands. At first, the heat was not bad as the caravan passed into the grasslands. A nice breeze had welcomed them. He had quickly stripped off his jacket and long sleeve tunic, leaving his arms bare. The touch of the breeze was cool and refreshing though it was not as brisk and chill as his home. His jacket was of thick wool and not suited for warm weather. The grasslands then turned into rolling hills of sand. The sight had mesmorized Onyx but now he was ready to get out of the desert.

"What I wouldn't give for a swim in a mountain lake," Onyx exclaimed as he dug around in his saddle bags for a hand cloth.

Soja appeared unaffected by the heat as he still wore his Saber uniform. His horse plodded beside beside Onyx's at an equal pace. Soja bent forward to pat the horse's neck. "Lavan is not too far ahead. We can take a relaxing swim in one of their oasis pools. Water so clear, you can see every stone and grain of sand on the bottom. It's pretty neat."

"How do you know what Lavan looks like? You've never left our homeland," Onyx asked, doubtful.

"I am a Saber, schooled in swordsmanship, sneaking around, and geography. I am more than a warrior," Soja replied, hinting at his extensive education. He winked. "Lavan is known for more than its crystal pools."

Onyx had tried to learn as much as he could about his surroundings for the journey to Crossroads. His Saber guard had proven to be extremely knowledgable at each step. Soja never lost his cool confidence and eager excitement. Most of the time, he rode dutifully at Onyx's side and told him stories. The Saber regaled his Prince with tales of strange creatures, Spiritborn history, and his personal favorite story called 'The March of Shadow Night.' Soja turned out to be a masterful storyteller and was very animated in his delivery. He swung his hands and arms, acting out the motions. Onyx laughed with him as he shared jokes, some being quite filthy in their subject matter. It amazed Onyx how un-Saber like Soja was and how bold his personality could be.

"So what is Lavan known for?" Onyx asked as the caravan mosied along at a slow but steady pace.

"The city is directly west of the Fireborn capital and acts as major trade center on the edge of the Red Desert. It has some of the best produce markets east of the River Shadow. Now that can be surprising. How could a desert city sustain such a market? Well, it contains the widest variety of peppers and citrus fruits you will ever see. And the very air smells of fresh spices. The food is legendary!" Soja excitedly explained. He sniffed the air deeply. "My father and my mother vacationed in Lavan after he retired from the Sabers. I was born nine months later if you catch my meaning."

Onyx shuddered but he had to admit Soja's lively personality made sense. "You don't speak of your mother much."

"I don't see a reason to. Like you, my mother died and I live each day for the glory of her memory. I'd like to think that she would be proud of me," Soja replied with a shrug of his shoulders. "My father doesn't always show it but I believe he is proud of me too."

Soja's words made Onyx think about his own parents and he withdrew into himself. The dry heat made him sweat even more and his vest clung to his body. He wiped his brow with a hand cloth and shielded his eyes from the bright sunlight. Up ahead loomed the sprawling city of Lavan where Onyx saw more of the strange plants Soja called palm trees. Palm trees were so different from the mountain pines he was used to. The enclosing wall was a light tan mud brick piece of architecture with designs carved on the surface. As Onyx came closer, he saw images of Fireborn running with lions, Dragons breathing fire, and solar symbols. He found the artwork fascinating.

Hayden Abendroth rode up to Onyx as the caravan slowed to a stop. "Come with me, your Highness. The mayor of Lavan wishes to welcome you and your father to the city." He turned back briefly and nodded towards Soja. Soja responded with his own nod.

Onyx followed the Saber Captain up to the front of the caravan where he dismounted. A groom took his horse upon Hayden's order but not before giving Onyx his royal crown. He set it on his Prince's head, bowed, and led the horse away. The metal of the crown was hot against Onyx's forehead. He hated wearing it. He tried to brush and tame his black hair to no avail.

His father was already at the city gate, supported by Kaiser and Morin. The crown he were looked like a heavy weight on his head. His clothes hung on his skeletal frame and his eyes bore no luster or shine. Onyx frowned at Morin as he moved close to his father's side. Morin stepped back to stand behind Kaiser. Onyx continued frowning, directing his glare towards Kaiser as he took his father's left arm. After a few tense seconds, Kaiser bowed his head and stepped away.

"Welcome to Lavan, Lord Aku and Prince Onyx. This is my dear wife," the flame haired mayor said proudly as he gestured towards a woman with long strawberry blonde hair at his side. She curtsied as her husband bowed. "Myself and the people of Lavan have prepared festivities in honor of your visit."

"Your kindness pleases both my father and I. We are both excited for our visit," Onyx stated dutifully. He bit back a comment about the intolerable heat.

"Come. Let me personally show you to your quarters. My wife shall send ahead for the cooks for bring some refreshments," the mayor declared with a smile.

Onyx was relieved to get out of the sun and extreme heat and found his chambers to be quite cool. The receiving room was light and airy with thin linen curtains separating it from the bedroom. It had high ceilings with intricately woven tapestries hanging on every wall. The stone was a glittering white marble with specks of silver and gold. In contrast, the furniture was made out of a dark wood and reeds. Shades of red was the other dominant decorating theme.

"Not too bad, your Highness," Soja commented as he turned around on his feet.

"I did not really expect all this. I thought that it would still be hot inside," Onyx said as he studied one tapestry. It was of a battle scene with a large Dragon.

Soja stepped over to the window. "See this tan brick? It has wards etched in the surface to hold heat and turn it away. Sure the Fireborn can manipulate fire but they can also manipulate heat. They can draw it in to keep warm or expel heat to cool themselves."

"So what now?" Onyx asked after he stepped over to the window. He ran his fingers over the brick, feeling the warmth.

"The mayor has organized a banquet and entertainment in honor of the visit. Good food, lively music, and beautiful dancers," Soja said, rubbing his hands together and grinning. "At sundown, we shall party!"

Thankfully, when the sun set in the Red Desert, the temperature dropped to a more comfortable cool. Onyx relished the chill that reminded him of home. He adjusted the collar of his dinner jacket as the chamber groom combed back his dark hair under the silver crown. The groom smoothed the wrinkles on the jacket with a careful hand. Onyx took one final look in the mirror and nodded. He thanked the groom who in return bowed deeply. He headed straight towards the chambers set aside for his father. Morin leaned against the stone wall opposite the door looking more like a bored guard than the High Commander of the Armed Forces. When Morin did not immediately salute, Onyx frowned.

"Is my father ready for me?" Onyx asked flatly. He crossed his arms tightly.

Morin jumped up and awkwardly bowed. It was more a reaction of surprise than of respect. "Your royal father is inside," he stated as he gestured towards the door.

Onyx stepped forward to look Morin in the eyes. Now he was tall enough to do so and at eighteen, he was even heavier than the Commander. He was growing well into his Silvanus frame. "I certainly hope that you are more observant around my father. I would hate to tell him that you are being lax in your duties."

"Of course, your Highness," Morin stumbled to say. He smacked his forehead with an uncoordinated salute. Onyx snorted before he entered his father's chambers.

Inside the receiving room sat his father in a tall reed chair, dressed in his black robes. Kaiser stood nearby, describing some of the various Fireborn dishes. His servant was nowhere to be seen.

"Out," Onyx ordered in a stern voice.

Kaiser stopped talking and looked up. He smirked as he laid a hand on the back of Aku's chair. He was dressed in a black long coat trimmed with silver brocade. "As Lord's Chancellor, I wanted to be sure that his Lord and Majesty was prepared for the evening."

"As Crowned Prince, I can take care of my father. Go and make sure our seats are ready before we arrive. Take the Commander with you," Onyx ordered. Kaiser latched his hands behind his back and bowed deeply. "I will lead my father to the banquet hall."

"As you wish," Kaiser said politely. As soon as he stepped into the hallway, he snapped his fingers. Morin immediately jumped to attention and followed after Kaiser.

Onyx let out a deep sigh once the dark wood door slammed shut. He eased himself down on the reed footstool before his father. Aku looked back at him as if he was not truly there and lost in some unknown distant world.

"I am worried, Father. Everyone will be looking at us and they will wonder," Onyx started to say as he took Aku's hand. He stopped himself and dropped his head. Part of him had been worrying about portraying an image of strength since leaving Cross. No one openly admitted it but the throne was sitting in a weak position. The Shadow Council had even debated on allowing Aku to make the journey to Crossroads but Kaiser had convinced them otherwise in the end. "I suppose I should thank him at some point. I would rather have you with me than left behind in Cross."

Aku's face appeared to soften in response to his son's voice and his one good eye lit up. The scars on the left side of his face pulled on his skin as he smiled. "My boy," he said with a thin raspy voice. His bony hand squeezed Onyx's with a light but firm touch.

A sense of hope filled Onyx's heart as he escorted his father to the banquet hall. The room was massive with high ceilings and a large chandelier that hung from the center by a system of chains. Tables were set up next to the walls with benches only on one side. Upon a raised dais with the royal banners of the Fireborn and the Shadowborn hanging above was the royal table. Onyx helped his father sit down before taking his own seat. The energy in the room was festive and lively as the crowd settled at the tables, talking excitedly about Crossroads. Food and wine was distributed liberally by the team of servants at a busy but calculated pace.

"How's the food, your Highness?" Soja asked, sliding into place beside Onyx. He swiped up a piece of flatbread and began to munch on it.

Onyx picked at a mixture of peppers that had been set on his plate with a dollup of cream. "It's spicy and I don't think I have tasted a cream like this before."

Soja dipped his flatbread in the cream on Onyx's plate and took a bite. He considered the taste for a moment. "Cool with a hint of herbs. A Fireborn speciality. You should try the goat cheese when it comes around. It's heaven on the bread."

It became a game between Onyx and Soja to try each and every dish that was presented to the royal table. As his Saber guard had told him, peppers and spice dominated the cuisine. The primary meats were goat, lamb, and pork. Vegetables of all kinds were spread out among the dishes with a variety of citrus fruits mixed in. Onyx found that he loved the taste of lemon with its sweet and tart flavor. Whenever he found something he liked, he shared it with his father in hopes of bringing him out of his listless state.

The meal service quieted down and the loud conversation diminished to a low volume. People turned their attention to the center of the room as a team of scantily clad dancers waltzed into the space. They were dressed in red and gold cloth that hinted at their slender bodies and curves. Onyx found the dancers' attire to be highly inappropriate and was about to say something to Soja until he saw that his Saber guard was making eyes at one dancer. The dancer returned Soja's glance by kissing her hand and blowing the kiss towards him. He played at catching it over his heart.

"Are you serious? You are a Saber," Onyx declared.

Soja only laughed. "And you are a Prince that is almost a man who has grown up around men. Live a little, your Highness," he stated with a big smile. "I kissed my first girl at ten years old. I intend to make sure you don't hit twenty one without kissing a girl."

Onyx's posture tightened with an overwhelming sense of nerves. Women and romance was something he had never given any attention to. He sank in his seat as the dancers began to shake their hips and wave their arms in the air. At first, the group of ten women performed their intricate dance together, matching each other move for move. After a while, the dancers began to separate, spinning and waving sashes of thin red fabric. They moved among the diners who clapped with the timing of their footsteps. The same dancer that had blown a kiss at Soja paused before the royal table. She hooked a finger to beckon the Saber forward. Before Onyx could protest, Soja pulled Onyx out of his seat and down on to the floor.

As the dancers continued to perform with those they had pulled out of the audience, Kaiser slid into Onyx's vacated seat and set a hand on Aku's shoulder.

"It must make your heart leap with such joy to see your flesh and blood enjoying life. See how he is fawned over. You must be proud," Kaiser stated as he squeezed Aku's shoulder. He leaned in closer to whisper in Aku's ear in a barely audible voice. "I would not do or say anything that could endanger his precious life."

Aku shuddered beneath Kaiser's tight grip. "Please..."

Kaiser smirked as he knew that his threat reached Aku's sensitive spot for his child. "Oh my dear Lord. Do not think that anything you do escapes my sight for I am always watching. Now let that weary soul of yours rest. You must be so tired after leaving Cross."

The dancers continued to move in perfect rhythm as they danced around Onyx, Soja, and the other pulled members of the audience. They laughed and joked with their new partners. Soja laughed the loudest as his dancer trapped him by wrapping her sash around his neck. Onyx was nervous and tight at first but slowly began to relax. As he started laughing with joy, he did not see his father weeping.

THE GATES OF CROSSROADS

Onyx had thought he had seen it all when the caravan stopped in Lavan but nothing prepared him for the grandness of Crossroads. As his horse crested the hill, the high white stone walls rose up from the green fields before him. It was such a stark contrast in colors that Onyx had to turn away from the brightness. Once his eyes had adjusted, he looked upon the city again. He could now see a set of massive wood and iron doors set within the walls. Scattered in the green fields were grand manors and farmhouses boxed in by carefully laid fences. The sight of Crossroads screamed of immense wealth and luxury for everyone who lived there. It was magnificent and Onyx found himself breathless from amazement.

"Ah yes. The great and grand Capital of the Northlands," Kaiser said cooly as he pulled on the reins of his horse. The horse stopped beside Onyx's clean limbed mount and shook its head vigorously.

"I never thought such a place could exist. Is there no poverty or ill here?" Onyx asked as he glanced at Kaiser.

"The city layout is laced with Spirit wards that forbid ill will and suffering within its walls. One of the Daylord's last acts before he disappeared south," Kaiser replied before gesturing towards a distant crystalline obelisk. "That is the source of the Daylord's power in Crossroads. It is what gives the city its defense against the Darklands."

Onyx studied the distant object, seeing how the sun beamed

upon its surface. Rays of light transformed it into a sparkling structure. "Lord's Chancellor, you are of an age to remember a vast stretch of history. What was the city like before the Daylord?"

"It was a shadow of what you see before you. I came here with my father when I was a boy to bear witness to the anointing of the Gryphons' new ambassador. That same Gryphon still lives in Crossroads though now as the acting King in the Daylord's absence," Kaiser explained as his horse shifted beneath him. "Yes, Proto Avis. The one soul in the Northlands who knows the Daylord's mind best."

As the caravan had gotten closer to Crossroads, the fireside stories turned more to topics like the mysterious origins of Bane Arlis the Daylord. Onyx regularly joined the camp bonfire to listen each night. At first the stories were grand and far reaching when the soldiers told them. Eventually, they begged Kaiser to describe his experiences as he was the only person in the entire caravan who had actually met Bane. At first, he graciously declined, blaming his relative youth at the time of his encounter. When Onyx asked him directly in front of the crowd, Kaiser finally told his story. It was a story that captured everyone though nothing like his first story regarding the death of his father. It was clear to Onyx that Kaiser was a fantastic story teller.

"Perhaps when I become Shadowlord, I will name a suitable and noble ambassador," Onyx mused as he studied the natural features of the land before him.

"I am certain that whomever you choose will bring your crown great honor," Kaiser placated in a subserviant tone. A smirk played across his face. "Perhaps your bastard cousin if I may make a recommendation."

"No, I do not think that I would name him to represent my people abroad. I would not want someone who runs from his place of birth for parts unknown," Onyx replied after some thought.

Kaiser bowed his head. "He is known to live in Crossroads. Allow me to deal with him so that you and your father will have peace and good cheer."

The fate of his bastard cousin had become a weight in Onyx's mind the closer he came to Crossroads. He was a threat to the throne Onyx was born to due to his greater age and experience. And then there were the rumors regarding his strong Silvanus looks that some claimed made him look like Shadow Night reborn. The thought was unsettling and Onyx shook his head to free himself of it. Kaiser was right in his suggestion. Crossroads was about celebration and positive energy, not dealing with royal bastards.

"Do as you see fit so long as my father's name is not

dishonored," Onyx finally said as he jerked on the horse's reins to get it moving again.

"Of course," Kaiser replied with a bow of the head.

Onyx's horse plodded along at a slow pace towards the city walls. At first, he rode alone at the head of the caravan but as the road started to widen and the farming estates came closer, his shoulders dropped. Almost immediately, Onyx found his faithful Saber guard Soja at his side. The Saber smiled with some sort of hidden delight which Onyx attributed to the joyful atmosphere of the celebration that waited for them.

"So what do you think?" Soja asked cheerfully.

"What?" Onyx said, not really paying attention to anything but reviewing the proper state protocols that Kader had taught him.

"What do you think of Crossroads? Isn't it huge?" Soja asked, raising his voice a little to catch his Prince's attention.

"It's the biggest city I have ever seen. I thought Lavan was big sitting amongst those sand dunes but this? It's incredible!" Onyx answered with excitement.

Soja reached over and patted Onyx's shoulder. "If you thought Lavan was fun, just wait until you see the city on the other side. I can't wait to go cliff diving!"

"I did not see cliff diving on the itinerary. Are the Airborn hosting it?" Onyx asked as he reached back to dig around in his saddle bags.

"It's just a bit of fun, your Highness. Just like those lovely ribbon dancers," Soja teased with a soft laugh. With one hand on the reins, he mimicked the flowing movements of the Fireborn. He laughed louder when he saw Onyx's face flush red. "Come on, your Highness. You have to admit those fine ladies were quite beautiful and very lovely companions."

Onyx shuddered with nerves. Another fact that became clear to him on the journey was that the Shadow Council planned to find him a suitable wife. He did not know the first thing about girls and romance. How was he supposed to find his mate for life in just a few days in a strange city he had never been to before. He had managed to avoid Soja's promise of kissing one of the dancers by hiding in his father's quarters in Lavan. Crossroads would be totally different as he would be on display more than ever. He was the Crowned Prince of the Shadowborn, a son of Shadow Night's bloodline. A lot was expected of him, especially if his father's poor health forced him to take his place in the events.

"Do I really have to?" he grumbled as his shoulders dropped.

"It's all a part of life. My father met my mother in Crossroads while he was Commander of the Sabers and she was the representative from Twilight, our northern city on the shores of the Sea of Truth. He said that despite his vows as a Saber, he promised to marry her as soon as he could. Nothing in the Saber handbook says we can't love another during our active service and my father is proof of that," Soja stated, smiling with a big grin. "Maybe I will have the same luck. Maybe even you too but who you end up with has greater implications."

"Implications?" Onyx asked nervously.

Soja nodded. "You are a future Shadowlord. Your eventual wife will be a Queen of the Shadowlord. You two will have sons and daughters, one of which will become the Shadowlord after you. You have a throne and a legacy to maintain."

"And all I thought was I would just wear a crown and wield a sword once I took the throne. I never really thought much beyond that," Onyx admitted in a sheepish voice.

The roadside soon became crowded with spectators ranging from the tall beastial Gryphons to the various members of the Spiritborn tribes. The Waterborn men and women looked up at Onyx on his horse with haughty expressions. Onyx was immediately mesmerized by their blue hair. There seemed to be no factor that determined how dark or how light their strange hair color would be. When he saw streaks of white in some of the Waterborn's hair, he decided that they were of an older generation. The few Airborn and Lightborn present in the crowd bore the same expressions as the Waterborn. Every single Airborn had white hair, making it difficult to determine age. The Lightborn all had golden hair that shimmered in the sunlight. Everyone of the Earthborn bowed their heads towards him since he was a blood relative of their Lord Palani. Typical of their hot blooded nature, the Fireborn danced and cheered.

Onyx was most amazed by the large variety of Gryphons he saw in the crowd and perched on the rooftops. Passing under an archway, a burly looking Eagle Gryphon with golden brown feathers flapped down to the ground before him and the caravan. The Gryphon bowed his head once and turned around for the caravan to follow him. It shocked Onyx to see that this Gryphon was as tall as his horse with great broad wings that he held up in the air.

"Now that is a big Gryphon. My guess is that he is a Mountain Eagle Gryphon," Soja whispered as he leaned over towards Onyx. "Each caravan must be getting an escort into the city."

"I have never seen a Gryphon before. I did not realize they came in so many colors and sizes," Onyx stated as he spotted a family of Vulture Gryphons with bald red heads.

The fanfare for the Shadowborn caravan grew in volume and

energy as it approached the city gates. Flower petals and streamers floated down and coated the roadway. Earthborn spectators tossed bright green leaves before Onyx and cheered loudly. Onyx began to smile and his nerves quickly became an afterthought. He raised his hand in the air and waved which elicited a roaring cheer from the crowd.

*****

Proto Avis sat upon a ledge that overlooked the roadway by the city's northern gates. He smiled at seeing the arrival of the Shadowborn caravan, pleased that their journey had been safe and uneventful. The collection of horse bound riders, carriages, and wagons trailed past the Northern Archway but were making good time in its approach. His eyes scanned the crowd, seeing their enthusiastic reaction. He rolled his shoulders when they started to ache, loosening the muscles. He rustled the feathers on the nape of his neck when he saw who he was looking for: Kaiser Adonis. The Shadowborn was riding next to a masked man wrapped up in tan and white. With a nod of his head, a Red Hawk Gryphon and a beefy Fireborn in a white collared leather cuirass weaved their way to the edge of the crowd towards Kaiser.

"Can I help you?" Kaiser asked, raising one eyebrow as he pulled the reins to stop his horse. His servant noiselessly did the same.

"Lord Proto Avis wishes that you wait outside the city walls until he is able to meet with you personally," the Fireborn said firmly.

"My duty is to the Shadowlord and I am under his command, not the Lord of Crossroads. I will remain at my Lord's side unless he tells me otherwise," Kaiser promptly declared.

The Hawk Gryphon and the Fireborn looked at each other and whispered under their breaths for a brief moment. The Fireborn brought his expression back to Kaiser. "The Lord of Crossroads acts under authority of the Daylord. As such, he knows the city to be safe and he trusts that the Shadowlord's son will look out for him in your place."

Kaiser's horse stamped back a step before he swiftly pulled it back into place with a tug on the reins. "Until the Daylord himself comes to command me to stay, I will follow the Shadowlord inside."

The feathers on the back of the Gryphon's neck bristled and his leonine tail swished and snapped behind him. The Shadowborn caravan continued to stream on past them, completely oblivious to their conversation. For all anyone could guess, it was a negotiation between the Shadowborn Lord's Chancellor and city emissaries.

Proto looked down upon the small group, studying the Gryphon's reaction carefully. It quickly became clear that his kinsman was getting agitated. He let out deep breath as he slowly stood up on all fours. His bones creaked in protest as his joints ached with age. He frowned in rising determination as he opened up his wings. He edged his front paws forward, gripping the edge of his perch with his right paw. Waiting until the last of the Shadowborn caravan passed through the gates, Proto flapped his wings and glided down to the roadway. He landed hard but did his best to brush off the throbbing pain.

"Ah, I see that the Lord of Crossroads has decided to greet me personally. Me who has attended every celebration since the Immortal Truth was written," Kaiser snapped with a growl towards the Red Hawk Gryphon and the Fireborn. The two stepped back in distress from his tone.

Proto sauntered over, holding his head up high and wings flared in a threat display. His companions parted so he could pass them by and stand before Kaiser. "You do not deserve any of my kindness, traitor of truth."

Kaiser rolled his eyes. "Why does everyone keep calling me that?"

Proto's body tightened and his talons dug furrows in the dirt beneath his feet. He glanced back over his shoulder and nodded towards the Gryphon and Fireborn pair. Both of them edged back to give him and Kaiser privacy but not so far back that they couldn't jump to defend him.

"Normally, I would say that someone who denies such talk is either ignorant or arrogant. I do not see you as ignorant so you must be arrogant," Proto growled. He contemplated snapping his beak at Kaiser's horse.

"Then I am flattered, Lord Proto Avis," Kaiser said in a long drawn out tone. He snickered as he glanced at his masked servant.

Proto followed his gaze and frowned. He did not like the feeling his heart got from Kaiser's servant. The man was tall and thin in his frame but beyond that, he could not discern any physical details. "My people do not believe in pride as a virtue and I am also not ignorant to what is said about you from all corners of this world."

"You are also old and brittle while I am strong and capable," Kaiser smirked.

"Enough! You will not enter Crossroads so long as I command it. And if you think to disobey my order, Vorin will be waiting with his hottest Dragon fire to roast you!" Proto snapped, his hackles bristling with anger.

"Fine. I'll stay out of Crossroads so you don't pop your feathers and make a mess," Kaiser said with an exacerbated sigh.

*****

Kaiser and Rache watched as Proto was escorted towards the city gates by the Red Hawk Gryphon and the Fireborn. He cocked his head, letting out a deep breath.

"Just a thought but he looked flustered and afraid. He stank of fear," Rache commented as his Demon eyes studied Proto. "Why would anyone think of a Gryphon as ferocious with the wings raised?" he added as he flapped his arms like a pair of bird wings. He then burst out laughing.

"Shut up," Kaiser snapped. "What makes him think that I can't find my own way into the city? I don't need his permission."

Rache shivered. "The Spirit wards might not stop you but they could stop me."

Kaiser waved him off. "There is nothing for us to worry about." He sneered as the gates slammed shut with a loud thud. "I hate that blasted puff of feathers and fur. Someone should end him."

WELCOME TO THE CITY

Remembering his place, Onyx had to uphold himself with grace and nobility amidst the heavy fanfare. Various flowers and green plants were tossed in his path as he and his father left the caravan. Aku had been unusually quiet and more diminished since leaving the gates as he used Onyx's arm to keep standing. Onyx supported his father while still trying to stand tall. He had to appear strong while his father was unable. With a careful pace, Onyx led his father into the grand hall of the citadel.

Great banners symbolizing every nation present hung from the high vaulted ceilings. A sky light constructed of iron bars and pristine glass let in the sunlight in the massive hall. Columns held up the heavy roof. Onyx compared the hall to a throne room though there was no throne present. In the exact center was a slanted slab of light colored marble with smoothed out scratches.

A Tawny Eagle Gryphon attendant directed the pair to stop before rejoining his comrades at the slab. Onyx steadied his father's posture and looked around at the other six assembled groups. He quickly recognized his uncle Palani, the Lord of the Earthborn, standing with his family across the room from him. To his left was a pair of Gryphon Lords with their families.

From what Onyx remembered, the Gryphons were led by two leaders instead of one. Paladon, the Osprey Gryphon, was the Lord of Peace and Stellaris was the Lord of War. He was a heavily built Sea Eagle Gryphon and dwarfed his fellow Lord. Gryphon politics meant that Paladon was the current decision maker since it was a time of peace. Unlike the other royals who wore crowns on their heads, the Gryphons wore collars to symbolize their status.

Everyone quieted as they heard the skylight creak open and in flew two Gryphons: a ghost like Barn Owl Gryphon and a cream colored Desert Falcon Gryphon. Onyx looked up to see the two flying in an intricate twisting pattern. They darted and flapped close enough to grasp talons and turn around in a violent spin before parting. The Owl Gryphon flew towards the north end of the grand hall and the Falcon Gryphon flew towards the south end of the hall. They slowed their speed with careful flaps and turned around to face eachother as they hovered. Onyx covered his ears when they both screeched. The Gryphons then flew directly at each other as if on the attack. For a moment, Onyx thought that they were going to crash right into each other. At the last possible moment, they altered their direction and flew straight up, disappearing through the open skylight. The skylight then slammed shut.

As soon as the display ended, people turned their attention to a passageway behind the Lords Paladon and Stellaris. The royal Gryphons parted to allow Proto Avis to walk through, bowing their heads in respect to the old sage. He walked to the slab and climbed up, gathering everyone's attention to him. He held his head up high.

"This day, we gather as kin of the Northlands to celebrate that sacred oath, the mighty Immortal Truth, and renew our promise to guard against darkness and protect innocence. We shall celebrate for seven days with parades, bonfires, combat matches, games, and plays. Then we will all assemble in the ritual hall to renew our promise to the Immortal Truth. Tonight at sun down, the celebration shall begin. I have brought you here to extend an official welcome to Crossroads," Proto stated looking each lord in the eyes. "As stated over a thousand years ago, our Daylord and King has left his command under my and Lord Vorin's authority in Crossroads. Misconduct will not be tolerated as we are here in peace." He stood up tall and flared his wings. "In Truth, I welcome you to Crossroads!"

As practiced, each person and Gryphon present nodded their acceptance. The Gryphons would never disobey their own kin and all bowed even lower in respect. Proto was pleased and descended off of the slab. The six Tawny Eagle Gryphons set up point around their sage and left the hall, the Gryphon royals in tow. Each nation's royal attendants were then allowed to enter. Onyx noticed that Kaiser was not present as Morin strode in. He then swiftly took Aku.

"I shall escort your father to his quarters now. He needs his rest before tonight's events," Morin said, having received no objection from Aku. Aku appeared listless at his side, silent and bearing a distant expression. "In the event he is unable to perform his duties, you will be expected to continue on in his place."

Onyx rolled his eyes. He did not like Morin all that much. "I know my place. You do not need to lecture me, Commander," he stated as he crossed his arms tightly.

Morin frowned. "Until Kaiser returns to your father's side, I shall act as liaison and you will be expected to follow orders. You are not the Shadowlord yet, my Prince," he growled. He turned his attention to Aku. "Come now, my lord. Let me get you to a quiet place to rest," he said as they walked away.

A golden haired young man from his uncle Palani's side ran over with an eager expression. "Come on. Everyone is heading to the cliffs."

"Ummm, who are you?" Onyx asked in confusion. He was not used to people running up to him and starting a conversation as if they were best friends. He leaned away from the young man.

"Officially, I am Crowned Prince Flynn Kano. But you can call me Flynn, cousin," the young man said with a wide smile. "Also known as the golden hair short Earthborn Prince in some circles. Let's get moving before we get stuck with a stuffy lecture or something. The cliffs are waiting!" Flynn said as he pulled on Onyx's wrist.

Onyx ripped his wrist from Flynn's grip and glared back at him. He was also not used to people grabbing at him and trying to pull him away. He could see Soja approaching with a hand at his belt.

"Ready to go cliff diving?" Soja asked jovially as he stopped beside Flynn. "Or is he still reluctant to have a little fun?" He set his hands on his belt. "Hey shortie."

Flynn waved back and bowed his head. "Saber," he said formally before he burst out laughing with Soja.

"Cliff diving? Soja, you mentioned this when we were entering the city. What exactly are you talking about?" Onyx asked, still wanting to smack his overly eager cousin for trying to drag him.

"The Waterborn and Airborn started the tradition many celebrations ago," Soja explained as he and Flynn moved to the hall entrance. Intrigued, Onyx followed. "Every celebration here at Crossroads, we the younger and more adventurous generation hold our own jumping contest. The last contest was won by an Airborn."

"Cliff diving sounds like a fun thing to do," Onyx said as he listened to his cousin and Soja rambled on about famous jumps from years past.

Soja turned to look at his Prince. "Something bothering you, your Highness?"

Onyx shrugged his shoulders. "It's nothing really," he stated meekly as he tried to ignore the probing words.

Flynn nodded as if he understood Onyx's problem. "There is another tradition that occurs at Crossroads every celebration. Betrothal of the unmatched royal heirs. I'm sure you told him about that, Soja."

The idea was an uncomfortable one for Onyx to think about. His nerves returned full force and he dropped his head. "Yea, he told me."

"My father is thinking of talking to Lord Aves again about matching me to his youngest daughter. Seli is nice and all but too quiet for my tastes," Flynn commented as the three passed by the edge of the giant city square where workers began to pile up logs and blocks of wood for the evening bonfire.

"Isn't she only fourteen?" Soja asked.

"Newly so," Flynn replied. "How about you, Onyx? Who do your people think you should be matched with?"

Put on the spot, Onyx stuttered for an answer. "I... I don't know..."

Soja put a hand on Onyx's shoulder as he looked at Flynn. "There is a bit of talk of matching him to a Fireborn Princess. Argos does have several daughters. I know his heir is already matched and due to marry in the new year. I think the Shadowborn could use a Queen of their nature to liven things up."

Onyx felt incredibly small and tried to put off his answer. To distract his thoughts, he looked about the city as they walked, seeing workers from every nation setting up decorations. Earthborn delicately placed flowers in elegantly shaped pots as a Waterborn carried a water can, sprinkling each newly planted blossom. Small Hawk and Falcon Gryphons sped about with messages and orders in halting words and chirps while Airborn translated. Fireborn and Lightborn worked together to set up lanterns on every street corner. Whenever he passed a Shadowborn worker, they immediately dropped to their knees and bowed their heads.

"What if I don't want to marry a Fireborn?" Onyx asked once they passed out of sight of the city square.

Flynn stopped Soja from answering. "We as Princes must do our duty. You especially as the future Shadowlord."

"But the Daylord isn't married," Onyx shot back feeling even more uncomfortable with the discussion.

Soja nodded towards Flynn who then took a few quick steps forward to give the two Shadowborn some distance to talk amongst themselves. Flynn gave Onyx a thumbs up to encourage him that everything will be ok.

"We all have duties and responsibilities in this world. The Daylord has chosen to give his entire life to the service of the Immortal Truth," Soja explained. "You're lucky that you even get to be married someday. Sabers are forbidden to marry until they complete their service. Many of them serve for life instead of retiring like my father did."

Onyx recognized that Soja was trying to help him but it wasn't working. "Can I just be the Shadowlord?"

"It's not like the Shadow Council plans on making an ill-suited match. Besides, Crossroads is a glorious place   There are plenty of lovely ladies here," Soja said as he spread his arms out wide, closed his eyes and let out a deep breath.

"Sabers can't marry. Why is that?" Onyx asked haltingly.

Soja chuckled. "A Saber's first love is to Lord and country. Doesn't mean I can't love or have fun while wearing the black and leathers. Being a Saber isn't all seriousness just like being a Prince isn't all stuffy ceremonies."

Onyx fell quiet and began to think that cliff diving may not be such a good idea. Being social was something he had never been comfortable with and growing up, he had rarely associated with anybody his own age. He rubbed his arms despite the warmth in the air. He ignored the bowing Shadowborn who murmured praise in the name of the Shadowlord as he passed. At first he was surprised to see so many of his people spread out through the city but now, he wished that he could escape their attention. He looked at his cousin Flynn who nodded and offered words to every Earthborn he saw and felt a sense of jealousy rise within him. Even Soja was more at ease, bowing his head and offering a polite wave of the hand.

The city of Crossroads was spread out over a low plain with two twisting rivers. It was a deceiving design as it sat at the top of the high cliff walls that separated the Mortal lands from the Immortal ones. It was a shining white beacon to the Mortal grasslands below. Having seen the city only from the north side, Onyx was excited to see the view over the Mortal lands. To him, Crossroads was a wealthy, clean city worthy of being the capital of the North. Everywhere he looked, people were gracious and full of joy. It was a huge change to his home city of Cross.

"Hey Soja. You think Ryder will come to the cliffs?" Flynn asked as he twisted around, walking backwards to speak to the Saber.

"He might but it depends on how the Arena matches are turning out. The qualifying round is going on right now," Soja answered.

"Now that is something I would pay to see," Onyx said excitedly. He loved watching combat matches and to see fighters other than Shadowborn battle each other. Lavan had already offered a preview of how the Fireborn would be fighting with their Flame Shots and staves.

"We royals get a special box seat and no one pays to watch," Flynn corrected. "I have my bets on Captain Oaken winning."

"Of course an Earthborn would cheer for his own countryman. I heard a Waterborn tote the skill of their Crowned Prince. What do you think, your Highness?" Soja asked Onyx directly.

Onyx shrugged. He did not know much about the Earthborn captain and the Waterborn Crowned Prince but he had heard many things about his bastard cousin. Everyone in Cross whispered about his street smarts and harsh nature as a fighter. A few questioned his honor and sanity. He had even heard Kaiser express interest in bringing Ryder Coba back to Cross. Onyx decided that he wanted to meet his estranged cousin and Shadowborn resident of Crossroads to see if he lived up to the hype.

CLIFF DIVING

The three reached the edge of the city where several other heirs and attendants had already gathered. The crowd was a mixture of Spiritborn and Gryphons who lounged about in the sun. A medium sized pile of broken boulders served as a perch for the Gryphons not stretched out on the grass. Several of the beasts had spread out their wings to warm them. Again, the Earthborn showed their respects to Flynn while the lone Shadowborn looked on with a stern expression. Unlike the others Onyx had come across, this Shadowborn did nothing to acknowledge him as a Prince. Onyx watched as the Shadowborn turned to the large gray and black Eagle Gryphon lounging beside him, saying a few words under his breath. The Gryphon nodded.

"Is that Ryder Coba?" Onyx asked quietly, directing Soja's eyes over to the Shadowborn.

"Looks like he will be joining us after all. Wonder how the qualifying round went," Soja said scratching his chin. "That is," Soja began to say. He suddenly snapped his fingers. "That is the son of the Gryphon Lords' great Commander Nova. His name is Harper. And over there is..."

Onyx listened to Soja as he introduced every one of the Gryphons and Spiritborn present. When he questioned him on how he knew everyone's name, Soja told him that he would not have been a proper guard if he did not know. Soja also added that while Onyx had been in the grand hall for the welcome, he had made a point of visiting the cliffs to prepare and learn who all would be there for cliff diving. Onyx shook his head, smiling and silently thanking Soja for his forethought. He reviewed everyone's names by looking back around at them and sorting through his guard's introductions in his head.

"Crossroads was built here to overlook the Mortal territory so technically we are jumping into that territory. But we have a few young Gryphons who like to jump too. They will fly us back to the top," Soja explained with lively gestures while Flynn jumped into the crowd, chatting with one of the Gryphons.

Onyx watched as a black and white Osprey Gryphon burst from the cliff's edge and landed on the grass. It shook its body as soon as its rider hopped off, thanking her in return with a bow of the head. The rider was an Earthborn girl with wavy brown hair now slick with water, her skin glistening. Her laughter was pure and full of joy as several others congratulated her on her jump. She curtsied and twirled with grace. There was something about her that left Onyx feeling light as air.

"Soja!" she called out coming over, slowing her steps once she saw Onyx. This silenced the others as well. She curtsied demurely in his presence. "Honored am I to meet the Crowned Prince of the Shadowborn," she said keeping her gaze down.

"Good. We know each other. Your Highness, this is Luna Artemis of the Earthborn. The Gryphon she came back with is Pala, daughter of Paladon. Her twin brother, Palas, is that one over there," Soja said pointing to another Osprey Gryphon. "He will inherit his father's position as Lord of Peace."

"Hi," Onyx squeaked out in response, looking upon no one other than Luna. She smiled in return.

"Have you come to cliff dive with us?" Luna asked in a jovial tone.

"Of course. It's his first trip to Crossroads and it is my job as his guard and friend to show him how to have a little fun. Care to assist me?" Soja asked, slapping Onyx on the back.

Onyx lurched forward and nearly tumbled into Luna, regaining his balance at the last second. Luna only laughed as her wet hair clung to her shoulders. He felt himself smile at the sound. He didn't even register Soja's shout towards a Fish Eagle Gryphon and his trotting footsteps away from his side.

"I can certainly show a newbie how to cliff dive properly," Luna said smugly as she twirled around towards Pala, skipping lightly on her feet. She spun around laughing. "First you will need a Gryphon partner."

Palas stood up on his perch and flapped down to the ground. He stepped forward slowly towards Onyx, on equal ground with him as an heir. The Osprey Gryphon was taller than him on all fours. His tawny gold eyes were surrounded by a black mask, intensifying his gaze.

"I shall fly you," the Gryphon Prince said in perfect calm. His beast accent was barely noticeable. Onyx suddenly felt himself dwarfed by the Gryphon as Palas looked down at him.

"I accept, heir of Paladon," Onyx finally said, remembering the proper set of words. He pulled off his shirt and boots, rolling the cuffs of his pants to his knees. Looking to his right, Onyx saw a brown and white breasted Eagle Gryphon approaching Soja who greeted him as Voci. He let out a deep breath as he went to stand by Luna at the edge with Palas behind him. Soja and Voci were quick to take the plunge, whooping wildly at the exhilaration. He looked over at Luna who smiled back at him.

"Something tells me Soja has done this before," Onyx commented as he leaned over to watch Soja fall. He shuddered at the height and stepped back.

"Don't worry. Each and every one of our parents has done this at least once in their lifetime," she said with a kind voice. "Just take a deep breath and let go."

Onyx gathered himself, taking another deep breath. Without further word, he leaped over the edge and began falling. His immediate thought was that this was the greatest height he had ever jumped from. He twisted his body around to have his head rushing towards the water below. Keeping his arms tight to his side, he glanced over to see Palas diving beside him. The Gryphon had his wings tucked tightly against his body, front limbs pressed to his feathered chest. His leonine tail blended in with his back legs. His form mimicked Onyx's. Onyx then found himself smiling as he thought to race Palas to the water. He looked towards his left side, finding Luna basking in the thrill and found himself moved by her enthusiasm.

The water was cold once he dove in and he found himself pushed to the bottom. Bunching his leg muscles, he pushed himself back up, shooting to the surface. He flung his head back, hair slapping against his shoulders. To his surprise, he found himself laughing with a joy he hadn't felt in years. He felt as if the jump had caused him to let go of something inside. And he felt good.

"See? Now tell me that wasn't fun!" Soja shouted as he floated nearby. "You think he did ok, Luna?" he asked across him. Onyx glanced back over at Luna.

"Not bad for a Prince," she giggled as she swam towards the shoreline where Palas, Pala, and Voci were shaking the water from their bodies. Soja quickly got up onto the sand and lay out on his back, a big smile on his face. Onyx came to the shore, feeling the gritty sand beneath his bare feet. "Most first timers aren't as calm as you," Luna said coming to his side, wringing water from a thick lock of her hair.

"What did you do?" Onyx asked now curious.

"I screamed the entire way down," she answered honestly.

Onyx turned to look back at the high cliff. "It must be taller than the fortress at Cross."

He looked towards the left and right of the spot he had just jumped from, seeing that it was in fact a split between two rumbling waterfalls. Onyx then turned to face south, looking over the Mortal territory. It looked very similar to the territory of the Spiritborn with forests, rivers and open grasslands. Off in the distance, he even spotted a small town on the banks of a river where farmers were hard at work tending their livestock and fields.

"One would think that they are oblivious to us here with such a set of cliffs guarding the border but I think they know," Luna said, seeing the same town. "They have the Daylord."

Onyx sighed deeply as he remembered the countless number of stories regarding the famous Bane Arlis. The most well-known story of them all was when Bane first appeared to the world in all of his grand, mythological glory. "The battle was sure to be lost but out of the lost ages of the Eastlands arrived Bane Arlis, born of nameless parents with Immortal greatness. Wielding a tremendous power..."

"He won the battle with a pass of his great sword," Luna finished as she turned to look Onyx. "And sealed the Darklands forever."

"That story has been told to me as far back as I can remember," Onyx stated. "Kind of like tradition," he added with a shrug of the shoulders.

Both he and Luna shuddered under a wave of cold water that splashed them. Zipping up out of the pool with majestic grace was the Gryphon named Harper. He landed on the shore and shook out a spray of chilling water. His slate gray feathers rippled from the motion as his wings flapped furiously. Beside the Gryphon rose up Ryder. The way his bastard cousin moved mesmerized Onyx. Every step was powerful and confident. His body was tall and strong with a plethora of tattoos and scars that told a story of many battles won and lost. He and the Gryphon exchanged a nod of approval at the successful jump.

Onyx went to the edge of the sand, seeing another drop further below to the grassland. The wind picked up a bit by the precipice, whipping his hair around lightly. He had never been in such a place before where the land stretched out to the horizon. Even Lavan could not compare. Something about the sight opened his mind even further.

Ryder came to his side and Onyx realized that his cousin was taller than him. He was built more heavily like a hardened soldier. There was an air of youth about him and yet, Onyx could see a wealth of experience in his expression. It was cold and hard. Onyx couldn't help but stare at his cousin's obvious strength and martial prowess. He then heard a soft chuckle and saw that Ryder was watching him.

"So we finally meet," Ryder said turning to look at Onyx. He crossed his thick arms tightly.

"You know about me?" Onyx asked, quickly realizing how stupid his question sounded. He took a step back.

Ryder chuckled softly. He then untangled his arms and extended a hand forward. "Ryder Coba the Silvanus bastard."

Onyx hesitated before reaching out to shake his cousin's hand. "Onyx Silvanus," he said before drawing his hand back. His mind was suddenly overwhelmed with questions. He withdrew into himself and returned his gaze to the land beyond the cliffs.

"Hey Ryder! Long time no see!" Soja boisterously greeted. He planted his fists on his hips.

"Oh goodie. A Rokar," Ryder stated with a roll of his eyes. He crossed his arms again.

"What's wrong with him being a Rokar?" Onyx asked in Soja's defense.

Ryder let out a deep breath. "Long story."

Onyx was grateful that he had the Mortal lands to distract him. He put all of his focus on the small river town. He watched the farmers as they tilled their fields. Even with his Immortal sight, he could not see what crops they were planting. His gaze passed to the river side where a collection of fisherman hauled in their catches. It was such a peaceful sight.

"I wonder if Bane is watching," Onyx stated as he studied the people in the fields.

"Trust me. He knows," Ryder said thoughtfully. "The Spirits of Terra tell him everything he could wish to know of the Northlands."

"The Spirits of Terra?" Luna asked.

"Manifestations of the Spirits of creation and messengers from the Spirit World. Omu the Great Wolf for example was the Spirit of Shadow," Ryder explained as his gaze shifted to the faraway fields. He pointed to the collection of buildings by a bend in the river. "That is Garhune, the closest Mortal town to the cliffs."

"How do you know so much?" Onyx asked. He quickly realized how insensitive his question was.

Ryder frowned. "I may be a bastard but I am an educated one."

The slight was embarrassing and Onyx shrank down in his posture. He then heard Luna scoff.

"Who wouldn't be with Proto Avis as a teacher," came her smart reply. Onyx regained his mirth and straightened out his back. He was starting to like Luna's bold nature.

"I bet Vorin the Dragonlord tells the best stories. I wonder if it is hard to understand him," Soja wondered out loud. He and Onyx looked at each other and shrugged. They both were wondering about the same thing.

"Though I have not personally spoken to him, we of the Gryphons understand Dragonspeak perfectly well," Palas stated as he approached the group from behind. He locked eyes with Ryder. "Master Coba here can understand Dragonspeak."

Onyx, Soja, and Luna jerked their heads around to look at Ryder. All of them waited for him to answer or make a comment about Palas' claim.

"I learned the Dragon tongue from Lord Vorin," Ryder finally said, sounding like he was unwilling to divulge more information about himself.

"Well you learn something new everyday," Soja said slapping Ryder on the back.

In a heartbeat, Ryder grabbed Soja's arm and threw him into the pool. Soja fell with a great big splash. He popped up from under the water with a look of shock on his face. Everyone but Ryder and the Gryphons were surprised at how quickly a Saber was outwitted and out maneuvered. Ryder nodded towards Harper and he quickly mounted the Gryphon's back. With a burst of energy, Harper took off and flew up towards the top of the cliffs.

"I think it's time for another jump," Luna stated before walking towards Pala. She paused and turned to look at Onyx with a teasing smile. "I think someone needs to perfect his jump first."

Onyx smiled back as he ran his fingers through his hair. He was ready to accept her challenge.

A REPORT FROM CROSSROADS

"I say we blast that bird beast for not letting us into the city," Rache said as he played with the coals of the fire place. He picked up coal after coal, letting each one burn his fingertips before setting them back down.

Kaiser sneered. "Stop that before you really hurt yourself," he grumbled, eyes watching the Demon. He shook his head as Rache continued to play with the coals. He then leaned back on the lounge and aimlessly reached out to a silver plated food tray. "At least, I am well provided for," Kaiser stated as he plucked a small cluster of green grapes. He pulled a grape off and popped it into his mouth. "You sure you don't want one?"

"I don't like grapes. Even wine is barely tolerable," Rache said as he briefly looked up from the fire place.

"Suit yourself," Kaiser replied as he proceeded to devour the fruit. "His refusal to allow me into Crossroads is really an insult but then I do not need his permission to enter the city." He chuckled as the last grape disappeared into his mouth.

"Why do you think he denied you entry? Just my opinion but I think he did it out of fear. He is afraid of you and your reputation," Rache asked as he grasped the metal fire poker and pushed around the remnants of an oak log.

Kaiser smirked with a big grin. "He is right to be afraid of me. He can hardly stand on his own feet let alone raise one of his talons to strike me down."

"What if it had been the Dragonlord who denied you entry?"

the Demon wondered aloud. Even he was aware of the massive reptilian beast that was in Crossroads for the celebration.

"It would have been so tiresome to confront him and I have not rested properly in days. But then I would have earned my reprieve if I had had to destroy him. Such a pity since he is the last Dragon," Kaiser replied, acting as if Vorin was no threat.

Rache stood up, brushing his hands together. A cloud of soot wafted down to coat the tips of his boots. "I can always creep into the city and slay the ragged bag of feathers while he sleeps. All I would have to do is waltz in and shout boo!" He went through the motions and laughed heartedly, pressing a hand to his torso to settle himself.

Kaiser shot Rache a doubtful look. "I may want to kill him and certainly he is ready to die at any second but I have not decided when and how," he answered as he fingered the food on the tray. He selected a wedge of yellow cheese and began munching on it. "I do not make rash decisions so far from my home base."

The Demon rolled his eyes as he stepped over to the window and pulled back the curtain. The street outside the inn was bustling with excited energy as people streamed in and out of the city. Farmers shouted to friends with boisterous welcomes and offers to try out a sample of their recent harvest. A small group of young Owl Gryphons trailed behind what looked like an instructor of their race. The older Gryphon was a big gray Owl Gryphon with a large round head and small golden eyes. At the tail end of their group was a Falcon Gryphon with rust colored wings. A pair of Lightborn dressed in cream linen robes jogged up and down the street passing out pamplets.

"Sounds like you are afraid," Rache commented as he let the curtain fall back into place. Suddenly he dropped to the floor, grabbing his head and slamming his eyes shut. He gasped and struggled for breath for several intense seconds before the pressure abated.

"Be careful what you say, Demon," Kaiser warned, pressing a finger to his temple.

Rache looked up at Kaiser through squinted eyes. He snarled, flashing his fangs and curling his lip. The pressure returned with a vengeance but he was able to keep his eyes open to see Kaiser smirking. As soon as Kaiser's finger left his temple, the pressure abated again and Rache was able to stand.

"I am just being realistic. The Gryphon may have the Dragonlord at his back here but that is not the only weapon he has. The Daylord left him with the power to rule in Crossroads. Who's to say that he did not leave some sort of alert system in place should he feel threatened?" Rache shrugged as he threw his arms out to the side.

Kaiser dropped the half eaten cheese wedge on the tray and dabbed his mouth with a napkin. He tossed the napkin over his shoulder, looking at Rache as if he expected him to pick it up. Rache rolled his eyes as he stepped over to grab the napkin from the floor. The Demon then tossed it onto the coals.

"I met the Daylord in my youth. His power lies in his mystery. No one alive is truly aware of what he is capable of. I wonder how a complete stranger has managed to mesmerize the entire Northlands. No one knows who the real Bane Arlis is," Kaiser mused as he looked up at the wood beam ceiling. "Some say he is greater than my ancestor Begin Anu and that is saying a lot."

"Never met the Daylord so I wouldn't know," Rache stated as he sat down in a nearby chair. He leaned back in the seat, mimicking Kaiser's relaxed posture. "What is he like?"

Kaiser scoffed. "He is quite serious and unforgiving. Very astute in his observations," he said, pointing upwards to emphasize his statement. "But very distracted."

The sound of footsteps racing up the distant stairs and pounding down the hallway was soon answered with Morin bursting through the door and into the room. The door slammed shut behind him as he bent over, hands on his knees.

"Yes?" Kaiser asked as he closed his eyes.

Morin took a moment to catch his breath before he stood up straight. "The bastard is definitely in the city." When Kaiser did not immediately answer or acknowledge his statement, he continued. "I saw him heading towards the cliffs after the Arena qualifying rounds."

"Of course he is here. Did he see you?" Kaiser asked as he opened his eyes.

Morin shook his head. "I don't think so."

"Or he did see you and did not think you were worthy enough to acknowledge," Rache snickered. "I certainly don't."

Kaiser waved the Demon off with a gesture of his left hand. "The bastard is a much more fearsome warrior than you are, Commander Win. I do not doubt that he was quite successful in his preparation for the Arena."

Morin frowned like a child ready to have a temper tantrum. He clenched his fists tightly. "I am a fearsome warrior. I bet that I could teach the bastard a lesson or two."

"Yea, about how to lose!" Rache roared with laughter.

Morin stepped forward to launch himself at Rache in anger. "Enough!" came Kaiser's furious shout.

Rache and Morin shuddered from the force of Kaiser's voice. They both quickly jumped to attention as Kaiser slowly pushed himself up from the lounge, his black bedroom robe dropping into place around his tall, lean body. He wore no shirt underneath, exposing his muscled torso. As old as Kaiser was, his body held on tight to a youthful appearance. He latched his hands behind his back and paced back and forth before Rache and Morin. His sharp gaze missed nothing as he pulled at Morin's shoulder pauldron to resettle it over the joint. He patted the steel with a grin.

"Commander Win, are you implying that my grandson is weak?" Kaiser asked, holding the grin on his face. He brought his face close to Morin's and the Commander gulped.

"Not at all, sir. He is truly mighty like you," Morin studdered to say.

Kaiser let a pleasant expression pass over his face as he grasped Morin's chin. He forced the Commander to stare him straight in the eyes. "Let me remind you that you are only where you are because of me. Not because of some perceived talent. Insult me or my blood again and I will skin you alive and set your entrails on fire. Got it?" Morin nodded quickly. Kaiser patted his face before striking him in the stomach, denting his steel armor.

Rache knew better than to laugh at Morin's misfortune for fear of Kaiser doing the same to him. Morin collapsed to the floor and rolled around, holding his stomach in the fetal position. He watched out of the corner of his eyes. He held his head up high, exposing his throat. His breath caught in his chest and refused to move. His heart thumped hard.

"Oh, don't be afraid, my Demon. I have a task for you," Kaiser said like a patronizing parent. He looked down at a groaning Morin. He swiftly kicked him to get him to stop. "For the both of you. Now get up."

Morin was slow to rise, grunting and moaning until he was finally on his feet. He grimaced in pain as his breath came in ragged succession. "I am at your command," he managed to say, his voice weak.

Kaiser nodded once. "Commander Win, I need you to scout out the Arena facilities under the pretense of security for your Shadowlord. I do not intend to sit and watch the matches amongst the dirty, disgusting riff raff." He rolled his eyes, feigning annoyance. He then set his hands on Morin's shoulders. "I am completely counting on you. Don't let me down."

The Commander managed a sheepish nod. "As you wish." He then turned around and was slow to leave. He waddled through the door and disappeared down the hallway.

"He is such an idiot but at least he will do what I say," Kaiser stated as he cocked his head. He then shot Rache a dangerous look. The Demon immediately stiffened. "And now for you."

Rache swallowed hard, worried that Kaiser was going to invoke their unholy bond. "I am at your command, Master."

"I need you to deliver a message to a certain Earthborn royal's son. And I'm hungry. Make yourself useful and get me some roast chicken from the kitchen. Hopefully the wine is decent and doesn't taste like horse piss." He popped his shoulders forward in a subtle roll. "Umbra wine is so much more hearty and robust."

BONFIRE

Onyx knew that his clothing had been laid out with care but he could not help but think of cliff diving and being in a pair of worn pants, preparing for the next jump. He ran his fingers over the rich black velvet dinner jacket with fine silver embroidery. The inside of the jacket was a soft cream silk. He put the jacket back down on the bed and set his hands on his hips. He glanced over at the side table where the finery of his station sat on feather pillows. The silver and moonstones shimmered from a recent polishing.

His father was not well enough to attend the dinner and bonfire so the crown upon his head would be heavy this evening. It was depressing to think of how sick he was. For a long time, he had tried to be hopeful about his father's condition but it was becoming clear that his recovery was slowing down. Part of Onyx knew that Aku was Shadowlord only by name and not by authority. The rest of him still wanted to hold on to the belief that his father would get better. He had to be realistic though and it hurt him to think that way. By the laws of his homeland, he could only become the Shadowlord by Shadowborn command though Onyx wondered if Proto Avis and the city of Crossroads had the authority to name him. He let out a deep breath as he tightened his belt. The leather band molded around his waist in a snug fit.

Onyx first pulled on the dinner jacket, smoothing out the wrinkles on the sleeves with a sweep of his hand. He tugged at the cuffs and secured the cuff links. The jacket was comfortable and not too tight. He turned to look at himself in the mirror. Smiling, he fastened up the front of his jacket and admired himself again. One thing about Shadowborn clothing was that even out of armor, it made the wearer look strong and powerful. Onyx had to admit that he liked what he saw in the mirror. He was becoming something more than a child Prince. He was becoming a man worthy to be the Shadowlord.

It only took a few more minutes before Onyx was fully dressed in his event attire. "Have to put on a face tonight," he mumbled to himself as he straightened his collar and smoothed down his dark hair. He stepped in front of the floor mirror one more time.

"Are you finished admiring yourself? I'm hungry," Soja said as he leaned against the door frame, arms crossed. He was still dressed in his Saber leathers and cloak.

"I was just thinking," Onyx replied, not wanting to appear vain.

"When are you not?" Soja stated with a laugh. He waved Onyx through the doorway and in to the hall. "I know you worry about your father. I do too and it's not just because I am a Saber."

Onyx's shoulders slumped. "Thank you for your support. It is comforting to know that the people care deeply about my father's well being."

Soja laid his hand on Onyx's shoulder. "Don't forget that we care about your well being too. You are the future Shadowlord after all."

"Perhaps the journey here was too much. Maybe it should have just been me," Onyx supposed as they passed by walls covered in selections of artwork. The many paintings depicted scenes from Spiritborn history ranging from terrific battles to portraits of grand leaders and generals.

Soja patted him on the back. "Why not go to him after the bonfire and tell him what you have seen? Surely he would enjoy hearing about the cliff diving."

The memory of the afternoon relaxed him as Onyx thought about the thrill of the jump and Luna. The way she laughed. The sound of her sweet and kind voice packed with sass. Her sparkling eyes...

"Hello in there," Soja said waving a hand in front of Onyx's face. "Do I need to tell you again who is hosting the dinner and bonfire? Or do you plan on figuring it out for yourself?"

"No, go ahead," Onyx replied, embarrassed that he had drifted away from their conversation.

Soja let out an exacerbated sigh. "The Lightborn are hosting the bonfire and the Earthborn, your kin, are hosting the dinner. The Ladies of Flora will be the servers, each assigned to a guest of honor. As the son of the Princess Nuru, you will be seated with the Kano family. But have no fear, I shall be seated with you as well," Soja explained.

Somehow the evening played perfectly into his desires. Luna was an Earthborn.

"Seriously, your Highness. Stop drifting off. You nearly ran into the wall," Soja stated as he pulled Onyx through the doorway. Onyx then realized how close he came to running straight into the doorframe.

He was led to the city square where tables and chairs had been set up for the Earthborn hosted dinner. The lamps had been lit as colorful streamers were tied between them. Laughter and conversation were heavy in the air. Soja weaved his way through the crowd to a long table where Lord Palani and his family were already seated. Flynn immediately jumped up.

"Good. You are here," his cousin said jovially as he pointed to the empty seat next to him.

Onyx sat down and slid himself forward. Soja moved to stand behind him, speaking to a Shadowborn attendant. The attendant quickly wrote the message down and darted away.

"I don't think we have ever had such a celebration at home," Onyx commented as he looked about.

"Nothing compares to Crossroads and how they party. Imagine if the Daylord were actually here. The celebration would never stop!" Flynn said with a happy shout. "You should come to a Harvest Festival at Cascade. Now that is a party!"

"Harvest Festival? I guess that would be pretty self explanatory," Onyx wondered.

Flynn nodded. "It happens in the fall when the wheat fields before Cascade are harvested. The air smells of fresh bread and sweet buns for days and then there is the Harvest Festival Ball. It is strictly an Earthborn celebration but you are half so maybe you can come to the next one."

"Planning for the next Harvest Festival begins when the previous one ends. My council has already discussed the collection of funds for the event. Formal invitations will go out after the first of the year. It would be wonderful to have my dear sister's son attend," Palani said leaning over from his seat.

"Why is it just for Earthborn?" Onyx asked looking in his uncle's direction.

Palani cleared his throat. "Each of the world's cultures have their own native traditions. For example, the Shadowborn have their Winter Solstice Ball. I don't think I need to tell you about that grand event." Onyx shook his head. "Consider the Harvest Festival as its equivalent in importance for the Earthborn. We celebrate what we hold most dear."

"Like the Winter Solstice Ball, it is where daughters and sons are formally presented into society once they have come of age," his aunt stated with a warm smile. She then made eyes at Palani and gave his right hand a squeeze. "It is how I first met your father, Flynn."

Flynn rolled his eyes and slid down in his seat. He quickly sat up when Palani nudged his foot hard. He sheepishly shrugged as if to apologize. Palani glared at him and gestured towards the bonfire to remind him that as host, they had to look and act their best. Flynn's mother softly chuckled, no where near as serious as her husband.

A pair of haughty looking Earthborn stepped into view of all of the diners, wearing crowns of ivy on their heads. The man bowed as the woman curtsied to each other before they turned towards the crowd with arms wide open. They repeated the greeting several times before standing up straight.

"As the sun sets upon the first day," the woman began, her voice surprisingly lyrical and light to hear.

"So we have come to say," the man continued, his voice just as light as his partner.

"By the grace of our Lord," the woman said as she turned towards Palani and curtsied.

"And by the hands of his court," the man followed. He smiled as he bowed towards Palani.

"A fine dinner and show," the woman said without skipping a beat.

"So sit back, relax, and Ladies of Flora. Let's go!" the man declared, the woman joining him at the very end.

Everyone applauded as the servers began to fan out with cups, decanters of wine, and pitchers of various drinks. Onyx could smell the overwhelming scent of wine but instead of the heavy kind he was used to, the variety of wine offered smelled of flowers and fruit. Laughter and conversation soon filled the air as toasts rang out with the sound of cups knocking against each other. Onyx watched as the servers ran about the circle, never coming near the royal table. He immediately thought that was odd.

Soon the Ladies of Flora arrived on the scene. He watched as they began darting about with drink pitchers in hand. They wore crowns of white flowers and green leaves. Their gowns were a flowing pastel green that stopped at their knees. They sang songs and danced around, not spilling a single drop. His heart leaped into his chest when he saw Luna. She hopped and spun, holding tightly to the metal pitcher in her hands, with a big smile on her face.

"Good evening, your Highness," Luna said politely as she poured a clear yellow liquid into his cup. She curtsied once she finished. "As a Lady of Flora, I am honored to serve you tonight."

Onyx smiled dumbly, entranced as she smiled back. Her perfume was a pleasant floral scent and her light brown hair floated in waves at her shoulders. He watched as she danced away, spinning into a lively formation with two other ladies. There was something about her that held on tightly to him.

"Your Highness?" Soja asked, shaking his shoulder.

Onyx snapped out of his trance. "I'm... I'll... I'm ok," he replied in a stutter. He reached for his cup and drank deeply.

Luna returned with a tray of golden crusted bread and a pat of butter. She deftly balanced it in her hands as she skipped about on light feet with a song on her tongue. Onyx smiled again as her sweet voice reached him. He watched as she sashayed up to another Lady and they both joined their voices together before erupting in a fit of giggles.

"Fresh from the ovens," Luna said, still laughing as she set the bread and butter down.

"Your song is so lovely. What is it about?" Onyx asked, wanting to keep her near him.

"It is a silly tune about a rabbit and a fox that play tricks on each other," she replied with a demure curtsy, eyelashes fluttering. She looked back up and smiled before taking the tray and once again dancing away.

He had never felt so light and happy in his life as he watched Luna dance and sing, carrying her tray and spinning around. Her laugh was pure and filled Onyx with a sense of joy. He wanted so much to join her.

"Your Highness, are you feeling ill? You have barely touched your food," Soja pointed out.

Onyx sighed deeply as he leaned back in his seat. "I've never felt better," he replied before reaching for his fork.

With the other Ladies of Flora, Luna danced away to retrieve the next course. Her balance amazed Onyx as not a drop of food fell despite the rigorous dance moves. She spun around and stopped in front of Onyx, curtsying before she set the new plate down before him.

"Roasted root vegetables and potatoes in a dill butter sauce with a hint of sea salt and ground black pepper," Luna described as she held her tray against her.

As she danced away, Onyx took a bite and immediately loved the course. It had an earthy and rustic flavor that reminded him of home but it was not as heavy as anything the Shadowborn normally prepared. He devoured it quickly and dabbed his mouth with a napkin.

His heart leaped when Luna reappeared with the next course. She came into view, arm in arm, with another Lady of Flora, singing a light hearted song about flowers trying to hide from the sun. The two girls partially acted out the song. Luna's companion knelt down, raising her tray over her head while Luna danced on the tips of her toes. Her companion then burst up, deftly balancing her tray, and the two girls spun around each other to arrive at the royal table.

"Spice rubbed pork with an apple berry glaze," Luna told Onyx as she switched out the plates. She curtsied with a playful smile on her face.

"Thank you. Everything is delicious," Onyx said before he started eating.

Luna giggled. "Just wait until dessert. You have not had sweets until you have tried what I am going to bring you next. If you will excuse me." Onyx smiled as she danced away.

"No one does sweet like the Earthborn. I hope the dessert has chocolate in it!" Soja said as he tore into the pork.

"Chocolate? What is chocolate?" Onyx asked, perplexed enough to set his fork down.

It was Flynn who answered. "It comes from the eastern region of the Earthborn homeland. The palace cook told me once how it is made. Take the cacoa beans, mash them up, boil them down, cool, and repeat. You do that enough and the impurities are removed and you are left with a sweet earthy liquid. Mix with a few other ingredients and poof! Chocolate!"

Much to Soja's delight, the Ladies of Flora came back with the rest of the serving team carrying a chocolate dessert. Onyx was surprised that it was a cold dessert as he expected it to be warm.

"I am have been dying to try ice cream! And with strawberries? You Earthborn know how to cook and make some delicious food!" Soja squealed as he dove in to the dessert.

Once he had taken a bite, Onyx understood Soja's enthusiasm. They both looked at each other as they scraped out their bowls. Dropping the spoons, they sat back with hands on their stomachs. Although he started the meal with his nerves at the forefront, Onyx now felt relaxed and at ease. He watched as the Ladies of Flora assembled for a final song and dance in front of everyone. Unlike their previous songs, they sang a more somber one with flowing dance moves to accompany their voices. It was a beautiful and captivating display that had Onyx entranced. He sat on the edge of his seat watching with delight.

Once all of the courses had been served and the performance had finished, Luna and the rest of the Ladies of Flora danced their way back to their charges. She stood with her back to Onyx, hands at her side. She briefly looked over her shoulder.

"Now the Lightborn and Vorin the Dragonlord will light the bonfire. Then we shall dance the night away!" she giggled.

Onyx had forgotten how poor of a dancer he was when he realized that he would be dancing with her. She was such a fabulous and captivating dancer that he could never hope to compare. It then crossed his mind that the moves in his sword work, while more aggressive and sharp, could double as dance moves. He hoped that would be enough to impress her.

Soja grabbed his Prince's shoulder and shook him. "I don't think we Shadowborn could ever capture that kind of beauty."

"Every Earthborn is taught some form of dance. Much like every Shadowborn is taught some form of combat," Palani stated as a servant refilled his wine glass. He raised his glass in thanks and the servant bowed before stepping away.

Flynn's mother then shushed her husband and directed the table's attention towards the center of the square. A double line of hooded Lightborn in golden robes slowly streamed towards the large pile of wood. They walked with their hands pressed together and their heads bowed in a solumn expression. The two lines split apart to surround the wood pile in a circle. The Lightborn then stimultaneously spun around on their feet to face the crowd.

Heavy wing beats brought everyone's attention skyward as a dark red scaled Dragon hovered over the square. The Dragon's serpentine neck arched back as a loud rumble built up in its chest. Suddenly, a red flame erupted from its jaws, lighting the bonfire. The Dragon roared before lifting up back into the night sky. Cheers and shouts of joy filled the air as Onyx stood up to applaud with everyone else. Soon people jumped out of their seats to dance, leaping over the tables to reach the square as a lively drum beat began playing.

"Shall we?" Onyx asked with no hint of nerves as he came around to the front of his table. He extended his hand towards Luna.

The surprise was clear on her face but she quickly recovered. "I am honored," Luna replied as she laid her soft hand in his.

Soja watched from his position on the side of the circle, completely understanding the exchange. "Well, well, my Prince. And here I thought that you did not like girls," he chuckled, clapping his hands with the beat of the music.

WRITTEN IN BLOOD

"Seriously, Father? A lesson this late at night?" Flynn groaned as he followed after Palani, arms drooping and his back bent.

"Straighten up. Your posture is horrendous," Palani said sternly as he slowed his pace to correct his son. "As the future Lord of the Earthborn, there is always opportunity to learn something new. The art of statecraft is an ever evolving skill that a future leader must have."

"But I'm tired," Flynn argued.

Palani suddenly stopped and whirled around to face Flynn. "Flynn, I don't do this to make you miserable. I only want to make sure that you are prepared for the role ahead."

Flynn sighed deeply as he looked into his father's eyes, seeing the pain of loss. He frequently saw that expression whenever he whined about his lessons. It always made him feel awful for complaining. The loss of his older brother and sister obviously still weighed heavily on his father's mind. "I'm sorry."

Palani set his hands on Flynn's shoulders. "I just want you to be ready to face anything when I am not there to help you. You are my only child left and I don't want to lose you too."

They both let out deep breaths. Palani then gestured towards the right hand bend of the hallway. They left the top of the grand foyer staircase, passing a servant who was putting out flaming lanterns. The servant paused in his work and dropped to one knee to show respect. Palani and Flynn bowed their heads to acknowledge the servant.

The study was the last door on the right, labeled with a metal plate. Flynn took one last look down at the foyer floor seeing a brown Wood Owl Gryphon preening its left wing feathers. His father went on inside the study, leaving the door open behind him. Flynn continued to watch the Gryphon bend itself around to tend to each feather. It amazed him how limber the big creature was. He stifled a snicker as the Gryphon leaned too far over and tumbled onto its side. He turned away from the railing and followed after his father.

Upon entering the study, Flynn saw his father standing with his back to him. He halted when he saw his father's shoulders shaking. He ignored everything else and focused all of his senses on him.

"What is it, Father?" Flynn asked in hesitation.

He heard the distinctive sound of paper being crumbled. Flynn watched as his father bent his head and held a piece of paper to his brow. Palani closed his eyes and seemed to be fighting back tears. Coupled with their earlier conversation, Flynn knew immediately that something terrible was written on the paper for nothing else could upset his father.

"Father, speak to me," Flynn begged as Palani remained tight and unmoving.

After a painfully long wait, Palani finally unclenched and handed his son the paper. Flynn uncrumpled it and smoothed it out before reading. "You are being watched from every shadow where true darkness lurks. Silence is your salvation," Flynn read aloud. He quickly looked up at his father with a confused expression that was laced with worry.

"Finish it," Palani ordered without emotion.

Flynn gulped before returning his attention to the paper. "Death awaits those that break their promise. No mercy. No hope. Only the world that which no one can return from."

An otherworldly chill permeated the air in the study. The glass on the windows and balcony doors frosted. Even the bright colors of the wall paintings dimmed. Flynn looked around, his ragged breath turning to a cold mist. He looked back down at the paper and was surprised to find that the ink was a vibrant red. The sight immediately horrified him. Before he could toss the note away, Palani grabbed it from him.

"This was written in the blood of a Waterborn. Their Spirit is trying to warn us," Palani stated as he looked towards the frosted glass.

"Warn us of what?" Flynn dared to ask as he drew close to his father.

Palani folded the paper and held it tightly in his right hand. "Something terrible is coming. I can feel it but I do not have the skill to interpret the signs. Flynn, summon the Gryphon Togra." When Flynn hesitated, Palani gestured towards the study door. "The Gryphon you saw in the foyer. I need to get a message to Proto Avis."

"Yes, Father," Flynn stated as he bowed his head.

He rushed outside and slammed against the railing, nearly toppling over it from the force. He struggled to remember how to address the Gryphon. "Master Gryphon of the Night, Lord Palani of the Earthborn wishes to see you at once!"

The Gryphon immediately looked up and bowed its head. With three wing flaps, the beast was air borne and twisted up towards the second floor. With a skill only acquired through much practice, the Gryphon slipped between the railing and the low ceiling to land beside Flynn.

"Lead me to him," the unmistakably male Gryphon said with a deep voice. A soft whistling hoot followed and Flynn understood it to be an indication that the Gryphon would keep his secrets.

Flynn led the Gryphon into the study where his father was waiting. The Owl Gryphon quickly eased himself into a respectful bow. Palani gestured for him to rise.

"Are you strong and true, Togra?" Palani asked sternly.

"I am strong and true, good Lord," Togra replied bowing his head and stilling his leonine tail.

Flynn watched as his father hastily wrote something on the same ominous note. He rolled it up and held it out towards Togra. The Gryphon looked at it with careful eyes. "A Spirit has touched this parchment. I know that you can sense it. I need this to be given directly to Lord Proto Avis and no other. Tell him and any who doubt your mission this: The Earth speaks the Truth."

"Yes, good Lord," Togra said before taking the note in his beak. He dipped back down into a bow before turning around and leaving the study.

"What did you write to Lord Avis?" Flynn asked, still staring at the door Togra just passed through.

"I will not say," Palani said after a long moment of silence. "It is better that you not know until I am sure of your safety. For now, we will both continue as if this note never came to us and we never saw its words."

THE CROSSROADS ARENA

"Welcome one and all to the Crossroads Arena where fighters and would be champions will battle it out for supremacy and the title! A title that will stand for one hundred years! Do you hear me, people of Crossroads? One hundred years!"

The mixed crowd of Spiritborn and Gryphons cheered and shouted with delight at the announcer's introduction. Gryphons of all shape and sizes flared their wings and threw back their heads to cry out with fervor. Gryphon chicks squeaked alongside their parents as they tapped their small feet.

Onyx and Soja made their way to their seats in the royal box, greeting the other spectators. The Shadowborn Prince was dressed in black pants with leather boots freshly shined and a light silver long sleeved tunic. His dark shoulder length hair was tied back in a small ponytail. As always, Soja was in his Saber uniform with his head uncovered and a big smile on his face.

"How did you ever become a Saber? I thought you were supposed to be a hidden guard," Onyx asked as they found their seats and sat down. He turned around to wave at his golden haired cousin Flynn. His heart jumped with unexpected joy upon seeing Luna seated dutifully nearby. She bowed her head in response.

"All part of my act, your Highness," Soja replied. "You see, people assume I won't be worth a challenge so that when they finally raise their sword, BAM! They won't know what hit them." He pounded his fists together.

Onyx shook his head, laughing. He turned around toward

his cousin, seeing his uncle and aunt. He bowed his head in respect.

"How is your father, nephew?" Palani asked in an inquiring voice. "I do not see him here."

"It was thought best for him to remain in his quarters to rest. The journey from Cross was hard on him and the Arena would have stressed him too much. I am here in his place," Onyx replied solemnly. His head dropped. He gathered his resolve. "But I did promise to regale him with stories of the fights. I know he will appreciate that."

Palani smiled and nodded as his wife took his hand. He briefly looked at her and whispered a sweet nothing. Flynn rolled his eyes and leaned forward to whisper in Onyx's ear. "I think I am going to be sick. These matches better start soon."

"Who do you think will win? My bet is on Ryder Coba. I hear Vorin the Dragonlord is cheering for him," Soja stated with a degree of absolute certainty.

"No way a rookie will beat an Earthborn veteran. And Eru is no slouch either. He is the defending champion," Flynn declared. He sat back with his arms crossed. "I'll take that bet."

Palani smacked his son across the back of the head. "You are a royal Prince of the Earthborn. You do not gamble," he admonished as Flynn rubbed his head.

The announcer continued by introducing each of the Arena finalists with a booming voice. Vendors scaled the rows of seats, hawking snacks, drinks, and pennants representing the fighters. A thin Airborn man worked with a team of Kestral Gryphons to pass out programs among the crowd. Banners flapped in the soft breeze. The mood in the air was full of excitement and anticipation. The announcer held up his hands to gather everyone's attention to him.

"Please welcome to the Crossroads Arena the defending champion and my kinsman, Eru the Wind Rider!" the announcer cried out at the top of his lungs.

Everyone rose to their feet clapping and shouting Eru's name. Gryphons beat their wings and screeched loudly. Pennants were waved back and forth. The lean Airborn champion waved to the crowd with his sinewy arms, basking in their praise. In a gesture of goodwill and sportsmanship, he turned around and shook his opponent's hand. His opponent was a tall, burly Earthborn with a bushy brown beard and thick shoulder length hair. On his left shoulder was a green inked tattoo of a stag.

"That is Oaken, the Captain of the palace guards," Flynn pointed out. "Too bad your Saber Commander did not come to Crossroads. He had a long standing challenge from the last ceremony for a rematch."

"I remember now. Commander Parahazur said he had 'thumped' your captain in the Arena qualifiers," Soja teased in a playful voice. "Maybe Ryder can act in his place and 'thump' Captain Oaken for him."

"Eru is a masterful fighter and the pride of Lord Aves' soldiers. His speed and agility will be hard to match but I have faith," Palani said proudly. He sat up straight. "Watch carefully, son. Captain Oaken will want a report from you when this is all over." Flynn let out an exacerbated sigh. "Training never stops for a future Lord of the Earthborn."

Onyx laughed as he understood his cousin's reaction. His mind drifted to his many lessons with his old teacher Kader Erebus where he was constantly reminded of his future. He looked up briefly to see Luna and another Lady of Flora speaking to his aunt. His aunt smiled and nodded, gesturing towards a pair of empty seats behind him. The two girls made their way to the seats and sat down, giggling at a private joke. He smiled as he turned himself around to visit with them.

"This isn't cliff diving but it is just as exciting," Luna commented with a teasing smile. She wore a plain forest green dress with a sewn in pink flower at her shoulder. Her brown hair was braided and decorated with green ribbons. "Are you cheering for your cousin? He is the only Shadowborn competing in the finals," she asked Onyx directly.

Onyx shrugged. "He's not exactly fighting as a true Shadowborn representing his nation. The announcer said he was Ryder Coba of Crossroads, not Cross."

"He's from Umbra, your Highness," Soja corrected.

"Really? I always thought he was from Cross," Onyx exclaimed with surprise.

Soja leaned in closer. "My father said he was born in Umbra where his mother was from. Despite being the bastard son of the reigning Shadowlord, he was not raised in Cross."

"Ssh! The match is starting!" Flynn quickly said, directing their attention to the Arena floor.

Dressed in a tan leather cuirass with matching bracers and boots, Eru looked calm and regal, the rest of his clothing a glittering white. His black tipped short white hair hinted at his extensive past as a soldier in the royal army. He held a long, thin sword in his right hand, the tip dragging against the dusty ground. His steps were careful and calculating. His left arm hung at his side, loose and ready. Oaken paced, carrying his heavy claymore tightly in his hands, forty feet away.

"On my mark!" the announcer cried out as he held his right

arm high in the air. The entire crowd silenced in fevered anticipation. Eru and Oaken stopped and faced each other with hard expressions on their faces. "Fight!" the announcer shouted, throwing his right arm down.

As soon as the signal had been given, Eru exploded into action. He jumped up in a twisting leap, turning his body around in a full circle. He kicked his legs around to gain an even stronger momentum as he swung his sword arm in a wide circle. He kept his left arm against his body at a tight angle. His body spun around, nearly parallel to the ground. Once his back was to Oaken, Eru swung his left arm out to slide down the sword blade. As he landed on his feet, he unleashed a blast of wind directly at Oaken.

The Wind Blast kicked up a cloud of dust that sped for the Earthborn. Oaken planted his feet, a snarl on his lips as he brought his two handed sword around in front of him. Eru's attack slammed into him full force just as he stabbed his sword into the ground. It tore at his hair and flung dust into his eyes. He grunted as the wind pushed him backwards. He tightened the grip on his sword as he dropped his head.

Eru was not one to sit still as he spun again and again, throwing more Wind Blasts at his opponent. With each successive spin, he edged closer. He cried out with a ferocious shout as he spun twice in a row, using a single foot to keep his balance, and charged up his power again. On the final revolution, the blast was thrown forward, kicking up a dust cloud that reached high into the sky.

Oaken, though rendered immobile by Eru's constant attacks, had not been idle. His own Spirit energy, guided by his sword, sped out from him through the ground. A plan had been formulating in his mind to disrupt the Airborn's Wind Blasts and enable him to go on the offensive. He roared as he ripped his claymore free and the ground shuddered violently.

"It's a masterful Earth Shift by Oaken to counteract the Wind Blast of Eru!" the announcer shouted as ten rock solid pillars rose up from the Arena floor with a thunderous sound.

The entire Arena shook but Flynn shouted with joy. "Go Captain Oaken! Show him how a real Earthborn fights!" he cried out at the top of his lungs. He leaned over Onyx's seat. "See that? See that? I'd like to see a Shadowborn do something that powerful!"

Onyx laughed at his cousin who furiously pointed towards the pillars. He had to help Flynn back to his seat when he fell forward. His cousin chuckled loudly while his parents shook their heads, smiling. Onyx was so used to seeing combat and contests of strength and power but he decided Flynn had never seen such an event. He figured that the Earthborn primarily focused on archery contests and tree climbing.

Luna's pure laugh and rigorous applause turned Onyx's attention to her. Her fellow Lady of Flora nudged her and subtlely pointed at the Shadowborn Prince. Luna smiled. "Have you ever seen what an Earthborn can do?"

"Nothing like this. I almost wish Commander Parahazur was here to see this," Onyx commented, resting his arm on the back of the seat.

"You are half Earthborn. With the proper training, you could perform an Earth Shift yourself someday," Luna stated, gesturing her head back towards the Arena.

It was a fact that Onyx forgot often. Though he identified himself as a Shadowborn, he was in fact only half blooded. Onyx thought of his uncle Palani's words about carefully watching the match to his cousin. He turned back around to focus on Eru and Oaken.

The dust cloud had settled, revealing ten rough cut stone pillars that Oaken had brought forth. He was hidden amongst them while Eru stood outside. The applause of the crowd had quieted as well as everyone waited eagerly for the next move. Eru scrutinized the change to the playing field for a brief moment before charging head first into the stone maze. He entered with such speed that he carried a burst of air at his back. The nimble Airborn leaped and pushed off of the pillars to gain height.

Oaken tracked Eru's movement through his sensitive connection to the earth. As soon as he saw his opportunity, he took it. Just as Eru made to land on a pillar to his left, Oaken swung his sword with all his might. The heavy blade cut through the stone with a resounding crack, the steel throwing off sparks. Eru's foot hit the unstable pillar and he was quickly thrown off balance. He tumbled towards the right, spotting a smirking Oaken on the ground below.

For the first time since the fight began, the two warriors met in close combat. It was Eru's speed and agility against Oaken's sturdy strength. The Airborn darted and jumped about on light feet, using his environment to avoid Oaken's heavy handed strikes. They battled each other, Eru bouncing around the remaining nine pillars, with a strange dance intent on besting the other. Oaken cut down another pillar as Eru threw yet another Wind Blast. The collapsing stone fell into the line of fire and dispersed the attack.

Instead of being dismayed, Eru leaped higher to the top of a neighboring pillar. He remained still for just a moment before he pushed off with his powerful legs. The Airborn shot high into the air. Oaken took the opportunity to follow, pushing off the collapsing pillar. He dragged his sword behind him.

"Can it be? Will Eru unleash his powerful... YES! YES! He is winding up the mighty Wind Storm! Hold on to your hats, folks! This is going to be a doozy!" the announcer shouted with delight.

Eru had soared high into the air before he finally twisted himself around in a more exaggerated form of his Wind Blast. Only this time, he was rapidly spinning his sword as he spun. With a powerful shout, he threw the rapidly spinning sword at Oaken. The spinning blade pulled down the clouds as it descended, forming a funnel cloud. Eru fell with the funnel cloud like a diving falcon. He reached out to grab the sword hilt and spun his body to bring the full force of Wind Storm down on Oaken. Without his connection to the ground, Oaken was at the mercy of the powerful Airborn attack. It slammed into the Earthborn head on and threw him on a collision course for the ground.

The crowd cringed as Oaken hit one of his risen pillars back first, crashing through the stone. Many covered their eyes but Onyx remained completely focused and excited. He gripped the edge of the box wall in eager anticipation as Eru landed on the top of a pillar. Oaken crashed into a pile of stone, throwing up a cloud of dust.

"Now remember folks. If Oaken can not rise, Eru will be declared the winner. The Earthborn captain is a hardy soul but Eru's Wind Storm hit him dead on. We wait for word from the Arena floor officials," the announcer explained from his call box.

A team comprising of a Waterborn and two Earthborn rushed out to the pile of stone. The Earthborn quickly began pulling stone pieces away to uncover Oaken. When enough rubble had been cleared, the Waterborn went to Oaken's side and checked him. Eru leaped down to the pile of stone to help. The Waterborn whispered a few words to the Earthborn pair who then promptly signaled that Oaken was unable to continue.

"Eru the defending champion has bested Captain Oaken of the Earthborn!" the announcer shouted.

The crowd erupted in cheers as Eru helped the Waterborn get Oaken to his feet. He shook his head as if he was dazed and unsteady. The two competitors exchanged kind words of praise for the other's skill.

"Now, Flynn. Why did Captain Oaken lose the fight?" Palani promptly asked his son.

Onyx had already figured out the reason but watched as his cousin squirmed, trying to decide on an answer. He stifled a laugh as Flynn's face contorted with frustration. His uncle then looked at him and nodded for him to answer. "By going into the air, Captain

Oaken lost his connection to the ground and his stability to defend himself against Eru's attack."

"Correct, nephew," Palani stated with a small smile. "You better not have helped him, Miss Luna."

Luna shook her head. "No, my Lord," she replied with a respectful smile.

Conversation about the upcoming matches soon dominated the audience in the royal box. It became clear that Ryder was the youngest participant and even Palani expressed doubt about his experience. Only Soja defended Ryder, being careful not to mention his royal blood as a reason for his strength. The royal box was fairly evenly divided on whether Alton the Waterborn Prince or Ryder the Shadowborn bastard would win by the time the Arena floor was cleared.

Once the last of the floor workers disappeared down a tunnel, the announcer stepped up to the front of the call box. He put his hands in the air, bringing the crowd to silence. His volumous sleeves swung in the breeze.

"And now, the second match in the Crossroads Arena! I give you for your fighting pleasure, Alton, Crowned Prince of the Waterborn!"

As expected, the gathered Waterborn cheered the loudest for their Prince. They waved blue pennants vigorously in the air. Onyx looked to his right, seeing the rest of the Waterborn royals seated nearby. They paid him no heed as they shouted Alton's name. He looked back to the Arena floor, seeing the tall Prince. Alton had long limbs that were covered in glistening armor to match the steel plate cuirass on his torso. Like the rest of his family, he had ice blue eyes and hair the color of the deep ocean with streaks of white. Onyx thought the look to be mysterious, enough to challenge the dark looks of the Shadowborn. He sported a long spear in his right hand that was as long as the Waterborn was tall.

"Fighting his Highness is..." the announcer declared before furiously beating the front wall of his call box like a drum player. "The Shadowborn Ryder Coba!"

The crowd's reaction was fairly mixed. Many cheered but others held back, wary of disrespecting the royal opponent. Soja jumped to his feet, shouting Ryder's name. Onyx dragged him back to his seat in a swift motion and gave him a stern look. They both shuddered when Vorin unleashed a mighty roar. The Shadowborn Prince looked up to the left side of the Arena where Vorin perched his enormous bulk. The ring of Gryphons along the top of the Arena complex were all on their feet, cheering for Ryder with high pitched whistles and cries. Even Proto Avis who was perched next to Vorin the Dragonlord's right side was on his feet. It was very clear who they were cheering for in the match.

Ryder walked out onto the Arena floor, a broadsword strapped to his back. His wavy black hair was loosely tied back with a small leather band. With his stubbled jaw and weather beaten leather cuirass, he looked dirty in comparison to the more heavily armored Alton. He wore a sleeveless tunic under his cuirass, revealing his brawny arms. Like Eru, the only other armor he wore was a pair of bracers, studded at the knuckles, and boots.

The crowd quickly hushed once the announcer put up his hands. As he waited for a small group of Hawk Gryphons to quiet, Alton spun his spear around in wide arches. His ice blue eyes bore into Ryder with simmering anger.

"I will enjoy defeating you, bastard. Consider it a kinder act than dragging you off to the ocean cells of Lough for what your father did to my people," Alton growled as he pointed his spear at Ryder who stood only twenty feet away. It cast a long shadow.

Ryder spat on the ground much to Alton's shock and disgust. "Suit yourself."

Alton roared with fury just as the announcer called out the start of the fight. He spun around, gritting his teeth as he swung his spear. Once Alton made the full revolution, he jabbed his spear forward. His breath caught in his throat as he discovered that Ryder had disappeared. Before he could even think to panic, Ryder appeared in a leaping spin behind him. He swung his leg around, kicking Alton hard in the head. The force of Ryder's strike sent Alton flying into the far wall.

Everyone was stunned into absolute silence as Alton crashed and fell in a broken heap. The same team that had assisted Oaken rushed to his side as Ryder landed right where Alton had just been standing. The Waterborn dropped down to his knees and took Alton's head in his hands. He breathed a very visible sigh of relief but he did shake his head to his two Earthborn companions. It was a clear signal that the Waterborn Prince was unable to continue.

Onyx, along with the rest of the spectators in the royal box, was completely shocked at how quickly the match ended. Even Soja's jaw dropped open, for once being rendered completely silent. The Waterborn quickly exited the royal box to go to Alton's side.

"Did that just happen?" Onyx managed to ask.

Soja slowly nodded. "He took him out with one blow. I mean I knew he was strong but that? I don't even know what that was."

"I have never seen a Shadowborn like him before. Perhaps," Onyx heard his uncle Palani utter before falling silent. He then felt

Luna's small hand on his shoulder.

"To think that he is your cousin. Guess I know who I am cheering for now," she admitted before she sat back.

*****

Proto folded his wings as he settled back down beside the massive Vorin. A smile played at the corners of his beak. He looked down at Ryder with bright eyes.

"The Silvanus bastard is stronger than I thought. Call me crazy but in that single act, I saw a man that could surpass Shadow Night and the Daylord," Vorin's deep voice rumbled. He arched his long neck. "That man right there is the true Shadowlord."

"Even if Ryder cannot see it yet, he is the heir of his forefather or I am a chicken," Proto said with a degree of playful pride.

"And I am a tiny lizard," Vorin replied. "I bet that even Kaiser Adonis would fear him.

Proto's eyes zeroed in on the tunnel Ryder had exited. He felt a glimmer of darkness as Ryder passed out of sight. "He better learn to fear Ryder Coba before the day is done."

THE SHADOWBORN WARRIOR

Ryder stood in the entryway of the Arena's North End, leaning against the frame of the tunnel opening. He picked and pulled at the ties of his leather bracers. His brow was furrowed in concentration as he thought about different combat strategies. He knew that he was fighting Eru the Airborn soldier based on the announcer's boisterous shout at the end of the previous match. The crowd now was shouting his and Eru's name at the top of their lungs in fevered anticipation. Ryder had to admit that he enjoyed hearing his name. When he had entered the Arena for his first match against Alton in the quarter finals, no one was calling his name. By his semi final match, people were eagerly anticipating what he would do. Now the final match was about to begin. The energy was high.

In his quarter final match, Ryder had stunned the crowd by knocking out his opponent in a single hit. He chuckled as he thought about the look of shock on Alton's face when the Waterborn Prince had realized he had disappeared into Shadow Slide. Ryder had not planned on using Shadow Slide to start the match but when the opportunity to do so presented itself, he took it. He could have easily killed Alton had his kick struck the Prince an inch higher but such an act would have not won him any points with the audience.

His semi final match against a Lightborn was a bit more of a challenge though not in the manner that the crowd anticipated. Ryder purposely did not use any Spirit energy and overwhelmed his opponent with his greater strength and experience. He laughed when he thought about how frustrated the Lightborn was when his Spirit attack powers had no effect on him. Ryder knew going into the match that a Lightborn would try to blind him at the first possible moment. He knew exactly how the Lightborn would move and generate the necessary energy. Ryder spun underneath the Lightborn's attack and struck him in the chest with the pommel of his broadsword. The Lightborn stumbled back, gasping for breath until Ryder swept his feet out from under him. In two moves, Ryder had defeated his semi final opponent.

The coming match against Eru would be different for Ryder intended to put on a show. He had fought enough Airborn soldiers in his time to learn how they moved and reacted to different situations. He had even tricked an Airborn combat master to teach him all of their Spirit techniques. The combat master had huffed and puffed about teaching a Shadowborn something he said could never be learned by anyone but an Airborn. Ryder proved him wrong in their first session. It was the same reaction he got from every combat master. How could a pure blooded Shadowborn learn and master non-native Spirit powers?

"Because I am different," Ryder said to himself in the entryway. In reality, it was the truth. He was different but he would never tell anyone why.

"I suppose I should be proud that you have made it this far," Kaiser stated as he leaned against the wall further down the tunnel.

"What do you want?" Ryder asked as he bent down to stretch his back. He set his palms on the ground before pushing himself back up to his full height.

"Like everyone else in that stadium, I want to see the real Ryder Coba fight. I want to see what a son of my bloodline is made of against such a noble champion," Kaiser mused.

Though his tone spoke of honest support, Ryder knew better. "I do not need your respect and hollow words of adoration to know that I am going to win," Ryder said flatly as he rolled his shoulders and shook his arms to loosen the muscles.

Kaiser slowly stepped over to Ryder, hands latched behind his back. "You should be thanking me for your great skill. As I am sure you remember, I did provide for all of that excellent training in your formative years. So can a grandfather wish his grandson good luck?" he asked as he stopped to stand before Ryder.

Ryder sneered though he was glad that he was a few inches taller and much stockier than Kaiser. He scoffed. "That depends. Do you actually care what happens to me out there? When I win, are you going to run out there and embrace me like you actually give a damn about my well being and success?"

"Doesn't sound like something I would do," Kaiser said after some thought. He looked Ryder up and down before reaching out to pat his arm. "To think, you could have been Shadowlord. You still could be if you come back to Cross."

Ryder jerked his arm away and glared at Kaiser. "Touch me again and you will lose that hand."

Kaiser grinned as he bunched up his shoulders. "I always love our little chats."

With an absent wave of the hand, Ryder brushed Kaiser off before returning his attention towards the Arena floor. A team of Earthborn were quickly sweeping and cleaning up the debris from the previous fight. From the South End of the Arena, Ryder could see Eru with a pair of foot soldiers who were helping him with his armor and weapons. Every once in a while, one foot soldier would step back to check out their progress before going back to helping Eru prepare. He supposed that the defending champion was given the honor of aides before a match. Ryder scoffed at the thought. A true warrior like him prepares alone. He locked eyes with Eru as soon as the aides stepped away. They both nodded.

"Ladies and gentlemen! Gryphons and Dragon! Here it is! The final match of the Crossroads Arena!" the announcer cried out, raising his hands up high in the air. The crowd roared with delight as they knew that the final match was coming. "Without further ado, I give you the defending champion of the Arena Eru!"

Eru walked out with his hands in the air, turning and waving towards the crowd. It was clear to Ryder that the Airborn basked in the attention. Such a display did not suit him. All of his focus had to be on his opponent and nothing else until the fight was over. Ryder was going to prove to Eru and the world that he was a superior fighter. That he was more than the royal bastard.

"Facing Eru is the warrior to watch Ryder Coba!" the announcer cried out and the volume of the crowd grew.

Ryder turned around briefly to glance at Kaiser who offered a small wave. "I'll show you a true warrior."

"With your bloodlines, I expect nothing less. You and the world may hate me but at least make this fight interesting. I'm tired of watching finesse and agility matches. I want to see true power," Kaiser stated with a tilt of the head.

Ryder smirked. He was ready to prove everyone wrong. He turned towards the entryway and stepped out onto the Arena floor. Kaiser did not matter. The world did not matter. What mattered was the fight to come and he was completely focused.

The announcer continued on with a recap of the day's events, weaving a tale of power and triumph. He spoke of Eru's delicate finesse and Ryder's hard hitting power. "Now, let's see who will win today! Are you ready, Crossroads?"

Eru slowly pulled his twin swords free from the sheaths on his back. He spun them in a slow circle just as Ryder came to a stop twenty feet away. Eru was wearing the same armor, freshly repaired, from his quarter final match. Ryder was still wearing his leather cuirass, bracers, and boots but he added pauldrons to better protect his shoulders. His knotted arms were still bare.

"I am glad to see you before me in this final match. I saw you during the qualifiers and I was quite impressed," Eru said with a degree of admiration. "Do not expect to defeat me so easily for I watched your matches carefully."

Ryder let out a deep breath. "I expect nothing less." He popped his shoulders to loosen the sword in its scabbard. A smirk played on his face. Eru had no clue what was coming. It was all tough talk coming from the defending champion.

"Fighters, are you ready?" the announcer asked at the top of his lungs. The crowd silenced as if to wait for their answers. Eru and Ryder nodded. "Fight on!"

Both fighters slowly walked towards each other, increasing speed as they got closer. By the time they reached a distance of ten feet, Eru and Ryder were in a full charge. Eru held his swords out behind him, a ferocious snarl on his face. Ryder gripped the hilt of his sword with both hands. His expression was that of utter calm and confidence. The Airborn then leaped high into the air above Ryder who quickly slid to a stop. Coming down with one sword before him and one sword behind him, Eru struck. Ryder took the blow of the forward sword, bending to accept the force. Eru's forward sword pressed hard against Ryder's sword. He then swung his back sword down to try to cut at Ryder's arms. Ryder then threw all of his weight back over his shoulder, throwing Eru behind him. Eru fell to the dirt and rolled to absorb the impact. He quickly jumped back up and charged Ryder.

The exchange of blows peeled and bounced off the Arena walls with a high pitched metallic sound. Eru darted and stabbed with blinding speed. Ryder met each strike with equal speed and agility. Unlike Eru, Ryder kept his feet on the ground, sliding them in the dirt in grand sweeping motions. The intricate dance of swordplay elicited oohs and awws from the eager crowd coupled with cheers for their favorites.

"What a fantastic match we have here! The speed of the Airborn Eru. Is it too much for the Shadowborn Ryder Coba? He has yet to attack the defending champion who has had him on the defensive since the beginning," the announcer called out as he addressed the crowd.

The words of the announcer rang in the back of Ryder's mind and he decided to change things up. When Eru charged in for his next attack, Ryder quickly went into Shadow Slide. Eru stumbled forward but quickly recovered. His eyes darted around as he searched for Ryder.

"You can't hide in your Shadow Slide forever!" Eru shouted as he spun around.

"Wasn't planning on it!" Ryder yelled as he came out of Shadow Slide in a full leap. He flipped over Eru's head, slashing his right shoulder before disappearing again.

Eru sneered as blood poured from his shoulder wound. He gripped his swords until his knuckles were white from the pressure. He shuffled back a few steps when Ryder appeared again, cutting at his torso as he spun around. Ryder disappeared in a shadowly mist just as Eru sliced and stabbed with his swords. Instead of uselessly cutting at the empty air, Eru weaved a current of air around his arms and down to the tip of the sword blades. The current twisted like a concentrated tornado.

Protected by Shadow Slide, Ryder saw what Eru was doing and immediately began formulating a plan. He zipped around, following his dirt track and leaving a Shadow Trail behind. He then burst out of Shadow Slide, coated in a silvery fire. He roared a battle cry in the Dragon tongue with his sword raised high over his head. Eru twisted around and crossed his swords just as Ryder brought his down. His sword cut through the crossed blades like hot metal through a block of wood. Eru immediately threw the pieces away, jumped back to the middle of Ryder's dust trail, and set himself up for a counter attack.

Ryder charged inside the trail and immediately every line lit up, pulling the silver fire away from his body. He slowed to a stop before Eru, crossing his arms tightly. "Spirit Fire? You like?"

The Airborn snarled but a hint of nerves passed in his eyes. As if to prove he was still courageous, Eru whipped the arm tornadoes around. Ryder chuckled as he watched Eru attack the flames with relentless fervor. He scratched his chin as Eru huffed and puffed in his efforts.

"What is this unyielding flame? Some Shadowborn technique of the highest order?" Eru demanded, still trying to sound tough.

Ryder shrugged. "You could say that. It all works because you decided to just keep hitting at me with your swords," he said, gesturing towards the tracks in the ground. "When I was in Shadow Slide, I left a trail of Spirit energy called Shadow Trail. Normally that technique is used for tracking and following. I tweaked it a bit to suit me and my needs." He pointed at Eru.

"And I saved it just for you."

"I am not done yet, Shadowborn!" Eru shouted before he crouched down and then vaulted into the air.

"Neither am I, Airborn," Ryder smirked before jumping up after him.

The announcer hung over the edge of his box in complete shock. "And Eru rises out of the fire for the Airborn's greatest technique. He last executed the Wind Falcon to win the title one hundred years ago. But what is Ryder Coba doing? I have never seen this silver fire before and by the heavens!"

The lines of fire followed Ryder and whirled around him like a roaring Dragon. The serpentine head curled out of the flames and arched its neck to roar. Broad wings licked with hot fire unfolded and flapped, pressing down with a warm current of air. Even Vorin sat up straight in amazement from the sight. Ryder's Dragon charged for Eru's Wind Falcon and quickly engulfed it, creating a booming thunderous sound. A great burst of light illuminated the entire Arena and many spectators had to avert their eyes to avoid being blinded.

The crowd slowly uncovered their eyes as the fiery light dissipated. Ryder came down out of the sky and landed perfectly balanced on his feet. He started walking back towards the tunnel entryway just as Eru crashed behind him. Ryder paused and chuckled, shaking his head. Out of the east tunnel, the referee team rushed out to Eru as Ryder started walking again. The crowd had fallen deathly silent, half waiting to see if Eru would get up and the other half hesitant to acknowledge Ryder's victory. The announcer watched with anxious anticipation, biting his nails. The Waterborn physic in the referee team looked up at the announcer and shook his head. Eru was unable to continue.

Already knowing the result, Ryder raised his right fist in the air and bowed his head. The crowd cheered at the top of their lungs and applauded vigorously. They jumped to their feet, shouting Ryder's name. Ryder raised up his other arm, quite pleased with himself.

"Our new champion of the Crossroads Arena, Ryder Coba!" the announcer finally bellowed. Ryder walked into the tunnel entryway with arms in the air before finally dropping them, basking in the sound of the crowd. No one was going to look at him the same ever again.

Kaiser smirked as he slowly clapped. "That was quite a show."

"Oh. You're still here," Ryder grumbled as he pulled a hand towel off of the bench Kaiser was sitting on.

"But of course. I haven't seen a Spirit Fire or Spirit Dragon in quite some time. I know that you would pull something like that out of your bag of tricks. You are my blood after all," Kaiser said with a smug expression. He then paused and raised a finger. "Question is who taught you for I do not remember sending you to such teachers."

Ryder wiped the sweat and dirt from his arms and face before throwing the towel at Kaiser's face. Kaiser snarled as he pulled the towel away and threw it on the ground. "Like you, I have my secrets."

Kaiser cocked his head and looked Ryder up and down. "You are more an Adonis each time I look at you. Tall, strong, and devious. You led that Airborn on into believing he actually had a chance. That sounds like something I would do."

"I am nothing like you," Ryder snarled though he had to admit to himself that Kaiser was right about his battle plan.

"Whatever helps you sleep at night," Kaiser said with a shrug of the shoulders. He gestured towards the open entryway, the roar of the crowd still as great as when Ryder's victory was declared. "Listen to that applause for Ryder Coba the royal Shadowborn bastard. A bastard of purer blood than the actual heir to the throne. A warrior of greater power than the sitting Shadowlord. Now, I don't know about you but I find that quite wrong."

"Just like how you consider yourself the heir of Begin Anu? It must be so awful looking at the sons of Shadow Night sitting on your throne," Ryder mocked with a snicker. He crossed his arms and watched as a vein twitched on Kaiser's temple. "You're not the only one with the snarky remarks."

Kaiser slowly stood up and looked Ryder deep in the eyes. "Like I said, you are more like me than you think, Peredur Adonis Coba-Silvanus." He snorted towards Ryder. "You can't hide behind a name like Ryder Coba forever. One day, they will know the truth and one day, they will hate you as much as they hate me."

Ryder leaned towards Kaiser, their faces within inches of each other. "And one day, I will destroy you. You have only seen a glimpse of what I was capable of. I can do so much more."

Kaiser grinned smugly, flashing a bright smile. "Get in line behind the others that wish me dead. I can't wait for that momentous day when I get to rip you to shreds. Should be fun."

"I look forward to it, Grandfather," Ryder mocked as he mimicked Kaiser's smug expression.

"See? You do look like a proper Adonis," Kaiser said as he backed away. "There is no escaping your bloodlines."

Ryder frowned. "I hate you." He turned towards the tunnel entryway. "Now leave. I have a victory to celebrate."

"Yes. Go and celebrate with the masses. Maybe I shall raise my glass in your honor too," Kaiser mocked as he raised his hand like he had a glass already. "To my grandson, a man living in his carefully constructed lie that will soon break."

ORDERS

Ryder basked in the glory of his Arena victory for the rest of the afternoon but was glad to return to his quarters for a well deserved rest. A banquet was planned that evening in his honor and though he normally did not care for formal events, it put a smug confident expression on his face. Before he could even wash out his hair, Soja came to him with a summons from Proto Avis.

"Since when are you running messages for the Lord of Crossroads? Don't you have a Prince to attend to?" Ryder asked as he looked up from the note.

"I serve the Silvanus family," Soja said confidently as he latched his hands behind his back. "Including you."

Ryder crumbled up the note and threw it at Soja. "Will you give it a rest?"

Soja managed to keep a pleasant expression on his face as he picked up the crumbled note and set it on a nearby desk. "Anyway, Lord Avis thinks extremely high of you. I can't think of anybody but a Commander or a Lord that affords the same respect."

"I have fought for that respect. I wasn't born to it like Argos or Palani," Ryder argued as he peeled off his sleeveless tunic, exposing his muscular upper body. He quickly pulled on a clean black linen shirt that he left untucked. "You still did not answer my question," he added as he smoothed his hair down and tied it back.

"A Falcon Gryphon named Lana gave me this note. She did

not speak our tongue well but I got the feeling that Lord Avis gave her the job and she did not want to see you," Soja explained.

Ryder chuckled as he thought of the young nervous Gryphon messenger from Coal. "Gryphons do not forgive insults so easily."

"Somehow I am not surprised. Should I step outside while you finish getting changed?" Soja asked as he made to turn towards the door.

"No, I'm ready," Ryder stated.

The two strode towards Proto Avis' quarters in silence though Soja fought the urge to speak at every step. He would raise a finger and start to open his mouth before Ryder glared at him and he stopped. They quickly climbed a tall grand staircase up to the top floor of the citadel. The top floor was expansive and open with tall columns holding up the ceiling. At the far end of the floor was a set of oak doors, baring entrance to the only room.

"Most people are dressed in formal wear when they go to meet with the Lord of Crossroads," Soja commented as they left the stairs. "But then you have all the bearing of a great Lord without even trying."

"Will you just drop it?" Ryder snapped as he and Soja walked across the long surface, the scent of fresh cut flowers heavy in the air.

Ryder was dressed informally in faded dark leather boots, scuffed on the toe and heels that tapped the marble floor in regular rhythm. His faded black wool pants were tattered and frayed. Even his long sleeved shirt was wrinkled. His dark hair was tousled despite some of it being pulled back from his face. His strong jaw was lined with the beginning of a beard. As dirty and frayed as he looked, Ryder still had a royal bearing with head held high and shoulders squared proudly. His appearance was a contrast to Soja's clean cut Saber uniform.

"You act and move like a Shadowlord more than Lord Aku or Prince Onyx. You showed everyone with your victory in the Arena that you are powerful and mighty. I know that you are aware of the troubles in Cross. You could reverse them if you came home," he pleaded, gesturing with his hands.

"I will not take the throne so tell your father to stop pushing the issue," Ryder said firmly.

"But you are still," Soja started to say before Ryder shot him a glare. Soja took a deep breath to gather himself. "You know the truth about Kaiser Adonis."

"There are a lot of things that I know about Kaiser Adonis. Things the world knows and things the world doesn't know. Things that the world does not need to know. But so long as he has the

Shadow Mirror at the border, he is in control and there is nothing I can do to save the throne," Ryder stated as he kept his focus on the doors.

The massive oak doors at the end of the hall were flanked on both sides by three Tawny Eagle Gryphon guards. Each one looked fearsome with sharp talons and beaks, ready to tear a trespasser apart. Soja stopped in his tracks but was surprised that Ryder continued forward undeterred. He was even more surprised to hear Ryder speak in the Gryphon tongue with such a confident degree of fluency. The first Gryphon to the right of the door quickly answered him in what could only be described as a hushed tone. When he bowed his head, the other guards followed suit. This was the universal sign from a Gryphon that one was allowed entrance. And for someone like Ryder Coba, it was a great honor to be allowed a private audience with Proto Avis.

*****

Ryder strode into Proto's receiving chamber with head held high, not even flinching when the oak doors shut with a deep thud. Before him was Proto Avis resting on his cushioned lounge perch, front limbs crossed. To Proto's left was Stellaris and to his right was Paladon. His senses told him that Vorin was nearby, ready to listen in on the coming conversation. Ryder came to a stop, bowed his head and swung his arms out to his side in the traditional greeting between Spiritborn and Gryphons. He waited for his turn to speak.

"First and foremost, congratulations on your magnificent victory in the Arena. We of the Gryphon nation were right to accept you into our culture for you have shown us that you are strong and noble," Stellaris said in his accented baritone voice. He and Paladon looked at each other and nodded.

"You are mighty, Peredur. Should you return to visit our homeland, my kin and I would like to honor your victory with a proper Gryphon celebration," Paladon said graciously. He spoke the common tongue with no accent.

"I am honored by your kind words," Ryder said as he latched his hands behind his back and bowed his head.

The three Gryphons murmured in their own tongue amongst themselves. Ryder could tell that they were discussing something of great importance in a volume so low that he knew that they did not want him to hear what was being said. Proto was speaking the most as his decisions carried the greatest authority. The two Gryphon Lords eventually bowed their heads.

"I am smart enough to know that I was not called to a personal audience with three Gryphon Lords just to receive their praise," Ryder reasoned as he straightened his back. He tilted his head, indicating the likely direction of where Vorin was patiently listening in. "If this is a matter of state where the Lords of the Northlands wish to congratulate me, where are the six Spiritborn Lords?"

"Because this meeting is just between us. I was just finishing business with my kin here," Proto Avis admitted with a bow of the head. "I also bear more trust for my kin than the Spiritborn Lords."

Both Stellaris and Paladon stiffened at the admission of the beloved sage. "To best clarify Lord Avis' words, we do not trust how you say," Paladon said before falling silent. It was clear he was having difficulty with translating his thoughts.

"You do not trust the eyes and ears around them like you trust your own kin," Ryder stated in the Gryphon tongue before returning to speaking the common tongue. "You are not alone. I do not trust the Spiritborn Lords either."

"A coded message reached me the night prior from Lord Palani of the Earthborn regarding his concern for safety from a malice that lurks in the shadows. I do not need to say the name for you to know who I speak of," Proto declared with a hint of restraint in his voice. "The malice that has followed him here to Crossroads."

Ryder scoffed much to the chagrin of Stellaris and Paladon whose hackles bristled in warning. "You mean Kaiser."

"I mean your grandfather," Proto said with a sense of utter finality. Stellaris grew more wary as his eyes never left Ryder. "Now you understand why I did not also call the Spiritborn Lords here. I can imagine that they would not take too kindly to you sharing his blood."

"You better not be thinking that I brought him here to Crossroads though I do not doubt my presence attracted him. I would sooner snap his neck than declare any allegiance to him," Ryder growled, growing agitated. He hated talking about his blood relation to Kaiser. "I suppose Lord Vorin told you of his suspicions before the celebration."

"He did and he extended his protection to protect you from us," Proto admitted as if the idea was humorous and light hearted. A soft whistle trilled in his throat. "No one but an Anu can look in the eyes of a Dragon without fear. Even then, one can not look into the eyes of Vorin if he has true darkness in his heart. He would have burnt you to a crisp had he seen such in you."

"I am glad that he didn't," Ryder stated as he crossed his arms tightly and leaned on his right leg. Part of him thought that he would have hated to fight off Vorin and his blistering fire.

"Vorin is the lone soul of us all to have known Begin Anu in any great detail and he told me that you remind him of the Farlander hero. A living, breathing hero before us," Proto stated with a soft smile in his eyes. He raised his right paw to silence Ryder before he could object. "That is why we have picked you to do something no one else has been able to do in a thousand years."

Ryder looked at the three Gryphons in confusion until it dawned on him. They wanted him to confront Kaiser. "I am no Begin Anu or Bane Arlis. I am no hero to be called on..."

"Let me stop you, Peredur," Proto interuptted using Ryder's proper name like Paladon had done. The Gryphons had always used it over his nickname of Ryder when they wanted to honor him or ask him to do something of great importance. "The stars have shown me that Bane is not answering our calls to bring him home to face Kaiser. Vorin would face the traitor if he could but the sacrifice of his kind when the Immortal Truth was written left him as his race's sole survivor and keeper of Terra's memories. You however are true in sight and powerful in Spirit. It may go against the law of Crossroads but we ask you, no we order you, to kill Kaiser Adonis for the good of the world."

He had begun to suspect that the three Gryphons and Vorin had discussed the idea of assassination long before the celebration. Most of the world likely thought that killing Kaiser would end their problems. But Ryder knew things about the man that no one else did. He knew about his practice of Blood Magic, his raising of Rache by the means of murder and sacrifice, and his darkest secrets that he was afraid to even think about for very long. A deep seeded hate for Kaiser that Ryder normally had suppressed in the back of his mind flared up as he thought about how he found his dying mother and how she warned him. He gripped his upper arms tightly, digging his fingernails into the muscle.

"I'll do it," Ryder finally admitted after a painfully long wait.

Proto immediately let out a sigh of relief along with his Gryphon kin. "Should you succeed, you will have more than the thanks of the Gryphons and the last Dragon. You will have the thanks of the world." The three Gryphons bowed their heads. "Go with our blessing, Peredur. We wish you strength and true aim."

Ryder unclenched his arms and repeated his Spiritborn to Gryphon bow. He spun on his feet and headed back towards the oak doors. He paused when he felt Vorin's great mind pressing down on his. He smiled and nodded as he felt a similar affirmation of blessing and hope.

*****

The young Saber was still waiting for him outside of the doors. Soja ran towards Ryder once the doors slammed shut.

"You serve the Silvanus bloodline, correct?" Ryder asked him as they started back towards the stairs.

"With all of my soul and being," Soja said enthusiastically. He slapped his clenched fist across his chest and bowed his head.

"Then I need a favor."

A BUDDING FRIENDSHIP

Luna looked at the message with hesitation as she paced around the common room of the Earthborn apartments. She stumbled when she ran into a cherry wood couch with green cushions. Another couch of the same detail faced it with a short coffee table placed in between them. Steadying herself, Luna reread the message. It was printed on stark white parchment and written in Onyx's own hand with his royal Shadowborn seal.

"He is extending a hand of friendship," Soja said as he stood off to the side with hands latched behind his back.

"I... I am flattered but what would the future Shadowlord want with an Earthborn court servant?" Luna asked, struggling to find her voice. She read the note again.

Soja took a step forward. "I cannot speak for him."

Her heart fluttered in her chest as she placed a hand over it. She had told no one what she thought of the young Shadowborn Prince since the day they met at the cliffs. "If it pleases your Prince, I accept," Luna finally said, handing Soja the note.

"That note was meant for you," Soja declined. "But I will convey your reply," he added with a bow before he left her.

Luna was shocked into silence. A Saber bowed to her! No one bowed to her. She was a court servant and not the daughter of a noble. Her father was a low level courtier and his father had been a low level courtier. She slid back into a velvet chair, trying to catch her breath. It all seemed so surreal to her to have a royal Prince ask to spend time with her. Or as the note said, to walk the city. She was suddenly at a loss at what to wear. She did not want to appear low and frumpy before Onyx. If she was going to be in the public with the Crowned Prince of the Shadowborn, she was going to look her best and represent the Earthborn court with dignity. But then she decided that she could not look any worse than she did after cliff diving and soaked to the bone.

But the note stirred in her the feelings she had buried deep inside since leaving the cliffs. Onyx was a handsome Prince and everyone whispered about his looks. All of the young Princesses present in Crossroads talked and giggled about the eligible bachelor. She had first thought it silly to fawn over someone they had never met. Lord Palani's son was equally as eligible as Onyx but he was a slender sapling to the Shadowborn prince's tall and mighty frame. Luna had been prepared to brush all of the talk out of her mind until she had actually met Onyx. Her heart jumped in her chest and she felt weak at the knees. He was handsome and his nervousness made him adorable to her.

After dressing herself in a knee length grass green frock, Luna felt ready as she finished braiding her hair. She tossed the styled lock over her shoulder. She looked one more time in the mirror and gathered her courage.

Just as the note said, Onyx was waiting by the pond in the Earthborn quarter's courtyard. Luna could immediately tell that he was nervous as she watched him wring his hands. She smiled as she leaned against the column. He was dressed in short sleeve black tunic that showed off his strong arms. A thick leather belt was cinched in at the waist.

"Do the Shadowborn only wear black?" she asked laughing as Onyx's entire outfit was one color.

Onyx immediately examined himself to see if anything was out of place. Luna thought his nerves were endearing as she approached him. She curtsied demurely before him.

"I guess we do," Onyx replied once she stood up. "I don't think I would look good in anything else though the coronation robes have a lot of silver and white in them."

Luna tried to imagine Onyx in the royal attire. "You should try a little green. Might spruce things up."

Onyx laughed at himself, more from nerves than actual mirth. But his confidence was growing. His shoulders relaxed and his smile was cheerful. "Shall we?" he asked as he extended the crook of his arm.

Luna hesitated. The gesture was that of a gentleman but it would set the entire city to talking. She had heard ahead of his arrival to Crossroads that the Shadowborn's royal Council intended to find him a bride. But she couldn't ignore the kindness in his eyes that she loved and the soft smile on his face. "Thank you, kind Prince," she teased as she took his arm. They both started laughing.

The marketplace was bustling with sights, sounds and smells of all sorts. Vendors shouted about their wares for sale, boasting their quality. Bakers set out rows and rows of bread, pastries and other fantastic treats. Onyx and Luna paused long enough to each pick a citrus pastry, wondering about the taste. When Onyx tried to pay for the treats, the baker graciously declined. "A gift to the Crowned Prince of the Shadowborn and his Lady."

The taste was sweet and tart as sticky syrup dripped down their fingers. Onyx and Luna laughed again at each other when their lips puckered from the tangy taste of lemon.

"Not bad," Luna said as she wiped her hands together.

"Definitely something I have not had before. Must come from the lands of the Fireborn though I do not remember tasting it in Lavan," Onyx commented. "I know that there is a Shadowborn food stall somewhere. Want to try something from my homeland?"

That was their game for the rest of the morning as they went about trying different and strange foods. Luna discovered that she really enjoyed the hearty meat pies the Shadowborn food stall offered. Onyx found a liking for the rustic spiced slices of chicken on flaky slices of bread from the Earthborn. They moved on to the goods that varied from jewelry to weapons and bolts of fabric. Luna found a shimmering black cloth that she wrapped over her head, twirling around to show it off to Onyx. She giggled as she let it drop to her shoulders.

"A fine cloth, my Prince. The weave was inspired by the colors of your homeland," the vendor said proudly. He lifted a finger to have them wait as he pulled out a soft silver cloth that was light and flowing.

Luna was immediately drawn to the fabric, fingering the lines of sewn in gems. She bit her lip as she wanted so much to have both the black and silver fabrics.

"I'll take both," Onyx said and Luna's heart leaped in her chest. Without thinking, she spun around and jumped up to hug him. She dropped and danced with excitement. She had never had such nice fabric before. She took them graciously in her arms after Onyx paid the vendor who thanked him profusely.

"Thank you!" Luna said over and over.

"You have been kind to me here. Take it as thanks from me," Onyx said as he offered to carry the paper wrapped fabric.

Luna danced around with excitement. All of her nerves were forgotten. She twisted around to look back at Onyx who smiled back at her. He whispered something to the vendor who promptly nodded, promising to take the fabric to the Earthborn court quarters. He then stepped back from the stall and offered the crook of his arm again which Luna took gladly.

"So what else would you like to see today?" Onyx asked.

"The gardens. My people brought some of the most beautiful blooms to help decorate for the celebration," Luna replied before breaking away from Onyx. She reached out a hand. "Come and I'll show you the one I brought."

Onyx followed Luna at a jogging pace towards the eastern side of the city where a large garden spread out over an acre. They passed under a white stone archway into a vibrant green space full of colorful flowers. Hummingbirds buzzed from blossom to blossom as butterflies fluttered and twisted in a dance above their heads. The floral scents were soothing and the grass smelled as if it had been freshly trimmed.

Luna bent down to remove her slippers. "The grass is very soft to walk upon."

The Shadowborn Prince removed his boots with a little tugging and dropped them beside Luna's cream colored slippers. He followed her off the sandy path and immediately felt the springiness of the grass. He paused for a moment, bouncing on his heels. It was so different than the stone pathways and wooden floors of Cross. And he liked it.

"Wow, this is so soft," he commented as he bent down to run his hand over the top of the shorn shoots.

"Did you honestly think an Earthborn would lie about the quality of a garden? I am a Lady of Flora. Not only do I tend to the royal ladies of the Kano family, I tend to their private gardens. I know how to raise the most beautiful flowers," Luna exclaimed with a toss of her hair. "An Earthborn would not be a true Earthborn if they did not know how to tend flowers."

"Is that a gibe against me since I am half Earthborn?"

Luna laughed as she spun around like a dancer. "My good Prince, I only speak the truth."

Onyx followed Luna to a corner of the garden where a stone grotto had been built with a small cascading waterfall. The waterfall spilled into a crystal clear pool, churning the water in a wave of ripples. Surrounding the back wall of the grotto was a menagerie of green ferns and delicate flowers. Luna brought him to a small patch of white orchids, gently lifting up a blossom to reveal a silver sunburst pattern. Tiny drops of water sparkled like starlight.

"This is the moon orchid that blooms to its full splendor during the long winter nights but when coaxed, it will open up during the daytime. My brother said that my father presented my mother with a bouquet after my birth. My mother loved the flowers so much that she wanted to name me after them," Luna explained with a serene expression. She bent down to sniff the flower.

"What is that one?" Onyx asked pointing at a single flower that grew in a bed of ferns to the left of the waterfall.

Luna stepped around him and spied the bejeweled flower. "That is the Emerald Rose. My Lord Palani brought it here in honor of his sister and your mother."

A moment of silence fell between them as they both stared at the shimmering flower. The leaves and stalk were of a beautiful emerald while the petals were a smooth pearl white. Onyx had never seen anything like it and to know that it was for the memory of his mother was a calming thought. There was nothing this beautiful in his homeland and he wished that there was more beauty. He decided silently that once he was Shadowlord, he would start a beautification project that remove the serious and dark perception of his people. And he would do it in honor of his mother.

Onyx walked Luna back to the courtyard he had met her in, still embroiled in his thoughts of his future reign. He bowed and kissed her hand like a gracious Prince before bidding her good evening. They locked eyes and smiled at the same time before Onyx watched her go inside with an extra bounce in her step.

HELPING A FRIEND

Ryder followed Soja to his quarters that he shared with the Sabers in the Shadowborn caravan. His presence with a Saber did not escape notice from the courtiers and servants who were preparing for the evening events. Many of them stopped what they were doing to whisper and watch Ryder as he passed by. Though Ryder did not make a show of it, he heard every whisper and felt every pair of eyes on him. Regardless of his purpose, Ryder's presence in the Shadowborn temporary residence was huge for until then, he had avoided the Shadowborn entirely. At least the Sabers practiced discretation and avoided making their interest known. Soja ignored everything entirely as they finally reached his bedroom. The small bedroom had two canvas covered cots with a white pillow and black wool blanket folded up at the foot. Soja stepped over to the oil lamp and twisted a knob at its golden base.

"Even I think it gets too dark in here. They could have least set me up in a room with a view," Soja grumbled as the small flame in the lip flickered to life. He stepped around Ryder to go and stand by his cot. "You honestly think switching a few articles of clothing will fool the kind of hunter you say Kaiser's servant is?"

"First rule of hunting: know your target," Ryder stated as he pulled off his shirt. He dropped it on the end of the cot. "Kaiser's servant is a Demon though very few know the truth. Demons track by using their senses melded into one. That allows them to hunt their targets by their auras. Now that may seem like an impeccable skill but it can be deceived."

The idea that he was going to lead a Demon on a wild goose chase unnerved Soja. He had no experience dealing with the dark and black hearted creatures beyond the fireside stories his father told him as a child. Dealing with Demons was the historic responsibility of the Shadowlord and his kin. But Soja reminded himself that it was his duty as a Saber to protect and serve the royal family even if the blood member before him was unwilling to accept his birthright. Soja pulled off his leather armor, dropping the pieces at his feet before putting on Ryder's shirt.

Ryder picked up a freshly laundered black cotton shirt and put it on. The lavender scent immediately masked the smell of combat that lingered on Ryder's skin. He then grabbed a scuffed leather cuirass he had borrowed from a store of armor. Soja looked at the design on the chest and saw a faded hooded cobra with its tail wrapped around a dagger. It was the crest of the now defunct Coba family.

"Guess it is only right that you wear that," Soja said pointing at the cobra on Ryder's chest. Ryder shrugged as he laced the matching bracers over his forearms.

It annoyed Soja that Ryder put so little belief in his family heritage. He was immensely proud to be a Rokar and was delighted to continue his family legacy as a Saber. By comparison, Ryder did not care. But then Ryder was constantly reminded by everyone who his family was. Soja started to tug and fiddle with the borrowed shirt.

"God, you Silvanus bloods are massive. This shirt hangs off of me," Soja said as he lifted his arms to show the loose sleeves.

"And you Rokars are tiny by comparison. Perhaps I should have asked your Saber captain Hayden Abendroth for his leathers. At least he matches me in height. This armor might be too obvious," Ryder said as he pulled on the bracer ties to loosen them. "I just need the ruse long enough to complete the job."

"Is Lord Avis really that confident that you can assassinate Kaiser? In Crossroads of all places?" Soja asked as he pulled on the fabric of his borrowed tunic. He bent down to pick up his Saber cuirass.

"I did just win the Arena fights, didn't I?"

Soja pulled on his cuirass, grunting at the extra fabric making it a tight fit. "Kaiser is nearly ten times older than you and I am sure he has failsafes in place to guard against assassins."

"I know him better than most, even Lord Vorin. But I do not know everything. I can not face both Kaiser and his servant at the same time so I am depending on you to distract the servant. Kaiser is at least smart enough not to attempt his own killing here for a small part of him believes that any malicious death will bring the

Daylord in the instant. But of course the arrogant part of him won't admit that he fears retribution from the Daylord," Ryder explained as he rolled his shoulders, throwing his arms back and forth. "But then that is only a guess on my part."

"How do you know that? How do you really know what Kaiser is thinking?" Soja inquired as he fumbled around with his sword belt.

Ryder turned his back to Soja, looking out of the window of the small bedroom. He latched his hands behind him. "You do not need the distraction. Focus on giving his servant a chase and do not engage him."

"I may be a Saber but even I know that this is dangerous," Soja pointed out as he slid a sword into the sheath at his left hip. "What will you do once Kaiser is dead? Will you take the throne?"

"I already told you a thousand times. I do not want the throne," Ryder growled. He crossed his arms tightly, his entire body tense.

"Why not!" Soja demanded.

Ryder held his breath for a moment, trying to contain his anger. "I have made my decision. It's time you and your father accepted it."

"You are still of royal blood. Maybe if this all works out, you can be a Saber for the future Lord Onyx since you don't want to deal with the throne yourself," Soja said, putting a hand on Ryder's shoulder. He dug into his belt and pulled out a small steel knife with a black leather wrapped handle. "Maybe this will help. My father gave it to me before I started my Saber training and it always brought me good luck. Maybe it will bring you good luck."

Ryder took the small weapon in his hand and turned it over in examination. The steel blade was pristine with no markings. There was no cross guard and the handle was capped with silver of fine quality. He bounced the knife on his palm, testing the weight.

"Best throwing knife out there and does well with the darker arts of combat," Soja stated as he crossed his arms. "Sure you can use it?"

With a snap of the wrist, Ryder hurtled the knife across the room before it thudded into the wall. The point was buried in a map right on the location of Kaiser's quarters in Crossroads. "I think I've got it. Just remember your part."

Soja nodded with a salute. "Imagine Kaiser's reaction to seeing you holding a Rokar knife before plunging it into his heart."

The optimism of the young Saber was uplifting but Ryder was more practical in his thinking. Kaiser was not a known warrior but he was a trained in the military arts courtesy of his father. It amazed him how people seemed to have forgotten that Kaiser was the son of a general. He looked down at his hand, imagining the weight of Soja's knife again. He curled his fingers as he reviewed in his head all of the body's vulnerable spots. Part of him wanted Kaiser to suffer and not have a quick death. Ryder then wondered if Kaiser even had a heart.

"People assume that my future is already decided. Does the bastard son of Akakios take the throne of the Shadowborn? Does Ryder Coba come home to Cross? Well, I have never put much credence in worrying about the future because it is the present that matters," Ryder stated as he turned to face Soja. "Let's go in the name of truth and justice."

THE MIND OF RACHE

Perched on a high rooftop, Rache scanned the city with his sharp senses. His eyes narrowed as he sorted through the different energy trails he detected. The fire red heat of the Fireborn was the first he pushed to the background of his mind. The cool blue of the Waterborn was next. The earthy green calm of the Earthborn and the brisk white of the Airborn quickly followed. He sneered as he phased out the bright yellow of the Lightborn.

The world suddenly grew dark but that was how Rache preferred it. It made the search for the elusive Shadowborn even easier. He gritted his teeth at the menial job of finding a worthless soul that clearly meant a big deal to Kaiser. Rache knew that Ryder was his grandson and had met him many times over the years but he could not understand his worth. Kaiser had never declared Ryder's mother as his daughter nor had he declared Ryder to be his grandson. If Ryder was worth anything, Rache believed that Kaiser should have openly claimed him as his heir. Part of him was intrigued by Ryder, a man whom Kaiser had helped shape into who he currently was: the Crossroads Arena champion. He had wanted to follow Kaiser to the combat matches but Kaiser said that Vorin the Dragonlord would have spotted him in a heartbeat. He sneered at the thought.

He skulked down, sliding quickly until he reached the street. He landed without a sound and stood up tall. A small crowd remained and took no notice of the tattered and veiled Rache while they bustled about for another night of celebration. A spectacular play was being hosted by the Waterborn and the Earthborn that would depict the history of the wretched Immortal Truth. A Fireborn had been picked to depict him as they both shared the same red hair color. It was an insult but the idea amused him. He debated on storming the stage during the final act.

The outdoor stage had been built on the northern edge of a city square on the eastern side of Crossroads. Lights made of small glass balls with candles tucked inside were strung up between lamp posts and tall wooden poles. A sizable crowd had already assembled, standing before the stage and talking about the play to come. They laughed over warm tea drinks and pastries served by Earthborn vendors that had set up shop. Four Waterborn walked among the crowd with brochures about the play and actors for sale. Rache looked to a tavern rooftop to see a small family of Screech Owl Gryphons waiting for the play to begin. He scoffed at the two chicks who could barely sit still, wondering to himself if they gave good sport.

"My dear kin of the North! I welcome you to a dramatic interpretation of that great moment in our history: the life of the Farlander Begin Anu!" an Earthborn dressed in green robes shouted as he took center stage with a blue robed Waterborn. The Waterborn held a conductor's stick for the drums, strings, and wind instrument band in the orchestra box to the left of the stage.

The Demon rolled his eyes as the crowd clapped with eager anticipation. A pair of Fireborn standing three feet in front of him chattered about the actor portraying that they described as 'the evil Demon Rache.' Rache smirked at the irony of the situation, considering he was that very Demon standing in the crowd.

"I first want to thank our master of music, Sir Myst of the prestigious Lough Music Academy," the green robed Earthborn stated proudly before beginning a round of applause. Sir Myst smiled and bowed. "He has composed a rousing yet beautiful symphony for tonight's play."

The crowd continued to clap with each introduction until the Earthborn host waved his hands to silence them. Both he and the music director bowed before leaving the stage and the curtains slowly began to rise. The Waterborn Sir Myst stepped to his post before the band and began waving his conductor's stick. The string, horn, and drum band began to play a slowly building piece of music that hinted at a lost age of Terra with the drum beats of war and the horns of battle cries.

Rache watched as a mock fight played out on stage between actors dressed as Demons in black and red with spikes and actors dressed as armored soldiers. In the midst of the costumed Demons rose up the Fireborn pretending to be him. Rache had to laugh as the actor cried out in what he likely believed to be a terrifying voice. The armored soldiers cowered in pretend fear, dropping their wooden prop swords to emphasize their state of mind. False Rache shouted for his Demons to attack, pointing angrily towards the soldiers. The whole scene was amusing to the real Rache while those in the crowd watching cried for mercy and justice.

The play continued to be an entertaining farce of what Rache had truly experienced. In truth, he was the terrible force that stormed the battlefield, intent on fighting until every last enemy was dead. When the play reached the death of Begin Anu, the actors glorified it with gold and silver cloths draped over his body as they carried the false Begin Anu off stage. False Rache was draped in black and dragged away, screaming. The music drove the emotion of the crowd as it reached a crescendo before dropping into a subtle chord of strings. Once it ended, the crowd cheered and clapped.

Rache snaked his way around the people towards the actors' tent. The actors congratulated each other with pats on the back and handshakes, unaware of the approaching danger. The Demon caught sight of the Fireborn who had played him and decided to act like the adoring fan.

"Good Fireborn, I was most enthralled by your portrayal of the Demon," Rache complimented in a placating tone. "Might I thank you for your masterful performance with a drink?"

The Fireborn grinned as he bowed his head. "That would be delightful." He briefly turned back to wave to his fellow actors before following Rache down a side street. "So what part of my performance did you like best?"

Rache smirked before throwing the actor into a dark alley between two closed shops. The actor groaned as he pressed a hand to his forehead. Rache bent down to his eye level, pulling his mask away from his face. His smirk revealed his fangs as his eyes turned blood red. Rache pressed a hand to the actor's throat, rendering him unable to speak. He took his other hand and pulled back the actor's shirt collar, bending in close to his ear. "The part where you died."

The actor did not have to die, Rache thought, but it was his Demon duty to remove those that mocked him. He stood up from his kill, blood staining his mouth before wiping it away with the back of his hand. He smacked his lips, savoring the spicy taste of the Fireborn's blood. Pulling his mask back over his face, Rache stepped out of the alley.

Rache scanned his surroundings, focusing all of his keen senses onto the task of seeking his prey. His body tightened as he felt the pull of the power of Crossroads. It was draining and he hated it. Even the very layout of the streets was constructed as a ward against Demons. He tightened his fists as his search continued.

The city was bathed in the golden light of torches and street lamps. The white stone buildings glowed with the brilliance of daylight. It was if the sunlight was captured in every surface of the city and with the rainbow colors of the banners and flowers, anyone could appreciate the sight. Red and white climbing roses wrapped around massive garden arbors that stretched across the street. Street performers dressed in black and gold costumes danced around, passing out sweet treats and fire poppers to the children, laughing as they bounced away. The boys and girls whooped with excitement as a vendor passed out sparklers that when lit, flashed blue and green.

"Focus," he muttered under his breath to remove the distraction of his surroundings.

He mingled among the crowd, unnoticed and unquestioned. The freedom to be in the streets would only last so long as he did not try to cross the city seal. He turned his gaze about, trying to catch a hint of Ryder Coba whether it be a whisper of his name or the beat of his heart. Most of the passersby recounted his match against Eru, marveling at his strength against the Airborn's speed. Hearing such words made Rache excited and more eager to begin the chase. Ryder would be a worthy opponent.

The steady hum of beating hearts broke into his senses. His mouth watered from the sound of blood rushing through veins. He stopped walking and took a moment to take a deep breath. He smirked. Memories of the past flooded his mind as Rache thought of the days where he was a walking terror. He then sneered as he thought about what he was now. A growl threatened to escape his throat until he caught a hint of his target's aura signature. Rache slipped into an alleyway and leaped up to the rooftop. The aura was stronger but fleeing away from him.

"So that is how you want to play, bastard."

The target's signature was still eluding Rache as he stalked around and scaled rooftops. He slid onto a slanted roof, hanging onto the edge with one hand. A frown crossed his face and he dropped to the street below. The joyous feeling in the air was stifling to one of his nature and he sneered. Why a few pieces of faded rock were so important was beyond him.

Rache was familiar with the Immortal Truth and would have read it when it was set in stone but it was guarded by a strong power. Demon wards and blood written promises gave strength to those who followed its words. Madness, Rache thought, as the world seemed worse with the Immortal Truth around.

A spark shot through his melded senses and he brought his hands up to press against his temples. He took a few steps back and the pain in his head subsided. Looking down at the street, he saw the rim of the seal of Crossroads. A curse escaped his lips.

He returned to the rooftops in a single bound and the power of the seal diminished. It was expected that the city center was protected by a ward but Rache had not expected it to be strong enough to repel him. He was a Demon that predated the building of the city.

"I will not be denied," he growled. If there was one thing he knew about Demon wards, they were powered by the presence of a Shadowlord through the twisted spells of the Immortal Truth. And if Kaiser was right, that person was Aku. Killing him would be simple and it would weaken the power of the Demon wards. Rache smiled at the thought. Aku was a shell of what he used to be, lifeless and easily guided. Getting rid of Aku would be too easy.

He landed on the balcony of the Shadowborn royal quarters and pushed open the ornate glass doors. He threw his cloak to the floor and stepped inside. Sitting on a parlor lounge was Aku who stared blankly into a mirror. He was dressed in royal attire and his hair was neatly styled. Despite the finery, Aku bore a haggard and sickly appearance.

Aku finally turned to face Rache, having seen him approach from behind. The look in his eyes was tired and his skin was a pasty white.

"My dear Aku, you do not look well," Rache said in a placating voice. "Perhaps you should lie down and rest."

"Yes... rest..." Aku whispered. His voice cracked as he spoke.

In a heartbeat, Rache had him pinned down with his left hand clamped around his throat. Aku did not struggle and only looked back into his eyes with a blank expression. This Aku could easily be commanded. No wonder Kaiser had such fun being a puppet master.

"I suppose it would be merciful of me to kill you. I'm sure you are tired of being a dead puppet," Rache said as he tightened his grip. "I don't know why Kaiser keeps this husk of dried out flesh around... perhaps for his amusement..." He leaned in close, his breath hot with anticipation of the kill. "Once I am done with you, I am going to kill the Silvanus bastard and then your precious princely brat of a son..."

Rache was thrown from the lounge, crashing into the far wall. Glass, wood and porcelain rained down in pieces from the impact. He shook his head a few times before jetting up to his feet.

Debris fell in a pile at his feet. He looked up to see Soja standing between him and Aku. It was a shock to him that a Saber like Soja could sneak up on him. But this was a different Soja Rokar. His childlike enthusiasm was now transformed into steely resolve.

"I will defend my sovereign Lord to the death even if it means my own," Soja snarled as he drew his blade and pointed it in Rache's direction.

Rache growled, his eyes shifting to blood red in building rage. "I will rip your head from your neck!"

"Go ahead. I am not afraid," Soja said stoically as he held tight to his sword hilt.

"Do you even know who I am? I have killed dogs bigger than you!" Rache threatened as he clenched his fists tightly.

Soja twisted his sword hand. "I know exactly who, and what, you are," he said firmly.

"You're Rokar's brat. Oh this will be fun. I shall take much joy in presenting him with your head," Rache gloated as he took a step forward.

"Then I will know that I died an honorable death," Soja stated without fear. He had long pushed away the warning from Ryder not to engage the Demon servant. Even he knew that he was no match for one as powerful as Rache but he was going to protect Lord Aku no matter the cost.

Rache frowned. He knew that Sabers were fearless and brave in the face of overwhelming force but Soja was barely a sizable threat. Where did his courage come from? He then noticed that he was not in his uniform. He sniffed the air and immediately knew Ryder's scent. He had been tricked! A roar exploded from his chest in fury. When he saw Soja's knowing grin, that only made Rache even angrier.

"Oh, did I make the Demon mad?" Soja teased.

Admitting that he had been deceived was the last thing Rache wanted to do. No one played him for a fool. He could barely find the words in the tongue of the Spiritborn to curse the young Saber. Instead curses and threats in his own tongue tore out of his mouth before he charged forward.

THE ASSASSINATION ATTEMPT

Ryder crouched on the rooftop of a building across the street from where Kaiser was staying. The light of the street lamp glowed just beyond the reach of his shadow. He eyed the string of banners that wavered back and forth in the breeze; the subtle flap of the canvas was annoying and he gritted his teeth in response. A breeze though capable of hiding footsteps would carry a scent to unwanted parties. Ryder had planned for this and rubbed the street dust all over his person to disguise his scent.

He had to admit that he wanted to see Kaiser die and he especially wanted to be the one to strike the killing blow. Ryder felt no family love for the man who called himself his grandfather. Growing up, he had first known him as the wealthy benefactor, representing his royal father and providing for his upbringing and education. But as he grew older, Ryder started to suspect that Kaiser was more than that. Kaiser paid a great deal of attention to every aspect of his life, directing it down to the smallest detail. It seemed too much even for a royal bastard. He was twenty one when he finally confronted his mother and grandmother for the truth. They admitted it reluctantly and from then on, Ryder felt his life change in a new direction. Grandfather or not, Kaiser was dangerous to all around him. His hand gripped the edge of the roof as he fought a long buried memory of his last time in Cross facing Kaiser. One that he had hoped to never revisit again and especially in the moment before he would kill the man.

*****

Ryder stood before the empty high back chair made of ebony wood and draped with a jewel encrusted silver cloth and a wide strip of crimson fabric. The chair was placed in a position of power upon a raised stone dais that granted whoever sat upon it a wide view of the throne room. He studied the throne and wondered if he was capable of sitting upon it like his forebears. It was against Shadowborn law for anyone but the Shadowlord to sit upon the throne and Ryder was no Shadowlord. Yet. He glanced at the scrap of paper crumbled in his right hand and unfolded it to reread the scribble.

"Are you considering Master Rokar's offer? I think it is rude of him to push his agenda while you are still mourning your dear father," Kaiser said as he sauntered up to Ryder from behind.

"Who let you out of jail?" Ryder snapped as he crumbled the paper and shoved it into his pocket.

"It seems that the Shadow Council has more things to worry about than watching little ol' me," Kaiser joked as he stepped up on the dais. "You however are in a very powerful position. If the people agree to legitimize you, you will become Shadowlord. You will sit upon your father's throne."

Ryder's eyes narrowed as he watched Kaiser run his fingers along the top of the arm of the chair. "I have not made a decision."

"Obviously or the Council would not be so desperate to recall Shiloh Silvanus back to Cross," Kaiser mused as he considered the supple and expensive fabric on the chair. "Now why would they even consider legitimizing a bastard when a perfectly legitimate son of patrilineal descent is still living?"

It certainly was a good question to ask. Yes it made sense because Ryder was in Cross as Shiloh was out on a mission to the distant reaches of their homeland. Ryder knew Shiloh hated Cross for the political machinations. He had begged Ryder to stay in Cross instead of going after the Mirror Sea Pirate. Shiloh was more than willing to volunteer to go in his place. Ryder had thought it foolish for Shiloh to leave while his father Akakios was facing justice for his failed war against the Waterborn. But then what standing did a bastard have against a true born Silvanus Prince?

"Why does it matter? You may be out of jail for now but I do not doubt that whoever sits on that throne will throw you back in," Ryder warned as he turned to face Kaiser.

The noble feigned innocence with an expression of surprise. "Dear grandson, I am here for a mission of goodwill for my dearly departed Lord's only child and heir. Surely you are not the only one who is grieving." He reached out a hand and laid it on Ryder's shoulder.

Ryder shook himself free. "We are not family!" He took a few steps back.

"You share my blood. I think that qualifies as family," Kaiser stated.

"If you claim to care so much about family, where were you when Akakios was executed. Oh I know! Languishing in prison or whatever dark depths you allowed the Shadow Council to put you in. You and that Demon servant of yours. If you think for one second to placate me and earn a place back in my court, well keep dreaming. I will never take this throne so long as you breathe," Ryder snarled viciously, pointing accusingly at Kaiser. He snorted as he stood up straight and squared his shoulders.

Kaiser tapped his chin to make a show of thought. "I would not make such a decision rashly, dear Peredur. You know as well as I do that Shiloh does not want the throne and it is your responsibility not to leave it abandoned. You are next in line regardless of your birth."

The blowhard noble was infuriating and Ryder could not think clearly enough through his rage towards Kaiser. "If you think for one second that you can control me, you are dead wrong. When Shiloh returns to Cross, I am gone and I will not return."

*****

He knew Kaiser was a shrewd thinker and brilliant strategist when it came to recognizing his physical surroundings. Ryder reached a hand forward to grab the rooftop edge, arching his back. His moment to strike would be brief as he waited for Kaiser to turn his back to him. Kaiser lounged across a red velvet bench, a leather bound book in one hand and tall glass of clear wine with a single floating cranberry in the other hand. He was dressed for bed in a house coat of black cloth, his midnight hair lying unstyled and messy. Kaiser appeared deep in study with an intense expression in his eyes. Patience was key to Ryder's mission as it made for a good hunter. He was prepared to wait but only for a small amount of time. Soja could only keep a Demon like Rache occupied for so long. His heart skipped one beat when Kaiser stood up, leaving the book on the bench. He downed the wine in one gulp and turned his back.

It was a split second before the knife flew towards Kaiser, Ryder following with Shadow Slide. The window split apart, the frosted glass pieces sparkling on the sill and floor. Kaiser turned around to the source of the noise, raising a hand to guard his eyes. The knife altered its course ever so slightly, the blade barely grazing across the back of his hand. Kaiser snarled as he realized what was happening. He threw a heavy fist forward to catch Ryder in the chest. Ryder went flying backwards through the broken window. He managed to catch the edge of the window sill before falling and slamming up against the outside wall. The glass cut deeply into his hand.

With a surge of his muscles, Ryder threw himself up and over the window sill, landing heavily on the floor. Kaiser did not seem the least bit put out by the sudden interruption to his evening. Instead of openly questioning his attitude, Ryder renewed his attack. He was going to kill Kaiser no matter what it took. But it infuriated him to see Kaiser so relaxed and he gritted his teeth tightly. With a flicker of thought, he tapped into his innate Spirit energy and unleashed Shadow Shock, throwing the sparkling black bolt at Kaiser's head. Kaiser casually lifted his left hand in time to catch the bolt and brush it away. The crackling energy blasted a nearby bookcase into pieces. Shreds of paper and splinters of wood floated down like rain drops during an evening storm. Ryder charged forward, this time combining Shadow Shock with his silver Spirit Fire into a battering ram.

Kaiser picked at his fingernails, ignoring the ferocious charge until the last possible second. He then grabbed Ryder's fire licked fist and laughed. He laughed as he crushed Ryder's fist, the force of his grip shattering the bones of Ryder's hand, wrist, and forearm. Kaiser then shifted his grip onto Ryder's broken arm, fingernails digging into his flesh, and twisted the useless limb. He pulled Ryder forward and kneed him in the gut before shoving him backwards.

"Amateur," Kaiser said as if it was an inconvenience to expend the least bit of energy in their encounter.

Ryder stumbled back, pain radiating from the hard hit. He spat out globules of blood as he tried to recover enough strength for a counterattack. He coughed violently, spitting up more blood. He then shot Kaiser a dangerous look. The Shadowborn noble only yawned and returned to picking at his fingernails. Ryder gritted his teeth as he clenched his left fist, ignoring the massive pain in his broken right arm. He charged forward again. As he did, Kaiser threw back his cumbersome cloak in a swift motion, revealing a long knife strapped to his leg. He ripped it free from its sheath.

"I laugh when people say that I am not a warrior. That I am just a Demon summoner and too old to be worth much of anything on the battlefield," Kaiser said as he held tight to his weapon. "Well, everyone is sadly mistaken."

Ryder rolled to his right, barely avoiding Kaiser's arcing slash. He gripped a large jagged piece of glass in his left hand and cut his palm open. Blood gushed from the wound. He ignored the pain as he pitched the shard at Kaiser's unprotected torso. It shattered into a shower of tiny pieces only a few inches away.

"What the..." Ryder managed to say before he had to dart out of the way from another slash. He flipped up to his feet and grabbed Kaiser's wrist to stop his forward attack. For a moment, it seemed as if Ryder would overpower Kaiser but as the seconds passed, it was clear that Kaiser would not yield.

"Oh, you actually think you can win?" Kaiser mocked before his free hand twisted hard on Ryder's left arm and snapped the bone. Ryder stumbled back, both of his arms now useless, and gritted his teeth.

"I am not so easily beaten," Ryder snarled, his breath hissing. He planted his feet and forced a current of Spirit energy through his shoulders and down to the palms of his hands. The cracking and resetting of bone was sickeningly audible and soon Ryder had healed the broken limbs.

"Hmm. Seems you learned a little something about healing from the Waterborn. I do wonder if your non-Shadowborn trainers had an inkling of your bloodline when you succeeded in learning their techniques. A Shadowborn that could master the other Spiritborn powers," Kaiser supposed in a mocking tone. He twirled the knife in his hand before pointing it at Ryder.

Renewed by the self healing, Ryder rushed forward. He initiated a close combat fight with Kaiser who was just as fast and limber as his much younger grandson. Ryder threw punches from all angles and attempted hard hitting kicks to knock Kaiser off of his feet. Kaiser remained steady and utterly calm, fighting in silence. The lack of emotion from Kaiser blinded Ryder with rage and he began to charge up another Spirit Fire attack. He rolled his left shoulder back, putting his body at an angle to Kaiser.

"I will kill you!" Ryder shouted with venom as he charged up the necessary Spirit energy.

Kaiser smirked and plunged his knife deep into Ryder's chest at an angle, hitting his left shoulder joint. The Spirit Fire immediately died. Kaiser quickly ripped the knife out before Ryder could retaliate and stabbed him again, this time aiming closer for his heart.

"I am sure you want to kill me but I don't want to kill you. Not yet," Kaiser said as he twisted the knife and brought Ryder down to his knees. He gripped Ryder's right shoulder tightly. "Your command of Spirit energy is impressive, grandson. But next time, don't challenge someone who is more skilled than you in wielding it." He leaned in closer to whisper in Ryder's ear. "Time to go back home where you belong."

DECISIONS

Rache growled as he faced Soja, who stood between him and Aku. The Saber proved more of a road block than he had imagined. Every time he would advance towards Aku, Soja struck like an annoying little insect. Rache wanted to smash him. Soja was small but fast and darted around like a hummingbird. His sword would shoot forward like a stabbing spear. It was infuriating to the Demon.

"Come on and fight me like the ruthless Saber you are!" Rache snarled, having just received a slash across the right side of his face. He felt the fury rising quickly within him, his power still diminished by the wards of Crossroads. The inner beast fought desperately to break free.

Soja had barely said a word since their initial and brief conversation, his focus resolute. It was the famous manner of the Sabers who fought in complete silence. Rache knew that this Saber was a talker and in the direct service of the Prince. His family had bought him that position. He was sure of it. Rache knew the Rokars were a powerful family who had thankfully been left behind to run the Shadowborn homeland. He did not care for the suspicious Zoras Rokar and now his son was annoying the Hell out of him. He snarled viciously as he prepared for another attack.

A stinging sensation brought Rache's attention to his left hand. A light red line appeared on the back on his hand and he immediately knew that this chase and encounter was a ruse. Someone was trying to kill Kaiser. Too bad they did not know

Kaiser could not be killed. Rache at first was angry but now he smiled, his white fangs gleaming.

"This has been fun, child, but I now have some important business to attend to," Rache said with a deep mocking bow, one arm across his back. He stood back up. "I shall kill you another time."

Soja saw the change in the Demon's expression and could barely question it before Rache burst out of the room. He quickly turned to check on Aku to see that he was suffering from a Demon burn across his throat. It was black and oozing blood. It smelled horribly vile. He tore a strip of fabric from his borrowed tunic and tried to clean the wound.

Aku's voice cracked as he tried to speak. "Protect... my... son..." The sound was dry and broken.

It surprised Soja that Aku had spoken and even given him an order. "My Lord, I will hold my Saber's oath and see that your family suffers no longer," Soja said as he strengthened his resolve. He stepped over to the door and threw it open.

A guard was posted at the end of the hallway and immediately came running upon seeing Soja. Sabers had seniority over court guards and Soja knew he could issue the right order. "Protect the Shadowlord with your life. A Demon of terrible power tried to kill him. I will spread the alarm."

The guard gasped and stammered for words. He slapped his right arm across his chest and bowed his head. "No one will be able to come near his Royal Highness without my sword to answer to, mighty Saber."

Soja let the guard pass into the room before he took off down the hallway. He planned on telling every guard to be on alert though he would not tell them just yet that it was Rache who attacked Aku. For the time being, he had to push Ryder's likely fate out of his mind. Coming across another guard, Soja ordered him to Aku's quarters in a command. The guard nodded and rushed away without question.

He burst into the courtyard and found a large Horned Owl Gryphon pacing the gateway. The beast held its head up high, looking fierce and imposing. Sliding to a stop, Soja got the Gryphon's attention with a wave of the hand. "I need a message delivered to Lord Avis at once."

"Lord Avis is resting," the Gryphon started to say as his ear tufts lifted up from his round skull.

"A Demon attacked my Lord," Soja interupted in a low voice. The Gryphon's hackles rose up. "I need to see him immediately."

Without hesitation, the Gryphon burst in the sky, flapping his large wings hard. Soja watched as he dipped out of sight.

Taking a deep breath, he calmed himself, relaxing his nerves as best he could. He twisted around to find Morin, still in his bed clothes and hair in a mess.

"Are you saying that Lord Aku was attacked by a Demon?!" the Commander demanded.

Soja hated the man who served Kaiser so loyally. "I fought the Demon monster myself," Soja stated firmly. "Seems like your beloved master has finally turned as my father always said he would. Maybe now you will remember who the Shadowlord is, if he survives the night," he added in a warning growl.

Morin frowned. "You dare question my loyalty?"

"Such is my duty to make sure the Shadowlord has trustworthy servants," Soja snapped. He did not have much pull over Morin's Commander position. He had to find the Saber in charge to issue his final order. "Until such time as Aku recovers or dies, the Crowned Prince is the Shadowlord. Get out of my sight." He truly hated the man and rushed away, not wanting to wait to hear his response.

Hayden Abendroth was barking orders left and right when Soja found him in the foyer. The Saber Captain had quickly taken charge of the rising chaos. Soja's message of the attack had carried farther and faster than he could have hoped. Soja bowed his head and waited. "Everyone out!" Hayden shouted. The room cleared, leaving only Hayden and Soja.

"I defended our sovereign Lord to the best of my ability though I wish I had killed the beast," Soja said in a subordinate tone.

"You did your duty in the face of evil. I shall recommend a promotion to Commander Parahazur upon our return to Cross," Hayden said as he paced nervously. "Are you harmed?"

"I will live but I fear for Lord Aku," Soja replied.

Hayden sighed deeply as he ran a hand over his face. "The Daylord will have to come now if the Shadowlord is no longer safe."

"I know the Crowned Prince is young but I vote to his rising as Shadowlord as soon as possible. Let us forgo the succession rules here in Crossroads so we may protect our people," Soja suggested after a moment of silence.

"It goes against tradition but I support the decision. I will gather all Shadowborn present in the city to vote upon it should Lord Aku pass into the Spirit World. However, I do not want to lose hope yet for his healing and survival," Hayden replied. "We can not name another Shadowlord while one still lives."

"Should we even include Kaiser?" Soja dared to ask.

Hayden spat venomously on the floor. "I will not include that scheming...!" He could not finish his curse of Kaiser as the anger gripped him.

"Lord Avis will know of this. He will make sure a message is sent to the Daylord and then we can end this storm," Soja stated with confidence. The Daylord would shake Kaiser's blasted arrogance.

"You will return to Cross at once. Your father must be told immediately. I will see to the safety of our Lord and Prince. Tell no one of your journey," Hayden promptly ordered. "The rebellion must be told."

"The border is sealed against me," Soja stated, remembering what Ryder had told him of the Shadow Mirror. He then told Hayden what Ryder had said.

"Find a way through," Hayden snapped. "We could certainly use the bastard in our fight. Do you know what has become of him?" Hayden asked looking Soja straight in the eyes.

Soja shook his head. "I can only hope our need reaches him as it should reach the Daylord. We will need all the help we can get before the end."

Hayden sighed deeply as he ran his fingers through his hair. He looked around the foyer. "We must do what we can. Speak honestly to Lord Avis. The truth must be told," Hayden declared.

The young Saber saluted his superior and whirled around to rush towards the citadel in the cloak of Shadow Slide. His desparate need drove him to unparalleled speed and he reached the massive fortress within seconds. He came out of Shadow Slide just before the gates, stumbling from the sudden change in speed.

The same Desert Falcon Gryphon he had met with earlier in the evening was speaking to the Horned Owl Gryphon in their native tongue. The Horned Owl Gryphon spotted Soja and issued him forward with a bob of the head. Soja jogged towards him, still trying to catch his breath and save energy for the race home.

"Mistress Lana says Proto Avis is resting in preparation to watch the stars . She will bear your message the rest of the way," the Owl Gryphon said in the common tongue. His accent was heavy and Soja could barely understand him. He at least spoke with more confidence than the Falcon Gryphon had when they last met.

"I must swear you both to absolute secrecy for your own safety," Soja told them, gesturing with his hands to emphasize his point. He waited as the Owl Gryphon quickly translated for his kin. Lana nodded though Soja could tell that she was nervous. "Rache..."

Both Gryphons cried and immediately began speaking to each other in the Gryphon tongue of whistles, chaws, and chirps. It was apparent that they knew the name of the Demon quite well.

It surprised Soja then when Lana stepped forward to look him in the eyes.

"Saber, I will fly your words," Lana said, her accent whistling through the translation. She said something to the Owl Gryphon in their native tongue and he bobbed his head.

"Make sure my Lord and his son are cared for. It pains me to leave them in this troubling time," Soja pleaded.

The Gryphons nodded with dips of their big heads. "We shall not fail you. We will both take an oath to protect all of the Silvanus bloodline," the Owl Gryphon stated. Apparently forgetting Ryder's unknown insult, Soja saw that Lana stood and held herself in the same manner as her kin. She was equally prepared and ready to hold to the declaration.

"Thank you," Soja said as he dipped into the Spiritborn to Gryphon bow. Even if it was not necessary, he was honestly grateful for their promise. The Gryphons in turn mimicked his bow. Without a second thought, Soja shifted into Shadow Slide and began his rush back home to the north.

*****

"This can not be. This absolutely can not be. I saw him fall myself," Vorin managed to say in disbelief. He snaked his head around to face Proto who was still in shock from the news. "Proto?"

The old Gryphon sat slackjawed, his wings draped on the ground. He did not have the strength to hold them up. His chest heaved as he struggled to find the words. His thoughts were racing with questions that ranged from Ryder's fate to how Rache was still alive. "Are you sure that he died?"

Vorin nodded. "Begin Anu and Rache exchanged fatal blows to the heart. I used my Dragonfire to burn Rache's body to ash. There was nothing left!" He looked about the room as if he was reliving the distant memory. The look in his eyes wavered between disorientation and rising anger. Vorin then snarled, smoke pouring out of his nostrils. "Get me Kaiser Adonis!"

KAISER'S STRANGLEHOLD

Kaiser strolled through the empty streets of Crossroads with a smug grin on his face. He was dressed in his finest clothes. He wore a pair of leather boots, black wool pants, and a luxurious coat lined with silk. A chain made of moonstones and silver rested across his shoulders. Despite his pristine appearance, his hair was tousled from the breeze. Kaiser reached up to smooth it down. He started to whistle an upbeat tune.

Following the events of the previous night, no one dared to step outside. The idea that Rache was alive frightened everyone from the smallest Spiritborn child to the largest Gryphon. Everyone except Kaiser. He was amused by the fear, pleased that he had a part in its cause. It did not even matter that the Lords of Crossroads sent his own blood to kill him or that Rache was led on a wild goose chase. Every part of last night played right into his hand. Ryder was back under his control. Rache threatened Aku with death and now he had earned his terrible reputation back from the depths of the past.

He stepped under an archway, dragging his hand over the chiseled stonework. Kaiser smirked as he saw Vorin and Proto Avis turn around to face him. The Dragon snarled, baring his sharp teeth. He snorted out puffs of black smoke.

"Dear, Dragonlord. Too much smoke might suffocate the delicate lungs of your Gryphon friend," Kaiser chastised as he walked between Vorin and Proto. He stepped up to the edge of the Wall of Crossroads. "Ah such a wonderous sight to look upon each day. I envy you."

A roar built up in Vorin's chest. "I want to know how you did it. I know that you had a hand in Rache's resurrection."

Kaiser pressed a hand to his heart as he turned around. "I would say that I am flattered but you know as well as I do that no one is capable of raising the dead." He chuckled softly as he latched his hands behind his back. "Not even the mighty Bane Arlis."

"Correct me if I am wrong but are you an expert on Demons or not?" Proto asked, his courage bolstered by Vorin's presence.

Kaiser swung back and forth on his feet. "I might be."

In that instant, Proto wanted to claw Kaiser's eyes out. His toes dug into the stone, dulling the tips of his talons. He wanted desparately to lash out but part of him feared that he would not be able to do much damage. He mashed his beak together as he watched Kaiser pick at his fingernails, acting as if their meeting was a casual conversation between dignitaries. Kaiser's look was deceiving. He was more than capable of tearing an old Gryphon like Proto apart. But Proto was secure in the knowledge that he had his friend Vorin at his side.

Vorin thumped his thick tail on the rock, kicking up a cloud of dust. "Do not think to lie in front of me. One snap of my jaws and you will be dead."

Kaiser chuckled and shook his head. His expression then turned dark. "You know nothing of death."

"And you do?" Proto asked, jerking his head back. He had not expected the statement. "You dare to make that claim in front of Lord Vorin?"

"Yes. Yes I do. Your kin chose to sacrifice themselves for the Immortal Truth. They chose death," Kaiser directed towards Vorin, lifting an eyebrow and crossing his arms.

"Don't you dare insult the name of my kin and their sacrifice! It is because of them we have the Immortal Truth!" Vorin roared. He shot his head forward within inches of Kaiser's face. Kaiser did not even flinch. "It is because of them that we have the Daylord."

Kaiser waved them off. "Clearly he does not respect the Immortal Truth as you think he should. Otherwise, he would have been here to defend poor sick Aku from Rache. Maybe I could have faced the Demon myself but you two banned me from Crossroads. I bet that I could have even killed Rache and saved you all of this trouble."

Both Vorin and Proto leapt up to their feet and hissed. The wind coming up from the Southlands plains whipped across the rockface as if the world was angry too. Kaiser seemed oblivious to their anger as he turned his back on them to look over the distant grasslands. Vorin started to growl louder, spitting out jets of flame. Proto flared his wings in a threat display.

"You sent my own flesh and blood to try and kill me. For the record, that was not very nice," Kaiser commented. He then slapped his hands together. "At least now I get to spend time with dear Peredur."

The two Lords of Crossroads were suddenly reminded of Ryder's fate. "Where is he?" they both demanded.

Kaiser turned around and waved a finger back and forth. "I must protect my family from the machinations of others. He has suffered so much over these years. He is no longer your concern."

"Then perhaps you do deserve to be burned by Lord Vorin's Dragonfire," Proto warned with an edge to his voice. Vorin roared in agreement, spitting out flames from between his teeth.

Kaiser burst out laughing. "Are you serious? I have already been through Hellfire and back. Dragonfire will just tickle my skin." He pretended to shiver.

In a gigantic burst of Dragonfire, Vorin bathed Kaiser with his great flame. He had had enough of Kaiser's arrogance and wanted him dead with every fiber of his being. He pushed more and more heat into his breath, lighting the sky with a burst of red, orange, yellow, and white. Kaiser disappeared under the brightness. Proto had to shield himself behind Vorin's right wing to avoid being burned. The air sizzled from the heat.

"Oh enough of this!" Kaiser shouted, his voice tearing across the roar of the flames. He twisted his hands in a circle before pushing them forward. The Dragonfire separated around him and burst out over the distant grasslands before the Wall. Not a hair or thread on Kaiser's person was singed.

Vorin closed his mouth and jerked his head back in shock. He snarled ferociously before blasting Kaiser with another burst of fire. Kaiser laughed out loud, repeating the same hand twisting motions to separate the flames.

"It did not work the first time so what makes you think that it will work the second time," Kaiser mocked. He backed up to the edge and threw his arms out wide. Kaiser chuckled with a mischievous smirk on his face. "You can't kill me with Dragonfire."

The Dragon lurched forward, raising a paw to swipe at Kaiser. It was Proto that stopped him by stepping in front and blocking a potential strike. He drew his wings in, the bones in them achy from holding them up so long. His tail swished behind him, dragging across the top of Vorin's planted paw.

"Do not think to hide behind your carefully constructed façade any longer. You may think that you are invincible but you are not for everyone has an end. If you do not fear the Immortal Truth then fear the Covenant of Spirits. It destroys people like you," Proto hissed.

Kaiser snicked. "You know what? Shadow Night said the exact same thing before he died. What a coincidence!"

Proto and Vorin had long suspected that Shadow Night was dead for it had been too long since anyone had heard or seen him. Had anyone else claimed to know his last words, the reaction would have been respect and sadness. Proto and Vorin were horrified and angry. Vorin shot forward, putting his jaws within inches of Kaiser's face. He snorted a cloud of smoke and growled. Kaiser smiled back.

"I am not afraid of you, Dragon," Kaiser politely said. "Go ahead and snap my body in two with your mighty jaws. I might even enjoy it."

Proto could not stop Vorin from opening his great maw and rushing to grab Kaiser. He fell back in shock when Kaiser set his hands on Vorin's open jaws. Kaiser held Vorin's mouth open to the point that Vorin was struggling to continue going forward. It was like Vorin had set himself against a solid mountain. He threw his strength into breaking Kaiser's hold, jerking his head back and forth. Spittle sprayed all over both of them. Vorin finally managed to break free once Kaiser let go. Kaiser shrugged as if to apologize for the inconvience, flinging the hot saliva from his hands.

"It did not work for Shadow Night and it will not work for you," Kaiser admitted as he dropped his shoulders. "It's a terrible thing that no one has believed me all these years. That I am a force to be reckoned with," Kaiser snarled. He took a step forward, forcing Proto and Vorin back. "Yes, I did raise Rache back from the dead. Yes, I have killed hundreds. Perhaps even thousands over my life time. And you know what? I enjoyed every second of it. So continue playing your game of 'let's kill that son of a bitch so the world will be safe,' and I'll continue playing mine. Except this time, I have one of your best players on my side. Try to take him back or try to kill me, I'll take another and kill them like I did your precious Shadow Night Silvanus. Ta ta!"

Kaiser sauntered past a flabbergasted Proto and Vorin, absently waved his hand in a farewell gesture. They watched as he disappeared under the archway and back into the city, listening to his boisterous laughter.

SHAKEN

Onyx paced the hallway outside of his father's quarters, his mirth from the celebration forgotten. He held the crown of the Shadowborn in his hands, rolling it between his palms. His emotions wavered between worry and fear to stern resolve. His father had been attacked by a Demon and the only person capable of healing his pain was Kaiser Adonis. He was surprised that Proto Avis had let Kaiser back into the city so quickly but he was grateful. No one knew Demon burns and injuries like Kaiser. He nervously walked back and forth, scuffing his boots on the stone floor. His ears strained for any word or cry of pain from inside where Kaiser was working on his father. His heart raced even faster as time went on.

The Saber Captain Hayden Abendroth stood at attention nearby, watching Onyx carefully. "Your Highness, I have postponed the meeting with our national representatives as requested. Is there anything else I can do?"

"I don't know," Onyx nervously said as he continued pacing back and forth. "What exactly did Soja tell you about the Demon?"

Hayden shifted his weight. He had already told his Prince but obliged him anyway. "The Demon was alabaster white with blood red hair and a terrible look in his eyes. He was thin but his body was compact with muscle. Rache is truly fearsome creature, your Highness."

It did not matter how many times Hayden described the Demon attacker. It just made Onyx pace even faster to the point that he was wearing down the heels of his boots. He twisted and twirled the crown faster in his hands as he could not help but stare at the door.

"What is going on in there? What is taking him so long?" Onyx blurted out as he paused by the door. He pressed his palms on the crown even tighter.

"The Demon touched your father's neck and left a terrible burn. Kaiser said that the wound goes deep and exposes his windpipe. He is taking great care to seal the wound," Hayden explained cautiously.

Onyx resumed pacing, keeping his head down and mumbling to himself. This was not how he wanted to become the Shadowlord. He wanted to have a proper coronation in Cross before a crowd of his kinsmen, not as an emergency in Crossroads. He wanted to finish his training in statecraft. The weight of command was something he was not prepared for, especially so far from home. He began to doubt his decision and ability to rule. He was only eighteen. What did he know about ruling the Shadowborn? What experience did he have? His thoughts strayed towards his bastard cousin and he frowned. Ryder was experienced. He was worldly. He was everything people said he was to be a proper Shadowlord. He was more capable and ready.

"I want to see my father," Onyx demanded harshly without really meaning to. He paused to look up at Hayden.

The dutiful Saber bowed his head and stepped over to the door. Onyx set the crown on his head and strengthened his resolve. He told himself that no matter what he saw inside, he would remain strong. Hayden opened the door for him and followed his Prince inside. Kaiser was busy snapping at Morin to pull open every curtain and open every window to get as much light and fresh air in the room as possible. The Shadowborn noble's hands were wrapped with cloth that was stained with blackened blood and pieces of burnt skin. It did not appear to bother him. Morin darted around with a pair of Sabers, ripping open the curtains and pushing open the windows. Kaiser barked another order to fetch a basin of hot water. The pair of Sabers nervously jumped at the order and rushed out of the room to fetch the basin.

Onyx stiffened at the sight of his father on the lounge, a cold gray palour on his skin. His mind flashbacked to the memory of when Aku was brought back half dead to Cross and he shuddered. Tears welled up in Onyx's eyes but he quickly squelched them. Kaiser stepped over to Aku's side, running a damp cloth through his hands.

"The Prince is here to see his father, Master Adonis," Hayden said sternly.

Kaiser paused as the cloth slapped down on his left hand. He silently gestured for Onyx to come forward but a glare forbade Hayden from following. Onyx gulped before he came to his father's left side, sitting down on a footstool. He hesitated to grab Aku's hand.

"How is he?" Onyx struggled to ask, the pain of his previous memory fresh and raw in his heart.

"Your noble father suffered greater when he was attacked on the hunt those years ago," Kaiser said in a flat tone. "He is weak but he will pull through."

The admission was a relief to Onyx and he let out a deep breath. He took his father's hand and found his touch to be icy cold. He looked up quickly at Kaiser. "He's so cold."

"A Demon's burn works to draw all heat in the body to where the monster touches. When treating such an injury, one must wrap their hands to avoid any lasting effect. The poison of a Demon's touch can linger for hours after contact," Kaiser explained as he showed Onyx his wrapped hands. "Do not worry, good Prince. I have already drawn most of the poison from your father. Another few hours and it should be gone from his body."

Onyx gulped as he held onto his father's hand. He stroked the back of it with his thumb, moving it in small circles. "How do you draw the poison away?"

"A secret art, good Prince. One I can teach you about later when your mind is more settled," Kaiser replied. The two Sabers burst back into the room and quickly set the large basin of steaming water by Kaiser's side. He waved them back and dipped the cloth in the water. He pulled it back out and twisted the cloth to remove excess water. "My mother taught me when a Demon had seen fit to claw my father's shoulder during a raid."

The admission about his past surprised Onyx. Kaiser was rarely candid about his long dead family, referring sporadically to them and even then, it was mostly about being the son of General Cian. It made Kaiser seem almost humane and kind and Onyx felt his fear abating.

"Master Adonis, who is responsible for the security of the Shadowlord on this trip?" Onyx asked.

"Commander Win, your Highness," Kaiser answered as he dabbed the wet cloth around Aku's face.

Onyx looked over his shoulder at Morin and curled his lip. He let go of his father's hand and stood up. Morin immediately stiffened as Onyx approached with clenched fists.

"Commander Win, where were you when my father was attacked?" Onyx demanded harshly.

"I was in my bedchamber resting," Morin admitted

nervously. He looked over at Kaiser.

"Don't you look at him! I am the one talking to you. Why was my father attacked on your watch by a Demon?" Onyx demanded in a louder voice.

Morin appeared to stammer and struggle for the right words to say. "Your Highness, this is Crossroads. Until last night, no Demon had set foot inside the city walls in over a thousand years."

"And yet one did, Commander," Kaiser interrupted in a forceful tone. "If you will pardon my interruption, your Highness."

"No, go ahead since you too were attacked on the Commander's watch," Onyx said as he returned to his father's side.

Kaiser handed Onyx the wet cloth and stood up. He rounded the lounge and came to stand before Morin. He then slapped him hard across the jaw, knocking him to the ground. Morin squeaked with shock as he rubbed the spot. "You have failed the Shadowlord by holding to a false belief that a Demon would not attempt to walk the city since one had not since the signing of the Immortal Truth! You have failed your Prince and you have failed me!"

The Commander looked up at Kaiser utterly frightened of him. "But..."

Kaiser struck him again. "You know the state of the throne and you risked it failing by not protecting your Lord! Now get up and beg the Prince's forgiveness for failing him and causing him pain."

Onyx watched as Morin crawled over to him. The Commander kissed the floor at his feet, his chest heaving with fear. He mumbled a line of words over and over with a shaky voice. Onyx jerked his foot away, his confidence swollen from Kaiser's strong words.

"If it pleases you, your Highness. I will recommend to the Shadow Council that Morin Win be relieved of his command and stripped of all titles for his failure," Kaiser suggested as he shot an angry glare down at Morin. Morin shuddered and pressed his brow to the floor.

"It pleases me greatly unless Commander Win can redeem himself and prove that he is worthy to lead the armies of the Shadowlord," Onyx replied as Kaiser took the cloth back. He stood up straight and looked down at Morin. "Master Adonis, make sure my father is well cared for. I will tend to his duties here in Crossroads."

Kaiser bowed his head. "As you command, your Highness." He gestured towards Hayden which surprised the Saber Captain. "I would recommend keeping Captain Hayden close at hand until this Demon is stopped. Both Lord Vorin and Lord Proto Avis have asked me to investigate."

"Then they have chosen well, Master Adonis," Hayden stated through gritted teeth.

Hayden's reaction was not lost on Onyx. "What is the problem? If the Lords of Crossroads trust Master Adonis with the investigation, then I do too. From what I have been told, Rache is a creature not to be triflied with. I have also been told by several people that Master Adonis has fought many Demons and no one knows them better than him."

At that moment, Aku coughed weakly, spewing a small spray of blood. Kaiser bent down to his side, speaking softly to him and wiping his forehead with the warm cloth. Everyone paused to watch him, some eager to see Kaiser's healing power in action. Kaiser left the damp cloth on Aku's forehead and took the cloth bindings off his hands. He then reached for the cloth that had covered Aku's burn. Onyx covered his mouth to avoid vomiting and was shocked to see the extent of his father's injury. Hayden laid a hand on the young Prince's shoulder. The room fell completely silent as Kaiser took the cloth from Aku's forehead and dropped it in the water basin.

Kaiser set his left hand on Aku's forehead and wrapped his right hand over Aku's neck wound. Onyx spotted a strange twisting mark on the back of Kaiser's right hand.

"What is that tattoo on Master Adonis' hand? I do not remember seeing such a mark before," Onyx whispered to Hayden.

"Blessing or curse, unseen by eyes, forever true, let the power rise," Hayden quoted. "It is a Spirit Mark, your Highness. An ancient magic. Very difficult to come by. Master Adonis' power is true. He really can heal Demon burns," Hayden explained, his voice changing from tactum reverance to amazement.

Onyx watched as the black mark on Kaiser's hand began to glow with silver light. The light pulsated, following the map of blood vessels under his skin. It spread to Aku's neck and Aku immediately started to struggle. Kaiser pressed his hand tighter on Aku's forehead, looking him directly in the face. Aku appeared to settle after a minute of shivering.

"Be at peace, dear Aku. The Spirits are with you," Kaiser murmured before he passed his left hand over Aku's eyes. "Rest now and regain your strength." He slowly pulled his hands away from Aku.

Aku's neck wound finished shifting in color from black to red just before Kaiser began to dress it with bandages. He briefly looked up and gestured for Onyx to come forward. Onyx gulped and swallowed hard. Hayden nodded his head and encouraged him to go to Aku's side. Onyx nodded back and slowly stepped over to his father's side, his nerves racing.

"I have drawn the last of the poison from your father's body. He should be able to rest and heal more comfortably now," Kaiser said in a low voice.

Something dawned on Onyx. "But where did the poison go? Did it go inside of you?"

Kaiser chuckled lightly. "Do not fear for me, your Highness. I know how to dispel the poison in a way that causes no harm. So long as your father is well, I will confront any pain that comes my way."

It was hard to comprehend what Kaiser was trying to tell him but Onyx was relieved to see his father peacefully sleeping. Still, it worried him that Rache had gotten so close. Crossroads was supposed a fortress against Demons. It even had wards built into the city design to repel them. Onyx took Aku's hand as he considered this conundrum. He had always been told that Rache had died in the same battle that Begin Anu had died. A battle that had occurred thousands of year ago.

"Master Adonis, if it was truly Rache that attacked my father, how is he alive?" Onyx asked Kaiser directly.

Kaiser let out a deep breath. "Look to the Covenant of Spirits, your Highness. It would seem that someone has thought to use it for their own dark ends. I would be afraid of such a person."

*****

A feeling of unease fell over the city of Crossroads as whispers permeated the air. The whispers spoke of the dangerous Demon lurking in the shadows, ready to attack at any moment. The celebration had transformed from a joyous affair to one of decorum. The streets grew unusually quiet without the energetic shouts of revelers and squeals of excited children. It seemed as if a dark cloud had settled over the city, casting a dull gray depression on everyone. No Gryphon flew in the open and if they dared to, they never went without a partner. No Spiritborn, even the Shadowborn, walked alone. It seemed as if danger was lurking around every corner and they was no indication of when it would reveal itself again. The Demon's prescence had taken hold of the city.

THE RITUAL

Once evening started to fall, Crossroads fell into a reverent and quiet atmosphere. Royals and dignitaries of note were dressed in their finest formal wear complete with jewels and crowns on their person. Guards from each nation lined the street on both sides, an unofficial sign that where they were was the way to go. Gryphons perched on rooftops, feathers and fur freshly washed and shimmering in the emerging starlight. None of them cried out or spoke in loud voices, self relegated to soft whistles and hoots amongst themselves. Lanterns burned brightly to light the way to the ritual hall.

Onyx walked at the head of the Shadowborn company, dressed in black and silver cloth. A silver and moonstone collar studded with diamonds rested across his shoulders. He bore a haughty expression as his father leaned heavily on his right arm, dressed in the same finery. Both of their crowns gleamed and sparkled against their dark hair. While Onyx had a sword belted on at his left hip, Aku had been given an ebony and silver cane to aid in his walking. The shuffling of their feet mixed with the tapping of Aku's cane. Together they represented the blood of Shadow Night Silvanus in his noble glory.

Behind the Shadowborn walked the Lightborn with Lord Evander at the front. He wore robes of bright gold that rippled with each of his steps. His blonde hair fell upon his shoulders and down to the middle of his back. Streaks of white hinted at his great age but the Lord of the Lightborn's face was smooth and had no wrinkles. His crown was made of crystal and yellow gems. Unlike the Shadowborn, the Lightborn carried no obvious weapons.

Two Owl Gryphons of snow white pelts waited at the doorway to the hall. The Gryphon on the left of the doorway shuffled its paws to stand in front of Onyx and Aku while allowing the rest of the Shadowborn to pass. The Gryphon on the right did the same for Evander and the Lightborn. Both creatures eyed Kaiser who had walked at the very end of the Shadowborn. The Shadowborn noble wore a cloak of black cloth, the hood drawn up over his head. A collar of silver and black diamonds sat across his shoulders. Kaiser wore no visible weapon and instead carried a silver crescent moon in his hands. A Lightborn man stepped back from his kin and came to stand beside Kaiser, wearing a similar get up but in the colors of his nation. He held a golden sun in his hands.

The Owl Gryphon ushers then escorted their charges inside the ritual hall. Onyx saw that most of the seats were already filled by the other Spiritborn except for three on the left frontside and two on the right frontside. Onyx, Aku, and Evander followed their escorts past the rows and Fireborn that stood in the aisles holding candles. Evander was quickly seated on the right side and the Shadowborn royals were seated on the left side. Onyx fought the urge to look around and see where his mother's family sat. As his usher passed in front of him, he stole a look back over his shoulder. Four rows of Shadowborn nobles and dignitaries were immediately behind him. Behind them were the Earthborn royals and their entourage.

His uncle Palani was dressed in vibrant greens, his golden brown hair held back by a crown of emeralds and silver in the shape of ivy leaves and twigs. His aunt sat next to her husband in a sumptuous gown of green and white. Her crown resembled a band of pink flowers. Flynn sat dutifully next to his mother though Onyx could see him twitching in his seat and bouncing his legs. A sharp look from both of his parents settled him. Onyx chuckled softly as he turned back around. He set his left hand on his father's hand and gave it a squeeze as he smiled.

At the front of the hall stood Proto Avis, his great wings outstretched accentuating his form. Before him on the altar was a basin lit by Vorin's own Dragon Fire, since at his great size, he could not fit inside the hall. Unlike before when he saw the old Gryphon, Proto's feathers were bright and supple. His fur was brushed and trimmed of any stray hairs. Proto looked strong and glorious like a Gryphon should, Onyx told himself. His talons and beak were shined to hold a bright sheen. Onyx began to imagine that Vorin was also not in the hall because his deep red scales would have glittered so brightly that no one would have been able to see. He hoped to see the Dragon after the ceremony was finished.

A low rumble of drumbeats sounded from the back of the hall. The rhythm was at first slow and steady, accompanied by no other instrument. Then, a chorus of voices began singing in a low ominous tone, vocalizing more than saying the actual words of a song. Onyx immediately knew that the voices came from an Airborn choir for there were no better singers in the Northlands. The first round of voices were the deep baritones of men but as the drumbeats sped up, another round of voices joined them. The sweet and soft tones of the female Airborn singers were haunting and yet inviting. As the combined sound of the drums and chorus grew in volume, several flutes joined in to add a playful and positive feeling to the song.

The song built in volume and sense of an epic history that was about to be told. From the back of the room, a team of dancers from each of the Spiritborn tribes began their routine, dressed in the colors of their nation. The Waterborn dancers led the way with their fluid movements. They waved their arms like the ripples on a pond and the treacherous surge of a stormy sea. Right behind the Waterborn pair were two Airborn who bounced on their feet and acted like a twirling breeze. Onyx then saw two Ladies of Flora behind the Waterborn and immediately recognized Luna. Green ribbons and white flowers were tied to strands of her hair. Unlike the last time she danced, her expression was serious and focused. Behind Luna and her Lady partner were the athletic Fireborn dancers, charging and dancing with powerful movements. The Lightborn moved in time with the Fireborn but rose their arms higher as if to lift themselves up to the sky. At the end of the dancing troupe were two Shadowborn whose moves were confident but somber.

The column of dancers split into two groups as they reached the front of the hall. The wide aisle was empty for a space until Stellaris and Paladon stepped forward. Each Gryphon wore the effects of their station. Their wings were raised in an upstroke flying position. Stellaris walked on the right with one of his dark brown flight feathers in his bill. Paladon walked on the left with a sprig of greenwood in his bill. The two Gryphons walked in time with each other as if they were marching.

Behind the Gryphons and the final souls of the procession were Kaiser and his Lightborn counterpart. Kaiser was taller and more proud in his bearing, the hint of a smirk playing on his face. Onyx wondered about the expression as his father's Chancellor passed by. Onyx watched as Kaiser and the Lightborn stepped up to the basin of Dragon Fire. The Shadowborn noble waited as Proto Avis gestured for the Lightborn to drop the golden sun in his hands. The Lightborn man nodded and quickly but reverently dropped the object into the basin. The Dragon Fire burst up and snapped, letting off a wave of heat that drove back Proto Avis and the Lightborn. Kaiser remained and did not lean away from the heat. After the moment passed, both returned to the basin. Proto Avis nodded towards Kaiser. Kaiser stepped forward and stuck his hand in the fire to drop the crescent moon.

Everyone, including the Fireborn, cringed as Kaiser kept his hand in the fire. Proto held his breath as Kaiser lifted his gaze to him, smirking. The Shadowborn noble slowly pulled his hand back, showing that the fire had not touched and burned him. He bowed his head before turning around to take the seat next to Aku. Proto's animal gaze did not leave Kaiser for a long time.

"Tonight, we come together to honor the great and powerful Immortal Truth! Shadow and light, rise as the champions of Immortalia Terra to battle the dark! Earth, Fire, Water, Air! The call of the Spiritborn!" Proto's voice shouted with command once he finally looked up at the assembled crowd before him. "Spirit and Beast, we own the North so the South may be free! May the next one hundred years be blessed and may we have cause to hope that peace will permeate the air and bring forth life, love, and happiness. Long live the Immortal Truth!" he cried out in a jubilant tone. He allowed a moment for the room of occupants to cheer. He grew silent, steading his breath, before he proceeded to recite the entire Immortal Truth from memory.

> *Lift up the Immortal Powers*
> *With voices singing of ages long past*
> *Lift up the Mortal Spirit*
> *Innocence of the future to come*
>
> *Shadow, light, air*
> *Earth, water, fire*
> *Feather and scale*
> *Blood and darkness*
>
> *We once lived in fear at the time of birth*
> *With no guidance before a terrible foe*
> *But a shining light came from afar*
> *To cast down a Demon monster*
>
> *Shadow against evil*
> *Master of the night*

Crowned by the moon
Praises sung by the wolf

The champions are named by all
Shadowlord and Daylord
Guardians of truth and mercy
Warriors of power and heart

Light against evil
Master of days
Crowned by the sun
Praises sung by the dove

United the bloodlines come together
To write a bond of truly great power
A promise is made to protect the innocent
And to make a code of laws...

The oath that began the Immortal Truth was in of itself an incantation to open one's mind to their deepest memories. For the youngest people present in the audience, the words stirred a feeling inside them about the past that they did not understand. For the oldest, it was more vivid and real. The song that started the ceremony fell into a low and haunting melody. Everything accented Proto's voice as he recited the oath in the common tongue.

Duty in times of war
We are the sword
We are the shield
We are the guardians against the dark

Duty in times of peace
We are the word
We are the song
We are the teachers of the light

Life is sacred
Life is precious
Death is endless
Death is forever

Proto then began reciting the governing laws written within the Immortal Truth's words. Onyx listened with great interest. Like every Spiritborn from the lowliest peasant to the royal Lords, he had read the Immortal Truth many times over. He had not been interested enough as a child to memorize it word for word but he made a silent promise to himself to do so before his hopeful winter coronation. He wondered if his father had to memorize it and he was sure that Kaiser knew the entire Immortal Truth by heart.

The recitation continued long into the night as Proto's voice kept its strength and power without stopping. Some of the laws seemed too simple to warrant inclusion, Onyx thought, but he decided that if his ancestor believed them to be important, then he would too. The Shadowborn Prince then began to wonder how the Immortal Truth would sound in Vorin's deep reptilian voice.

By these words shall we live
By these words shall we die
The Spirit reigns
The Immortal Truth reigns

At the stroke of midnight, Proto finished his recitation and the Dragon Fire burst into the air. The column of flames reached for the ceiling, spreading out in a star like pattern. The fire shifted through an entire rainbow of colors before exploding into a rain of glistening energy. The drops descended to the sound of great applause and several people jumped up from their seats to catch the sparkling light.

"Long live the Immortal Truth!" Proto crowed at the end of his recitation.

The room cheered their praise and the music started up again with a joyous tone. The dancers began an aggressive and bounding routine back down the aisle, followed by the singers and musicians. They led a jubilant parade out into the streets where those who could not be inside the ritual hall were able to see them. Vorin roared and spit out a jet of fire up into the night sky and everyone cheered with a vigorous round of applause.

RACHE AND RYDER

The room was dark except for a slowly approaching torch light that flickered. It smelled of wet earth, cold stone, and... blood? Ryder groaned as he grimaced at the sickening smell of his own blood that soaked the floor near his head. His skull throbbed with a dull ache that radiated from back to front. Even the smallest beam of light burned in his eyes. His chest burned with the slightest of breathing. His arms felt weak and limp with only a miniscule amount of strength left to let him know that they were still attached. A throbbing pain pulsated out from his left shoulder in waves. He tried to center himself to attempt a healing technique the Waterborn taught him but he could not sense his core and grasp on it long enough to call forth the necessary Spirit energy.

"How long have I been out" was the first thought that crossed his mind as he lay prone on the floor. He wondered how he got to the dark room.

It took nearly every fiber of his will to get his body to move. As he raised himself up to his knees, his wrists suddenly stopped moving with him. He fell back down, slamming his chin on the floor. He gasped before spitting out a globule of blood. With even greater effort, Ryder forced himself to his knees and did not attempt to move further. He slumped downward, his weight pressing down on his hips. He was thankful that his mind was no where near as bad as his body. He redoubled his efforts to reach for his Spirit energy.

The torch light continued to move closer to what Ryder now

saw was a wood door with a small steel barred window. He still could not see the torch bearer but as the light came closer, his soul felt the overwhelming darkness of an ancient Demon. And if he was correct, that torch bearer was Rache. Ryder's assumption was proven correct when the door swung in and Rache stepped inside the room. He watched as the demon set the torch in a bracket on the wall.

"So you are awake. Kaiser feared that perhaps I had hit you too hard and killed you," Rache said as he held a crudely spiked whip in his hands, small blades dangling from its tails.

"It will take more than a crack over the head to kill me, foul beast," Ryder growled. He would not let the pale skinned monster scare him.

"Now, now. Did I come in here calling you names? If it helps, I know plenty," Rache answered as he leaned against the door frame.

Ryder gritted his teeth. "As do I..."

The whip came fast and struck him on his left shoulder, leaving four deep bleeding lines. It stung mercilessly and the grating sound of the blades scraping across the floor made his head pain worse. He slumped towards his left, gritting his teeth so tight that he thought that he would shatter them. Even the attempt to breathe gave him agony. The Demon snickered as he slapped the whip handle into his right hand. The sound was grating on Ryder's ears.

Rache tenderly rolled the whip back up, letting the blades dangle. He admonished Ryder with a wave of his cruelly clawed finger. "I'm here for a chat with legend in the making Peredur Adonis Coba-Silvanus."

"Fine then. What does the mighty Rache have to say to me? It's not like you have had opportunity all these years following Kaiser around like a mindless servant" Ryder confidently said.

Rache's accuracy with the whip was unfailing as he landed another blow on Ryder's left shoulder. The blades cut through the major muscle and exposed the underlying bone. The pain was terrible as blood poured from the wound. Ryder slammed his eyes shut to avoid tears streaming down his cheeks. Rache struck again, this time hitting Ryder's right shoulder and creating the same wound.

Ryder's entire body heaved from the effort to hold back the pain. His torso flexed in the effort to keep steady. Copious amounts of blood ran down his body, staining his skin. His heart thumped hard against his chest wall in a sporadic rhythm.

"Yes, a Demon of my caliber. I am skilled in more ways than the hunt. I can strip a man of his flesh without spilling a drop of blood but since I don't like you, I will spill as much blood as I please," Rache sneered with pride. He gestured in a direction that Ryder assumed was pointing toward Kaiser. "I would gladly take you apart if he would issue the command. But this stupid fucking bond prevents me! Because you share his blood, I can not kill you!"

Ryder felt relieved at the admission though he did not doubt that Rache would still beat him within an inch of his life. He had to find out more about the bond that the Demon shared with Kaiser. "If I were his son, yes, but I am just a grandson. Blood relation is diminished with each successive generation."

Rache pointed at him with the whip. "But you still share his blood. You are still an Adonis, a descendent of Begin Anu. The blood of a Farlander runs in your veins as freely as it does his. Time does not diminish it. It strengthens it or do you know nothing of the power of a Farlander."

"I have an idea of it," Ryder said carefully. He had to keep Rache talking so that he could learn as much as he could and to regain some strength.

"Do you know the story of Begin Anu? Of why he came to the Spiritlands?" Rache asked, acting like he thought Ryder was stupid and uneducated.

The memory of the story was buried deep within his mind and once Ryder tapped into it, the images of the story rushed into the forefront. It was such an intense flood that Ryder withdrew from it and the images faded. He took a moment to gather himself before he spoke. "I know what I was told. No Farlander blood exists in the Spiritlands except in his line and that of his children."

"You and Kaiser are the last of Begin Anu's eldest child. Perhaps the last of his entire bloodline. The key to it all. But you! You also bear the blood of Shadow Night Silvanus, the mighty Shadowlord. You could have it all," Rache mocked as his hands twisted around the whip.

Ryder could tell that the words Rache spoke were not his own but that of Kaiser. He decided to latch on to that observation. "You hate him as much as I do."

"Of course I hate him! The entire world hates him! The only person that likes him is himself!" Rache roared. He snarled before snapping the whip forward and cutting long tracks across Ryder's torso. "And for some reason, he finds you worthwhile though you have long proven your hate."

"He finds you worthwhile. Perhaps we are alike," Ryder said in between hard fought breaths. He kept himself conscious by latching on to every hint of life with the full force of his mind.

Rache nodded. "Perhaps we are for we are both under the

power of Kaiser Adonis. At least I will eventually be free of his influence. You however will never escape it. You are an Adonis by blood. He is a part of you now and forever."

It was a fact that Ryder hated to acknowledge and it was one of the reasons why he ran from Cross. He began to hate Rache for pointing that fact out. A flicker of Spirit energy welled up in his heart and he grabbed onto it. He held it tightly, drawing it out from the depths of his core in small amounts. It was a paltry amount to what he could normally touch.

"If you are bound to his blood by your unholy bond then you are bound to me as well. However I will not seek to command you. Only to kill you and rid this world of your blight," Ryder promised with a smirk.

Rache sneered as he began to pace around Ryder. He slapped the whip in his hands as he slowly walked in a circle. He then began to laugh. "Do you know what people say about you? You are Shadow Night Silvanus reborn in the flesh. That you are his true Spiritual heir. Well, I say they are wrong. I say that you are the heir of Kaiser Adonis." He slid a hand over Ryder's head like he was a pet dog. "An Adonis finally and legitimately on the throne of the Shadowlord."

"I am still a bastard no matter what Kaiser tries to promise and if he thinks to control me, he is dead wrong," Ryder snapped.

Rache grabbed Ryder's hair and pulled his head back, exposing his throat. He squatted down, setting one knee on the blood soaked floor. He leaned in and sniffed Ryder's neck, running his tongue over his lips.

"You don't know how powerful you truly are. Kaiser could show you and teach you everything he knows," Rache whispered before he released his grip. Ryder's head fell forward from the force. "But then, I would trust nothing he says," the Demon added as he slowly rose to his feet.

Ryder rested his chin on his chest before lifting his head to watch Rache. His entire body shuddered from the weakness of bloodloss. The Spirit energy would only sustain him for so long before he would fall unconscious. "I trust no one but myself."

"Good. I would hate to think that I had beaten the wisdom out of you. I don't much like the idea of watching over someone stupid. They are only amusing for so long," Rache said as he came to stand before Ryder.

"So this is what you have been reduced to: a jailor? You seem apt to remind me of what I am. How about I remind you of what you are. You are Rache, the great and terrible Demon General of the Darklands. Answerable to no one save your own desires. You are so much more than my babysitter," Ryder said looking up at Rache with a flat expression.

The whip came faster and harder than Ryder had ever felt. The blades cut deeper and deeper, hitting bone and tearing through muscle. Rache beat Ryder down until he fell to the floor, barely hanging on to his consciousness.

"You are right! I am the great and terrible Rache of the Darklands! The darkest terror this world has ever seen! I have seen death! I have passed into the void of no return and yet here I am! Beating the shit out of a lowly bastard!" Rache roared, his voice laced with rage. His eyes were now blood red and his teeth now sharp like a beast's fangs. He finally threw the whip down in an angry huff.

Ryder's eyes fluttered as his senses began to withdraw from his control. He gulped hard, his heartbeat slowing down. He was coated in his own blood and he did not know how much he had left in his body. Rache had said that he could not kill him but that did not mean he could not die. Before he fell unconscious, he thought of the one thing in his life that gave him comfort and peace.

DANCE OF HEIRS

The entry hall where Onyx had first been greeted in the city had changed dramatically for the Heirs Masquerade Ball. The banners representing each nation seemed to shine in the abundant candle light. The skylight had been opened for the starlight and moonlight to shine through. At every pillar was a massive iron candelabrum full of glowing candles. Wrapped around every stone monolith were cloths of red and black, symbolizing the traditional hosts for the event. Great drapes of the cloth had been carefully hung from the high ceiling between each pillar.

The slab of marble in the middle of the room had been left bare except for a small flag pole bearing the symbol of Proto Avis. The crest was similar to the Gryphon nation in that it depicted a Gryphon, drawn by a Gryphon artist with his talon tips, but its claws were retracted and its head bowed. It was a fitting symbol for the peace loving sage and Lord of Crossroads.

Onyx adjusted his mask, made to look like a wolf and etched with silver on the black base. The fur crest was scratching against his forehead and he itched the spot as he looked around the room. He searched for the lion masks that would be worn by the Fireborn. In particular, he looked for the red and gold lioness of Argos' eldest daughter. Heir to the Fireborn throne, Ilana was a flame haired beauty with a spitfire personality to match. She was older than him and already bethrothed but as tradition called, he was to dance with her to formally open the ball.

Everyone had masks on except for the Gryphons who wore

crowns of gold. Palas' crown wrapped around his head with delicately etched details and had a ridge that went across his skull to symbolize his status as heir. Beside him was Lord of War Stellaris' massively built son with spikes instead of a ridge on his crown. Both bore fearsome expressions.

His favorite masks were worn by the Earthborn. They resembled deer with delicate details of silver on the green base. Men of that nation had an additional feature to their masks: silver antlers. Every mask had been elegantly made with the finest forest green velvet.

"My Lord, if you please," a lion masked Fireborn asked with a gesture towards the open space that had been designated for his dance with Ilana. He saw one of his own entourage doing the same for the Fireborn Princess.

They were both led to the open space and left alone with everyone watching. Onyx bowed as Ilana curtsied just as the soft music began to play. They joined their hands together without a word and moved in their carefully choreographed dance. While concentrating on his steps, Onyx began to wonder what would have happened if either his nation or the Fireborn did not have the expected dancers. The string and drum band played on in careful rhythm.

Ilana was a skilled dancer but Onyx had been surprised at how tall she was in comparison to a girl like Luna who was rather short. He himself was tall and had broad shoulders, typical of a Silvanus blood relative. But Ilana could almost look him in the eyes. He then realized how rough her hands were and wondered if she was as good a warrior as her father.

He was relieved when the opening dance finished and others joined in with the same slow style. Ilana curtsied as he bowed and turned to take the open hand of a Waterborn wearing a sea serpent's mask. Suddenly alone in the crowd, Onyx felt awkward. He made his way to the side of the room until he was stopped by a small Earthborn woman. She curtsied even lower than Ilana.

"I would be honored to dance with you, Shadowborn Prince, if it pleases you," came the request.

Of course it was rude to refuse so Onyx made his bow and extended out his hand. A soft hand was laid in his as the girl stood back up. Her flowing gown of light green settled back into place. Onyx then spotted a silver and pink jeweled broach pinned at her left shoulder.

"Are you a Lady of Flora?" he asked.

The girl smiled. "I am, good Prince." There was something knowing about her tone. It was almost like she was about to laugh. It made him smile and feel more at ease. "You didn't think I wouldn't try to have at least one dance with my new friend."

It was Luna! Onyx found himself chuckling at how he didn't figure it out sooner. He felt the tension leave his body as he relaxed. He had been so worried about Soja's disappearance that he had forgotten about her. The same light as air feeling he had when they first met days ago returned. He had often thought about why he felt that way as he had met plenty of girls since the trip started. Onyx even thought that at one point he was more connected to his Earthborn heritage than that of the Shadowborn. It reminded him of what Kader had once said: "You have your father's looks but your mother's Spirit."

Onyx rejoined his father when there was a pause for the Gryphons to dance in their unique manner. He focused in on a pair of Falcon Gryphons, both with white and gray pelts. They faced each other with their wings slightly flared and bowed deeply, the tips of their beaks touching the floor. The Gryphons then brought their heads back up. They stamped their feet before jumping up into the air with several quick flaps to direct them to land to the side. Both Gryphons circled each other as they bobbed their heads until they stood at their partner's original position. Feet slapped the floor again and they jumped back in the direction they had come. Onyx was amazed at their dexterity and grace as the Gryphons twirled around in place to return to where they started. The routine began again as more Gryphons joined in. Luna remained with him at his request, holding gently to the crook of his arm.

"Father, I would like you to meet..." Onyx began before Luna stopped him. She stepped away from his side and curtsied low to the floor. "I would like to introduce you to Lady Luna Artemis, a friend who has been most kind to us and our throne," he finished.

"Come closer, child," Aku's voice cracked as he waved his hand for Luna to come forward.

It had been so long since he had heard his father speak. Onyx was filled with elation and nearly jumped to embrace Aku. He held back as Luna stood back up to face the Lord of the Shadowborn. She was regal in her bearing but submissive at the same time. "You remind me of my fair Queen. It pleases me that my son has found such a soul in this city," Aku stated, his voice weak. Beneath his wolf mask, he was smiling.

"I am honored, great Lord," Luna replied with a deep and nervous curtsy.

Aku waved Onyx forward. "If you please, a moment with my son," he said to Luna.

"Yes, great Lord," Luna said politely before rejoining the crowd.

Onyx sat by his father and leaned towards him, eager to listen. He quickly glanced towards Luna who offered a fleeting smile as she stood with several Earthborn.

"I feel a new strength in me that I haven't felt in many years," Aku began, his voice slightly stronger. "This city..." he said looking around. "It has a power that heals and protects."

Onyx followed his gaze and found that he was watching Kaiser. "Father?" he asked.

"I need you to be strong where I cannot be. I fear our throne is in danger," Aku's voice faltered for a moment.

Kaiser came forward with Morin at his side, laughing at a private joke. "My Prince, you have a role to play," he chastised.

Onyx frowned as he stood up tall. He looked Morin in the eyes. "As does the Commander if he chooses to remember it. See that no harm comes to my father," he said harshly. Morin held his breath and kept close to Kaiser's side.

Just before midnight, the respective rulers were to dance in the same manner as the heir's dance. As his father was physically unable, Onyx took his place. He looked at Argos' queen, a flame haired ravishing beauty not unlike her daughter Ilana. She had a more delicate and tall frame. Her dancing was more refined than her eldest daughter's moves.

Midnight came and everyone removed their masks. Attendants darted about the room, collecting the masks and offering food and drinks. Onyx slipped out to the front stairs for some air and space to think. What did his father mean? And what did Kaiser have to do with it? And where was Soja? He wished the Saber was not missing.

"Are you ok?" Luna asked as she held her mask in her hands. The silver and green ribbons dangled as she fingered the seams of silver thread along the edge.

"Can I speak to you... honestly?" Onyx asked frankly. Luna nodded. "Normally, my Saber Soja Rokar would be my sounding board but... well, I don't know where he is."

Luna stepped a little closer to him. "What's wrong?"

Onyx sighed deeply. "My father hasn't spoken in such a long time. He said the throne is in danger. The Silvanus family has suffered more than its fair share of tragedy. Everyone knows that. My grandfather's death, my mother's death, the attack that nearly killed my father. The list goes on."

"A Lord always worries about his throne. My Lord Palani has kept your cousin close in recent years. This is the first state visit in over ten years," Luna stated with a heavy sigh.

"I remember that when my mother died, he sent a letter of regret for not attending the funeral. If a Demon has infiltrated my home, how could anyone trust that it is safe? Especially if it is Rache..." Onyx said before taking a deep breath and letting it out slowly.

Luna had hesitated at first but eventually laid a comforting hand on his arm. "So what do you think he meant?" she asked calmly.

"Whatever the danger may be, it's closer than a wild Demon would be... I don't know. It's not like I trust Kaiser enough to ask him. He is an authority on the ways of the Demons but how can someone know so much about Demons without being affected by them," Onyx replied.

"Can't imagine anyone that does escape any ill effects. The poison alone causes terrible pain when the body is subjected to it," she pulled her hand away and shivered.

Onyx shrugged. "Something is clearly up and I intend to figure it out. If I am to be a good leader for my people, I must protect my throne first."

"My brother is a scout! He can help you!" Luna suggested, eager to help.

"That is very kind of you but we have only known each other for a few days. I cannot place you or your family in danger," Onyx stated with regret. His shoulders slumped from the admission.

"A Prince need allies," she said, sounding more like her role as a Lady of Flora. "And when I said I was your friend, I meant it." Her tenacious Spirit showed through in her tone.

Oynx reached under his tunic collar and pulled out a thin silver chain with the symbols of his mother's house: the twin leaves and crystal sphere. Also attached to the chain was the wolf's tooth and crescent moon. He removed it from his neck and dropped it in her open hand. "In my homeland, it is customary to give a new friend a symbol of trust. I choose this which was given to me by a man I had trusted. Bear it well, Lady Artemis as you have been nothing but a kind soul to me here."

Luna was speechless as she held the precious charms in her hand. On the spur of the moment, she quickly stood up on her toes and kissed Onyx on the cheek. She dropped back down to her feet slowly as she saw his stunned reaction. Both of them flushed red.

"I am so sorry. I'm going to go and pretend that never happened," Luna stammered to say as she gestured back to the door. She slowly stepped back and started to turn.

"Wait," Onyx softly said as he grabbed her wrist. Luna halted and turned to look back at him. "Promise me that we will find each other again."

"I promise," Luna replied.

A WAY TO GET IN

Soja crashed into the river bank with a heavy thud, splashing the slow moving water. He groaned as he turned around to face the invisible wall, seeing the energy ripple dissipate. His head and back throbbed with pulses of pain that spread into his limbs. Ready to give up, Soja leaned against the sandy bank and looked up into the night sky. The stars flickered like small torch lights while a puff of clouds slowly moved to reveal a waxing moon. Once again, he tried to decipher an opening pattern or some sort of mystical mark. But it was helpless and of no use to waste any more energy.

Under the power of Shadow Slide, Soja had managed to traverse the distance between Crossroads and the border of his homeland in record time. It was foolish of him to have done so and dangerous as well. Sai's warning roared back into his mind. If a Saber stayed in Shadow Slide too long, he would be pulled across the veil and into the Spirit World, never to return to the land of the living. Soja shivered from the deathly chill the power of Shadow Slide left behind, feeling no heat of life in him.

"Father would have beaten me for such a foolhardy action. And for getting so dirty in my leathers," Soja told himself as he looked at the dirt that caked his uniform. Even his short black hair was under a cap of brown river mud. He quickly brushed the muck from his head and face.

The River Shadow flowed on in silence, unaware of Soja's attempt to cross it. Soja kicked at the water in protest before he pushed himself to his feet. He studied his surroundings again, counting the trees that lined the top of the bank. Beyond the trees was his homeland and he could not get to it no matter how hard he threw himself at the invisible Shadow Mirror.

"There he is! Get him!"

Soja turned around to see Rothe and two Sabers take aim with steel tipped arrows. They stood upon the eastern river bank, dressed in their pristine leathers and supple cloaks. He could hear the stretch of the bow strings being pulled. All three stared at him with a deadly gaze behind their masks. They were intent on killing him!

"So much for comradery and loyalty!" Soja joked with a small degree of sarcasm. Seeing Rothe now with an arrow pointed at him was the confirmation of him being a turncoat. His words fell on deaf ears. His already sore and tired muscles bunched in preparation.

Rothe's two companions fired first, aiming for Soja's heart. Soja leaped into the air, flipping backwards as the arrows sped right through where he just was. He landed and managed to lean to the right in time to avoid a direct hit from Rothe's shot. The arrow grazed his upper arm, cutting a deep gash into the muscle. Soja had no time to consider the burning pain as he jumped over a collapsed chunk of the river bank and ran. The three Sabers were quick to follow, sliding down the high river bank and following in hot pursuit.

Blood poured from the gash but Soja ignored it as he ran south. Water and mud stained his boots in increasing amounts. Arrows continued to fly past him as Soja trusted his senses to protect him. He spied a low hanging branch covered in gray moss approaching fast. With a split second decision, Soja gripped the branch and vaulted up high onto the top of the bank. He spun around to hide behind a thick oak trunk. He stifled a laugh as he heard the three Sabers slide and crash into each other, cursing violently. Soja then began running northbound.

The curses continued as the Sabers followed, now covered in as much dirt and grime as Soja. They scurried up the sandy ridge to catch up. Soja picked up his pace, batting aside branches and vines as a dust cloud rose up in his tracks. He fervently hoped the Sabers were out of arrows. His left arm was growing numb despite all of his efforts to keep his adrenaline pumping.

"Running won't save you, traitor!" Rothe cried out as his footsteps came closer. Speeding along through the canopy were the other two Sabers as they tried to move within attack range.

Soja moved to turn and shout back a mocking curse when his right foot caught on an upraised tree root. He flew forward and skidded ten feet before coming to a stop. The dust cloud settled heavily around him, clearing just as Rothe approached with a broad sword drawn. His companions landed behind him, pulling out their own sharp blades. Soja wondered if his wit and charm could save his life. All he was certain of was that he would never join Kaiser's cause.

"You're an Abendroth! Captain Hayden's nephew!" Soja stated trying to unnerve Rothe with the mention of his uncle.

Rothe and his companions laughed out loud, snickering and brandishing their swords. "So? What does blood truly mean other than a sign of death!" He slashed at Soja's torso, cutting a thin line across his cuirass. "Next cut will be deeper," he warned.

Soja pressed his eyes shut, not wanting to see the Wolf Spirit Omu who came to a Saber about to die. Or so his father had warned him before he graduated into the ranks. He had warned him about a great many things and Soja wished that he could remember them all. He kept waiting for the death blow. Nothing came.

His eyes shot open as he heard a heavy creak on the branches above them. A horse sized Owl Gryphon with gleaming white feathers burst through the foliage, beak open in a loud screech of attack, talons bared. He fell upon Rothe in a terrible fury, throwing him to the ground to Soja's right. The beast was quick to snap a powerful kick to one of the remaining Sabers. The other, in a state of shock and indecision, did not notice a shadowy figure approach from behind. A glint of cold steel was all Soja saw as the figure cut the Saber's throat. Soja watched as the figure went over to the Gryphon whose hackles were bristled with rage.

"The Immortal Truth does not forgive traitors who laugh at its sacred words," the figure said with no remorse. He nodded towards the Gryphon who promptly bit down on Rothe's throat.

The Gryphon in his attack was a fearsome foe Soja thought to himself as he watched the beast raise up his blood soaked face from his kill. He wondered if he was next. The night seemed to be determined to make sure he did not live to see the dawn. Soja expected the Gryphon to turn his fury upon him. But just as he was sure that Rothe was going to kill him, the Gryphon did nothing to indicate that he was going to finish the job. His companion extended a hand towards him and Soja took it, being pulled up from the ground.

"I am Haro Artemis, Scout of the Earthborn. This is my partner, Arik Barr of the Gryphons," the figure said just as a cloud drifted past the moon, basking him in a soft light. He was dressed in forest green cloth and earthy brown leather that served as light armor. A green head band was tied around his skull, a silver leaf threaded onto the forehead. Light brown hair was pulled back in a loose ponytail.

"Soja Rokar, Saber of the Shadowborn," Soja stated, feeling that he could trust the pair. He told himself that if they had wanted to kill him, they would have let Rothe do it and then attack.

Arik the Gryphon jumped down to the river water and began washing his face. Haro seemed distracted by his partner, a smile on the edge of his lips as he set his hands on his hips. A breeze shook the moss laden oak limbs above the forest path. Branches creaked unseen in the towering pine trees that reached above the canopy. Off in the distance, an owl hooted back and forth with its neighbor, staking its territorial claim. Soja then wondered if Arik could understand the words of their conversation and if it meant anything to him.

"So why were those Sabers chasing you? To my knowledge, Sabers are a brotherhood of loyalty," Haro asked with an inquiring voice.

What was loyalty to Rothe Abendroth and ultimately Kaiser Adonis? The scout's question made Soja laugh unexpectedly. It took him a moment to calm down. "In the old days, loyalty was a treasured quality. In these dark times, I can only be certain of my own loyalty."

"Then something must be truly amiss if Sabers attack other Sabers," Arik stated as he climbed up the river bank. His face was clean and shining from the water.

"There are a lot of things wrong with this world and chief of all calamities is him," Soja stated, swinging his arm in the direction of Crossroads.

"Kaiser Adonis," Haro and Arik said at the same time before Soja could state his name. "We know all about him and his dark ways," Haro continued as Arik turned his attention to the bodies of the dead Sabers.

"I need to get to Cross immediately and warn my father," Soja shouted in desperation.

Haro shook his head. "You and the entire Northern Alliance but there is no crossing over the River Shadow into your homeland."

"I cannot even fly over the water," Arik piped in as he dragged Rothe's body to the side.

"Ryder said no one could cross the Shadow Mirror," Soja grumbled in frustration. He looked to see Haro and Arik whispering in low voices that he could not hear what they were saying. They knew something!

"There is much to be said, Saber Rokar, but we will not say it here. Come with us to Agin and speak with one who can tell you more," Haro suggested in a cautious but authoritative voice.

Soja wanted to argue but he had to admit to himself that he had not rested since leaving Crossroads many days ago. The distance travelled in that short of time had pushed him to the limit and he was in need of sleep and food. Sabers were hardy when the situation called for extreme tests of will and he was still a young man. Soja knew that his father would reprimand him if he knew, even under the circumstances. He nodded his acceptance.

Agin was a small Earthborn town, nestled in a grove of tall pines and hardwood trees. But what made it unique was that it had buildings both on the ground and in the trees. The bottom level was a thick wall made of weathered tree trunks that circled a large clearing. The second level was the soldiers and guards walkway with buttress like arches to support the third level. The final level of the outer wall served as the quarters for the city guards and visiting soldiers. Soja had to admit as he, Haro, and Arik approached that the design was impressive. The only disruption in the symmetry of the wall was the main gate.

The main gateway into Agin consisted of two heavy doors with narrow slits for windows. It was ugly and looming at first glance but as Soja came closer, the doors were etched with intricate designs that he could now see. He was given no time to appreciate them as bowmen lined the second level and drew back on their bowstrings. Soja stopped at the edge of the forest road but Haro, pulling out his scout's seal, continued forward with the symbol raised up high. Arik sauntered at this partner's side, wings raised up proudly.

"Haro Artemis of Cascade with Arik Barr of the Gryphons!" Haro loudly announced. "I come with Soja Rokar of Cross, Saber of the Shadowborn!"

The bowmen relaxed and one shouted for the gates to be opened. Soja stepped forward as the hinges creaked and groaned, the doors slowly swinging open.

"Even the Earthborn are cautious in these times. To assure those who have granted you entry, I will walk in first and Arik will come behind you. Walk with your palms forward to show that you come unarmed. Like this," Haro explained before he showed Soja what he meant.

Soja followed Haro through the gate, acutely aware of the bowmen glaring at him with caution. They whispered in low voices before turning their attention back to the forest. It was unnerving for him to be looked upon as a threat despite being a Saber. But then the Shadowborn were used to the sight of a Saber slinking around like hunting cats. Soja then wondered if the Earthborn had an equivalent to his order. More importantly, he wondered what gave the Earthborn cause to worry in his presence.

Once inside the wall, Soja could see a small collection of buildings situated around thick tree trunks. Some were even part of a tree, carved within the largest and sturdiest wood. The streets were covered with a thin layer of leaves and pine needles. Torches flickered, bathing the town in a low and warm light. It was a comfortable sight despite the few Earthborn who looked at him with a mix of surprise and worry. Haro led him to the centermost building that was carved out of a massive pine stump.

The most unexpected person stepped outside and embraced Soja like he was a dearly missed son. It was Kader Erebus, alive and well. He looked very much as Soja remembered even in the standard Earthborn green robes. His black hair was thinner but it still hung down to his shoulders. His silver eyes still bore the wise gaze Soja always knew. Soja returned the embrace, grateful to see the old sage again.

"Come. Let me tend to your wounds. We have much to talk about," Kader stated before turning to Haro and Arik. "I'll take it from here."

Soja followed Kader inside, finding a cozy sitting room with a fire blazing in the hearth. A cup of mint tea and a small bowl of roasted nuts were placed on a side table that was positioned next to a velvet arm chair. Book shelves were stacked with scrolls and leather-bound tomes. A woven fiber rug covered the floor. Kader directed Soja to sit down before disappearing down a hallway.

"This is the home of the Mayor of Agin. He is currently eating dinner with the captain of the guard," Kader explained as he returned with a basket of bandages and salves. He pulled the other chair forward and sat down. He gestured for Soja to remove his cuirass and tunic. "Come now! Hurry up before these wounds fester and rot. You don't want to scar now do you?"

"It is only my left arm. I'll survive the bumps and bruises," Soja said before ripping off the left sleeve of his tunic. His arm was bare from his forearm bracer to the shoulder sculpted pauldron.

Kader first reached for a damp cloth and began cleaning the blood and dirt away. His sharp silver eyes worked methodically with his careful fingers to remove the debris. Blood flowed more freely but Kader was quick to staunch it with a medicinal powder. He then applied a cool salve, which smelled of aloe, spreading it over the wound and surrounding tissue. "The Earthborn taught me how to make this salve," Kader said before laughing for a moment. "We Shadowborn are good for war and killing. Earthborn are good for peace and healing."

"Kaiser told us that you were dead. Overwhelmed by grief," Soja mentioned after a long pause.

Kader scoffed as he finished tying the bandage around Soja's arm. "Of course he would say that. He could not tell the truth that he tried to have me killed by the Shadowlord's own Sabers." He shook his head. "I still can't believe an Abendroth defected to him."

"No need to worry about Rothe anymore. The Gryphon killed him," Soja stated.

"I'm sure his noble uncle will not be surprised. Rothe was always quite rebellious. Blood did not mean much to him," Kader replied as he pushed back his chair and sat down. "Tea?" he offered.

Soja shook his head. "What does blood mean in these times other than pain and death?"

Kader smiled. "It means different things to different people. It is all about interpretation. Take your loyalty to the Silvanus family. Whether or not a blood member sits on the throne, you still support them and protect them. I am of the same mind for all members of the family no matter how close or far they are to me."

"I just wished I had not failed Ryder. I feel like I have failed Shadow Night by not being able to protect him too," Soja mumbled as he sunk down in his chair.

"Ryder Coba?" Kader asked. Soja nodded before proceeding to tell Kader all that had transpired in Crossroads. Kader kept his silence until Soja had finished. "Ryder is a brave man to face Kaiser alone. It says a lot that Proto Avis and Vorin believed in Ryder enough to ask him to kill Kaiser. What do you have to say on the matter?"

"Ryder does hate Kaiser and I mean he really hates him. Granted, Kaiser was involved in the downfall of his father so I guess he has that reason. Kaiser seems to have an abnormal interest in him but I have to be honest and say that of all the Silvanus relatives we know about, Ryder is the strongest," Soja explained, acting as if admitting his thoughts was shameful.

Kader let out a deep breath. "So Kaiser has Rache at his side for protection. The border remains sealed."

"Ryder said it was something called a Shadow Mirror," Soja interjected.

A thought crossed Kader's mind and he picked up a book from beside the tea kettle, waving it briefly. "Then I am glad that my hard work will be worthwhile. Over the last six years, I have been compiling every bit of research and observation about the Shadow Mirror's power. I will say that all such work originates from Adonis Anu's private journals with various interpretations over the centuries."

"Well does it say anything about repeling Sabers and native

Shadowborn because it was more than willing to throw me back," Soja exclaimed as he sat back and crossed his arms.

"Yes it is strange how this wall of energy has the ability to choose who passes and who doesn't. Or more to the point, Kaiser controls it like some sort of gate keeper. I would like to speak with Ryder Coba. It would at least be an interesting conversation," Kader mused. He leaned his head back and closed his eyes, deep in thought. His eyes then snapped open. "No one but the Daylord and the Adonis family know how to raise a Shadow Mirror. It is a power not found in any bloodline native to the Northlands." He sat up in his chair and leaned forward. "I know it is not said often but Kaiser is a descendent of Adonis Anu though I do believe his ancestor would curse him. Anyway, to know the Shadow Mirror. To understand it, Ryder would have to be related to Kaiser."

Kader burst up from his seat and began to pace in the small room. He paused and set his hands on his hips. "Do you happen to remember the name of his mother?"

"I think it was Aylin," Soja said, remembering how his father had told him when he first discussed the royal bastard with him.

"Yes, Aylin. I remember her now. A beautiful Shadowborn woman with a noble's bearing and the shrewd mind of a diplomat. Not afraid to speak her mind and probably the only person her son listened to without question," Kader stated as he resumed pacing. "Yes it does make sense."

"What are you saying, Master Erebus?" Soja asked. "That Ryder is a descendent of Kaiser?"

"He is Kaiser's grandson through his mother. It is the only thing that fits with this Shadow Mirror business. Oh if I could talk to him," Kader said as he sat back down. He slid forward to sit on the edge of the cushion. "If what I said is true then the border is not completely sealed. There is a way to get in and Ryder Coba is the key."

THE RETURN HOME

He thought that coming back to Cross would remove the weight of his thoughts from his shoulders but Onyx was unable to leave the questions at the border. So much had happened at Crossroads that could not be ignored. He rubbed his temples as his head threatened to burst from the overwhelming desire for answers. For a split second, Onyx wanted to throw the crown from his head and gallop away. He let out a tense breath as he readjusted his grip on the horse's reins. The horse protested with a loud snort.

To his left rode the Saber Captain Hayden Abendroth, his back straight and stern gaze directed on the road before them. To his right rode another Saber whose face was so well covered that Onyx could not even tell if they were a thin man or a small woman. Behind him was his father's carriage surrounded by even more Sabers. It was such a change from when the caravan had left Cross. Now everyone was on edge. Everyone except Kaiser.

Onyx could not help but be confused as he thought of his father's Lord's Chancellor. How could he be so calm about everything? He did have a degree of sympathy for the man as Kaiser had been attacked. Kaiser was almost cocky about the entire situation, praising his masked servant for rescuing him from Rache. Unlike his father, Kaiser was uninjured from the encounter. Aku was left with a burn around his neck as if the Demon tried to choke the life from him. The wound was gross to look upon and Onyx held back from staring at it. Thankfully,

Kaiser had cleaned the wound and covered it for the return home.

The road to Cross stretched out before him, beckoning the young Prince home. Ancient pines loomed along the roadside, dropping needles whenever a breeze brushed through the branches. Birds hidden in the canopy called out in various songs as if to welcome the caravan. The air was cool and Onyx felt soothed by it, taking a deep breath and slowly releasing it. A strip of blue sky peeked through the trees as the forest began to thin out.

Onyx looked ahead, seeing a glimpse of the farmland that surrounded the city of Cross. Riding at the front of the caravan, the field workers would be able to clearly see him. Messengers had been sent ahead to announce their arrival and Onyx imagined Zoras Rokar furiously preparing a welcome ceremony that would honor the return of the royals. He was then suddenly reminded of his missing friend Soja.

What was he going to tell Zoras about the fate of his son? Onyx knew nothing but he suspected that Hayden did and wasn't going to tell him. He thought about ordering the Saber to reveal what he knew for as the Crowned Prince, Hayden would be obligated to answer him. But as Sai had told him during his training, Sabers acted in secret to protect the throne from harm and the burden of thought. Onyx then remembered that Zoras was a former Saber Commander and likely already knew what Hayden was hiding. Sabers seemed to know a great deal more than they let on. Soja was certainly proof of that despite his unconventional nature.

One thing that urked him about Soja was his loyalty to Ryder Coba. Onyx had no doubt that his friend was loyal to him as his personal guard and future Shadowlord but there was something more honest and mysterious about Soja's love for his bastard cousin. He hated Ryder for it. Here he was, the legitimate born Prince of the Silvanus bloodline, and a bastard dared to command more respect than he deserved. Even Vorin the Dragonlord and Proto Avis held Ryder in high esteem as if he had not been born a bastard. Onyx's mind screamed in frustration for a small part of him was jealous of Ryder's great power. He felt threatened by Ryder's obvious strength when his father was so weak. Would the Shadowborn people want Ryder on the throne over him? Onyx wanted to scream out loud but held back. He let his feelings about Ryder simmer in burning anger. One consulation was that the Waterborn hated the bastard son of Akakios.

"See how the people welcome you, your Highness," Hayden suddenly said. Onyx looked up from his mental wanderings to see field workers cheering and raising their tools.

Onyx wondered if Hayden had sensed his chaotic thoughts

and had sought to relieve the tension. He looked over at the Saber, his face betraying nothing. Indeed as the caravan pulled out of the pine forest, more and more farmers abandoned their field work to stand along the roadside and watch. Onyx went through the motions; bowing his head, offering thanks and kind words, a wave of his hand. In comparison to his fine clothes, the farmers wore faded garments of cotton and wool that had seen better days. Their hands and forearms were wrapped with worn leather straps to protect against thorns and sharp branches. Many of the men sported full beards while the women all had their long dark hair in braids that bounced on their backs. Each one of the common folk wore bright smiles on their faces.

The admiration of his people rejuvenated Onyx's spirit. Only a trueborn Prince could garner this kind of love. Onyx straightened his back and squared his shoulders in response. There was no way that his bastard cousin could match this kind of reaction from the Shadowborn. Ryder had abandoned them for parts unknown. Onyx had not and that made him feel proud. He grinned at the thought.

The mountain wall of the Heights soared ahead and Onyx could now see his castle home. Banners bearing the royal Silvanus crest flapped in the wind all over the city. More and more people crowded the roadside, waving and cheering. No one seemed to mind that work had been abandoned for they were welcoming their Prince home. As he was the most visible, Onyx heard his name shouted more than he heard his father's. People pressed against fences, leaned out of windows, or stood on rooftops to shout and catch a glimpse of the returning caravan. Even their dogs howled with delight.

Seeing all of the support made Onyx more certain that taking the throne was the best thing he could do. Part of him was worried about his abilities to be an effective leader but Onyx told himself that he was strong. His thoughts drifted to his ailing father and instead of feeling sad, he felt happy. Soon his father would not be burdened with the responsibility of being the Shadowlord and that perhaps, Onyx hoped, he could get better. Then his father could watch him lead the Shadowborn people into a golden age.

A thought that refused to stay in the deep recesses of his mind was that of the Earthborn girl he had met in Crossroads. Luna may have only been a Lady of Flora, a lady in waiting to his aunt, but to Onyx there was something greater about her. Her smile could melt ice. Her laugh could shake stones free from their mountain prisons. He smiled as he thought how her jokes could make someone even as prudish as Zoras laugh. He had not understood the flighty feeling at first, for he thought it was just nerves but Onyx decided that he had connected to her warm Spirit. It reminded him of the brightness his mother had borne before her passing. Onyx made up his mind as the caravan passed into the inner city to invite Luna for a visit.

Standing on the steps of the council building was Zoras Rokar, tall and proud, dressed in supple robes of black and silver with a wolf fur lined cloak around his shoulders. Sai Parahazur stood to his right in his Saber armor, head uncovered with his eyes watching the wide square before them.

"What do you see?" Zoras quietly asked. He made eyes at Hayden and nodded.

Sai repeated the motion with Hayden. "I see a Prince's triumphant return home. I also see a great deal of change."

"I do not see my son at the Prince's side and rarely have so many Sabers ridden openly into Cross. Something happened in Crossroads," Zoras stated as he searched the caravan for Soja.

"I will speak to Hayden as soon as time allows. He will hide no truths from me," Sai stated with a bow of the head. "I would like to smack that smug expression right off of Kaiser's face."

Zoras laid a hand on Sai's shoulder. "Peace for now, Commander. We must properly welcome our Prince and Lord home."

The applause and cheers grew louder as Onyx dismounted. He did not wait for a groom to take his horse's reins as he stepped over to his father's carriage. Zoras noticed Morin jumping back with a degree of shock as Onyx forced him away. Kaiser appeared to calm the soldier as he pulled Morin back and gestured for Onyx to continue. Onyx assisted his father out of the carriage, keeping him close to his side as the two royals walked forward. Zoras, Sai, and the rest of the councilors descended the stairs and dropped to their knees in a deep bow. Everyone in the crowd fell to their knees and the raucous noise died down.

"The people of Cross welcome you, Lord Aku and Prince Onyx, with open arms and resounding voices," Zoras said once he lifted his head. Everyone stood up as he did. "We are most happy to have you home again."

Onyx set his hand on his father's. "We are happy to be back. The journey was long but well worth it."

The formality in Onyx's voice surprised Zoras though he did not show it. Something indeed had happened in Crossroads.

"Commander Parahazur, would you escort my father to his chambers?" Onyx asked with emerging order and command. "I wish to speak to Master Rokar alone."

"As you wish," Sai replied with a bow of the head. He stepped forward to take Aku, lending his sturdy strength to support him. Sai gestured to a team of Sabers to follow him.

"I am at your command," Zoras stated as Sai and the Sabers led Aku away under a round of applause from the crowd.

"On the morrow, I want the Shadow Council to assemble to discuss impending matters of state. See to it that no one is absent. No excuse will be accepted," Onyx ordered in a firm, confident tone.

Zoras bowed his head deeply. He could now see that this was not the Prince that had left for Crossroads. He was colder and less innocent. Zoras had seen such change before in young Sabers who had seen their first combat. The youth of boyhood was gone and a man had emerged.

A QUESTION OF LOYALTY

Onyx stood up from his seat, the chair sliding backwards as he laid his hands on the table. He wore his full royal regalia, a shining crown on his head. His expression was stern and commanding as he looked over the members of the Shadow Council. Courage soared through his heart as he thought about what he was going to say. He looked at Zoras Rokar who sat at the other end of the table, his hand wrapped around a gavel handle.

"Before the journey of Crossroads, I expressed a desire to take my father's throne. I do it not out of a desire for power and to usurp his authority. I do it out of charity. I am not blind to my father's condition. I know that he is unwell and not likely to recover. It is my hope and belief that upon my ascension to the throne, it will give him the chance to heal in peace without the stress of the crown," Onyx explained in a commanding tone of voice.

"A noble sentiment that all of your forebears would approve of. It takes courage to do what you must in a difficult situation," Zoras said with an approving nod. "We are also not blind to the poor health of Lord Aku."

Every one of the other councilors nodded save for Kaiser who only shrugged when Zoras glared at him. "The art I used to bring him back is not exact and its effect over time is uncertain."

"I do not accuse you of failure, Master Adonis, for he would have been dead otherwise. I must thank you for your efforts to save my father," Onyx stated. Kaiser smiled and nodded. "I think we must all be thankful for your vast knowledge of Demons. The throne is better protected with someone like you nearby."

Zoras and Sai rolled their eyes. Their action immediately caught Onyx's attention. The Prince lifted a questioning eyebrow. Zoras briefly glanced at his compatriots before sliding forward in his seat. "My good Prince, there are those of differing opinions regarding the loyalty of Kaiser and the protection he offers."

Onyx turned to look at Kaiser. "What do you have to say to this, Master Adonis?"

Kaiser remained in a reclined position in his seat, tapping his palms on the arm rests. "I have given bad advice to previous Shadowlords and members of your family. Suggestions that I thought would curtail the hint of madness but sadly my suggestions failed. I must live with my failures and I am forever trying to prove myself to the world."

"At least we do not have the hint of murder that surrounds us," Zoras snapped, gripping the gavel.

Without missing a beat, Kaiser replied. "At least I am not trying to steal the throne right out from under a legitimate son by throwing support behind the bastard of Akakios. Or have you not told everyone how you have tried to legitimize the bastard to become Shadowlord. We all know how you support him with unwavering loyalty."

The admission set the entire room to talking and slowly into arguing. Kaiser and Zoras stared each other down, ignoring the shouts and harsh words around them. Onyx slammed his fist on the table and everyone silenced.

"Is this true? Are you trying to legitimize the bastard so that he may usurp me? Onyx demanded.

Zoras remained in a tight silence for a long time before he replied. "It was once considered before the rule of your grandfather."

"Oh please! You are lying to the boy's face! You Rokars live and breathe for the bastard more than you do the Lord Aku and his honorable son," Kaiser laughed loudly. "I think it would be best that you explain yourself before this Council can continue."

"Madhuri Coba was a dear friend of the Rokars and as such, we promised to look out for each other and our respective families. As his grandson and the last of the Cobas, I still hold to my promise. As a Saber, I also swore loyalty to protect the entire Silvanus bloodline and that oath does not end with those upon the throne. He may be a bastard but he is a royal bastard," Zoras explained. He then gestured towards Onyx. "Your Highness, it is my hope to have him serve as your ambassador. If his birth is legitimized, he would have the respect and nobility necessary to serve you."

Onyx wanted to tell himself that Zoras' argument made sense. It certainly explained Soja's behavior in Crossroads towards Ryder. His cousin was a full grown adult with a vast amount of experience. But his presence would be a threat to his own power on the throne. Onyx did not want to be endlessly compared to Ryder.

"Until he decides to come back to Cross, he is simply a Shadowborn man who has abandoned his homeland. Should he come back, he will answer to his conduct. Right now, we have more pressing matters," Onyx said sternly as he leaned over the table. He took several deep breaths. "If I am to rise to the throne, I want to be crowned on the night of the Winter Solstice. I want the transfer of power to be as smooth as possible. I do not want to cause my father any more stress. Am I understood?"

Each councilor acknowledged his statement with a hearty affirmative. Even Kaiser agreed. Onyx watched as Kaiser punched Morin in the shoulder to get him to follow suit. Morin cringed from his touch and his voice was shaky in his response.

"As per the laws of this land, are you of age and the correct state of mind for the crown that awaits you?" Zoras dutifully asked.

"I am of age and sound body and mind," Onyx replied.

"Until you are crowned, you will be the Regent of your father's throne. Laws of regency for those who do not recall is normally a matter for the Shadowlord to decide. Considering his infirmity and increasing inability to serve, leadership falls to his heir if he is of age or to the Council until the heir is of age to ascend to the throne," Zoras explained, tapping the table briefly.

"I do not see the Shadowlord here," Kaiser piped in from the other side of the table. "How can we decide on this matter without his input?"

"I would have to agree with the Lord's Chancellor," Morin chimed in.

Onyx frowned. "I speak for my father as no one else here can. Not even you, Lord's Chancellor."

Kaiser shrugged. "It is as you say, your Highness. I was only quoting the law to make sure my kinsmen here understood fully the matter at hand."

"By the law of Shadow Night Silvanus, the heir is the voice of the Shadowlord from the time he is named. He may listen to our advice but if he deems it unfit to follow, he does not have to abide by our words. I am of mind to give his Royal Highness the same courtesy that I would give his father," Zoras stated, keeping his eyes on Kaiser.

Sai then leaned forward in his seat. "The Sabers will follow you to the very end, your Highness. I will assemble the Captains and let them know of your coming ascension. At the crowning ceremony, we will all bend the knee and swear our loyalty for everyone to see."

"I shall do the same with the armed forces," Morin quickly said. He shuddered when Kaiser stared at him and sunk down in his seat.

"I seem to remember Commander Win of your failures in Crossroads. You were responsible for my father's security and under your watch, he was attacked by a Demon," Onyx growled harshly. He planted his fists down on the table top. "I have yet to decide if you are still worthy of your vaulted position."

Kaiser raised his hand a short distance. "If I may, your Highness, might I recommend that Commander Win keep his position until a suitable replacement is found? I do have some military know how that I learned from my father."

"I trust that you will find this nation a more capable Commander of the Armed Forces," Onyx said before returning his stern gaze to Morin. "Unless you can prove yourself to me."

"I will do anything to assure you of my loyalty, your Highness. Let me prove to you that I am worthy," Morin pleaded. His skin was pale white with fear of failure and losing his power.

Onyx stood up straight, keeping his eyes on Morin. Each of the councilors stood up and Kaiser shuffled over to Onyx.

"Your Highness, we will plan for you a grand coronation ceremony. You can trust the Shadow Council to do what is best and worthy for you," Zoras promised though he kept his eyes on Kaiser.

Zoras dismissed the Council and everyone began to exit the room. Kaiser remained by Onyx's side as Morin was still sitting down. As Zoras passed them, he glared at Kaiser who only smirked in return. Once the room emptied, Kaiser stepped over to Morin's chair and slapped his hands down on the Commander's shoulders.

"I think now is the time to answer for your failures," Kaiser said as he leaned in closer. "Prove to us how deep your loyalty is."

"I will do anything," Morin blurted out. He jumped out of his seat to fall on his knees before Onyx. He pressed his forehead to the floor. "Anything you ask, your Highness."

Onyx stepped back. "Get up. This is not becoming of a Commander." He looked towards Kaiser. "What do you suggest?"

Kaiser smirked as he latched his hands behind his back. "I can take care of Commander Win for you, your Highness. I will make sure that he knows who to be loyal to."

KAISER'S CONFIDENCE

"He is a child who thinks that he has power," Kaiser said as he slid a few papers to the right side of his desk. He set a silver moon paperweight on top of the stack. "And you let him frighten you. He is not even a pure blood Shadowborn."

Morin gulped. "I am not afraid of the Prince. He is not the one who struck me in Crossroads." He rubbed his jaw, still sporting a bruise that had turned to a mottled yellow and purple.

Kaiser scoffed. "Seems I did hit you across the jaw in that city. You deserved it but my act has served its purpose. The Prince believes I support him. That I am looking out for him." He turned his attention back to the papers before him for several minutes before he looked back up. "You have nothing to fear from the boy. You have more to fear from me for you are only still alive because you are remotely useful to me."

Had those words been spoken by any other person, Morin would have felt relief and reassurance. Instead he shivered in fear and uncertainty. "I am a good Commander for the Armed Forces."

"I'm sure that you believe yourself to be. You have yet to command all of the soldiers' respect under your authority. If you want to be a good Commander, you have to make them respect you. Make them fear you if they disobey your orders. I might be persuaded to give you a little advice," Kaiser suggested as he looked up at Morin and tilted his head to the side. "I did learn a few things as a general's son."

"Anything, my Lord. I will do anything to earn your respect

as Commander of your Armed Forces," Morin promised, his eyes wet with tears. A cloth hit him in the face and slid into his hands.

"Stop your weeping," Kaiser growled. "It ill becomes you."

Morin wiped his eyes dry before he peered over at the paper Kaiser was writing on. "What are you doing?"

Kaiser paused in his writing and snorted loudly. He then set the goose feather quill aside in the inkwell and sat back in his seat. "The affairs of state are not your concern. Your duty is to convince the soldiers to follow you without question. I have taught you a few necessary skills to achieve that. Unless you don't think that you are capable. If so, I will recall your cousin from his search to take your place."

The Commander gulped as he twisted the cloth in his hands. His breath became erratic as his nerves grew more intense and unsettled. Kaiser returned to his writing, ignoring Morin's anxiety. He wrote quickly in his flowing script, stopping when the ink on his quill had dried and he had reached the bottom of the paper. With deft hand movements, he dipped the quill, scraped off the excess ink on the lip of the well, and began writing again on a fresh sheet of paper.

"Why are you still here?" Kaiser asked, not stopping in his work.

"You have not dismissed me," Morin nervously said, still wringing the cloth in his hands.

Kaiser snapped the fingers on his left hand and Rache stepped out of the shadows. Morin froze as he watched the Demon approach. Rache paused before him, smiling with fanged teeth, before snatching the cloth out of the Commander's hands.

"Now you may go," Kaiser said sternly. He chuckled when he heard Rache growl at Morin who could not leave the room fast enough.

"Shall I follow him?" the Demon asked as he slapped the cloth in his hands. He brought it up to his nose to sniff it.

Kaiser waved him off. "Don't waste your time. Morin may be stupid but he is loyal."

"He is worthless but," Rache started to say.

"But what," Kaiser growled as he glared at him.

"His family has no worth and there is no prize to be won with his loyalty," Rache said as he dropped the cloth right on the paper Kaiser was working on. "Doesn't your family have more trustworthy, more capable allies?"

"I am all that is left of the Adonis bloodline save for my hateful grandson. Have you succeeded in breaking him?" Kaiser asked as he pushed the cloth aside and continued writing.

"He is your hateful grandson so he is equally as stubborn

and difficult as you are," Rache laughed as he crossed his arms tightly.

"Are you growing soft too?" Kaiser asked as he pulled a new set of papers towards him. He picked up a quill and dipped the tip into an inkwell. "Should I find some other Demon to break him?"

Rache scoffed as he dropped his arms. "You insult me. I will break him."

The soft scratching sound of the quill going across the paper filled the silence of Kaiser's office. He bent over a piece of parchment, writing line after line. Dropping the quill into the inkwell, Kaiser sat back to survey what he had written.

"You told Morin that you were working on matters of state. Is that true?" Rache asked as he came to lean over Kaiser's shoulder.

"These are indeed matters of state for I must continue my lovely façade. I must keep myself informed of the goings on in this nation. I do have a rebellion to crush at some point so I must know all the details from the smallest barter in a village market to the movements of every Shadow Council member," Kaiser said proudly. He reached up and scratched his skin, fingers dragging over the emerging stubble. "Draw me a basin of hot water and soap. I do not like the idea of wearing a beard."

The Demon sneered. "I'm sure Axum has not been dormant in his fight and chase with the Daylord. I wonder how his efforts are progressing. Has he sent word?" Rache asked as he reached over to pick up the cloth.

"His last message bore few words of consequence. He finds that by following the mad Aday Silvanus around, he is able to avoid open confrontation with the Daylord. He says that the Daylord seems preoccupied with some unknown trouble. Perhaps the mighty warrior from the Eastlands is not as great as everyone thinks," Kaiser stated. He tapped his chin then pointed a finger like he had an important thought cross his mind. "Aday's half breed bastard is now a century old, proving that he inherited his father's Immortal blood. The other half breed bastard shall reach his thirtieth year of age next spring."

"What did you tell him?" Rache asked as he stepped back towards the privy closet and began preparing the basin.

"I told him to keep a careful eye on Aday and his sons. Aday is beyond saving in his madness which I have to applaud myself for," Kaiser smiled. "It is amazing what Shadow Blind does to open the mind to manipulation. As for his sons, the elder is under careful watch and the younger I am not too concerned about. I told him to end the younger son should he show a hint of power since I have more important matters here."

Rache laughed as he stepped out of the privy closet and gestured to Kaiser that the basin was ready for his use. Kaiser bowed his head before getting up and stepping inside to shave. For a time, all that could be heard was the scraping of a blade over skin and the sloshing of water in a bone china bowl. After several minutes, Kaiser came out with a clean shaven face.

"Much better," Kaiser said with a smile as he returned to his desk.

Rache paced around the opulent office, running his fingers over the silver and gold inlay of a display table. Sitting on an ebony wood sword display was the Silvanus family blade. He reached for the leather wrapped hilt.

"I wouldn't do that if I were you," Kaiser said as he bent over a new sheet of parchment.

Rache scoffed as he wrapped his hand around the hilt. He jerked back as a shock ran up his arm. He looked at the blade in disgust. He sneered at it as he brought his arm back down.

"I warned you," Kaiser said as he looked up. "That sword was forged for Shadow Night Silvanus upon his enthronement by Odin Kano with the fires of Vorin the Dragonlord. Add a little touch from me and I get to have a nice little artpiece," he explained before he returned to his writing.

A growl escaped Rache's throat. "I fear no sword or weapon."

Kaiser chuckled. "If you think that sword is nothing to worry about then Bane's great sword should simply be a worthless piece of steel."

The Demon whipped around and rotated his right arm just enough to expose a long twisted scar on his pale skin. The scar ran from the outer side of Rache's shoulder muscle, curved around his bicep towards his elbow and down to his wrist. The scar was black in color and had been made by a sword point. "One day I will rip that damned... I'll rip Bane's head from his neck..." he growled on the edge of fury. "I have not forgotten his sword. I can't believe it did not leave a scar on you."

"A scar or lack there of does not mean Bane's sword did not cause me pain. I wish him dead just as much as you," Kaiser stated as he continued writing, pausing only to switch to another sheet of paper.

Rache glared at the sword as he turned away from Kaiser. He clenched his right hand tightly. "I want the glory of destroying the Daylord before all those that love him," he fumed after a long silence. "What is your next command, my Lord?"

Kaiser gathered himself and thought in silence for a few minutes. "You are hungry for some blood, my good servant, and I still have a lot of paperwork and negotiations to take care of. Why don't you have the night off?"

Rache smirked, feeling the burning hunger in his throat. He grabbed his coat from the back of a chair and put it on. Drawing up his hood and mask, he laughed with a devilish expression in his eyes. "Tonight Cross shall rain with blood."

THE SABER SPY

Under orders from Zoras, Sai had done his best to keep an eye on Kaiser and an ear to whatever the Shadowborn noble was bound to say. He settled a degree of his command to Hayden Abendroth so he could focus on his watch. Hayden was the sole Saber Captain he could trust with all of his being and he had ordered him to monitor and decide if the other officers could be trusted. He hated having to spy on his own Saber brothers and sisters. In this day and age, Sai could trust no one like he used to. Even so, Sai was glad and eager to spy on Kaiser. He wanted to prove once and for all that Kaiser was a traitor in more than just whispers and rumors. It was time that the world took control of its destiny from the machinations of Kaiser Adonis.

It stunned him to learn that Aday Silvanus was in fact alive and part of the reason behind the Daylord's absence. It floored him that Aday was a father of two half breed sons born seventy years apart from each other. The details regarding the older son intrigued him but Sai knew that he could not be certain of his allegiance. To Kaiser, it seemed as if the younger son was simply nothing to worry about. Sai thought that was foolish of him but if there was one thing Kaiser wasn't, it was foolish. The man knew exactly what he was doing and just who was in control every waking moment of his life.

Sai could not believe what he was hearing as he sat on the balcony roof's edge. From what Hayden had reported, Kaiser seemed to have gained the Prince's trust by healing his father and punishing Morin. But it was all just an act. It was all just a game to him. Sai steadied his heartbeat to calm himself as he thought about the other things Kaiser had revealed. Who was the bastard grandson? Was Loran Win really in Kaiser's service? He thought about the prison massacre that happened in Eclipse six years ago. He had gone to the city to investigate with Eclipse's Saber Captain and learned of the escape of the fearsome Mirror Sea Pirate. Sai had to laugh. Morin Win was a scared and poor excuse for Commander of the Armed Forces. His cousin would have been a better fit had he not been a black hearted pirate.

He eased himself forward, gripping the edge of the roof. He was careful not to make any sound for fear of alerting the Demon he knew was inside. If Kaiser treated this creature like a servant, Sai was uncertain of just how powerful the Demon was or even worse, how powerful Kaiser was. It angered him that the more he learned about Kaiser, the more questions he had.

Cross bustled with the approach of night. The market venders were boasting of last minute sales while tavern owners threw open their doors, welcoming in patrons. Smoke trickled out of chimneys as kitchen fires roared to roast the day's meat. He could smell the various spice rubs and his mouth watered. This was a city he loved with all his heart and he knew that no one was safe from Kaiser so long as the traitor was alive. Sai was prepared to defend his home with all of his being from the danger that lurked in the room below him.

In a silent move, he slipped down from the edge and landed on the roof of the walkway that led to the private quarters. He flipped through the open window and landed on the stone path. The guards at the entrance quickly bowed before opening the heavy oak doors. Sai nodded his head towards them in silent thanks.

"Is the Prince in his quarters at this hour or has he preceeded towards the dining hall?" Sai inquired with a bob of the head.

"He has decided to take his dinner in his quarters this evening. He complained of a headache earlier this afternoon and wished for peace and quiet to rest," the left hand guard reported. To Sai, it seemed that the guards were hesitant to let him pass but he knew that they were aware of the folly denying passage to the Commander of the Sabers.

"Then I shall be brief and not disturb his Highness any more than necessary," Sai stated with a confident voice. He bowed his head once the guards stepped back to let him pass.

Instead of using Shadow Slide, Sai walked openly to Onyx's quarters, displaying his strength and letting all know that he was there. Most Sabers moved in the shadows and skulked about in secret haunts on the throne's business. As Commander, he was the universal symbol and reminder that the Sabers were strong and mighty warriors. Each door warden, guard, and chamber servant bowed their heads towards Sai as he walked down the hallway, his head uncovered and his identity plain to see. He passed scores of paintings, tapestries, and weapons on display before he reached Onyx's rooms.

Sai came to a stop in front of the door warden. "I need to see his Highness in private," Sai stated firmly.

The door warden eyed him for a moment. "Your Highness, the Commander of the Sabers wishes for an audience," he said after knocking on the door.

"Let him enter and you may leave your post. I will be safe in his presence," came the answer from the other side of the door.

Sai found Onyx sitting by the window with a menu card in his hand. The Prince pinched the bridge of his nose and closed his eyes tightly for a moment. He then opened his eyes again and set the card down. Sai bowed in submission, one clenched fist across his chest. He then stood back up. Onyx gestured for him to sit on a nearby chair.

"To what do I owe the pleasure of your company, my Commander," Onyx asked sounding tired.

"I was told that you were unwell. Is that true?" Sai asked in concern.

"I did not anticipate a meeting with the Shadow Council giving me such a powerful headache," Onyx said with a tired smile.

"Matters of state can be taxing on the mind, your Highness. I too left that meeting with a headache. Try some ginger root tea. It will help to settle your nerves and your thoughts." Sai finally sat down and moved the chair to face Onyx. "Also, I recommend a good night's sleep."

Onyx smiled. "You are most thoughtful and kind, Commander. I shall be glad to have you lead the Sabers when I take the throne. Will you take supper with me?"

Sai shook his head. "I have business to attend to so I respectfully decline. Perhaps another time."

"Then do what do I owe the pleasure of this visit?" Onyx asked as he reached for the menu card.

"As is my duty, I watch over your Highness by watching those that claim to serve you with honesty, loyalty, and integrity. Especially in this time when we must be certain of one's loyalty. After the Council meeting, Master Rokar asked me to follow up on some information he received about the Crossroads visit. I spent the remainder of the afternoon doing as he asked by looking and listening." Sai cleared his throat. "Your Highness, I beg you not to trust anything Kaiser Adonis says or does. He is a liar for he says one thing and means another."

"What did you learn?" Onyx asked, perking up at the statement.

"I have learned so much. Most alarming is that he has a Demon in his service. I did not lay eyes on the creature but I felt the darkness in my heart," Sai stated as he pressed a hand over his heart. "It has to be that masked servant of his. That servant is a Demon!"

Onyx shuddered. "You are certain? How do we know that Kaiser's servant and the Demon are one in the same."

"That is what I hope to find out, your Highness. But I learned a great deal more. Aday Silvanus is in fact alive though he is beyond the point of madness. He has two half breed bastard sons that live in the Southlands. The elder is a century old and the younger will be thirty years of age next spring. Kaiser himself claims to have a bastard grandson that is under the Demon's watch and he has the Mirror Sea Pirate in his service," Sai explained in full. As he spoke, he saw the alarm rise in Onyx's expression. The menu card dropped from the Prince's hand and fell to the floor at his feet.

"You have never given me cause to doubt your word, Commander, but what you have revealed is troubling," Onyx admitted, a hint of his youth breaking through as he shuddered.

Sai reached a hand forward and set it on Onyx's shoulder. "Your Highness, let me investigate further and raise those that I know are truly loyal to you and your father." He fell silent for a moment, debating with himself.

"Who do you speak of?" Onyx asked cautiously when he saw Sai's hesitation.

"The rebellion against Kaiser Adonis," Sai said in a low voice. "It has been brewing for many years and it pains me to admit that this secret has been kept from you. We of the rebellion had hoped to fight him without endangering those of the Silvanus bloodline. Perhaps in the end, we shall have need of you."

He expected Onyx to show some degree of fury. Instead, Onyx looked to be deep in thought. Sai looked at Onyx and saw a boy coming of age into a tough situation. He could read the worry in the way Onyx slumped his shoulders and held his eyes in a downcast gaze. The way Onyx greeted him was informal and vulnerable and yet it showed Sai that the Prince trusted him completely. The Saber Commander after all was present with Aku at the time of Onyx's birth and was the one who told him that Nuru had delivered a healthy son. Sai loved the young Prince like he was his own flesh and blood and was prepared to give his life for him.

His Saber oath was more than a reciting of words. It was a promise.

"Always you have worked in the best interests of the throne. You have been with my family for as long as I can remember. Surely, you have your own family to tend to," Onyx mused as he looked out the frosted glass of the window. Sai could tell that he was avoiding thinking too much and exacerbating his headache.

"My younger sister and her family live near the south gate of Cross. I have two nephews and a niece. I honor the Parahazur name by my service to you and your father," Sai answered without hesitation.

"They must be proud of you," Onyx commented as Sai handed him the dropped menu card.

"Take your meal in good faith, your Highness. Your Commander of the Sabers will serve you by investigating all that has been said. Take care not to confront Kaiser alone should matters come to a head," Sai said before he stood up. He saluted and bowed before heading towards the door.

INFORMATION

At first, Sai was not sure where to start in his investigation. It was not from lack of fore knowledge or confusion. Sai knew that investigating Kaiser in any form or fashion invited danger and if Madhuri's fate was any indication, it also invited death. In fact, speaking out against Kaiser was dangerous. Kaiser would just smile in the face of criticism, not moving or firing back with an equally damning claim. Sai had seen it many times during a Shadow Council session when Zoras spat and snarled at the noble. As much as he personally hated Kaiser, he admired his ability to remain calm. But as everyone in the rebellion knew, what Kaiser did not say or do was even worse. Sai knew that he would have to chance death if he was going to find out the truth.

Sai knelt down to the floor of his bedroom and reached under the bed. Placing one hand on the side of the mattress, he pulled hard on a cold iron handle. Out came a long dark wood trunk, covered in dust. He undid the latches and lifted the lid. Inside was his Saber leather armor, dull from being in storage. He smiled as he thought of when he had received it from his predecessor. It was a fond and proud memory of his Saber graduation. He ran his fingers over the layers and stitching lovingly.

It took longer than Sai would have liked but he did not want to rush oiling the leather. Now the leather armor gleamed as if it was brand new. Sai pulled and tugged at the ties, snapping buckles into place. The cuirass was tighter than he remembered especially around his shoulders.

"You were right, Master Erebus. A Saber grows into his armor," Sai chuckled, remembering Kader's blessing words at his graduation.

"My Commander," came a voice in the hallway. Sai let out a deep breath and went outside room to find Donovan Shunga.

Donovan was a high ranking Saber and similar in build to Sai with broad shoulders and thick arms. Just as it was with Sai, his size did not diminish his speed. He took up the pace beside Sai as he handed him a slip of paper.

Sai quickly read the short note before handing it back. "It angers me that we have been so blind to what Kaiser has had at his side."

"Well it's not like he flaunted that servant of his everywhere. And if that servant is truly a Demon, he is a lot smarter than your typical lowlife," Donovan stated. "And a lot more dangerous."

"No matter. We as Sabers must be ready to face the same enemies our ancestors did to protect all that we love and hold dear. We must put ourselves at risk. As Commander, I will put my life first before those of you and our comrades. Should my investigation result in my death, I want Captain Hayden to meet with Zoras Rokar about taking my place," Sai explained.

"Are you that worried?" Donovan asked with great concern. He stopped Sai with a touch on the shoulder. "Be honest, Commander."

Sai let out a deep breath. "To admit fear is to show courage for you recognize both weakness and strength within you to go forward. I swore an oath to serve Lord, land, and the Immortal Truth. If I must give my life to fulfill that oath, I will gladly give it."

Donovan smiled as he patted Sai's shoulder. "Then I am honored to follow you, Commander, wherever your path may take you. Whatever you need, you can trust in me."

"Thank you, Donovan. I am glad that there are still a few Sabers under my command that I can trust," Sai replied, returning the gesture. "I trust you now to deliver my message to Hayden should I not return. Until such a time, keep watch over Lord Aku," Sai added with an encouraging smile.

Donovan nodded. "To Lord, land, and the Immortal Truth."

"You know what? I had a very similar conversation with my predecessor. He told me that he was proud to be a Saber even if Lord Shiloh chastised him constantly for his big mouth," Sai laughed.

"It is sad that he died trying to run away with the bastard. Some say that Ryder led him to his death but I do not believe such slanderous words. No true Saber would do what he did without a very good reason," Donovan stated.

A thought dawned on Sai and a curious expression spread across his face. "Commander Sorin," Sai started to say as he tried to find the words for his thoughts. "Wasn't he close to Master Erebus?"

"It doesn't matter. Both Commander Sorin and Master Erebus are dead," Donovan quickly pointed out.

"Dead or alive. It does matter," Sai stated as he pulled away and turned around. "Remember your orders and keep to the Truth!"

Sai disappeared into Shadow Slide as soon as he turned away from Donovan. His focus was so intense that that he saw nothing but where he wanted to go. He shifted his energy to the east. He quickly moved through the streets like a dark ghost, completely unseen by the people. Even if they did see the moving shadow, they knew to ignore it. Sabers were masters of the Shadow Slide, a technique that transformed a Shadowborn into a speedy shadow to move about; it served its purpose both in combat and in intrigue. The only downside was that it left the user very cold once he returned to himself. None of the effects mattered to Sai. He had his mission and he was going to succeed.

The northeast section of Cross was poor and less extravagant in design than the area close to the palace. The city was not without its share of thieves and cutthroats and in this section was where they congregated when not committing crimes. Sabers regularly patrolled in the area with soldiers so his appearance would not be unexpected. He returned to form in the middle of a small square amidst stunned onlookers. One man in the middle of stealing a loaf of bread dropped his pilfered prize and ran in fear. Sai may have been in his old leathers but his fierce expression was unmistakable. The Commander of the Sabers had arrived.

After a quick survey of his surroundings, he stepped forward towards a run down two story building that appeared to have been an inn for the poor. The plaster of the outer walls was covered in a gray foul smelling mold. The wood beams of the frame were rotten and splitting. As Sai looked up to the second story, the building appeared to be leaning over the street. His stride was confident and powerful until his boot landed in a puddle of dirty water, splashing all over his foot. He silently sneered at the stench in the air and vowed to bring the area to the attention of the Council. People averted their eyes and kept their mouths shut as he passed.

Inside of the inn was no better as Sai let the door close behind him. The air smelled of sickness mixed with healing herbs.

A fire burned low in a blackened stone hearth. Of the seven cots crammed in the small room, five were occupied with pale and sickly patrons.

"Ah, Commander. Have you come with the healing touch of our Lord?" a sweaty thin man asked as he wiped his hands with a dirty cloth. He had his shirt sleeves rolled up to his elbows and his dark hair tied back.

"I need to speak to a Shadowborn named Den," Sai said as he looked at the sick people.

The thin man sighed deeply. "I am he."

"We are Immortal. What is this illness?" Sai asked, stunned to see such poor health in his fellow Shadowborn. He looked around, trying to discern what injury or disease was affected the unwell.

Den looked around the room, eyeing his two nurses who tended the ill. "These five were found nearly drained of their lifeforce and Spirit energy not too long ago. I had heard of losing one's connection to their Spirit energy but never where it affected their lifeforce. I am at a loss."

Sai frowned. This was not normal under any circumstances. Immortals were immune to the diseases that afflicted the Mortals. "I ask you again. What is this illness?"

The man sighed deeply and gestured for Sai to follow. He led him to a back room that was more private and shut the door. Sai found himself surrounded by jars of herbal concoctions and sprigs hanging from the ceiling as they dried. The small work table had pieces of various plants that Sai could not identify scattered around a cutting board.

"I wish that I had a straight answer for you. After the first incident, I had a mind to investigate. But then more people afflicted by this illness were discovered and I did not have the time. Most have died after a while. Thankfully, those that did die were so lost in their own minds that they did not feel the pain of their bodies shutting down. It was horrible to watch," the man started to say. He had to pause to gather himself.

"How did you know that they had lost their Spirit energy?" Sai asked with a quick look in the direction of the common room. He laid a hand on his right side where a knife lay hidden. He turned his attention back to Den who wiped a tear from his eye.

"Master Erebus made sure to teach those of his order how to use Shadow Call. Unlike Earth Call, we Shadowborn use it to detect Spirit Energy within each other and direct it properly. I used the power on those I came across," Den explained before pausing again. Sai saw that whatever Den had experienced was causing him great sadness. He set a hand on Den's shoulder, encouraging him to continue. "I could not sense their Spirit energy. Not even a glimmer or spark. All I felt was that they were lost and wandering on the edge of the void. It was as if they stayed in Shadow Slide too long and were dying. Even before I arrived, many more have been found dead and left to rot in the gutters," Den stated as he looked despondent. He wiped his brow with the cloth he had been twisting around in his hands.

Sai was horrified to hear of such suffering and again promised to bring the area to the attention of the Shadow Council. "Cross is the jewel of the Shadowborn. How could such destitution exist without my knowledge?"

Den quickly cleaned up the table. "We told our Council delegate several times. When we did not see him for a month, I thought that perhaps he and the Council were in negogiations for aid. But then the inn nightguard found his rotting corpse in a ditch behind the building." He tossed the plant debris in a trash basket behind him.

"How can the murder of a city delegate go unreported even to a tax collector? This is completely outrageous! I can assure you that I will bring the entire Council myself to address the problems here," Sai promised. "Completely unacceptable."

"I thank you, Commander. Now you wished to speak with me? I will gladly give you my time in exchange for your service to the Council," Den asked as he started wiping down the table with a tattered cloth.

"You were of Kader Erebus' order, correct?" Sai asked for confirmation.

Den nodded. "He is the one that taught me the healing arts though my training was suddenly ended six years ago."

"Yes, when he died," Sai mused as he looked away and tried to collect his thoughts.

"He did not die, Commander," Den nervously said before quickly looking over his shoulder.

Sai jerked his head around to stare at Den. "Repeat that."

"Kader Erebus did not die, Commander. He fled the city under duress with Sabers on his trail. He urged myself and two other students to disband the order and run to the halls of the other Spiritborn Lords. This is the first time I have spoken of this since that night," Den said, sweat beading on his brow. He gulped hard. "When I went to my quarters, I found the other students... I found..."

It was clear to Sai that Den was deathly afraid and on the verge of a nervous breakdown. Sai's thoughts immediately turned to Kaiser. He wanted to convince the Shadowborn man that he was safe but Sai did not know if he could truly promise to protect him.

Kaiser was everywhere. He could barely trust his own shadow if Sabers had turned their loyalty to the traitor. He clenched his fists tightly in anger.

"I will not stand for Sabers under my command going against their oath. As soon as I find them, I will strip them of their leathers and have them imprisoned for treason!" he declared in a loud voice. "Do you remember the Sabers from that night?"

"I did not see their faces but there were six of them," Den said as he continued to wipe down the table though it was now perfectly clean. He kept his gaze down and away from Sai's penetrating eyes. His chest heaved in fright.

Sai stepped back to the table and forced Den to look at him until he calmed. "What else did Master Erebus tell you before he fled?"

"That we were to warn anyone who would listen about Kaiser," Den said with some effort before his voice broke.

"Has Kaiser or anyone representing him come to see you since that night?" Sai quickly asked.

Den gulped. "That servant of his. Always his face is covered but those eyes. I will never forget those terrible eyes."

Sai slapped his other hand a little too hard on Den's shoulder. He held Den to steady him enough to speak. "Tell me what you saw."

"Blood red. They were blood red. It was like looking into the face of a Demon so ancient and powerful that my entire being went cold. Please do not make me say more!" Den cried before tearing himself away. He fell up against the wall and curled up in the fetal position, shivering violently.

He did sympathize with Den for a Demon was a terrible force to behold. But he already knew that Kaiser's servant was a Demon. He had even heard the Demon speak though the voice did not have the same effect as the knowledge of his identity. Sai was too trained to let such a thing frighten him. He bent down to Den's level. Den pulled away as if he was frightened of Sai.

"I am not here to harm you, Den, but I need to have my questions answered. This is a matter of great importance for our Lord Aku. I must know the identity of Kaiser's servant. Is there anything, any detail from those afflicted with the loss of Spirit energy to the servant himself, that led you to believe..."

"Commander Win said that Rache would kill me if Kaiser ordered him to!" Den shouted before sobbing. His skin gained a ghostly white palour. "Commander Win came after the delegate was found dead. He recognized me from Master Erebus' order and said that it was too bad I got away and that if I wanted to live, I would keep my mouth shut. He said that what Rache would do to me would be even worse than what Kaiser did to Commander Sorin for taking the bastard away."

A shifty army Commander and traitorous Sabers hinted at deeper terrors within the Shadowborn lands. Sai had already known about Morin and his loyalty to Kaiser but he did not think of him as a murderer or even much of a threat. But Sai had to wonder how Rache came to Kaiser's service when all stories said that he was dead and gone. Sai had to ask himself why Kaiser had such an intense interest in Ryder Coba. This went more than just him being a royal bastard. A plan began to formulate in his head. If he was going to break the lock around Kaiser, he was going to have to break Morin Win first. He would have to tread carefully now that he knew that Rache was Kaiser's masked servant.

"For all these years, you have been good to the Sabers and to the Shadowborn people. I will do everything within my power to make sure that those who presume to threaten good people like you are brought to justice. I will start with Morin Win," Sai promised with absolute conviction.

A VISIT WITH SPIRITS

Onyx carefully walked down the mountain path to the hallowed tombs. He held a burning torch in his left hand so not to scorch the low hanging branches of the trees. The trees rustled in the soft breeze letting him know how close he was to the edge. The path continued to descend, winding through the greenery until it turned around a corner of stone. Onyx could now see his grandfather's tomb with torch lights still burning ever since he had been buried. They were kept lit from dusk until dawn every night. In a nearby gnarled tree hooted an owl and Onyx looked up to see the white faced bird perched on the edge of a branch. It hooted again when they locked eyes.

"Master of the night," Onyx said honorably. Owls were second to wolves in Shadowborn culture and were welcome as good omens in graveyards. The bird scuttled back to the tree trunk and settled in to watch him. It hooted one last time before falling silent.

Onyx turned his attention to his grandfather's tomb, a great stone barring the doorway. Etched on its face was his grandfather's name, years of life, and his title. He knelt down and stabbed the end of his torch in the dirt before him. The glade was suddenly and completely silent save for the flickering noise of the torches.

"Grandfather, since your passing, I have not been able to see my purpose," Onyx began to say before the tomb. "I know that I was born Onyx Shadow Silvanus, son of Aku and Nuru, Prince of the Shadowborn. I followed what was expected of me, learned the law, and ways of the sword. But never in my heart did I know what that all meant," He fought back a tear. "I am afraid, Grandfather. So afraid of the future."

A chill overcame Onyx as the torches burned brightly. He pulled his cloak around his body. "The more my eyes open to the world, the more I question it and all who live in it. I start to question myself and what my role is. I thought I knew who I was before Crossroads but I was wrong. I do not know who I am. Am I truly ready to take the throne when there are others out there more capable than me? Am I capable of defending the throne when danger is so close? I vow to remove the danger to the throne and learn to see the truth in the world but I wonder if I can even do it. I can't do this alone. If you hear me, please, I ask for guidance. Some word or sign that the Spirits are with me." His mind turned to Luna. "Help me keep my promise."

Onyx closed his eyes and steadied his breathing. He put his hands together and bowed his head to pray. He prayed for guidance. He prayed for wisdom. But most of all, he prayed for peace. His heart slowed to a steady beat as he whispered his prayers over and over to himself, keeping his hands clasped. The chill wind came again and Onyx's body shivered. His eyes opened.

"Grandfather, as you once told me, the Spirits have the power to help change the world. I do believe that they led the Daylord to our homeland to fight alongside Shadow Night and break the Demons' hold. I believe that they helped create a beautiful and peaceful world. I believe that they can help me in these troubled times. Ask them to guide Commander Parahazur and those that fight in this rebellion. Ask them on behalf of me," Onyx pleaded, pouring his confused emotions into every word.

The chill wind rushed through the tree tops and the branches creaked as they knocked into each other. The owl hooted a shrill call in protest. Onyx found that the sound was strangely distant. He closed his eyes as a cloud of dust spun and turned in a small twister towards him. Once the stinging storm of dirt receded, Onyx opened his eyes again.

Where was the tomb? Where were the trees? He looked around at the grey mist in confusion. Getting to his feet, Onyx turned around to see more of the strange mist. He spotted the tree that the owl had perched in only that it was bare of leaves. Sitting beneath its branches was a large black wolf with gold eyes.

"Child of Shadow," the wolf said without moving its mouth. It then stood up and took several steps forward.

Onyx froze in place as the wolf came towards him. It was as tall as a horse at the shoulders with jaws that could snap his body in two. The wolf circled around him, breath visible in the chill air.

He gulped as it came eye to eye with him, an ancient expression in his eyes. "I have come at your call," came the same deep voice.

"I did not call anyone," Onyx said as he felt dwarfed in the presence of the wolf. "Did my Grandfather send you?"

"Your heart spoke of your need," the wolf spoke. "I am Omu."

"The Spirit Wolf..." Onyx managed to say.

A smile came to Omu's eyes. "Indeed I am."

It was a moving moment to the young Prince to be faced with such an ancient and powerful force. Kader's stories of the great wolf ran through his mind as he felt his body grow weak. He found himself at a loss for words. Omu sat down before Onyx and studied him with his golden eyes.

"I have been watching you as I watch all since you entered this world. I have seen it grow darker and darker with no ability to halt the growing shadows. Never has my desire to walk among you and your kin been so strong as it was when Akakios fell," Omu said with a grave voice.

It surprised Onyx that Omu mentioned the fallen Shadowlord that had preceded his grandfather's rule. It was an odd reference and yet, he knew that a Spirit would say something without good reason. He waited for Omu to continue but the Spirit appeared to hesitate. In fact, Omu looked reluctant.

"I can say nothing more about Akakios to anyone but his heir. Only he can learn of his father's secrets and memories," Omu dutifully said. He briefly looked down but Onyx could tell that the Spirit was looking away. He was fighting some unknown force.

Onyx did not know what to say or ask. He felt that something was wrong but could not identify the source of the feelings. The chill wind rushed through the glade again and he shivered. Off in the distance, he heard an owl hooting a strange and haunting song.

"I miss this world," Omu suddenly said. He looked around and appeared to smile. His golden eyes lit up with a warm glow. "It warms my heart to see it again. People like your dear grandfather have told me much about it."

"What do they say?" Onyx dared to ask.

"It depends on who you ask but many say the same thing: a danger unlike anything is growing and taking root," Omu said, starting with a knowing tone and finishing with a growl. His hackles bristled and his lips curled. He then turned his fierce gaze upon Onyx.

Onyx shuddered under Omu's intense and beastly face. Though he grew up with stories of Omu's benevolence and kindness, Omu was still a powerful Spirit. He was a guide for the dead and an omen of darkness. He tried to edge himself away from the mighty Spirit Wolf but found himself unable to move. He fought against the invisible force holding him to no avail. The wind grew colder and Onyx worried that he was being drawn into the Spirit World.

"What is happening? Why can't I move?" Onyx shrieked, hoping to get Omu's attention.

"The Spirit World is angry and I am doing much to shield you from their rage," Omu snarled as he looked around. He roared in defiance, the sound bouncing and shaking off the stone and trees. The chilly wind appeared to die down and Onyx felt a degree of warmth returning to his limbs.

"Are the Spirits angry at me? What have I done to dishonor them?" Onyx squeaked. He had never felt so helpless and weak in his life.

Omu shook his head and relaxed his posture. "No, they are not angry with you nor have they abandoned you. But they can not tell you who you are. That is something you must discover for yourself. You must find your own strength and determine where it will lead you."

Onyx immediately deflated at Omu's words. He wanted to hear what he needed to do or what to say. He wanted to hear that the Spirits blessed his goal to become the Shadowlord. Onyx quickly reminded himself that the Spirits were never direct on purpose. Picking apart each of Omu's words, Onyx tried to discern a hidden message, something that would give him more hope.

"You have grown into a fine young man," the wolf said with a warm smile in his eyes. "There are many that are proud of you and continue to watch over you with pride."

"Like my mother? Is she proud of me too?" Onyx asked in earnest.

Omu nodded. "She is proud most of all."

Happiness welled up in Onyx's heart and he felt immediate relief. He wanted to rush forward and wrap his arms around Omu's furry neck but wondered if he would tumble through the Spirit and hit the ground. He resorted himself to smiling. The wolf bowed his head, holding the position for a few seconds before lifting it again.

"It is in you to be great but you must discover it for yourself. Do not let others control you. Learn from your elders and accept that the truth can hurt and heal," Omu stated.

Onyx realized that Omu's form was dissiappating into a thin mist and his voice was becoming distant. He rubbed his eyes from the strain of trying to see Omu. When Onyx opened his eyes again, he was back in the glade before his grandfather's tomb. He spun around, looking for Omu. He nearly jumped in shock when the owl hooted breaking the silence. It then flapped its wings a few times before flying off and out of sight. He tried to make sense of what just happened. Did he really meet with Omu the Wolf Spirit or was it just a hallucination?

CONFRONTATION

Onyx turned around and froze. On the edge of the glade, Kaiser stood with his servant. For once in his life, Kaiser did not look polished and clean. He sported stubble on his jaw that was speckled with black and gray. His usually coifed hair was loosely tousled. Underneath his black coat, Kaiser's white linen shirt was untucked. Kaiser's servant carried a torch in his left hand, dressed in his usual tattered clothes.

"Ah, fancy finding you here. Out here late at night and so alone. Where is your Saber?" Kaiser asked. He innocently looked around. "I do not think your father would appreciate his only son and heir walking around unprotected."

"Considering your history of military know how and prowess, I have a feeling that a Saber would be superfluous. Besides, we are deep within Cross and beside my grandfather's tomb," Onyx said as he gathered his nerves. He was still reeling from his encounter with Omu.

Kaiser smiled as he gestured towards the torch in his servant's hand. "Someone must keep the torch by Akakios' tomb lit. No one else will so I have taken it upon myself to keep up the tradition. Well in absence of his son of course. Normally it would be his duty but you know." He shrugged.

There was something about Kaiser's demeanor that unnerved Onyx. He watched as Kaiser silently gestured towards the left, directing his servant to leave down the shaded pathway. His servant bowed his head and left without a word.

"Why aren't you going?" Onyx asked.

"I can not leave you alone. Besides, he knows the way," Kaiser said. He sauntered over to Onyx's side. "Still thinking about your decision to take the throne? Is that why you are out here?"

Onyx let out a deep breath, his shoulders weighted down by his thoughts. "I want to believe that what I am doing is the right thing. Do you support my aspiration to take my father's throne."

Kaiser set his hand on Onyx's shoulder. "If you believe in something strongly enough, you can make anything happen. Just know that the road will be difficult. I know that you think taking the throne would be a mercy to your father and indeed it would be from the struggles of sitting upon it himself. But then his worry turns to you and his desire to see you succeed. Not everyone will be as welcoming and accomendating to a youth."

The statement regarding his young age reminded Onyx that he was in fact only eighteen years old. A man to some but a child to many. He deflated at the thought until Kaiser gave his shoulder an encouraging squeeze.

"With someone like Ryder, why would anyone even consider me worthy? He's proven himself a warrior beyond compare. He is worldly and smart. What am I?" Onyx openly questioned.

"I think you need to ask who you are before you ask others what you are," Kaiser politely suggested.

"What would you do in my place?" Onyx asked as he turned to look at Kaiser. "What would you say?"

Kaiser appeared to think for a moment. He let out a deep breath. "I would tell them that I am Kaiser Adonis first and the son of Cian second."

"But isn't that the same thing?" Onyx asked doubtful about the interpretation of his original question.

"The same and yet different. I have not let myself be defined by those who have come before me. I created my own identity and though there are those that disagree with it, it is who I am," Kaiser replied. He pressed a hand to his heart. "I am after all eleven hundred years old. The closest in age at the court of your father is half my great number of years. I was born in a different era and thus my ways are a little strange and more abrasive than the delicate customs bred under the rule of your grandfather."

What Kaiser said made sense. He was from a different time, the same as the most ancient souls still living in Terra. It had to be strange for him to walk among people so much younger than him. He also did not make a show of his history as a warrior which led many, including Onyx, to believe that he was not much of one at all. One thing that Onyx did know was that Kaiser was an experienced healer, the best in the Shadowborn lands. He had seen Kaiser in action on several occasions, bringing his father back from the brink of death. In those moments, Kaiser had worked without complaint, staying awake through the days and nights and showing no signs of weariness.

"How do you do it?" Onyx asked in earnest.

Kaiser tilted his head. "Do what?"

"Not to sound insulting but you are so much older than everyone else. Does it feel strange to be around people that are practically children in your eyes?" Onyx shrugged. He felt embarrassed for even asking.

"I have grown used to it. At my age, you become numb to those around you dying to the point that you accept it as the nature of things. I live knowing that I am the last of my line," Kaiser mused. He closed his eyes and let out a deep breath.

"But Sai said that you admitted to having a bastard grandson," Onyx blurted out. Kaiser's eyes snapped open.

Kaiser slowly turned his head to look directly at Onyx. The look in his eyes was so unnerving that Onyx gulped. "Did he now? I wonder what gave him the notion that I have procreated a child that produced a grandson. Have I ever been married?"

"Well no but," Onyx started to say.

"Have I ever courted a lady with the intention of marriage?" Kaiser fired quickly, lifting an eyebrow.

"I don't know but," Onyx tried again to answer.

Kaiser was too quick for him. "The answer is no. I have never done any such thing. Do not be so quick to believe what others say. As you have pointed out, I do not have the most savory reputation and there are many who would spread rumors and lies to discredit me."

In a way, Onyx felt like Kaiser was angry at him for making a claim that he had a grandson. Kaiser's tone was stern and unforgiving. His response to Onyx's words was quick and to the point. It made Onyx feel like the child he was. He dropped his head and stared at the ground. The glade seemed like it was closing in around him and he shivered from an imagined chill. Kaiser's hand dropped away from his shoulder, removing the sense of comfort.

"I trust Commander Parahazur more than I trust you. I believe what he tells me and I have no reason to believe that he would lie to me," Onyx finally said, gathering his courage. He turned on his feet to face Kaiser. "You however have much to answer for."

"And just what do I have to answer for?" Kaiser asked in annoyance.

"Your servant is a Demon. That I know Commander Parahazur would not lie about. And now that same servant is walking around the graves of my ancestors, desecrating them with his presence," Onyx growled. He clenched his fists tightly.

Kaiser shook his head, laughing. "You should not believe everything you are told. Of course the Saber Commander would want to discredit me by claiming my servant is a Demon. It is only because he believes that my reputation is so horrible that no one but a Demon would agree to serve me."

Onyx felt hot blood on his palms and unclenched his hands. "He has never given me reason not to trust him. Unlike you. People speak of you like you are the very name of treachery."

"I simply tell the truth, your Highness. I speak reality and hide nothing from others. I am plain and not hidden," Kaiser said matter of factly. He gestured towards himself. "Of anyone in this city, you can always trust me to be as you see me."

"What about that which I do not see? How can I be certain you are not lying to me now?" Onyx warned.

Kaiser scoffed. "If you want to be a proper Shadowlord, you must learn how to tell a lie from the truth. You would find no better teacher in that art than me. It is easy enough to believe that what you see, hear, and sense is true but," Kaiser raised a finger. "Spirits can shield whatever they wish and say whatever they want to convince you otherwise. The skill to see beyond reality of the world and into the nature of Spirits is a skill obtained with age."

"Spirits can lie?" Onyx asked, now drawn into Kaiser's revelation.

"They are the worst liars of all. They can distort your senses, possess a man into madness, and make you think against what is in your heart. It takes a walk within their world to strip them of that power. It takes a man of true power to return from their world. Bane Arlis the Daylord would be an example of such a man who has seen the truth as it was meant to be seen," Kaiser explained. "If you want to be great, you will have to follow his example."

Onyx began to doubt his own worth with each word Kaiser said. His body slackened and he looked down at the grass by his feet. His heart began to beat in an erratic rhythm. He swallowed hard.

"I want to be a great Shadowlord," Onyx managed to say.

"An honorable sentiment. You recognize your own faults and see room for improvement. You are on your way," Kaiser smoothly said. He gestured around the glade with his hand. "The world has no time for weakness and doubt. It will devour you and spit out your bones for the carrion crows to feed on."

The grand vision that Kaiser had weaved suddenly shattered and Onyx felt naked and bare before him. His heart hammered in his chest and he struggled to steady his breath. He looked at Kaiser who stared back with a studying gaze.

"I am sorry that I must be so harsh but you must open yourself to the reality of the world. It is cruel and unforgiving. However I do see courage in you. Hold on to that and use it to find greatness," Kaiser emphasized by grabbing at the air, making a fist, and shaking it.

Onyx felt like the glade was closing in on him. The air seemed stale and he began to miss the cold breeze from his experience with Omu. The nearby trees creaked more from age and settling earth than from a brisk wind. He wanted to look around for the owl but with Kaiser watching, he was too afraid to turn away. There was something in Kaiser's face that drew him in. Something behind the penetrating gaze that gave him pause. Onyx swallowed hard.

"Can I ask you a question?" Onyx inquired.

"You just did but go ahead," Kaiser chuckled lightly. The spark in his eyes changed from cold and mysterious to warm and inviting.

"Why would the Spirit World be angry?" Onyx asked.

Kaiser let out a deep breath and nodded as if to say he was considering the question with great thought. "As much as the Spirits want, they can no longer walk among the living as they used to. Should a soul rise up to threaten the balance of the world, they can only watch and wait for a need strong enough to call them through the void. They have the power to act but are helpless to do so. I would imagine anyone in that position would be angry."

"Are you the soul they fear?" Onyx blurted out.

"Heaven's no!" Kaiser laughed but there was nothing pure and good in the sound. "I am but one old man."

Everything in Kaiser's statement put Onyx on edge. "Sometimes it only takes a single soul to change the world. Think of the Daylord. He tipped the battle in favor of the Northern Alliance a thousand years ago."

Kaiser scoffed. "It also can take a single soul to destroy the world whether it is their intent to do so or not. Or it can take the will of many to wage a war against one, disrupting peace all for an imagined threat. Let us say a rebellion?"

Onyx froze. He wanted to ask how Kaiser knew about the rebellion. Surely Kaiser knew the identities of his critics. Zoras Rokar was one of them. So was Commander Parahazur. Onyx even remembered his old teacher Master Erebus acting suspicious in Kaiser's presence. But how could Kaiser cause so much hate when he had saved Onyx's father on many occasions? There was no other person capable of the specialized kind of healing needed for Demon wounds. No one near as skilled as him. Onyx looked over at Kaiser and imagined a predator lying in wait. Waiting for an opportunity to strike. He stumbled back a few steps.

"I will admit that I followed you here. At first, I had thought to make sure that you had proper protection but then a thought crossed my mind. I have grown tired of placating your ill father with hollow threats of killing you. I find that you are no longer of use to me," Kaiser warned as he stepped forward.

"I want you gone from Cross immediately. You and your servant," Onyx ordered in a shaky voice.

"You do not yet wear the crown therefore I respectfully decline," Kaiser said as he edged another step forward. He shrugged his shoulders as if to say he was sorry.

Onyx gritted his teeth, biting back feelings of fear and anxiety. "I now speak with my father's voice. And I think that I am being rather kind by letting you leave than executing you for every crime you have committed."

"Kind? I could have killed you when you were a squalling babe in the cradle. I think that I have been kind in letting you live so do not presume to threaten me. You are a child in a man's world," Kaiser answered.

Onyx did not want to lose his cool but fear was starting to get the better of him. He quickly took a deep breath to calm himself. "I am a grown man now and no longer a child. I am the blood of Shadow Night and you will obey my command."

Kaiser laughed. "Your command? You are a child, a nothing to me. Only an annoying fly. Worthless and ill suited for the destiny pounded into him since birth. Do you honestly think you can threaten me, boy? I do not need a sword to slay a man. That is what my servant Rache is for."

As if called out to by name, Rache slipped out of the shadows, unveiled and laid bare. "So finally we have a proper meeting," Rache stated with a smirk. He turned to Kaiser. "He's rather thin for a Shadowborn prince. At least his father was worth something before I tore his heart out."

"It was you!" Onyx shouted and he fought every fiber in his being not to leap forward and attack Rache. He knew that any act would be foolish against a Demon well known for slaughter and destruction.

"I am not sure why your grandfather thought I could raise him from the dead. No one goes to the Spirit World and comes back unscathed. Save maybe the Daylord but we all know how busy he is nowadays," Kaiser said, laughing heartily.

Onyx was filled with rage. "Get out of Cross and maybe I won't command my soldiers to kill you."

Kaiser leaned forward. "Issue that command and he destroys your dear father. Him and anyone else you so happen to care about. And who is to say he will stop?" he said pointing at Rache beside him.

"Yes I do tend to get a little out of control," Rache snickered as he crossed his arms tightly. "Let's see there was that ravishing bar wench two nights ago. And that guard at the southern gate. I could go on but it would take a while," he stated as he counted out the number of people he killed. "Ten Sabers during last winter and Madhuri Coba right before your grandfather's funeral! Haha! He wasn't even a worthy challenge!"

Kaiser snapped his fingers and Rache instantly had Onyx pinned against the stone wall next to Shiloh's tomb. Kaiser sauntered over to Rache's side. "You are a child, a worthless child, and even the bastard surpasses you in worth and greatness. I think it is high time that you look upon reality and see the world for what it truly is. You will learn the same lesson I did when I was a child: the world is cruel," he added, slapping Rache on the shoulder.

Onyx felt the vomit rise up in the back of his throat. The Demon smelled of death and blood. He began to choke when Rache wrapped a hand around his throat. "You made a pretty new friend in Crossroads. I would hate to have to kill her," Rache threatened.

He knew that he had to get away. He had to run as far as he could. He was no longer safe in Cross. But Rache's strength was overwhelming and there was no hope for escape.

POWER SHIFT

"What the Hell are you doing in my quarters!" Morin shouted in anger upon seeing Sai in his rooms. The Saber Commander was aimlessly sifting through a desk drawer, picking and pulling at sheets of paper.

Sai looked up to see Morin stagger in. Morin was dressed a luxurious dinner jacket and had a dagger belted on his left hip. He set the note he was reading down on the desktop. "The real question is how low did the High Commander of the Armed Forces have to sink to win Kaiser's approval," he said as he turned to face Morin. "I think we both know that you are not truly qualified to lead an army and I highly doubt that Kaiser recruited you for your martial skills."

Morin sneered. "You have no business here. Get out," he growled as he stared Sai down.

"I make it my business to find out why our Prince questions the loyalty of his Commander," Sai replied coolly.

The fury was plain in Morin's tight expression as he shook from it. He pointed at Sai. "Saber or not, I still have a right to my privacy."

"That right ended when you sold yourself to Kaiser's service. Given a hint of power and you are transformed into nothing more than a bully. Kaiser's bully on puppet strings for him to play with. You honestly think he cares about who you are? I am at least granting you a chance to repent your sins and pledge your loyalty to the throne, where it belongs. Will you not take it?" Sai asked politely.

Morin fumed as he looked about his study. He saw the open drawers of his desk and the disarray of his shelves. Cushions had been shifted on his chairs and bench. Several of them had been ripped at the seams, spilling out a mess of white down feathers. Curtains had been thrown open to let in the maximum amount of light. Every weapon and piece of armor was missing. He turned his gaze back to Sai, seeing that he stood between him and the door to his private quarters. The Saber Commander was dressed in his leathers, looking calm and collected in his expression.

"You have destroyed my room! Where is the shield that hung over the fireplace? My father gave that to me!" Morin demanded as he rushed about the room, digging through the mess for the heirloom.

Sai chuckled. "You will need more than a shield to protect you from not only your Master's wrath but that of the Shadowlord. Least of all me for I do not deal with treachery lightly."

Morin threw down a torn cushion and stamped his feet. "Is this just because I am a man of low birth compared to the great and wonderful nobility of the Parahazurs?" he sneered. He spat on the floor at Sai's feet. "Or perhaps you are jealous of my good fortune?"

"Morin, I have never been jealous of you. In fact, I pity you. You had such talent and ambition and you wasted it in your service to Kaiser. Your drive has left you alone in this world and I do not doubt that no one would mourn your death. I believe even your cousin would not care," Sai stated as he stepped around the desk, shoving a stack of papers and a full ink well to the floor.

The look on Morin's face was full of scorn and hate. He looked like a child that had just had his favorite toy taken away from him. "I want that shield. It belonged to my grandfather," he growled harshly.

"A shield? Is that all you care about?" Sai asked incredulously.

"It is the only thing that is left of him and my family. I'm sure you have never thought about what it is like to scrouge around for food. To sell your precious belongings just to feed yourself or gain the services of a healer. My family suffered in the aftermath of the Battle of the North for many years until Kaiser found us and offered us his patronage. But you," Morin snarled, pointing an accusing finger at Sai. "You grew high and mighty within the walls of Cross, never to fear anything than perhaps not having the best sword or the finest jewels."

"If that is what you truly think of me, then I am glad you

will not live to see the same heights. You are not deserving of any nobility to your name or person. At the next Shadow Council, you will be formally stripped of your command. You will be placed under arrest and have all of your assets seized. Your fate will be left for the Shadowlord to decide," Sai stated with great formality.

Morin seemed to struggle to catch his breath as he looked about. He gripped the hilt of his dagger, fighting the urge to pull it free of its sheath. "You can not do that."

"I just did," Sai said with amusement.

Morin ripped the dagger out of its sheath and charged at Sai with an angry shout. His movements were heavy and uncoordinated. Sai quickly disarmed him by grabbing his weapon arm, twisted it behind his back and forced him to drop the dagger. The steel blade hit the floor with a metallic ping. Sai gripped Morin's left shoulder as he held his right arm behind his back. He then let got and shoved him forward. Morin tripped over a chair leg and fell flat on his face. He quickly twisted himself around to reach for his dagger but Sai kicked it far out of reach. Morin scrambled on his hands and knees to go after it.

"This is pathetic, Morin. No Commander of the Armed Forces should be crawling like a child. Get up," Sai said. He grabbed the back of Morin's jacket and lifted him to his feet. "Perhaps the next Commander will be lenient and let you rejoin the army and rightfully earn your place."

The idea that he was not going to keep his title horrified Morin as he lost all color in his face. He stumbled away from Sai, looking around and arguing with himself. He grabbed his head and looked ready to burst into tears. Sai knew that he was too unsettled to center himself and summon Spirit energy. That had been the Saber Commander's aim for he did not want to feel the pain of Shadow Shock again. He did not really think that he would find anything of note in Morin's quarters. Kaiser was too smart to trust anything to his lackey besides a word of mouth order. With Morin so unsettled, Sai knew that he would be easy to break for information.

"I know that Rache is Kaiser's Demon servant. Who is the bastard grandson?" Sai demanded as he carefully Morin's nervous breakdown.

"I can't tell you," Morin admitted, his voice breaking.

"Why not?" Sai asked flatly.

Morin gulped hard. "He will kill me."

Sai slapped both of his hands down on Morin's shoulders. He looked him straight in the eyes. "Consider it your just rewards. Now who is his bastard grandson? You can tell me."

"I can't! All he talks about is taking control of the Sabers and the soldiers under my command. Says he plans on combining the two commands under one person: his grandson," Morin blurted out quickly on the verge of tears.

"His grandson! Who is he? Where is he?" Sai asked, fully interested in discovering the identity of the mysterious relative. He shook Morin when a sob overwhelmed him.

"Peredur!" he shouted and Sai let him go. Morin dropped to the floor in a heap, weeping with fear.

Sai did not know Ryder very well but well enough to know who his mother was. Everyone knew that Akakios was Ryder's father but few knew that his mother was named Aylin. She was a spirited woman from Umbra with a noble's bearing and proud countenance. No one knew who her parents were thus everyone assumed they were of no importance.

"How do I know that you are not lying to me? Ryder looks nothing like Kaiser," Sai exclaimed.

"His eyes. Look at his eyes and you will know," Morin said. "He can summon Spirit Fire. I saw it for myself!"

"Spirit Fire?" Sai asked as he bent down to Morin's eye level. "He can summon more than the Spirit powers of a Shadowborn? That's impossible."

Morin swallowed hard, almost too afraid to speak anymore. It took him several minutes before he attempted a reply. "He has the blood of a Farlander in his veins and it comes from Kaiser. Please don't make me say more."

Sai grabbed Morin's shoulders again. "Where is he?"

By now, Morin was inconsolable with the prospect of both losing his command and his death overwhelming him. The pasty white color of his skin now had hints of sickly gray.

"Where there is no light in the shadows. He is cold and alone for the dead do not talk. It's where he and his servant are spending the night," Morin said with a distant and detached voice.

At first, Sai had no clue what Morin was talking about and it was clear that he was not going to say anything else. He began to work through each word until the answer became clear: the tomb of his reviled father. The tomb of Akakios was the sole tomb in the hallowed grounds that did not have a burning torch by the opening. Sai stood up, leaving Morin curled up in a ball at his feet.

"May the Spirits have mercy on you, Morin Win, for Kaiser Adonis and the Shadowlord will not."

Sai made to leave but he heard Morin start to mumble. He paused to listen, keeping quiet so he could hear Morin's low voice.

"I have grown tired of the boy and pulling his father's strings. Perhaps I will end him tonight once and for all. Maybe I will even make my dear grandson watch as Rache slaughters his royal cousin..."

Sai did not wait around to hear more before jumping into Shadow Slide. His Prince was in danger. He had to get to him before Rache did.

SAI AND RACHE

Onyx spit out a mouthful of grass and dirt, coughing violently. His sides burned like a fire had been set inside of his body. He managed to wrap his arms around his torso in an attempt to stabilize the pain. Blood poured from the corner of his mouth, caking on his chin. Onyx was sure that his back had to be broken from being thrown against the stone door of his grandfather's tomb. Intense relief flooded him as he felt his toes scrapping the inside of his boots. He coughed again, his head swimming in a haze.

"Oh poor sweet child. I am sorry that it has to be this way," Kaiser whispered softly. He bent down and set a hand on Onyx's shoulder.

At first, the touch was soft and gentle. Before Onyx could seek out its comfort, Kaiser dug his nails into the round muscle. Onyx gasped and inhaled a clump of dirt. He coughed again, shuddering under Kaiser's powerful grip.

"Do not be frightened. Death will bring you a peace that you could never hope to find in life. No longer would you place second behind your glorious cousin. No longer would you have to worry about upholding the mantle of your illustrious ancestors. You would be free," Kaiser murmured. He released Onyx's shoulder and grabbed his chin. He snapped Onyx's head hard enough to make his ears pop. "I can free you."

It took everything within him for Onyx to look Kaiser in the eyes. Though his snarl was pathetic, garbled through the mouthful of dirt and blood, Onyx fired back. "Never."

Kaiser smirked before releasing Onyx's chin and easing away from him. He spun on his feet and started to walk away. He snapped his fingers. Immediately, Onyx was pulled off his feet by Rache. The Demon held him up with his right hand, waving with his left.

"Rache, it seems as if my lesson is not getting through to him. Please remind the Prince to respect those stronger than him," Kaiser politely ordered in a sing song voice.

"Can I tear off his sword arm first?" Rache eagerly asked. He ran his tongue over his lips and snapped his fangs close to Onyx's face.

"Bring him to me," Kaiser ordered, gesturing with his hand.

Rache snickered with evil delight as he started to walk towards Kaiser. He teased Onyx by loosening his grip and tightening it. It was as if he was daring him to escape and give chase. Onyx wanted to escape with all of his being but Rache's grip was so tight that he could barely breathe. His senses were hazy. He wondered if this was how Demon poison worked.

"Run, your Highness!" shouted Sai as he burst onto the scene. The Saber threw himself at Rache, tackling both Onyx and the Demon to the ground.

The fall broke Rache's grip and Onyx fought to pull himself away from the tangle of limbs. He rolled away, knocking into Kaiser's feet. As Onyx looked up, Kaiser wiggled his fingers in a wave, a cruel smile on his face. Despite injury, Onyx jumped up to his feet and bolted towards the mountain pathway.

"Oh no. He is getting away. Whatever shall I do?" Kaiser halfheartedly exclaimed as he slowly turned to face Onyx. He watched for a few seconds before raising his left hand. He stretched out his fingers with a sudden snap.

Onyx slammed into an invisible wall of energy and fell back. His body hit the ground with enough force to knock the wind out of him. He felt a crack in his right shoulder, rendering his sword arm useless. Not that it mattered for he did not have a weapon. Onyx never believed for a second that he should be carrying a blade in his own home. He wished that he had as the Sabers did. Pain radiated out from his shoulder as he attempted to roll over.

Kaiser nudged him in the back with his boot, hitting Onyx just below the ribcage. He smirked when he saw the Prince in obvious pain from the smallest touch.

"I am glad that I waited to kill you. Doing this now is so much more fun than if you had been a child," Kaiser mused.

Nothing Kaiser could say would make Onyx feel any less in danger of dying. All Onyx knew was that he had to listen to Sai and run as fast and far as he possibly could. But with his growing number of injuries, Onyx was not sure if running was even an option for him. He could not even ease his body away from Kaiser. The cold ground provided minimal relief.

Kaiser studied Onyx for a moment before reaching down to grab the back of his tunic. Onyx grunted and spat out blood as Kaiser dragged him back towards the glade. "Come now, child. Let us watch dear Rache rip Commander Parahazur to shreds. It is truly a thing of beauty and not to be missed."

*****

Sai had lost track of Rache after a heated exchange . He had done everything in his power to knock Onyx free from Rache's grip, throwing his strudy weight against the Demon. They had crashed and rolled, snapping sapling trees, crushing funeral wreaths, and even splitting several head stones. Rache had quickly disappeared after that but Sai knew that the game had only just begun. He knew that the Demon was watching him from a safe distance, studying him and deciding on his next attack. Sai trudged carefully through the tall grass, keeping his senses sharp. He was treading close to the tomb of a disgraced Shadowlord. He kept a loose but ready grip on his preferred weapon: the double bladed pole arm. He spun it around once, testing the weight of the weapon.

Rache slid into view as he perched on top of the great stone blocking Akakios' tomb. A grin with a mouth full of gleaming white fangs shone in the low light. He looked like a hunting cat ready to pounce. His teeth shifted back to a more normal if not ghastly appearance.

"Cheers to the mighty Saber Commander who lost two Shadowlords under his command with a Prince soon to join his kin. I must applaud you for I do not think I could have done it better. Congratulations," Rache snickered as he clapped slowly.

The Demon's words stung Sai's pride and sense of duty. Yes, he had failed Shiloh and Aku. One was dead and the other was lost. But that did not mean that he was going to stop protecting the Silvanus family. He tightened his grip on the pole arm. "Failures or not, I will continue to serve until my last breath. Even then, I will use my Spirit to champion the cause against Kaiser Adonis and all those that oppose him," Sai vehemently promised.

Rache leapt down to the ground and strode towards Sai. His tattered tan and white clothes blended in with his pale skin. His crimson hair framed his sharp featured face. As he came forward, Rache wiggled his fingers, transforming them in wicked claws. Blood dripped from the tips of his newly erupted talons.

"Do you honestly think that the royal brat will escape Kaiser? Even if he manages to, he will never escape the border for all those who wish my master harm can never cross it. Save one," Rache admitted with a shrug. "It is a small setback that only Kaiser's blood can cross through the Shadow Mirror. Much like your Prince, he is not going anywhere unless Kaiser wills it."

"Not under my watch!" Sai shouted.

The Saber Commander spun around, kicking up a spray of dirt and chopped grass. Rache jumped back and covered his eyes to avoid being blinded. In an instant, Sai was on the attack, full of determination to kill the Demon monster he saw before him. Sai leapt forward in a twisting spin, swinging his doubled bladed weapon in a wide arc. Rache did not remain still, snapping his back like a whip and rolling to the left to avoid the downstroke. He swept under the attack, shooting up to his feet to slash at Sai's back. In a heartbeat, Rache's sharp talons collided with the blade of the Saber Commander's weapon. He snarled.

Amused by Rache's response, Sai smiled and shoved hard with all his weight. The Demon stumbled back, clearly the smaller of the two. Not wanting to give his opponent any chance for a break, Sai charged forward, leading with his left shoulder and weapon pulled back. Rache turned at the last second to avoid taking the full force of Sai's attack. Anticipating the maneuver, Sai suddenly slid to the right and brought his pole arm up in a quick cleaving motion. The tip of the blade tore at Rache's tunic, ripping a wide swath of fabric and exposing his lean torso. A thin red gash appeared on Rache's chest, leaking blood. Though he knew that Rache was a Demon, it surprised Sai to see how normal his build was.

The resulting snarl was entirely unlike anything Sai had heard. It was one of a bloodthirsty beast that had broken free from a deep, dark prison. A creature ready to unleash its fury on the world. The snarl built into a ferocious roar that echoed off the rock walls and trees. It shook the branches and cracked the stone. Sai had to duck and shield his head from a rain of stone fragments.

*****

"Rache does not sound too happy," Kaiser commented as he looked towards the west.

Onyx kept his hands clamped tight over his ears. The sound of Rache's roar pulsated in his skull to the point that he was feeling ill. Through hazy eyes, Onyx looked up at Kaiser who appeared unaffected by the noise. He watched as Kaiser scratched his chest. A wave of nausea rolled through his body and Onyx fought the urge to vomit. He groaned, a stream of blood leaking from the corner of his mouth.

*****

Rache's retribution for a minor injury was just as fierce as if he had received a grievous wound. His behavior became more primal and vicious. The Demon engaged Sai in a dance that mimicked a hunter pursuing a worthy and wild prize. Rache darted around, leaping and bouncing off tree trunks and embedded stones. He hissed like a cat whenever he laid eyes on Sai.

"I would have thought that you would bark, considering how your dear master orders you around. You're like a dog on a leash ready to break!" Sai laughed as he fended off Rache. He threw Rache back.

"Then we are both dogs for very different reasons," Rache snarled as he stopped sliding back in the dirt. He spit out a jet of saliva. "Unlike you, I bite back!"

"I think my pole arm would beg to differ," Sai retorted as he spun his weapon around as a show of strength.

Rache reflexively reached up to touch his chest wound. The gash had stopped bleeding and was now smoking. The smell was stomach churning. "Go ahead! Strike me where others have failed!"

"Save one," Sai stated with out skipping a beat.

As soon as the words left Sai's mouth, Rache roared again and charged forward. He stabbed and slashed with his claws, snapping his fangs when he drew close enough to Sai. The Demon's rage fueled his strength and speed in a way that surprised the Saber Commander. He parried Rache's flurry of attacks, shifting his feet to keep up with the Demon's speed. Sai then started to recognize a style to Rache's fighting that reminded him of a Saber under his command: the speedy but strong Soja Rokar. Sai's heart swelled with pride.

Rache slid underneath a sweep of Sai's great weapon, knocking down a graveside torch. The tall grass crackled and caught fire. In an instant, the fire spread through the dry leaf litter, transforming into a raging inferno. Rache cackled with delight. He danced among the flames, basking in the burning warmth. He swept his hands through the fire, caressing the ever changing curves.

Sai was horrified to see that the fire was not burning Rache's skin. In fact, it seemed to invigorate the Demon. He watched as Rache walked through the flames to prove that fire could not touch him.

"I am a creature of shadow and fire. No blaze can harm me, even those that burn within the belly of a Dragon. You, however, can still get burned. Let me give you a taste of Hell!" Rache shouted. He twisted and weaved his hands, directing the fire to his will. Soon, he had formed his own weapon with a whip shaped fire.

Sai jumped to the left to avoid Rache's body cleaving strike. In the effort to avoid the attack, Sai's weapon took the fire whip full force and snapped in two. He rolled for several feet before popping up to his feet. All around him was an inpenetrable wall of fire. The heat was unbearable and Sai was sweating through his armor. He looked around for an escape route.

"Is this what your master wanted? Burn a Commander of the Sabers alive?" Sai yelled over the roar of the flames.

"A life for a life," Rache's voice wavered from a distance.

"His life or yours? I get the feeling that you'd rather snap his neck?" Sai said as he pulled out his long knife.

"Oh, believe me. I'm first in line. But until that time comes, I'll make do with yours instead," Rache said before charging forward.

Sai softened his posture and released the tension in his body to absorb the impact of Rache's body who drove his shoulder into Sai's chest. The pair burst through the flames back into the glade before Shiloh's tomb. The Demon wrapped his arms around Sai as he tackled him to the ground. Rache released, pushed off from the ground, and flipped over in a full body spin to land behind Sai. Sai whipped around, knife in hand once he was steady on his feet. Quicker than lightning, Rache slashed at Sai's chest with his claws. Sai thought his knife would cut off the Demon's hand. Instead, to his surprise, the knife's blade snapped off at the handle upon hitting Rache's bony wrist.

Rache's claws dug into Sai's left shoulder and he stumbled back from the impact. He twisted his body away from the beast's grasp to tear himself free. The pain was intense and burning as blood poured down the front of his cuirass. Using the mental discipline learned from his Saber training, Sai blocked out the pain with a flicker of thought. The pain was relegated to a dull ache in the back of his mind. Bereft of his weapon, Sai prepared for a tough fight against Rache. At least now he knew that Rache preferred hand to hand combat as a test of strength.

Rache struck again in rapid succession, claws slicing through the leather cuirass. When Rache drew back for another damaging blow, Sai took the opportunity to slip into Shadow Slide.

"You can't delay any longer, Saber! Your little trick will only protect you for so long!" Rache shouted as he turned around in a circle. He held his arms open. "I have faced greater warriors than you and killed them without breaking a sweat! So I shall be polite and give you a free hit!"

Sai surged forward, coming out of Shadow Slide from behind Rache. He held the broken knife blade in hand, blood streaming from his palm where the edge had dug in and he drove it deep into Rache's neck. Suddenly, he was thrown back against the great stone blocking Shiloh's tomb, snapping his spine from the force. Rache laughed as he pulled the blade out, licked a glob of blood from the flat surface and tossed it aside. He smacked his blood stained lips and laughed maniacally. With no feeling from the chest down, Sai struggled to center his focus.

"Kill him," Kaiser ordered in a cold voice. He kicked Onyx when the Prince cried out for Sai.

As Rache bent down to place a heavy hand around Sai's neck, he spoke. "Let me tell you a little secret, Saber. I am no mere Demon in service to a disgraced noble. You and everyone else have no clue who the real Kaiser Adonis is."

Sai coughed from the pressure on his neck. The world around him grew so black and cold that he knew his death was coming. When he spied the faint outline of Omu behind Rache and heard his low growl, he knew it was true. The Spirit had come to escort the Saber home. He gasped as his vision began to fade. "You won't win..."

Rache scoffed before snapping Sai's neck. "They all say that." He drew his hand back and let out a deep breath. "At least Rokar proved a meager challenge. I expected more from the Commander of the Sabers. But then you did not have the wards of Crossroads to protect you from my power. Do not worry. I'll make sure that he joins you soon enough."

Kaiser applauded while Onyx wailed for Sai's death. "You see, your Highness? This is what happens when a Saber dies in your service. Be grateful for Commander Parahazur's sacrifice. You get one more night to live."

FATHER AND SON

"Another dies and departs this world for the home of the Spirits. Another life falls before a darkness too terrible and strong to stop," Ryder mused in the silence of his prison. "Another noble Commander of the Sabers gives his life. May the Spirits protect you, Sai Parahazur, for you died a true Saber's death."

The death of Sai reminded Ryder of his predecessor who had also given his life in service of the Silvanus bloodline. Two souls whose courage and loyalty stayed with them to the end. Ryder found that he was angry and jealous of both Sorin and Sai. Sorin and Sai had exemplified what it meant to believe in something strong enough to fight to the death for it.

"I can not be what the world wants me to be," Ryder admitted, his chest heaving.

The weight of everything Ryder had felt the day he left Cross dragged his Spirit further into the darkness. It held his heart in an icy grip for over one hundred years but now the wall was threatening to break. In the pitch black of his father's tomb, Ryder began to entertain the idea of death. He was not afraid of death; he actually welcomed it. Unlike many, he was not blind to the true nature of the world.

"I suppose that makes me a horrible son," Ryder spoke out loud as he sat back against his father's stone coffin. He rested his left arm on his bent knee, the cold shackle pulling at his wrist until it bled. "The last of a once noble bloodline..."

His voice trailed off into silence. Ryder told himself that he was a realist and had never really paid attention to the matter of Spirits. Being a bastard growing up in a world where bloodlines meant a great deal had made him stoic and unforgiving as a man. Spirits did not matter to him but he found himself wanting their company. Maybe it was because his father's corpse rested close by. It was the first time Ryder had seen his father's tomb since witnessing his execution years before.

The interior of the tomb was crude in its decoration. There were no murals depicting Akakios' life. No jewels or treasures had been packed away. The small cave had been hastily excavated. The only hint that the occupant was anything but a commoner was the carved effigy on the coffin. Ryder pushed himself to his feet to look upon his father's likeness.

The effigy of Akakios was incredibly lifelike though it was covered in a heavy layer of dust. Arms had been carved to where they were crossed across his chest. Ryder set his hand on the clenched stone fist as he looked at the face. Even the cold stone could not hide the strong resemblance between father and son. Both shared the same rugged jaw and refined nose. Their gazes matched perfectly. But Ryder could tell that there was a degree of softness in his father's eyes that he did not share. Ryder's stern gaze was a feature of the Adonis blood that flowed in his veins. Everyone thought it was an expression reminiscent of Shadow Night Silvanus but Ryder knew better. He hated to think about it but it was one thing in Kaiser that he saw in himself. Ryder slid back down to the floor.

"The world would have no love for me if they knew," he mumbled to himself. "I am nothing but a pawn to those who seek to control me."

His mind drifted from memory to memory, never spending longer than a few seconds on each one. He thought about when he left Cross and his mental wanderings stopped. The sound of recent combat just outside of the rolled stone door brought back the vivid sights and sounds. He drew up his knees and wrapped his arms around them. He shivered from the chill in the stale air.

"It was a fool's errand to come here, Sai," Ryder said aloud as he turned and set his head on the side of the coffin. "I am just a bastard. I am worth nothing. You did not need to die for me."

It was something that Ryder never understood. Why were the Sabers, elite guards to the royals, risking their lives for him? There may have been those who thought otherwise but Ryder told himself that he was never going to sit on the throne. So why were the Sabers wasting their time? One Commander had already died to help him escape Cross. Now another had died in the attempt to rescue him. What did everyone see in him that he could not? Yes, he was a royal bastard. Yes, he heard how everyone said he was the second coming of Shadow Night for he was not blind. The weight of it all threatened to overwhelm him.

For the first time in his life, Ryder did not know where his path was going to take him. Two options were before him: death or service to Kaiser. Technically speaking, Kaiser could take the throne and name him his heir. Ryder so much as gathered that from the last time Kaiser came to speak with him. Kaiser had tried to offer Ryder his protection in the coming war but Ryder staunchly refused. He knew that Kaiser was not going to give up so easily on whom he called his beloved grandson. Ryder managed a grin as he remembered how he spit in Kaiser's face. He laughed softly as he thought of the look of disgust on Kaiser's face as he wiped the spit away.

Ryder's mood became more morbid and dark. "What would you say to that, Father? Your bastard son on the throne you failed to keep. They did take your head and would probably take mine if the world could bring themselves to kill another Silvanus. Why they did it in the first place when you were just the puppet... I do not think we will ever know." He dropped his knees and arms to his side. "What does it matter? You've never been there for me and now I could lose my life or I could lose my soul."

*****

The great ebony wood doors to the throne room remained tightly closed with steel armored soldiers on guard to both sides. The six soldiers stood with blank expressions on their faces and pole axes held tightly in their hands. A single Shadowborn man, dressed in embroidered finery, stood with a short wooden staff clutched under his hands in front of the doors. Only he showed any degree of emotion as he studied the pair before him. Like everyone else, he was curious.

"Remember, do not speak unless spoken to," Aylin said as she smoothed down the black hair of her son. She stepped back to admire him. "All of those men and women in there are your superiors so you must pay them proper respect."

"Says who?" Ryder asked with a degree of harshness.

"Says society. You can be a bit headstrong and stubborn and this is no time to be offending anybody," the lithe Shadowborn woman stated, attempting an encouraging smile. She then stood to Ryder's right. He silently offered the crook of his arm. "Just remember your manners."

"I don't even want to be here," Ryder grumbled as his mother took his arm.

Aylin's sharp eyes darted up to meet her son's. "I know you would have preferred to live a nameless life in Umbra but when the Shadowlord summons you, you do not ignore him." She tightened her hands on his muscular arm.

"It was Kaiser Adonis who summoned us to Cross. The Shadowlord's mouthpiece, not the Shadowlord himself," Ryder pointed out. He was growing impatient with the whole affair.

"He is your father. He told Master Adonis that he wanted to meet you officially and formally present you to the court," Aylin snapped.

"You mean that asshole you call a father. Why doesn't he claim you as his daughter? I am sure that he has considered the glory of having a Silvanus grandson. Why now after all this time? Why is a bastard worth the Shadowlord's time? Why should any of them care?" Ryder argued as he watched the team of six soldiers move back. The doors began to creak loudly as they slowly opened. "Why should I care?"

The Shadowborn who had been facing them turned around and squared his shoulders. He picked up the short staff and held it loosely in his hands. It was obvious that he was trying to look noble and proud.

"Forget about Kaiser and focus on the Shadowlord. By right of birth, you are your father's heir. Ryder, you are not the only one being judged here," Aylin said under her breath. "I am the woman who birthed the royal bastard. The sordid details of my life are no longer private." She fell silent as she held his arm.

He could now tell that his mother was nervous. She was trembling. It was a stark contrast to her normal stoic nature where nothing bothered her. Ryder began to think that her nerves would have been worse if he was a young child and not a grown man. Instead of being small and fragile, he was tall and strong. He sighed deeply as he laid his free hand on hers, giving it an encouraging squeeze.

The Shadowborn man stepped into the throne room, paused, and tapped the wooden staff on the stone floor three times. All conversation stopped as everyone looked towards the open door. "Lords and Ladies of Cross! Your Highnesses and Your Majesty! I present to you the Lady Aylin and Peredur Coba-Silvanus of Umbra!"

Ryder escorted his mother inside the throne room as soon as the Shadowborn man stepped to the side. He kept his head held high, mirroring the posture of his mother. Though he did not show it, Ryder could see the surprise on everyone's faces. They too must have been expecting a child instead of a man. Here he was, a young adult several inches past six feet in height with a powerfully built frame carefully sculpted from years of hard training. The leather cuirass he wore, though scratched and worn, did nothing to diminish the aura of strength he put off.

Ahead of Ryder and Aylin stood the people of highest rank in the room. To the right of the throne stood Madhuri Coba and his wife the Silvanus Princess Mali. Ryder first studied the Commander of the Armed Forces, seeing a physicality that he immediately respected. Ryder preferred the obvious military power of the man that was his grandfather by Akakios. His grandmother Mali, dressed in a flowing gown of silver and white jewels, was tall and noble with a matching crown on her head. Both of his grandparents studied him carefully before Mali broke off eye contact to whisper to her husband. Madhuri then nodded.

To the left of the throne stood Kaiser Adonis, Kader Erebus, and Zoras Rokar. With his sharp raptorian gaze, Kaiser was easily the fiercest of the three Shadowborn men but he was by no means the biggest. Kader watched Ryder with a degree of hungry interest. The looks coming from the shorter wiseman unnerved him. Zoras Rokar gave Ryder the same sense of physicality as Madhuri though he was dressed in the formal wear of a politician instead of the armor belonging to a warrior. He still however exuded the ferocity only obtained from his years as Commander of the Sabers.

In the very center was Akakios, Lord of the Shadowborn and his birth father. Ryder immediately saw that he matched him in height but he was more heavily built than his father. Akakios' black hair was swept back from his face revealing a surprisingly soft expression. He was no hardcore warrior as his bloodline suggested. Ryder picked out features in his face that matched his own. Though Ryder had complained about coming to Cross, he was genuinely curious about his birth father. In particular, he wondered how Akakios would react before the entire court.

Akakios studied Ryder with the same careful eye. He slowly stepped away from the throne. Aylin and Ryder halted but she urged her son forward. Everyone in the room remained painfully quiet.

"It is like looking at myself in the mirror," Akakios uttered as Ryder slowly stepped away from his mother's side. When Ryder attempted to bend his knee in respect, Akakios quickly pulled him back up to his feet. He left his hands on Ryder's shoulders. "For tonight, I am not your Lord. I am simply a man looking upon his son for the first time."

The tension in the room went out like a breath held in for far too long and people relaxed, dropping their shoulders. Ryder knew that the entire event was just for show and was a way to publically announce him as the bastard of Akakios. Kaiser had actually suggested the whole affair though part of Ryder wished he hadn't. He felt awkward as Akakios embraced him tightly to a round of applause. The applause slowed when it was clear that Ryder was not moving to return the embrace.

In truth, Ryder did not know how to truly react. He had long known that Akakios was his birth father and as a boy, he wanted so badly to meet him. The times that he did, it was always private and unofficial. Back then, it was if the powers that be did not want Ryder to be more. As he grew older, Ryder decided that the same powers that be wanted Akakios to marry a proper wife and birth legitimate children. As the years passed with no royal marriage or true born children in sight, there was more attention given to the royal bastard. As a man, his heart was more uncertain. There were just too many unanswered questions. For now, he decided to play the part and returned Akakios' embrace.

*****

Ryder found himself angry as the memory faded away. Every part of him was flooded with the deep seated rage he had kept locked away since before he ran from Cross a century ago. He looked up towards the low stone ceiling of the tomb as if to will it to break apart and collapse on top of him. A flicker of thought was all it would take according to the Earthborn who taught him how to harness the power of the earth. He closed his eyes as the idea faded.

"Do you doubt your worth so much that you would end your life in order to keep running?"

Ryder's eyes shot open at the sound of the voice. He was certain that he truly heard it and it was not in the confines of his mind. His senses sharpened from countless years of wary practice. His muscles tightened in preparation.

"What is Peredur afraid of?"

His head jerked around and he pulled against his chains. He slid his legs towards him. "Who's there?"

Ryder watched with breath that frosted in the chilly air as a mist materialized before him. It took the form of a man sitting up against the wall facing him. The dim sparkling mist cleared revealing Akakios, mirroring Ryder's posture. He was dressed in faded garb belonging to a prisoner, a tattered shirt billowing around his thin torso. The front of the shirt was soaked in blood from a grievous neck wound. The image of the execution quickly replayed in Ryder's mind.

"I thought your head had been cleaved from your neck," Ryder stated firmly.

The Spirit shrugged though he stretched his wounded neck to reveal how deep the wound went. Ryder grimaced at seeing the cracked bone that peeked out from the edges of a thick metal ring. "Those who prepared my corpse made sure to at least bury me with my head attached precariously to the rest of my body."

Ryder had to admit to himself that the sight grossed him out. His mother had taught him as a child that the Spirits of the dead appeared as they did at the moment of their death. Those Spirits of stronger individuals could alter their appearance in minor ways to appear less gruesome. He was at least grateful that Spirits did not retain an odor of rotting death or the salty scent of blood. If the Spirit of his father had, he would stink of blood and sweat. Ryder forced his eyes from the neck wound.

"It's not like I had the power in life to change how my Spirit would appear to you. I was barely even a century old at my death," Akakios stated as if the problem did not really bother him. It was odd how nonchalant the Spirit was.

"Why are you here?" Ryder asked cautiously.

"Because my son is troubled," came the simple reply.

"I do not need the help of the dead. Leave me!" Ryder demanded with a growl.

Akakios was unphased by his son's ferocity. "I did not ask to come but your heart called out to me just the same. One thing the living do not realize about Spirits is that we do hear your cries. But when a heart calls out for us, we are compelled to answer no matter the reason or understanding." He shrugged slowly. "And I can not leave until your trouble is unraveled."

"How do I know that Kaiser did not raise you up to haunt me? You have never spoken without his voice," Ryder pointed out. The chill in the air began to seep into the metal chains, numbing his hands.

"As powerful as Kaiser is, he does not have absolute control over the nature of Spirits. Take the fate of my cousin Aku as an example. Kaiser reanimated a corpse using the soul of a Demon. From this side of the veil, it is horrible seeing Aku's Spirit trying to return to his body only to grow weaker and fade faster," Akakios replied, looking genuinely sad.

The expression in Akakios' eyes was so raw and pure that Ryder was convinced that it was his father speaking. He found that he did not know how to react.

"Yes, I can see the shock in your eyes. You have never seen me without Kaiser's influence. Unlike you, I was not strong enough to resist him," Akakios said with a deep sigh. "And it cost me my life."

"I already figured that out. Are you done yet with your

spiritual intervention or must I continue to suffer?" Ryder snapped.

"That depends on whether or not you choose to keep running from the truth," Akakios pointedly said.

The reply was direct and not hidden by any words meant to disguise its intent. Akakios meant to unnerve his son. Ryder immediately hated the Spirit for it. Before he could answer back, Akakios spoke again.

"You are a descendent of Shadow Night Silvanus and Kaiser Adonis. You are my one and only son. You are not only running but hiding from that truth. You could put as many miles as you want at your back but you will always be who you are no matter where you go. Leaving Cross did not stop those who believed in you from wishing for your return. It did not absolve the Sabers of their duty to the Silvanus bloodline. Even if you never come to the throne, they will always give their lives to protect you. They will die to protect against the utter ruin of Shadow Night's bloodline."

"But why is a bastard worth it?" Ryder asked in earnest.

Akakios got a knowing look on his face. "You mean why is the son of Kaiser's daughter worth it. Yes I learned of your mother's father upon my death. I learned a great deal when I entered the Spirit World. You are not afraid of the throne. You are afraid of him. You are afraid of the shared blood in your veins. You care of the sanctity of life but can others look past your Adonis blood to see that?"

The Spirit of his father was doing what Ryder could not do: admit his fear of the truth. It had always been a thought in the back of his mind but he would throw himself at the next challenge to avoid addressing it. He ran from Cross under the perception of escaping Kaiser when in reality, Kaiser was in control. He was always in control. So long as Kaiser was alive, he could never escape or run far enough.

"Ryder, so long as he breathes, no one is safe. Not even you. Of all the people on Terra, you are the only who shares his blood. You are his heir as much as you are mine. You also bear the blood of Begin Anu and as such, you are his heir above all else. You are strong in a way that I could only dream of. You can bring the world hope," Akakios stated, addressing his son by his nickname. He smiled warmly. "Sometimes a person is called to greatness even if they do not want it. Given the choice, I would have never taken the throne. But I knew it to be right deep inside. Fate can be cruel but it is also kind. Perhaps you would have never been born had I not."

The feeling and emotion in his father's words touched Ryder deeply within his heart for he also heard his mother's voice in them. For a long time, he did not dare to speak. He finally let out a deep breath. "Did you ever love my mother?"

Akakios nodded. "Kaiser's influence was not so great that I was incapable of loving her. When the executioner's blade was mere moments from my neck, all I thought of was you and her. I knew then that my Spirit would not rest until I knew both of you could be saved." The Spirit began to fade. "You have a chance, a power to do what others can not. You are worthy of honor and might. Worthy of being a hero like Begin Anu or Shadow Night. All you have to do is rise up and take it."

As the Spirit of Akakios faded into nothingness, Ryder found that he desparately wanted his father to stay. He wanted his father to tell him how to defeat Kaiser. Ryder reached out towards the space where the Spirit had just been, feeling nothing but the cold.

SORROW AND FEAR

Onyx stormed into his quarters, full of rage and sorrow, past injuries forgotten beneath his emotions. He kicked at the furniture and threw chairs into the wall. He ripped down tapestries, curtains, and anything that he could get his hands on from the walls. He threw books, ripping pages from their spines. The torn pages rained down around him as he collapsed onto his knees sobbing. Sai Parahazur was dead. His grandfather and mother were gone and his father was a living corpse. Everyone he had loved and had been loved in return was gone. He was trapped in Cross, a prisoner of Kaiser Adonis. He gripped his chest with his left hand as he tried to contain the overwhelming heartache. Tears poured from his eyes in waves. His voice cracked from the sobs.

"Who is left?" he asked himself. In his heart, he knew there were no more heroes left in his homeland. Everyone feared the power held by Kaiser and his Demon servant. The Demon was now revealed as the terrible Rache, ancient killer of heroes. He briefly thought of his bastard cousin, trapped and hidden, imprisoned in some unknown location. Who indeed was left? Who was brave enough and strong enough?

Stories about the Daylord crept into his mind and Onyx began to feel a sense of calm. Bane was known by all to wield extraordinary power and he had even saved his ancestor Shadow Night. His sudden appearance on the battlefield brought hope and courage to the beleaguered Shadowborn troops. He slayed so many Demons that he appeared unstoppable before the Spiritborn. He then raised up a Shadow Mirror on the borders, cutting off the Darklands from the rest of the world. If there was one person that could help him, it would be Bane.

But finding Bane meant leaving his homeland and Onyx suddenly was afraid. Everyone had said Bane was deep in the Mortal lands fighting a Demon. He did not know where to even begin. He let out a deep breath, his shoulders sagging.

"Where are you, Omu? I need your guidance!" he shouted to the emptiness of his room. He pounded the floor with his fists. "Tell me what is right!"

It seemed as if that his loud shout would shake the room and bring the Wolf Spirit to him. He desparately pressed his need and desire as far as his senses could go. Nothing.

"You have abandoned me! You have abandoned me to death! You told me to face my fears and it failed! Now, I am to die and so will the throne of Shadow Night! The world will crumble before Kaiser and no one will be left to stand against him!"

Again there was no response coming. His emotions rushed through in torrential cycles of despair and hopelessness. He pressed his forehead to the ground, crying hot tears in an endless stream. He sobbed for what seemed like hours until his chest dry heaved violently from the effort. Exhausted, Onyx rolled over onto his right side, hugging his stomach. He felt numb to the world and he wondered if this was what it was like to have nothing left to live for.

Luna. The name bounded across his senses with revitalizing energy. Flynn. His uncle Palani. Even Ryder his bastard cousin. As Onyx thought deeper about them, he unfolded his limbs and relaxed the tension in his body. There were still people that mattered. He still mattered. And that thought gave him strength.

"Maybe I am not afraid of him," Onyx wondered as he thought about his last encounter with Kaiser.

It was hard to think of Kaiser as anything but frightening. Rache certainly qualified as frightening. Onyx thought back on Omu's exact words but they did not yield up an answer. He pushed his mind to the limit as he tried to come up with different interpretations. A question then dawned on him: what was he truly afraid of? It was hard for him to think about because it meant he had to admit to himself his own faults. He was afraid of failing everyone's expectations of being a good Shadowlord. He was afraid of dying. Most of all, he was afraid of losing his father. Onyx realized that because of that fear, Kaiser had had a tight hold on him since Aku was brought back a broken mess. Kaiser was controlling him through the condition of his father. Once Onyx had acknowledged the fear, he thought about how to overcome it and it was a road he did not want to go down. He was going to have to let his father go. And he had to wonder if there was any other option to letting his father go other than killing him. It horrified him to think about taking another person's life. To take his father's life was beyond inconceivable. He was not a killer. He had never taken a life in all his eighteen years.

The idea put Onyx in a daze for he had no strength in his heart or his body to do the deed. His fear of Kaiser and Rache was paralyzing him and taking his courage away. The pain of his injuries roared back to the forefront and he was prepared to cry for a healer. He needed help to deal with his pain, both physical and emotional. He needed help to fight the destructive pair of Kaiser and Rache. He needed Bane, Ryder, his uncle, anyone to help him take down Kaiser Adonis. He knew that he could not do it alone. He also knew that if he wanted their help, he was going to have to leave Cross. A part of him felt horrible about abandoning his city and his people to Kaiser. Onyx wondered if the Shadowborn would understand his intentions. Even he had to admit that he did not fully understand the decision. Was this what it felt to make a sacrifice for the good of his people and that of the world?

"A Shadowlord must do what is right even if it hurts," Onyx said to himself as he sat up straight. He got to his feet, his confidence growing. He searched the debris in his quarters for a knapsack, finding it under a broken chair. He then darted around, shoving a long sleeve shirt and travel pants into the bag. Pausing for a moment, he then set the bag down on the bed and he searched for his weapons. He tossed his travel jacket on to the bed as he pulled his weapons trunk out from under the bed.

After changing into his travel clothes, he strapped on his sword belt and slung his knapsack over his shoulder. He locked the door and strode over to the window bench. He opened the window doors and leaped up to the edge. Onyx strengthened his resolve, again pushing his pain away.

"I will return and I will free this land," Onyx said as he looked around at the stone wall of the Heights. He took a deep breath and jumped, slipping into Shadow Slide.

RYDER'S ESCAPE

Ryder's head jerked to the side as he sat up on his knees, wrists chained to the floor. Pain throbbed from his bleeding cheek as the cold scent of the tomb mixed with blood entered his senses. His breath settled back into a steady rhythm as he returned his gaze to Rache.

A sneer came from the Demon's lips. "Why won't you die?" he growled, flexing his right hand.

"I think in some strange way that your bond with Kaiser protects me," Ryder stated. "Perhaps being his grandson is not so bad after all."

"So an accident of nature gives you the power to cheat death? You are a worthless bastard!" Rache snapped angrily.

"I am an Adonis line bastard as well as a Silvanus line bastard. I am worth a great deal. You choose who cares for my blood more," Ryder teased with a grin.

Rache's brow furrowed as he grabbed Ryder's chin and forced him to look in his face. "You look like a man. Stink like a man. I am certain you can curse just like a man. I do not see what is so damn special and worthwhile about you. At least the royal brat in the castle was worthwhile. Aku's Spirit would do anything Kaiser asked just to protect his precious son."

"I highly doubt that Kaiser is being altruistic in keeping me alive. I am not so blind to know that what he does is in his interests alone. It's very Demon like if you ask me," Ryder declared.

Rache threw Ryder down and his skull hit the floor hard. He skulked away from Ryder's side and leaned against the wall, crossing his arms tightly. "You are at least not a total bore."

"Glad that I can entertain you but surely my dear grandfather is more interesting than me," Ryder seethed through gritted teeth. "Would you have chosen to follow him if the bond was not present?"

"Our desires for this world criss cross a great deal. Gratitude is not a feeling a Demon normally possesses but I suppose I have to be thankful that he lifted me from the abyss to walk this land again," Rache replied with a shrug.

Ryder pushed himself up to a sitting position as he settled his breath. His head swam and he felt himself wavering. "Seems Kaiser is acting more like a Demon than you are."

"I hate him for the bond but it could be worse. I could be stuck bonded to you. Your heartbeat is too pure and annoying. His heartbeat is always steady and strong," Rache stated with a glimmer of praise for Kaiser.

"You have known Kaiser for a very long time. I guess it is safe to say he has always been an arrogant self important person. I'd say soul but I doubt that he has one," Ryder supposed with a shrug of his shoulders. His old injuries twinged in protest.

A silence fell between them and Ryder knew it was not from a lack of what to say. It had surprised him how much Rache talked for he hid nothing about his character. Was this the true nature of a Demon or was this attitude the result of a thousand years being chained down in servitude? Were Demons more than what the stories told? Ryder was happy when Rache finally struck him out of frustration for his predicament. The Demon hit him across the right side of his jaw, the force throwing him to the side but thankfully not all the way to the floor.

Rache snarled harshly behind gritted teeth. "You are more like Kaiser than you think. I have never met another Spiritborn, Gryphon, or Dragon that would converse so willingly with my kind. Like him, you do more than curse me."

"Maybe I inherited his intelligence. I certainly did not get it from my father."

"Given a little effort and you might be able to speak my native tongue as smoothly as your dear grandfather. You actually could learn a lot from him. And from me," Rache suggested halfheartedly.

"No thanks. I am doing quite well on my own," Ryder declined after shaking his head. "Unlike you, I have the choice to accept or decline Kaiser's service if I wish to."

Rache's lips curled in simmering anger. "I hate you."

Ryder chuckled, tasting blood in his mouth. "Everyone does, Demon, so get in line. The Waterborn would probably shoot me on sight if I ever set foot in their lands."

Rache paced forward a few steps and put his hands out to the side. "We are both trapped here. However, I will get to leave this place alive and you will be buried with your father if I get my way," he said pointing at Akakios' effigy. "I wonder if he even cares that you are here."

"I doubt it," Ryder replied after he spit out a globule of blood. He was not about to show that the Spirit of his father had opened his eyes and given him a new and different kind of strength. He cringed as he stretched out his back. It was sore from his long captivity.

The Demon looked at him curiously. "Do you care?"

Ryder shrugged his broad shoulders. "People seem to think that I should care about Akakios. He didn't care about me. Why should I care about him?"

"A fitting answer from a royal bastard. You know what? I knew Akakios once. Full of ambition just like his Silvanus mother. But he wasn't cut out to rule," Rache started to say. "Now your grandmother, she was a master at the political game but Shadowborn law forbids daughters from ruling while a son lives. Rather archaic if I say so myself."

"I know my history. Why else do you think I left Cross?" Ryder asked, feeling annoyed. This was the game that they constantly played in their conversations.

Rache leaned against the wall, arms crossed. "The Shadowborn are in decay. This very city smells of death."

Ryder scoffed. "I'm sure you and your master are to blame." He twisted his arms in a small rotating motion.

The lowlight of the torch cast a dark glow on Rache's face. "Maybe we are. Kaiser has been at work for a very long time."

"Kaiser is a power hungry and delusional fool. You may be a famous Demon but you placed yourself on the losing side yet again," Ryder said with confidence. "You are a dog to be kicked around just as my father was. He cares nothing about you. You are only his pawn. He only cares from himself!"

Rache roared with laughter before he advanced forward, holding a crooked knife blade under Ryder's jaw. "You can't rile me up again. I have learned your tricks, bastard," he seethed in a dark tone. He used the blade to caress Ryder's cheek. "I think perhaps in another life, we might have even been friends. I shall surely miss our banter." He grinned. "I borrowed this from Parahazur's failed attempt to rescue your pathetic cousin. Perhaps he even intended to rescue you too."

"That explains the noise," Ryder stated. He hid his sadness at another Saber Commander dying needlessly for him.

Rache drew the blade back. "It was fitting of him to die as a Saber wishes in service of the royal family. Don't they all wish that?"

"I wouldn't know. I'm not a Saber," came Ryder's careful reply.

Rache looked around the dim candle lit tomb. The walls were carelessly chipped and carved with no care to the occupant. There were no golden treasures or precious jewels. It was a bare and cold place. A thick layer of dust coated every surface. "It's pitiful to imagine what you could have been and what you are now."

"Perhaps we will never know!" Ryder stated as he ripped the chains in half with a targeted Shadow Shock and immediately slipped into Shadow Slide.

Rache roared in fury as he threw his knife point down into the ground. His eyes darted around following Ryder's Slide. Ryder reappeared by the great stone door. Rache snarled, lips curling around sharp fangs.

"It seems that I do not hate my father after all for his Spirit has given me the strength to break free of you," Ryder said with a mocking salute. "And even in another life, I still wouldn't like you enough to be friends." He grinned before slipped back into Shadow Slide and escaping.

THINGS FALL APART

"You are an idiot! Worthless! Stupid!" Kaiser roared, his face red with rage. "You let a bastard child outsmart you!"

"No, I let an Adonis bastard escape because this bond of ours prevents me from killing him. I bet the high and mighty Kaiser Adonis did not see this coming. Perhaps if you had not spawned that daughter of yours then you wouldn't have her son to deal with," Rache snarled in defense.

Kaiser slapped him hard across the face, leaving a blistering red mark. "You know nothing of the true power of the bond. Look at me!" He jerked Rache's face to look into his own. "I do not care that he escaped. I can always find him again. I do care that you allowed him to subvert your true nature and outwit you. He is a better Demon than you are and he does not even have that blood type in his veins."

Rache remained stern as Kaiser let go of his chin and stalked away. "This does remind me of your story."

"What story?" Kaiser asked flatly, pausing in place.

"The one where your father...Rache started to say before Kaiser struck him so hard that his jaw cracked from the force.

Kaiser sneered until his posture slackened. "Yes, there is a certain degree of irony. But I now have command over those that seek to make my end. The bastard shall never have command over me."

"I would not be so certain. He is like you in many ways and claims to have inherited your intelligence. I do not think this world could handle two of you," Rache stated in a careful tone.

"Peredur. Ryder. Whatever he chooses to call himself has a heart and sense of justice. In his current state, he is an opposing force for he does not realize how great he could truly be. And I don't mean the whole second coming of Shadow Night Silvanus that the world seems to think of," Kaiser said as he resumed his track back towards his desk. Rache watched as he suddenly turned and came to a stop before the royal sword. "He is the heir of my bloodline whether he chooses to acknowledge it or not. I think nothing of it but he fears what the world would think if they knew. He is already disliked for his father and bastard status. He will be driven into oblivion if they knew that he was my blood. I could declare him now."

"Why don't you?" Rache asked.

Kaiser chuckled as he dragged the fingers of his left hand down the length of the sword. "I do not wish to share the spotlight."

It was hard to tell for Rache if Kaiser was still blisteringly angry. The Shadowborn was capable of shifting his emotions in the span of a heartbeat from calm to explosive violence. Rache gave up a long time ago trying to predict his master's moods. He then thought about Ryder. Kaiser's grandson was more predictable but still it was difficult to see if he would be just as shifty. Both men were such a contrast to what he knew as a Demon. Demons had no middleground and bounced from one extreme to the next as if it was an innate skill to master by adulthood. Rache began to think that he had been around Kaiser for too long for his ability to emote was becoming muddled.

"But now, I must expend energy I had reserved for future endeavors to bring my grandson back home to me. I really wish you had been smart enough to know when you are being played," Kaiser said as he turned to face Rache. The glimmer of rage was back in his eyes.

Rache stood strong before the angry Kaiser. He crossed his arms tightly. "I seem to remember that you let Onyx escape."

Kaiser's face twisted in fury. He jabbed a finger in Rache's direction. "You were outwitted by a bastard who used your pride against you," he seethed as he rounded the desk. "I thought you were the best the Darklands had to offer."

"I am the best," Rache growled as he stared back at Kaiser.

Kaiser curled his finger and looked down for a moment. His breaths were quick and hard with his anger. His long throat scar glowed black. "You have failed me," he struggled to say before looking back up.

The black scar on Rache's arm started to burn and he

gritted his teeth in response. He sucked in his breath as the scar fire increased in intensity. Blood vessels swelled in a spidery map under pale skin. His temples throbbed in increasing pain as his throat burned.

"Are you going to end me over a mistake?" Rache asked under great strain.

Kaiser looked him straight in the eyes, grabbing and holding Rache's chin. His hand slipped down to Rache's neck. He then applied a choking pressure and Rache gulped hard.

"I shed Shadowborn blood to bring you forth," Kaiser said sternly. "I expect you to shed it in return for the gift I have given you." He threw Rache back and turned around.

Rache rubbed his throat as he regained his balance. He coughed hard as he stood up straight to face Kaiser. He was afraid. "I will bring you the bastard and the prince's heads."

"You already brought me the Saber's," Kaiser stated as he stroked the skull of Sai Parahazur on his desk. It had been dried and bleached white. "I just wish his memories had been easier to read. I am of a mind to do a little extermination but I must know where to strike before bringing my will to bear."

"The older a soul, the tighter the lock on their Blood Memories. Sai was a royal purist and though he knew of your grandson as a royal bastard, he did not give him the same kind of respect he gave to those born legitimately. It is easy to break a bone. It is not easy to break through strong emotions like loyalty," Rache explained with a shrug of the shoulders. He had learned the ins and outs of blood memories very early on in his life.

"Sai Parahazur has a sister in the city. Why don't you pay her a visit and bring her news of her precious brother?" Kaiser suggested as he picked up the skull and dropped it into Rache's hand. "Slay who you must but leave no one alive. Bring me the information I seek. If the rebels want to make war, let me bring it to their door."

"Finally something worth my time," Rache said with a smirk.

Kaiser scoffed as he sat back down in his desk chair. "It's time to step out from the shadows," he said as he leaned back in his chair. "It's time to make our proper war."

MARTIAL LAW

Zoras looked down at the map on his desk as he sipped a mouthful of red wine. He crossed his arms, holding the wine glass in his left hand. His eyes traced the entire length of the River Shadow from edge to edge. He set his glass down and pulled open a desk drawer to take out a straight edge and a compass. Placing the compass aside for the time being, Zoras took the straight edge and laid it on the center of the map. He pushed and moved the instrument until one end sat on the mark that indicated the capital city of Cross and the other end rested on the bottom edge of the map. He bent over his desk, marking the desired route with a sharpened pencil. He stood back up to check his work.

Zoras reviewed a map of the current system of roads in the Shadowborn lands. At the last Council, the Master of Roads had proposed a plan to improve the roadways leading south out of the capital. Zoras had to agree as the roads south had been severely damaged during Akakios' reign and had laid in relative disrepair for far too long. He glanced at the notes the Master of Roads had given him. The paper had a series of figures and measurements provided to the council by the Mayor of Horizon, a city on the southern coast.

Despite his normal duties of effectively running the country, Zoras had other reasons to worry about roadway conditions. In the back of his mind, he was planning for an inevitable war. The seemingly inpenetrable borders still unnerved him so reinforcements would be few and far between. Part of him hoped that such power at the eastern border did not extend to the coastline. One of his war plans included enlisting the aid of the mighty Waterborn Navy but Zoras knew they would not help if Ryder was involved. Even long after they had gotten justice with the execution of Akakios, the Waterborn wanted nothing to do with Akakios' bastard son. To get them to even consider helping, Zoras would have to find the legitimate Prince, Onyx, and considering his recent escape, he did not know where to start looking.

"Look past your prejudice and focus on who the actual enemy is," he grumbled. He picked up his glass and downed the rest of the wine in a single gulp. "I need allies."

Zoras had learned of Sai Parahazur's death that morning from Donovan Shunga. The information regarding his demise was scant but Zoras had a strong suspicion that Kaiser was involved. He sneered at the thought. It confounded him how Kaiser always managed to worm his way in and out of trouble. This time, he believed, Kaiser was the cause. He still had Donovan's hastily written note in his pocket, telling him:

'Sai dead. Ryder unknown.'

It was news he did not want to receive. Sai was a purist when it came to who sat on the throne but he was a staunch supporter of the rebellion. Losing him wounded Zoras' cause and sense of Saber brotherhood. But with questions surrounding Ryder's whereabouts, Zoras had ordered Donovan to further investigate. He could not afford to lose more allies and supporters. In particular, he could not lose Ryder to Kaiser. Zoras leaned his fists on the top of his desk, studying the map in the faint hope of it revealing hidden answers.

The door to his study slowly opened and Zoras looked up to see Kaiser walking in. The ever cocky Lord's Chancellor wore a long coat whose hem stopped at his ankles. The coat's fabric was a soft black, fibers woven closely together to make it soft to the touch. Zoras thought for a moment if Kaiser wore anything but black. He himself was dressed in an untucked white linen shirt with sleeves rolled up to his elbows. His own cloak was laying across the back of his desk chair.

"To what do I owe the pleasure?" Zoras asked without really meaning it. His gaze returned to the map.

Kaiser puffed up his chest. "I take it that the Lord's Regent was informed of the passing of Sai Parahazur. We are now without a Commander of the Sabers."

"That absence is already weighing heavily on my mind. You may inform Lord Aku that I intend to find a suitable and proper successor by the next morning," Zoras cooly replied as he gripped the edge of his desk. The wood cracked from the pressure.

"Might I make a suggestion?" Kaiser innocently asked.

Zoras looked up at him and frowned. "The naming of a new Commander is for Sabers only. I do not need your help nor do I want it. You have never been a Saber and know nothing of what it takes to command such a noble order."

"Then his Majesty expects nothing less than perfect and with your aid, I am sure a proper successor will be found," Kaiser praised.

The tone in Kaiser's voice spoke of insult and arrogance. His body posture was surprisingly relaxed and confident as if he was untouchable. As if he knew something that Zoras did not. Zoras watched as Kaiser's eyes drifted around the spacious office.

"Say your piece and be done with it. I do not have the time to deal with you," Zoras snapped.

"I would imagine so. Our laws name you the temporary Commander of the Sabers. I do wonder why you ever retired from such a noble position," Kaiser expressed with curiosity.

Zoras set his callused hands on his hips. At Kaiser's prompting, his thoughts did turn to when he had resigned his command and retired from the Sabers. He had served as Commander of the Sabers since Sin Silvanus sat on the throne and only left during the ill fated reign of Akakios. It took him many years to sort through his reasons for retiring. Though he had managed to escape Akakios' fall, the sense of abandoning his Lord weighed heavily on his broad shoulders. His sense of duty followed him and he thus transferred his loyalty to Akakios' son. He sighed deeply, maintaining a stern expression as he looked back at Kaiser.

"That is my own business," Zoras stated firmly, biting back a snarl.

Kaiser nodded as if he understood. "Probably for the best. Based on your successors, I would imagine the curse of leadership would have ended up killing you too." He scoffed. "And I was actually starting to like Parahazur."

That was enough! Zoras snarled in the face of Kaiser's blatant arrogance. A truly uncouth and nasty curse formed on his lips but Zoras managed to gather his control. He let out a deep breath to calm himself. He looked to see that Kaiser had started pacing around his office, always careful to keep his left side facing away from the desk. The man's eyes went up and down the walls, studying the multitude of weapons and shields on display. Zoras did not like how casual Kaiser was acting as he stepped around the dark wood furniture.

"Go ahead and speak your mind. You would end me in a

heartbeat if you had the nerve," Zoras growled. He was dropping all pretenses in front of Kaiser.

"Good because pretending I give a crap about you is such a hassle," Kaiser exclaimed as he dropped his shoulders. He looked back at Zoras with a smirk. "And I could have been rid of you a long time ago but even you have your uses."

Zoras was not surprised by Kaiser's reply. He slid his hand down towards his belt where a dagger sat in its scabbard. His untucked shirt thankfully hid the sheathed weapon. He kept his eyes on Kaiser while mentally taking note of a heavy broadsword on display. Zoras had received the weapon as a gift from his friend Madhuri Coba when he had been named the Lord's Regent. The sword rested on a wooden rack on a table behind a couch that faced away from him. It was on the other side of the room but Zoras was confident he could retrieve it before a fight could break out.

"You don't like me and I don't like you. Can we at least agree on that?" Zoras asked, acting cautious while being blunt.

Kaiser nodded as if he understood. "Of course, child."

Zoras berated himself silently. He needed to throw Kaiser's confidence off balance. "I am not the fool you think I am. I know my successors died at your hands."

Kaiser pressed his right hand to his chest as a feigned look of hurt and ignorance crossed his face. "I never touched them with hand or blade. How dare you accuse the Shadowlord's most loyal servant of murder when you yourself head a rebellion against his rule?"

"You loyal? Ha! My support of Ryder Coba maybe well known but I would never betray the throne," Zoras declared with a boastful laugh.

"Yes, you are still young," Kaiser mused as he lifted the royal blade into view. His left hand gripped the hilt while the blade rested in his right hand. He gently tapped his palm with it a few times before pointing the sword at Zoras. "You presume to imagine that I have done terrible things in the Shadowlord's name. Well let me tell you a little something you might find important. You kill me and every Silvanus will drop dead by my last heartbeat. That is if you actually can kill me."

The threat in Kaiser's voice was deadly. Zoras held on to the dagger hilt tightly as he slowly stepped around his desk. He kept his eyes on Kaiser, searching for a hint of action or decision to strike. One thing was certain to him. If Kaiser wanted him dead, he would have not engaged in conversation. He would have just acted.

"Try to kill me and I will have you thrown out of Cross,"

Zoras started to say.

Kaiser quickly laughed. "Is that supposed to pass for a threat? Who out there is brave enough to act against me?" He followed Zoras' path with the point of the sword. "I have not lived this long only to fall to a pack of rebels. You will have to do better than that."

He stepped forward and pinned Zoras agains the wall. The sword point pressed against the center of his chest. A small drop of blood stained his shirt.

"Go ahead. Raise the bastard's banner. Ignite the flames of the war you seem so desparate for. But before you do, let me tell you a little secret," Kaiser dared with a warning in his voice. He twisted the sword to cut deeper. "He is my daughter's bastard."

The idea that Kaiser had ever been a father made Zoras laugh out loud. "What an outrageous claim!" He laughed again when he saw how his reaction caused Kaiser to furrow his brow.

Kaiser then scoffed and Zoras stopped laughing. "Ask him yourself." He quickly ripped the sword away, slashing Zoras' shirt open and leaving a long gash across his front. "From this point on, I am declaring martial law for the whole of the realm. Go and tell your fellow rebels that should you raise arms against me, I will destroy you. My claws are so deeply embedded that you will see that there is nowhere for the rebellion to hide. I will find you."

"The rebellion is more than a few Shadowborn. It is the world and you will have to kill many to stop us," Zoras said as bravely as he could. He was thankful that the bleeding was not worse as he pressed a hand over the deepest part of the wound. "I am not the only one who wants you dead."

"Oh and I am sure that you think you have someone capable of killing me. Well then, I await the assassin's blade with eager anticipation," Kaiser replied confidently. "Now you better run to your rebel friends to deliver my message before I come knocking down the door to tell them myself."

Zoras squared his shoulders and snorted towards Kaiser. He quickly grabbed his cloak and threw it on. "You will regret turning your back on the Immortal Truth."

Kaiser chuckled as he watched Zoras leave the office. "I am sure I will." He smirked with all hint of impending danger. "I suppose that I will let you live until I tire of you breathing. That you can be sure of."

REUNION

Ryder came out of Shadow Slide, stumbling a few steps as he fell against a moss covered tree trunk. He slid down to the ground, arms and legs limp from exhaustion as he tried to catch his breath. All of the pain he had blocked out during his torture came back with a vengeance as his body tensed up. He closed his eyes tightly, feeling the returning warmth of his own blood, seeping out of his wounds. It took a moment before Ryder had gained enough control over himself to stand back up.

The village lay just beyond the trees in a wide clearing. Each building had walls of stone and dark wood with gray slate roofs. The iron street lamps gave a cozy feel with their soft light. It had been a hundred years since Ryder was last in this small village on the East Road and he could tell that there was a nervous feeling in the air. He pilfered a large coat from a laundry line and slipped it on. The mess on his body stuck to the cloth in an uncomfortable way. Smearing a handful of mud on his face to disguise his identity, Ryder stepped into town looking like a beat up forest drifter.

Forest drifters were solitary and houseless Shadowborn who felt at home in the wilds and away from the city. Their clothes were tattered and worn due to years of wandering. When they did come into town, it was usually to gather news at the local tavern. Ryder headed for a popular tavern called the Dark Night Inn. The evening was already beginning to come to life as the sun was slowly setting. Ryder spied the lamp lighters fanning out with torches to light the street lamps. One sneered at him as he passed, momentarily distracted by Ryder's filthy appearance.

"Take a bath," one passerby shouted as he pulled his demurely dressed wife closer to him.

Ryder brushed the comment off with a shrug of his broad shoulders, stepping into the gutter to let the couple pass. The gutter water splashed upon his dark brown leather boots and pants. The cool moisture was soothing on his heated skin so he welcomed it. He chuckled as he took one final look at the well-dressed couple. His disguise was working. But Ryder quickly reminded himself that he may have had a famous name and face but few could put the two together. He began to wonder how many people actually knew who he was beyond a royal bastard.

The Dark Night Inn was already bustling as people streamed in for the evening cheer and food. The smell of roasting meat made Ryder's mouth water. It had been too long since he last had a decent meal. He fumbled around in the coat and in his pockets for any coins.

"Your kind is not welcome here, drifter," a brutish looking thug in crude steel plate armor growled. His beefy hand rested on the hilt of a broad sword at his waist.

Ryder stopped his forward pace and glanced through the smoke stained windows at the activity inside. More of the unofficial door guard's kind were inside, drinking and telling crude jokes. There was something about the scene that put him on edge. And the greeting he received at the door didn't help.

"Since when, child," Ryder snapped in a low and shaking voice. Forest drifters tended to be from an older generation so Ryder had to keep up with his ruse.

The thug wrapped his hand around the sword hilt. "Since the Border Act was set in law ten years ago," he laughed.

Ryder bit back a snarky comment. "The Immortal Truth is the law of the Shadowlord's land."

Suddenly the thug pulled out his sword and set the tip under Ryder's chin, pointed towards his throat. Ryder looked down at the shining blade, seeing a pristine and clean edge. Either this swordsman took good care of the weapon or he had never used it. Ryder then looked back at the thug and realized his size was not from muscle but from excessive fat. He then grinned.

"What are you smiling about?" the thug grumbled. His wolf shaped steel helm slid down on his head nearly blocking his vision. "Answer me!" he demanded.

Ryder slowly put his left hand on the thug's wrist, wrapping his fingers around it. He then quickly gripped it tightly and pulled down, snapping the thug's bones. The sword immediately dropped and clattered on the stone sidewalk as the man fell back, screaming in pain. He cried like a baby who had been pinched too hard. It was a pathetic sight. Ryder then decided he would have more luck going to the back door where the kitchen staff threw out the scraps to the dogs. At least he wouldn't have to fight his way to the bar for food and information.

A wood pile stood as a small barrier to the back door, hiding the tiny dirt yard from the view of the street. The two chickens that were pecking around the sparse grass scattered into the bushes when Ryder drew close. The kitchen door opened just as he turned the corner and out stepped a young black haired man with tawny skin, apron tied around his waist. His eyes widened when he saw the battered Ryder and started to turn and shout. Ryder tackled him to the ground and shushed him, placing a hand over his mouth. The kitchen worker shook with fear. He then started studied Ryder's face, a questioning look in his eyes but a look of recognition behind them.

"Promise you won't shout?" Ryder asked in a low voice. The kitchen worker nodded and Ryder removed his hand. They both sat up, covered in dust and pieces of grass.

"You're Ryder Coba," the worker said, brushing his short locks back from his face. A smile quivered on his lips. He was not certain if he was happy, surprised, or scared.

Ryder nodded for he would not deny a correct guess. He tried to figure out if he knew the young man for he did not appear much older than Soja. He suddenly felt defensive and ready to fight. "How do you know me?" he asked despite it being a stupid question.

"Everyone knows what Lord Aku and Prince Onyx look like. I can tell that you have Silvanus blood in you so you can be no other than the bastard of Akakios. My name is Den," the worker replied, trying to alleviate Ryder's fear of discovery. "Plus there are few who act openly against Kaiser's allies here in the village. Former nobodies have taken up the sword in Kaiser's name looking for glory and reward." Den looked back towards the door, the sound of angry shouts in the background.

"The Mayor should not have let this happen," Ryder commented. He watched as Den shook his head.

"The Mayor was murdered in his bed ten years ago and the city hasn't been the same since. The good souls who have remained have petitioned the Shadow Council over and over but their voices have fallen on deaf ears. I left Cross to see what I could do to help on my own when Commander Parahazur was killed," Den started to explain but shrugged his shoulders. "We are losing hope that the Shadowlord will ever come. The Shadowborn have been abandoned to ruin."

Ryder found it utterly painful to hear such words from one of the commonfolk. For once, it was a stranger, someone who had never met him, that accused him of abandoning his people even if Den did not name him. A sense of duty began to rise up in Ryder's heart though he could not say why. All of the emotion from the day he left rushed into him and it combined with the strong desire to act that was surging through his entire body. It had to be the influence of his father's Spirit. Despite lingering questions, Ryder hardened his heart and stood straight up, ignoring all protests of injury and pain.

"Go inside," Ryder ordered as he looked back towards the street. Den didn't hesitate to scramble through the door and pull it shut. The lock clicked with a shudder.

The thugs had no one to fear as an enemy when Kaiser was there to back them up. They had no faith in the throne unless Kaiser was seated upon it. And that thought made Ryder angry. He was going to send a powerful message to Kaiser: Peredur Coba-Silvanus was back and ready to fight him. Even the thought that his return would embolden those who supported him as the Shadowlord did not deter him from action. He stood up tall and closed his eyes, putting all his focus and emotion into his core. A sense of calm coursed through him as he felt his mind opening up to a deep power.

Behind him unnoticed rose up the Spirit of Akakios and Omu the Spirit Wolf, each with determined smiles shining in their eyes. His midnight fur sparkled with starlight as a mist sheltered him from view. They had heard Ryder's silent call and had been more than ready to answer. In the call was laced the voice of Shadow Night, a whisper from the past guiding them to the present. They slowly stepped forward following Ryder out to the street, a trail of impenetrable shadows following them. The wolf looked at Ryder seeing not the dirty royal bastard, but instead a pure Shadowborn clad in shining silver armor. The image was fleeting but Omu knew that this once unwanted son was on his way to becoming what he was born to be. The wolf looked to Akakios and both nodded with pride.

"Come out of your shadow and lay yourselves bare before your Lord!" Ryder commanded in a booming voice. His voice was amplified with a deeper sound behind it, the growl of a wolf enunciating his words. It was hard to tell who was truly speaking though Ryder only heard his voice.

Ten thugs barreled out of the Dark Night Inn, their injured comrade at their backs. All were clad in an assortment of steel armor and baring an array of weapons. When they turned to see

Ryder, each of them saw what Omu had first seen: a noble warrior in silver armor, his face veiled by shadows. Ryder's eyes were glowing white like a dark phantom out of the Spirit World. They also saw Omu at Ryder's right side, body bristling in anger. A misty form appeared on Ryder's left side. All were afraid for they saw what appeared to be Shadow Night Silvanus, back from the dead to haunt them. Each one stammered and shivered with fright.

"You have betrayed the law of the Immortal Truth and dishonored those who fought for your freedom. The path you have chosen will only bring you death, not glory. Kaiser has given you empty promises and keeps all power for himself. If you are true Shadowborn, you will denounce him now and curse his name," Ryder stated with the utmost authority though he did not know where the words came from. But still the words and feelings that came grew stronger within him.

The street and buildings faded into the mist that Omu commanded as it spread. A chill was heavy in the air. Together with Ryder he said, "Leave this place and beg for your master's forgiveness only to face certain death. Or you can join with the truth and be reborn!"

Crying like newborn children, the thugs immediately threw down their weapons and fell on their knees. The mist began to dissipate and the street lamps relit with the departing darkness. Omu faded, pleased that Ryder had indeed returned home. He looked to Akakios just before the Spirit mist dissipated. A crowd had begun to form, people slowly coming out of their homes to surround Ryder and the thugs who cried and begged forgiveness. A wave of exhaustion threatened to topple Ryder as he returned to himself, not fully aware of what had transpired. He had felt a vast well of experience and powers enter him in the alley. He could not explain the feeling.

Pushing through the edge of the crowd was Hayden Abendroth, Saber mask thrown back to reveal his expression of shock. He shouted towards the four soldiers that had followed him into the circle. With slices of his hand and pointing his finger, Hayden directed the soldiers to take the blubbering thugs into custody. Once they were under control, he approached Ryder with his right hand wavering over his knife. Like everyone watching, he too was cautious. But there was no reason to be as Ryder's eyes rolled back into his head and he fell forward, Hayden catching him at the last second.

The next thing that Ryder could remember and sense was the cool dampness of a cloth being rubbed across his skin. His wounds were numb from some sort of salve he could not identify.

Bandages were wrapped tightly around his torso. He strangely felt comfortable as if he was lying back on a bed with a blanket drawn up to his waist. His vision began to clear as his senses slowly sharpened. A shadow passed into his view.

"Welcome back," came Hayden's even voice. Ryder turned his head, spotting the Saber's distinctive lean frame. He appeared to be smiling. "I'll take my leave with your permission."

"What? You don't answer to me," Ryder started to say in confusion.

"Says one of the last Princes of the Silvanus bloodline."

Though Ryder had expected to come across her at some point, Haven's delicate but sharp voice hit him hard and his heart leaped into his chest. A surge of energy lifted him forward but a hand pushed him back down to the bed. And there Haven was, revealed to him as she had always appeared in his memory, in leather armor and chainmail.

"Stay down. You have taken a few too many knocks to the skull," Haven said as she dipped the cloth in the bowl of water next to her. She wrung it before softly padding his forehead. She looked back briefly to Hayden and nodded. Hayden bowed his head and left the small room.

Ryder didn't argue though he wanted to jump out of the bed and embrace her tightly. He did not realize that he would have missed her as much as he did in that moment. His head rested against the feather pillow, eyes only for the Shadowborn woman in front of him. He smiled warmly.

"I have missed you," Ryder said softly.

"And yet not enough to come back sooner. It took a Demon dragging you to Cross for you to come home," Haven curtly stated. She tossed the cloth into the bowl of water with a splash.

Her response had been unexpected. Ryder had imagined that she had missed him terribly. "What did I do?"

Haven frowned, bouncing her trademark long braid back over her right shoulder. "You left me. You left Cross. You left your homeland for one hundred years." She pushed away from his bedside and picked up the bowl.

"Don't leave me," Ryder tried to say as he reached out to grab her arm.

Haven slapped him hard across the cheek. She angrily threw down the bowl, the water splashing on the floor. "Did you honestly expect me to be waiting for you with open arms? Did you honestly think the few notes you sent were enough?" she shouted with fury. "I am not the same Haven Ombre that YOU left behind to escape the people who wanted to put you on the throne."

"I did not leave because of Zoras' plans," Ryder said, trying to defend himself. He found himself upset that his onetime love had rejected him.

"You could have fooled everyone with that show you just put on. Only a Silvanus could call Omu and put the fear of the Spirit World into Kaiser's men," Haven accused as she stood and crossed her arms tightly. "Though I do not doubt that even that will drive them off for long.

"I did what?" Ryder asked as he sat up, trying to remember.

Haven rolled her eyes. "If you had truly rejected the throne, Omu would have spat at you and ignored your summons. But clearly part of you has entertained the idea of accepting Zoras' offer."

Ryder turned his head away for she spoke the truth to him like no one ever could. "That is not why I left." He watched as Haven came to sit beside him, her hand sliding over top of his right hand.

"Ryder, I know you better than anyone on Terra so you better tell me the truth. Didn't your mother always teach you to be honest?" Haven asked, her voice suddenly full of concern.

He turned to look her directly in the eyes and nodded. "She told me something that I did not want anyone to find out. And clearly telling me led to her death." His gaze dropped for a moment. "Swear that you will tell no one."

Haven nodded as she squeezed his hand. "On my family's honor."

It took a long time before Ryder spoke again. "Before my mother was killed, she told me that her father was..." He couldn't bring himself to say it. That he was a son of the Adonis family bloodline and directly related to the North's greatest enemy. It was easy to be strong before Kaiser who had never known him closely. But he was ready to break apart before Haven. "Her father was Kaiser. I don't want to become like him but I fear that it will happen anyway. Please save me."

The shock was immense but Haven did not want to show it before Ryder as he fell into her arms, trembling from all of the emotion he had locked inside since the day he left. She let him cry, knowing that he had done the same for her and would continue to do. For now, he was home.

RYDER AND HAVEN

Ryder lay back in the bed, his right arm behind his head as he stared up at the ceiling. The ceiling was constructed of heavy oak beams that spanned the width of the roof. White paneling spread out between each beam though there was evidence of previous storm damage. Cracks and tan water stains were everywhere. A stain had even crept down the wall just in front of the bed beside the room door. In an odd sense, Ryder felt like the detail of the room reflected exactly how he was feeling.

He found that no matter how hard he tried, he could not fall asleep. No matter the pain of his wounds, rest was eluding him. Ryder was physically exhausted from his long torture and imprisonment with Rache. He was borderline half dead from using Shadow Slide to escape from Cross and rush all the way to a village on the East Road. Ryder thought he could convince himself that he had been through worse but try as he might, nothing was worse than what had transpired between him and Haven. She now knew his greatest torment. She had also appeared to reject him or at least she was not as ready to fall in his arms as he was for her. Of all that had happened since his capture in Crossroads, her offputting reaction at their reunion hurt him the most.

His room door cracked open, the rusted hinges creaking in the slow movement. Ryder was preparing to jump out of the bed to defend himself when Haven's slender form appeared. She stepped into view, a blanket wrapped loosely around her body. A swath of cloth had fallen away from her right shoulder, exposing a patch of bare skin. Ryder relaxed, watching her carefully.

"I couldn't sleep," she said just above a whisper. She closed the door behind her but did not make any more effort to move forward.

"Me either," Ryder replied, hoping that Haven would come to his side. He laid his head back on the pillow.

Haven remained rooted where she was in front of the door. She pulled the blanket back up over her shoulder. Her long black hair fell in waves down her back. She appeared to be fighting back a painful emotion as she looked away from Ryder.

"What is it?" Ryder quietly asked.

Haven sniffled as a lone tear streamed down her cheek. She reached up to wipe it away. "I am so afraid that if I go to sleep, I will wake up and you will be gone again."

Ryder's mind instantly went back to the last time he had seen Haven. She was laying beside him in a deep sleep, the blankets tangled around her naked form. Her raven hair was pushed away from her face. He was facing her on his side, the sunlight beaming through the window across his bare back. He remembered reaching forward to caress her cheek one last time before pulling himself out of the bed and leaving her.

"I am here now," he said, trying to reassure her.

"But for how long? How can I be sure that you will not just leave again?" Haven fired back. "What if it is Kaiser that takes you away this time?"

"I will not let him," Ryder said sternly though a part of him did not believe he could hold off Kaiser for long.

Haven finally made her way over to the bedside. Ryder shuffled his body to make room for her, pulling back his own blanket for her to crawl under next to him. She was careful not to hit or press against his bandaged wounds as she pulled their shared blanket up over her shoulders. Her head rested next to his. He moved to lie on his side to face her, taking her right hand in his left hand.

"Ryder, I do not think I can ever get you to understand how much pain you have put me through for these last one hundred years. To wake up that morning to discover you had left was one thing. To realize that you were not coming back was another thing entirely. No one knew where you had gone. When the bones of the Saber Commander were found, I was worried that something terrible had happened to you. I spent years searching the borders for some sign of you. Some hope that maybe you would come back to me," Haven said before her voice faltered.

Ryder squeezed her hand in an attempt to soothe her. "There is no wound deeper that than the one I dealt myself in hurting you. But..."

"No. I won't let you blame Kaiser for everything. You made the choice to leave. He did not command you nor did he ask you," Haven interrupted her voice surprising strong. She took her hand away.

For a long time, Ryder and Haven laid beside each other in a tense silence. His eyes never left her face while she kept her gaze away from him. Each time he attempted to take her hand, she pulled it from his reach. Ryder wanted to reach out and comfort her by taking her in his arms and never letting go. But she kept her distance.

"He will try to destroy us both before the end," Ryder declared.

Haven finally looked into his eyes. Her eyes were red from crying. "He already has."

Her statement cut him deeply and his wounds twinged with shared pain. "I would have asked you to come with me but I know that you could never leave your family behind."

"No I wouldn't have. Not even for you," Haven staunchly replied. "Why did you leave, Ryder? Why did you honestly leave?"

Ryder slowly reached for her hand and she finally allowed for him to take it in his hand. He gave it a squeeze. He knew that for the time being, this was all Haven was going to allow. "I was afraid. I am of Kaiser's blood. What is to say that I will not become like him? I was already the bastard of an executed Shadowlord. The son of a supposed whore. The Shadowborn hated me just for that. Then Zoras was pushing the throne like it was my divine right and each time he did, it pushed me further away. In the end, the hate and fear was just too much to bear. I had to get away."

"Just like my pain, I doubt that I will understand your feelings before you left though I desparately wish I could. At least then, I could understand my anger towards you. Perhaps I could forgive you and move on," Haven said, getting better control over her tears.

"To who? Jarod? He's a self indulgent prick who only saw you as a piece of flesh," Ryder stated with a hint of jealousy.

Haven chuckled softly. "I think he learned his lesson after you knocked his teeth out. Your mother must have been furious for what you did."

"She was. She said, 'No son of mine will be making a fool of himself or me by hurting another. Even if they deserve it.' I had to do physical training and combat drills until my fingers bled," Ryder said as he reminisced on the memory. He let out a deep breath. "I will say Jarod never came near you again so mission accomplished."

"No he didn't. Few gentlemen did when they knew that you were not far behind to defend my honor. Even when you were gone, no one dared to try to court me into marriage. At first, my father was amused by it but as the years passed, he started to worry just as much as I did. My entire family did." Haven's mirth then disappeared as she hid her face again. Ryder reached to lift her chin up so that she was looking into his eyes. "They never stopped thinking of you."

"I guess that I have to earn more than just your trust again. I have to earn theirs back as well," Ryder said in a defeated tone. He lightly kissed her forehead.

Haven sighed deeply. "As mad as I want to be at you, I can't be angry at you forever. One hundred years is long enough to hold on to such feelings."

"It is a long time," Ryder said softly.

Ryder rolled onto his back and accepted Haven into his arms. She snuggled up against him, laying her right hand on his muscled chest. She was careful not to cause him too much discomfort.

"What are you going to do now?" Haven asked.

"I know what I want to do and what I have to do. If I want to live free, I will have to fight Kaiser."

"Will you make a bid for the throne? You are Onyx's elder in the royal line," Haven pointed out.

Ryder sighed deeply. "As much as people want me to sit on that throne, it is not where I am meant to be. I will only accept Zoras' offer if there is no other that could serve the Shadowborn and the world best. I can only hope that whatever I decide, you will be at my side."

"So long as you are at my side, Ryder," Haven said in affirmation. She then chuckled. "May the Spirit World strike you down if you ever leave me again. That is if I don't get to you first."

"Duly noted," Ryder replied as he wrapped his arms around her.

THE BORDER

The horses' hooves thundered down the dirt road at full speed. Both animals lathered at their bits but continued forward. They were as determined as their riders to reach the border. Their flanks were slick with sweat as their powerful muscles surged. They tossed their heads, their manes whipping in the wind of their pace.

"Do you think Soja will be at the bridge?" Haven called out as she lifted up a few inches in the saddle. The leather creaked as her boots scraped the sides.

"I don't know how to really explain it but I just know he will be close by. It's a trick I learned from the Earthborn. So long as he is on the ground, I can sense where he is if he is close enough to me," Ryder replied as he kept his eyes on the road. He tightened his grip on the reins.

Haven smiled and laughed. "I may be biased but you are much greater than you appear."

"You are biased," Ryder chuckled as he stole a look at her. He smiled when he saw that she had done the same. Her gray eyes sparkled, illuminating her pale skin. As soft as her expression was, Ryder was happy to have her at his side again for she was a skilled warrior. He did not allow his mirth to delude the fact that Kaiser had agents out trying to capture him. He had to keep all of his senses alert.

The road they were racing on led them away southeast from Dusk. It crossed under the eaves of an old pine forest that was being invaded by the gnarled limbs of hardwood trees. It was fairly straight with only the occasional twist and turn. Many smaller roads and paths split off for parts unknown. It had been over a century since Ryder had properly traveled the eastern territory of his homeland. It had in fact been Haven who directed their route. When he asked her how she knew the area so well, being from Umbra, she replied in a solumn voice that she had tried to find him when he first ran away.

"We should pass two roads that turn south before we reach the bridge. They are pretty overgrown but with me leading the way, you will not miss them," Haven stated with certainty. The south roads would lead them away from the bridge but at least provided an escape route if needed.

Ryder sighed deeply. He did not want to turn south if he could help it. The southern territory of the Shadowborn lands, in particular the southeast section, was sparsely populated. Most Shadowborn felt that a poison permeated the soil and air there in wake of Akakios' ill fated march to attack the Waterborn. He remembered the great exodus of people that migrated into the northern cities and the whispers of danger that spread. That was when people began to look at him with caution and scorn for being Akakios' bastard son.

"Do you remember when we first travelled to the border together? You said you were going to show me the lands of the Earthborn."

Haven's sweet voice brought Ryder out of his dark thoughts. "That was so long ago."

Haven chuckled lightly. "We are not old enough to say things like that. Not yet at least."

He was about to respond when the hint of a rushing chill swept across his senses. It was the unmistakable chill of someone in Shadow Slide. Ryder at first berated himself for not noticing the chill sooner but he told himself that even he did not have the power to read past the shadows of the night. With a sharp toss of the head, he got Haven's attention. He nodded once towards their rear, indicating silently that they were being followed. She nodded as she shifted the reins solely into her right hand. Ryder guided his speeding horse closer to Haven's. She held out her left hand, gripping both the reins and pommel of the saddle to maintain balance. He then tossed her the reins of his horse which she deftly caught.

As soon as Haven had a grip on his horse's reins, Ryder lifted himself free of the stirrups with the strength of his arms alone. The strain pulled on his still healing wounds but he bit back any hint of pain. He swung his feet to stand on the horse's back in a low crouch. Keeping his left hand on the front of the saddle, Ryder brought his right arm straight back to maintain balance. He spotted a thick low hanging branch up ahead. The chance to act would be small. He quickly locked eyes with Haven and nodded. She nodded back. Ryder then reached up and with perfect timing, swung himself up into the canopy of branches.

He quickly scrambled into the darkness as Haven rushed away down a game trail with his horse in tow. Ryder sharpened his senses as the Shadow Slide followers came closer. He held his breath as six Sabers shifted out of Shadow Slide and came to a stop under his hiding place. It was immediately apparent to Ryder that all of the Sabers looked nervous under the traditional leathers and light armor of their order. He watched as they looked about in confusion.

"We lost them," cried a short Saber who appeared to be drowning in the fabric of his cloak.

"Hush!" snapped the Saber who stood at the head of the pack. He had a husky tone to his voice. "Two horses and riders don't just disappear. They found out that we were following them."

"How? Shadow Slide is hard to detect by even..." an unusually thin Saber started to say before his meaty companion hushed him with a hand over his mouth.

The behavior of the Sabers embarrassed Ryder. It was clear to him that these were new recruits who were obviously looking for glory or pretending to be the royal agents to get undue respect. He guessed that none of them had actually ever been in a real life or death fight. Just as he was formulating an attack plan, Haven slid into view on a thick branch across from him. Her expression of pity told him that her thoughts about the Sabers matched his. He held a finger to his lips as the pack meandered beneath them.

"We have to capture him or Lord Kaiser will kill us," exclaimed the same short Saber. He looked to be the most frightened of the six.

The Saber at the head of the packed stomped towards him with a growl on his lips. "Shut up before they hear us!"

Just as he turned away to address the other five, Ryder swung down and grabbed the short Saber before quickly disappearing into the tree tops. When the lead Saber turned back around, he jumped upon seeing that the short Saber was gone. Immediately, everyone pulled out their swords, the sound of steel scrapping together unusually loud in the quiet of the forest. The leader shushed his companions with sharp hand gestures.

As the Sabers frantically looked around, Ryder pressed his left hand over their captured companion's mouth. He held him against the trunk of the tree he was perched in. The short Saber was barely half of Ryder's weight and immediately knew that there was no point in resisting. His eyes locked onto Ryder's deep penetrating gaze and he blanched. Ryder reached forward and pressed the thumb of his right hand to the center of the short Saber's forehead. Haven looked on as Ryder closed his eyes, murmuring a string of words under his breath. The short Saber slumped over like a dead weight.

With a heavy thump, the once disappeared companion of the Saber pack dropped to the ground in an unconscious heap. Each one of them jumped with shock and surprise. The leader shoved a Saber with thick brawny arms forward and he stumbled in response. Another Saber with an equally thick frame took a few cautious steps forward.

"Well, is he dead?" the leader snapped. He watched as the brawny armed Saber poked at their unconscious companion.

"He looks like he is sleeping," the Saber dared to answer.

"Care to join your friend or would the permanent sleep of death suit you better?" Ryder mocked once he dropped down to the road. He rose to his full height and squared his broad shoulders. He cocked his head as he waited for an answer.

It took the two Sabers a moment to realize that Ryder was unarmed before they charged forward. They leapt over their fallen companion, expecting the other three Sabers to join them. Like an unseen bolt of lightning, Haven jumped down onto the shoulders of the thin Saber. She quickly flipped him over, slamming him hard on his back and knocking the wind out of him. In the meantime, Ryder had sidestepped the thin Saber's meaty companion, allowing him to get within striking distance. With a strong kick to the torso, Ryder knocked him back full force, breaking half of his ribs. The meaty Saber tripped and fell on top of his winded companion in a heap. He cried out in pain.

"Hey, Haven! Catch!" Ryder called out as he kick up the dropped sword and tossed it towards her.

She snatched it out of the air and deftly whipped the sword around in a circle. "You're next!" she declared as she pointed her newly acquired weapon at the thick framed Saber who had stumbled back from Ryder.

Ryder ducked and dodged the attacks from the brawny armed Saber. A laugh was on his lips as he teased the Saber with openings to attack only to swiftly move out of the way. When he grew bored of the feint, Ryder dropped down and swept his right leg out in a wide arc. He knocked the Saber off of his feet but before he could hit the ground, Ryder grabbed him by the collar and pulled him close to his face.

"Get a good look. This is the face of the man your master

will face on the battlefield," Ryder declared with a confident smirk. "Are you afraid?" The Saber quickly nodded as his teeth chattered from fear. "Good."

With a hard throw, Ryder threw the Saber forward and he collided with the thick framed Saber. They fell in a tangled mass of limbs.

"Hey! I had him!" Haven snapped as Ryder set his hands on his hips.

"Fine. You can take down the captain," Ryder laughed as he gestured towards the shivering leader. His knees shook and knocked together as he proceeded to wet himself from fear.

"Yay!" Haven squealed with delight. She tossed the sword aside as she whipped around.

At that gesture, the leader took off down the road, shouting for help. Haven caught up with him quickly. She leaped forward, flipping over him, and landed directly in his path. The Saber slid to a stop, kicking up a cloud of dust. He tried to turn around only to run straight into Ryder. He fell back on his rear and started to hyperventilate.

Ryder squatted down to the Saber's eye level as Haven stood menacingly behind the Saber. "Now, I have been quite generous in not killing the lot of you. Though certainly any death I could give you would be a pin prick to what your supposed master would do to you. I believe in mercy for the innocent," Ryder stated as he pressed a hand over his heart. He then dropped it. "You and your companions are not fit to be Sabers. Becoming one was an empty promise. What I can offer you is the kind of glory you are truly seeking."

The Saber leader looked past Ryder at his groaning companions before returning his gaze to Ryder. He nodded slowly. "He said that if you are not captured, he will kill us."

"Sounds like the real Kaiser," Haven said as she crossed her arms tightly.

Before the Saber could look back at her, Ryder grabbed his chin and forced him to look directly into his eyes. "If you want to keep your life, and gain the glory you desire, you will go to Dusk and beg a true Saber for a chance to get your honor back. You will seek out Hayden Abendroth. Your short unconscious friend will ensure that you are believed." He tightened his grip on the Saber's jaw. "You are right to fear me for if you and your companions prove deceitful, I will hunt you down and kill you myself."

"A bit harsh," Haven commented as the Saber passed out from the threat. "I don't know if you realize it but you are kind of scary."

Ryder stood up, rubbing his hands together. "In today's

world, I have no time to be soft. I will be blunt if I have to be." He stepped over the Saber to stand at Haven's side. "And do remember who I said I was related to."

Haven untangled her arms and laid a hand on Ryder's left shoulder. She felt the thick cloth bandage beneath his shirt sleeve. She smiled softly. "You are the right kind of scary. Now let's go get Soja."

After fetching their bay horses from where Haven had picketed them, Ryder and Haven continued their fast paced ride to the border. They reached the bridge that crossed the River Shadow southeast of Dusk by midnight. The stone bridge reached between the two banks of the river like a hand reaching out for salvation. On the side that touched the Earthborn territory, vines twisted and held onto the gray stone in a tangled mess. The water rushed in its course a short distance below, splashing around rocks and exposed tree roots.

Ryder dismounted and studied the land on the other side of the river. A natural archway formed by oak limbs loomed over the space where the bridge met the bank. Beyond the archway, a road stretched east into the Earthborn lands and as Ryder knew, towards the city of Agin. He stepped away from his horse as Haven dismounted, grabbing the reins.

"It looks like anyone can just walk on through," she commented.

"The Shadow Mirror is not meant to be truly seen. It is a shield that hides in plain sight," Ryder mused as he slowed to a stop. He bent down and picked up a palm sized rock. With a flick of the wrist, he sent the rock flying. Haven expected it to sail right over the bridge and jumped when it slammed into an invisible wall. "See how the energy ripples? The Mirror is revealed when something contacts it."

"I still don't understand how this power works. I mean if no one can pass it, how are you supposed to?" Haven asked as she watched the bright silver energy dissipate.

Ryder stepped right up to where the rock revealed the Shadow Mirror. "It is an ancient power derived from the Spirit World. Vorin the Dragonlord once told me that it was a crude imitation of the seal that separates our world and that of the Spirits. Very few people have the power to raise a Shadow Mirror. The Daylord for example."

"And Kaiser," Haven pointed out.

Ryder nodded as he lifted his hands and pressed against the shield. Strands of silver energy crept out and wrapped around his arms. "The literature that is out there is scattered when it comes to the mysteries of the Shadow Mirror. A person that successfully raises a Mirror has command over what can pass through. However if a person is related by blood to the raiser, they can pass through without trouble." He began pressing forward encountering a small degree of resistance. "Don't be frightened if I disappear," he stated before he in fact did.

Haven could not help but squeak with shock. She stared at the spot Ryder had just passed through for a long time, straining to see past it.

*****

"Woah!" Soja cried out as Ryder tumbled into him. They both fell to the ground, stunned momentarily. They disengaged from eachother.

"I wasn't sure you would be here," Ryder stated as he brushed the dirt from his knees.

Soja rose up to his feet. "Call it my Saber instinct or that you are moderately predictable." He straightened the bracer on his left forearm. "Judging by the fact that you were able to pass..."

"Don't say it," Ryder growled in warning as he interrupted Soja. "It's hard enough just knowing."

Soja shrugged before he looked back at the Shadow Mirror. He crossed his arms tightly. "So how am I supposed to get through that?"

"Hop on my back. I'll carry you through," Ryder said. He gestured for Soja to hurry.

*****

Haven bit her lip as she saw the silver energy brighten and glow. With an audible snap, Ryder burst through with Soja on his back. He stumbled to regain his balance while Soja quickly rolled off. Soja jerked and swung his arms around, wiping his face.

"I told you it would feel strange," Ryder said, laughing at Soja's furious attempts to brush his body.

"It feels like I just walked through a thick net of spider webs! Please tell me they are not crawling all over me! I hate spiders!" Soja screeched as he continued to dance around and wave his arms.

Ryder laughed as he stepped to Haven's side. "He will break his arm if he whips it around any faster." Haven snickered as she fought the urge to burst out laughing. "You can ride with me now. Soja can take your horse."

"Ok but first I think he has to finish his spider dance," Haven giggled.

Soja harrumphed as he took the offered reins. He swung up on the saddle in a single fluid motion. He watched as Ryder mounted his horse before reaching down to lift Haven. She settled behind Ryder by wrapping her arms around his muscled torso and laying her head on his back. Soja shook his head before turning his horse around with a tug of the reins.

RACHE ATTACKS

Rache sauntered through the streets, a devilish smirk on his face. The hood of his cowl cast shadows that hid his blood red eyes. His muscles twitched with eager anticipation. He sniffed the air deeply, savoring the taste of blood and body heat. All around him the city was sleeping oblivious to the walking danger that lurked. The few stragglers that spotted him immediately slammed doors shut or disappeared down dark side streets.

"Halt," commanded a guard that stepped in front of Rache. The Demon cocked his head as if amused. "What matter of business do you have at this hour?"

Rache stared at the guard through the thin cloth of his mask. He locked eyes with him, slowing his breath and heartbeat into a soft murmur. The sound of the street faded out and the street lanterns dimmed into a lifeless flicker.

"Murder," Rache crooned.

The guard, caught in the illusion of the Demon's eyes, froze with fear. His teeth chattered as he struggled to keep a tight grip on the torch in his hand. When Rache took a step forward, the guard dropped the torch and stumbled back several steps. Rache stepped over the torch, snickering in a low, dark tone.

"What are you?" the guard shivered, barely able to get the words out.

Fear in anyone amused Rache as if it was an affirmation of his great power. "I am revenge."

He tore into the guard, throwing him to the ground. He

ripped the wolf's head helmet off and threw it through a nearby shop window. The guard made the attempt to scream but Rache grabbed his jaw and slammed his mouth shut so hard that he bit his tongue in half. Rache laughed even louder as claws grew out of his finger tips, scratching bloody lines on the guard's face. The guard coughed up a fountain of blood that splattered over Rache's right hand. He dipped a finger from his left hand in the mess and pressed the blood soaked tip to his tongue. A dark and terrible grin slowly formed on his face. He increased the pressure on the guard's jaw, slowly crushing the bone beneath his right hand. The guard began to thrash beneath Rache with diminishing strength as he choked on his own blood. A gurgle bubbled up in the dying guard's chest.

"Oh? Do you have something to say?" Rache mocked. He released the pressure and drew his right hand back. The guard's eyes fluttered before rolling into the back of his head. "I suppose not."

Rache straightened up to his full height and stepped over the dead guard, leaving the body and burning torch in the street. He flexed his right hand, drawing the claws back in. Blood dripped from his finger tips. He brought his hand up and proceeded to lick it clean from the gore. Though he never turned down the chance to consume blood, the blood of guards and low level soldiers tended to be thin and lacking in taste. The street guard he had just killed was no different though in his fear, his blood had a slightly sweet flavor that lingered on Rache's tongue.

The lanterns roared back to life behind him once he turned towards the right, following a twisting pathway to a modest manor home by the south western wall of the city. Rache paused at the edge of the shadows, seeing two gate guards playing a game of dice by firelight. They laughed and joked loudly, shoving eachother when a good toss of the dice was made. Rache smirked as energy surged in his muscles. In a heartbeat, the two guards collapsed dead as Rache paused to pick up a stray die that had been scattered from his quick strike attack. He studied it for a moment before crushing it between his fingertips. The gate was locked but Rache easily ripped it open, bending the metal beneath his grip. His heart began to beat faster as he drew close to the front door. He pulled the door knocker away from the wooden planks and slammed it hard enough to split the wood.

*****

Sasha Parahazur nudged her sleeping husband's shoulder once she heard the loud pounding at the front door. "Darling, someone is at the door."

Baron grumbled and pulled the bedcovers up over his head. He shifted to lay on his left side, avoiding Sasha's annoyed look. She pushed him again, this time shoving him in the back. "Who would call at this hour? It is the middle of the night."

"Perhaps it is my brother. Go check and see before the sound wakes the children," Sasha insisted in a loud whisper. When Baron did not move, she shoved him harder and he grumbled in a half awake groan. "Sai is at least respectful enough not to Shadow Slide his way inside."

Baron sat up on the edge of the bed, giving himself a moment to recover his senses enough to stand up. Once on his feet, he grabbed a house coat and threw it on. "Saber Commander or not, what is so important that he has to wake us up in the middle of the night."

"If it makes you feel any better, I'll come with you. Then we can both lose sleep over greeting my brother at the door," Sasha said before she rolled out of bed.

The couple crept through the upstairs hallway towards the staircase that led down to the family sitting room. Baron paused to pick up a lantern before they both walked into the small foyer. The knocking had ceased just as Baron reached for the door handle.

"It's just the Chancellor's servant," Baron said over his shoulder to Sasha. "How can I help you?"

"If I may enter, I bring your family news that is best said inside by the fire. There is quite the chill in the night air," Rache smoothly said, feigning a subservient voice.

Baron gestured for Rache to enter. Rache took a long step over the threshold before Baron closed the door behind him. He and Sasha led the Demon into the family sitting room where Sasha quickly got a roaring fire going. Rache remained on his feet, declining an offer from Baron to sit. Sasha joined her husband on the couch.

"What news do you have that it could not wait until morning?" Baron asked as Sasha took his hand.

Rache pretended to hesitate before answering. "The great and noble Commander of the Sabers was found dead before the tomb of Akakios."

Sasha fought the urge to wail out in shock while Baron set his arms around her in a tight embrace. He kissed her head in the attempt to comfort her.

"Once his identity was confirmed, the Lord's Chancellor ordered me to bring you the news as soon as possible," Rache said as he bent down. He set a hand on Baron's shoulder. "Despite the late hour, I could not wait."

"I thank you, kind servant. How did my brother in law come to his death?" Baron asked, trying to stay strong for his wife.

The Demon feigned even more sympathy as the memory of killing Sai played back in his mind. "It seems a terrible Demon has entered Cross and slain him."

For a long time, all that could be heard was the crackling of the fire and the restrained comforting of a husband for his suffering wife. Baron spoke softly to Sasha as tears streamed down her face. Her breathing became more ragged from the effort spent mourning her beloved older brother.

"How do we tell the children? They loved their Uncle Sai," Sasha squeaked, her voice weak with sorrow. She buried her head against Baron's shoulder as another series of sobs gripped her.

Dark thoughts entered Rache's mind as he subtlely sniffed the air. There were three children sleeping on the second floor: two boys and a little girl snug in their beds. "The late Commander of the Sabers will be given all honors due to his station for his funeral march," Rache stated in a kind voice. Immediately, the tone felt awkward to the Demon but it was all part of his plan.

"Do you know if he is suffered?" Baron asked as Sasha was incapable of speaking.

Rache's hand slid up to the skin at Baron's neck, revealing a deathly chill in his flesh. He reached around behind him and pulled out Sai's bleached skull. He glanced at it, smirking. "Why don't you ask his bones if he suffered when I snapped his neck." Rache crushed the skull into tiny pieces with the force of his grip. Sasha's face blanched before Rache ripped Baron from her. With a swift kick, the couch was sent flying and crashed into the far wall.

"Baron!" Sasha shrieked as she tried to drag herself from the debris.

Rache lifted Baron up with the inhuman strength of his left arm, keeping a tight grip on his throat. Baron thrashed his legs, hoping to kick the Demon in the knees while he gripped the corded arm. Rache roared with a laugh that shattered the glass mirror above the fireplace. Glass flew everywhere as the windows exploded next. Sasha reflexively covered her head to protect her eyes. Shards rained down on her as she stole a glance at her husband. The sight horrified her. Rache was laughing as Baron's face started to turn blue from lack of air. Courage suddenly welled up inside of her and Sasha leaped up from the floor, wielding a broken chair leg. She made to strike Rache across his back but the Demon reacted faster than she could. He threw Baron at her and both flew into the broken couch.

"Baron! Baron!" Sasha shouted as she slapped his face. She looked up at Rache, a hurt and angry look on her face.

Rache pulled back his cowl and mask, revealing his Demonic identity. He bent down to pick up a large shard, considering its sharp edges for a moment. The light of the fire cast across his body in ghastly shadows as he slowly stood up to his full height. He threw the glass piece aside. Almost as soon as it left his hands, claws erupted from his fingertips in a bloody mess. He stalked towards Sasha as she held Baron on her lap. She shivered with fear as Rache crouched down. He put a claw under her chin and forced her to look him in the eyes.

"Baron is dead, sweetie. I crushed his throat and what you see are his dying gasps. One of my many favorite things to see," Rache mused with a devilish grin. He let out a deep breath. He quickly dragged his claw back, cutting a gash in her chin. "I can bestow upon you the gift of death too if you wish but I have some business to attend to."

Sasha looked down at Baron, ignoring the bloody wound on her chin. Baron's face was a pasty blue. He gasped one last time before his eyes rolled back into his head. She snarled as she looked back at Rache. The Demon had disappeared.

The screams of her three young children in their dying throes echoed all the way downstairs. Sasha made the attempt to get up but collapsed. She looked down at her left leg, seeing a large piece of glass embedded into her thigh. The wound poured copious amounts of blood. Sasha cried profusely, feeling completely helpless to stop the Demon. She held onto Baron's body as she listened to the heavy footsteps that walked from room to room. Only when she had no more tears and her face was red, Rache returned with a devilish grin on his face.

"I thought you Parahazurs were supposed to be fighters until the very end," he mocked as he licked the blood from his fingers.

The sight horrified Sasha. "You monster..."

"But of course. I am Rache after all," came the dark, condescending reply. Rache gestured towards the upstairs. "They certainly saw me for who I am."

Sasha pushed all pain into the back of her mind as she struggled to find confidence. But in the face of Rache's fangs and claws, it was a difficult task. She couldn't help but tremble on the floor as Rache approached. He bent down to her eye level.

"You are so much like you precious brother. So tenacious but," Rache said stroking her cheek with a finger. He jerked it back, the claw cutting into Sasha's skin. He chuckled. "Well I'll stop playing now and just kill you."

"But what?" Sasha quickly asked without meaning to. She tried to push herself back away from him.

Rache held up a finger. "Bargaining for your life I see. What can you offer me?"

Blood dribbled down Sasha's chin as she struggled to collect her thoughts. She couldn't tell him what she knew. She cringed as Rache scraped some of the blood from her chin. He paused to consider the taste of it in his mouth.

"Oh," he said as he licked his lips. He then returned his gaze back. "You see. The blood is very powerful and can hold very important memories." He smacked his lips. "I thank you for your assistance. I think I will let you live a little longer." He held out his hand behind him and a torch from the fire flew to his palm.

The flames around the burning wood crackled hot as Rache brought it down. He touched the torch to the edge of Sasha's skirt and it caught fire. He then stood up and tossed the torch into the middle of the room. The rug lit up as the flames took hold. Rache saluted Sasha before turning to leave.

Rache pulled his hood and mask back into place as he stepped out of the house. He smirked as he heard Sasha's ear piercing screams of horror and pain. He would have preferred to draw out her death but he had bigger prey to take down. Behind him, the heat of the growing fire burst out from the broken windows, catching the nearby trees. The leaves and branches burned quickly and dropped smoulders to the ground. The dry yard grass crackled and popped before swiftly erupting into an uncontrollable fire. The house behind him crumbled as the flames reached into the sky. Behind his cover in a nearby alleyway, Rache watched as the fire brigade came running with buckets of water. He smirked as the flames took over the neighboring house.

"Now to pay a visit to the Rokars on this glorious evening," Rache said to himself.

SACRIFICE

"We have to take a stand against Kaiser and his monster! He has driven our Prince away and who knows what else!" Donovan Shunga shouted, pounding a fist on the heavy wood table. "It has been eight days since Ryder brought Soja over the border and we have done nothing!"

Zoras Rokar sat in his chair, fingertips pressed together as he considered Donovan's words. "We need to tread lightly for we do not know where his influence begins and ends. With the magic at the border, help cannot get to us and we cannot escape." He looked towards Ryder and his son Soja. He was thankful that Ryder had escaped captivity and brought Soja through the mysterious Shadow Mirror. It still confused him as to how Ryder was able to cross it and bring Soja back into the Shadowborn lands. He had his suspicions and strongly believed that both his son and Ryder knew the answer.

"Kaiser or a member of his bloodline are the only ones capable of unlocking the border and crossing it freely. He mimicked the blood key by providing his allies and loyalists with seals made of silver and his own blood," Ryder said with arms crossed tightly. He looked over at Soja and shook his head when the Saber tried to speak.

"If you have found a way through the border, we have to know," Zoras said sternly.

Though society said that Zoras outranked him, Ryder knew that Zoras still saw him as a royal Prince and the rightful

Shadowlord. "Passage through the border is not our greatest issue. Our greatest problem sits in Cross. You do not get to Kaiser without going through his Demon Rache. Unlike in Crossroads, there are no Spirit wards here to deter his power from releasing. Not even a Saber can hope to compete with him at his full strength."

"You could," Zoras said as he studied Ryder closely. Kaiser's revelations roared back into his mind. "Like the Demon, you are more than you appear."

Ryder shifted his weight between his feet. "Like Rache, you will not like what you find under the surface."

Zoras then turned to his son with a stern expression on his face. "If you know something that could put all of our efforts in jeopardy, you must tell us. I will not risk going forward without knowing all the facts about those who fight for the cause."

"It is not my place to say, Father," Soja said, looking down at his feet. He stole a look at Ryder.

It was frustrating the ex Saber Commander to no end. "If it were not for my damn loyalty to you, Ryder, I would order you to speak."

An uneasy silence fell between the four Shadowborn men as Ryder and Zoras held their standoff. Donovan and Soja looked back and forth in a mixed degree of worry and nerves.

"Do you want my help or not?" Ryder asked in a flat tone.

Zoras let out a tense sigh. "I will need answers first, Peredur Coba-Silvanus," he said using Ryder's formal name.

"Father, this is no time to be pressuring anyone willing to help us take down Kaiser. I trust that Ryder is acting with the interests of the rebellion close to his heart. You must trust in that," Soja said, jumping in to the standoff between the two men.

"Soja is right. There is a time and place for questions and answers but now is not that time," Donovan agreed.

"With Aku under his control, Kaiser can command the armed forces to do his will. I don't know how many Sabers have been swayed," Soja piped in, being one of two Sabers in the room. "Hayden Abendroth has already assembled a defense team with Lady Haven to stop the attacks on our people. But we need more under our banner."

The personal study of Zoras Rokar was that of a scholar; book shelves full of leather bound tomes and dusty parchment scrolls. Walls were covered in maps except for the space directly behind his desk chair. A large family tree occupied the space in a gold frame. The furniture with its elegant craftsmanship hinted at the wealth of the Rokars. It was the home office of the head of the council but now it served as a base for the rebel movement.

"How many are under your command, Donovan?" Zoras asked calmly.

"One hundred that would die for my family's service and that of the throne. There are others but I am not certain of their loyalty," he dutifully answered.

Zoras then turned to his son. "Are there any you can trust to our cause? Even a few Sabers would be helpful."

"The Abendroth Sabers. I would trust them with my life," Soja replied. "There are five of them not including Hayden now that Rothe is dead."

Zoras nodded as he calculated numbers in his head before turning to look at Ryder. "You are the sole Silvanus blood relative in our rebellion. That alone means a great deal."

"If you intend to raise me to the throne, I will not accept it," Ryder stated firmly.

Zoras held up a hand. "I have long understood your position, but there may come a day," he replied before drawing his hand back down. "As I was saying, you as a Silvanus blood relative can inspire the people that the throne has not abandoned them. In that, you are important to us."

"We are all important to this rebellion," Donovan pointed out as he took a step forward. "What will you have us do?" he asked Zoras directly.

A deep heavy hearted breath escaped Zoras' chest as he considered the options. He sat forward to study the map on the table. A thick line marked the magic bound border of the Shadowborn lands. He traced the eastern border with his eyes. He touched the tip of a finger on Cross and his home. He drew his finger back on the great eastern road.

"Gather as many allies as can be found. Have them meet here," Zoras paused to point to a spot that was northeast of Cross. "We must not engage our enemy just yet." Donovan, Soja and Ryder nodded.

"What of Onyx and Aku?" Ryder asked.

"I believe that Aku is lost to us. But we must rescue the young Prince. He is a youth but his presence will inspire all. Find him and be quick as I don't think we can delay our war for too long," Zoras said as he stood up from his seat.

"For truth," Donovan said putting a hand in.

Soja quickly followed. "For truth."

"For the throne," Zoras stated adding his hand.

"For peace," Ryder said. His hand then slipped to his sword hilt as darkness fell on his heart.

"I feel it too," Zoras quickly said.

The four rebels were all able to feel the close presence of

something terrible; Rache was coming. Zoras quickly began directing their escape in silence. Maps were folded up and notes were packed in Zoras' travel bag. Only nods and hand gestures were exchanged between them.

There was a chill in the air as Zoras directed the household towards the woods while Donovan looked around nervously.

"Where is the beast?" Donovan whispered.

"Close," Ryder said quickly. He put a hand on Donovan's shoulder. "If I must face this beast, take this letter to Haven."

Donovan sat a hand on Ryder's shoulder after pocketing the folded piece of paper. "Stay strong, Peredur."

Soja interrupted with a nervous expression. "We need to hurry."

"Too late, my dears," Rache said with a devilish grin. He sauntered forward, his pale skin gleaming in the moonlight.

Ryder pushed Donovan in the direction of the woods as he took up sword beside Soja. "Soja and I will distract Rache. Get everyone to the main base." Donovan nodded before disappearing into Shadow Slide.

"Remember your speed," Ryder reminded the young Saber at his side.

"And you, your strength," Soja replied.

Rache pouted. "Why do you have swords and I don't? It's not fair." He stamped his feet like a crying child before gathering himself. "Oh I remember!"

The Demon zipped forward with sharp claws extended. His crimson hair whipped around his face. With deadly speed, he covered the distance and attacked Soja first. Soja bent backwards at the waist to avoid Rache's sweeping arm. Just as the arm passed over him, Soja twisted his body and slashed with his sword at Rache's back. With unnatural agility, Rache slipped down into a drop kick and swung his left leg around, knocking Soja to his back. The impact of the ground jolted Soja and he lost his grip on his sword.

"Don't forget about me!" Ryder shouted as he tackled Rache to the ground. He released his grip and flipped over the Demon. He ripped his sword from its sheath and stabbed down at Rache's chest.

Rache snarled and rolled out of striking distance, flipping up to his feet. Soja had rearmed himself during the direction change with Ryder. Rache feigned submission with hands up as Soja and Ryder drew close. He then dropped his hands and snapped his fangs.

"You are but child's play. I have fought better opponents than a Saber child and royal bastard," he challenged boldly.

No answer came as Soja and Ryder rushed forward with swords held out to the side. They split at the last possible second and slipped into a simultaneous Shadow Slide. Rache rolled his eyes at the move as he quickly locked on to their aura signatures. Ryder's aura was a strong and powerful one while Soja's aura was sharp and quick.

Soja dashed in from Rache's right, slipping out of Shadow Slide. He brought his sword down in a sweeping arc, catching the tip on Rache's sleeve. He quickly went back into Shadow Slide as Rache turned to retaliate. Ryder appeared before him and in a pile driving tackle; he shoved his sword into Rache's torso. The force drove Rache back and he roared out loud, sweeping his right arm around. Claws met flesh as Rache tore at Ryder's left side.

Though in searing pain, Ryder slipped into the protective Shadow Slide to avoid a second strike. He held on tightly to his concentration and focus as he sped around Rache.

Rache stood up and looked down at the sword in his stomach. "Amateur!" he shouted as he pulled it free.

Soja flew in, sword held up to cleave Rache's head from his shoulders. He spun to Rache's right side, spinning and swinging his sword low to cut his legs out from under him. Rache twisted to his left, stabbing Ryder's sword towards Soja. The blade cut across Soja's right shoulder as he continued to spin, aiming his sword at Rache's left arm.

The two twisted and moved in an intricate sword dance. Soja's speed was his greatest weapon as he darted in and out of reach. His movements were both calculated and fluid. Rache's strikes were heavy and packed a lot of power. Whenever the swords collided, the steel sung a metallic screech as sparks flew.

Ryder then charged in after a glance from Soja. He wrapped his arms around Rache and tackled him again to the ground. The Demon roared with rage as he attempted to throw Ryder's heavy weight off of him. Like a wild stallion, Rache bucked and bellowed. Ryder shifted his right arm and pressed down on the Demon's shoulders.

Soja spun his sword around and laid the blade on the back of Rache's neck. "Rache, Demon of the Darklands. You are hereby committed to execution by the name of the Shadowlord."

Rache bared his fangs, eye turning blood red. "It will take more than a threat of execution to stop me!"

With a great burst of energy, Rache threw Ryder off his back. His skin bubbled as a map of red veins blanketed his skin. His bones cracked and realigned as muscles swelled. Huge claws replaced his fingers that were black as night and sharp as any sword. His jaws grew into a short snout that resembled that of a rabid wolf. Saliva dripped from the sharp teeth. He roared at the top of his lungs, the sound so loud that it shook the ground.

"Run!" Soja yelled to Ryder as he stood between him and Rache.

"No! I will not let another Saber die for me!" Ryder shouted back. He began to charge up a massive amount of Spirit energy for his Spirit Fire.

"I will not let you fall into Kaiser's hands again for you will never escape a second time. Now run! The bloodline must endure!" Soja roared with the cold confidence of his loyalty.

"No! I don't have a family! You do!" he argued.

"You have Haven. Now go! I swore my life to protect the Silvanus bloodline and that includes you!" Soja said as he shoved Ryder back. "I will die if I have to."

Ryder hesitated. He didn't want to leave Soja alone to face Rache. The Demon was certain to rip him to shreds. "What of your father?"

"Tell him I died a Saber in service of the Shadowlord," Soja said with absolute conviction. He began to step away towards Rache.

It was the hardest decision Ryder ever had to make when he left Soja. He knew that Soja was headed towards certain death. He ran hard and fast blocking out the sound of the fight behind him. His left side burned as his chest heaved from the extreme effort. He then heard the running footfalls of a great wolf.

"Follow me!" Omu ordered when he came in close to Ryder. "Now is your time, son of Shadow Night!"

Though he did not truly understand why Omu came to him, Ryder matched his pace with the Spirit Wolf until both slipped into Shadow Slide.

COUSINS MEET AGAIN

Onyx looked down at the tattered map in his hands, trying to make sense of it. He quickly realized that knowing how to read maps was one skill but applying that skill in a real situation was something else entirely. He groaned as he crumbled it up and tossed it aside. He slumped back against the tree trunk and slid down to the ground.

"This is my homeland. Why do I feel so lost?" he asked himself as he looked up through the tree canopy. Stars blinked through the heavy cloud cover. He let out a deep breath of exhaustion.

The decision to leave was so easy to make but Onyx felt that the act was the most difficult thing ever. He picked and pulled at the grass by his feet before tossing the shredded bunch aside. He reached for the crumpled up map and flattened it back out before him. With a finger, he retraced his path back to Cross before dragging his finger over to the River Shadow. He tapped on the bridge marker. That was where he had to go.

Thundering footfalls grew closer and closer. Onyx jumped up, grabbing the map and his pack. The tree branches shook just before a great wolf burst through and slid to a stop in the clearing. Right behind him was a Shadowborn that had been in a grueling fight.

The wolf straightened up. "Son of Shadow Night, we meet again." It was Omu!

Onyx was relieved to see the Spirit Wolf. "Well met, Omu,"

he replied with a bow of the head. He then turned his attention to the Shadowborn, realizing that it was his cousin Ryder.

Ryder bore a sense of hard experience and a tough nature in his eyes. It matched his soldier's frame that was a trait of a Silvanus blood relative. Onyx then saw long bloody gashes on the left side of Ryder's torso that exposed the muscle underneath. The wounds looked painful but his cousin showed no sign of hurt in his expression. If his clothes were not blood stained and his hair groomed neatly, he would have passed for a noble. He looked like a true Shadowlord and Onyx found himself jealous.

"There is no time for pleasantries. We have to get to the base before Rache comes after me," Ryder said with a hint of urgency.

"Peace, Peredur," Omu admonished. "I brought you here for a reason. No longer will the sons of Shadow Night's bloodline be divided in a time of great trouble." The wolf looked directly at Onyx. "You can not run now when your people need you."

"I'm not running," Onyx lied. He cringed when he saw both Omu's and Ryder's knowing gazes. He set his bag down at his feet as the great black wolf paced around the two. "I thought that you were being held captive somewhere in Cross or so Kaiser hinted at," he directed at Ryder.

Ryder sighed deeply. "By Kaiser's Demon in my father's tomb."

"A blasphemy to the peace of the dead," Omu spit out as the fur on his hackles raised up. He shook his big head, closing his eyes. A soft growl escaped his mouth. "You two are what is left of Shadow Night's blood line. It is the responsibility of both of you to secure the throne against that defiler."

"We need the Daylord. We can't hope to defeat Kaiser without him," Onyx reasoned.

"We can and we will even if I have to rip his traitorous heart out myself. You must learn to do what I did one hundred years ago: to not let your fear of him rule you," Ryder stated firmly. Onyx noticed a hint of sorrow in his voice.

"But I am not a warrior like you," Onyx said meekly.

Ryder touched his shoulder. Onyx flinched from the touch, his shoulder still in pain from Kaiser's beating. Without a word, Ryder delicately felt around the muscle before suddenly pulling Onyx's arm and shifting the joint back into place. Onyx shrieked from the pain but felt a sense of relief in his shoulder. "You can be if you try. Strength is more than physical being. It is the ability to decide when to raise the sword or the shield. That is something you will not learn in a trainer's classroom." He poked Onyx in the chest. "You have to see it for yourself."

"A magic barrier seals the border. Even now, I feel its draining effect," Omu said as he looked around at the night sky. "It is an ancient power much like that present in you two."

Onyx let out a deep breath as he thought of his poor father still in Kaiser's grip. But he did not feel ready to face him. "I can't," he admitted in a whisper.

"Remember what Master Erebus once told you. You have greatness in you. Both of you do," Omu stated as he looked first at Onyx and then at Ryder.

They watched as Omu dissipated into the blackness of the woods. Soon the only sound was the rustling of the leaves.

"In these times, our people look to the sons of Shadow Night. Without us, who will lead them out of darkness?" Ryder mused as he stared at the spot where Omu had been standing.

"But I can't face him. He is so much older and stronger than the both of us," Onyx repeated in defeat. He picked up his bag and slung it over his shoulder. "I can't hope to compete."

Ryder sighed. "You are right to be afraid but don't let your fear control you. I ran away from my home once because of fear. But now I realize my place is here." He closed his eyes and bowed his head. "And in my heart, I know it is right."

His cousin's speech was unexpected but moving. Onyx too then bowed his head and closed his eyes, thinking of everything and everyone that he loved. He loved Cross and the lively energy of the people. He loved his father and wanted him to feel free again. He wanted to show Luna the city he called home. He then thought of his promise to Luna. He put a hand over his heart as he remembered the pleasant memories of Crossroads.

"I hope you can Shadow Slide," Ryder said as he took a few steps towards the north.

"Of course I can," Onyx snapped without really meaning to.

Ryder scoffed. "You have probably never travelled any great distance in Shadow Slide. If you feel yourself slipping, focus on my Spirit. It will keep you tethered to the world so you do not become overwhelmed and descend into the darkness."

"Can't I just follow you in Shadow Slide?" Onyx asked.

"Obviously no one has taught you the finer points of using Spirit energy," Ryder chuckled softly as he set a hand on Onyx's shoulder. "You need to find a real teacher and you will certainly find one where we are going."

THE REBEL HIDEOUT

Ryder led Onyx north of Cross to a high mountain settlement surrounded by broken peaks. Only a small crooked path provided access. The trees were covered in faded bark with a crown of dry leaves. The air was chilling to the bone. Onyx thought to comment to his cousin about the conditions but could not spare his thoughts long enough to avoid taking a fall down the side of the rock face. He saw that Ryder walked with confidence and balance, finding the sturdiest footholds.

Up ahead was a sturdy gate made of petrified wood. Ryder and Onyx paused before it. A silver armored guard stepped forward out of Shadow Slide and looked them both up and down. He nodded and with a silent gesture of his head, he directed them forward through the gateway. Once they passed inside, the gate was quickly shut and locked behind them. Onyx hid behind Ryder as everyone in the open space looked over at them both. No one dared to utter a whisper.

"Follow me closely," Ryder directed in a low voice. He led Onyx to a stone building that connected to the back wall. With a bow of the head, the guards let them pass without question.

The room inside was set up like a command center and at the head of the table was Zoras Rokar. He looked up and immediately dismissed everyone else in the room. They left without protest, bowing their heads towards Ryder and Onyx. Once they were gone, Zoras' shoulders slumped and he bore a haggard expression.

"Kaiser has seen fit to gather his allies in force and strike out at anyone that opposes him even in the few days since we parted," the old councilor blurted out. He ran his fingers through his hair. "Do you know what happened to Soja? I have not seen or heard from him."

"Your son defended the bloodline of Shadow Night to the end and thus allowed for my escape," Ryder stated, not holding anything back. "I do not know his fate beyond that."

Zoras slumped back into his chair. The news weighed heavily on him. He then looked at Onyx. "Long have I tried to defend the throne of your ancestor from darkness. I have done much to make sure his bloodline would not die. Now it seems I am looking upon the last two sons of the Silvanus line. "

"My father is still alive," Onyx argued.

"Your father has been dead since Kaiser saw fit to kill him and make him a puppet. Kaiser's treachery is beyond anything the Immortal Truth could guard against," Zoras admitted.

The truth of his words hurt Onyx to the core. He nearly collapsed with the realization until he felt Ryder's strong hand on his shoulder. How could he have all the courage and confidence in the world when he had nothing. But Onyx realized that fact was what made his cousin so much stronger than him. Ryder ultimately had lost everything when Akakios was executed and his mother murdered. He had no siblings and no family that he was even remotely close to.

"Where are Donovan and Hayden?" Ryder asked, showing concern.

"Leading attack groups. Hayden is east of Cross and Donovan is on the outskirts of Umbra," Zoras reported as he flattened out the map before him. "Haven is here."

Ryder leaned over the map to the location Zoras pointed at. "Always eager to prove herself but no one knows that place better than her. I taught her well."

"A female Commander? One that you trained?" Onyx asked curiously for he did not know of many women in military office. He quickly noticed how Zoras looked to Ryder to explain.

"You have been surrounded by men. Yes, women can command our soldiers and few warriors are as deadly as her. Our allies are few against Kaiser. We take every loyal volunteer," Ryder explained. "We need a plan for Kaiser will not sit still for long with Onyx and myself outside of his reach."

"You have clearer insight into his mind better than most people. I look to you for advice," Zoras quickly said, looking at Ryder like he was a foot soldier before a general.

Ryder stood deep in thought, chewing on a fingernail. He

stopped to cross his arms tightly and stepped away from the table. Onyx watched as Ryder slowly paced back and forth. Ryder then paused and appeared ready to speak but quickly continued to pace. It was strangely fascinating to Onyx as he observed his cousin whisper to himself, discussing some plan or maneuver. Ryder really looked like a battle hardened commander who was careful in thought but quick in action.

"We need to strike at Kaiser deep within his own circle. We need to do it hard and fast before he can retaliate. But first, we need to get Aku away from him. I will take Onyx back to Cross and we will rescue Aku from Kaiser's imprisonment. Then we can formulate a more thorough battle plan with all the rebel commanders," Ryder finally said as he looked up, first locking eyes with Onyx and then with Zoras.

Onyx gulped. He had once thought himself a capable warrior but as he had been told multiple times, he was just a child. He was not ready for a real battle. But he was also not going to admit it. He wanted to prove to himself that he was just as much a Silvanus warrior as Ryder. And he desparately wanted to rescue his father.

"Only a son of Shadow Night's blood would be so bold," Zoras stated. "The guard outside shall see that you two are outfitted with proper armor and weapons," he directed with a gesture towards the door. "But first, you are deserving of rest."

*****

Once Ryder and Onyx had received their equipment, they carried the armor in silence and went to the sword smith to have the blades sharpened.

"I am afraid," Onyx admitted as the smith grinded and shaped with screeching accuracy.

"Then you are more sane than most. History has gifted us with Shadow Night's blood and the Shadowborn look to us whether we want it or not," Ryder said sternly as he tightened the bracer on his left arm, testing the fit. "Think of who you wish to fight for."

Onyx took a deep breath and let it out slowly. He thought of his father and Luna, the two people in the world that mattered most to him. If his father was indeed dead, his Spirit was trapped and it was his duty as his son to see that it was set free. But Luna was a different matter entirely. And the enemy he faced shook him to the core. He had thought that he had the courage to do what he must but now that moment seemed like a fleeting memory.

Ryder sensed his distress. "What I said earlier is still true. And we do not go to Cross without a decent plan. Rache is the greater force and I will fight him myself. It is up to you to rescue your father."

Courage was slowly returning to him but Onyx could not ignore his fear. He took another deep breath. "How do you do it? How do you fight and kill?"

Ryder sighed deeply. "Fighting is an expression of physical might and mental power. Killing is just an end result against a perceived threat. I do not enjoy it but I know it is right. Think of yourself as a Saber defending the throne to the utter end. They do it because they love their Lord and people."

"Then we are Sabers going to save the throne," Onyx said. Ryder nodded as he took his newly sharpened sword. His stomach then rumbled loudly. "I could use something to eat though."

"We can take this equipment to our quarters before joining Zoras. It is no use to storm Cross tired and on an empty stomach," Ryder pointed out. Onyx nodded and sheathed his sword.

The activity of the hideout was that of an army preparing for battle. Forges roared to life with sword and armor smiths crafting weapons, shields, and anything else that could be used in the coming war. Many of the Shadowborn dropped to their knees or bowed their heads when they saw Ryder and Onyx. Onyx accepted their respect with a trained bow of the head but Ryder appeared to ignore it entirely. It was only right since Onyx was the heir to the throne and his cousin was just a royal bastard.

"Can it be done if Rache is protecting Kaiser?" Onyx asked.

"Anything is possible so long as you have the courage to face what is to come," Ryder simply replied.

TRUTH AND LOYALTY

Ryder left Onyx with the armor smith so that a full suit could be fitted properly. He sensed his cousin's apprehension about going to Cross but more importantly, Ryder saw Onyx's jealousy. He would have to break his cousin of the mindset before they could leave. First on Ryder's agenda was to deal with Zoras in a long overdue meeting. As he walked towards the small office Zoras had greeted him in, his mind hardened with a mass of angry words that he could barely make sense of. There was a lot that Ryder wanted to say and needed to say. He had to clear his mind before going to Cross just like his younger cousin. Both of them, he believed, needed to be absolutely focused on the difficult task ahead.

As he expected, Zoras was still in the command office, leaning over a map that had been stretched out over the table. The old politician looked up and grinned. Ryder stopped on the other side of the table and crossed his arms tightly.

"To what do I owe the pleasure?" Zoras asked as he quickly marked a proposed rebel outpost.

"Like I am sure you told Kaiser, it is time to drop the pretenses and speak plainly. I know that he told you," Ryder said harshly.

Zoras let out a deep breath and slowly straightened his posture. "You are as astute as your grandfather for he indeed told me the last time we met. Given a few more minutes in his company, I might have lost my head such is his terrible threat." He looked over Ryder. "Are you here to finish the job?"

"In all the years you have known me, you honestly think that I am like him?" Ryder frowned, his fingers digging into his arms. He fought the urge to curse.

"Well you are his heir. You are the last of the Adonis line. Farlander blood flows as strongly in your veins as it does in his. You are both harsh and resolute when you have decided on a path. You are both frightenly strong and powerful in your bearing. About the only difference I can think of is that his kindness is false. Yours is at least remotely real," Zoras explained. It was obvious he had thought about the answer for a long time.

Ryder quickly picked up on Zoras' posture and movements. The old politician was clearly threatened by him. Zoras appeared as an arrow ready to be fired from a bow. His hand dropped to the hilt of a knife belted on his left hip. He was ready to defend himself against the perceived threat Ryder presented. At first, Ryder was angry for it was a sign that Zoras perceived him to be as dangerous as Kaiser.

"Knowing this full and well, you still allowed me into your presence. You still act as if you wish that I take the throne with your support. How can I trust you just like how can you trust me?" Ryder directly asked. He dropped his arms, immediately seeing Zoras tighten his grip on the knife hilt.

"Because you are still a Silvanus by the blood of your father," Zoras said as his fingers relaxed and dropped away from the knife. "No one is perfect, Ryder. You are not and I am not."

"Stop trying to placate me, Zoras. Stop trying to kiss up to me. If I have one thing to thank Kaiser for, it is the ability to know when someone is speaking with an alterior motive," Ryder growled harshly. "Ever since I was born, people have seen fit to determine what my future was going to be. Take a military assignment, become a Saber, or take the throne of the Shadowborn. Each one of these you have pushed on me and have never relented. Well it is time that you know what I really think. If you want me to fight with you and not against you, you will be wise and listen to what I have to say."

Zoras's hand drifted back to his knife hilt. He squared his jaw. "I understand that perhaps I have been..."

"No! You will not speak until you have heard everything I need to say!" Ryder shouted before regaining control of himself. "What you have desired of me for the last century is more than just assuming a title. You are asking me to give up my life to rule a nation not only as a politician but as a general. You are asking me to become Shadow Night. I am not Shadow Night and I never will be. You need to let go of this ideal that I am some kind of savior."

The tension in the room was so thick that it could be cut with a knife. Ryder appeared to grow in size while Zoras appeared to diminish and shrink. The candles dimmed to the point of barely illuminating their faces. Every hint of gold or silver dulled.

"I have to believe in something," Zoras admitted in a pained tone. "You only see that what I desire but you do not understand why."

Ryder immediately felt horrible for having yelled at Zoras. He had come into the room, determined to lay bare his thoughts on the Rokar family's constant pressure. For the first time, he began to think that there was more to the pressure than just stopping Kaiser. Kaiser had done a terrible amount of damage to his own life. It was like he was a virus infecting everyone he interacted with, causing them pain and madness before ultimately taking their lives.

"We all have reason to hate Kaiser. I know that he destroyed your father and murdered your mother. You need to know what he has taken from me," Zoras said. His hand dropped away from the knife hilt. "I lost my parents right after I became a Saber. They were returning to the family estate after the graduation ceremony when they disappeared. A moon cycle later, their remains were found. Lord Sin pulled Kaiser back into the fold to investigate as the top authority on Demons. I ran my own investigation alongside that of the throne, trusting only my instincts. Years went by with no answers. Right after I became Commander of the Sabers, Kaiser appeared to congratulate me with a warm embrace only to whisper in my ear about my parents' fate. I wanted to throttle him for I knew then that he was responsible. I tried to go to Lord Sin but Kaiser was always there. Everytime I tried to speak, the words never came though I knew exactly what I wanted to say."

"Shadow Blind. He must have casted it on you when he whispered in your ear," Ryder said knowingly. Zoras looked back at him to explain. "It's a forbidden Spirit technique that can disrupt one's senses."

"Somehow I am not surprised," Zoras exclaimed as he rubbed his forehead. "How else could Kaiser control so many people? I am sure there is more that you can tell me."

Ryder nodded. "I know that Kaiser is responsible for the death of your wife. He kills to intimidate."

"And now he has my son," Zoras managed to say before breaking down. It was a long time before he managed to get his emotions back under control. "I have to believe in something. Ever since I was a small boy, I was told of the noble might of the Silvanus family. With all of the hardships and losses I have suffered, I knew that I could depend on the throne to save me. So long as a Silvanus son sits on the throne, all will become right in the world. I want to hold on to that belief."

Ryder let out a deep breath. "I will not sit on the throne. Not unless there is no one else. Until then, I will help you fight this war."

Zoras then began laughing as he leaned over the map covered table. "It seems we have needed to have this conversation for a very long time. Perhaps we should finish it with a knock out brawl like most men but I have a feeling that I must get in line. I am certain that Haven wants to deal with you first."

"Do you honestly think that Aku can not be saved? How far gone is he?" Ryder asked.

"He is a dead soul walking. There is no saving him and I know that Onyx will have a hard time dealing with that fact. He will need all the support he can get," Zoras stated as he straightened up. "What is your plan for Cross?"

Ryder stepped towards the table and pulled over a diagram of the capital city. He stretched it out, setting a small wolf's head paperweight to hold down the edge. He scanned the grid patterns of the roads and alleys. Ryder quickly realized how long it had been since he had actually travelled the streets of Cross.

"This is the most current map of the city?" Ryder quickly asked.

"It was drawn last spring during the roadway review," Zoras answered. He pointed at the northeast section of the city. "Renovations are on the schedule for this part of Cross so there won't be as many people here."

"Which means a death or two will not be quickly noticed. My gut tells me that if I am to confront Rache, it will be here," Ryder stated as he scratched his chin. He looked back at the spot. "I will distract him long enough so Onyx can retrieve his father."

"I will assemble the rebel leaders here to plan for the next step. We will wait for your return to officially declare war," Zoras promised. He smiled and nodded in encouragement.

FAMILY BONDS

Both Onyx and Ryder welcomed a moment of rest though the expectations of what was to come weighed heavily on them. Onyx saw the storming of Cross as a daunting task considering he was only eighteen. Ryder looked at it as just another battle, fully aware of what he was facing. Onyx followed his older cousin through the rock tunnels, trying to figure out his thoughts. The deeper they went into the mountain, the heavier his heart became. He looked towards Ryder who walked with his shoulders straight and head held up proudly.

"How can you be so calm?" Onyx started to say before deciding he didn't want to ask. He hung his head.

Ryder chuckled. "You've never experienced a real fight before. Where your opponent wants to kill you. What you are feeling is natural and nothing to be ashamed of," he explained as he tightened his grip on the burning torch in his right hand. The skin on the back of his hand appeared dry and cracked as if it had been burned.

Zoras had found them quarters that kept them separate from the rest of the rebel soldiers and allies. He seemed to do whatever it took to please them, in particular Ryder. He acted like a blabbering servant despite his age and ranking as a former Saber Commander and member of the Shadow Council.

"How old are you?" Onyx found himself asking as they stepped inside the medium sized room.

Ryder set the torch in a bracket next to the door and walked around the room, lighting the oil lamps. "Older than you."

"Well I know that you are older than one hundred since everyone has said you left Cross a century ago," Onyx said as he sat down on one of the two available beds, testing how soft the mattress was. It was no feather bed but he knew he could sleep just as peacefully. He ran his hands over the blanket, noticing a pile of clean clothes that had been laid out for him.

Ryder pulled off his shirt, dropping the tattered and dirty piece at his feet. His back was to Onyx and he could see the extensive map of black ink across his shoulders and down his spine. Scars crisscrossed through the artwork, giving the appearance that Ryder had been whipped many times over. He then spotted a line of deep scars on the back of his right shoulder where it appeared that a Gryphon had attacked him.

"In Gryphon culture, an outsider is accepted after he is taloned in the right shoulder and does not shout out in pain. It is one of their rites of initiation," Ryder explained before he pulled on a clean linen shirt. "To commemorate the moment, I had a Fireborn artist tattoo my back with the wings of a Phoenix and my proper birth name: Peredur." He finished changing into the full set of clean clothes before sitting down on the opposite bed.

Onyx felt better once he was in clean and comfortable clothes and he lay back on the bed, staring at the stone ceiling. "How often do outsiders get the Gryphon rites of initiation?"

"Not often," Ryder replied as he rubbed the tension out of his legs. "To even be considered as an outsider, you have to be at least two hundred years old."

"You're really that old?" Onyx asked as he sat up.

Ryder smiled. "I'm two hundred fifty years old. I'm actually older than your father and mother."

"Wow. You are old. You must have never lost a fight," Onyx commented as he lay back down.

"Oh I have lost a few. The result of a fight is not about winning or losing. It is about survival," Ryder stated before rolling back his right shirt sleeve. His right forearm had a blackened hand print wrapped around it. He rolled his arm to reveal the back side where five deep claw marks sunk into the muscle. "I am lucky to have survived this fight against Rache."

Onyx sighed deeply as he listened to Ryder get up from the bed and step over to the wash basin. "I've never lost a fight."

Ryder scoffed as he scrubbed the blackened skin. Flakes fell off into the basin revealing a deep red scar. "You have never been in a real fight."

"I have too!" Onyx shouted as he shot up to his feet. "I've fought with Commander Parahazur!"

"Have you ever been in a fight where your opponent was trying his hardest to kill you? I doubt it therefore a training fight with the old Saber is not a real fight," Ryder challenged.

Onyx wanted to fire back with a comment that would tear at the hard veneer of his warrior cousin but nothing good enough came to mind. He frowned and crossed his arms tightly. The room now felt smaller and more like a prison cell instead of a relaxing oasis from the world outside. He tried to ignore the rumble in his stomach from hunger and the burn in his throat from thirst. He wanted to appear as tough and strong as Ryder. Especially since Zoras was treating Ryder like a respected royal. He wasn't a royal! He was a bastard son! He was supposed to be worthless! Onyx's thoughts yelled at him with fuming jealousy.

The jealous thoughts continued when he and Ryder met with Zoras for a small evening repast. He scowled in his seat, picking at his plate of roasted venison and root vegetables. Ryder had been given the distinguished seat at the head of the table with Zoras to his left and Onyx to his right. It was a clear sign that Zoras saw something great in the bastard son. It wasn't right since he was a legitimate born Prince and heir to the throne. Why did his cousin get the seat of honor? Was Zoras Rokar some sort of traitor?

"We are standing on the edge with nowhere to go but forward," Zoras stated as he leaned back in his wooden chair.

"Are we ready for open war against Kaiser? The entire north has been afraid to openly oppose him for so long that it makes me wonder if we are even capable of defeating him," Ryder reasoned before drinking the remaining contents of his mug.

"I seem to be looking at a few rays of hope here that I haven't had since the days of my childhood. My father used to tell me stories about Shadow Night Silvanus and Bane Arlis by the fireside. Such magnificent fighters," Zoras stated with reverence. He briefly leaned back to wave a server away. "I have two Silvanus sons here before me."

Finally! Some recognition! Onyx found himself smiling now that Zoras had acknowledged his royal rank. He sat up straighter and held his head up proudly.

"You have one Silvanus warrior," Ryder stated firmly. "Or more to the point, one with actual experience."

The good mood was gone as fast as it had appeared and Onyx sunk down in his chair. He lost his appetite and pushed his plate away from him. "The Commander of the Sabers and the Commander of the Armed Forces taught me how to fight."

Ryder laughed but Zoras remained silent. "Sai was a royal purist and wouldn't have harmed a hair on your head. Morin is

Kaiser's lackey and wouldn't have cut you unless his master ordered it. If you want to truly know how to fight, I can teach you."

Though he was frustrated with his cousin, he had heard plenty of stories about Ryder's travels and experience. Perhaps there was something he could learn from him. His jealousy started to decrease as he contemplated learning a fighting move from one of the other nations. Onyx began to wonder how people like the Earthborn or the Airborn fought.

"I can have the practice yard cleared for you," Zoras suggested as servers came to clear the plates and utensils away.

The practice yard was really just the open space between the stone buildings that were carved into the rim of the mountain. There was no roof which meant no protection from the elements. The space was nearly free of grass save for a few sparse patches. Any wood in the construction came from the lower slopes. The dirt was gray and held very little moisture on the surface of the ground. Boot prints ran off in trails of hurried and relaxed strides.

A lithe Shadowborn in light armor darted about with a torch, lighting the hanging lanterns. Zoras snapped his fingers for a weapons master to bring forth a rack of swords. Ryder stood a few feet from him, rubbing dirt on to his palms. He slapped his thighs to remove the excess before pulling off his shirt. Zoras took it and bowed his head. Onyx watched his cousin prepare, taking mental notes. He bent down to the ground to grab a handful of dirt to rub on his hands, thinking on whether to show off his body like Ryder.

"I can do this," Onyx told himself in a low breath as he pulled off his shirt. His skin was unmarked and pristine but still defined with his emerging adult muscle. He was no street fighter but he was trained. Confidence was his weapon in maintaining his focus.

Ryder rolled his broad shoulders, tossing his head back and forth to crack his neck bones. He took the offered sword from the weapons master, flipping it between his hands to test the weight. Nodding, he gripped the hilt in his right hand. He turned to face Onyx. "Ready for a lesson?"

Onyx nodded, eager to prove himself a worthy opponent. "I'm ready to show you that Commander Parahazur was a great teacher." He took a sword from the rack and turned his back towards Ryder, walking across the yard. With a sharp motion, Onyx turned back to face him, sword held down at his side. His heart jumped when he realized that Ryder was gone.

Just as soon as Onyx took in the observation, Ryder appeared before him out of Shadow Slide, struck his sword arm and twisted in to elbow him in the face. Onyx stumbled back, holding his nose and nearly dropping his sword. Blood poured from his nostrils. Angry, he rushed at Ryder with the intent of throwing his weight into him to knock him off balance. Instead, Ryder bent backwards a step to receive his smaller weight and Onyx tumbled head over heels behind him. He landed hard in the dirt on his back and found a sword pointed to his throat.

Onyx felt a roar building in his chest and he swung his sword out to knock Ryder's blade away. He rolled out of reach and flipped up to his feet. He smirked before he entered his own Shadow Slide.

"Here's something I bet Sai didn't teach you!" Ryder shouted, his voice distorted and distant from outside of Shadow Slide.

Suddenly Onyx was ripped out of Shadow Slide. He fell to his stomach, skidding a few feet and losing grip of his sword. He rolled onto his back and spun up to run for his weapon. Ryder already had a foot on the blade. Onyx stopped in his tracks, contemplating his next move. He growled, blood caking on his face. He then rushed forward, dropping down at the last second to slide and reach for his sword. Ryder laughed and landed a hard kick to his chest, sending Onyx flying to the side of the yard. He groaned as he slowed to a stop.

"In a real fight, your opponent sees an opportunity and takes it. If I had intended to kill you, you would already be dead," Ryder said as he balanced his sword with the flat against his right shoulder. "Formal training does not matter. It is experience in the field that counts."

Onyx gritted his teeth as he pushed his body off of the ground. His chest burned with throbbing pain. He watched as Ryder glanced towards Zoras and nodded. The old Saber picked up a sword from the rack and removed his heavy cloak. The weapons master helped him to remove his armor and strip him down to a similar look as Ryder. Zoras was not as heavily built as Ryder but looked just as dangerous with a perfectly sculpted body. A long thin scar ran down the length of his left arm.

The crowd that surrounded the open yard shivered with anticipation. Zoras was a well known Saber of the highest quality and experience while Ryder was the self taught Silvanus son. Onyx sat up rubbing the top of his stomach to free up the tension that had built up. He watched as Zoras and Ryder paced around in a circle, holding similar poses with swords held down at their sides. It was such a different start to his own fight with Ryder. Ryder had immediately launched into a sneak attack and used his greater frame to toss him about. There was nothing normal about that fight. It did not go by the rules Sai had taught him. A moment of realization hit Onyx. Maybe that was Ryder's point: that a fight ultimately has no rules.

Zoras rushed in first, sliding to Ryder's right side and swinging his sword out to cut at his knee. Ryder tucked his sword against his side and flipped forward with a hand spring. He spun around to meet Zoras' crushing strike. The collision of steel rang out into the night. They pushed against each other, neither willing to give way. Ryder then slammed his head forward, hitting his skull against Zoras' forehead. Zoras stumbled back two steps and Ryder shoved hard to throw him off balance. But the old Saber was quick to recover and recognized Ryder's next move. He lurched forward with his shoulder, pushing Ryder back.

Onyx studied the fight carefully, trying to understand the choices Zoras and Ryder made to attack and defend. As he thought about it, Ryder had used his inexperience against him, making him look like a fool before the crowd. But he did not feel as angry as he had when he fought his cousin. It was now just simmering.

The banging of swords and quick movements of booted feet mixed with cheers and clapping as Ryder and Zoras continued their battle. Ryder appeared to be smiling as he spun and twisted to meet Zoras' heavy handed strikes. It amazed Onyx that both fought without armor and still performed maneuvers that could break bones. He then noticed that Ryder had changed his attacks into forms more fluid and dancer like. He moved light on his feet, sliding his sword down the length of Zoras' blade before slamming the pommel on the back of his hand. Zoras lost his grip on his weapon and it dropped. He had no time to retrieve it as Ryder spun around to sweep his legs out from under him.

"I concede, my good Prince. That was a worthy fight," Zoras said as Ryder pressed his sword point to his chest. Ryder smiled big as he extended a hand to help the older Shadowborn up.

"He is not a Prince!" Onyx shouted as he leapt up to his feet. The crowd immediately fell silent. No one dared to say a word as Onyx stomped forward, dropping only to pick up his sword. He would suffer defeat if he had to but Ryder was not a Prince and not his superior in the family line. Zoras stepped back and Onyx pointed his sword at Ryder. "Again."

"Not while you are angry. You will not learn a thing blinded," Ryder stated before turning to Zoras to say something.

"I will not be denied!" Onyx roared as he swung his sword in a high arc. His strike was heavy handed and full of power. But Ryder saw what was coming and grabbed Onyx's sword arm. Onyx struggled to free himself only to be thrown on his back to the ground in a cloud of dust.

"You have a lot to learn about fighting and about me," Ryder said sternly. He took his shirt back from Zoras. "When you can figure out what I tried to teach you, then we can continue."

*****

Onyx sat by the small pool that served as the water supply for the mountain hideout. The pool's surface rippled as a tiny waterfall spilled into it. The sound was relaxing but Onyx still felt a heat wave of emotions. He felt angry, jealous, embarrassed and confused at the same time. He wished his father was by his side to help him figure his thoughts. But it was only Ryder who came to sit beside him.

"Leave me alone," Onyx grumbled as he hugged his knees and turned his face away.

"Unfortunately our day and age will not allow that," Ryder stated, patting Onyx's back. Onyx shrank away from him. "Have you figured out what I tried to teach you?"

Onyx sneered. His thoughts were too erratic to make a statement. Every terrible memory threatened to overwhelm him as he thought about his father in Cross. Suddenly he felt helpless and he shuddered. "I don't know."

"You harbor a lot of misplaced jealousy. I acted purposely to break you of it for jealousy and anger will cloud your thoughts and render you useless in a fight. When we first met in Crossroads, I knew that someday I would have to teach you this lesson," Ryder said.

"You saw that this entire time?" Onyx asked, immediately embarrassed and feeling small.

Ryder nodded. "Onyx, we are from different worlds and backgrounds. However, both of us have the same legacy to live up to. You are young and have yet to experience the world like me. And considering how unbalanced our world is right now, it will be even tougher."

"I'm supposed to be the Silvanus Prince. The heir to the throne. Not this," Onyx stated, turning to face Ryder.

"No one likes to admit that they are afraid, Onyx," Ryder said with a shrug of the shoulders.

"Are you afraid?"

Ryder sighed deeply. It took him a long time to answer. "After my father Akakios was executed, I was afraid of what my future would hold. Your grandfather was away from Cross at the time, trying to hunt for the Mirror Sea Pirate and I was the only Silvanus blood there. But I was a bastard and the son of a father declared insane. What faith would anyone have in me? But Zoras Rokar started a motion to have me legitimized so I would be legally eligible for the throne. It was expected of me to accept but in my heart, I knew that it wasn't the right decision for me."

"You could have been Shadowlord and you said no? Why?" Onyx asked.

"Like I said. It wasn't the right decision for me. I chose to stay away from Cross after that and lived in Umbra for many years. The Rokars have continued to be my royal supporters whether I like it or not. So don't be angry at them for calling me a Prince," came Ryder's explanation. He looked at his cousin like a wise mentor. "Your problem when you fight is that you are ruled by your emotions. There is no guide or focus to them."

It was true that Onyx's mind was all over the place, especially since leaving Cross. He wondered if there was ever stability to his thoughts. "How?"

"Think of those you care about. Think about what you are afraid to lose," Ryder said.

"Who are you afraid of losing? Both of your parents are dead," Onyx asked.

Ryder chuckled a little as he smiled. "Her name is Haven Ombre."

Now the presence of the female Commander made sense. "Is she your wife? I did not think you were married."

"I'm not married. My parents weren't so I see no rush to bind ourselves together. We do not need that affirmation to know what we both feel is right," Ryder replied. "She is my family now."

"Is she from Umbra too?" Onyx asked.

Ryder nodded. "My only connection to Cross is my father and his family. I would be content to live in Umbra with Haven to the end of my days but fate has chosen a different path for me."

"What would you have done if you weren't born a royal bastard?" Onyx asked, feeling like they were building a connection.

"I would be the same person before you. I would have still travelled the world, learned what I have learned, and people would still treat me the same," Ryder replied after a long moment of silence. "I would still be fighting to break free of what people expect of me."

Onyx was starting to see Ryder in a whole new light. Here was an example of someone who was born into one life and chose to take it and run down his own path. He could barely imagine the emotions his cousin had experienced over the years for his decisions. Ryder had done what Onyx was trying to do: he broke free.

"I'm ready to do what I must even if I am afraid," Onyx finally said. Ryder patted him on the shoulder. "I want to break free."

CAPTURED

The manacles slinked into place with a loud clang as the chains dangled and hit the floor. Soja was pushed on to his knees and forcibly shoved forward in a bow. The slack on the chains was released and he was able to sit up. Soja looked up to see Kaiser lounging on the throne. The light coming from the high window beamed down on him as if he was divinely chosen for a quest. But Soja knew better. No good soul would charge Kaiser with a great purpose to help the world. If anything, the light should have been red since he was chosen by Hell to kill and destroy. He frowned as he squared his shoulders to face the man.

Kaiser twirled his left hand, stretching his fingers before tapping his chin. A smug grin appeared on his face. "Soja Rokar, son of Zoras. Saber of the Third Class. Son of the former First Class Saber and Commander of your order. So much was expected of you."

Soja tried to understand Kaiser's aim. If it wasn't for his tone, Soja would have thought that Kaiser was trying to honor him. "Blood and rank mean nothing to you."

A chuckle escaped Kaiser's lips before he turned his gaze to the young Saber. "I think you are mistaken. Blood and rank mean everything to me. As well it should considering who my father was. I did grow up surrounded by the army and all of its influences."

"Clearly none of their moral teachings reached you," Soja taunted with a clear truth of Kaiser's character.

Kaiser ignored the jab as he shifted his position to sit up

straight. He put both hands on the arms of the throne and leaned back. He wore an outfit of black and dark leather, his trademark vest hugging his body. "The world is not a kind and loving entity. I have simply embraced that fact. There is nothing better than the truth."

Soja could see right through Kaiser's words and yet felt confused and uncertain by them. He felt that there was a lie somewhere in what he said. "The Immortal Truth..."

"Is just a code of laws powered by the sacrifice of a thousand Dragons. We are taught to believe that it is binding in our lives and actions. People blindly follow it without question. Well I was born into a world without the Immortal Truth and I am doing just fine without it," Kaiser interrupted with a sharp tone.

"Everyone hates you," Soja stated without missing a beat.

Kaiser laughed for a few minutes. "I do not care whether people like me or not. I will not go blindly in my life thinking that people truly care and respect me like the Silvanus family has. Even the Daylord knows that there are those who... dislike him."

He had a hard time trying to think of anyone that spoke against the Daylord. Even Soja thought the world of the ancient war hero. His eyes moved to the high window where a moon and sun had been set in stain glass. He used the image to give him peace of mind and calm to continue facing Kaiser.

"Wouldn't you lose faith in a hero that does not come when called?" Kaiser asked in a mocking sympathetic tone. He leaned forward on the throne. "Seems that is reason to lose faith in the Daylord and all that the Immortal Truth has named as champion."

The throne room, despite its wide floors and high ceilings, seemed to close in on Soja as he felt his will being shaken. He sat up as straight as he could, trying to exude confidence. He then noticed that the tapestries and Silvanus coat of arms were gone and that the room was bare of all personal effects. "I have faith in the Daylord and the Shadowlord."

Kaiser laughed again. "Certainly, maybe the Daylord but the Shadowlord is nothing more than a faded stain of blood on a sword. The Silvanus bloodline has been whittled down to a few broken pieces."

"Even broken pieces can be put back together," Soja reasoned.

"Really? Show me," Kaiser challenged before snapping his fingers.

A hard blow hit Soja in the back of the head and he collapsed forward on his stomach. He gasped from the sudden pain, his vision blurry. He managed to see Kaiser lift himself from the throne and stride forward with a confident pace. Kaiser gestured towards an unseen person but Soja instantly knew that it was Rache who had struck him. As if on cue, Rache slid into view, the knuckles of his right hand covered with blood.

"I am not going to play games with you, child. I have a war to fight. The one you and your father brought to my door. I have tried all these years to fight it peacefully and without the wide destruction you assume that I will cause. Besides, that is Rache's job," Kaiser stated before giving a quick nod to his servant.

Rache stepped behind Soja and grabbed his hair, pulling him up and baring his throat. Soja gritted his teeth doing his best to resist the pain overwhelming him. The Demon's fingers dug into his skull, pressing against the bone.

"Can I, boss?" Rache asked with an eager hunger in his eyes.

Kaiser waved him off. "I know that your father is the top leader for this supposed rebellion. He has never liked me very much so who else could it be? Aku is already dead. Onyx is a child that will not survive his next fight. Ryder? Well I have yet to form a proper opinion of him."

"There is still Sage Silvanus and Aday..." Soja choked to say as Rache jerked his head back.

"And I shall deal with them accordingly. In the meantime, you get to await your few hours left in a cell. You shall be executed on the morrow. Let's say at nightfall?" Kaiser leaned in close. "You shall get to die as a Saber should and your father will be so proud. I'll be sure to tell him goodbye for you."

*****

Soja collapsed in the dank and dark cell, the steel door slamming shut behind him. The heels of his hands were torn up by the ragged stone. He curled up into a tight ball in a futile attempt to contain his physical pain. After twenty minutes, he unfolded his limbs and lay flat on his back. He took several deep breaths to calm his thoughts and to ignore the throb from the back of his head.

The sense of failure threatened to overwhelm him but Soja hardened his heart and thought about his duty. His action allowed Ryder to go free. It was his duty as a Saber to protect the Silvanus family even if it meant the cost of his life. He had taken the oath and he was going to hold to it until death. There had never been any question about that. He sighed deeply as he realized that he had twenty four hours left to live. There was no hope of escaping with Rache on the prowl. At least that is what Soja told himself.

Rache had hit him hard enough on the back of his head

that Soja could no longer center himself enough for a Shadow Slide. The move was calculating and not just a way to cause him pain. He tried to consider what Rache's aim might have been when he attacked the rebel outpost. Did he intend to kill Ryder for Kaiser?

"No. Kaiser said he had no opinion," Soja told himself. But even as he said it, he did not believe it. Kaiser saw Ryder as something different and important. Sure Ryder was older and an experienced fighter when compared to Onyx but he was not to be controlled or told what to do. How was Ryder an easier target than Onyx?

"Because he is truly different," came a deep but soothing voice. "He is a key player in this war."

Soja turned his head to see Omu sitting on his haunches. The great Spirit Wolf appeared solid and whole, his golden eyes catching a glint of light. His black fur appeared luscious and soft to the touch. The sight was welcoming.

"If you are here, then I am a Saber about to die. I will not be escaping?" Soja asked, fear threatening to overtake him. He quickly beat it back down into the back of his mind.

Omu nodded. "It is a sad duty that I bear to the noble Shadowborn people. To guide them to the Spirit World upon their death."

"I know that I should be afraid to die. That somehow I failed in my duty but," Soja started to say before he felt himself unable to continue.

"Your heart knows what you have done in life is right and good. The absence of fear nor the presence of it is wrong. You have courage, Soja Rokar, and that is what has made you a great Saber," Omu said warmly. He lay down beside Soja, keeping his head up. "You have made your peace."

Soja had to admit that it made sense on why he did not feel any fear. He smiled. "I don't think my father would have handled death well."

"That I cannot tell you. You bear his nobility but your Spirit is all your own," Omu replied. "And the world has heard the call."

"The call? What call?" Soja asked, sitting up despite his protesting body.

Omu followed suit and sat straight up. "The world is rising with hope and courage like it hasn't seen since the days of Begin Anu. The true Shadowlord has returned and will soon reunite with the Daylord to aid you." If the wolf could have smiled, he would have.

"You mean Aku will recover?" Soja blurted out, his first thought to the current Silvanus on the throne.

"Have no fear for the war to come. Believe in what your

heart tells you and the truth will be revealed," Omu said as he started to dissipate into a ghostly mist.

Soja reached out in his direction just as the Spirit Wolf disappeared into the shadows of the cell. He lay back down and closed his eyes, trying to make sense of Omu's words. Someone was coming. And this someone could turn the tide of the war for good or for ill. And Soja would not live long enough to see him arrive. Tears filled his eyes and streamed down his cheek.

TORTURE

Soja began to think that perhaps it was foolish of him to believe that Kaiser would allow him peace in his last hours. It crossed his mind not for the first time that Kaiser was not a merciful person. He never had been and would likely never be. It confounded him how so many people could follow Kaiser so blindly and delude themselves into thinking loyalty to him was salvation. How could so many people turn their backs on the Shadowlord? Were people that desparate for glory?

He had to admit to himself that the throne he protected was weak and crumbling. People's sense of safety directly correlated to the strength of their leader. Lord Aku was a broken and sickly shell of his former self. There was no way to say that he was a strong, effective leader. Onyx, though physically strong, was young and inexperienced. Ryder was a totally different story. He was an experienced and powerful warrior but he was a bastard. Of the three, Ryder was the best person to be Shadowlord. But Soja knew that Ryder would not take the throne. Even if he wouldn't, Soja was going to protect his friend until the very end.

His end was fast approaching, he realized, as the two brutish guards grabbed his arms tightly. Neither of them spoke as they dragged him from his cell but their harsh expressions said it all. They were taking him to a place that was very unpleasant. An hour ago, the observation would have unnerved him. But as he had done then, Soja let the image of the wolf Spirit Omu fill his mind with peace. Omu's kind words of encouragement flooded his

heart and gave him courage against the horrible things that
awaited him.

The guards dragged the half clothed Soja down a spiraling
stair case that was poorly lit. Each bump and slap of his limbs
against the cold stone jolted his battered and bruised body. He
hated how he could not command his body anymore though his
thoughts ran a mile a minute. Even then, Rache's blow across the
back of his head had done more to Soja than anything else. He
could no longer use Shadow Slide or any other innate technique.
He could not center himself properly to even attempt a Shadow
Slide. The sense of helplessness threatened to overwhelm him
again but he quickly steeled his heart with courage.

The stairs descended deeper and deeper into the unknown
depths of the prison. Or the Heights, Soja could not tell. The level
of grime on the nearby walls indicated to him that the passage was
ill used. Soja tried to recall his lessons regarding the tunnels and
pathways that spread out through Cross. As his Saber instructor
had taught him, the network of tunnels aided the Sabers in their
secret wanderings. But for the life of him, Soja could not place
where he was. He was certain that the passage had been of use at
some point for at measured spaces, an iron bracket had been
secured to the wall above their heads. In contrast, only a few
brackets held a still burning torch. Their irregular placement did
not allow Soja's vision to settle and it made him nauseous in his
current condition.

After an almost unbearably long time, the stairs ended and
at the end of the landing was a windowless wooden door. A torch
burned to the left of the door. Without a word or change in pace,
the guards opened the door and pulled Soja inside. Once inside,
Soja immediately had an idea of where he was: a torture chamber
from the Second Dominion War. He had only ever heard rumors of
such a place but there was no questioning what he saw. The
jagged stone of the walls were coated in centuries of melted candle
wax, wicks sticking out all over the surface. In the many nooks
and crevices that scattered the walls were small burning candles.
Smoke stained the stone above them. The room was surprisingly
well lit.

"Secure him to the table," came Kaiser's calm order.

Soja caught a glimpse of Kaiser's back before the guards
lifted him and slapped him down on the table. His bare back hit
the table with enough force to split the already aged wood. Soja
gritted his teeth from the resulting pain. In his silent agony, he
barely noticed the guards pulling at his limbs, stretching them.
Cold iron shackles touched his skin and jolted him into awareness.

"You may leave," Kaiser said in a smooth voice. Soja

listened as his vision started to clear and he tried to watch the guards leave. The door slammed shut. "Good. Now we are alone."

The pain of being thrown onto the table subsided into a dull ache. Soja turned his head to where Kaiser was standing, his back to him. Kaiser was dressed in a body hugging black vest that blended into his black pants and boots. His sinewy arms were bare except for a silver ring on his left hand. Kaiser's right hand was hidden from Soja's sight.

"Do you know this place?" Kaiser asked as his right hand drifted over a set of cruel and sharp instruments. The metal clinked together in a strange song.

Soja strengthened his resolve before answering. "I know of it." He did not want to give Kaiser any satisfaction with a shaky, uncertain reply.

Kaiser chuckled. "It is so much more than what you are thinking," he said as he held up a thin tool with a jagged blade. He turned it back and forth examining its features. "I taught two Silvanus Princes the art of Blood Magic and the true power of the Spirit World in this room. Such a terrible art to learn but all the more useful if mastered." He set the tool down and returned his attention to studying another strange instrument. "You obviously know that the blood in our bodies is more than a salty red liquid. It is life. It is power. It is memory."

The muscle in Soja's right shoulder began to twitch. He had to pull on his right arm harder in order to turn enough towards his left. Kaiser kept his back to him. "It is love. It is loyalty. It is truth."

The dark Shadowborn scoffed. "And so the story goes but blood is so much more. Aday Silvanus failed to understand and it drove him mad. I tried to teach Akakios what his uncle failed to learn and well, we all know what happened to him." He lifted what looked like a long iron pen and set it in the flame of a nearby candle.

Soja watched as the metal turned red hot. "Is this how you teach Blood Magic?" he asked, indicating his current situation with his eyes.

"Oh no. This is just for fun," Kaiser replied as he lifted the heated instrument out of the fire and turned around. He stepped forward, smiling, until he reached Soja's left side. "I would not waste the intricacies of my art on the likes of you."

Kaiser's fingernails dug into the flesh of Soja's left side, drawing lines of blood. But that was nothing compared to the burning, stabbing pain of the red hot iron pen being dragged across his skin. Every muscle tensed as Soja arched his back. But Kaiser shoved him back down with a heavy hand. Soja took a few short breaths before he forced himself to look down at his torso. Kaiser had drawn a thin line across his stomach, cutting into the top layer of skin. Blood oozed out and traced the lines of his muscles. Soja had no time to consider what Kaiser was going to do next before the red hot pen touched him again.

"Torturing me to death will not stop the rebellion," Soja boldly declared as his body was shaking in bursts. Kaiser only scoffed as he continued to carve a cruel design with the heated pen. The pain burned through Soja's entire body and he fought the overwhelming urge to scream out loud. "I go to my grave knowing that..."

"And just how do you know that you are going to die?" Kaiser interrupted.

"Because Omu came to me. The Spirit World knows what you are doing and you will be punished for your crimes," Soja said with as much force as he could muster.

"If I am to be punished, why doesn't the great Wolf Spirit come strike me down right now?" Kaiser dared as he stepped back from Soja. He held out his arms and looked towards the stone ceiling. "You hear that, Omu? Come and kill me now!" he shouted with daring pride. After a pause of silence, Kaiser dropped his arms and smirked. "You see that? Even the Spirits have abandoned your cause." He turned his back towards Soja and picked up a long knife. He considered it for a moment before setting it back down on the tray.

For a moment, Soja's vision hazed over and he felt his senses pulling away from his body down a long, dark tunnel. The thought of Omu brought him roaring back to life. He furrowed his brow and snarled. "The Spirits have not abandoned me! They have abandoned you! They will inflame the hearts of those that seek to cast you down and kill you!"

"People seem to keep saying that like it is supposed to frighten me," Kaiser mused. "Well I have seen death. I looked it right in the eyes and I laughed." He snickered as his right hand alighted onto a small bowl with a brush laying across the rim.

The room darkened for a single beat of Soja's heart. It was fleeting but noticeable. What was stranger was that Soja felt his body shiver from the touch of cold air. It did little to soothe the pain of his wounds. He tried to steady his breath by focusing all of his mind on an image of the Wolf Spirit. A sense of warmth crept back into his limbs and he closed his eyes, smiling. It was if the pain did not matter despite what Kaiser had done and was likely to do. Courage was his weapon against it. He let that thought calm him.

"It is said that to laugh at death is to fear it. A true man accepts that someday his life will end. Even though we are Immortal Spiritborn, someday we will cease to exist," Soja said with a peaceful expression.

"A nice sentiment for those who are pathetic and weak," Kaiser said as he picked up a short, curved knife. He ran the thumb of his right hand along the edge of the blade. "You are more than welcome to believe in that. I will not stop you from doing so."

Soja watched as Kaiser began to paint a dark liquid over the edge of his chosen knife. The smell stung his nose and forced bile into the back of his throat. He swallowed hard. It was an odd but sickening odor that permeated the air. He equated it to the smell of rotting blood mixed with the ashes of burnt flesh. There was another item mixed in with the blood scent that Soja could not identify. It had him worried.

Kaiser took in a deep breath and let it out slowly. "I love the smell of Spirit Poison. Really opens up the senses. A dash of Demon's blood. A sprinkle of silver dust. A pinch of bone ash provided by a most willing volunteer," Kaiser snickered as he listed the ingredients of his concoction. "A drop of Farlander blood from yours truly and let's not forget my favorite: tears of a Dragon. Plus a few other little things."

It sickened Soja that Kaiser equated his Spirit Poison to that of a baker's recipe, listing ingredients as casually as a veteran bread maker would. He tried to pull on his restraints but found that he did not have the strength to make his limbs move. He tried again to no avail.

"It amazes me how much one can learn from a Demon. Perhaps you are one yourself!" Soja snapped.

"If what you claim is true, then that would make your dear friend Ryder a Demon blood too. Ryder. Where did he get such a ridiculous name?" Kaiser asked as he set the brush down in the bowl. He turned around, casually flipping the knife between the fingers of his left hand.

"His name is Peredur," Soja growled, his Saber sense of duty speaking for him.

Kaiser rested the knife's tip on his chin once he crossed his arms. He gestured with it as he shrugged. "I would have named him after myself. It would have been proper of his mother to name her son after her father." He shifted his weight. "No matter. What is done is done and he will simply have to be content to live with Adonis as his second name."

Soja's Saber instincts kicked in with such ferocity that he nearly leapt free from the table. Or at least he willed himself to but failed. He stared back at Kaiser with unwavering eyes. Kaiser came back to the table side, seeming to ponder a private question.

He switched the poison coated knife to his right hand and reached out for the center of Soja's muscled chest. Soja took the opportunity of their closeness to spit in Kaiser's face. Kaiser immediately froze as if shocked by Soja's action but the look on his face did not change. Instead, Soja saw a dangerous fire burning in Kaiser's eyes.

Faster than he could see, Kaiser gripped Soja's throat with an immeasurable strength. He snarled viciously. "Unlike your father, I have grown tired of you breathing and like your mother, I will carve out your heart and feed it to the flames!" He snapped Soja's head up so quickly that Soja thought his neck would break. "Yes, I am the one that killed your mother. It brought me such joy to see you and your so called mighty father weep. Now, he will get to cry over your grave!"

It came so quickly that Soja had no time to react. The absolute burning pain of the knife dragging across his skin rocked him to the core. It blocked out every sensation. The poison of the knife spread quickly through his system like a raging fire. Even more horrifying was the feeling of something being ripped away from him. As the agony continued, Soja thought of Omu, pushing his last conscious thought to the wolf Spirit to bring news of his coming death to the true Shadowlord.

RETURN TO CROSS

"Is that all you are going to wear?" Onyx asked as he buckled on his steel fronted shin guards. He tugged at the piece of armor to assure himself of the fit.

Ryder was dressed in the same light style leather armor he had worn during his final match in the Crossroads Arena. He threw his arms back and forth, rotating his shoulders. "If I was going into proper battle, I would wear a full set of steel armor. This is a rescue mission that requires stealth and speed. I need to keep Rache away from the castle for as long as possible. I won't be able to do that if I am weighed down by heavy armor."

They stood in the open yard just before the hideout gates. Only a few interested onlookers were present for Zoras had issued new orders. A trio of scouts conversed near the smith's forge. A thin Shadowborn darted around, lighting lanterns with a small flaming torch.

"You really think that we can do this?" Onyx gulped. He wanted to believe in his strength and his training but the task ahead was daunting to him.

"You mean do you think that you can do this," Ryder said as he turned to look at Onyx. Onyx sheepishly nodded. Ryder laid a hand on his cousin's shoulder. "I'll handle the Demon. You just have to get inside the castle and retrieve your father. If you are spotted, your position as the Crowned Prince will grant you greater access and command than if I went in. Also, your father will respond to your presence better than mine."

Onyx gulped again. Ryder's logic was sound but still he was worried. This was his first real combat experience or as Ryder had told him, his first real life or death combat experience. Even then, he was worried for Ryder who was going up against Rache, a Demon he knew to be of terrible power and strength. Was his cousin so confident that he could defeat Rache or was he just good at hiding his fear? He then spotted a Shadowborn woman, dressed in leather armor and chainmail, stomping towards them with a determined look on her face. Ryder turned around to face her just before she slapped him. Onyx's breath caught in his chest from shock.

"You're leaving me?!" the woman snapped as she stood back crossing her arms tightly.

"Technically, you left me right after we came back from the border," Ryder said before he was quickly slapped again.

"But not to face a Demon alone!" the woman said with a hint of desperation in her voice. She looked down briefly.

Ryder stepped forward, pushing her back so they could have some privacy. "Haven," he said in a soothing tone. The woman looked up at him, her expression changing from hurt to worry. Ryder wrapped his arms around Haven, pulling her close to him. Haven responded by untangling her arms and embracing him tightly.

"I don't want you to go. What if he captures you again?" she asked softly.

"I have to do this for Onyx and Aku," Ryder replied as he stroked the back of her head. She only tightened her grip on his torso. "I know that you want to come with me but I ask you to stay here. Zoras will need a capable fighter on hand while I am gone."

"You're an idiot," Haven grumbled as she pulled away from his embrace. She wiped a tear from her cheek.

"But I am your idiot," Ryder replied with a teasing smirk.

Haven then looked him directly in the eyes. "We are going to have a serious talk when you get back." She looked around Ryder to lock eyes with Onyx. Onyx shuddered under her gaze. "You better make sure he comes back."

Onyx stammered to give an answer as the Shadowborn woman walked away. Ryder slapped him on the back and he stumbled forward.

"Come on. We do not have much time. The sun is setting and it will only be night for so long," Ryder stated before he disappeared into Shadow Slide. Onyx took a deep breath to settle himself before following Ryder in his own Shadow Slide.

*****

Ryder and Onyx arrived on the outskirts of Cross, coming out of Shadow Slide at a wooded bluff. They kept low to the ground as they crawled to the edge of the overhang. The city laid out before them in a sleepy haze. Few street lanterns were lit and there were no spirals of smoke coming from the many chimneys.

"I don't like this," Ryder commented as he narrowed his eyes. "It has been a while since I have last been to Cross proper but even I know that this is not how the city should be at night."

"The taverns should be bustling with activity and the roast fires should be lit all over the city. The castle windows should all be glowing with golden light," Onyx said. He nudged Ryder in the shoulder and directed his attention towards the distant castle. "There should be guards at the main gate but I can not see any."

Ryder remained silent for a long time. He studied the network of buildings, searching for any hint of life. There was a subtle charge in the air that gave him a negative feeling. The more he looked towards the southwest, the more the negative feeling grew in his heart. The charge pulsated like a rumbling storm, escalating in volume with every thump of his heartbeat. He tensed up in response.

"What is it?" Onyx asked, sensing Ryder's distress.

Ryder laid a hand on Onyx's shoulder. "Center yourself like you are preparing for Shadow Slide but push your senses out like you are preparing to track auras."

Onyx closed his eyes and promptly did as Ryder told him. His eyes snapped open as soon as he felt the charge. "It feels like when people were getting excited for the Crossroads Arena. Kind of pulse pounding," he said, gesturing with his hand towards his heart.

The negative feeling in Ryder's heart transformed to one of worry. In the back of his mind, his thoughts turned towards Soja. To him, the pulsating charge indicated a raucous crowd begging for something terrible. He knew that he could deal with the worry but as Ryder knew, Soja was Onyx's friend and guard. If Onyx was going to rescue his father, he was going to have to focus fully on his mission and nothing else. Ryder saw Onyx as too fragile to handle both the burden of his father's condition and the likely fate of Soja.

"What does a Demon's aura feel like?" Onyx asked, breaking the silence.

"A Demon's aura bears a dark chill that causes apprehension and anxiety. It is like a poison to the soul, worming its way through your entire being," Ryder answered as he searched the city.

"Then how is it possible that Rache was so close and I never felt a thing?" Onyx asked, sounding a bit frustrated. He slid back from the edge and sat down, crossing his arms.

Ryder looked back over his shoulder at Onyx. He gestured for his cousin to return to his side and Onyx promptly did. "Just like you and I, a Demon can choose to mask his aura from others. It takes experience and intense training to understand the subtlties of auras and Spirit energy."

"Can you teach me?" Onyx asked, looking at Ryder intensely. "Can you teach me about Spirit energy and fighting?"

The request surprised Ryder and he laughed in response. "You mean become a trainer and mentor? What makes you think that I would be a good choice?"

Onyx shrugged, appearing uncertain. "Well you said that I would find someone at the base and who better than you? Everyone says how great a Shadowlord you would be so surely, you must be powerful in both body and mind. Even now, you show your great courage by facing Rache on your own."

Ryder laughed again as he leaned on his side, facing Onyx. "Asking me to mentor you makes me feel old."

"I don't think I would have come on this mission if I could not trust you not to lead me astray. Besides, we are family and at this point, it is something that I want to hold on to," Onyx replied as he picked at the grass. "I feel like this rescue mission will end with my father's true death and if given the choice, I don't think that I could raise the blade to grant him mercy."

The terror and sadness at such prospective loss was plain to see in Onyx's eyes. The young Prince dropped his head and furiously pulled at the grass to keep his attention diverted.

"In life, there are decisions to made. Some are easy and some tear you apart. Then there are the ones that never leave you no matter how hard you try to leave them. Remember what I told you earlier: think about those you care about. Think about what gives you calm and peace," Ryder said with encouragement.

"You mean like you and Haven Ombre?" Onyx asked, feeling a sense of stability returning to his thoughts.

Ryder nodded. "Do not let your emotions rule you but guide you in your mission. Do not think. Just feel and trust in yourself. In a fight, there is no time to question every move on whether it is right or wrong. You only have time to make the move."

"Is that my first lesson?" Onyx asked with a smirk.

Ryder chuckled. "Guess so." He shook his head, amused at the idea of training and mentoring Onyx. "If it is to be so, you must trust that what I say and do is for your best interests. But first, I have a Demon to distract and you have a father to rescue. Meet me upon the Heights before dawn. I will know when you have arrived there."

Onyx nodded, a feeling of confidence spreading through his body. As long as he held on to the feeling and the words of his cousin, Onyx knew that he could survive the night.

EXECUTION

The steady, slow drip of moisture woke Soja from his unconscious state as it fell on his cheek. He groaned as he slowly reached a hand up to wipe it away. The pain in his body was gripping as he struggled to move. He gasped when he turned over on his back, realizing the entire left side of his rib cage was broken. His vision was hazy as he opened his eyes, seeing the dark cold interior. More water dripped onto his face as his senses started to clear.

The prison cell was small, wet, and depressing with a dark stone wall and thick metal bars. The lone window was almost touching the ceiling, bars blocking any escape. Not that Soja was in any condition to make an attempt. After his torture session with Kaiser, Rache had beaten him so thoroughly that he was too broken to even need chains. The bones in his legs were gravel and he could barely feel the tips of his toes. Every time his heart thumped in his chest, pain pulsated and numbed his senses. Soja did appreciate the cold air as it seemed to lessen the sting of his injuries.

"Get up, traitor. It's time to end your rebellious ways," Morin sneered as the prison door creaked open. Soja felt himself being pulled up from the floor and dragged away from the small cell. The waves of pain from the hard motion made him tense and feel feverish. Morin's determined tight steps were unmistakable as he took charge of the group.

He led them out into the prison yard where onlookers

cheered and shouted angry names at Soja. Morin raised up his hands, eliciting more cheers as he smirked, thinking of what was coming. Once up the stairs, the prison guards laid Soja down on his back on the stone table, tying him down at his wrists and ankles. The torchlight and pyres flickered and cast a red glow over the yard. Morin then held up one hand, commanding silence as he stepped to the front of the platform.

"My fellow Shadowborn! Brothers and sisters most loyal to the mighty Kaiser Adonis! I bring to you today a traitor to his name!" Morin shouted before whipping around to point at Soja. "He conspired to kill our great Lord! He has spread lies and has incited a rebellion that threatens us all!" The crowd roared with even more jeering taunts directed at Soja. Morin turned back towards one of the guards taking an offered ragged dagger. "What do we do to traitors?" he asked in a lower tone as he walked over to the side of the stone table.

"Cut out his heart! Burn him!" the shouts from the crowd came. "Kill him! Kill him!" the crowd then began chanting as Morin looked down at Soja. He smirked dangerously.

"He has shown us where his loyalty lies and by his death, he will bring honor back to his people. By his dying screams, he will bring the blood home," Morin growled with a devilish grin. He leaned in close to whisper in Soja's ear. "You will bring him home."

The crowd of Kaiser loyalists roared with hate and jeers of disgust at Soja. They spat and cursed as several threw pieces of refuse onto the platform. Morin basked in the glow of his personal glory. He walked up to the front of the platform and threw his arms into the air. The crowd roared louder and begged him to finish Soja off.

"I am sorry but I must do as they wish," Morin said as he raised the dagger in one hand and used his free hand to press down at the top of Soja's chest. He then smirked. "Oh have I wanted to do this for a long time."

Soja gasped as his voice cracked with unspeakable pain while Morin drove the dagger blade in his chest just below his hand. Morin began pulling back, breaking through the rib cage as blood poured out. Soja's cries excited the crowd to an insane fervor. Letting the dagger fall to the side, Morin took his hands and broke open Soja's chest. He gripped Soja's weakening heart and tore it out. He held it high in the air as he walked over to the small pyre at the front corner of the platform. The crowd roared even more as Morin raised the heart over the flames.

"Tonight let Soja Rokar burn in Hell!" Morin shouted before dropping the heart. The flames sparked and crackled as they engulfed the still beating heart. The crowd roared and erupted in cheers, shouting Kaiser's name over and over into the night.

With Morin facing the crowd, arms out to the side, he did not see Ryder dropping down to the platform with sword raised. He only turned around when he heard the hushed intake of breath before Ryder cut him down. Morin crumbled as he gripped the bloody stump of what remained of his arm. He screamed out in pain and his cries sent the crowd into a panic.

Seeing the danger, the guards closest to the platform descended on Ryder. Ryder rolled over the table grabbing the dagger and a quick twitch of the wrist sent it flying. It plunged blade forward into the chest of one guard while Ryder took his sword to the other, vaulting back over the table. A quick slice of the long blade decapitated the guard, splattering blood across him. The remaining two guards charged at him at the same time. Ryder blocked the guard on his right by hitting the flat of his blade against the edge of the other sword. The action jolted the guard into dropping his sword. Ryder quickly snatched it up as he brought his sword back to block the second attack. He shoved both guards back and they nearly stumbled off of the platform. Ryder spun each of his swords in preparation for the counter attack.

The swordless guard ripped the dagger from his dead companion. He snarled a curse between gritted teeth while his partner took a step forward. Ryder spotted over their shoulders the approach of four more guards and instead of worry; he felt a powerful courage rise up in his heart.

"For Soja," Ryder growled as he tightened his grip on his weapons. He then charged forward, not wanting to wait for the guards to reach him.

The four guards in the crowd were just starting to climb up to the platform when Ryder burst over the side, swords stabbed through their two comrades. He crashed onto the cobblestones of the yard and rolled forward, ripping his swords free. In the blink of an eye, Ryder jumped back towards the platform. The guard at the bottom of the platform stairs had no time to react as Ryder tore into him. Ryder crossed his swords and pulled back quickly to decapitate the guard. He vaulted over the collapsing body to take on the next one.

With the thickness of the crowd, other guards had trouble pushing through the mass of people to help their comrades. People were both afraid and transfixed by the bloody fight. There was no stopping Ryder no matter how many guards came at him. He parried several strikes and stabs from his fourth guard opponent before swinging his left hand sword down to cut at the legs. The guard stumbled from the sudden change and toppled forward.

Ryder threw himself up against the platform to avoid being accidently tackled. His sharp eyes shot up towards the last two guards and in a heartbeat, his swords were bathed in silver fire. He charged up the remaining stairs. With blinding speed, Ryder passed them by and swung his swords, passing through the necks of the guards. As soon as the bodies dropped and tumbled down the stairs, Ryder threw his ruined swords away.

The crowd had fallen completely silent, watching Ryder as he ascended the stairs. He walked over to the stone table where Soja's body laid, chest tore open. He took Soja's hand and gripped it tightly. Morin groaned and Ryder shot his gaze around to the struggling Commander. Ryder stepped back from the table, pulling a torch free from its iron stand. Morin cringed at the sight of the raging Ryder as he approached like a predator.

"Now, it is you who must burn in Hell," Ryder said before pressing the burning torch onto Morin's chest. As Morin burned alive, Ryder stepped to the front of the platform. He looked about at the horrified faces that also spoke of confusion at what they had just seen. Everyone was stunned into silence. Ryder had gore splashed across his front with a splatter on his face. He then realized that they wanted him to speak.

"My name is Peredur Coba-Silvanus, son of Akakios, and bastard to the royal Silvanus bloodline. I am here to say that you have been lied to. There is no salvation in loyalty to Kaiser Adonis. There is salvation in loyalty to the Immortal Truth," Ryder shouted before pointing back towards the castle. "He has been lurking in the shadows all these years to destroy everything you hold dear! Now he says that he will wage a war that will win him power and might. Well I am prepared to fight a war to destroy him! Completely and utterly!"

He did not want to admit it but he was just as good a speaker as Kaiser. The people in the crowd were starting to murmur and act as if a barrier had been broken and they were seeing and hearing on their own for the first time. He was capable of infusing conviction into every word. The major difference was that Ryder was honest and true even if he wasn't to himself. "Denounce him! Curse him! Stand up and fight! Tell him no more will I run! No more will I cower in fear! I will rise and you will fall!"

The crowd started to speak loudly and some even began to applaud. The applause was slow but steady. Ryder could see that they were afraid. He had to get them to believe in the same courage he felt. He gestured back towards Soja's body. "This was a Saber who gave his life all because he believed in hope. He believed in his people and he believed in me." Ryder turned to look at the Saber. "Though I never told you, in life you were a friend. An honest and true friend. I hope to one day return the same kindness and respect you gave me."

"Here, here!" shouted a single man. With that single declaration, the full spell of Kaiser's might was broken. The crowd had turned for Ryder.

Ryder raised up a clenched fist into the air. "I have returned home and together, we will win."

THE RETURN OF IZTAL

A harsh, burning fire snapped and flickered, illuminating Kaiser as he paced around the edge of the room. Blood leaked down his right arm and streamed down the length of the sword blade in his hand. The tip of the sword painted the blood as he took slow, calculating steps. This was the same room he had wrested away from the Shadow Council before the journey to Crossroads. It was devoid of all decoration and furniture. Every window had been filled in with stone and mortar. At regular intervals on the wall were torches that cast sharp shadows. In the center of the room was a pyre surrounded by burning coals and wood logs.

Rache watched his master from the doorway, leaning back against it with his arms crossed. He kept well away from the blood circle knowing the power it held. Even though he was not standing inside of the circle, he could already feel his life force draining as a breathy hiss sounded in his ears. It was like the world of the dead was calling him back. He shivered, quickly rubbing his arms in reaction.

Kaiser finished with his blood circle and turned his back towards Rache. Scars tugged across the skin in ragged lines that were stained black. They spoke to Kaiser's long and brutal history and a damning secret. Fresh blood stained his right arm as it drained down from a wound on his bicep. The blood on the floor reflected the firelight in an eerie bronze sheen.

"I hear that my dear grandson has brought his cousin to

Cross," Kaiser said as he wiped the sword blade clean with a tattered cloth.

"The Prince is of little consequence but your dear grandson killed Morin Win and has incited a riot," Rache reported.

Kaiser faked a pained sigh. "Now who will entertain me from day to day." He glanced over at Rache, looking him up and down. "No, I need you to kill those that annoy me."

The fire hissed as Kaiser's blood reached it in its slow crawl. Its light dimmed to reveal Aku lying on the stone pyre. His eyes looked as if they had sunken into to his skull. His eyelids fluttered with his shallow breathing.

"He looks dead," Rache commented. He snorted when Kaiser threw the sword at him and he managed to catch it by the hilt before it could stab him.

"He is dead. He has always been dead. You try keeping a corpse animated for longer than a day," Kaiser snapped. "Idiot," he grumbled under his breath in a voice purposely loud enough for Rache to hear. The Demon growled in response.

A silence fell between them as Kaiser returned his focus to Aku and the fire. He closed his eyes and calmed his heartbeat with slow, steady breathing. The blood circle began to pulsate in time with his heartbeat. He slowly lifted his left arm, stretching out the fingers of his hand. Aku began to rise from the pyre, limbs drifting like lifeless wet rags. His own scars were glowing a light red color.

Rache paced to the other side of the fire until he faced Kaiser. "You really think Iztal will heed your call? The Demon is a twit."

Kaiser shot him an angry glare. "Hush! I must have silence!" he snapped. He twisted his hand around slowly, rotating Aku's direction. Closing his eyes, he began to speak in a low unintelligible voice.

The fire began to leap up and lick Aku's limp body. The smell of brimstone and ash was potent in the air. Kaiser produced a dagger from his belt and sliced open his left arm from his wrist to the crook of his elbow. Rache stumbled, grabbing his own arm and seeing the shared gash. Blood poured to the floor and moved quickly to the fire. The flames sparked higher and with more heat as the two bloods pooled in the coals.

"Blood of the ancient. Blood of the Demon..." Kaiser mumbled as his wound quickly closed, leaving a long pink line. He mumbled off a few more lines before raising his voice again. "I offer these to you, Iztal. Use them to enter the body of the Shadow and come forth to my call."

Aku's body then jerked to life as the flames rose higher. The color of the scars shifted from red to black as eyes snapped open.

The mouth opened in a soundless scream. Kaiser then quickly swept his right hand before him, killing the flames. He drew his left hand slowly back towards him before lowering it to his side. Aku's body responded to his hand motions and collapsed to the floor on unsteady feet.

Rache rounded the fire brazier, keeping a close eye on the revived body. "Iztal?"

A smile crossed Aku's face as Iztal asserted his control and took over. He then stood up straight as Rache came to Kaiser's side. "A Demon in a wolf's clothing, Master," Iztal said with a slow bow.

It was strange for Rache to be looking at Aku and hear Iztal's voice. But Demon possession was a tricky technique for a summoner. It depended on both the Demon and the possessed. And Kaiser knew things that Rache did not.

Kaiser snapped his fingers and Rache quickly ran over to him carrying a black vest. Kaiser pulled it on and waved Rache back several steps. He latched his hands behind his back.

"Welcome back, Iztal. How was the Spirit World?" Kaiser asked.

"This body does not fit the same," Iztal said, his voice wavering between Aku's natural voice and his own deep tone. His chest fluttered as his breathing grew stronger.

Kaiser studied Aku's reanimated body, watching as Iztal's power slowly took control. Veins bubbled down his limbs and across his torso in pulsating waves. The skin began to darken as hot blood spread beneath the surface to take away the pasty white palour of death. Muscles swelled with renewed strength. As bones cracked and thickened, Iztal began to stand up straight instead of bent over. The face filled in as the eyes shifted to a blood red color. With one last deep breath, Iztal had asserted his full control.

"Give it time," Kaiser said as he stepped forward. He put a finger under Iztal's chin and lifted it. "Ah, now we look more like a Demon and less like a wasting away Shadowborn corpse. Now how was the Spirit World?"

Iztal tensed up but Kaiser patted the side of his face, shooshing him in a smooth voice. "Demons do not reside like your kind in the Spirit World. We spend our eternity of death in an endless Spiral. I am glad to be free of it."

"Yes, that Spiral is not a pleasant ride. I am pleased that you were not so deep in it that you could not hear my call," Kaiser said as he drew his hand back.

Rache cringed at the mention of the Spiral. Within the Spirit World, there was a blackness set aside for the most horrible of souls. He shook his head free of the thought, not wanting to dwell on it any longer.

"So Iztal. This time around, I have employed Rache here to bring you forth for I have another task for you," Kaiser said as he drew up side by side with the Demon. He leaned in to whisper in Iztal's ear. "I want you to kill Aku's precious child."

Iztal turned his head and looked Kaiser in the eyes, a grin spreading across his face. "It could not please me more than to kill for you, Lord Kaiser."

"Where does that leave me?" Rache asked, hiding his jealousy behind a tight expression.

Kaiser turned towards Rache, smiling. "You get to bring me the bastard."

"Dead or alive?" Rache asked immediately excited. He wanted to test himself again against Ryder in the field of combat.

"Do whatever else you please but bring him to me alive. In one piece preferably," Kaiser replied.

The two Demons bowed with grins on their faces, eager for the task ahead. "Consider us unleashed," Rache and Iztal said at the same time.

UNDER ATTACK

A light rain fell, cooling the city and raising a wall of mist. Lightning flashed upon the Heights, illuminating the castle in an eerie light. Onyx gulped at the sight. It had been hours since he and his cousin had parted. He tried to tell himself that it was ok to be afraid. It meant that he had a heart. He gulped again. At least he was not going to face the Demon Rache like his cousin. Ryder had told him that he was going to keep Rache at bay so that he could enter the castle and rescue his father. What Onyx did not tell him is that he felt that to rescue his father meant killing him. He hoped that he could get his father away from the castle so that his cousin could do the deed. Ryder seemed to have no fear about taking a person's life.

The city streets were strangely deserted. During a normal night in Cross, guards were on patrol, traders arrived late from the East Road, and even thieves crept through the maze of buildings. Onyx saw no one. When he turned a corner towards the main causeway to the castle, a thin matted gray dog froze in midstep before bolting from view. He let out a deep breath but a sense of unease began to settle on him. It was different from his fear of what was to come. It caused him to shake and jump at any sound. He drew out his sword and gripped the hilt so tight that his knuckles turned white.

"Have to remain focused. Have to remember what I am fighting for," Onyx mumbled to himself. Ryder's advice played back in his mind and it forced him to think about the people that mattered to him most. It also reminded him of his promise to Luna. "I will find you again."

Rain drops accumulated on his armor and Onyx appeared to shimmer as he passed under the lantern light. The great doors of the castle, normally surrounded by guards, stood in complete silence. It was such a contrast to what Onyx knew and despite the lack of guards, the sight was inviting. He felt compelled to enter the castle. The door iron was cold to the touch as he lifted it and pulled the righthand door open. The inner entryway was just as empty of the normal hustle and bustle of servants, guards, and courtiers. Onyx slowly and cautiously made his way inside, the door closing behind him. It was eerie how deserted his home was. He began to wonder how long he had actually been gone.

His first priority was to get to his father. He crept towards the left wing of the castle, careful to avoid making too much noise. As inviting as the silence was, it also unnerved him. Every noise made him freeze in place until he was sure that the source had passed him by. Onyx wondered about using Shadow Slide but something told him that it was not a good idea. It was a great defensive and sneaking technique but one could not attack while still in its hold. Onyx also knew that he could not focus enough to properly execute it. He climbed the stairs that led towards the private quarters. Still no other living souls crossed his path.

Onyx thought back on what Ryder told him regarding Demons. A trained mind could sense the dark aura of a Demon's soul. A really trained mind could tell the difference between a younger Demon and an ancient Demon. It was a skill that came with experience for no Spiritborn could mimic the same aura as a Demon. He thought back to when he had foolishly confronted Kaiser and when he had met Rache face to face. It confused him as to how all this time, he did not realize that Kaiser's masked servant was a Demon and not just any Demon. Rache was infamous for his power and brutality. How could his cousin hope to compete with such an ancient and mighty beast? Onyx began to realize that his inexperience in judging others was showing. If he was going to be worth anything as a fighter, he would have to learn more about his prospective opponents. Ryder had tried to teach him that and showed him that an enemy could very easily take advantage of his inexperience.

"When this is all over, you are going to teach me how to really fight," Onyx whispered to himself. After saying it out loud, the goal of training under his cousin gave him the courage to keep moving forward. It gave him focus and confidence in light of his current task.

He was relieved when he finally reached his father's private quarters. By now, he was not surprised that the door was not guarded or had a door warden to announce visitors. Onyx opened the door as quietly as possible and closed it behind himself before he looked into the depth of the receiving room. The room looked as he remembered: a large crackling fire with a highbacked chair sitting before it. A side table next to the chair had a silver tray with a tea kettle and a single cup and saucer. The tea in the cup appeared to have been freshly poured as steam rose up in a small transparent cloud. Onyx stepped over to it and sniffed the cup. It was mint tea, his father's favorite. The scent relaxed him and brought forth pleasant memories of his boyhood, sitting by the fire and listening to his father tell stories. Onyx then spotted a folded note sitting on the seat cushion. He sheathed his sword and picked it up.

"Welcome back to your beloved home, your Highness. I also extend my hand towards your dear cousin for bringing you here. It has been such a long time since Cross has hosted so many sons of the Silvanus bloodline. I think that we should celebrate and raise our glasses to the might of your throne. From the desk of Kaiser Adonis," Onyx read aloud. He tossed the note into the fire where it quickly burned to a pile of ashes.

Onyx immediately knew that his father was not in his quarters and that Kaiser was fully aware of his and Ryder's movements in the city. At first, fear threatened to overwhelm him but he quickly battled it back down and let courage surge through his entire body. He took in a deep breath and let it out slowly to further calm himself. Last time, Onyx knew that his fear of Kaiser got the better of him. This time, that was not going to happen. He was going to be aware of his fear but he was not going to let it rule him.

Unlike before when he was creeping towards his father's quarters, Onyx travelled quickly using Shadow Slide to reach the throne room. He rose up from Shadow Slide just before the heavy ebony wood doors. He set his hands side by side where the doors met and shoved with all his might. Normally, it took a team of four to open the throne room doors. With Onyx's young developing strength, the doors creaked open as he stepped forward. Once he crossed the threshold, he let go and let his arms drop down to his sides. All of his focus then went forward towards the Shadowborn throne.

Reclined and stretched across the royal chair was Kaiser. He was dressed in a plain black house coat that lay open, exposing his lean muscled torso. His normally styled hair was tousled and messy. He even sported a five o'clock shadow. His blackened throat scar stretched and pulled across the skin of his neck as he laughed at some private joke. It was if he had dragged himself from bed and had made no true effort to look presentable before a Prince.

"Welcome, welcome, my dear Prince Onyx!" Kaiser boasted. He swung his legs around to sit up in the chair. "I am sad to see that your cousin did not follow you here."

Onyx slowed to a stop ten feet away. He clenched his jaw as his left hand settled on the pommel of his sword. "Only the Shadowlord can sit upon the throne," he growled.

Kaiser looked around from left to right and up and down before returning his gaze to Onyx. "I think that I can make it work for me." He bounced for a few seconds on the cushion. "Seems comfortable."

Onyx pulled out his sword and pointed it at Kaiser with an aggressive expression on his face. "That seat is for the sons of Shadow Night Silvanus only."

"Ah yes. The whole inheritance thing," Kaiser mused as he leaned forward, resting his elbows on his knees. He waved his right hand absentmindedly. "I happen to know a thing or two about heirs and bloodlines."

"Get off of that throne," Onyx snarled.

"Yada, yada, yada. Get off the throne. It's not yours. You're mean. You're nasty. I hate you," Kaiser mocked as he imitated Onyx's voice with a squeaky inflection. He sneered as he leaned back in the seat, resting his hands on the arm rests. "Put that sword away before you hurt yourself."

It was infuriating Onyx that Kaiser was not taking him seriously. He was the Crowned Prince of the Shadowborn, a direct descendant of Shadow Night Silvanus. He was born to greatness and he lived his life honorably. But as he thought about the declarations, he began to doubt what his role was. A flicker of memory in his heart brought him back to his senses. It was all part of Kaiser's game: to sow seeds of doubt with his clever wordplay.

"You can not fool me. Not this time," Onyx stated with confidence.

Kaiser feigned a look of defeat but soon smirked. There was a dangerous spark in his eyes. "Then let us talk like civilized men over a drink." He snapped his fingers once.

Out of the shadows beyond the royal chair came a hooded figure balancing a tray in his right hand with his left positioned behind his back. On the tray were two crystal glasses and a bottle of deep red wine. The newly arrived servant sauntered over to Kaiser and offered him the tray. Kaiser picked up the bottle and filled both glasses halfway. He traded out the bottle for one of the glasses. Onyx watched as the servant stepped back to Kaiser's right side, still balancing the tray in his right hand.

Onyx studied the servant, immediately seeing that it was not Kaiser's normal attendant. For starters, the new arrival was wearing black and red cloth that was torn and tattered. It was wrapped around his shoulders and torso in a loose fashion, leaving both arms bare. Because of the way the servant was standing in the mix of shadow and light, Onyx could only see his right side. The skin on the servant's right arm was pale and stretched tightly over corded muscles. It was clear that he was a hardened fighter. Nothing about him said young and inexperienced.

"Where is Rache?" Onyx asked.

Kaiser downed the wine in a single gulp before smacking his lips and setting the glass back on the tray. "He is busy so I asked this fine soul to assist me. I think he is doing quite well." He poured himself another glass of wine. "He is superb at obeying orders but curses like a Mirror Sea pirate. I find it to be a nice balance. Like this Umbra wine. Both harsh yet inviting to the tastebuds."

Trying to discern what exactly Kaiser was talking about was beginning to give Onyx a headache. "Where is my father?" he demanded.

"Such a loving son to worry about his dear father," Kaiser said as he stood up from the seat, grabbing the bottle of wine from the tray. He stepped down the dais and turned his head to glance at his servant. "He will tell you."

The servant slowly set down the tray on the seat cushion. He stepped around Kaiser and headed straight for Onyx in a slow walk. Onyx took a step back, holding his sword towards the servant. His grip tightened on the sword hilt. Kaiser swayed as he weaved around the dais towards the left, still carrying the glass and wine bottle. "Iztal, I'll be soaking in the hot springs. Let me know when you have finished with the royal brat."

A dark laugh and a sinister gleam sparked in the servant's eyes. The sound was unsettling to Onyx as it was both dark and familiar. It grew in volume as Kaiser disappeared into the left hand hallway. The servant slowed to a stop, the tip of Onyx's sword touching a swath of cloth on his chest.

"Lord Kaiser was right. You ask a lot of questions for a Shadow Child," the servant snickered. "Let me save you the trouble of a proper introduction. I am Iztal, slayer of Shadowborn and whoever my master commands me to kill."

It now dawned on Onyx that the new servant was a Demon and not just any Demon. It was Iztal. The Iztal. His father had told him the nightmarish story of when Sin Silvanus battled the

Demon before the smoldering ruins of Umbra. His great grandfather, after a long night of fighting that left his sword arm weak and useless, managed to slay Iztal by crushing the Demon's chest with a well placed kick. Onyx remembered how his father described Sin's heavy handed finishing move that knocked the wounded Demon to the ground so he ould wield a long knife with his good arm to deliver the killing blow. How was the one and only Iztal alive and standing before him?

As if he heard Onyx's mental question, Iztal pulled back his hood with his right hand and finally brought his left arm forward. It was grossly deformed with bloated red veins. The hand was twisted into monstrous claws. What was most horrifying to Onyx was that he immediately recognized the map of scars on Iztal's left side as his father's. It took everything within him not to stumble back in shock. He struggled to speak as his sword arm began to shake.

"How..." was all Onyx managed to say.

"Yea, sometimes I wonder how Kaiser does it but he does it and he does it very well. So here I am, back for a little revenge. Who better than a broken Shadowborn of Sin's line? How about the very Demon that killed his youngest son!" Iztal roared with pride. He laughed out loud, holding his stomach with his right hand until he calmed himself enough to speak again. "Surprise. I am the one that did in your grandfather and now, it's your turn to die."

FIGHT IN THE STREETS

Ryder had long put Onyx out of his mind though a sliver of thought hoped that his young cousin would succeed. A part of him envied the love Onyx had for his father for it was something that he never felt growing up. His mother Aylin was the dominating influence in his life up until her death. After she was gone, he felt abandoned and alone. He had turned to Haven and her family for solace. They had welcomed him with open arms. Her father thrilled in having him help in the forge, crafting swords and other weapons as an apprentice. Haven's mother taught him how to cook which he found both relaxing and challenging. Haven's three sisters adored him, treating him like a much loved older brother. At first, the transition from life with his mother to that of Haven's family was strange but he quickly adjusted. Ryder missed that life and now he was fighting to get it back.

He and Onyx had separated on a side street near the farmer's market. His young cousin headed towards the castle, leaving him to attempt to rescue Soja and search for Rache. Once he had broken the crowd at Soja's execution, he expected the people to be rushing to their homes for safety. The streets were abandoned of all people. Even the stray cats and dogs he expected to see were in hiding. Ryder immediately recognized it as the city's way of saying it was afraid. As he crept deeper into the city, the signs of fear became more intense. Street lamps were dim or completely void of a flame. A chill lingered in the air. To his trained eye, Ryder knew that Rache was nearby. No other entity could elicit such a reaction in the world than a Demon.

Ryder was not particularly fond of the idea of fighting Rache in a storm even though the Demon was gifted with a command over fire. It wasn't so much the rain itself that bothered him. It was the potential for blinding lightning strikes. He had been struck once before when traveling close to the northern borders of the Gryphon territory. The Sea Eagle Gryphon that had led him there waxed eloquently about storm flights and how only the Dragons could cross through the front that stretched out before them. Of the nine territories of the Northlands, Ryder had yet to visit two of them: the Darklands and the Dragonlands. Ever since that profound moment, Ryder was determined to become strong enough to travel through the storm front that guarded the Dragonlands. As such, he was experienced fighting in stormy weather but that did not mean that he enjoyed it.

"Where are you?" Ryder asked, mostly speaking to himself in a low whisper.

The gutters in the street had been transformed into miniature rivers from the rainfall. Dirt, market debris, and other assorted trash floated by. He spotted several buildings with poorly repaired roof tops and broken windows. Signs swung haphazardly from above doorways. Piles of refuse littered the sidewalks and spilled over into the streets. It made Ryder sneer at the thought that Kaiser had such control of the Shadow Council that the cleanliness of the city suffered. Cross may not have been his home but it was the capital of the Shadowborn.

He followed the dark warning in his heart towards the slums. Upon turning the corner, Ryder spotted a pale half dressed corpse. He sniffed the air finding the smell of decay hanging heavy. He quickly crossed the mucky cobble stone street to closely examine the body. The neck of the body appeared to have been ripped open down to the bone. A shredded flap of skin was folded back away from the wound. Ryder turned the body over from its face down position, finding the deceased man's face frozen with fear.

"His blood was rather thin and poor in quality," Rache said from the other side of the street. He leaned back against a lamp post, licking the blood from his fingers. The Demon smacked his lips. "People from this," he paused to absentmindedly gesture with a wave of his blood soaked right hand. "...Hell hole tend to be poorly fed and malnourished. Blood is blood though."

"I am sure with Kaiser in power that you have had your pickings of Cross' unsuspecting citizens," Ryder said as he slowly stood up. Rain streamed down his face.

Rache nodded. "People tend to notice when servants go

missing in the castle. What is surprising how little those in power care about even the smallest and poorest of souls within their city walls." He crossed his arms looking away from Ryder. "This city is infested with deceit and cruelty. I love it!"

Ryder stepped over the body, slowly pulling his sword free from its sheath. "Really? I see the source of the city's infestation before me."

"That is the nicest thing someone has ever said to me," Rache teased as he feigned gratitude. He pressed his right hand to his chest, pretending like he was about to cry.

"Cut the theatrics. I am not the idiot that Morin was and I am not the liar that Kaiser is," Ryder snapped.

Rache finally turned to face Ryder, revealing that he had a sword in his left hand. Blood streamed down the blade and dripped onto the ground. The Demon looked just as he did the last time Ryder saw him. His tattered shirt was ripped open from his right shoulder down towards his left hip. Ryder could see an open gash that was puckered and red in color but the wound was not bleeding. Blackened veins trailed around it in a strange web. On any other person, the wound would have been mind numbing and painful but Rache barely appeared to notice it. Blood and gore stained his clothes and boots.

"I must thank you by the way for killing that pathetic waste of a Shadowborn soldier. I think Kaiser only kept him around for his own personal amusement. I'll admit watching him squirm was entertaining." Rache paused to laugh softly. "I wonder who will entertain me now. Perhaps Kaiser's bastard grandson."

"You can't kill me," Ryder declared as he raised up his sword, gripping the hilt tightly with both hands.

"True enough but I can still beat you to within an inch of your life," Rache said. He started to take slow steps towards Ryder. "I am truly going to enjoy that."

Ryder smirked. "Then let this be a battle for the ages. Kaiser's Demon versus Kaiser's sole descendent. If people are going to remember this, let it be for the explosive power and insurmountable might."

"Glad we are on the same page. Perhaps I will get to see if you are actually worth Kaiser's time and maybe you are his superior in the ways of war," Rache said as he spun his sword around into attack position.

Though Ryder and Rache hated each other, both fighters were eager to test their strength against the other in a proper one on one match. This time, there were no wards within the city and no allies. It was just the two of them. Demon versus Shadowborn. Ryder knew that Kaiser wanted him back under his control so his objective in the battle would be two fold: keep from being captured and distract the powerful Demon long enough for Onyx to fetch his father. With Rache so desparate to beat him and bring him back to Kaiser, Ryder knew he could keep the Demon's attention for a long time.

Rache charged forward, ready to drive Ryder back against the ramshackled buildings. He held his sword arm back in preparation for a full force attack once he was close enough. Ryder dug his feet and prepared to take the weight of the Demon. He did not want to draw on his native Spirit energy unless necessary. Using Spirit energy too often could tire him much faster and make him much more vulnerable to capture. Ryder could at least count on Shadow Slide to pull him out of a sticky situation. Rache crouched down before jumping high into the air. The Demon brought his sword high over his head, a roar on his lips. At the last possible second, Ryder side stepped Rache's strike, spinning around to slash at his back. Rache twisted out of reach of Ryder's downstroke. Ryder slid three feet on the slick ground as Rache threatened to cleave him in two.

The intricate sword dance began once Rache twisted at the last moment, his sword meeting Ryder's with a clap of thunder. They shoved against each other before Ryder pushed Rache back hard. With his greater weight against the Demon's slighter frame, it was easy to knock Rache off balance. Rache was quick to recover and slashed his sword at Ryder's torso. Ryder cartwheeled to the right just out of reach of the attack. He vaulted off of a hitching post to stab at Rache's left shoulder. The point of his sword sliced open a deep gash, cutting into the muscle. Rache lurched forward and snarled. The Demon tossed his sword to his right hand and his left arm immediately distorted into a grotesque swollen limb. Long claws tore out of his finger tips in a bloody mess. The swollen blood vessels throbbed from the pressure of the growing muscle beneath them. The Demon chuckled darkly as he wiggled the claws.

"Time to change the game," he snarled, a devilish smirk on his face.

Ryder had already felt the bite of Demon claws and the old wounds throbbed to remind him of the pain they caused. It was if Rache had picked up another sword and armed himself. The Demon returned for a counter attack, alternating between stabbing with the sword in his right hand and slashing at Ryder with his claws. It kept Ryder on his toes and never allowed him a moment to rest or to consider his next move. He was forced to go on the defensive, using his sword to block and depending on his armor to protect him. The grating sound of Rache's sword bouncing off his steel bracer made him mash his teeth together. Ryder tried to cut off Rache's claws but found them just as solid and hard as his sword. The next time he crossed swords with Rache, the Demon slashed at Ryder's left forearm. A long claw dragged across the back of Ryder's hand, slicing through the protective leather. His grip slackened on his sword and Rache threw his weight forward. Ryder fell back onto the street, splashing in a murky puddle of water.

"This is where you belong, bastard. At my feet. When I drag you back to Kaiser," Rache started to say before Ryder interrupted him.

Ryder swung his legs around, wrapped them around Rache's legs, and knocked him off his feet. Rache's back slammed on the ground. Ryder rolled forward, snatched up Rache's dropped sword, and spun around to face him. "You will have to drag me back like the Demon you are."

Rache roared before he flipped up to his feet. The same change that transformed his left arm surged through his right arm. His upper body bulked up as his shoulders broadened. His neck and torso thickened to support the increased weight. "If that is how you wish to fight, bastard, then I will fight you like the Demon I am."

"Good because I would like to kill you for the Demon you really are," Ryder exclaimed as he spun the swords in his hands. "Shall we?"

"We shall," Rache snarled as he brandished his sharp claws.

Demon and Shadowborn traded strikes with sword and claw. Ryder turned into a furious storm of deadly steel, stabbing and cutting at Rache. The Demon struck back with brutal strength, slicing through tall street lanterns and stone walls. Thunder boomed in increasing volume. Lightning flashed, illuminating the entire sky. Rain continued to fall in heavy sheets. Ryder slung water off of his swords as he spun towards Rache. He waited until Rache reared back for a counter attack before slipping into Shadow Slide. Rache stumbled forward, roaring in fury.

"I hate Shadow Slide!" Rache bellowed.

Seeing Rache unsettled was amusing to Ryder. Through the protective coat of Shadow Slide, he surged around Rache in a wide circle. As soon as he came around to Rache's back, Ryder burst out of Shadow Slide. He drove both swords deep into the muscle, pinning Rache to the ground. The Demon bucked like a wild stallion, trying to throw Ryder off.

STEEL ON STEEL

No matter how many hours he had dedicated to combat training, Onyx felt completely unprepared in facing a Demon like Iztal. In fact, he felt utterly powerless. His only saving grace was that Iztal was teasing him with feigned attacks and toying with him by leaving obvious openings for a counterattack. Whenever Onyx moved in to stab Iztal with his sword, the Demon blocked him at the last possible second. Each attempt by Onyx resulted in Iztal's manic laughter. Onyx was giving everything in trying to break through Iztal's defense and each defeat added to his desperation.

"So this is the mighty power of the Silvanus bloodline? Ha! You can not even scratch me with that needle of yours," Iztal mocked after he knocked Onyx to the floor.

Onyx spat out a mouthful of blood and used the back of his hand to wipe a splatter of it from his chin. He gritted his teeth as he pushed himself up off of the stone floor of the throneroom. Iztal had punched him hard on the left side of his face and his jaw throbbed with pain. He was certain that the bone was not broken but another hit like that could shatter his jaw entirely. With his left hand, Onyx manipulated and rubbed the sore spot as he flexed his jaw. He spat out another mouthful of blood as he stood up straight, holding his sword loosely.

"I do applaud you for your tenacity. I suppose that it is your Earthborn blood that you have to be thankful for. Earthborn are always so stubborn and don't know when to die," Iztal stated. He bowed his head as if to show respect.

It was all just part of the Demon's act as Onyx had discovered. The false praise was meant to throw him off and mock him. The behavior reminded Onyx of Kaiser and the young Prince wondered if he had imbued a part of himself onto the Demons he raised from the dead. Onyx tightened the grip on his sword as he tried to strengthen his resolve.

"It seems Demons do not know when to die either," Onyx said tightly.

"Aww. It is just so adorable to see you act tough. You think that you are actually strong enough to compete with me," Iztal teased as he brandished his claws.

Onyx knew that a Demon's words were just as powerful a weapon as their sharp claws and fiery touch. He watched as Iztal sauntered towards him, slowly at first but gradually increasing his speed. Iztal's pace grew faster as he drew back his left arm and set his right arm before him at an angle. Onyx decided to meet Iztal's charge. He gripped his sword with both hands, tightening his hold before he took off towards the Demon. Both fighters easily cleared the distance between them in seconds. Onyx began to swing his sword in a maneuver to cut Iztal's torso but as soon as his sword left his side, Iztal pressed his hand to the blade and flipped up over him. The Demon twisted his body around to slash at Onyx's back with his claws. Onyx stumbled forward from the force as the claws dragged across his armor. They screeched as they cut the metal, pulling at the chainmail underneath. Onyx gritted his teeth and before he fully regained his balance, he twisted and swung his sword back around. Iztal parried the sword with his claws, stopping it in its tracks.

He smirked as he waved a finger. "You will not get at me that easy." His right leg then shot forward. Iztal planted his foot on Onyx's chest and kicked him backwards at full force.

Onyx went flying until his back slammed into a tall pillar that held up the ceiling of the throneroom. The stone cracked from the impact and Onyx collapsed to the floor. His sword hilt cut into the palm of his hand. Hot blood greased his hand and Onyx lost his hold on the weapon. He gasped and coughed, spewing blood with each breath. The pain in his back grew hot within the span of a single heartbeat and Onyx wondered if his back was broken. He reflexively tried to move his feet. He was immensely relieved when he could feel his toes scratching the inside of his boot. His chest plate was crunched in, digging into his skin, but had managed to keep Iztal's kick from shattering his breastbone. There was still enough pressure to render taking a full and deep breath very difficult.

He did not want to believe that he was this pathetic of a

fighter against a Demon that was as powerful as Iztal. The Demon was using his father's broken body after all so how could he have all of this strength? Onyx slid his bleeding right hand on the floor in an attempt to wipe the sticky gore from his palm. He coughed hard as he tried to take note of where Iztal was. His head throbbed painfully, blurring his vision and sense of hearing. Even his thoughts were becoming muddled.

"Earthborn are both stubborn and tough to break. Had you not had your mother's blood, your spine would have been shattered from the impact. Do you know nothing of what it is to have Earthborn blood?" Iztal mocked with a booming laugh.

As a Prince of the Shadowborn, Onyx had always identified himself as a Shadowborn though he was half Earthborn too. But why did Iztal care? Was it all part of the Demon's game to prove that no Spiritborn could survive a contest against him? Onyx reached out for his sword and held it as tightly as he could. He flipped up to his feet, ignoring the throbbing pain. If he was a stubborn Earthborn beneath his Shadowborn exterior, then he would never give up until Iztal was dead. He rushed towards the Demon, intent on cleaving his left hand from his arm to disable the deadly claws.

Iztal snickered, having anticipated the maneuver. He blew a breath on his right hand as if to wake it up and claws tore out of his finger tips. He brandished the newly erupted claws and charged towards Onyx. Blade and claw met in a booming collision of thunder. Iztal parried Onyx's cuts and slashes as if he was fighting with his own pair of swords. He laughed, stuck his tongue out, and teased Onyx with openings. At first, Onyx was falling for the false openings but the Shadowborn prince quickly learned to avoid going after them entirely. Iztal then jumped back one step as Onyx was in full swing, causing the Prince to stumble. He hopped back in close and slammed his pointed elbow down on Onyx's sword arm. The Demon was prepared to laugh out loud but before he could utter a chuckled, Onyx's reflexive punch slammed into the right side of the Demon's head.

Onyx managed to grab his sword before it could hit the ground in the fluid counterattack he had laid on Iztal. As Iztal stumbled back, Onyx slashed upward, cutting a deep gash across the Demon's front. He was prepared to celebrate the small victory until he heard his father's voice in Iztal's scream of pain. Instantly, Onyx's mirth and courage diminished. He froze in place, barely able to breathe.

"Remember, your Highness. It's not just me you are fighting. It's your dear old dad!" Iztal laughed darkly. "And it won't just be me who dies when you deliver the killing strike."

To actually face the idea of ending his father's life instead of just thinking about it horrified Onyx in a way that he could not imagine. He was not a killer. He was not an executioner. Kaiser was both of those things. Even his cousin Ryder had the fortitude to take a life. But not him. Onyx began to weep as the thoughts consumed him. All resolve was gone. All hope that he would survive the night disappeared in a heartbeat. He was going to die and Iztal was going to end him. His sword dropped from his hand and clattered on the stone floor. It was now useless to him for he no longer had the will to fight.

"Don't you dare give up!" shouted his father's voice.

Onyx looked around, his head jerking back and forth from wall to wall and floor to ceiling. His eyes then settled on Iztal who had both hands gripped his head. The Demon's mouth was contorted in a wordless scream. His blood red eyes shifted to Aku's gray eyed gaze. Blood vessels bulged on his throat as if he was choking.

"You must fight! You must save me!" screamed Iztal with Aku's forceful voice. The Demon finally threw his head back and screamed at the top of his lungs.

Onyx pressed his hands over his ears to shield himself from the noise. The full throated scream was so loud that it cracked the pillars. Dust and pieces of stone rained down upon them. Onyx felt his bones threatening to crack and he was driven to his knees. He mashed his teeth together so tightly that the left side of his jaw throbbed with even more intense pain than before. He fell over on his side, trapping his dropped sword beneath his body.

Iztal's scream finally split and he bent over coughing up blackened blood. He spit out several mouthfuls before looking up at Onyx and snarling ferociously. His eyes were blood red again and full of fury. As Iztal opened his mouth to roar, his fangs were stained with blood. The Demon's roar was dangerous in its tone but it was strained.

"No more games, you worthless piece of shit!" Iztal snarled, bloody spittle hurling from his mouth. He pointed at Onyx with his left hand, the claws now transformed into cruel serrated blades. The scars that criss crossed the limb pulsating alongside the swollen veins. "It's time to say goodbye to everything you think you love and hold dear. I will end you!"

Onyx grabbed his sword and rolled quickly out of the way of Iztal's charge. The Demon slid to a stop and snapped his head towards him. He snarled before he twisted his body to resume his attack. With a flicker of thought, Onyx pulled himself into Shadow Slide, hoping to use the temporary shield of his Spirit energy to regain ground. Something had happened to incapacitate Iztal, even if only for a moment. His father's Spirit had broken through. His father was fighting with him to defeat Iztal. The thought gave Onyx immense courage and hope that his cause was not all lost. His thoughts jumped back to his lesson with Ryder. His cousin had used his inexperience against him. It was a weakness that Ryder saw and exploited. And now, Onyx saw a weakness in Iztal that he too could use against the powerful Demon.

He burst out of Shadow Slide just long enough to shout. "I will save you, Father! I will save you!"

The effect was immediate as Iztal stumbled but the Demon quickly recovered. He shook his head as if to rid himself of an annoying noise. "He can not hear you! His Spirit is broken!"

Onyx was not about to believe the Demon this time. He came out of Shadow Slide again. "Father! I know that you are in there and I know that you can hear me! I will not only defeat this Demon prison you are trapped in, I will win this war against Kaiser. Ryder and I will raise our swords to cast him down!"

Again, Iztal stumbled but his recovery came quicker than before. "Against Kaiser, there is no victory! And don't forget that I possess your father's body and his power!"

Onyx did not think that a Demon could utilize Shadow Slide or any of the native Shadowborn powers but Iztal did. The Demon roared as black bolts of Spirit energy sparked and whipped around his body in a furious tornado. He then slammed his hands on the floor, unleashing a shock wave that tore Onyx from Shadow Slide. The force of the Shadow Shock Wave sent Onyx flying through a tall glass window and out into the terrible storm.

CRASH AND BURN

It was sickening to see the pleasure Rache got from licking his own blood off of the broken sword blade. Ryder had grimaced as the Demon pulled the piece of steel through his chest, fighting back bile as the suction popped once the metal was free. Rache laughed as if the action tickled him though blood poured down his front. After being thrown from Rache's back, Ryder had slid twenty feet down the street, gouging his hands on the stone. He remained in a crouching position, testing the grip on his remaining sword. He tossed his head to fling the rain water from his eyes, his hair slapping back against his neck and face.

"That almost hurt," Rache snickered before scrapping his tongue against the broken steel in his right hand. Blood dripped from the corners of his mouth. "Spicy with a hint of burning heat. I wonder what your blood tastes like."

"Why don't you come over here and find out!" Ryder declared before he launched himself forward.

The thunder boomed and the lightning flashed in the sky as Ryder charged towards Rache, his remaining sword gripped tightly with both hands. A ferocious snarl was on his lips, his eyes burning with the thrill of the fight. Rache bellowed with his own roar as he rushed forward to meet Ryder's attack. The whole sword and the broken sword met in a shower of sparks from the force of the impact. Steel screeched and screamed like a dangerous fight between two predators. Faster than the blink of an eye, Ryder and Rache traded blows that shook the ground and cracked nearby windows. In an explosion of glass, the lanterns burst from the force of their strikes. Flames snuffed out quickly in the pouring rain, trails of smoke reaching into the sky.

Ryder could not dwell on the people inside the nearby buildings who were likely cowering in fear with hands over their heads. The only thing that mattered was right before him. His only focus was to defeat Rache and rid Cross of Kaiser's favorite weapon. Rache in his long years of service to Kaiser was very familiar with how Shadowborn fought so Ryder knew he could not fight him as the Demon expected. He twisted and flowed like an errant wind, sliding under attacks like a rushing wave. It surprised Ryder that the Shadowborn were considered the best warriors when the Airborn and Waterborn understood so much more about a body's ability to move. But that flicker of thought passed as Rache swung his broken steel blade at Ryder's neck. He bent over backwards as the weapon passed over him before popping back up. He jabbed his sword forward at Rache's exposed chest.

"You are better than this, Rache. You are the flower of the Darklands. Ferocious and terrible. And yet you are losing to a child!" Ryder mocked, hinting at their age difference.

The jab at the Demon's strength worked as Rache roared in fury. Ryder jumped back just in time to avoid being smacked in the head with Rache's swinging arm. The Demon roared again, throwing the broken blade down. It shattered into a thousand tiny pieces from the force of the impact.

"I will find a way to kill you!" Rache bellowed, his voice laced with a deep roar.

Ryder knew that Rache's weakness was his pride along with his hate for Kaiser and he was prepared to use it against him. With the Demon infuriated, he was likely to make mistakes that he would never make if he was calm and in control. But Ryder knew he had to be careful. A Demon's rage could very easily get out of control.

Rache's body twisted and grew into a more monstrous form. The change that had occurred to his arms and upper body descended down to the bottoms of his feet, leaving him a huge mass of swollen muscle. Bony protrusions erupted from his heels as the bones of his foot cracked and stretched. More protrusions tore through the cloth covering Rache's back. His face contorted and stretched into that of a monstrous Hell hound, jaws full of long sharp teeth. His crimson hair grew into a thick mane that looked like a raging fire. He bent forward, roaring louder than the thunder.

Illuminated by the flashing lightning, Rache's true form was devastating to look upon. Ryder did not cower before the monstrous Demon for it had been his intention from the beginning to draw out Rache's beast form. He wanted Rache's greatest weapon out in the open. For several long seconds, the two faced each other in fevered anticipation as the storm raged around them. Rache in his new form towered over Ryder and outweighed him by several hundred pounds. Ryder looked like a small sapling before a collosal oak tree. Steam rose up from Rache's heated body in twisting spirals.

"Now you are fighting me like the Demon you are," Ryder said calmly. A rush of air and heat surrounded his right arm, bursting into the silver Spirit Fire that consumed his arm from shoulder to the tip of his sword.

The Demon's response was an earth shaking roar that cracked the stone street and shook the nearby building hard enough to split the walls. Rache began to charge forward, picking up a broken street lantern pole as a weapon. Ryder did not move but he watched carefully, slipping into Shadow Slide just as Rache swung the iron pole. It clipped him on the left shoulder before he could surge away. The pain was muted by the protection of Shadow Slide but Ryder knew that the bone was crushed. He whipped around Rache as fast as he could before bursting out of Shadow Slide. As Ryder raised his Spirit Fire licked sword, Rache rolled around and slammed his makeshift weapon into Ryder's torso.

Ryder went flying and crashed through a nearby storefront. The window shattered upon impact, cutting him all over his back. He collided with the back wall and collapsed to the ground. His head swam as his vision was completely gone. Even his hearing was distant and shaky. His hearing recovered first as he heard Rache tearing through the rest of the front wall, laughing darkly.

"Oh. Did the baby Shadowborn forget that I become faster too?" Rache tormented in a deep and horrible voice. "There is a reason I was able to kill Begin Anu and it was not because I am strong."

Ryder's vision began to clear as Rache loomed over him. The Demon's hot breath stank of rotting flesh. Coupled with his swimming mind, Ryder vomited, nearly choking on his own bile. His balance and ability to center himself was slow to return and he was desparate to get away. Rache's right hand clamped over Ryder's neck and he lifted him up from the debris. The Demon snorted in Ryder's face. It only took a single second of clear thought for Ryder to act. He plunging his melting sword into the meat of Rache's arm. Rache shrieked from the burning pain as he released Ryder, dropping him to the floor. As soon as his back hit the stone, Ryder managed to pull himself into Shadow Slide and escape from Rache's reach.

He stumbled as he reappeared outside in the streets, rain doing very little to cool his heated pain and calm his nerves. Rache continued to wail, fully focused on the burning metal in his arm. Ryder fell to one knee, holding his stomach with his right arm as he retched up a mixture of bile and blood. He wanted to tap into his Spirit energy to use a Waterborn technique of healing but he needed the energy more to fight Rache. The healing would also take too much time and it would be worse to be disrupted during the process. Such disruption could unsettle the focus necessary and send Spirit energy through him in a destructive wave, doing more damage. Ryder forced himself to his feet, gritting his teeth against the pain.

Rache howled one last time before he ripped the metal away, tearing his flesh. He turned around to face Ryder and snarled, spittle dripping from his jaws. "I may not be able to kill you but I will do everything in my power to make you wish that you were dead!"

Ryder steeled himself in preparation. He slipped into Shadow Slide as soon as Rache drew close and he sped around towards the Demon's right side. Unexpectedly, Rache grabbed him and ripped him out of Shadow Slide and slammed him into the ground. The Demon pressed down, crushing Ryder's abdomen while Ryder furiously clawed at Rache with his right hand. He reared his right hand back, igniting a burst of Spirit Fire and jabbed it into the metal burn wound. Rache howled and released the pressure. Ryder rolled towards his left and flipped up to his feet. He coughed heavily, spitting out blood.

The Demon's howl transformed into a low hearty laugh as he slowly turned his head to look at Ryder. The look in his blood red eyes was deadly. Ryder had to wonder how Rache was able to tear him from the shield of Shadow Slide when Demons were unable to use Spirit energy. They were not born or possessed the natural command necessary. They were creatures of blood. They were the masters of reading memories from the water of life. It then hit Ryder. Rache was raised by the blood of Shadowborn and bonded to Kaiser. The Demon had access to their power and who knew what Kaiser truly was capable of. Ryder instantly knew that he was essentially fighting Kaiser through the guise of Rache. This he had not anticipated.

"Now you are starting to see the true power of the bond I share with your grandfather. It may be a prison but what a wonderous prison!" Rache gloated. "You too could experience this power for yourself. Command the might of the Darklands with a pass of your hand. Command the entire North and bend everyone to your will."

Ryder had been tempted by the idea of taking the Shadowborn throne. There were so many that believed him the most capable to rule over any other Silvanus son. Everyone had always told him that he was the very image of Shadow Night. He clenched his fists, ignoring the screaming pain. Kaiser was offering him the chance to be his heir if he would only accept him. He could learn to command Demons like Rache to fight for him and protect him.

"No," Ryder growled. That was not the life he wanted.

"Fair enough but you will only get so many chances before Kaiser decides to kill you," Rache said matter of factly. He brandished his claws and curled his lips back to reveal jagged fangs.

Bereft of a sword, Ryder was forced to depend on his flagging speed and agility and shaky hold over his Spirit energy. But as he told himself from the beginning, his mission in Cross was to keep Rache occupied. He managed to dodge a heavy handed punch from Rache, disrupting his thoughts as he leapt away. Ryder grabbed the edge of a nearby overhang and swung himself back around to land on Rache's back. He gripped the largest of the bony spikes, using it as an anchor as Rache began thrashing and clawing at him. Ryder gritted his teeth and grimaced every time a claw scratched his body and soon his left side was torn up and bleeding profusely.

Rache suddenly pitched forward in a roll, crushing Ryder with his weight. The Demon finished his roll and reversed back up to his feet. He snarled in a teasing manner.

Ryder gasped for breath, his rib cage crushed in. The very spike he had been using as an anchor had pierced his body, leaving a gaping hole. The street water splashed against his sides as the rain continued to fall in heavy sheets. A shadow passed over his face, lightning flashing to reveal Rache's monstrous frame. The Demon began to smile and laugh.

HERITAGE OF THE EARTH

Instinct drove Onyx once he was out in the open space. His eyes darted around, desparate to find a shadow. As soon as he spotted what he was searching for, Onyx pulled himself into Shadow Slide. It was a messy attempt to avoid falling the hundreds of feet to the ground below. The Shadow Slide was immediately broken as soon as Onyx hit the side of the rock wall of the Heights. The stone was slick from the torrential downpour and Onyx nearly lost his grip on the tiny ledge. He slammed into the cold stone so hard that he lost his breath and heard the crack of several ribs. Stars danced before his eyes as the pain threatened to overwhelm him. It took Onyx several minutes to regain enough control over himself to open his eyes again.

Up above, Iztal stuck his head out to look for his prey, smiling when he looked down and spotted Onyx. The Demon crawled through the broken window like a grosteque cockroach, gripping the stone with surprising dexterity. He snickered and flashed his white fangs.

Onyx knew that he could not use his Shadowborn power against Iztal. Though the Demon himself could not summon Spirit energy, Iztal was in his father's body and privy to all of his abilities to call it forth. In truth, Onyx did not know everything his father had been capable of. He had always imagined him to be a superior warrior. What Silvanus son wasn't? His thoughts then turned to dismay as he thought about himself. Onyx did not feel he could count himself amongst such an elite group. Yes, he knew how to fight. He had been trained by the best and yet, his bastard cousin outclassed him. But as Ryder had told him, experience was what mattered in a fight. It was not enough to know how to use a sword, the act of actually wielding the weapon was a totally different understanding. And it was obvious that Iztal knew Onyx's true lack of skill. It was if the Demon could predict everything he was going to do before he could actually do it. Onyx's inexperience made him predictable and vulnerable to the combined force of Iztal and his father's mind.

The Demon's connection to Aku's mind was however a weakness that Onyx planned to exploit. As he had discovered, his father's Spirit was fighting with Iztal beneath the surface. He swung his right hand up to grip the ledge. The rock crumbled and Onyx fell backwards several feet before he managed to find another rock ledge to grab on to. The stone cut into his palms and the blood made his grip more precarious. Onyx looked up to watch as Iztal crawled down the rock face towards him. Lightning flashed behind the Demon, illuminating him like a black spider crawling down a wall. The look in his eyes was horrifying and deadly.

"I will smear your dirty blood all across this rock face!" Iztal declared with a booming voice. "Then your people will see how thin and weak you truly are!"

It was hard not to be shaken by Iztal's words. Onyx tightened his grip on the stone and gritted his teeth together. He still had his weapon. "I will not die, Father!"

Iztal froze in place and shook his head repeatedly as if to rid himself of a troublesome noise. He brought up his left hand to smack the side of his head.

"I will not give up!" Onyx bellowed as he reared his right arm back. He swiftly punched the rock face, shaking it with the force of his Earthborn Spirit energy.

The stone cracked and split, a crevice climbing up towards Iztal with alarming speed. He struggled to maintain his grip as the stone shook beneath him. A final jolt as the split in the rock face reached him threw Iztal into the open air. He tumbled over Onyx's head, thrashing and struggling to regain a secure hold. He found his hold before he could fall to the ground. Onyx seethed as Iztal's claws dug into his calf and nearly slipped himself as the Demon's full weight threatened to drag him down. Iztal tried to reach up with his right hand before thumping back against the wall.

"If I go down, you are going down with me!" Iztal shouted over the thunder. He began to pull Onyx down.

Onyx tightened his grip on the stone, the pain in his leg searing like a raging wildlife. He slammed his eyes shut. The pain became even worse as Iztal's claws dug deeper into the muscle. In a gut reaction, Onyx pulled himself into Shadow Slide, dragging Iztal with him. Despite the extreme danger, Onyx could not kick the Demon free in time. He surged for the top of the Heights, the Shadow Slide breaking in and out of focus. Onyx took one look over his shoulder just before clearing the ledge. A silvery form hovered over Iztal, trying to tear the Demon's claws free from Onyx's leg.

Both Demon and Shadowborn tumbled and rolled out of Shadow Slide. Onyx fought free of Iztal's grip, kicking him in the face. The Demon spat and snapped his fangs, blood dribbling down his chin. Onyx struggled to get to his feet, his right leg unsteady with his weight. He stumbled once before managed to maintain balance. He leaned heavily on his left hip.

Iztal snarled before launching himself off of his stomach and settling on his feet. Blood, mixed with rain, dripped down his body. The liquid mixture ran down his claws and fell to the stone at his feet.

"I bet that hurt," the Demon snickered, gesturing towards Onyx's wounded leg.

"Nothing you can say will hurt worse than what I must do," Onyx snapped, using the burning pain to fuel his courage.

"Oh? You mean kill dear old daddy? Yes. I suppose that would hurt. I can help you by tearing out your heart so it doesn't cause you too much pain," Iztal casually suggested.

Onyx clenched his fists tightly. In Shadow Slide, he knew that he saw his father's Spirit trying to help him. He could not see Aku now but Onyx knew that he was close. That gave him a sense of peace despite the obvious danger before him.

"At least there will those that shall mourn him. I wonder. Will anyone care if you die?" Onyx asked harshly.

Iztal shrugged. "I have already died once. Kind of like your father. Rache did such a good job that even I had to stand up and applaud him for his fine work."

Though the memory threatened to overwhelm his mind, Onyx forced it back down. "Whether or not I live, there are those that will tear you to shreds for ending me."

"Hmmm. I suppose that I should be worried about your bastard cousin. You might actually want to be worried too. He is Kaiser's grandson after all and I certainly would not trust anyone of that bloodline," Iztal said with a devilish grin.

Was that how Ryder was so much stronger and smarter than him? Was it because he was of Kaiser's blood? Was Ryder truly fighting to save the throne? The sheer amount of questions bogged down Onyx's focus and his balance wavered. He fell to one knee, seething.

"Awww. Got a booboo?" Iztal snickered as he lurched forward. "Let me help you with that."

Onyx managed to roll out of the way just in time to avoid his arm being sliced from his body. Iztal's claws screeched as they hit the stone, sending up a wave of sparks. The Demon snarled as he quickly turned his gaze on Onyx.

"Father! I know that you are near!" Onyx shouted upon seeing the blood red eyes.

Iztal shrieked and grabbed his head, spitting up a stream of blackened blood. "Stop it!"

Onyx did not know if Iztal was shouting at him or shouting at his father's Spirit but he pressed on. "Oh. Do you have a booboo too?" he mocked.

Iztal's answer came in a deafening roar as he reasserted his control. The Demon charged towards Onyx. Onyx stumbled on his injured leg, narrowly avoiding another of Iztal's attempts to rip into his arm. He knew that he could not depend on his physical power to fight with his leg so weak. His Shadowborn Spirit energy would only help him so much before Iztal broke through it again. Untrained, Onyx had only one choice: his Earthborn Spirit energy. His thoughts drifted back to the Crossroads Arena, seeing the magnificent power of Captain Oaken as he shifted massive stones. A flicker of worry halted him. What consequences did the Earthborn face if they tried things they were not ready for? Was it the same as the threat of falling into the void for a Shadowborn? Risk or not, Onyx had nothing left in his arsenal.

He thought about how Shadow Slide was initiated by sensing the cool of a shadow while centering one's core. Using it as a guide, Onyx focused inward, instead drifting to the warmth of his memories. He relived countless moments with his mother when she taught him about his Earthborn heritage. Everything she taught him, from the names of plants to the different types of rock, flashed in his mind. In the midst of his focus, Onyx found the invisible magnetic field that he knew the Earthborn could sense with ease. It was a strange and almost foreign feeling and yet it felt right. It felt like coming home to Onyx. When he opened his eyes, his mouth dropped open.

To each side of Iztal were the Spirits of his parents. His father's silvery form held the hand of his mother's light green essence. They both smiled with immense pride before slowing starting to dissipate. Onyx reached out to them, catching Iztal's attention.

"What are you looking at? Do you see death?" Iztal teased as he brandished his claws.

"No. I see who I am. I am the son of Aku Silvanus, Lord of the Shadowborn. I am the son of Nuru, Princess of the Earthborn. I am Shadowborn and I am Earthborn!" Onyx affirmed as he wrapped himself in the energy of the field.

The fight began again as the lightning flashed, illuminating the entire sky. Onyx used the field's energy to stabilize his wounded leg as he charged forward. Iztal was ready for him, slashing with his claws. He swung his deformed muscular arms to cut at Onyx but the Shadowborn Prince dropped down to his knees and slid underneath the attack. Once Onyx was behind Iztal, he flipped up to his feet in a spin. He drew upon the field energy again as he continued his spin, knocking Iztal down with a heavy kick. The Demon fell, hitting his chest on the stone. Iztal growled, swinging his legs in a spiraling spin to knock Onyx off of his feet. Onyx lost his balance and began falling backwards. He managed to get a hand on the ground to shove himself back into the air with an agile flip, narrowing avoiding another kick.

He landed heavy on his feet, cracking the stone, a plan forming in his head. "What do you think of me now, Father?"

Iztal snarled as his blood red eyes shifted back and forth to Aku's silver eyed gaze. Veins pulsated on his face from the extreme effort to keep the Spirit back. "I see a warrior in the making," came the double voiced reply. "I see my son."

Onyx laughed as he saw how Iztal struggled to regain control. It surprised him when he heard his mother's sweet laugh and he smiled. Both of his parents were looking out for him. Now he only needed to set their Spirits free.

KAISER'S GAME

The first thing that Ryder could sense was that he was swaying back and forth, his limbs smacking against each other. His senses were slow to settle but he quickly realized that he was walking. No, someone was carrying him and they were walking. For a second, the thought seemed completely odd and foreign. He was supposed to be fighting Rache in the streets under a stormy sky. The stony street should not be swaying beneath him though his head swam and his chest burned. But who was carrying him? Ryder's eyelids fluttered until he slammed them shut upon smelling the stomach churning odor of rotting flesh. Bile rose up in the back of his mouth.

The jolting motion of going down stairs sent waves of pain throughout Ryder and he gritted his teeth to avoid spewing. He groaned involuntarily. Rache jabbed his shoulder upward into Ryder's stomach to get him to shut up. The Demon snarled in warning against any further outbursts whether whispered or shouted. Ryder felt like that perhaps he had said or done something before to warrant the reaction. He then realized that Rache was no longer in his monstrous form and he could no longer feel the rain falling.

Why did he feel so confused? If he was inside, the rain would not be falling. Ryder groaned again as his head throbbed. Another jolt of the Demon's shoulder reminded him to be quiet. Ryder resorted himself to silence with no argument. He felt his senses start to settle out and decided to focus on counting the number of steps Rache was taking. It was sure to be an inaccurate number but Ryder hoped that he could use the count to figure out where the Demon was going. They were definitely descending but to where? Rache seemed absolutely sure but he was not going to give up answers easily.

Ryder's vision soon cleared enough to realize that the stairs were constructed of a dark stone. A fine mist clung to them. Grooves were cut into the stairs to prevent slipping. It suddenly occurred that these were the stairs that lead to the hot springs inside the rock wall of the Heights. It had been many years since he last visited the hot springs under very different circumstances. A dumb smile crossed his face as Ryder remembered showing Haven the space and the hours they spent in the water, her small body pressed against his body. The heat of the passionate memory gave Ryder a sense of warmth and steadiness.

He was suddenly dropped and he hit the stone floor hard. Curling up in a ball, Ryder fought back waves of pain with short breaths that only made it worse.

"Welcome back to Cross, dear grandson," came Kaiser's distinctive smug voice. A soft chuckle followed. "Have some wine. It will dull your pain."

Ryder forced his eyes open. Before him in the warm water pool was Kaiser sporting a five o'clock shadow of stubble on his face. His midnight hair was partially slicked back on his head by the moisture in the air though several strands clung to his forehead. He was reclined back against the stone ledge of the pool, his arms draped around the shoulders of two stunning women. In his left hand was a half full crystal wine glass. His right hand was pressed against the back of one Shadowborn woman's head, stroking her dark locks. He bent in to kiss her brow, keeping his dangerous eyes on Ryder. The woman moaned with delight and shuffled in to press her body against his chest. The other woman reached across Kaiser to wrap her arm around his neck and Kaiser turned to kiss her. When his lips left hers, he snickered with a devious smirk.

"Ladies, do not be shy. This is my grandson Peredur," Kaiser mused to the pair. He then looked back at Ryder. "Or do you prefer that ridiculous nickname Ryder?"

A third Shadowborn woman of equal beauty sauntered into view. She was wearing an oversized house coat and nothing else. Kaiser leaned his head back as she bent down, murmuring a sweet nothing. Whatever he said amused the woman as she stroked his hair, brushing back his bangs. Kaiser laughed in response. Both of the women in the water with him moaned, pressing themselves against him.

"Sweet girls, there is plenty of me to go around," Kaiser said as he set his glass down. The woman behind him picked it up and promptly drank the contents.

Ryder did not know whether to be disgusted by the sight or impressed. Kaiser had never appeared to be an attractive prospect though he was not lacking in his handsome looks. He was tall, finely built, and very wealthy. What woman would deny that? Ryder studied the three women draped around Kaiser, realizing that they were courtesans. They were undoubtedly much younger than the man they were fawning over. Though he wasn't completely certain, the women in the water were topless and very likely completely naked. Bile rose up in the back of his throat as he realized that Kaiser was equally unclothed. Something about the idea of Kaiser being naked made Ryder want to vomit.

"You're disgusting," Ryder grumbled as he tried to push himself up off of the floor. Rache pressed a foot to his back to force him back down.

Kaiser laughed. "I am just enjoying the spoils of war. Is that so wrong?" He waved his right hand for Rache to step back from Ryder. "Besides it is lonely here at the top and nothing soothes that feeling like the heat of a woman's flesh. I would think that with your lover, you would understand."

It did not surprise Ryder that Kaiser knew about Haven. He was however prepared to ferociously protect her. "You are still disgusting."

Kaiser raised a finger as if to make a point. "Just to remind you that your mother's mother was a whore. A very beautiful one but still a whore. At least I think she was. I did not really pay attention." He snickered as his hands drifted down the backs of the two courtesans, disappearing beneath the water. They then giggled with delight.

Ryder gritted his teeth as he tried to push himself up off of the floor. This time, Rache did not stop him. He shook his head and spat out a globule of blood. Out of the corner of his eye, Ryder saw that Kaiser finally lost his confident grin and was frowning. Ryder settled on his knees, taking careful breaths to calm his senses.

"And you call me disgusting? Look at you," Kaiser said, gesturing towards the blood and gore that covered Ryder. "You're filthy."

"If I am your heir, I think this is quite fitting. Unlike you, I do not hide the blood I shed," Ryder fired back as he pressed his hands to the stone floor.

Kaiser then smirked as the third courtesan began massaging his bare shoulders. "I hide nothing. I am who I am though the world is too afraid to see everything there is about me. I can not control what they see. You however hide everything. You are desparate to control what others see."

The three women giggled as Kaiser flattered attention on each of them with teasing kisses and fondling grabs. He pulled the two women in the water closer to his body, murmuring words that obviously pleased them. The third woman stroked his cheek, whispering something under her breath back to him. Kaiser leaned his head back into her lap, smiling. The woman bent down to kiss him on the lips.

Ryder could not stand the erotic display before him. He desparately wanted to rip Kaiser's confident smirk from his face. His fingertips dug into the stone, cracking it from the force of his touch. "What do you want from me?"

Kaiser gestured for the third courtesan to move back with a wave of his hand. She harrumphed and reluctantly slid away. The black house coat billowed around her in cloth waves. Kaiser snapped his fingers and she promptly began filling the glass with wine. Once she was finished, she handed Kaiser the glass. He took a sip and smacked his lips. The girl pressed against his left side took the glass and giggled before drinking a mouthful. She then passed it to the woman on Kaiser's right who finished off the glass of wine with a long draught. Still holding the glass, she bent in to kiss Kaiser.

"Ladies, I am trying to conduct business. Why don't you get dried off and wait for me in my quarters?" Kaiser suggested softly.

The courtesans frowned, reluctant to leave Kaiser. The two women in the water each took a turn to kiss him before standing up. Ryder had to admit that each girl was shaply and attractive with long limbs and curvy figures. Black locks of hair cascaded down to their shoulders and down their backs. Water dripped from their bodies as they stepped out of the pool. Kaiser slapped their posteriors with a devilish smirk on his face. The girls giggled as they each picked up a towel, wrapping the fabric around their naked bodies. They blew kisses towards Kaiser as they exited the hot springs through a dark passageway. The third woman dropped the house coat from her shoulders, revealing an equally beautiful body. She pirouetted slowly on her feet before sauntering after her two companions.

"Such fine beauties," Kaiser sighed deeply as he reached up to smooth his hair. "We should have some fun later."

"Sir," Rache started to say.

Kaiser brushed him off. "Not now. I am spending time with my dear grandson who I love with all my heart."

"That is utter bullshit," Ryder snapped.

"Hmmm. Perhaps it is. I doubt that I could ever change your opinion of me," Kaiser admitted with a shrug. He stretched out his arms to rest on the ledge of the pool. "But I do actually have business to conduct. First, let's chat."

"About what?" Ryder asked as he began to draw upon the latent field energy in the stone.

"About you," Kaiser started to say. "Peredur Adonis Coba-Silvanus. Better known as Ryder Coba. Son of Akakios. Son of Aylin. I know more about you than you think. I know you left Cross because of me, not because of Zoras pushing the legitimacy idea. I know the details of your world travels and what you have learned. I know your strengths and your weaknesses."

Ryder sneered as he continued to pull the energy into his body to strengthen his broken bones. "Do you?"

Kaiser nodded. "You and the others may not see it but my reach is further and deeper in the world than can be seen." He lifted up his left hand, making it seem like his fingers were claws. "Try to tear me free and the world will fall. But certainly even I have an end and every man must have a son who follows him. You and I are the last of the line of Adonis, Begin Anu's eldest."

"You know what? I do not care. People seem to think that blood is all that matters in this world. Who you are related to. How great and powerful your ancestors are. I will make my own destiny!" Ryder declared.

"You don't have to get angry," Kaiser said before he twisted around to lift himself out of the pool. For a man of Kaiser's advanced years, his body was still carefully sculpted with hard muscle. He quickly covered himself with his house coat, tying the belt around his waist. "Go ahead and leave. I have all the time in the world to bring you back. Run to your lover and embrace her one last time," he said absently waving with his hand.

Rache took one step away from the opening to the stairs, arms crossed tightly. He eyed Ryder as if to dare him to leave. He snapped his fangs once. A map of reddened veins surrounded his eyes. His bones appeared more prominent in the low candlelight.

"The next time we meet, I promise that I will be the one to end you," Ryder warned once he got to his feet.

Kaiser kept his back to Ryder, letting out a low dark laugh. He set his hands on his hips before looking over his shoulder. "It will be the last time I extend the chance for you to become my heir. For if you deny me, I will destroy you."

Ryder knew that Kaiser meant every word of the threat but he still could not understand why he was letting him go. With the field energy he had pulled from the stone, Ryder was able to maintain his balance as he stepped backwards towards the opening. Kaiser gestured for him to leave as if his presence was an annoyance. He glanced at Rache as he came alongside the Demon. Rache snorted, eyes flashing blood red in warning. The Demon was clearly angry though Ryder was not sure if Rache was mad at him or at Kaiser. Despite his apprehension, Ryder turned and quickly ran out of sight up the stairs.

*****

"Oh no. He's getting away," Kaiser said halfheartedly.

"Are you crazy? You wanted him captured alive. I brought him to you and you let him go? Why?" Rache demanded in a harsh tone. He swept his arms towards the opening where Ryder had just left. With a furrowed brow, he stared at Kaiser's back, silently demanding an answer.

Kaiser was not moved. He turned around to face Rache, rubbing his forehead. "You just do not get it." He dropped his hand and lifted up his eyes. "This is just a game and he is but a pawn. I intend to move the pieces as I please until I decide that they are no longer worth my time. Besides, without Morin, who else is there to entertain me?"

VICTORY?

Iztal was now fighting with more desperation and ferocity than Onyx thought possible. The Demon was angry, pushing all of his rage to the forefront. He slashed with his claws and snapped with his fangs like a cornered animal. It was if he knew that the Spirits of Onyx's parents were now allied with their son and fighting against him. Up until this point, the fight had been a trivial game. Now, it was about survival.

Onyx too thought about survival, the first true feeling that perhaps his inexperience was not a lost cause against greater opponents. He was capable of getting better. Maybe even good enough to compete with his cousin Ryder. The only thing that stood in Onyx's way was Kaiser, the one person that could end it all for everyone. Onyx knew that the first step in freeing himself from Kaiser's reach was to end his father's suffering. He hated himself and Kaiser each time his mind touched on the painful thought.

"It did not have to be this way," Onyx declared in a voice that threatened to break. He closed his eyes and bowed his head, clenching his fists tightly. With a deep breath, Onyx looked up at Iztal. "It does not have to be this way."

The Demon sneered. He flipped back up to his feet after tripping over an upraised stone. Brushing the dirt from his chest, Iztal steadied himself. He snorted as if the fall was a minor inconvenience. "Doubting yourself again? I am growing tired of it."

"Perhaps you fear my father's Spirit coming to knock you back down," Onyx stated with quiet confidence.

Iztal laughed heartedly. "I do not fear him or anything the Spirit World can throw at me. I have beaten death once. I can beat it again."

The thunder boomed as lightning flashed behind the Demon's deformed frame. Though the heavy rainfall had abated into a misty drizzle, the storm threatened to restart at any moment. It was if the bad weather ebbed and flowed with Onyx's courage and Iztal's wild confidence. The lightning flashed again, illuminating the stone in black and white.

"How can you be so sure? How can you be certain that Kaiser will bring you back?" Onyx asked, using any chance of conversation to learn more about his enemy.

Iztal spat on the ground. "Just as you are doubting your own power, you doubt Kaiser's true might. You and the rest of the world have no idea of what he is capable of."

It was disheartening to think of Kaiser being anymore dangerous and fearsome than he already was. Ryder seemed to have an inkling of it and if he was indeed of Kaiser's bloodline, perhaps he was privy to the same deep power. The questions threatened to overwhelm Onyx but he wrestled them back down into the depths of his mind. He had to focus.

"And what is Kaiser capable of? Killing thousands? Razing a city to the ground in a single night? He seems more content to sit upon the throne of my ancestors drinking wine and watching the world around him," Onyx fired back, remembering how drunk Kaiser appeared in the throne room.

The Demon only snickered as he took a step forward. "You will just have to find out from the other side!"

"Not if my father has anything to say about it!" Onyx shouted back with renewed courage. Surely if his father was on his side, maybe the rest of his ancestors were too.

As soon as the words left Onyx's lips, Iztal stumbled from an invisible assault. The Demon grabbed his head, his mouth dropped open in a wordless scream. The bloated veins pulsated in painful throbs as they threatened to burst from the pressure. For a moment, Onyx felt sad for Iztal, a Demon who was just a pawn for Kaiser. But then he felt a surge of anger for knowing how his father suffered from Kaiser's machinations and from Iztal's deadly possession. The heat of the field energy burned like a fire threatening to explode into a raging storm of destruction. It was if the stone beneath his feet was feeding into his anger, treating him as a vessel for its own rage. The world was no longer a sleeping giant.

Onyx flipped backwards, slipping into Shadow Slide as soon as his feet hit the ground. Once in the black veil, Onyx saw the inferno of the earth's rage. He embraced it fully and utterly, pulling the energy into his body and aiming it forward.

Iztal, still in the grips of Aku's Spiritual attack, roared as he tried to tear himself free. He started to claw at his eyes, tearing the flesh and shredding it into bloody furrows. He tore at his skull, ripping clumps of hair that stuck to his bloody hands. The veins swelled and began to burst.

Locked within Shadow Slide, Onyx charged forward like a battering ram. He heard the victorious shouts of an endless array of Spirits. When he opened his own mouth to cry out, a roar echoed within his voice following by a distant booming howl. The stone ground cracked and split as he started to rise up towards the Demon. Fragments surrounded him like a deadly shield, fit to protect him and ready to strike at his enemies. Onyx found himself smiling, his heart burning with courage and determination. The black veil of his Shadowborn power sparkled with green light as he passed out of Shadow Slide.

"Father, I set you free!" Onyx shouted, the roar of Omu's mighty wolf Spirit echoing with his voice.

Iztal screeched with an ear splitting shriek as he finally looked upon Onyx's powerful attack. The two collided with explosive force. The broken Demon could do nothing to halt or slow Onyx as the Shadowborn Prince drove him back. Bones shattered beneath the stone assault. Iztal screamed as Onyx twisted around, throwing the Demon over his shoulder. Iztal slid to the edge of the Heights. Onyx grabbed a swath of cloth and pulled Iztal back, the stones floating around him.

"What do you have to say now, Demon? Even if Kaiser ends me, the world is angry and it will find another to strike him down," Onyx snarled. He leaned in closer. "Both worlds are angry."

"He can not be stopped! He can never be stopped!" Iztal stammered to say before a fountain of blood poured out of his mouth. He struggled to catch a breath. "He will break the Immortal Truth and destroy the Covenant of Spirits!"

"How?" Onyx asked, momentarily intrigued. He heard only sparing words about the Covenant of Spirits. Iztal gulped, coughing when blood started to fill his lungs. Fear gripped him in such a way that Onyx did not think possible. What was so terrible about Kaiser that even Demons were afraid of him? "Answer me!"

"The gates! The gates!" Iztal gurgled before spitting up more blood.

It surprised Onyx to hear the Demon cry and to see tears of blood streaming down his mangled face. "What about the gates?!"

Iztal did not say more, uttering a pained cry before his red eyes rolled back into his head. His body began to swell. Onyx shoved the bloated body off of the Heights before stepping to the edge to watch it fall. With a sickening explosion, Onyx watched as what was left of the Demon burst into a cloud of blackened blood. The gore rained down on the castle roof below him.

In the end, the body looked nothing like his beloved father, having been completely overwhelmed by Iztal's Demonic power. Onyx still found himself weeping and he fell to his knees. His father was now completely gone. He was alone. He froze when he felt cold arms embrace him. Looking to his left and right, Onyx saw a shimmer of Spirit energy that replaced his stone shield. He felt warmth seep back into his limbs. His sorrow was brushed away like leaves in the wind and replaced with love and hope. For a long time, he wept with a smile on his face.

Onyx watched as the sun crept up over the horizon, barely visible behind the lingering storm clouds. The sight was both beautiful and foreboding. He had survived the night. He had survived his first fight with a Demon. Onyx threw his arms up into the air as if to declare to the world that he was still alive. He turned his head back when he heard footsteps.

"Ryder!" Onyx shouted with relief. He jumped to his feet and jogged over to his cousin.

Ryder held out a hand to stop Onyx from embracing him. "I feel worse than I look."

Onyx dropped his arms. Ryder looked worse than Iztal had before his death. His cousin held his left arm across his stomach, his hand pressed over a grievous wound. It appeared as if every inch of him was stained with blood and gore.

"Is Rache dead?" Onyx quickly asked.

Ryder shook his head. "Demons of his power are tougher to kill than you might think." He glanced over Onyx's shoulder towards where Iztal had fallen. "Iztal is a foot soldier to Rache's general."

"Wait. You knew I was fighting Iztal?" Onyx asked, taking a step back. He followed his cousin's gaze before quickly turning to look at him. "Did you know that Kaiser used him to possess my father?"

Ryder let out a pained breath. "There is a lot I know, Onyx. Things I have not told you though I would not be surprised if Iztal did."

"You mean like how you are Kaiser's grandson?" Onyx stated as he took another step back.

The words appeared to deflate Ryder. His shoulders dropped. "It would have been better that I told you myself than for you to hear it from a Demon. But would you have agreed to come to Cross if I had?"

Onyx shrugged. "Probably not. Everything that Kaiser has a hand in seems to be corrupted."

"I do not claim to be untouched by Kaiser's influence as his grandson but I will never let him rule me. Kaiser is but one of my forebears and it is through him that I am a direct descendent of the Farlander Begin Anu. He left his home to make his own destiny and I intend to do the same," Ryder explained.

"So you can command the six Spirit energies like him?" Onyx asked as he remembered the many stories told to him about the ancient war hero.

Ryder nodded. "One of two Shadowborn who can."

"Kaiser is the other one," Onyx supposed. "And he has had a thousand years to develop his power."

"That is what we are up against in this war. I was wrong to leave Cross when I did and as your cousin, I am sorry that I abandoned the throne of our ancestor Shadow Night. Even if it takes me ten thousand years, I will make it up to you and the Silvanus family," Ryder promised with a warm smile in his eyes.

Onyx set a hand on Ryder's right shoulder and returned the smile. "We both will." He then remembered Iztal's words before he fell. "Iztal said something about Kaiser destroying the Covenant of Spirits and gates. What could that mean?"

"Nothing good," Ryder said swiftly as he looked around. "We need to get out of the city before too many people find out that we are here."

"Can you even move?" Onyx asked, taking note of Ryder's bruised and battered form.

Ryder scoffed. "I got up here didn't I? I'll need your help though to go the rest of the way. Can you Shadow Slide us both?"

"Won't going into Shadow Slide be too dangerous for you right now?" Onyx asked.

"Looks like I will have to teach you something about Spirit Anchors. Don't worry about me. Just do it," Ryder said like he was amused by the question.

"Ok," Onyx said as he made sure he had a hold of Ryder's shoulder. With a thought, both he and Ryder disappeared into Shadow Slide.

IT'S NOT OVER

Unlike the last time Onyx was in Shadow Slide, the dark and faded world appeared as it always had. No distant Spirit voices could be heard and there was no ethereal sparkle of energy. Onyx did see the outline of his cousin though the silver glow surrounding Ryder's body appeared faded. What surprised him was that every so often, the glow brightened until he realized it was brightening and fading with Ryder's heartbeat. Onyx felt Ryder's powerful mind pressing against his mind, acting as a guide towards their destination. As Onyx touched upon their mental connection, he sensed a hint of relief and warmth.

Onyx knew that had Ryder not been with him, he would have never found the rebel hideout again. It was Ryder who prompted him to pull out of Shadow Slide. Onyx remained standing as Ryder stumbled to his knees, holding his hand tighter over his open wounds.

"I told you it wasn't safe," Onyx said as he bent down to try to help Ryder.

Ryder gritted his teeth. "Shadow Slide dulls pain."

"Ryder!" shouted a woman with a clear but worried voice.

Onyx looked up to see a Shadowborn woman rushing towards them. She was clad in light leather armor and had a dagger sticking out of her left boot. She completely ignored Onyx, practically pushing him out of the way as she slid to kneel before Ryder. Onyx graciously stepped back, the twinge of his leg wound reminding him of his own battle injuries. He looked around the bare patch of dirt and grass, seeing the familiar sights of the hideout. Slowly, Shadowborn armed with various weapons and equipped with leather and steel armor stepped into view. Soon Zoras Rokar appeared with Hayden at his side.

"You idiot. You should not have left me behind to face the Demon on your own," the Shadowborn woman admonished as she held Ryder's face in her hands. She pressed her forehead to his.

Ryder reached up with his right hand to caress her cheek. "I suppose sorry will not be good enough."

Both Zoras and Hayden rushed over to Onyx and Ryder. Zoras slid down to Ryder much as the Shadowborn woman had while Hayden inspected Onyx with a careful eye.

"Come on, your Highness. Let us tend to your wounds and then we shall talk of many things," Hayden said, offering for Onyx to lean his weight on him.

Onyx gladly took the chance to pull his weight off of his injured leg. Hayden slid his arm across Onyx's back to support him while the Prince laid his arm across the Saber's shoulders. As he leaned on Hayden, the pain of broken bones, deep cuts, and bruises began to throb back into his awareness. Hayden led him away though he took one last look over his shoulder at Ryder. He watched as Zoras and the Shadowborn woman worked together to lift up his cousin.

*****

"I need to know what happened in Cross," Zoras asked once Ryder was laid down on the bed that was set against the right side of the room.

Haven spun around on her feet to stare back at the ex Saber Commander. "Not until he has had a chance to heal. You will not set foot within a hundred feet of him until he can stand on his own," she snapped.

"Haven," Ryder said softly as he winced in pain.

She ignored him and promptly slapped Zoras across the face. "Could not spare any warm bodies to storm Cross? Is that the excuse you gave him? Or were you too afraid to take up the sword yourself against Kaiser."

Zoras rubbed his cheek and frowned. "Were you any other soldier in this war, this insubordination would not be tolerated."

Haven pointed an accusing finger at Zoras. "You want me to smack you again?"

"Enough!" Ryder said with more force. He grabbed Haven's right arm and pulled her down to sit beside him on the bed.

The room fell silent save for Ryder's pained breathing.

Haven pulled herself from his grip and massaged his muscular right arm with a soft stroking touch. She did not appear to care about getting blood all over her hand.

"What is your command then?" Zoras asked as he dropped his hand from his face.

"Just go," Ryder grumbled.

"The healers should here any moment," Zoras started to say.

Ryder seethed when Haven's hand moved to the gaping hole under his ribs on the right side of his torso. She pulled back the shredded remains of armor.

"I will tend to him," Haven said as she locked eyes with Ryder. "Have the healers leave their supplies at the door."

Zoras glanced at Ryder who nodded. He threw up his hands and turned around to leave, closing the door behind him. A knock came a few minutes later. Haven got up from Ryder's side to answer it. She spoke a few curt words to the trio of healers before they handed her their supplies. She thanked them before closing the door.

"Would be easier if I could submerge myself in water," Ryder suggested with a pained breath.

"I don't know how the Waterborn heal themselves or what they taught you but I doubt even they could heal a Demon wound like this," Haven said as she paused to fill a small basin with water.

Ryder settled his head on the feather pillow, doing his best not to cry out in pain. Haven came back to his side, sitting on the edge of the bed. She dipped a cloth that she found in the healers' supplies in the basin. Squeezing the excess water out with a tight twist, Haven proceeded to wipe the gaping wound clean. Ryder winced and gritted his teeth at every touch no matter how soft or gentle Haven was.

"I'm surprised you are still alive after the beating Rache gave you," Haven commented before she dug her fingers in the wound to pull out a congealed globule of blood.

Ryder whimpered at the contact, gripping the bed mattress tightly with both hands. His back arched but Haven gently pressed his body back down. Though breathing was painful, Ryder managed to settle himself. Haven then resumed cleaning the wound. He resorted himself to quietly watching as she mixed up a poultice of healing herbs.

"We need to stop spending time like this," Ryder finally said after Haven had packed the wound with her poultice. They both looked at each other and smiled.

"It would be nice but we have a war to fight," Haven replied as she turned to set the cloth in the basin. The water in the basin quickly turned red. She paused and set her hands in her lap. "Promise me one thing, Ryder."

"Anything," Ryder said as he set his right hand on her hands.

Haven wrapped her hands around his, holding on to it tightly. "That you will never leave me again."

Ryder pushed himself to sit up, pulling himself close to Haven. He touched his forehead to hers as he set their tangle of hands over Haven's heart. "You are my Spirit Anchor, Haven. I could never leave you for fear of hurting you." He paused for a minute. "When this war is over, I want us to start our lives as husband and wife."

"Do you really mean it this time?" Haven asked. Ryder nodded. "Then I am yours," she murmured with a sweet smile before their lips met.

*****

Onyx was very grateful for the work of the healers for now he was able to rest without pain. But in the solitude of his small quarters, his mind drifted towards the sorrow that his father was gone forever. He tried to convince himself that it was Iztal he had killed though the image of the Demon possessing his father was hard to ignore. The Demon had distorted his father's features to the point of being unrecognizable. But he could still see his father in the monstrous face.

"I am sorry, Father," he said out loud as he stared up at the stone ceiling. He felt like he was enclosed in a cave. "Can you forgive me for what I had to do?"

His head jerked towards the wooden door when he heard a knock. He swung his legs around to sit up on the edge of the bed. Pressing his right foot to the ground, he tested his ability to bear weight on his leg. Part of him was proud of the wound that Iztal had dealt him. It proved that he fought a Demon and had survived. The scars would forever be a reminder of the battle.

"Come in," Onyx stated, not wanting to push himself just yet.

The Shadowborn woman he had seen earlier stepped into the room first, followed closely by Ryder. His cousin appeared sturdier on his feet and even looked upbeat. The woman sat down on the bed facing Onyx's bed, Ryder sliding in to sit beside her.

"You're looking better," Onyx commented, seeing that Ryder was now cleaned from the blood and gore and wearing a fresh set of clothes.

Ryder chuckled as he hooked his right arm around Haven's

neck, pulling her in close. "My lady does a good job as a healer," he said as Haven fought to free herself.

"So you must be Haven Ombre," Onyx stated gesturing towards her.

Haven pushed herself free and glared briefly at Ryder. Ryder only offered a shrug as an apology. She bowed her head. "Haven Ombre of Umbra, your Highness. I at least remember a sense of decorum," she said before slapping the back of Ryder's hand when he attempted to set it on her thigh. She glared at him again. He chuckled in response.

Onyx had to admit that Haven was a beautiful woman even though it looked like she was more comfortable in armor than in a dress. Her black hair was tied back in a loose braid that rested on her shoulder. She was obviously smaller and shorter than Ryder but Onyx believed that she could fight as well as his cousin.

"I don't think I have ever seen you happy before, Ryder," Onyx pointed out. "You kind of give off this vibe that you are all business."

Haven and Ryder looked at each other for a moment. "Don't you even dare," Haven warned as she leaned back away from Ryder, holding onto her long braid.

Ryder laughed as Haven shook her head to still let him know not to mess up her hair. "For once in my life, I know what my future will hold because I have decided what will be and what will not be. She will tell you that leaving Cross was the stupidest decision I have ever made. In the end, my leaving taught me something I don't think I could have learned by staying: what is really and honestly important in life."

"Family," Onyx said, remembering what Ryder had previously said about Haven.

Ryder patted Haven's left knee. "With your permission, your Highness, I would like to say a few words to the people here."

It surprised Onyx that his cousin used the formality of his Princely title. He stammered for a moment, trying to find the right words to respond. "Of course," he said, standing up with Ryder and Haven. "But I think for now, you can just call me by my name. Until the throne is won, we are cousins. Nothing more and nothing less."

Ryder held out his hand. "Agreed."

They shook each other's hand vigorously as if to confirm their pact. Haven even smiled when Onyx offered his hand to include her. She shook it graciously though she fought the urge to curtsy before him.

"I think it is only right that I include you too, Haven," Onyx said confidently. He gestured toward Ryder. "You are his lady after all."

"Thank you," Haven replied politely as she pulled her hand back.

Onyx refocused his attention on Ryder. "You are older and more experienced in the ways of the world than I am. That much I know to be true. If you choose to lead this rebellion, I will gladly follow you."

Ryder scoffed though he held an approving smile on his face. "We have much to do in the days to come and we all must be prepared for what faces us."

*****

Every rebel, from scout to guard to healer, assembled in the yard underneath the open sky. Loyal Shadowborn of all backgrounds, size, and gender gathered in a wide circle facing the entrance to the stone headquarters. Zoras stood to the right of the ebony doors while Hayden stood to the left. Conversations were whispered amongst the group about why they had come together and ideas were tossed about in regards to what happened in Cross. Everyone fell silent when the doors opened. Haven stepped out first with Ryder and Onyx in tow. She went to stand beside Zoras, latching her hands in front of her and waiting patiently. Onyx stood to Ryder's left and looked to him to speak first.

Ryder cleared his throat before glancing around the crowd. "I know that I do not need to tell you who I am for surely you can see it. I know that I do not need to introduce my cousin. But you see us now before you, bruised and battered. Last night in Cross, I faced the Demon Rache in battle and Onyx here fought against the Demon Iztal." Ryder gestured towards Onyx. "Your Prince defeated Iztal and sent him back to the Spiral. He has shown himself to be a true Silvanus son to you, strong and courageous in the face of evil."

The crowd clapped and cheered, praising Onyx's victory. At first, Onyx was embarrassed but as the volume grew, so did his delight at being recognized. He bowed his head, smiling wide.

"I however have not been a true Silvanus son to you," Ryder suddenly declared. The crowd immediately fell silent. "I abandoned you a hundred years ago to suffer this ruin when I could have stayed to help cast it down. I will forever be apologizing to the end of my days. Many have suffered but many will continue to suffer if we do not all rise up as one. I am no true Prince but I am a warrior and I ask you now. If I take command, will you follow me?"

The people murmured amongst themselves, slow to respond. Onyx saw his chance and took it. "I am not the warrior my cousin is but I have seen him fight against the greatest in the Northlands. He is the Champion of the Crossroads Arena and I put my trust in him to lead our people to victory. Who else would go to face Rache knowing he might not come back? He did it to help me and he did it to protect you. I will follow him."

Slowly, similar declarations were spoken, growing in volume until the people were shouting and cheering. Zoras then took center stage, holding up his hands to quiet the crowd.

"In the absence of a proper Shadow Council, it is my duty as Lord's Regent to say that we are now at war. So long as a Silvanus son breathes, we will fight Kaiser for the throne of Shadow Night. I too will follow Ryder," Zoras declared, glancing towards Ryder with a bow of the head.

Both Ryder and Onyx were pleased that the crowd cheered them on. Onyx turned to embrace his cousin, illiciting further shouts and declarations.

"You would make a great Shadowlord," Onyx said once they parted.

Ryder sighed deeply. "As would you in due time. Greatness is in us and the Shadowborn need us both to lead them in this war."

A MESSAGE

Proto Avis' eyes searched the stars, head turning in all directions. His far reaching gaze studied the cloud patterns with care. In his mind, he reviewed the different names of cloud types in both his native language and in the common tongue. He quickly identified each constellation, taking note of their position in the sky. He shuffled his wings, rolling his shoulders when they started to ache.

"Lord Avis," the Airborn attendant said before dropping down to one knee and bowing his head.

"Can you see it? Can you see what the sky is saying?" Proto mused. He let out a deep breath, his feathered chest rising and falling slowly.

The Airborn rose up to his feet and looked up at the night sky. He turned about on his feet. "I'm sorry, my Lord. All I see are stars in a clearing of clouds."

Proto chuckled softly. "That is exactly it. The clouds are pulling away at the moon's command, letting the stars shine through." He closed his eyes. "Can you feel their light beaming down upon you?"

"My Lord, something has happened to the Immortal Truth," the Airborn blurted out in a tumble of words.

The Gryphon's eyes popped open and he brought his head down. "The crack has grown?" he asked with genuine curiosity.

The Airborn nodded. "Something... odd has happened."

Proto turned around and focused on the young Immortal

man. "How odd?"

"The words in the stone are glowing like veins of silver," the Airborn reported.

"Silver," Proto said, thinking deeply. "It makes sense now."

"What does if I may ask?" the Airborn wondered as he latched his hands behind his back.

Proto lifted his head towards the sky. He gestured with his right paw, tracing a line of stars. "See how the stars are aligned, leading towards the moon from a wisp of dark clouds. One, two, three, four, five, and six. Six bright stars like a pathway taking a soul home." He tapped a talon in the air as he counted. "Yes, there are six stars."

As the old Gryphon spoke, the clouds thinned out even more. They transformed into a transparent mist. Even more stars sparkled as if they were relieved to be out of the darkness. The entire sky took on a life of its own. The wind moved like a restless breath, rustling Proto's faded brown feathers. He closed his eyes, embracing the touch of the moving air. The Airborn did the same, smiling with a soft expression.

"The wind is talking to me in a way that I have never heard before," the Airborn said as he opened his eyes. "It's singing."

"You hear it too. It is a Spirit song for a lost soul that has been found after many years of wandering. I had almost forgotten what it sounded like," Proto recollected. "It is one of the most beautiful sounds in the world."

As both Proto Avis and the Airborn attendant knew, Spirit songs were carried by the wind. The words were sung by wandering souls who had finally found their way. It was impossible to remember anything from the song but the sense of happiness and peace that filled one's heart. The mystical tones inspired the Gryphons' Feather Whisper for carrying messages. As the feathers were from living creatures, they could be charmed into holding a person's voice. One breath from a Gryphon activated the latent Spirit energy. The bigger the feather, the more words the energy could hold. Another breath from a Gryphon spelled the Feather Whisper to release the spoken words only to the intended recipient.

"Can the stone of the Immortal Truth hear the Spirit song? Is that why the runes are glowing?" the Airborn asked.

"You would have to ask an Earthborn if stones can hear," Proto stated. He then stood up on all fours. "Take me to the cavern before my old bones give out."

The path from the compound to the cavern entrance was long and tedious but Proto dared not stretch his wings. The long years had not been kind to his aging bones though his mind remained sharp as a knife. His fur and feathers lost their shining luster of youth and were now gray with age. Proto was relieved when he reached the rocky ledge. He took in a deep breath of mountain air and let it out slowly.

A white flash zipped into view as Arik Barr the Barn Owl Gryphon flew hard and fast. He twisted his wings around to quickly turn towards the cavern. Avoiding a gust of wind with a sharp dip, Arik flared his wings and swung his tail to steady his descent. He landed on the ledge, taking several hurried breaths.

"An urgent message, my Lord," he chawed in the Gryphon tongue as he bowed in respect. Proto bid the Airborn to go without him into the cavern. The attendant bowed in Spiritborn to Gryphon fashion before disappearing into the darkness of the opening. "News from the border!"

"You have flown far and fast. Where is your scout Haro Artemis?" Proto asked. He knew the names of every Gryphon and Earthborn scouting pair.

Arik took a moment to steady his breathing, letting his great chest rise and fall until the pace slowed. "Kader Erebus heard a Spirit song." He gulped once. "He said it held the voices of Aku and Akakios, speaking a declaration of courage and hope. The song was 'I am coming home. My sons are coming home. Child of shadow and earth. Man of the far Spirit. We are coming home.' Kader knew that the only one who could interpret the words would be you and he sent me. My partner Haro is running to Cascade to bring the song to Lord Vorin before he leaves for Crossroads."

Proto thought hard for a long time. "Have the fastest Gryphon you can find meet me in my chambers at once."

Arik nodded. "As you command, my Lord." In silent and fluid motion, Arik lifted into the air and dove down into the valley.

Keeping his wings folded tightly against his body, Proto walked through the tunnel to where the stones of the Immortal Truth were kept. His claws clicked on the stone floor, the sound echoing off the walls.

The tunnel soon opened up into a large stone cavern with a skylight. Moonlight beamed down onto the center of the room. Pillars of white granite held up a ring around a central pedestal. The walls were covered in runes and glowed with a soft light.

"My Lord Avis," the keeper said, directing Proto's attention to the pedestal. "I have never seen this in all of my years."

Proto looked down at the tablets of the Immortal Truth, feeling the familiar pull of its power. "How long have the runes been glowing?"

"Since the storm has stopped. I am not certain what to make of it," the keeper explained, scratching his head.

"When the words were bound to the stone, the power of our

souls were bound too," Proto said, touching a claw to his signature. "I suspect the trouble in the lands of the Shadowborn has something to do with this."

"Trouble?" the keeper asked.

Proto shook his head. "Much is on the move. Keep to the truth, good keeper. I fear the world is changing and we must be prepared."

His wings ached in anticipation of the flight back down. But Proto needed to get a very important message out to a very important person. He bid the keeper goodbye and left the cavern, deep in thought. The high mountain air had a calming effect once he reached the ledge. He took a deep breath and lifted off the ledge. Using the air currents to cushion his wings and body, the flight down was smooth and not as taxing as he anticipated. He landed and immediately rushed to his chambers.

Upon entering his chambers, he found Arik with a hard muscled Falcon Gryphon. The Gryphon's white plumage was speckled with black spots. His fur was supple and shimmering in the moonlight.

"My Lord Avis, this is Gyr," Arik introduced. The Falcon Gryphon bowed his head. "He was preparing to fly out on a training lesson with the new mountain recruits."

"I am the fastest and truest flyer of my family, Lord Avis," Gyr said with a deeper bow.

Proto gestured with a toss of the head for Arik to leave him and Gyr alone. Arik bowed his head in respect before departing. "It relieves me that a descendent of Mistress Gia is who I will be sending. Sure flight and strong nature." He walked over to his bedding and lay down. "If you will pardon my need for rest. Flying is not what it used to be for me."

"Then I will fly for you," Gyr said confidently.

Proto settled into the soft cushions. "The world is changing and we need all of the noble souls that can be found. What I am about to ask you is dangerous for no other messenger has been able to fly to the Southlands and return home."

Gyr stood up straight and squared his shoulders. He bore a stern expression in his raptorian eyes. "I was born upon the high mountain peaks during the winter. I spent my youth flying through the most terrible of blizzards."

"I am quite serious. I know firsthand that our enemy has been killing any Gryphon that flies beyond the Wall of Crossroads. I know that you are confident and proud of your skills as a flier but this mission is more than flying a message," Proto stated firmly. Gyr finally loosened up and settled in to listen closely. "Fly with all of your might. Find our hero and bring him home to us."

"No Feather Whisper?" Gyr asked as he sat on his haunches.

"No, no Feather Whisper," Proto stated. "You are to seek out Bane Arlis the Daylord and convince him to return to the Northlands. Aid him if you must in his trials but bring him back. Tell him that Proto Avis sends for him in a dark hour."

Gyr sat up straight and proud. "Then I shall bring our great champion home if I have to tear out the Demon's eyes myself."

THE HUNTERS

Rache pushed open the double doors into Kaiser's private quarters. The receiving room was sumptuous in its décor with gold and silver leaf frames on the wall and black velvet furniture. To Rache's right was a circle of chairs around a finely carved mahogany table. On the table was a half finished meal that was clearly meant for four people. The Demon rolled his eyes as he spied a courtesan's lacy dress lying across the back of a nearby couch. He stepped further inside, his hand brushing across a standing globe that served as the centerpiece for the room. The globe shifted and spun beneath his touch. He looked up at the floor to ceiling window, the curtains pulled back to let in the moonlight. Stepping to the window, Rache set his hands on his hips and looked through the frosted glass.

A heavy creak to Rache's left took his attention away from the scene outside and towards the bed chamber. He sneered as he looked towards the open ebony door. Rache did not need to see the courtesans to know that they were present though he was relieved that their heartbeats were sedate and not sped up by any hint of passion. It sickened him to think of Kaiser wasting his time, indulging his lust and proving his desirability. The Demon could not figure out why Kaiser was indulging himself with women. Was his master trying to produce a son to mold to his will?

Kaiser had never given him the impression that he desired a family life. The Shadowborn was the most selfish, arrogant bastard of a man that Rache had ever encountered. Kaiser knew that he was intelligent and believed himself to be smarter than everyone around him. Rache had to admit that he admired that about his master. It certainly would have been boring to serve a stupid individual who could not lie and could not manipulate others on his whim.

He stepped through the open chamber door, finding Kaiser asleep on a four post bed. The three women from the hot springs were draped around him in a deep slumber. Rache knew better. Kaiser's mind never stopped even when he was asleep. He was capable of jumping to alertness within a heartbeat. Rache watched as Kaiser's bare chest slowly rose and fell. The black scars on his throat appeared subdued though a large blood vessel throbbed and pressed against it. Not for the first time, Rache wanted to squeeze the life out of Kaiser for the prison he called a Spirit Bond.

"Your summoned guest is here," Rache said in a low voice.

Kaiser let out a deep breath, turning his head to the left. His forehead pressed against the top of the courtesan's head. Her long eyelashes fluttered as she smiled from the contact. The courtesan on the right shuffled in closer and settled against the crook of his shoulder. His right arm reflexively reached up to wrap around her naked back. The third and shortest of the three women laid on top of Kaiser, her head resting on his chest. Her wavy black hair was splayed across her back in a tousled mess.

"Later. I'm busy," Kaiser murmured. His eyes remained closed.

Rache crossed his arms and sneered. The room stank of sweat, spilt wine, and the flowery perfume of the three courtesans. The bed sheets were twisted and wrinkled. Kaiser looked like a man who had won a great victory, his arms wrapped around the spoils of war.

"Your bedwarmers can wait. Your guest can not," Rache said a little bit louder.

Kaiser's eyes snapped open. "Fine."

"Please tell me you have some clothes on underneath that blanket," Rache pleaded as he leaned back against the door frame.

The three women murmured in soft voices, not wanting Kaiser to leave. Kaiser whispered back to them in an enchanting voice before he sat up. The woman across his front slid to the side and frowned with sleepy eyes. Kaiser then slid to the right side of the bed, dropping to the floor. He bent out of view briefly before standing back up, belting on a pair of black pants.

"Happy now?" Kaiser asked flatly as he stepped around the edge of the bed, carrying a pair of leather boots. He paused to pull them on, gesturing with a toss of his head for Rache to hand him a linen shirt. Rache picked up the white shirt from the back of a chair set by the fire place. He tossed it towards Kaiser who deftly caught it. "I was having such a nice dream," he added once he had the shirt on.

"You can return to your bedroom escapades later. You told me to wake you when he arrived. I did. Don't get angry at me for doing what you told me to do," Rache growled.

Kaiser grabbed his black and silver brocade jacket and quickly put it on, leaving it open. He began to smooth out his hair as he followed Rache out of his private quarters. "While I am meeting with my guest, I need you to do a little cleansing of the masses."

"I'm listening," Rache said, intrigued by the statement.

"I have grown tired of the cries coming from the northeast part of this city. Silence them," Kaiser ordered with finality.

"With pleasure," Rache grinned.

Kaiser and Rache came to a stop when Loran stepped away from the shadows of a side entrance to the throne room. Loran, dressed in Saber leathers, bowed before Kaiser. He followed Rache with his eyes, never looking away for a moment. Kaiser stepped past Rache, patting him on the shoulder. The Demon and Loran continued their staring contest until Kaiser stepped between them.

"Rache, you have work to do," Kaiser reminded the Demon in a curt voice. Rache curled his lips, flashing his white fangs. A low growl rumbled in his throat as he turned away, leaving Loran and Kaiser. Kaiser poked Loran with a finger to get his attention. "Leave it. You also have work to do."

Loran bowed his head. "I'll bring your guest in."

Kaiser walked into the empty throne room, his boots clacking against the stone floor. He quickly made his way up to the royal chair, pausing when he saw the swath of crimson cloth draped across it. He snarled as he ripped it away, throwing it aside before sitting down. As soon as his hands cupped the ends of the arm rests, the distant double doors were thrown open. Loran came in first, followed by a shabby cloaked figure. He gestured for him to halt ten feet from the raised dais before stepping aside to Kaiser's right. The figure then threw back his hood.

It had been centuries since Aday Silvanus last stood before the throne of his ancestors. In the ensuing years, he had diminished from tall and proud royal heir to a haunted shadow of his former self. He stood hunched over, stringy black hair hanging in his face. His dull eyes had sunk in to his skull. His body shuddered from the effort to remain standing.

Kaiser leaned to one side, one arm upon the arm rest, fingers rapping the edge with concentration. "Welcome back to Cross, Aday. I hope that your journey here was not too trying for you."

"All for a noble purpose, my Lord," Aday said as he swept into a deep bow. He stood back up and nodded his head.

"Good," Kaiser said as he pressed two fingers of his left hand to his temple. He then pointed at Aday. "I have given you the necessary gifts and power. I trust that your hunting skills will accomplish what I desire."

"Who is it that you wish me to hunt, my Lord?" Aday asked, his voice sounding distant and haunted.

"As we speak, there are still six Silvanus sons not confirmed dead. Three are within my sphere including you. One is hidden. Two roam the Southlands," Kaiser explained, counting out the number on his left hand. "Aday, I am sending you south to get rid of your halfbreed spawn and perhaps make a stand against Bane."

There was no reaction. Kaiser had just ordered Aday to kill his own sons. It amused the dark noble that Aday was too far gone to express fatherly love. Kaiser did not think that Aday would be able to succeed against Bane. To him, it was a win win situation. Either Aday would be killed or Bane would be killed thus removing a potential enemy to take up arms against him. Kaiser gestured with a wave of his hand that Aday was dismissed. Aday bowed before disappeared into Shadow Slide.

Loran sauntered back to the front of the dais as soon as the double ebony wood doors closed. "Why send him away from Cross? Aday would have been a valuable ally to sow seeds of doubt among the Shadowborn. He would have been of better use than Ryder. Everyone thinks Aday is dead. Lost to the depths of time."

Kaiser slowly got up from the chair. He descended the dais and walked towards Loran until he stood in front of him. He locked eyes with the Shadowborn until Loran averted his gaze. "I move as I wish, Loran. I do what I want and say what I want. I do not fear what others will do or say. When I have obliterated the last of the sons of Shadow Night, I will turn my sight to the distant land of my ancestor. Within the Farlands lies my true heritage." Kaiser stepped closer to Loran to whisper in his ear. "Remember your poor cousin, Loran, and do not question me again. I do not need a sword to rip a man to shreds."

Loran gulped at hearing the clear danger in Kaiser's voice. The sound was chilling to the core. He fell to his knees and lowered his head. "Forgive me, my Lord."

"Oh dear Loran," Kaiser mused as he patted Loran's head like a dog. "At least you can see what it is that I intend to do." He lifted Loran up with a finger under his chin. "I intend to tear down the very foundations of the world and show everyone the true nature of order and rule." The look in Kaiser's eyes then turned deadly. "And I will watch it all burn."

APPENDIX A

NOTE

With Book 2 and Book 3 still to be revealed, I have included as much information as possible without spoiling story secrets. More information will be revealed with subsequent books.

RACE AND CULTURE

In Flight of the Broken, there are many different types of races and cultures that all originate from the Spirit energy of Terra. Each is unique in their values. Since it may not be easy to see the basic details within the text, I am providing them here for you.

GRYPHONS

LANGUAGE: When they speak their language, it consists of the sounds birds can make. They use sound rather than words. When speaking the common tongue, transitioning from sound to spoken word is difficult. It takes a lot of practice to speak in the common tongue and usually a Gryphon speaks with an accent. It takes many years of repetition to speak without an accent. It is very difficult to learn the Gryphon language though it can be done. Gryphons can also understand the nonspeaking avian species of the world and converse with them.

NAMES: Names come from real world bird scientific names and usually from the corresponding species of bird of prey. Family group names come from the genus but are usually not shared outside of Gryphon society. Most Gryphons are called by their birth names (first name). Parents name their children when they hatch out from the egg. Some Gryphons will acquire nicknames based on deeds or environment and will go by them throughout their lives.

SOCIETY AND BEHAVIOR: Gryphons are essentially animals with a few human traits and characteristics. The lion part influences the desire to live in groups but Gryphons are perfectly happy and capable of living alone. They mate for life and if a mate dies, the survivor usually doesn't live much longer afterwards. Children are highly prized as vectors to carry on the family legacy and for their purity and joy. Both parents participate in raising children (usually 1-3 per nesting period). Children age similar to how normal birds of prey do and then when they hit maturity, they start training in various services. Usually after the Gryphon graduates their training, courtship begins between young Gryphons. Courtship can take a while and a male will present a gift to the female's parents when he has chosen her as his mate and is seeking their blessing. Gift is usually a small wreath of personal feathers and flowers which is later worn by the female during the mate ceremony.

POLITICS: Leadership is held by two Gryphons chosen to be the Lord of War or Lord of Peace. When the world is as war, the Lord of War is the primary decision maker. When the world is at peace, the Lord of Peace is the primary decision maker. They balance each other out to ensure that no rash decisions are made.

HOMELIFE: Gryphons do not wear clothing but may wear pieces of light armor, crowns and jewelry. They fancy trinkets and nature made gifts. Steps and furniture are not very common in Gryphon homes and very few read and write non-Gryphon books.

VALUES: Gryphons are closest with Dragons and Airborn and hold high regard to those who have proven their worth. They respect other Lords and sages. They dislike those that seek to dominate others and will defend friends and allies fiercely. They can be slow to act when old or quick to act when young. Gryphons do have faults in how they interact with the Spiritborn and they seem haughty and unsociable. Since they depend on instinct, they are seen as good judges of character but they can be fooled if a person is a good enough liar.

DRAGONS

LANGUAGE: Dragons speak with guttural sounds, growls, and vocalizations. Only Vorin, the only named Dragon, is known to be capable of speaking the common tongue of the Spiritborn and understanding the Gryphon tongue.

NAMES: Names are given based on appearance, deeds and bloodlines. It is unknown if surnames are granted, when birth names are given, and if names differentiate between genders.

SOCIETY AND BEHAVIOR: Dragon society operates in a similar manner to the Gryphons in that they are beasts and not of the humanoid race. They are known to be distant from Spiritborn society. Dragons are usually very independent but fiercely loyal to those they consider friends.

POLITICS: The only known fact about Dragon leadership is that when the Immortal Truth was written, Vorin was elected to survive the Dragon race's sacrifice.

HOMELIFE: Unknown

VALUES: Vorin is considered to be the last Dragon alive and has adapted to living with Gryphons and Spiritborn to where his original instincts have been buried deep within his mind.

DEMONS

LANGUAGE: Unknown but it is believed that when Demons speak, the words sound harsh and dark. The timbre of their voices cause non Demons to feel afraid.

NAMES: It is not known how true Demon names are given out but Spiritborn society names them according to the terrible deeds they were known for.

SOCIETY AND BEHAVIOR: It is the goal of all Demons to destroy the good people of Terra as they believe themselves to be the rightful rulers. Independence and treachery run rampart and leaders last only as long as they can fight off challengers. Demons kill or harm each other in power struggles. They are opportunistic and will participate in any possessions, rituals, or invocations so long as it ultimately benefits them. There is no true organization to their society.

POLITICS: Generals would be chosen to promote and advance the Demon race's idea of conquest and rule. Fear and promises of power are the few things that can motivate a Demon to follow a group and obey orders.

HOMELIFE: Demons are most often nomadic with few permanent settlements. Nothing is known about family dynamics if any exist. All Demons have various levels of power and all can transform into a monstrous beast form. Many Demons will drink blood as a sense of control over the weak. They do get some sustenance from it and can read blood memories. They can eat and drink normal meals. Attire can be anything as they regularly take from their victims. Armor and weapons tend to be sharp and cruel in appearance.

VALUES: Demons value power and dominance. Loyalty is not highly valued and most Demons will fake loyalty until a better opportunity arises. Intellectual learning is a low priority and skills in war are prized. Demons are not particularly book smart but are very street smart.

SPIRITS/GHOSTS

LANGUAGE: Spirits will speak the language of the person they are visiting with fluency. It is unknown if they have a separate language of their own.

NAMES: Names are derived from what the Spirit was in life. There is no true naming system.

SOCIETY AND BEHAVIOR: All Spirits live in the Spirit World, a realm that borders the land of the living. It is difficult to cross over but if the call is great enough, a Spirit can walk in the land of the living. As no one ever comes back from the Spirit World, the structure of their society is unknown. It is believed that Spirits carry on their lives as if they had never died. Older Spirits act as guides to the living.

POLITICS: Unknown

HOMELIFE: Unknown

VALUES: Values depend on the nature of the Spirit of the deceased but most Spirits tend to be good hearted.

SPIRITBORN

LANGUAGE: The common tongue is spoken universally among the six tribes. It is the primary language of politics, negotiations, and the economy.

NAMES: Names can vary among the six tribes. Many are named for future hopes, environment at time of birth, virtues, in honor of ancestors, family, and friends, deeds or whatever the parents like.

HISTORY: The six tribes were at one time one unified race. As spirits were born into flesh, the environment they entered into influenced the separation of the original race. Each tribe can breed with each other and produce mixed children. It is very rare to find a pure family line that have members capable of expertly controlling their respective element. Many of the Spiritborn tend to have at least one different tribe member in their background. All of the tribes are related to each other but have differences based on their home environments. But there are always exceptions within an individual tribe.

SPIRITBORN: SHADOWBORN

NAMES: Though the Spiritborn can have a name of their choosing, most Shadowborn tend to have either their first name or middle name relate to the following words: shadow, night, black, silver, wolf, moon, and dark.

SOCIETY AND BEHAVIOR: The Shadowborn come from the high mountain forests. Many Shadowborn are serious and focused. Men are fiercely protective of what they care about and normally do not admit their inner feelings. Women are very similar if confronted but are more compassionate. Both men and women participate in a warrior based society though men predominate in the militaristic orders. Men tend to have first preference in inheritance however daughters can inherit if no other male family exists. All Shadowborn are capable of tapping into their shadow Spirit energy and using the innate power. The most common technique is Shadow Slide.

POLITICS: The Shadowborn are led by the Silvanus family

as Lord of the Shadowborn and Lady of the Shadowborn. The throne is usually inherited by the eldest son though sometimes it falls to the next available son of the Silvanus bloodline. It is believed that should the Silvanus family fail, Shadowborn society would collapse. The royal family is beloved by the people as symbols of strength and stability. Military order commanders hold an equal amount of respect. The Shadow Council that advises the royal family and consists of fourteen members: the Shadowlord, Lord Regent, Lord's Chancellor, Master of Trade, Master of Roads, Master of Homeland, Treasurer, Master of Shadowborn Affairs, Commander of the Sabers, Commander of the Armed Forces, Master of Justice, Master of Education, Master of Spiritual Affairs, and the Ambassador.

HOMELIFE: Black, silver, and armor dominate everyday attire and many Shadowborn carry some form of a blade on their person at all times. Shadowborn tend to wear clothes suited for the cooler mountain weather. All Shadowborn are eligible for military services and to become a Saber, one of the personal guards to the royal family, though nobles are usually picked over lower born people. However, if a Shadowborn has proven him or herself, their efforts are rewarded with favors and positions. All Shadowborn have black hair and most have silver eyes.

VALUES: Loyalty to the throne, the Immortal Truth and family are some of the most important values to an average Shadowborn. Respect and admiration are common for warriors who have proven themselves. When considering the Silvanus bloodline, there are some Shadowborn who believe that only a legitimate born son can inherit the son. Others believe any son of the line, legitimate or not, can inherit so long as he has proven himself strong and worthy.

SPIRITBORN: LIGHTBORN

NAMES: Similar to the Shadowborn naming rules but first or middle names relate to the following words: light, bright, shine, gold, yellow, sun, and star.

SOCIETY AND BEHAVIOR: The Lightborn come from the grasslands and tend to be aloof and distant. Men and women are equals and any child regardless of gender can inherit. They hate the idea of killing and murder and prefer to disarm opponents. Most Lightborn seek intellectual pursuits and try to understand the workings of the world.

POLITICS: The current leader of the Lightborn is Evander. Teachers and scribes make up the advisory council.

HOMELIFE: Attire consists of airy robes of white or lightly colored cloth. Most Lightborn have blonde to stark white hair. Education is a top priority for children and both sexes participate.

VALUES: They value learning and despise war. They are the ones most concerned with what will happen in the future and are believed to have knowledge gifted to them by the ancient Spirits of Terra.

SPIRITBORN: FIREBORN

NAMES: Similar to the Shadowborn naming rules but first or middle names relate to the following words: fire, heat, red, desert, lion, coal, and burn.

SOCIETY AND BEHAVIOR: Fireborn come from the desert and tend to have vivacious and fiery personalities once they get to know others. They are cautious when first met. They are hotheaded but fierce warriors loyal to protecting what they care about. They love celebrations and parties. Men and women are equal and can inherit as the eldest regardless of gender.

POLITICS: The Fireborn are led by Lord Argos and his queen.

HOMELIFE: Attire is light, sun protective and appropriate for desert life. Hair is almost always a shade of red.

VALUES: Fireborn value good cheer and enjoy the company of others. Feats of strength, control and speed dominate their society and they don't value learning as much as other Spiritborn.

SPIRITBORN: WATERBORN

NAMES: Similar to the Shadowborn naming rules but first or middle names relate to the following words: water, cool, blue, ocean, ice, river, and flowing.

SOCIETY AND BEHAVIOR: Waterborn love to be in or near any source of water, finding comfort and protection. Most are serious and quiet in their dealings with the other nations. Warriors tend to be experts when fighting in and around water. When on land, they tend to be clunky in their movements.

POLITICS: The leadership of the Waterborn belongs to Lord Marinus after the failed war with the Shadowborn.

HOMELIFE: Waterborn commonly wear robes and clothes of blue, gray, and white. They feel at home when around water and become nervous when away. Hair is usually shades of blue, blonde or white.

VALUES: They value learning and the healing arts. However, they have withdrawn from Immortal society after Akakios' failed invasion and currently have a hard time trusting others. The main target of their animosity is Akakios' bastard son.

SPIRITBORN: EARTHBORN

NAMES: Similar to the Shadowborn naming rules but first or middle names relate to the following words: earth, nature, wood, rock, green, and forest.

SOCIETY AND BEHAVIOR: Earthborn come from the forests and tend to be carefree and loving. Men and women are equal in society and can inherit as the eldest child regardless of gender. Scouts and healers predominate but there is a standing army of bowmen and swordsmen. They are very agile and fast but not particularly strong. They use their environment in everyday life. Though different classes exist, discrimination is a rare occurrence and the crowds mix together without trouble. Earthborn also work with the Gryphons in scouting pairs separated into day time patrols and night time patrols.

POLITICS: The Earthborn are led by the Kano family. The royals are well loved and their names are held sacred after death.

HOMELIFE: Festivals and balls are common social events that all Earthborn can attend. Families tend to live close together or in the same house. Children are encouraged to see the world as part of their education.

VALUES: They value family, friends, nature, and protecting the innocent. Earthborn like to believe the best in people and that all bad souls are capable of being saved.

SPIRITBORN: AIRBORN

NAMES: Similar to the Shadowborn naming rules but first or middle names relate to the following words: air, storm, thunder, white, flight, bird, or sky.

SOCIETY AND BEHAVIOR: Airborn come from the high mountains and tend to be quiet and thoughtful. They are effective assassins and spies as they can move in silence. Men and women are equal and can inherit as the eldest regardless of gender. They are the lore masters and guardians of the original Immortal Truth for Terra. They live and share the mountains with migrant Gryphons and are the only Spiritborn competent with speaking the Gryphon tongue.

POLITICS: Aves and his queen rule the Airborn with equal power. Because the Gryphons share and participate in Airborn society, they serve on the advisory council with native Airborn.

HOMELIFE: Attire can vary depending on where Airborn travel. If they are in the high mountains, they tend to wear heavy cloaks and robes. If they are travelling in the lower valleys, they are usually seen wearing tribal style outfits. Hair is always white with streaks of gray and black. Airborn like to wear feather ornaments.

VALUES: Airborn are respectful of others and the world like the Earthborn and distant like the Lightborn. They prefer to make observations and consider all actions, rarely acting without reason.

MORTALS

LANGUAGE: The Mortals speak the same language as the Spiritborn but the tone of their voices is even and unremarkable.

NAMES: Mortals have a similar naming system to the Spiritborn but they do not use the environment or the elements as inspiration. Carrying on the name of ancestors is the most common method for naming. Mortals use surnames as badges of honor to promote their interests.

SOCIETY AND BEHAVIOR: Mortals see Immortals as otherworldly super warriors and they hold the Daylord in the highest regard.

POLITICS: Each Mortal settlement has a mayor or leader that is answerable to the capital city of Arken.

HOMELIFE: Information to be revealed in Book 2: Flight of the Lost.

VALUES: Information to be revealed in Book 2: Flight of the Lost.

APPENDIX B

CHARACTERS MET OR DISCUSSED BY OTHERS

GRYPHONS

- Lord Proto Avis- An ancient Eagle Gryphon known for his great intellect and wisdom. Lives in Crossroads.
- Arik Barr- A young Barn Owl Gryphon in the scout patrol. Partnered with Haro.
- Stria- Day captain of the Western Scout Patrol.
- Whisper- Night captain of the Western Scout Patrol.
- Lana- A desert Falcon Gryphon and messenger between the Fireborn and Crossroads.
- Savanna- A desert Falcon Gryphon and trainer of messengers in Crossroads.
- Grinus- A gray Falcon Gryphon general mentioned by a Gryphon messenger.
- Paladon- An Osprey Gryphon and the current Lord of Peace.
- Stellaris- A large Eagle Gryphon and current Lord of War.
- Pala- Daughter of Paladon. Twin sister of Palas.
- Palas- Son and heir of Paladon and twin brother of Pala.
- Voci- A fish Eagle Gryphon in the company of Palas and Pala.
- Nova- A gray crested Eagle Gryphon and top level commander. Sometimes Regent of the Gryphon homeland.

- Harper- Son of Nova. Friend and traveling partner of Ryder Coba.
- Razila- Harper's mate.
- Togra- A Wood Owl Gryphon in service of the Earthborn during their stay in Crossroads.
- Gyr- A white Falcon Gryphon messenger sent south to alert the Daylord.
- Gia- Ancestor of Gyr as said by Proto Avis.

DRAGONS

- Vorin- Dragonlord and friend of Proto Avis.

DEMONS

- Rache- Kaiser's Demon servant.
- Iztal- A low level Demon in the service of Kaiser. Possesses Aku when summoned.
- Axum- An ancient Demon general in the service of Kaiser. Currently terrorizing the Mortal people.

SPIRITS/GHOSTS

- Omu- The Wolf Spirit of shadow and guide to the Silvanus bloodline.

SPIRITBORN: SHADOWBORN

- Shadow Night Silvanus- The ancestor of the Silvanus bloodline and first Shadowlord.
- Lord Shiloh Silvanus- Former Shadowlord and father of Aku.
- Kaiser Adonis- A pure blooded Shadowborn from Umbra with aspirations for power. Antagonist.
- Madhuri Coba- Former Commander of the Armed Forces and husband to Mali Silvanus. Father of Akakios Coba-Silvanus.
- Lord Aku Silvanus- The broken soul and current occupant of the throne of the Shadowborn. Father to Onyx Silvanus.
- Akakios Coba-Silvanus- Son of Mali and Madhuri. Father of Ryder
- Morin Win- The new Commander of the Armed Forces and henchman of Kaiser Adonis.
- Peredur Adonis Coba-Silvanus- Bastard son of Akakios and

Aylin. Unnamed heir of Kaiser Adonis. Commonly known as Ryder Coba.

- Kader Erebus- Former Lord's Chancellor and rebel leader against Kaiser.
- Onyx Silvanus- Son of Aku Silvanus and Nuru Kano. Of Shadowborn-Earthborn origin.
- Sai Parahazur- Commander of the Sabers and rebel leader against Kaiser.
- Sin Silvanus- Second son of Shadow Night Silvanus and father to Aday, Mali and Shiloh.
- Zoras Rokar- Former Commander of the Sabers and current Lord's Regent of the Shadow Council. Father of Soja and rebel leader.
- Soja Rokar- Personal Saber guard to Onyx and son of Zoras. Friend to Ryder.
- Mali Silvanus- Mother to Akakios and wife of Madhuri Coba.
- Sage Silvanus- Youngest son of Shadow Night.
- Aday Silvanus- Eldest son of Sin and older brother to Shiloh. Believed to be insane.
- Den- Former student to Kader Erebus and Saber informant.
- Rothe Abendroth- Saber of middling rank and nephew to Saber Captain Hayden. Servant of Kaiser.
- Donovan Shunga- Former Saber guard to Aku and rebel leader under Zoras.
- Haven Ombre- A lowborn girl from Umbra and rebel fighter. Ryder's lover.
- Cian Adonis- Former General of the Northern Border and father of Kaiser.
- Anu Silvanus- Eldest son of Shadow Night Silvanus. His death served as inspiration for the creation of the Sabers.
- Hayden Abendroth- Saber captain and uncle to Rothe. Rebel captain under Zoras.
- Sasha- Sister of Sai Parahazur and wife of Bard.
- Baron- Husband of Sasha and rebel informant.
- Khan Adonis- Younger brother of Kaiser Adonis.
- Adonis Anu- Eldest son of Begin Anu and ancestor to the Adonis Family.
- Loran Win- Cousin of Morin. Called the Mirror Sea Pirate.
- Aylin Adonis- Mother of Ryder.
- Jarod- Former suitor of Haven Ombre.
- Commander Sorin – Former Commander of the Sabers.

SPIRITBORN: LIGHTBORN

- Evander- Lord of the Lightborn.

SPIRITBORN: FIREBORN

- Forges- First Lord of the Fireborn.
- Argos- Lord of the Fireborn. Has five daughters.
- Ilana- Eldest daughter and heir to Argos.

SPIRITBORN: WATERBORN

- Nereus- Former Lord of the Waterborn.
- Marinus- Current Lord of the Waterborn.
- Sir Myst- Music master of Lough.
- Alton- Crowned Prince of the Waterborn.

SPIRITBORN: EARTHBORN

- Nuru Kano Silvanus- Mother of Onyx and wife to Aku. Daughter of Oren and Willow and sister to Palani.
- Oren Kano- Former Lord of the Earthborn and father to Palani and Nuru.
- Palani Kano- Current Lord of the Earthborn and uncle to Onyx. Father of Flynn and two deceased children (a daughter and son).
- Haro Artemis- Scout of the Earthborn and partnered with Arik. Older brother to Luna.
- Willow- Wife of Oren Kano and mother to Palani and Nuru.
- Avani- Captain of the Western Scout Patrol.
- Luna Artemis- Lady of Flora in service to Gaia. Younger sister to Haro and friend to Onyx.
- Flynn Kano- Son of Palani and cousin to Onyx. Crowned Prince of the Earthborn.
- Odin Kano- First Lord of the Earthborn and ancestor to the royal family.
- Gaia- Daughter of Odin and former leader of the Earthborn.
- Captain Oaken- Earthborn captain of the palace guards.

SPIRITBORN: AIRBORN

- Aves- Lord of the Airborn.
- Seli- Daughter of Aves and Princess of the Airborn.
- Eru- A champion fighter that Ryder defeats in the Crossroads warrior matches.

MORTALS

- None named or met in Flight of the Broken.

OTHER

- Bane Arlis- An Eastlander known as the Daylord.
- Begin Anu- An ancient war hero that came from the Farlands. Killed by Rache.
- Sando Ateru- A prophet of mysterious origins.

APPENDIX C

PLACES VISITED, DISCUSSED, OR SEEN ON MAP

REGIONS

- Terra- The name of the world where the book takes place.
- Spiritlands- The name of the landmass where most of the Immortal and Mortal races live.
- Farlands- A mysterious and distant land south of the Spiritlands.
- West Gatelands- A small group of islands to the west of the Spiritlands.
- Stormlands- A group of islands between the Spiritlands and the Farlands.
- Darklands- A desolate land where the Demons live.
- Northlands- Home of the Immortal races.
- Eastlands- A wild and untamed land where Bane Arlis comes from.
- Southlands- Home of the Mortal races.
- Dragonlands- Home of the Dragons protected by a stormy sea.
- Spirit World- A mysterious realm where the Spirits of the dead roam.
- Spiral- A dark and endless path full of torment for evil Spirits.

CITIES

- Tempest- Capital city of the Airborn. Guards the cavern where the stones of the Immortal Truth are kept.
- Cross- Capital city of the Shadowborn. Home of Onyx Silvanus and many others.
- Crossroads- Capital city of the Northlands. Home of Proto Avis.
- Cascade- Capital city of the Earthborn. Home of the Kano Royals.
- Coal- Capital city of the Fireborn. Home of Argos and his family.
- Lavan- City of the Fireborn. A major trade center.
- Garhune- A Mortal city visible from the Wall of Crossroads.
- Lough- Capital City of the Waterborn. Home of the royal family.
- Dusk- City of the Shadowborn. Twin city of Agin.
- Eclipse- City of the Shadowborn. Notorious for pirate raids.
- Twilight- City of the Shadowborn. Birthplace of Soja's mother.
- Branch- City of the Earthborn.
- Moor- City of the Shadowborn.
- Horizon- City of the Shadowborn.
- Agin- City of the Earthborn. Twin city of Dusk.
- Range- City of the Earthborn.
- Mys- City of the Waterborn.
- Umbra- City of the Earthborn. Birthplace of Kaiser Adonis and Ryder Coba.
- Blaze- City of the Fireborn.
- Isle- City of the Waterborn.
- Forde- City of the Waterborn.
- Coast- City of the Waterborn.
- Fog- City of the Waterborn.
- Roar- City of the Fireborn.
- Arken- Capital city of the Southlands.

LANDMARKS

- Demon's Eye- Lake in the Darklands.
- Daylord's Shadow Mirror- The magical barrier between the Darklands and the land of the Shadowborn.
- Sea of Truth- The northernmost body of water that borders the Spiritlands.

- The Mirror Sea- A western body of water notorious for pirates and barbarian raiders.
- Shadow Point- A piece of Shadowborn land that juts out into The Mirror Sea west of Eclipse.
- Howling River- A river in the Shadowborn lands.
- North Bend- Outpost to the Western Scout Patrol.
- The River Shadow- A river that serves as the border between the lands of the Shadowborn and the Earthborn.
- The Heights- A high wall of mountains surrounding the city of Cross.
- Kaiser's Shadow Mirror- The invisible barrier that has sealed the Land of the Shadowborn.
- Water's Eye- An island in the Waterborn lands.
- Red Desert- A desert in the Fireborn lands.
- West Shadow- The western branch of The River Shadow near Crossroads.
- East Shadow- The eastern branch of The River Shadow near Crossroads.
- Wall of Crossroads- Rock wall between the Northlands and the Southlands.
- East Road- The main roadway out of the city of Cross towards the border.
- Northern Forest- Forest north of Cross.
- Site of Ascension- Place north of Cross where Shadow Night first was named Lord of his people.
- Crossroads Arena- A place for combat matches and training in the city of Crossroads.
- East Road Bridge- The bridge over The River Shadow that leads towards Agin.

APPENDIX D

RULES

THE NATURE OF SPIRIT ENERGY

All abilities come from a Spiritual origin. Some have a stronger connection to that innate power than others. The Immortals have the strongest connection while Mortals have the weakest connection. Everyone is capable of using Spiritual power to manipulate their environment except for Demons. The Demons lost the ability to tap into their own Spirit energy and their anger resulted in the First Dominion War. The power and how great it can be is directly related to bloodlines. Blood is a powerful element with which to transfer memories, seals, and magic. When one signs in blood, they are bound to what they signed and promised. The world will otherwise functions without a person's manipulation. Very few can affect the world on a big scale. Only the oldest of souls can do so. Sometimes the world and Spirit World act as one to create and destroy. That is when a miracle or a cataclysm can happen.

THE SPIRIT POWERS

- SHADOWBORN
  - **Shadow Mirror**- A power exclusive to Begin Anu and the Farlander bloodlines. To raise a

Shadow Mirror, a summoner uses their own lifeforce to draw up a shield that can only be breached by those the summoner wishes. Anyone of the summoner's bloodline can cross through with no trouble. Only the summoner's command or death can break a Shadow Mirror.

- **Shadow Shock-** To produce Shadow Shock, a Shadowborn must tap into the electrical energy of their heartbeat and guide it to the dominant hand. Shadow Shock can have a paralyzing effect when one is struck by it.
- **Shadow Wolf-** A Shadowborn projects their Spirit energy in the shape of a black wolf. The ability can be amplified based on level of rage and requires extreme focus.
- **Shadow Slide-** The most basic skill available to a Shadowborn. To go into Shadow Slide, a Shadowborn must center themselves by aligning their heartbeat to the cool pulse of a shadow. The ability becomes easier to use as one practices and gets older. Shadow Slide is an evasive defense move and one cannot attack while in it. Inside, it can dull pain and have a chilling effect but if one stays in too long, they risk being pulled into the Spirit World. It allows a Shadowborn to move quickly across great distances.
- **Shadow Shield-** A technique that can mimic a Shadow Mirror and cut off another's ability to project or send out Spirit energy. It can directly lead to a contest of wills until one person gives up.
- **Shadow Shade-** A Shadowborn can project images of themselves to fool or misdirect others. A fully trained Shadowborn can project any number of Shadow Shades to train for combat matches.
- **Shadow Trail-** A basic power where a Shadowborn leaves behind a trace of Spirit energy as a signal to others or to direct more complex techniques.
- **Shadow Blind-** An outlawed technique where a trained Shadowborn can alter or block part of another's mind and senses. It can be used to create an army of loyal followers. Difficult to break.
- **Shadow Sleep-** Another questionable technique that causes others to fall unconscious. Two fingers of the caster's dominant hand must be pressed to the center of the receiver's forehead in order to direct the

thread of energy.

- o **Shadow Shock Wave-** A more powerful version of Shadow Shock using both arms.
- o **Shadow Guide-** A stabilizing ability used in Shadow Slide to guide others and keep them from being pulled into the Spirit World.
- o **Shadow Break-** A technique meant to force someone out of Shadow Slide. Requires extreme concentration on the natural pulses of one's surroundings.
- o **Shadow Draw-** A power meant to pull shadows closer to the Shadowborn for use in other Spirit energy shadow abilities.
- o **Shadow Call-** By placing a hand over the heart and the forehead, a Shadowborn centers themselves and uses the focus to detect Spirit energy in another person.

- EARTHBORN
    - o **Earth Touch-** A basic Earthborn skill to touch and sense the invisible magnetic field in the earth.
    - o **Earth Call-** A basic Earthborn power where an Earthborn can use their connection to the natural field to send out a signal with Spirit energy.
    - o **Earth Command-** An intermediate technique where an Earthborn can direct stone or plants to move and act. It can be used for artistic or combat purposes.
    - o **Earth Shift-** An ability that requires great strength to execute. An Earthborn acts as the focal point, using Spirit energy to move large stones. They must remained connected to the ground to maintain power.
    - o **Earth Strike-** A basic skill where an Earthborn charges up Spirit energy in their dominant hand and punches stone hard enough to break it.
    - o **Earth Draw-** A basic technique where an Earthborn taps in the natural pulses and pulls them into their body to stabilize injuries or provide added strength.

- AIRBORN
    - o **Air Push-** An Airborn manipulates the air flow around them to push and pull people and objects.
    - o **Wind Blast-** A technique used primarily in combat. An Airborn must begin charging Spirit energy while executing a spinning jump. The air then must be directed with the dominant hand towards the target.
    - o **Wind Storm-** An advanced power where an Airborn

leaps high into the air in a full spin. The continuous spinning charges up Spirit energy that pulls air into a large funnel cloud. The Airborn then flips around and dives at the opponent at full force. The entire thing looks like a tornado.

- o **Wind Spiral-** A technique where an Airborn directs their Spirit energy to twist around one or both arms. The twisting air can be used to attack or deflect.
- o **Wind Falcon-** An advanced, more stylized version of Wind Storm. Spirit energy is projected out to look like a large falcon.

- FIREBORN
  - o **Fire Shot-** A very basic power where a Fireborn charges up Spirit energy to combust the heat in the air. Commonly used alongside staves to direct the shots.
  - o **Heat Ward-** A simple charm used to hold heat or turn it away.

- WATERBORN
  - o **Water Heal-** A basic ability using water to heal surface injuries on contact. The more a Waterborn concentrates, the more thorough the healing is. Uses a cooling effect to dull pain or ice over broken bones.

- GRYPHON
  - o **Feather Whisper-** A practice where a Gryphon charms a feather with a single breath to hold voices. The breath activates the latent Spirit energy. The bigger the feather, the more words the energy can hold. Another breath from a Gryphon will charm the feather whisper to release the spoken words only to the intended receipient.

- DRAGON
  - o **Dragon Fire-** Dragons produce their fire by combusting the acid in their stomachs to blistering temperatures. They then suck in air to shoot out a stream of flames from their mouth. They have a very hot core of Spirit energy with which to tap into at will.

- DEMON
  - o **Demon Fire-** A remnant of the days when a Demon could use Spirit energy, they transform their rage into a malleable force. A fire must already be present in the environment for a Demon to use their rage to direct it. They can not produce a flame by

themselves.

- o **Demon Ward-** A mysterious charm crafted by Bane Arlis to protect the city of Crossroads from Demons. The strength of the ward is believed to be influenced by the presence of the Shadowlord.

- SPIRIT
  - o **Spirit Energy-** The invisible power of Terra that was left over from the days before the Covenant of Spirits separated the world of the living and the world of the dead.
  - o **Living Memory-** A phenomenon that can occur to an individual when entering a space that has been charged by latent Spirit energy. A vision of the individual's past is brought to life right before their eyes.
  - o **Spirit Ward-** A harmless technique where an individual crosses their heart in a form of protection from coming into contact with too much Spirit energy.
  - o **Spirit Call-** The ability to sense an individual's Spirit energy and compel them to move towards the caller.
  - o **Living Map-** A map that has been ensourced with Spirit energy to depict the world with realistic detail.
  - o **Spirit Roar-** A higher form of Spirit Call utilized by Spirits to summon allies or frighten enemies.
  - o **Spirit Fire-** A technique where Spirit energy is directly combusted into a silver or golden flame for combat purposes.
  - o **Spirit Dragon-** A more advanced, stylized version of Spirit Fire where the caster projects the form of a Dragon.
  - o **Spirit Poison-** A darker practice that utilizes various ingredients to create a toxin that can block Spirit energy.
  - o **Spirit Anchor-** The sign of a truly deep connection between two souls where each person is aware of where their partner is and if they are living or dead.
  - o **Spirit Song-** A phenomenon where the world declares that a wandering Spirit has found its way to the Spirit World. Hearing a Spirit song leaves a listener with a sense of peace and happiness thought they do not remember the words.
  - o **Spirit Bond-** A phenomenon that occurs between a Spirit of Creation and a living bloodline. The connected Spirit will come to an individual when the

need in their heart is great enough.

- BLOOD
  - **Blood Memory-** A natural phenomenon that occurs in both the Immortal and Mortal races. When the blood of an individual is tasted, a taster is privy to the individual's power and strongest memories. The clarity of the blood memory increases when the number of blood relatives decreases in an act of preservation.
  - **Blood Magic-** An outlawed and forbidden dark practice involving torture, poisons, and mental manipulations.
  - **Blood Seal-** A method created by Kaiser Adonis to help his followers bypass the Shadow Mirror. He imbues traces of his blood in metal pendents to mask and surpress the Spirit energy of a carrier.
- COMBINATION
  - **Shadow Shock Spirit Fire-** A technique invented by Ryder Coba combining the paralyzing power of Shadow Shock and the burning Spirit Fire.
  - **Shadow Quake Line-** A power invented by Onyx Silvanus combining the speed of Shadow Slide and the power of Earth Strike.
  - **Demon Shadow Rise-** A dangerous summoning ritual created by Kaiser Adonis using the blood sacrifice of his three Shadowborn family members to bring forth Demons.
  - **Demon Shadow Bond-** Another technique created by Kaiser Adonis to bind his summoned Demon in a powerful bond to protect himself from injury.
  - **Shadow Mirror Mist-** A defensive maneuver invented by Kaiser Adonis in which a small bone shattering shield of air and water is created before him.

THE IMMORTAL TRUTH

The Immortal Truth is an ancient code of laws governing the Immortal races and their interaction with Terra. It names the Shadowlord and the Daylord as Champions of Truth. It first addresses how the world of Terra was created and the Spiritual origin of the Immortal races. It gives a history of the world up until the sealing of the Darklands. At this point, the code of laws begins. The role of the Champions is first stated and the role of all Immortals to protect the short-lived and innocent is detailed. All

Immortals are to defend against the Demons of the Darklands. These are the high laws of Terra. The lower laws are more targeted to each individual race's day to day lives. Though the Immortal Truth is the law of Terra, each race has their own laws within their border regarding their innate powers, religion, celebrations, and general courtesies. The Immortal Truth was signed in blood by a member of each good Immortal race, imbuing the words with power. This power becomes a ward and barrier against the dark powers. If one of the signer bloodlines fails, the ward is broken and the terror of the Dominion War will return in full force.

ACKNOWLEDGEMENTS

I have been working on this dream for what seems like a very long time. I can not describe the feeling of awe and happiness holding a book I wrote in my hands. To my editors and those who listened to my creative brainstorming, I can not thank you enough.

Ashley Causey

FLIGHT OF THE LOST

His words are like poison to the soul. His presence on the battlefield is an immediate omen of doom. So walks Kaiser Adonis clad in armor and carrying a blood soaked sword. He smiles when he hears cries of pain and laughs at the sight of death. But hidden amongst the lost and shattered voices in his wake are whispers of hope.

However, hope is hard to come by for those of the rebel resistance. Even with the addition of Ryder Coba and Onyx Silvanus, the struggle for survival is real. Cities are being burned to the ground. The innocent are screaming for salvation. The pressure to halt Kaiser's attack on the world is mounting. Sooner or later, someone is going to break.

A glimmer of hope lies in the mission of the Gryphon messenger Gyr to find the legendary Daylord. The proud Gryphon soars for parts unknown with nothing more than his wit and determination to guide him. What secrets do the Southlands hide? What will Gyr discover when he finally meets the real Bane Arlis?

The shadows are getting darker for the most terrifying enemy is the one inside.

ABOUT THE AUTHOR

Ashley Causey writes and lives in South Carolina. For more news and updates, go to Facebook and visit the Flight of the Broken Official page.